MALCOLM

GEORGE MacDONALD

BETHANY HOUSE PUBLISHERS

Bloomington, Minnesota 55438

The Novels of George MacDonald Edited for Today's Reader

Edited Title	**Original Title**
The Curate of Glaston (3 in 1) includes:	
The Curate's Awakening	*Thomas Wingfold*
The Lady's Confession	*Paul Faber*
The Baron's Apprenticeship	*There and Back*
Malcolm (2 in 1) includes:	
The Fisherman's Lady	*Malcolm*
The Marquis' Secret	*The Marquis of Lossie*
The Poet and the Pauper (available June 2002) includes:	
The Baronet's Song	*Sir Gibbie*
The Shepherd's Castle	*Donal Grant*
A Scottish Collection (3 in 1) includes:	
The Maiden's Bequest	*Alec Forbes of Howglen*
The Minister's Restoration	*Salted With Fire*
The Laird's Inheritance	*Warlock O'Glenwarlock*
Stories that stand alone:	
The Baron's Apprenticeship	*There and Back*
Maiden's Bequest	*Alec Forbes of Howglen*

MacDonald Classics Edited for Young Readers
Alec Forbes and His Friend Annie

———

Discovering the Character of God by George MacDonald
Knowing the Heart of God by George MacDonald

MALCOLM

GEORGE MacDONALD

Edited for Today's Reader by Michael R. Phillips

BETHANYHOUSE
MINNEAPOLIS, MINNESOTA

Malcolm
by George MacDonald

Copyright © 1982
Michael R. Phillips

Previously published in two separate volumes:

The Fisherman's Lady © 1982 by Michael R. Phillips. Originally published in Great
Britain under the title *Malcolm* by Henry S. King Publishers, 1875. Published in the
United States by George Routledge & Sons, New York, and by J. B. Lippincott,
Philadelphia, circa 1875.

The Marquis' Secret © 1982 by Michael R. Phillips. Originally published as *The
Marquis of Lossie* in 1877 by J. B. Lippincott and Co.

Cover illustration by Bill Graf
Cover design by Jen Airhart

Published by Bethany House Publishers
A Ministry of Bethany Fellowship International
11400 Hampshire Avenue South
Bloomington, Minnesota 55438
www.bethanyhouse.com

Printed in the United States of America

Library of Congress Cataloging-in-Publication Data

MacDonald, George, 1824–1905.
    Malcolm / by George MacDonald ; edited for today's reader by Michael R.
Phillips.
       p. cm.
The fisherman's lady was originally published as Malcolm, and The marquis' secret
was originally published as The Marquis of Lossie.
    ISBN 0–7642–2559–6 (pbk.)
    1. Christian Fiction, Scottish. 2. Scotland—Fiction. 3. Fishers—Fiction.
I. Phillips, Michael R., 1946– II. MacDonald, George, 1824–1905. Marquis of Lossie.
III. Title: Fisherman's lady. IV. Title: Marquis' secret. V. Title.
    PR4967 .M27   2001
    823'.8—dc21

                                                           2001003977

The
Fisherman's
Lady

Preface

I first heard of George MacDonald ten or twelve years ago when a friend read me the following quote from an old out-of-print book he was reading: "Anyone who has enjoyed the writings of C. S. Lewis will quite naturally want to move on eventually to George MacDonald."

My first reaction was very near shock.

"How dare she say—even hint!—that *anyone* can compare with C. S. Lewis?" I said to myself. "Not to mention the implication that this MacDonald, whoever he is, could have produced writings beyond his; why, the thing's preposterous!"

I was a totally committed C. S. Lewis devotee—still am! I was jealous of any insinuation threatening Lewis's position in my mind as the greatest writer of all time. And to say you could "move on" from Lewis to someone else—implying Lewis to be the lightweight, MacDonald the heavyweight—that was a premise I could never allow, no matter who MacDonald was!

Yet somehow I couldn't get that quote out of my head. And eventually I had to find out who George MacDonald was and what he had written.

When I found MacDonald's two Princess and Curdie fairy tales in our local library, my Narnian appetite for top-notch fairy stories coupled with Christian allegory was quite naturally aroused. And upon completion I did have to admit, "Hmm, these are pretty good—a definite addition to the Narnia tradition."

I continued to seek out other MacDonald works, for by now I could see that he held definite promise. I found *Gibbie* and *North Wind* and enjoyed them as well. I was discovering in MacDonald the very thing that had always made Lewis so special—the ability to include insightful principles and profound spiritual wisdom in a top-flight, well-written, compelling story. And MacDonald seemed to share Lewis's wide-ranging gifts and abilities as a writer. He was not limited to one or two particular styles or genres. I found adult fantasies, children's fantasies, adult novels, children's novels, realism, allegory, short stories, daily devotions, poetry, sermons, essays, translations and history. And in whatever he did I sensed the same wisdom coming forth, the same penetrating spiritual perception concerning intensely practical concerns.

After reading the few MacDonald's I could find, my curiosity was kindled to learn what I could about the man. And what should I discover first but that he had been Lewis's favorite author! He was to C. S. Lewis what Lewis had always been to me. So highly did Lewis feel indebted to him, in fact, that he compiled an anthology of selections from MacDonald's works, in the foreword of which he made the statement: "I have never concealed the fact that I regarded him as my master." And, indeed, wherever I went in the writings of Lewis from that time on, I began to find hints of this very thing: His letters often mention various MacDonald books he was reading at the time. In his autobiography, *Surprised by Joy*, Lewis credits MacDonald's *Phantastes* with starting him on the road toward conversion to Christianity, and in *The Great Divorce* Lewis has MacDonald act as his guide through heaven.

I wondered how I could have missed all this before!

Clearly, though MacDonald had been dead for three quarters of a century, he was nevertheless a literary force to be reckoned with; his books seemed to have a profound influence wherever they were read. Yet as I began to delve more deeply into the life of this nineteenth-century Scotsman, I quickly discovered that though he had written over fifty volumes, less than ten were currently in print or available.

So I began a long search—through old bookstores dealing in used books, out-of-print search services, obtaining copies from other loyal fans—and gradually unearthed many more of MacDonald's books which I had not read. What I discovered was that his most common form of writing was the lengthy Victorian novel, much like those of his friend and contemporary Charles Dickens. Though none of his full-length adult fiction was then in print, it had been by far MacDonald's most frequently used format.

And as I began to read these novels, something very similar to the aura surrounding the Narnian tales settled upon me. But it was different. I was transported, not to a make-believe fairy world, but to the solid reality of Scotland, where the raw force and beauty of nature—the peat moors, the rugged seascape, the high mountains, the icy streams—and the simple, strong and passionate natures of the Scottish people of MacDonald's creation captured my heart and fancy just as thoroughly as had the talking beasts, the green meadows and the ocean's warm salt spray of Aslan's Narnia.

Great writers have the gift of creating a world in the imagination of their readers. Tolkien has given us middle earth; for his readers Lewis brought Narnia, Malacandra and Perelandra to life. MacDonald's contribution is a Scotland where the heroes are as real and captivating as Sam, Frodo, Caspian or Lucy. Who could meet David Elginbrod, wee Sir Gibbie, Donal Grant's mentor—old Andrew, or the piper Duncan and be the same afterward? Because the fairy-tale allegory is in such high vogue today is no reason to overlook the traditional novel as being able to yield equal fruit in the imagination. For though MacDonald's created world is solid and real—an actual place—it is nonetheless vivid and enchanting, and his characters nonetheless powerful to move our hearts and change our lives. Surely his heavy impact on the writing and ideas and created worlds of Tolkien and Lewis and others speaks for itself.

It is my hope to introduce you to the world of George MacDonald's fiction. This is, in my opinion, one of MacDonald's most pleasurable novels. It is a thriller in every sense of the word. Yet, as you will see, it contains far more than mere plot.

I can truthfully say that if you enjoy fiction, and especially if you enjoy the writings of C. S. Lewis, you will want to move on to George MacDonald—not because MacDonald is necessarily better than Lewis, but because he offers more of the same. What is great in Lewis is also great in MacDonald.

Snuggle up cozily to a warm fire, let your mind drift off across the miles to MacDonald's homeland, and allow that man of wisdom and spinner of yarns to envelope you in his tale.

I hope you enjoy your journey into MacDonald's world as much as I have!

Michael Phillips
Eureka, California
June 1980

Contents

•••••••••••••••••••••

Introduction

*A*n interesting frontispiece appears in a 1935 edition of a book[1] dealing with nineteenth-century authors: a composite photograph of a group of eminent Victorian writers—J. A. Froude, Wilkie Collins, Anthony Trollope, W. M. Thackeray, Lord T. B. Macaulay, E. G. Bulwer-Lytton, Thomas Carlyle, Charles Dickens and George MacDonald. The modern student of the period might easily do a doubletake at first glance, asking, "Who is George MacDonald, and what is *he* doing there?"

But as MacDonald's biographer has pointed out, "Such a question would not have occurred to most of MacDonald's contemporaries. Instead they might have expressed surprise to learn that he would be largely forgotten by the middle of the twentieth century. For throughout the final third of the nineteenth century, George MacDonald's works were bestsellers and his status as a [writer and Christian] sage was secure. His novels sold, both in Great Britain and in the United States, by the hundreds of thousands of copies; his lectures were popular and widely attended; his poetry earned him at least passing consideration for the laureateship; and his reputation as a Christian teacher was vast. This . . . popularity alone makes MacDonald a figure of some significance in literary history."[2]

And though in certain ways he had to cater to the public, MacDonald was not the ordinary "popular" writer who is successful in the marketplace but is not taken seriously by qualified critics. "In his own time MacDonald was esteemed by an impressive roster of English and American literary and religious leaders. He was among the closest friends of John Ruskin [Lewis Carroll, Lady Byron] and Charles Dodgson; and he moved as a peer in the company of Alfred Tennyson, Charles Kingsley, F. D. Maurice, R. W. Gilder, Harriet Beecher Stowe, Oliver Wendell Holmes, Mark Twain, and Henry Wadsworth Longfellow. All of them respected, praised, and encouraged him, yet his reputation has nearly vanished while theirs survive. . . .

"[It is not] that MacDonald has been entirely ignored in the twentieth century. Indeed, although he is little known among the general reading public, MacDonald has received considerable scholarly and critical attention during the past twenty years. G. K. Chesterton was among the earliest twentieth-century critics who found MacDonald's 'message' of importance in a

---

[1]*The Victorians and Their Reading* by Amy Cruse. A copy of the photo is found on page 353 of *George MacDonald and His Wife* (1924) by Greville MacDonald, George, Allen, & Unwin, London. Repr. Johnson Reprint, N.Y., 1971.
[2]*George MacDonald* by Richard Reis, Twayne Publishers, N.Y., 1972, p. 17.

post-Victorian [world]. Chesterton once referred to MacDonald as 'one of the three or four greatest men of the nineteenth century.' "[3]

Perhaps the most important of MacDonald's modern admirers was C. S. Lewis, who repeatedly acknowledged MacDonald as one of the most important inspirers of his own fantasies and Christian theological writings. In his own autobiography, *Surprised by Joy*, Lewis describes how reading MacDonald's *Phantastes* began a process of conversion from skepticism to Christianity. In *The Great Divorce*, Lewis makes MacDonald his guide and mentor. Another Lewis volume, *George MacDonald: An Anthology*, is a formal acknowledgment of the debt Lewis felt toward MacDonald and consists of selections from his works. In its preface Lewis says of MacDonald, "I have never concealed the fact that I regarded him as my master; indeed I fancy I have never written a book in which I did not quote from him. But it has not seemed to me that those who have received my books kindly take even now sufficient notice of the affiliation. Honesty drives me to emphasize it."[4] And throughout Lewis's various published letters are sprinkled brief informal glimpses of the importance MacDonald's writings played in Lewis's personal reading program and spiritual growth. "I have read a new MacDonald since I last wrote, which I think the very best of the novels. . . ," he wrote to Arthur Greeves in 1931.[5] In response to a letter in 1939, he asked, "Do you know George MacDonald's fantasies for grown-ups. . . ?"[6] In 1951, in reply to a question posed him, he began by saying, "As MacDonald says. . . ."[7] And to his friend Sister Penelope in that same year he spoke of "My love for G. MacDonald. . . ."[8] Indeed, though it was in 1915 when he first discovered MacDonald ("I have had a great literary experience this week . . . the book is Geo. MacDonald's *Phantastes*. . . ."[9] he wrote excitedly to Arthur Greeves in October of that year), he was still reading him with relish and enthusiasm more than forty-five years later.

Though it has now been nearly twenty years since his death, the writings of C. S. Lewis are presently more widely read than ever. Indeed, Lewis is without a doubt the most diversified, widely read Christian writer of this century, perhaps of all time, with the exception of the New Testament authors. Yet though MacDonald's deep influence in the roots, literary tradition and spiritual background of C. S. Lewis is primary and unquestionable, were he alive today Lewis might well remark, as he did in 1946, that those who have received his books do not take sufficient notice of the MacDonald affiliation. It is therefore impossible for the modern follower of the writings and ideas of C. S. Lewis to obtain anything but a fragmentary picture of his thought without at the same time delving into the works of George MacDonald.

It is not only with Lewis that he is associated. MacDonald's name appears with uncanny frequency in published discussions from the writings of

[3]Ibid., p. 18.
[4]*George MacDonald: An Anthology*, ed. C.S. Lewis, Geoffrey Bles, 1946, p. 20.
[5]*They Stand Together*, ed. Walter Hooper (Macmillan), 1979, p. 402.
[6]*Letters of C.S. Lewis*, ed. Walter Hooper (Harcourt, Brace, World, 1966), p. 167.
[7]Ibid., p. 231.
[8]Ibid., p. 232.
[9]Ibid., p. 27.

the various other "Oxford Mythmakers" such as J. R. R. Tolkien, Owen Barfield, Dorothy Sayers, Charles Williams, and others. There is evidence, for instance, that he was a favorite also with Tolkien and also was influential in his writing.[10] He is increasingly coming to occupy a key position in the growing body of literature surrounding these and other imaginative Christian writers. His works, in all their editions, are included in the Marion E. Wade Collection at the Wheaton College Library which is dedicated to the interest and preservation of such writings.

George MacDonald's life (1824–1905) spanned the greater part of the nineteenth century. He was a devout Scotsman from a race of bards, pipers, intense loyalties, clan feuds, and steeped in history. His Celtic roots yielded writings full of romance, vision, nature, heather moors, peat fires, high mountains, storm-tossed seas and rugged coastlines. He was drawn to the ministry and studied toward that end. But after a brief stay in the pulpit, his warm, human, imaginative and progressive ideas were increasingly found to be unorthodox according to the rigid and backward standards of the religious establishment of his day, and he was forced to leave it. He thus turned to writing; and in the following forty-two years of his active writing career, the enormity of his output was staggering. He produced some fifty-two separate volumes of immense variety which may be roughly categorized as: three prose fantasies, eight fairy tales and allegories for children, five collections of sermons, three books of literary and critical essays, three collections of short stories, several collections of poetry (which, along with the short stories, in succeeding years came out in many different editions by scores of publishers), and some twenty-five to thirty novels (depending on the definition and method of classification). And among the most amazing aspects of his prodigious career is the fact that many of these (indeed, most of the novels) were over 400 pages in length and some ranged over 700. In addition to writing, MacDonald also lectured widely. He made a tour of the United States in 1873 during which his lectures were highly acclaimed and eagerly attended.

Though MacDonald may be judged a "success" as a writer and public figure by just about any standards, poverty was nevertheless never far from him. And he suffered as well from poor health, first with tuberculosis, then asthma and eczema. Unlike best-selling authors today who receive large royalties for their work, such was not true for George MacDonald. Though his works were serialized in scores of magazines and though his books were sold in Britain and the United States in phenomenal quantities, he received very little for his efforts. Royalties were small and many of his works were illegally pirated and sold without his ever receiving a cent from the proceeds.

Because his life was one of constant financial peril and physical adversity, MacDonald's writing was for him a practical way to earn a living. He had a large family to care for and had to provide for them however he could—by writing, lecturing, tutoring, occasional preaching, and odd jobs

---

[10]Richard Carpenter, *The Inklings* (Houghton, Mifflin, 1979), p. 158.

that presented themselves. Though it can no doubt truthfully be said that MacDonald's first loves lay in the areas of preaching, poetry, and fantasy, he recognized that on the whole the audience representing the potential "market" was made up mainly of middle-class Victorian men and women who fed on dramatic fiction. Out of necessity, therefore, he became a novelist, convinced that he could convey his deep spiritual convictions to a larger audience of readers through fiction. He turned to the novel in the early 1860s, and it became his primary form of published work. And because of the immense popularity of his novels, it was for them he was primarily known.

There is a peculiar quality in a MacDonald novel that has great power to move its reader. For MacDonald was no ordinary man. He had a powerful vision of the meaning of life; his spirit was in close union with the Spirit of God; and he had unusual insight into the application of spiritual principles in daily life situations. And it is this wisdom and spiritual perspective which set his stories apart from those of his contemporaries, most of whom wrote simply for the market. For though MacDonald had to sell books to an audience desiring action, plot, suspense, intrigue, drama and romance, he nevertheless was even more concerned with the novel as a means to an end. There was a message of God's love burning inside him which he had to express.

It is this very desire to spread the reality of God at work in men's lives which undoubtedly contributes to the fact that MacDonald is not known today as is his contemporary Dickens, though during their lifetime such would not have been the case. Today's "average" reader is vastly different in world outlook than his or her counterpart of a century ago and is not nearly so concerned with spiritual matters. This is a new era of literary taste; happy endings are no longer in vogue as they were then. Yet these shifts in the public appetite must not keep us from George MacDonald's work. His writings deserve careful consideration in our own day as well. For not only is his influence on his own contemporaries unquestioned, so is his impact on many well-known authors of recent times.

It is interesting to note, however, that until very recently there has not been a single one of MacDonald's conventional novels in print. And even with today's renewed interest in his works, only a few are now available in expensive limited edition reprints ranging from $50 and up. Yet the novel was his primary form of written expression. To understand MacDonald at all, one needs to experience his novels.

When the reader does, however, two problems are immediately encountered in MacDonald's writing style. First of all, MacDonald frequently used lowland Scots dialect for the dialogue between his characters, which few now understand at a glance. And, secondly, MacDonald's tendency toward preaching and rambling often erupts without warning, and he lapses into off-the-subject discourses which slow up the story line considerably.

For the loyal MacDonald follower, such idiosyncrasies lend a certain charm and flavor. But when the average person is reading a novel, he wants to move through the drama without having to stop and wade through a sermonette or to unravel and decode a passage in Scotch dialect. When these difficulties are overcome, a MacDonald novel is truly elevated to the first rank. For there is much excellence in his stories—shrewd characterization, lively drama, suspense, authentic dialogue, intricate plots, captivating realism.

Besides the stories themselves, MacDonald's novels are enhanced by spiritual truths woven in and throughout the characters whose lives open before us. MacDonald was so thoroughly a Christian that God's wisdom simply came forth from his pen almost in spite of the story line. It is as though he were continually weaving two parallel stories—that of the "plot," and that of the partially submerged spiritual journeys being traveled in a parallel plane by those characters involved in the story. And MacDonald moved freely from one level to another. To the knowledgable reader who recognizes the dual purpose of his writing and who is aware of MacDonald's spiritual vantage point, the travels back and forth from level to level make the plot all the more meaningful and the spiritual truths that much more alive. C. S. Lewis commented on the principles one can uncover in a MacDonald novel by saying they "would be intolerable if a man were reading for the story [alone] but ... are in fact welcome because the author ... is a supreme preacher. Some of his best things are hidden in his dullest books."[11]

The novels of George MacDonald are therefore intriguing to the modern Christian reader. Nearly every one contains in the narrative a strong vision of a loving God gradually revealing himself in the lives of men and women through nature and daily circumstances. As the various facets of the plot unfold, MacDonald carries on a commentary of spiritual observation (level two) through the characters, their growth and interaction, and the action of the drama itself (level one). The characters responding to their circumstances provide a rich source of insight into why people think and behave as they do. The plot is the skeleton around which the characters and truths come to life.

"In developing his vision of life creatively through the imagined real worlds of the various novels, MacDonald moves to authenticate his theological convictions, thereby avoiding a danger confronting the pure theologian. It is easy for students of theology to become people given too much to abstractions, content to handle life at a comfortable distance and to minimize the concrete quality of human experience. But in the novel, broad pronouncements concerning the human situation and human conduct will not suffice. MacDonald, not unlike his great contemporary Dostoevsky, knew that the novel provides a means of testing the validity of theological principles, a means the like of which the seeker after Truth can hardly afford to ignore. For a serious novel presents life as it is lived by men in their daily courses."[12]

And it is just at this point that MacDonald's novels excel. His characters are alive; you feel with them; you accompany them as they are opened to

---

[11]Op. cit., *George MacDonald: An Anthology*, p. 17.
[12]Roland Hein, *The Worlds of George MacDonald* (Harold Shaw Pubs.), p. 8.

the principles of God and His love. Before long you are one of the characters yourself on Level Two as you sit back to reflect on some nugget of wisdom you have just unearthed from a conversation between two characters.
But then suddenly you will find yourself jolted back to Level One, roused in
anger at the villain, breathing with heart-pounding gasps as the heroine
rushes to escape through the newly discovered secret passageway of the old
castle!

To get at the true George MacDonald, you must get into his world. And
his world is revealed through his fiction. Nearly every novel contains much
autobiography sprinkled through it. Not only is he a superb storyteller and
weaver of fantasies, but at the same time he *is* the central character—and if
not himself surely someone he has known.

Throughout all his stories, one can see that he ever loved the Scotland
from which he had come. As Lewis said, "All that is best in his novels carries
us back to that 'kaleyard' world of granite and heather, of bleaching greens
beside burns that look as if they flowed not with water but with stout, to the
thudding of wooden machinery, the oatcakes, the fresh milk, the pride, the
poverty, and the passionate love of hard-won learning."[13] When feeling with
MacDonald the wind blowing from a high northern mountain or from a
storm-tossed northern sea, you are sometimes overcome with the sense that
the wind is from someplace higher still. There is a special world captured
by MacDonald in his novels, a world perhaps not fully present in any particular one but toward which each makes its own contribution. And it is a
world worth seeking out.

The difficulty, however, as mentioned before, is that MacDonald's novels
are often out-of-print and, when available, are long and many times unintelligible to the fast-paced reader. My proposal with this reprinted edition of
one of my favorites is to once again open this world of George MacDonald
to modern-day readers. What I have done is to cut the original by about half
by removing disgressions from the story and by condensing some of the
"wordy" portions. In addition I have "translated" the Scots' dialect, an ex-
ample of which follows, into English:

> "Ye hae had mair to du wi' me nor ye ken, an' aiblins ye'll hae mair nor yet
> ye can weel help. Sae caw canny, my man."
> "Ye may hae the layin' o' me oot," said Malcolm, "but it sanna be wi my
> wull; an gien I hae ony life left i' me, Is' gie ye a fleg."
> "Ye may get a war yersel': I hae frichtit the deid afore noo. Sae gang yer
> wa's to Mistress Coorthoup, wi' a flech i' yer lug."

(Some dialect of certain characters has been retained for authentic "flavor.")

The original was published as *Malcolm* in 1875. Something of the immense popularity of the book can be appreciated from the fact that after its
serialization in magazines, it was published in more than a dozen different
editions in the few years following its release.

The story is set in northern Scotland on the coast of the shire of Banff,

---

[13]Op. cit., *George MacDonald: An Anthology*, p. 12.

an area with which George MacDonald's ancestors had long been associated and of which MacDonald was very familiar; he was raised in Huntly,
some twenty miles south of this particular stretch of coastline. For this and
other reasons (which will become clear as the story progresses), the story
can be seen as a window into the background, heritage and character of
George MacDonald's Scottish past. But whatever autobiography, allegory or
symbolism we discover in the reading, we do well at the same time to read
for pure enjoyment's sake. After reading one of MacDonald's stories, his wife
once asked him for "the story's meaning." He replied, possibly to us as well
as to her, "You may make of it what you like. If you see anything in it, take
it and I am glad you have it; but I wrote it for the tale."

Michael Phillips

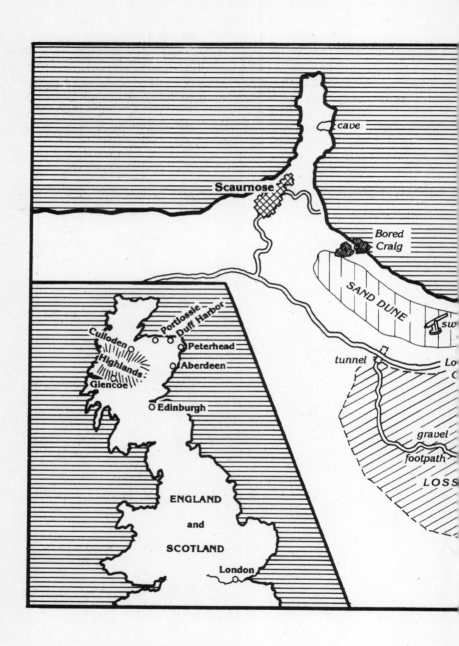

cave

Scaurnose

Bored
Craig

SAND DUNE

sw

tunnel

Lo

gravel

footpath

LOSS

Portlossie
Duff Harbor
Culloden
Peterhead
Highlands
Aberdeen
Glencoe
Edinburgh

ENGLAND

and

SCOTLAND

London

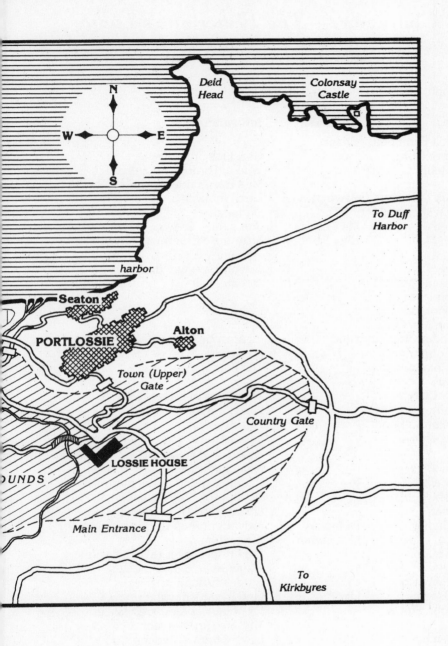

Characters—*The Fisherman's Lady*

(In Approximate Order of Appearance)

Name	Nickname	Information
Griselda Campbell	Grizel	
Margaret Horn		Griselda's 3rd cousin
Mrs. Mellis		Wife of Portlossie merchant
Jean		Miss Horn's housekeeper
Barbara Catanach	Bawby, Bobby	Local midwife
Watty Witherspail		Undertaker
Stephen Stewart	Mad Laird	Son of Mrs. Stewart
Joseph Mair	Blue Peter	Scaurnose fisherman, Malcolm's friend
Phemy Mair		Joseph's younger daughter
Mrs. Annie Mair		Joseph's wife
Malcolm		
Lady Florimel		
Duncan MacPhail		
Alexander Graham	Sandy	Ex-preacher, schoolteacher
Mrs. Courthope		Lossie House housekeeper
Lord Colonsay of Lossie		The marquis of Lossie
Hector Crathie		The factor of Lossie House
Mr. Cairns		Parish minister
Jonathan Aulbuird		Parish sexton
Johnny Bykes		Lossie House gatekeeper
Will		Assistant gamekeeper
Mr. MacPherson		Head gamekeeper
Lady Bellair		Countess-friend of the marquis
Lord Meikleham		Nephew of Lady Bellair
Mr. Stoat		Lossie House horseman, groom
Meg Findlay	Partaness, Meg Partan	Neighbor friend of Duncan and Malcolm
Annie Mair		Blue Peter's sister (also his wife's name)
Charley Wilson		Annie's husband
Lizza Findlay	Lizzy	Meg Partan's daughter
Mrs. John Stewart		Proprietor of Kirkbyres estate
Tom		Mrs. Stewart's servant
Mr. Glennie		Lawyer from Aberdeen
Mr. Soutar		Lawyer from Duff Harbor
Mr. Morrison		Justice of the peace

1

••••••••••••••••••••

The Corpse

*T*hough the day would soon grow warm, the early coastal chill cut straight to the bone. The rising sun would have to work to thaw the damp earth, nearly frozen from the hours of darkness. Likewise, as the sun began to beat down on certain inhabitants of the surrounding neighborhood, it met a similar resistance to its warmth. For they too had been in darkness— but of a different kind.

Dawn was about to break in upon Portlossie and its people. But none would have imagined the light that would gradually engulf them, would spring from one whose light had just gone out and who now lay dead in an upper room of an old house overlooking the Seaton from the town above. Griselda Campbell had been a little-known and even lesser-understood enigma who had lived the past twenty years of her lonely life as a virtual recluse with a distant relative. Her passing in the very prime of life was greeted by those few who knew her not so much with mourning as with curiosity.

Griselda's life was shrouded in mystery. But hers was not the only past kept carefully shielded from would-be intruders. As she had long ago with-drawn into the seclusion of her inner thoughts, so had several others. And now it seemed the secret which bound them all together would go quietly to the grave with poor Griselda. For she alone had held the missing piece to the puzzle without which none of the others would ever know the full scope of the truth. Indeed, it *was* a cold morning and would have been colder still had anyone known the extent of Griselda's long and painful silence.

Margaret Horn shivered and pulled her sweater more tightly around her broad shoulders as she closed the door to the empty room where rested the body of her departed third cousin. She turned back to the room on her right to rejoin her early caller, whom she had left for a moment. How bitterly cold a corpse can be, she thought to herself. And on this particular morning the sun was having unusual difficulty warming the heart of Margaret Horn which was steeling itself against all intrusions, especially the one most feared of all—the feeling of grief.

"No, no. I've got no feelings, I'm thankful to say. I never knew any good to come to them," she said as she returned.

"Nobody would have ever accused you of them, mem," said her visitor, Mrs. Mellis, the wife of the town dry-goods dealer who had called ostensibly to console her, but in actuality to see the corpse.

"Indeed, I've always had enough sense just to do what I had to do without interfering," went on Miss Horn. A brief silence followed.

"Ah, she was taken young," sighed the visitor with long-drawn tones.

"Not that young," returned Miss Horn; "she was nearly thirty-eight."

"Well, she had a sad time of it, anyway."

"Not that sad, as far as I can see—and who should know better? She had sheltered quarters here, and would have, as long as I was seeing to it."

"But she was a patient creature with everyone," persisted Mrs. Mellis, not to be foiled in her attempt to draw out some word of acknowledgment from the former companion of the deceased.

"Indeed she was that! And a bit too patient with some. But that came of having more heart than brains. Now *she* had feelings! But it's a pity she didn't have the judgment to match, for she never doubted anybody enough. But it doesn't matter now, for she's gone where all that's less important. For one that has the harmlessness of the dove in this wicked world, there's a flock of them that has the wisdom of the serpent. And the serpents make sad work of the doves."

"Well, you're right there," said Mrs. Mellis. "And as you say, she was easy enough to persuade. I have no doubt she believed to the very last he would come back and marry her."

"Come back and marry her! What do you mean? I tell you, Mistress Mellis, if you dare to hint at another word of such gossip, you'll be less familiar with this side of my door from now on!" The hawk eyes of Miss Horn glared.

Mrs. Mellis's voice trembled with something like fear as she replied, "God guide us, Miss Horn! What have I said to make you look at me like that?"

"Said!" repeated Miss Horn. "There's hardly no gossip in all the country-side but what comes from you. And it's all trash. It's small thanks you'll get for it here! And with her lying there just in the other room as she'll lie till the judgment day. Poor thing!"

"I'm sure I meant no offense, Miss Horn," said her visitor. "I thought everybody knew she was sick over him."

"Over who, in the name of the father of lies?"

"Oh, that long-legged doctor that set out for the Indies and died before he was across the equator. Only folks said he wasn't dead and would be home again when she was married."

"It's all lies from head to foot."

"Well, it's plain to see she pined away after he left and was never herself again—you don't deny that?"

"It's all heresay," persisted Miss Horn in a softened tone. "She cared no more about the man than I did myself. She pined, I grant you. And he went away. But the wind blows and the water runs, and the one has little to do with the other."

"Well, I'm sorry I said anything to offend you. And now, with your leave, I'll just go and take one last look at her, poor thing."

"Indeed, you'll do nothing of the kind! I'll let nobody glower at her that would go and spread such gossip, Mistress Mellis. To say that such a dove as my Grizel, poor, soft-hearted, winsome thing, would have looked twice at any such serpent as him! No, no, mem. Go your way and come back straight from your prayers tomorrow morning. By that time she'll be quiet in her coffin and I'll be quiet in my temper. Then I'll let you see her—maybe."

Mrs. Mellis rose in considerable displeasure and with a formal farewell walked from the room, casting a curious glance as she left in the direction of the room in which the body lay. She descended the stairs slowly as if on every step she deliberated whether the next would bear her weight. Miss Horn, who had followed her to the head of the stair, watched her out of sight below the landing. She then turned back into the parlor, but with a lingering look toward the opposite room, as if she saw through the closed door what lay white on the bed.

"It's God's mercy I have no feelin's," she said to herself. "To match up my poor Grizel with such a flighty man as that! Ah, poor Grizel. She's gone from me like a knotless thread."

Miss Horn's thoughts were interrupted by the sound of the latch of the street door, and she sprang from her chair in anger.

"Can't they let her sleep for five minutes!" she cried aloud.

But after a moment's reflection she thought, "It'll probably just be Jean coming in from the pump."

But hearing no footsteps along the passage to the kitchen, she concluded, "No, it can't be her, for she goes about the house like a new-shod colt." She went downstairs to see who might have thus presumed to enter unbidden.

In the kitchen, the floor of which was as white as scrubbing could make it and sprinkled with sea sand, sat a woman of about sixty years of age whose plump face to the first glance looked kindly; to the second, cunning; to the third, evil. Her deep-set, black, bright eyes, glowing from under the darkest of eyebrows, had a fascinating influence—so much so that at first meeting one was not likely for a time to notice any other of her features. She rose as Miss Horn entered, buried a fat fist in her soft side and stood silent.

"Well?" said Miss Horn.

"I thought you might be wanting one of my calling?"

"No, no. There's no hand that lays a finger on the bairn but my own," said Miss Horn. "I've had it all finished before the light of day. She's lying quiet now—very quiet—waiting on Watty Witherspail. When he brings the coffin, we'll lay her into it and be done with it."

"Well, mem, for a lady born and bred like yourself, I must say you're taking it unusually composed."

"I'm not aware, Mistress Catanach, of any necessity laid upon you to speak your mind in this house. I don't expect it. And anyway, why shouldn't I take it with composure? We'll all have to take our turn before long, composed as we have the grace to be, and go out like a dying candle—yes, and leave our memories behind us."

"It's not that much of a memory I expect to leave behind me, Miss Horn," said the woman.

"The less the better," murmured Miss Horn, but her unwelcome visitor went on.

"Them that's most in my debt knows least about it. It's God's truth, I *know* worse than I ever *did*, mem. A person in my trade can't help falling in among bad company once in a while, for we're all born in sin and brought forth in iniquity, as the Book says. But you know the likes of me mustn't tell tales. All the same, if you don't take the help of my hands, you won't refuse me the sight of my eyes, poor thing?"

"There's none shall look upon her dead that wasn't a pleasure to her living. And you know well enough, Bawby, she couldn't bear the sight of you."

"And good reason she had for that too, if what goes through my mind before I fall asleep nights when I'm thinking to myself be the truth. Of course it may be no better than an old wives' fable dreamt up by my imagination."

"What do you mean?" demanded Miss Horn sternly.

"I know what I mean myself, and one that's not content with that is ill-prepared to be a midwife. I would just like to get a certain fancy out of my head that's been in my memory many a long year. But, please yourself, mem, if you don't be neighborly. I'll just have to harbor my suspicions privately yet a while longer."

"You'll not go near her!—not to save you from all the ill dreams that ever gathered about you," cried Miss Horn.

"Gently, gently," said Mrs. Catanach. "Don't anger me too much, for I am but mortal. Folk take a lot from you, Miss Horn, that they'll take from no one else. For your temper's well known. But it's an ill-fared thing to anger the midwife—so much lies with her. And I'm not in the mood to put up with it today. I wonder at your being so unneighborly—at such a time too, with a corpse in the house."

"Go away. It's my house!" said Miss Horn, in a low, hoarse voice, restraining herself from rising to tempest pitch only by the consciousness of what lay in the room just above her. "I would as soon let a cat into the dead-chamber to go loping all over the corpse as I would let you into it, Bawby Catanach. And there's to you."

At this moment the opportune entrance of Jean afforded fitting occasion for Miss Horn to leave the room without encountering the dilemma of either turning the woman out—a proceeding which Mrs. Catanach, from the way in which she set her short, stout figure squarely on the floor seemed ready to resist—or of herself abandoning the field in discomfort. She turned and marched from the kitchen with her head in the air and the gait of one who has been insulted on her own premises.

She was sitting in the parlor, still red-faced and wrathful, when Jean entered, closed the door behind her, and drew near to her mistress. She bore a narrative of all she had seen, heard, and done while "out on the town." But Miss Horn interrupted the moment she began to speak.

"Is that woman out of the house, Jean?" she asked, waiting for an affirmative answer as a preliminary condition for all further conversation.

"She's gone, mem," answered Jean—adding to herself in a wordless thought, "I'm not saying where."

"She's a woman I wouldn't have you go around with, Jean."

"I don't know anything wrong with her, mem," returned Jean.

"She's enough to corrupt a churchyard," said her mistress with more force than fitness.

Jean, however, was on the shady side of fifty and was more likely to have yielded already than to be liable to a first assault of corruption. And little did Miss Horn think how useless was her warning or where Barbara Catanach was at the very moment. Trusting to Jean's cunning, as well she might, she was in the dead-chamber and standing over the dead. She had folded back the sheet—not from the face, but from the feet and raised the night dress of fine linen in which the love of her cousin had robed the dead for the repose of the tomb.

"It would have been better for her," she muttered, "to have spoken fair gto me. I'm not used to being treated so foul like that. But I'll get even with her yet, I'm thinking—the old goat! . . . Losh! And praise be thanked! There it is. A bit darker, but the same—just where I could have laid the point of my finger on it in the dark. Now let the worms eat it," she concluded as she folded down the linen of shroud and sheet. "And no mortal knows of it but myself and him that would have been behooved to see it, if he was a bit better than Glenkindie's man in the old ballad."

The instant she had rearranged the garments of the dead, she turned and made for the door with a softness of step that strangely contrasted with the ponderousness of her figure, indicating great muscular strength. She opened it with noiseless circumspection to an inch, peeped out from the crack and, seeing the opposite door of the parlor still shut, stepped out with a swift, noiseless swing of person and door simultaneously, closed the door behind her, stole down the stairs and left the house. Not a board creaked, not a latch clicked as she went. She stepped into the street as sedately as if she had come from paying to the dead the last offices of her composite calling.

2

The Witch

It was forenoon of a day in early summer. The sun was gradually working its will on the countryside. The larks were many and loud in the sky above Mrs. Catanach as she made her way down the street. As she gazed northward, the cloudless blue sky stretched over an all-but-shadowless blue sea. Two bold and jagged promontories, one on each side of her, formed a wide bay. Between the one on the west and the sea-town at her feet lay a great curve of yellow sand, upon which the breakers, born of last night's wind, were still roaring from the northeast, although the gale had now sunk to a breeze. But Mrs. Catanach was looking neither at nor for anything, for she had no fisherman husband or any other relative at sea. She was but revolving something in her unwholesome mind.

As she thus stood, a strange figure drew near, approaching her with step almost as noiseless as that with which she herself had made her escape from Miss Horn's house. At a few yards' distance from her it stood, and gazed up at her as intently as she seemed to be gazing on the sea. It was a man of dwarfish height and uncertain age, with a huge hump on his back, features of great refinement, a long, thin beard and a forehead unnaturally large over eyes of a pale blue which had a pathetic dog-like expression. Decently dressed in black, he stood with his hands in the pockets of his trousers, gazing immovably at Mrs. Catanach's face.

Becoming suddenly aware of his presence, she gave a great start and exclaimed, "Preserve us! Where did you come from?"

"I dinna ken whaur I come from,"* he replied immediately, his cheeks flushed and his eyes glowing as he gazed out to sea. "Ye ken 'at I dinna ken whaur I come from. I dinna ken whaur ye come from. I dinna ken whaur onybody comes from!"

"Hoot, laird! No offense!" returned Mrs. Catanach. "It was your own fault. What do you mean standing there glaring at me without telling me you was there?"

"I thocht ye was luikin' whaur ye came from," returned the man in tones apologetic and hesitating.

"What do I care where I came from, so long as—" and here Mrs. Catanach hesitated.

"So lang's what, if ye please?" pleaded the man with a childlike entreaty in his voice.

"Well, if you must have it, so long as I came from—my mother," said the woman looking down on the man with a vulgar laugh.

The hunchback uttered a shriek of dismay, turned and fled. And as he turned, his long thin white hands flashed out of his pockets and pressed themselves against his ears. With marvelous swiftness he shot down the steep descent toward the shore.

The name she had given the hunchback was no mere nickname. Stephen Stewart was indeed the laird of the small property and ancient house of Kirkbyres, of which his mother managed the affairs. Although she hardly managed them *for* her son, seeing that beyond his clothes and five pounds a year of pocket money, he derived no personal advantage from his possessions. He never went near his own house, for, from some unknown reason, he had such a dislike for his mother that he could not bear to hear the word "mother" or even the slightest allusion to the relationship.

Some said he was a fool; others, a madman; some, both. None, however, said he was a rogue, and all would have been willing to allow that whatever it might be that caused the difference between him and other men, through-

---

*Scotch dialect—"I don't know where I come from."

out the disturbing influence blew the air of a sweet humility.

The way the laird now pursued lay along the sandy beach toward the great and rocky promontory which closed in the bay on the west. It was nearly low tide and the wet sand afforded an easy road for his flying feet. Where the curve of the waterline turned northward at the root of the promontory, six or eight fishing boats were drawn up on the beach. Near where they lay a steep path ascended the cliff; thence through grass and some plowed land it led across the promontory to the fishing village of Scaurnose.

Leaving the flat beach behind, his way was now very rocky and difficult, lying close under the cliffs of the headland. He passed the boats, going between them and the cliff without even a glance at his friend Joseph Mair, at work on one of them. Several of the men ceased their work for a moment to look after him. His flight toward the rocks was also observed by a child of about ten from the bottom of a ruined boat nearby the others. She was the daughter of Joseph Mair—a fisherman who had been to sea in a man-of-war and who had, in consequence, acquired the nickname Blue Peter. Having saved a little money by serving on another man's boat, he was now building one of his own. Unlike many of his fellows, he was a sober and, indeed, thoughtful man, ready to listen to the voice of reason, one of the most respectable inhabitants of the place. They were, in general, men of hardihood and courage, encountering as a mere matter of course such perilous weather as the fishers on a great part of the coasts would have declined to meet.

The mad laird was a visitor at the house of Joseph Mair oftener than anywhere else. On such occasions he slept in a garret accessible by a ladder from the ground floor, which consisted only of a kitchen with fireplace and sleeping quarters. Little Phemy Mair was therefore familiar with his appearance, his ways and his speech, and she was a favorite with him.

Scarcely had the laird vanished from view of the boats when Phemy scrambled out of hers and pursued him down the coast, along the base of the promontory. She soon came within sight of the laird just as he turned into the mouth of a well-known cave and vanished.

When Phemy entered the cave some moments later, the laird was nowhere to be seen. But she went straight to the back of the cave, rounded a projection, and began an ascent which only familiarity could have enabled such a child to accomplish. She passed through another opening and reached the floor of a second cave.

As his hands were still pressed to his ears, the laird heard nothing of Phemy's approach. She stood for a while staring at him in the vague glimmer with no apparent anxiety as to what would come next. Presently she fancied she saw something glitter away in the darkness—two things—they must be eyes! The eyes of an otter or polecat of which creatures the caves along the shore abounded. Seized with sudden fright, she ran to the laird and laid her hand on his shoulder crying, "Look, laird, look!"

He started to his feet and gazed bewildered at the child. She stood between the wall and the entrance, so that all the light was gathered upon her pale face.

"Whaur did ye come from?" he cried.

"I came from the old boat," she answered.

"What do ye want wi' me?"

"Nothing, sir. I only came to see how you was getting on. I wouldn't have disturbed you, but I saw two eyes of something glaring away yonder in the dark and they scared me."

"Well, well. Sit ye doon, bairnie," said the mad laird in a soothing voice. "The polecat won't touch ye. Ye're no afraid of me, are ye?"

"Eh, no!" answered the child. "Why should I be? I'm Phemy Mair."

"Eh, bairnie! It's you, is't?" he returned in tones of satisfaction, for he had not recognized her until now. "Sit ye doon, sit ye doon."

Phemy obeyed and seated herself on the nearest ledge. Nothing disturbed them now but the sound of the rising tide. Phemy sat beside the laird in the glimmering dusk, without fear and without a word spoken. As evening crept on, she at last fell asleep on his shoulder. After a while the laird gently roused her and took her home, on their way warning her to say nothing of where she had been; for, he said, if she exposed his place of refuge, wicked people would take him and he should never see her again.

3

· · · · · · · · · · · · · · · · · · · ·

The Lady

The next day's sun had been up for some time in a cloudless sky. The wind had changed to the south and blew soft country odors to the shore, in place of the usual scents of seaweed and broken salt waters, with now and then a suspicion of icebergs. From what was called the Seaton, the sea-town, of Portlossie—a crowd of cottages occupied entirely by fisherfolk—a solitary figure was walking westward along the sands which bordered the shore from the root of the promontory of Scaurnose to the little harbor which lay on the other side of the Seaton. Beyond the harbor the rocks began again, bold and high and, after a mighty sweep, shot out northward and closed in the bay on the east with a second great promontory. The long, curved strip of sand was the only open portion of the coast for miles; the rest was all closed in with high rocky cliffs. At this one spot the passing vessel gliding by gained a pleasant peep of open fields, belts of wood and farmhouses, and sometimes managed to see a great house glimpsing from amidst its trees. In the distance one or two bare, solitary hills rose to the height of over a thousand feet.

On this open part of the shore, at some distance beyond the usual high-water mark and parallel with the shoreline, the waves of ten thousand northern storms had cast up a long dune of sand terminating toward the west within a few yards of a huge, solitary rock. The sand on the inland side of the dune was covered with short sweet grass and, in the warmer seasons, with the largest and reddest of daisies. Over this grass came the figure just mentioned, singing. On his left the ground rose rapidly to the high road; on his right was the dune, interlaced and bound together by the long clasping roots of several coarse brush-plants. It shut out all sight of the sea, but the moan and rush of the rising tide sounded close behind it. At his back rose the town of Portlossie, high above the harbor, with its houses of gray and brown stone, roofed with blue slates and red tiles. It was no highland town, yet down from its streets on the morning air now floated the sound of bag-pipes—borne winding from street to street and blown loud by the piper to wake the sleeping inhabitants and let them know it was now six o'clock.

The man on the dune was a youth of about twenty, with a long swinging, heavy-footed stride which took in the ground rapidly. He was rather tall and large-limbed. His dress was that of a fisherman, consisting of blue serge trousers, a shirt striped in blue and white and a Guernsey frock which he carried flung across his shoulder. On his head he wore a round blue hat, with a tuft of scarlet in the center.

His face was more than handsome—with large features, not finely cut, and a look of mingled nobility and ingenuousness, amounting to simplicity or even innocence. The clear outlook from his full and well-opened hazel eyes indicated both courage and decisiveness. His dark brown hair came in large curling masses from under his hat. It was such a form and face as would have drawn eyes in a crowded thoroughfare.

About the middle of the long sandhill, a sort of wide opening was cut in its top, in which stood an old-fashioned brass swivel-gun. When the lad reached the place, he sprang up the sloping side of the dune, seated himself on the gun, drew from his trousers a large silver watch, regarded it steadily for a few minutes, replaced it, took from his pocket a flint and steel with which he kindled a bit of touch-paper which he applied to the vent of the swivel. A great roar followed.

Its echoes had nearly died away when a startled little cry reached his ears. Looking to the shore, he discovered a young woman on a low rock that ran a little way out into the water. She had half risen from a sitting posture and had apparently just discovered that the rising tide had sur-rounded her. He rushed from the sandhill, crying out as he approached her, "Don't move, mem! Wait till I get to you."

He ran straight into the water and struggled through the deepening tide—the distance being short and the depth too shallow for swimming. In a moment he was by her side, scarcely saw the bare feet she had been bathing in the water, and heeded as little the motion of her hand which waved him back. He caught her in his arms like a baby and had her safe on the shore before she could utter a word. Nor did he stop until he had car-ried her to the slope of the sandhill where he set her down gently without the least suspicion of the liberty he was taking and filled only with a passion of service. He proceeded to dry her feet with the frock he had dropped there as he ran to her assistance.

"Let me alone, pray!" cried the girl with half-amused indignation, drawing back her feet and throwing down a book she carried that she might better hide them with her skirt. But though she shrank from his devotion, she could neither mistake it nor help being pleased with his kindness. Probably she had never before been immediately indebted to such an ill-clad individual of the human race, but even in such a costume she could not fail to see he was a fine fellow.

"Where are your stockings, mem?"

"You gave me no time to bring them away, you caught me up so—so rudely," answered the girl half angrily, but in such lovely speech as had never before greeted his Scottish ears.

Before the words were out of her mouth, he was already on his way back to the rock, running with great strides. The abandoned shoes and stockings were in imminent danger of being floated off by the rising water, but he dashed in, swam a few strokes, caught them up, waded back to the shore and, leaving a wet track all the way behind him, he carried the rescued clothing at arm's length back to their owner. Spreading his frock out before her and observing that she continued to keep her feet hidden under the skirts of her dress, he turned his back and stood.

"Why don't you go away?" asked the girl, venturing one set of toes from under their tent, but hesitating to proceed any farther in the business.

Without a word or turn of his head, he walked away.

Either flattered by his absolute obedience and persuaded that he was a true squire, or unwilling to forego what amusement she might gain from him, and certainly urged in part by an inherent disposition to tease, she spoke again, "You're not going away without thanking me?" she said.

"What for, mem?" he returned simply, standing stock-still again with his back toward her.

"You needn't stand so. You don't think I would go on dressing while you remained in sight?"

"I was as good as gone away, mem," he said, turning to look at her but then casting his eyes on the ground.

"Tell me what you mean by not thanking me?" she insisted.

"They would be empty thanks, mem," he said, "that were given before I knew what for."

"For allowing you to carry me to shore, of course."

"Be thanked then, mem, with all my heart."

"Don't keep saying 'ma'am' to me."

"What am I to say then, mem?—I beg your pardon, mem."

"Say 'my lady.' That's how people speak to me."

"I thought you were bound to be somebody out of the ordinary, my lady. That must be why you're so bonny," he returned, with some trembling in his tone. "But you must put on your hose, my lady, or you'll get your feet cold, and that's not good for the likes of you."

The form of address she prescribed conveyed to him no idea of rank. It but added to his notion that she was a lady as distinguished from one of the women from his own segment of life.

"And, pray, what is to become of you?" she returned, "with your clothes as wet as water can make them?"

"The salt water knows me too well to do me any harm," returned the lad. "I go wet to the skin many days from morning to night—when we're herrin' fishin', you know, my lady."

"Tell me," she asked, changing the subject, "what made you fire that gun in such a reckless way a little bit ago? Don't you know it is very dangerous?"

"Dangerous, mem—my lady, I mean? There was nothing in it but a pennyworth of blasting powder."

"It nearly blew me out of my small wits, though."

"I'm very sorry it frightened you. But even if I had seen you, I would still have had to fire the gun."

"I don't quite understand you. I suppose you mean it was your business to fire the gun?

"Just that, my lady."

"Why?"

"Because it's been decreed in the town council that at six o'clock every morning that gun's got to be fired, at least as long as my lord the marquis is at Portlossie House. You see, it's a royal burgh, this, and it only costs about a penny, and it's grand to have a small cannon to fire. And if I was to neglect it, my grandfather—who you heard with his bagpipes before I fired the gun—would go on and on playing his pipes and wouldn't know when to quit."

By the time the conversation had reached this point, the lady had gotten her shoes on, had taken up her book from the sand and was now sitting with it in her lap. No sound had reached them but that of the tide, for the screams of bagpipes had ceased the moment the swivel was fired. The sun was growing hot, and the sea, though far in the cold north, was gorgeous in purple and green. The glow of a young summer morning pervaded earth and sky and sea, and swelled the heart of the youth as he stood in unconscious bewilderment before the self-possession of the girl. She was younger than he and knew far less that was worth knowing. Yet she had a world of advantage over him—not merely from the effect of her presence on one who had never seen anything so beautiful, but also from the readiness of surface thought and polish of her speech which gave her an assurance of superiority over the man she now favored with her passing conversation. As to her personal appearance, the lad might well have taken her for twenty; for she looked more like a grown woman than he, strongly built and tall though he was, looked like a man. She was rather tall, slender, finely formed, with small hands and feet. Her hair was of a dark brown, her eyes of such a blue that no one could have suggested gray, and her complexion was fair—a little freckled which gave it the warmest tint it had.

The description I have here given may be regarded as occupying the space of a brief silence, during which the lad stood motionless, like one awaiting a further command.

"Why don't you go?" said the lady; "I want to read my book."

He gave a great sigh as if waking from a pleasant dream, took off his hat with a clumsy movement and descended the dune, walking away along the sands toward the sea-town.

When he had gone about two hundred yards, he looked back involuntarily. The lady had vanished. He concluded that she had crossed to the other side of the dune; but when he had gone so far on his way to the village as to clear the eastern end of the sand dune and there turned and looked up its southern slope, she was still nowhere to be seen. The old highland stories of his grandfather's came crowding to mind and, altogether human as she had appeared, he almost doubted whether the sea, from which he thought he had rescued her, was not her native element. The book, however, not to mention the stockings and shoes, was against the supposition. Anyhow he had seen a vision of some order or other, as certainly as if an angel from heaven had appeared to him.

Of course no one would dream of falling in love with an unearthly creature, even an angel. And as to this girl, the youth could scarcely have regarded her with a greater sense of far-off-ness. Still, he walked home as if the heavy boots he wore were wings at his heels.

"Such a girl!" he kept saying to himself, "and such small white hands! and such a bonny foot!"

4

The Piper

The sea-town of Portlossie was as irregular a gathering of small cottages as could be found. They faced every which way and were divided from each other by every sort of unpredictable street and passage. Close behind the Seaton, as it was called, ran a small road which climbed high to the level of the town above. In front of the cottages lay sand and sea. Eastward the houses could extend no farther for the harbor, and westward no farther for a small river that crossed the sands to the sea.

Avoiding the many nets extending long and wide on the grassy sands, the youth walked through the tide-swollen mouth of the river and passed along the front of the village until he arrived at a house whose window was filled with a curious collection of things for sale—dusty looking sweets in a glass bottle, tin covers for tobacco pipes, toys and tapes and needles and twenty other kinds of things all huddled together. But as he went in at its open door, it lost all appearance of a shop, and the room with the tempting window showed itself only as a poor kitchen with an earthen floor.

"Well, how did the pipes behave themselves today, Daddy?" he inquired as he strode in.

"Ah, they kept themselves in line, they did," returned the tremulous voice of a gray-haired old man who was leaning over a small peat-fire on the hearth, sifting oatmeal through the fingers of his left hand while he stirred the boiling mess with a short stick held in his right.

It had silently grown to be understood between them that the pulmonary condition of the asthmatic old piper should be attributed not to his internal but to his external lungs—namely, the bags of his pipes. Both sets had of late years manifested strong symptoms of decay and, in the case of the latter, decided measures had had to be taken to keep it musically alive. The youth's question, then, was in reality an inquiry into the condition of his grandfather's lungs, which grew more and more asthmatic. Notwithstanding, old Duncan MacPhail would not hear of giving up the dignity of being town piper to sink into the imagined indignity of being a mere shopkeeper.

"That's fine, Daddy," returned the youth. "Shall I finish with the porridge? I'm thinking you've had enough of hanging over the fire this morning."

"No, sir," answered Duncan. "I'm perfectly able to make ta parrich myself, my poy, Malcolm." And as he spoke Duncan lifted the pot from the fire and set it on its three legs on the table in the middle of the room, adding: "Tere, my man—tere's ta parrich!"

This settled, the two sat down to eat their breakfast; and no one would have discovered from the manner in which the old man helped himself nor from the look of his eyes that he was stone-blind. It came neither of old age nor disease—he had been born blind. His eyes, although large and wide, looked like those of a sleepwalker—open, but with a shut sense and their color was pale.

"Have you had enough, my son?" he said when he heard Malcolm lay down his spoon.

"Ay, plenty thank you, Daddy, and it were right well made," replied the lad.

As they rose from the table a small girl suddenly burst in and hastily said in a thoughtless screech, "Mister MacPhail, my mother wants some oil as soon as possible."

"Fery coot, my chilt. Put young Malcolm an' olt Tuncan hasn't said their prayers yet, and you know fery well tat I won't sell pefore prayers. Tell your mother I'll bring ta oil when I come to look at ta lamp."

The child ran off without response. Malcolm lifted the pot from the table and set it on the hearth, put the plates together and the spoons and set them on a chair, tilted the table and wiped it hearthward, and took down a Bible and laid it on the table. The old man sat down on a low chair by the chimney corner, took off his hat, closed his eyes, and murmured some almost inaudible words, then repeated in Gaelic the first line of the hundred and third Psalm—"O m'anam, beannich thusa nish—" and raised a tune of marvelous wail. No less strange was the singing than the tune—wild as the wind of his native desolation or as the sound of his own pipes. It seemed all but lawless, for the multitude of so-called grace notes hovering and fluttering endlessly around the center tone made it impossible to unravel from them the air of a known tune. It had the same kind of liquid uncertainty of sound which had hitherto made it impossible for Malcolm to learn more than a few common phrases of his grandfather's native speech.

Malcolm read a chapter of the Bible, plainly, after which they knelt together and the old man poured out a prayer, beginning in a low, scarcely
audible voice, which rose at length to a loud, modulated chant. Not a sentence, hardly a phrase, of the utterance did his grandson understand, nor
was there more than one inhabitant of the place who could have interpreted a word of it. It was commonly believed, however, that at least one
part of his devotions was invariably a prolonged petition for vengeance on
Campbell of Glenlyon, the main instrument in the massacre of Glencoe.[1]

Devotions past, Duncan said, "Give me my pipes, my poy," and reached
out his hands as eager to clutch the instrument as the miser is to finger his
gold. "Listen to me as I play, and you'll soon pe able to play too, dance or
coronach with ta pest piper petween Cape Wrath and the Mull o' Cantyre."

Duncan played tune after tune, until his breath failed him, and an exhausted grunt of a drone in the middle of a coronach, followed by an
abrupt pause, revealed the emptiness of both lungs and bag.

"Now, Malcolm," he said, offering the pipes to his grandson, "you play
tat after me." He had of course learned all by ear and could hardly have
been serious in requesting Malcolm to follow him through such a succession of musical mazes.

"I haven't the memory for that, Daddy. But Mr. Graham's been teaching
me flute music and maybe that'll help me a bit. Wouldn't you better be
taking Mistress Partan's oil, as you promised her?"

"Surely, my son. I should pe keepin' my promises."

He rose and, getting a small stone bottle and his stick from the corner
of the room, left the house to walk with unerring steps through the labyrinth
of the village, threading his way from passage to passage. His eyes, indeed
his whole face, seemed to possess an ethereal sense of touch, for he was
ever aware of the neighborhood and proximity of material objects nearby.

He was a strong figure to look upon in that lowland village, for he invariably wore the Highland dress. He had never had a pair of trousers on his
legs and was far from pleased that his grandson clothed himself in such
contemptible garments. He especially made the best of himself on Sundays
when he came out like an aged butterfly with his father's sporran purse in
front of him, his grandfather's dirk at his side, his great-grandfather's little
black-hafted knife stuck in the stocking of his right leg, and a huge round
brooch of brass on his left shoulder. In these adornments, he would walk
proudly to church, leaning on the arm of his grandson.

"The piper's considerably ill-off this morning," said one of the fishermen's
wives to a neighbor as the old man passed them, the fact being that he had
not yet recovered from his second revel in the pipes so soon after his morning's duty and was consequently coughing and more asthmatic than usual.

"I don't doubt he'll be slipping away some cold night," said the other. "It
sometimes sounds as though he's got no breath left."

"Ay, he does have to work at it, poor man. But it's extraordinary how he's

---

[1]See Appendix 1, page 227.

managed to live and bring up such a fine lad as that Malcolm of his."

"Well, providence has been kind to him. And, too, he's been a diligent creature—for a blind man, as you say, it's just extraordinary."

"Do you remember when he first came to the town, lass?"

"Ay, what could keep me from remembering that? It's not been all that long."

"Well, Malcolm, who's such a fine lad now, they tell me he wasn't much bigger than a small haddock then."

"But the old man was an old man even back then. Though it's no doubt he's grown much older since."

"A doctor's child the lad . . . at least, that's what they say."

"Ay, they say. But who knows? Duncan could never be gotten to open his mouth even a peep as to the father or mother of him, and so it may well be as they say. It's nigh twenty years now, I'm thinking, since he made his first appearance."

"Some folk say the old man's not really named MacPhail, and he must have come here in hiding for some rough business he was mixed up in somewhere else."

"I don't believe no such gossip about such a poor, harmless man. Someone who makes his own living, without eyes to guide him, can't be all that bad. God guide us! We have to answer for ourselves without passing judgment on anyone else."

"I was but telling you what folk told me," returned the other.

"Ay, ay, lass. I know that, for I certainly know there's plenty of folk around here to spread such things."

———

As soon as his grandfather left the house, Malcolm went out also, closing the door behind him and turning the key but leaving it in the lock. He ascended to the upper town and turned to look back for a few moments. The descent to the shore was so sudden that he could see nothing of the harbor or of the village he had left—nothing but the blue bay before him and the filmy mountains of Sutherlandshire in the distance to the left as the coastline gradually swung around northward. After gazing for a moment he turned and continued on his way, through Portlossie and out beyond through the fields. The morning was glorious, the larks jubilant, and the air filled with the sweet scents of cottage flowers. Across the fields came the occasional low of an ox and the distant sounds of children at play.

His road led him the direction of a few cottages lying in a hollow. Beside them rose a vision of trees bordered by an ivy-grown wall from amidst whose summits shot the spire of a church. These cottages were far more ancient than the houses of the town; and it was from one of them, rather larger than the rest which stood close by the churchyard gate, whence had come the noises of children. For this was the parish school and these cottages were all that remained of the old town of Portlossie, which had at one time stretched in a long, irregular street almost to the shore. The door of the school was partially opened, and flowing out from it was the gentle hum of the honeybees of learning. Malcolm walked in and had the whole of the busy scene at once before him. The place was like a barn, open from wall to wall and from floor to rafters to thatch, browned with the peat smoke of vanished winters. The children were seated at their desks toward the back half of the large room, and toward the front sat only the master's desk.

Alexander Graham, the schoolmaster, descended from his desk and met and welcomed Malcolm with a kind shake of the hand. He was a man of middle height, very thin, and about forty-five years of age. He looked older, however, because of his thin gray hair and slightly stooping shoulders. He was dressed in a rather shabby black tailcoat and clean white shirt. The rest of his attire was noticeably gray and shabby also. The quiet sweetness of his smile yielded a look of composed submission. This was attributed by some townsfolk to his disappointment at still being but a schoolmaster whose aim, they thought, was a pulpit and a parish. But Mr. Graham had been released from such an ambition years earlier, if indeed it had ever possessed him, and had for many years been more than content to give himself to the hopeful task of training children for the true ends of life. He lived the quietest of studious lives, with an old housekeeper.

Malcolm had been a favorite pupil and the relation of master and scholar did not cease even when Malcolm saw that he ought to do something to lighten the burden of his grandfather and so left the school to live the life of a fisherman.

"I've had an invitation to Miss Campbell's funeral—Miss Horn's cousin, you know," said Mr. Graham in a subdued voice. "Could you manage to take the school for me, Malcolm?"

"Yes, sir. There's nothing to keep me from it. What day's the funeral?"

"Saturday."

"Very well, sir. I'll be here plenty early."

This matter settled, the business of school began again, in which, as he often did, Malcolm had come to assist. Only a pupil of his own could have worked with Mr. Graham, for his mode was peculiar. He would never contradict anything but would oppose error only by teaching truth. He presented truth and set it face-to-face with error in the minds of his students, leaving the two sides and the growing intellect, heart and conscience to fight the matter out. To him the business of the teacher was to rouse and urge this battle by leading fresh forces of truth onto the field.

Toward noon, while he was busy with an astronomy lesson, explaining partly with the blackboard and partly with two boys representing the relation of the earth and moon in front of the class, the door gently opened and the troubled face of the mad laird peeped slowly in. His body followed as gently and at last his hump appeared. Taking off his hat, he walked up to Mr. Graham, touched him on the arm, and standing tiptoe, whispered softly in his ear as if it were some painful secret, "I dinna ken whaur I come from. I want to come to the school."

Mr. Graham turned and shook hands with him, respectfully addressing him as Mr. Stewart, and got down for him the armchair which stood behind his desk. But with the politest bow the laird declined it and, mournfully repeating the words, "I dinna ken whaur I come from," took a place among the other students surrounding the astronomically symbolic boys.

This was not his first appearance there, for every now and then he was seized with a desire to go to school, plainly with the object of finding out where he came from. This always fell in his quieter times, and for days at a time he would attend regularly. He spoke so little, however, that it was impossible to tell how much he understood, although he seemed to enjoy all that went on. He was so quiet, so sadly gentle, that he gave no trouble of any sort; and, after the first few minutes of a fresh appearance, the attention of the scholars was rarely distracted by his presence.

The way in which the master treated him awoke like respect in his pupils. Boys and girls were equally ready to make room for him, and anyone who managed by some kind attention to awake the watery glint of a smile on the melancholy features of the troubled man would boast of their success. The peculiar sentence the laird uttered was the only one he invariably spoke with definite clarity. In most other attempts at speech he was liable to be assailed by a recurring impediment during which he could get out but one word here and a word there and therefore often betook himself to the most extravagant of gestures to supplement his words.

Mr. Stewart remained in the school all the morning, taking full part with the students in all they did, and sitting perfectly still except that he murmured to himself now and then, "I dinna ken whaur I come from."

When at noon the pupils dispersed for dinner, Mr. Graham invited him to go to his house to share his homely meal; but with polished gestures and broken speech, Mr. Stewart declined, walked away toward the town, and was seen no more that afternoon.

5

• • • • • • • • • • • • • • • • • •

The Cannon

Mrs. Courthope, the housekeeper at Lossie House, was a good woman who did not lord it over her acquaintances because of her position, as small rulers are apt to do, but cultivated friendly relations with the people of the sea-town. Some of the rougher women took pleasure in finding flaws in her and despised the sweet outlandish speech she had brought north with her from England. But she was not the less in their eyes a great lady, for to them she was representative of the noble family on whose lands they and their ancestors had been settled for ages, the last marquis not having even visited the place for many years, and the present one having done so only lately.

Duncan MacPhail was a favorite with her, and she seldom visited the Seaton without looking in on him. So that when Malcolm returned from the

Alton, or Old Town, where the school was, it did not in the least surprise him to find her seated there with his grandfather. Apparently, however, there had been some dissension between them, for the old man sat in his corner strangely wrathful, his face in a glow, his nostrils distended, and his eyelids working as if they were trying to speak.

"We are told in the New Testament to forgive our enemies, you know," said Mrs. Courthope, heedless of Malcolm's entrance.

"Inteed, I will not pe false to my shief and my clan," retorted Duncan persistently. "I will *not* forgife Cawmil of Clenlyon!"

"But he's been dead a long while, and we may at least hope he repented and was forgiven."

"I'll pe hoping nothing of the kind, Mistress Kertope," retorted Duncan. "But if, as you say, God will pe forgifing him—which I do not pelief—let tat pe enough for ta greedy plackguard. For it will matter little whether poor Tuncan MacPhail will pe forgifing him. Anyhow, he must do without it, for he shall not haf it. He is a fillain and a scounrel, and so I say, with my respects to you, Mistress Kertope."

His sightless eyes flashed with indignation; and perceiving it was time to change the subject, the housekeeper turned to Malcolm.

"Could you bring me a nice mackerel or whiting for my lord's breakfast tomorrow morning, Malcolm?" she asked.

"Certainly, mem. I'll bring it to you bright and early, the best the sea'll give me," he answered.

"If I have the fish by nine o'clock, that will be early enough," she answered.

"I wouldn't like to wait so long for my breakfast," remarked Malcolm.

"You wouldn't mind it so much if you waited asleep," said Mrs. Courthope.

"Who could sleep until such a time of day as that?" exclaimed the youth.

"You must remember, my lord doesn't go to bed for hours after you, Malcolm."

"And what can keep him up so late?"

"Oh, he reads and writes and sometimes goes walking about the grounds after everyone else is in bed," said Mrs. Courthope, "he and his dog."

"Well, I would rather be up. I so like to be up and out in the quiet of the morning before the sun's up to get the day going." Malcolm continued on at some length with such thoughts in the hope of affording time for the stormy waters of Duncan's spirit to assuage. Nor was he disappointed, for if there was a sound on the earth Duncan loved to hear, it was the voice of his boy. And by degrees the tempest sank to repose.

Mrs. Courthope had enough poetry in her to be pleased with Malcolm's quiet enthusiasm and spoke a kind word of sympathy to his views as she rose to take her leave. Duncan rose also and followed her to the door, making her a courtly bow.

"She's a coot woman, Mistress Kertope," he said as he came back, "and I'll not pe plaming her for forgifing Clenlyon, for he did not kill *her* creat-cran'mother. Put it's not coot to tell me I should pe forgifing ta rascal. Put she's a woman and she'll not pe knowing petter."

Then, changing the subject, he went on, "You'll pe minding you pe firing ta cun at six o'clock exactly, Malcolm. For all Mistress Kertope says, my lord, chust come home to his property, will want things chust as tey haf peen. And, inteed, I vonder why he hasn't peen sending for old Tuncan to pe gifing him a song or two on his pipes, for he must haf coot Highland plood in his own feins. So, mind you, fire ta cun at six, my son."

For some years, young as he was, Malcolm had hired himself to one or another of the boat proprietors of the Seaton or of Scaurnose for the herring fishing. He had thus earned enough to provide for the following winter so that his grandfather's little income as piper and other small returns were able to accumulate (in various concealments about the cottage) for the future. Until the herring season should arrive, however, Malcolm made a little money by line-fishing. He had bargained the year before with the captain of a schooner for an old ship's boat and had patched and caulked it into a sufficiently serviceable condition. He sold his fish in the town and immediate neighborhood where a good many housekeepers favored the handsome and cheery young fisherman.

As a result he would now often be out in the bay long before it was even time to wake his grandfather, in his turn to rouse the sleepers of Portlossie. But the old man still always waked about the right time, and no one yet had any complaint. Duncan was the cock which woke the whole yard; morning after morning his pipes went crowing through the streets of the upper region until the sound of the gun-signal.

When Malcolm meant to go fishing, he always loaded the swivel the night before; and about sunset the same evening he set out for that purpose. Not a creature was visible on the border of the curving bay except a few boys far off on the gleaming sands whence the tide had just receded: they were digging for sand eels. But on the summit of the long sand-hill the lonely figure of a man was walking to and fro in the level light of the rosy west. As Malcolm climbed the near end of the dune, the man was turning back at the far end. Halfway between them was the embrasure with the brass swivel, and there they met.

Although he had never seen him before, Malcolm perceived at once it must be Lord Lossie, and lifted his hat. The marquis nodded and passed on, but the next moment, hearing the noise of Malcolm's proceedings with the swivel, turned and said, "What are you about there with that gun, my lad?"

"I'm going to clean her out and load her, my lord," answered Malcolm.

"And what next? You're not going to fire the thing?"

"Ay, tomorrow morning, my lord."

"What will that be for?"

"Oh, just to wake your lordship."

"Hmm," said his lordship, with more expression than articulation.

"Shall I not load her?" asked Malcolm, throwing down the ramrod and approaching the swivel as if to turn the muzzle of it again into the embrasure.

"Oh, yes! Load her by all means. I don't want to interfere with any of your customs."

There was something in Malcolm's address that pleased Lord Lossie—the mingling of respect and humor, probably, the frankness and composure, perhaps. He was not self-conscious enough to be shy and was so free from design of any sort that he doubted the good will of no one.

"What's your name?" asked the marquis abruptly.

"Malcolm MacPhail, my lord."

"MacPhail? I heard that name this very day . . . Let me see—"

"My grandfather's the blind piper, my lord."

"Yes, yes. Tell him I shall want him at the House. I left my own piper at Ceanglas."

"I'll bring him with me in the morning if you like, my lord, for I'll be over with some fine trout tomorrow morning. Mistress Courthope said she's going to fry one for your lordship's breakfast. But maybe that'll be too early for you to see him."

"I'll send for him when I want him. Go on with your brazen serpent there, only, mind you, don't give her too much supper," said the marquis as he turned and resumed his walk.

Malcolm lifted his hat and again bent to the swivel.

The next morning he was rowing slowly along in the bay when he was startled by the sound of his grandfather's pipes, wafting clear and shrill on the breath of a southern wind from the top of the town. He looked at his watch; it was not yet five o'clock! The expectations of a summons to play at Lossie House had so excited the old man's brain that he had waked long before the usual time, and Portlossie must wake also. The worst of it was that he had already, as Malcolm knew from the direction of the sound, almost reached the end of his beat and must even now be expecting the report of the swivel. Until he heard it he would not cease playing, so long as there was breath in his body. Pulling, therefore, with all his might Malcolm soon ran his boat ashore and in another instant the sharp yell of the swivel rang among the rocks of the promontory. He was still standing watching the smoke flying seaward when a voice, already well known to him, said close at his side:

"What *are* you about with that horrid cannon?"

Malcolm started. "You scared me, my lady!" he returned with a smile and a bow.

"You told me," the girl went on emphatically, "that you fired at six o'clock. It is not nearly six."

"Didn't you hear the pipes, my lady?" he rejoined.

"Yes, well enough. But a whole regiment of pipes can't make it six o'clock when my watch says it's not yet five."

Thus compelled, Malcolm had to explain that the motive lay in his anxiety lest his grandfather should over-exert himself seeing he was subject to severe attacks of asthma.

"He should stop when he is tired," she objected.

"Ay, if his pride would let him," answered Malcolm and turned back toward the beach, anxious to draw the fishing line he had so hurriedly left.

"Have you a boat of your own?" asked the lady.

"Ay, that's her down yonder in the water. Would you like a row? She's nice and quiet."

"Who? The boat?"

"The sea, my lady."

"Is your boat clean?"

"Of everything but fish. But no, it's not fit for such a pretty dress as that. I wouldn't let you go today, my lady. But if you like, be here tomorrow morning. I'll be here at this same hour and have my boat as clean as a Sunday suit."

"You think more of my dress than you do of me," she returned.

"There's no fear of yourself, my lady. You're well enough made not to spoil. But I wouldn't want to think of the dress after only an hour in the boat with the fish jumping about. But indeed, I must go; I must say good morning, mem."

"By all means. I don't want to keep you from your precious fish."

Feeling rebuked without knowing why, Malcolm accepted the dismissal and ran to his boat. By the time he had taken his oars, the girl had vanished.

His line was short, but twice the number of fish he wanted were already dangling from the hooks. It was still very early when he reached the harbor. At home he found his grandfather waiting for him and his breakfast ready.

It was hard to convince Duncan that he had waked the royal burgh a whole hour too soon. He insisted that, as he had never made such a blunder before, he could not have made it now.

"It's ta watch 'at'll be telling ta lies, Malcolm, my poy," he said.

"But the sun says the same as the watch, Daddy," persisted Malcolm.

Duncan understood the position of the sun and what it signified as well as the clearest-eyed man in Portlossie, but he could not afford to yield.

"It was some conspeeracy of ta cursit Cawmils, to make me lose my poor pension," he said. "Put never mind, Malcolm. I'll make up for it tomorrow mornin'. Ta coot peoples shall haf teir sleep a whole hour later tan usual."

6

· · · · · · · · · · · · · · · · · · ·

The Salmon Trout

*M*alcolm walked up through the town with his fish, hoping to part with some of the less desirable of them and so lighten his basket before entering the grounds of Lossie House. But he had met with little success and was now approaching the town gate, as they called it, which closed a short street at right angles to the principal one, when he came upon Mrs. Catanach— on her knees cleaning her doorstep.

"Well, Malcolm, what sort of fish do you have?" she said without looking up.

"How did you know it was me, Mistress Catanach?" asked the lad.

"Know it was you?" she repeated. "If there be but two feet at once in any street of Portlossie, I'll tell you whose head is above them with my eyes closed."

"Hoot! You're a witch, Mistress Catanach," said Malcolm merrily.

"That's as may be," she returned, rising and nodding mysteriously. "I've told you no more than the truth. But what made you blast us all out of our beds at five o'clock in the morning today? That's not what you're paid for."

"Indeed, mem, it was just a mistake of my poor daddy's. He had been afraid of sleeping too long, you see, and woke up too soon. I was out fishing myself."

"But you fired the gun before the stroke of five."

"Ay, I fired the gun. The poor man would have burst himself if I hadn't."

"The devil'd have had him if he had burst himself—the old Highland beggar!" exclaimed Mrs. Catanach spitefully.

"You shouldn't even think such words about my grandfather, Mrs. Catanach," said Malcolm with rebuke.

She laughed a strange laugh.

"*Shouldn't!*" she repeated contemptuously. "And who's your grandfather that I should take heed of what I say about his righteousness?"

Then with a sudden change of her tone to one of would-be friend-liness—"But what'll you be asking for that little salmon trout, man?" she said.

As she spoke she approached the basket and would have taken the fish in her hands, but Malcolm involuntarily drew back.

"It's going to the House for my lord's breakfast," he said.

"Hoots! Just leave the trout with me. You'll be asking sixpence for it, I reckon," she persisted, again approaching the basket.

"I tell you, Mistress Catanach," said Malcolm, drawing back now in the fear that if she once had it, she would not yield it again, "it's going up to the House."

"Hoots! There's nobody there that's seen it yet."

"But Mistress Courthope was down last night and wanted the best I could hook."

"Mistress Courthope! Who cares for her? The affected old woman! Give me the trout, Malcolm. You're a good lad and you'll be the better for it."

"Indeed, I couldn't do it, Mistress Catanach—though I'm sorry not to be able to help you. But I committed myself, you see. But there's a fine haddock, and a nice small cod, and a gray gurnard."

"You'll leave the trout with me," said Mrs. Catanach imperiously.

"No, I can't do that. You must see yourself, I can't."

The woman's face grew dark with anger.

"It'll be the worse for you!" she cried.

"I'm not going to be frightened. You're not such a witch as that," said Malcolm, irritated by her persistency, threats and evil looks.

"Don't push me too far, Malcolm," she returned, her pasty cheeks now red as fire, and her wicked eyes flashing as she shook her clenched fist at him.

"And why not?" he answered coolly, turning his head back over his shoulder, for he was already on his way to the gate.

"You misbegotten foundling!" shrieked the woman and waddled hastily into the house.

"What ails her?" said Malcolm to himself. "She had to have seen that I was bound to give Mrs. Courthope the first offer."

By a winding carriage-drive, through trees whose growth was stunted by the sea winds, Malcolm made a slow descent. The air was full of sweet odors on the ascending dew and trembled with a hundred songs at once, for here was a very paradise for birds. At length he came in sight of a long, low wing of the house, and went to the door that led to the kitchen. There a maid informed him that Mrs. Courthope was in the hall and he had better take his basket there, for she wanted to see him.

The house was ancient, mainly of two sides at right angles, but with many gables, mostly having corbel-steps—a genuine Scottish dwelling, small windowed and gray, with steep slated roofs and many turrets, each with a conical top. Carved around some of the windows in ancient characters were scripture texts and antique proverbs. The oldest part of it was said at one time to have been a monastery. In front was a great gravel-space, in the center of which lay a huge block of serpentine from a quarry on the estate, being the pivot, as it were, around which all carriages turned.

On one side of the house was a great stone bridge stretching across a little glen in which ran a brown stream spotted with foam—the same that entered the firth beside the Seaton. It was not muddy, for though it was dark it was clear—its brown being a rich transparent hue gathered from the peat bogs of the great moorland hill behind. Only a very narrow terrace-walk with battlemented parapet lay between the back of the house and a precipitous descent of a hundred feet to this rivulet.

The hall door stood open and just within hovered Mrs. Courthope, dusting certain precious things not to be handled by a housemaid.

"Good morning, Malcolm," she said. "What have you brought me?"

"A fine salmon trout, mem. And if you only could have heard how Mistress Catanach scolded me 'cause I wouldn't give it to her! At first she was almost flattering, but when I wouldn't yield, in no time she was yelling and cursing me."

"She's a peculiar person, Malcolm. Those are nice whitings. I don't really care about the trout. Just take it back to her as you go."

"I doubt she'll take it, mem. She's an awful vengeful creature, folk say."

"That reminds me, Malcolm," returned Mrs. Courthope, "that I am not at all at ease about your grandfather. He is not in a Christian frame of mind at all—and he is an old man too. If we don't forgive our enemies, you know, the Bible plainly tells us we shall not be forgiven ourselves."

"I'm thinking it was Someone even greater than the Bible who said that, mem," returned Malcolm who was an apt pupil of Mr. Graham. "But you're no doubt referring to Campbell of Glenlyon," he went on with a smile. "It can't matter that much to him whether my grandfather forgives him or not, seeing as how he's been dead now for a hundred years."

"It's not Campbell of Glenlyon; it's your grandfather I'm anxious about," said Mrs. Courthope. "Nor is it only Campbell of Glenlyon; he's equally fierce against all his clan and posterity as well!"

"They don't even exist, mem. There's not even such a person on the face of the earth as a descendant of *that* Glenlyon."

"It makes little difference, I fear," said Mrs. Courthope, who was a skilled logician. "The question isn't whether or not there's anybody to forgive, but whether Duncan MacPhail is willing to forgive."

"That I do believe he is, mem. Though he would be as astonished to hear me say it as you are yourself."

"I don't know what you mean by that, Malcolm."

"I mean, mem, that a blind man, like my grandfather, can't know himself really rightly because he can't know other folk right. It's partly by knowing others that you come to know yourself, mem—isn't it, now?"

"Blindness surely doesn't prevent a man from knowing other people. He hears them and he feels them and indeed has generally more kindness from them because of his affliction."

"From some of them, mem. But it's little kindness my grandfather has experienced from Campbell of Glenlyon, mem."

"And just as little injury, I should suppose," said Mrs. Courthope.

"You're wrong there, mem. A murdered great-grandmother is certainly a great injury. But even supposing you are right, what I say is still to the point. But I must explain just a bit. When I was a young laddie at the school, I once heard that a certain boy was mocking my grandfather. When I heard that I thought I could have just cut the heart out of him and sunk my teeth right into it. But when I finally found him and got a grip of him, and the rascal turned up a frightened dog-face to me, I just couldn't drive my clenched fist into it. Mem, a face is an awful thing! There's something look-

ing out from inside that just prevents you from doing what you might otherwise like to it. But my grandfather's never seen a face in his life—let alone
Glenlyon's that's been dead for so many a year. If he were looking into the
face, even of that Glenlyon, I do believe he would no more drive his knife
into him—"

"Drive his knife into him!" echoed Mrs. Courthope in horror.

"No, I'm sure he wouldn't," persisted Malcolm. "And one thing I am certain of—that by the time he meets Glenlyon in heaven, he'll not be that far
from letting bygones be bygones."

"Meets Glenlyon in heaven!" again echoed Mrs. Courthope, who knew
enough of the story of the massacre to be startled at the taken-for-granted
way in which Malcolm spoke. "Is it probable that a wretch such as your
legends describe him should ever get there?"

"Don't you think God's forgiven him then, mem?"

"I have no right to judge Glenlyon, or any other man. But as you ask me,
I must say I see no likelihood of it."

"How can you complain about my poor blind grandfather for not forgiving him then?—I have you there, mem!"

"He *may* have repented, you know," said Mrs. Courthope feebly, finding
herself in less room than was comfortable.

"In such a case," returned Malcolm, "the old man will hear about it the
minute he gets there, and I've no doubt he'll do his best to persuade himself."

"But what if he shouldn't get there?" persisted Mrs. Courthope in pure
benevolence.

"Hoot, mem! I wonder to hear you. A Campbell let in and my grandfather kept out! No, things go another way up there. My grandfather's a good
man even though he does look at things more in line with the Law than the
Gospel."

Apparently Mrs. Courthope had at length come to the conclusion that
Malcolm was as much of a heathen as his grandfather, for in silence she
chose her fish, in silence paid him his price, and then with only a sad
"Good-day," turned and left him.

He would have gone back by the riverside to the sea; but Mrs. Courthope
having waived her right to the fish, he felt bound to give Mrs. Catanach
another chance. So he returned the way he had come.

"Here's your trout, Mistress Catanach," he called aloud at her door,
which generally stood a little ajar. "You can have it for the sixpence, and a
good bargain it is too, for its size."

As he spoke he held the fish in the door, but his eyes were turned to the
main street where the factor's gig was at that moment rounding the corner.
Suddenly the salmon trout was snatched from his hand and flung so violently in his face that he staggered back into the road. The factor had to pull
sharply up to avoid driving over him. From the house came a burst of insulting laughter and, at the same moment, out of the house rushed a large, vile-
looking mongrel with hair like an ill-used doormat and an abbreviated nose.
He caught up the trout and rushed with it toward the gate.

"That's right, my child!" shouted Mrs. Catanach to the brute as he ran, "Take it to Mrs. Courthope! Take it back to her with my compliments."

Amidst a burst of malign laughter, she slammed the door and from a side window watched the young fisherman.

As he stood looking after the dog in wrath and bewilderment, the factor, having recovered from the fit of merriment into which the sudden explosion of events had cast him and having succeeded in quieting his scared horse, said as he slackened his reins to move on, "You sell your fish too cheap, Malcolm."

"The devil's in that dog," rejoined Malcolm. And, finally, seized at last by a sense of the ludicrousness of the whole affair, burst out laughing and turned to go.

"No, no, laddie. The devil's not away in such a hurry. He remained behind at the house," said a voice behind him.

Malcolm turned again and lifted his hat. It was Miss Horn who had come up from the Seaton.

"Did you see all that, mem?" he asked.

"Ay, I saw it all as I came up the street. But don't just stand there. She'll be watching you still, like a cat watching a mouse. I know her! She's a cat-woman and I can't abide her. She's not safe. She's up to no good with her evil and her secrets. Come with me. I want a small fish. I can't eat with her lying dead in the house. But I must get some strength in me before the burial. It's God's mercy I was made with no feelings, or what would have become of me! But what's the good of grieving? It's not worth the salt in the water, Malcolm. It's an evil world. Yet it might be a good one if it weren't for evil men."

"I'm thinking more about evil women at this moment, mem," said Malcolm. "Maybe there's no such thing. But yonder's certainly an awful lot like one. As beautiful a salmon trout as you ever saw, mem! It's all I'm able to do to keep from cursing that foul dog of hers!"

"Hoot, laddie! Hold your tongue."

"I will. I'm not going to do it, you know. But such a fine trout as that— the very one that you would have liked, mem."

"Never mind the trout. There's more where that came from. What made her angry at you?"

"Nothing more than that I was obligated to give Mistress Courthope the first choice of my fish."

"The woman's not even worth your notice, except to stay out of her way, laddie. And that you'd better do. Don't you anger her again if you can help it. She has an evil look and I simply can't abide her. Here, there's your money. Jean, take in this fish."

During the latter part of the conversation they had arrived at Miss Horn's and had been standing at the door while Miss Horn ferreted the needed pence from a pocket under her gown. She now entered, but as Malcolm waited for Jean to take the fish, she turned on the threshold and said, "Would you like to see her, Malcolm?— A good friend she was to you, so long as she was here," she added after a short pause.

The youth hesitated. "I never saw a corpse in my life, mem—and I'm just a little afraid," he said after another brief silence.

"Hoot, laddie!" returned Miss Horn in a somewhat offended tone. "That's what comes of having feelings. A nice corpse is the most beautiful thing in creation—and so quiet! You ought to see a corpse, Malcolm. You'll have to do it before you're one yourself. And you'll never see a prettier one than my Grizel."

"If you insist, mem," said Malcolm resignedly.

At once she led the way and he followed in silence up the stair and into the dead chamber.

There on the white bed lay the long, black, misshapen coffin, and, with a strange sinking at the heart, Malcolm approached it.

Miss Horn's hand came from behind and withdrew a covering. There she lay, awful, yet with a look of entreaty that strangely drew the heart of Malcolm. The tears gathered in his eyes, and Miss Horn saw them.

"You must lay your hand upon her, Malcolm," she said. "You should touch the dead to keep you from dreaming about them."

"I couldn't," answered Malcolm. "And besides," he went on, "she would be too pretty a dream to miss. Are they all like that?" he added, speaking under his breath, "so beautiful?"

"No, indeed," replied Miss Horn with mild indignation. "Would you expect Bawby Catanach to look like that? No—I beg your pardon for mentioning the woman, my dear," she added with a sudden divergence, bending toward the still face and speaking in a tenderly apologetic tone. "I know well that you can't stand the very name of her, but it'll be the last time you'll hear it till eternity, my dear." Then turning again to Malcolm—"Lay your hand upon her, I tell you," she said.

"I dare not," replied the youth, still under his breath, "my hands are not clean. I wouldn't touch her with fishy hands for all the world."

The same moment, moved by a sudden impulse whose irresistibleness was veiled in his unconsciousness, he bent down and put his lips to the forehead.

As suddenly he started back erect, dismay on every feature.

"Eh, mem!" he cried in an agonized whisper. "She's so cold!"

"What should she be?" retorted Miss Horn. "Would you have her buried warm?"

He followed her from the room in silence, with the sense of a faint sting on his lips. She led him into the parlor and gave him a glass of wine.

"You'll come to the burial on Saturday?" she asked, half inviting, half inquiring.

"I'm sorry to say, mem, but I can't," he answered. "I promised Mr. Graham to take the school for him, to let him go."

"Well, well, Mister Graham's obliged to you, no doubt, and we can't help it. Give my regards to your grandfather," she said.

"I'll do that, mem. And he'll be pleased, for he's awful grateful for any such attention," said Malcolm, and with the words took his leave.

7

·····················

The Funeral

*T*hat night the weather changed and grew cloudy and cold. Saturday morning came with a dismal drizzle and a cold northern wind. All was gray—enduring, hopeless gray. Along the coast the waves roared on the sands, persistent and fateful.

In spite of the drizzle and the fog blown in shreds from the sea, a large number of the most respectable of the male population of the burgh, clothed in Sunday gloom, made their way to Miss Horn's, for despite her rough manners she was held in high repute. If she spoke loud, she never spoke false or gossiped in the dark. What was chiefly responsible for the respect in which she was held, however, was that she was one of their own, her father, minister of the parish, having died some twenty years before. Comparatively little was known of her deceased cousin, who had been much of an invalid and had mostly kept to the house. But all understood that Miss Horn was greatly attached to her, and it was for the sake of the living mainly that the dead was thus honored.

As the prayer drew to a close, the sounds of trampling and scuffling feet bore witness that the undertaker, Watty Witherspail, and his assistants were carrying the coffin down the stair. Soon the company rose to follow it and, trooping out, arranged themselves behind the hearse, which, horrid with nodding plumes and gold and black paneling, drew away from the door to make room for them.

Just as they were about to move off, to the amazement of the company and the few onlookers, Miss Horn herself, solitary in a long black cloak and black bonnet, came out and made her way through the mourners until she stood immediately behind the hearse, by the side of Mr. Cairns, the parish minister. The next moment, Watty Witherspail addressed her in half-whispering tones of expostulation,

"You're not thinking of going yourself, mem?" he said.

"And why not, Watty, I would like to know?" growled Miss Horn from the vaulted depths of her bonnet.

"The like was never heard tell of!" returned Watty, with the dismay of an orthodox undertaker, righteously jealous of all innovation.

"Well, it'll be told of from now on," rejoined Miss Horn, who in her rising anger spoke aloud, caring nothing about who heard her. "Do you think that I've been a mother to the poor young thing for so many years only to let her go away at last with the likes of you and your company?"

"Hoot, mem! There's the minister beside you."

"I tell you, you're but a bunch of rough menfolk. There's not a woman among you to keep things decent, except I go myself. I'm not begging the minister's pardon either. *I'll go.* I *must* see my poor Grizel to her final bed."

"I dread that it might be too much for your feelings, Miss Horn," said the minister who, being an ambitious young man of lowly origin and very shy of the ridiculous, did not in the least wish her company.

"Feelin's!" exclaimed Miss Horn in a tone of indignant repudiation. "I'm going to do what's right. I'm *going*, and if you don't like my company, Mr. Cairns, you can go home and I'll go without you. If she should happen to be looking down, she should see me with her to the end."

And before the minister could utter another syllable, she had left her place to go to the rear. The same instant the procession began to move toward the grave and, stepping aside, she stood erect, sternly eyeing the irregular ranks of two, three and four as they passed her, intending to bring up the rear alone. But there was already one in that solitary position, with bowed head—Alexander Graham walked last and single. The moment he caught sight of Miss Horn, he perceived her design, and, lifting his hat, offered his arm. She took it almost eagerly, and together they followed in silence, through the gusty wind and monotonous drizzle.

The schoolhouse was close to the churchyard. An instant hush fell upon the scholars when the hearse darkened the windows, lasting while the horrible thing slowly turned to enter the iron gates. The mad laird, who had been present all the morning, trembled from head to foot, yet rose and went to the door with a look of strange, subdued eagerness. When Miss Horn and Mr. Graham had passed into the churchyard, he followed.

With the bending of uncovered heads in a final gaze of leave-taking over the coffin at rest in the bottom of the grave, the ceremony of burial was fulfilled. Though the wind blew and the rain fell, no one left the churchyard until the mound of sheltering earth was heaped high over the dead by the hands of many friends assisting with the spade and shovel.

As soon as the labor was ended, Mr. Graham again offered his arm to Miss Horn, who had stood in perfect calmness watching the whole with her eagle eyes. But though she accepted his offer, instead of moving toward the gate she kept her position in the attitude of a hostess who will follow her friends. When they reached the schoolhouse she would have had Mr. Graham leave her, but he insisted on seeing her home. Contrary to her habit, she yielded and they slowly followed the retiring company.

"Safe at last," sighed Miss Horn as they entered the town—her sole remark on the way.

Rounding a corner, they came upon Mrs. Catanach standing at a neighbor's door, gazing out upon nothing as was her habit at times, but talking to someone in the house behind her. Miss Horn turned her head aside as she passed. A look of low, malicious, half-triumphant cunning lightened across the puffy face of the "howdy." She cocked one busy eyebrow, setting one eye wide open, drew down the other eyebrow, nearly closing the eye under it, and stood looking after them thus until they were out of sight. Then turning her head over her shoulder, she burst into a laugh, soft and husky with the general flabbiness of her corporeal conditions.

"What a couple the two of them make!" she said and burst again into gelatinous laughter.

As soon as the churchyard was clear of the funeral train, the mad laird peeped from behind a tall stone, gazed cautiously around him, and then with slow steps came and stood over the new-made grave where the sexton was now laying the turf to make it look trim for the Sabbath.

"Whaur is she gone to?" he murmured to himself. He could generally speak better when merely uttering his thoughts without any attempt at communication. "I dinna ken whaur I come from, and I dinna ken whaur she's gone to. But when I go mysel', maybe I'll ken both. I dinna ken . . . I dinna ken whaur I come from."

Thus muttering, so lost in the thoughts that originated them that he spoke the words mechanically, he left the churchyard and returned to the school.

The next day, after services and a lazy Sabbath afternoon, Malcolm again made his way in the evening to the Alton to visit Mr. Graham. Malcolm found his friend seated on a stone in the churchyard.

"See," said the schoolmaster, "how the shadow from one grave stretches like an arm to embrace another. In this light the churchyard seems the very birthplace of shadows." A brief silence followed. "Does the morning or evening light suit such a place best, Malcolm?"

The pupil thought for a while.

"The evening light, sir," he answered at length, "for you see the sun's dying like, and death's like falling asleep, and the grave's the bed and the sod is the bedclothes, and there's a long night ahead."

"Are you sure of that, Malcolm?"

"It's the way most folk sees it, sir."

"Come here, Malcolm," said Mr. Graham, and took him by the arm and led him toward the east end of the yard.

"Read that," he said, pointing to a flat gravestone covered with moss, but the inscription nevertheless stood out clearly: "He is not here; he is risen."

While Malcolm gazed, trying to think what his master would have him think, Mr. Graham resumed: "If he is risen—if the sun is up, Malcolm—then the morning and not the evening is the season for the place of the tombs; the morning when the shadows are shortening and separating, not the evening when they are growing all into one. I used to love the churchyard best in the evening, when the past was more to me than the future. But now I visit it almost every bright summer morning and only occasionally at night."

"But, sir, isn't death a dreadful thing?" asked Malcolm.

"That depends on whether a man regards it as his fate or as the will of a perfect God. Its obscurity is its dread. But if God be light, then death itself must be full of splendor—a splendor probably too keen for our eyes to receive."

"But there's the dying itself; isn't that fearsome? It's that I would be afraid of."

"I don't see why it should be. It's the lack of a God that makes it dreadful, and *you* would be greatly to blame for that, Malcolm, if you hadn't found your God by the time you had to die."

They were startled by a gruff voice near them. The speaker was hidden by a corner of the church.

"Well, she've covered now," it said. "But a grave never looks right without a stone, and her old cousin would hear of none being laid over her. I said it might be set up at her head where she should never feel the weight of it. But no, no, none for her."

It was Watty Witherspail who spoke, with a deep and rather harsh voice.

"And why wouldn't she have a stone?" returned the voice of Jonathan Aulbuird, the sexton. "No doubt it was the expense."

"How am I to tell why it was?"

"She was doubtless thinking that a stone would be too heavy for such a work-worn creature to lift when the trumpet is blown," said the sexton with a feeble laugh.

"Well, I don't doubt that my boxes are a little too well made for the use they're put to," responded Watty. "They shouldn't be that hard to open, though, if all is true that the minister says. You see, we don't know when that day will come, and there may not be time for the wet and worms to drive the boards apart."

"Hoots, man! It's not your long nails and screws that'll hold down the redeemed even if the judgment were tomorrow morning," said the sexton. "And for the rest, they would be glad enough to stay where they were. But they'll be coming out too, have no fear of that."

Malcolm and Mr. Graham listened silently to the sound of their retreating footsteps.

"How close together come the solemn and the grotesque, the ludicrous and the majestic," said the schoolmaster. "Here, to us lingering in awe about the doors beyond which lie the gulfs of the unknown—to our very side come the wright and the gravedigger with their talk of the strength of coffins and the judgment of the living God!"

"I'd been thinking to myself," said Malcolm, "that it is strange to have a woman like Mistress Catanach be the one who sits receiving little babies into this life, like the gatekeeper of the world. It doesn't promise too well for them that she lets in. And now here's Watty Witherspail and Jonathan Aulbuird as the porters to open and let all that's left of us back out again. Just think of such as them having such a hand in such solemn matters."

"Indeed, some of us do have strange porters," said Mr. Graham with a smile, "both to open for us and to close behind us. Yet even in them lies the human nature which, itself the embodiment of the unknown, wanders out through the gates of mystery, to wander back, it may be, in a manner not altogether unlike that by which it came."

In contemplative mood the schoolmaster spoke in a calm and lofty sustained style of book-English, which strangely contrasted with that in which Malcolm kept up his side of the dialogue.

"I hope, sir, that it'll be no sort of celestial Mistress Catanach that'll be waiting for me on the other side, or for my poor daddy who could hardly stand being tossed about on *her* knee."

Mr. Graham laughed outright.

"If there's one to act the part of the nurse," he answered, "I presume there will be one to take the mother's part too."

"But speaking of the grave, sir," pursued Malcolm, "I wish you could drop a word that might be of some comfort to my daddy. It's plain to me, from what he says, that instead of leaving the world behind him when he dies, he thinks he's going to lie all clammy and wet in the ground just trembling at the thought of the sudden, awful roar of the brazen trumpet of the archangel. I wish you would look in on him and say something to him some night. It would be no good mentioning it to the minister; he would hardly understand. And if you could just slide in a word about forgiving his enemies! I made light of the matter to Mistress Courthope because she only makes him worse. She does well with what the minister puts into her, but she has little of her own to mix up with it, and so what she says carries little weight with my grandfather. Only you mustn't let him think you called on purpose."

They walked about the churchyard until the sun went down in what Mr. Graham called the grave of his endless resurrection—the clouds on the one side bearing all the pomp of his funeral, the clouds on the other all the glory of his uprising. After the twilight was gone they once more seated themselves and talked and dreamed together of the life to come. There were also long periods of silence. For the master believed in solitude and silence. Say rather, he believed in God and he believed that when the human is still, the Divine speaks to it, because it is its own.

8

•••••••••••••••••••

The Marquis

The next morning rose as lovely as if the mantle of the departing resurrection day had fallen upon it. Malcolm rose with it, hastened to his boat and pulled out into the bay for an hour or two's fishing. When his watch bore witness that the hour was at hand, he rowed lustily to shore, fired the gun, rowed back to the Seaton, ate his breakfast, and set out to carry the best of his fish to the House.

The moment he turned the corner of her street, he saw Mrs. Catanach standing on her threshold. She seemed forever about the door, on the lookout at least, if not on the watch.

"What's in your basket today, Malcolm?" she asked with a peculiar smile which was not sweet enough to restore vanquished confidence.

"Nothing good for dogs," answered Malcolm and was walking past.

But she made a step forward and with a laugh said, "Let's see what's in it anyway. The doggie's away on his travels today."

"Indeed, Mistress Catanach," persisted Malcolm, "I can't say that I like to have my own fish flung in my face, nor to see an ill-fared tyke run away with it right before my eyes."

After the warning given him by Miss Horn and the strange influence her presence always seemed to have on his grandfather, Malcolm preferred keeping up a negative quarrel with the woman.

"Don't call names," she returned; "my dog wouldn't take well to being called an ill-fared tyke, or to have names flung in *his* face. Let's see what's in your basket, I say."

As she spoke she laid her hand on the basket, but Malcolm drew back and turned away toward the gate.

"Lord save us!" she cried with a yelling laugh. "You're not afraid of an old wife like me?"

"I don't know; maybe I am and maybe not—I won't say. But I don't want to have anything to do with you, mem."

"Malcolm MacPhail," said Mrs. Catanach, lowering her voice to a hoarse whisper while every trace of laughter vanished from her countenance, "you have had more to do with me than you know, and no doubt you'll have more yet than you can help. So speak your mind gently, my man."

"That may be," said Malcolm, "but it won't be with my will. And if I have any life left in me, I'll give you a fright."

"Hoots, man!" she said in rising temper, "go your way to Mistress Court-hope with a flea in your ear. I wish you luck—such luck as I would wish you!"

Her last words sounded so like a curse that Malcolm had to force a laugh to keep from being overcome by a creeping chill.

The cook at the House bought all his fish, for they had had none for the last few days because of the storm. As he was turning to go, he heard a tap on a window and saw Mrs. Courthope beckoning him to another door.

"His lordship desired me to send you to him, Malcolm, the next time you called," she said.

"Well, mem, here I am," answered the youth.

"You'll find him in the flower garden," she said. "He's up early today, for a wonder."

He left his basket at the top of the stairs that led down the rock to a level of the stream and walked up the valley to the garden. It was a curious old-fashioned place, with high hedges and close alleys of trees, where two might have wandered long without meeting, and it was some time before he found any hint of the presence of the marquis. At length, however, he heard voices and, following the sound, walked along one of the alleys till he came to a little arbor where he discovered the marquis seated and, to his surprise, beside him the white-robed lady he had twice met on the sand dunes. A great deerhound at his master's feet was bristling his mane and baring his teeth with a growl, but the girl had hold of his collar.

"Who are you?" asked the marquis rather gruffly, as if he had never seen him before.

"I beg your lordship's pardon," said Malcolm, "but they told me your lordship wanted to see me and sent me to the flower garden. Shall I go or stay?"

The marquis looked at him frowningly for a moment, and made no reply. But the frown gradually relaxed before Malcolm's modest but unflinching gaze and the shadow of a smile slowly took its place. He kept silent, however.

"Am I to go or stay, my lord?" repeated Malcolm.

"Can't you wait for an answer?"

"As long as your lordship likes. Shall I go and walk about, mem—my lady, till his lordship's made up his mind? Would that please him, do you think?" he said in the tone of one who seeks advice.

But the girl only smiled, and the marquis said, "Go to the devil."

"I must ask your lordship for the necessary directions," rejoined Malcolm.

"Your tongue's long enough to inquire as you go," said the marquis.

A reply in the same strain rushed to Malcolm's lips, but he checked himself in time and stood silent, with his hat in his hand. The marquis sat gazing as if he had nothing to say to him, but after a few moments the lady spoke—not to Malcolm, however.

"Is there any danger in boating here, Papa?" she said.

"No more, I dare say, than there ought to be," replied the marquis listlessly. "Why do you ask?"

"Because I should so like a row! I want to see how the shore looks to a mermaid."

"Well, I will take you some day if we can find a proper boat."

"Is yours a proper boat?" she asked, turning to Malcolm with a sparkle of fun in her eyes.

"That depends on my lord's definition of 'proper.' "

"Definition!" repeated the marquis.

"Is it too long a word, my lord?" asked Malcolm.

The marquis only smiled.

"I know what you mean. It's a strange word to come out of a fisherlad's mouth, you think. But why shouldn't a fisherlad have a smattering of logic, my lord. For Greek or Latin there's but little opportunity for exercise in these parts. But for logic, a fisherman can have a hand in that."

"Have you been to college?"

"No, my lord—which is a pity. But I've been to school ever since I can remember."

"Do they teach logic there?"

"A kind of it. Mr. Graham sets us to try our hand at it, just to make us quick and keen, you know."

"You don't mean you still go to school?"

"I don't go regular. But I go as often as Mr. Graham wants me to help him, and usually I learn something or another."

"So it's schoolmaster you are as well as fisherman? Two strings to your bow—who pays you for teaching?"

"Oh, nobody! Who would pay me for that?"

"Why, the schoolmaster."

"No, that would be an affront, my lord."

"How can you afford the time for nothing?"

"The time comes to little compared with what Mr. Graham gives me in the long evening—in the winter time, you know, my lord, when the sea's much too contemptuous to be meddling with."

"But you have your grandfather to support?"

"My grandfather wouldn't be pleased to hear you say it, my lord. He's terribly independent. And what with his pipes and his lamps and his shop, he could keep us both. It's not that much the likes of us needs. He won't let me go too far fishing, so that I have more time to read and go to Mr. Graham's."

As the youth spoke, the marquis eyed him with apparently growing interest.

"But you haven't told me whether your boat is a proper one," said the lady.

"Proper enough, mem, for what's required of her. She takes good fish."

"But is that a proper boat for me to have a row in?"

"Not with that dress on, mem, as I told you before."

"The water won't get in, will it?"

"Not more than's easily gotten out again."

"Do you ever put up a sail?"

"Sometimes a little lug-sail."

"Nonsense, Flory!" said the marquis. "I'll see about it." Then turning to Malcolm—

"You may go," he said. "When I want you I will send for you."

Malcolm thought to himself that the marquis had sent for him this time before he had wanted him; but he made his bow and departed—not without disappointment, for he had expected the marquis to say something about his grandfather going to the house with his pipes.

There was in Lord Lossie a true heart and a certain generosity which all the vice he had shared in had not completely quenched. Overbearing, he was not yet too overbearing to appreciate a manly carriage and had been pleased with what some would have considered the boorishness of Malcolm's behavior—such as could not perceive that it had the same source as the true aristocratic bearing, namely, a certain unselfish confidence which is the mother of dignity.

The marquis had been a spendthrift, hence he had never been out of financial difficulties. And so when a year or so ago he succeeded to his brother's marquisate, he was, despite his large income, too deeply in debt to hope for an immediate rescue. His new property, however, would afford him a refuge from troublesome creditors. And there too he might avoid expenditure for a while and perhaps rally the forces of a dissolute life. The place was not new to him, having some twenty years before spent nearly twelve months there, of which the recollections were on the whole pleasant. So here he was at Lossie House.

He was about fifty years of age, more worn than his years would account for, yet younger than his years in expression, for his conscience had never bitten him very deep. He was middle-sized, broad-shouldered but rather thin. He was fond of animals—he would sit for an hour stroking the head of Demon, his great Irish deerhound, but at other times would tease him to a wrath which touched on the verge of the dangerous. He was fond of practical jokes and would not hesitate to indulge himself even in those that were not in the least refined, the sort that had been in vogue in his merrier days; and Lord Lossie had ever been one of the most fertile in inventing and loudest in enjoying them. If he was easily enraged, he was readily appeased. He could drink a great deal but was no drunkard. His creed was that a God had probably made the world and set it going, but that He did not care a brass farthing, as he phrased it, how it went on or what such an insignificant being as a man did or left undone in it.

The mother of Florimel had died when she was a mere child, and from that time she had been at school until her father brought her away recently to Lossie House. She knew little, that little was not correct and, had it been, it would have yet been of small value. At school she had been under many laws and had felt their slavery. She was now in the third heaven of delight with her liberty.

Her father regarded her as a child, of whom it was enough to require that she should keep herself out of mischief. He said to himself now and then that he must find a governess for her; but as yet he had not begun to look for one. Meantime he neither exercised the needful authority over her nor treated her as a companion. His was of a shallow nature. With a lovely daughter by his side, he neither sought to search into her being nor to aid its unfolding but sat brooding over past pleasures lost in the dull flow of life. But, indeed, what could such a man have done for the education of a young girl? As a father he expected qualities in her which in other women he had never taken the slightest notice. And because of such he had done much toward destroying his right of claiming such from her.

So Lady Florimel was running wild, and enjoying it. As long as she made her appearance at meals and looked happy, her father gave himself no trouble about her. How he managed to live in those first days at Portlossie without company—what he thought about or speculated upon, it is hard to say. All he could be said to do was to ride over the estate with his steward, Mr. Crathie, knowing little and caring less about farming, or crops, or cattle. He had by this time, however, invited a few friends to visit him, and expected their arrival before long.

"How do you like this dull life, Flory?" he said as they walked up the garden to breakfast.

"Dull, Papa?" she returned. "You never were at a girls' school or you wouldn't call this dull. It is the merriest life in the world. To go where you like and have miles of room! And such room! It's the loveliest place in the world, Papa."

He smiled a small, satisfied smile and stopped to stroke his Demon.

Malcolm went down the riverside, not overly pleased with the marquis; for, though unconscious of it as such, he had a strong feeling of personal dignity. He arrived at his cottage and found Duncan seated in a corner with an apron over his knees occupied with a tin lamp. He had taken out the wick and had laid its flat tube on the hearth, had emptied the oil into a saucer, and was now rubbing the lamp vigorously to clean it.

Duncan had brought the germ of this ministry of light from his native Highlands, where he had practiced it in his own house, no one but himself being permitted to clean, fill or trim the lamp. He must have had some feeling of a call to the work; for he had not been a month in Portlossie before he had installed himself in several families as the genius of their lamps, and he gradually extended the relation until it comprehended almost all the houses of the village.

It was strange and touching to see the sightless man thus busy about light for others. A marvelous symbol of faith he was—he not only believed in sight but also in the mysterious and even unintelligible device by which others saw, which he had made his livelihood. Even when his grandchild was the merest baby he would nightly kindle the brightest and cleanest of train-oil lamps. The women who at first looked in to offer their services would marvel at the trio of blind man, babe and burning lamp, and some would expostulate with him on the needless waste. But neither would he listen to their words nor accept their offered assistance in dressing or undressing the child. The sole manner in which he would consent to accept their help was to leave the baby in charge of this or that neighbor while he went his rounds with the bagpipes. When he went lamp-cleaning, he always took Malcolm along.

He had certain days for visiting certain houses and cleaning the lamps in them. The housewives had at first granted him as a privilege the indulgence of his whim. But by and by when they found their lamps burned so much better from being properly attended to, they began to make him some small return. And at length it became the custom with every housewife who accepted his services to pay him a halfpenny a week during the winter months for cleaning her lamp. He never asked for it; if payment was omitted, never even hinted at it; received what was given him thankfully; and was regarded with kindness and, indeed, respect by all.

A small trade in oil arose from his connection with the lamps and was added to the list of his general dealings. The fisherfolk made their own oil, but sometimes it would run short; and then recourse was had at Duncan's little store, prepared by himself chiefly from the livers of fish caught by his grandson. With so many sources of income, no one wondered at his getting on.

9

·····················

The Storm

*L*ooking at Malcolm's life from the point of his own consciousness, it was pleasant enough. Innocence, devotion to another, health, pleasant labor, love of reading, leisure, a lofty-minded friend—bathed in such conditions and influences, the youth's heart was swelling like a rosebud ready to burst into blossom.

But he had never yet felt the immediate presence of a close relationship with a woman. He had never known mother or sister, and although his voice always assumed a different tone and his manner grew more gentle in the presence of a woman, he had found little individually attractive among the fisher-girls. There was not much in their circumstances to bring out the finer influences of womankind in them; they had rough usage, hard work at the curing and carrying of fish and the drying of nets, little education, and but poor religious instruction. At the same time any shortage of virtue was all but unknown among them. It had never come into Malcolm's thoughts that there were live women capable of impurity. Mrs. Catanach was the only woman he had ever looked upon with dislike—and that dislike had generated no more than the vaguest suspicion. It followed that all the women of his class loved and trusted him; and hence in part it came that, absolutely free of arrogance, he was yet confident in the presence of women. The tradesmen's daughters in the upper town, however, spoke to him with a kind of condescension that made him feel the gulf that separated them. But to one and all he spoke with the frankness of manly freedom.

But he had now arrived at that season when, in the order of things, a man is compelled to have at least a glimmer of thought about the life which consists in sharing life with another. Though confident, Malcolm was in no way conceited. He was capable of neither airs nor inferiority. Thus he had not even begun to think of the abyss that separated Lady Florimel and himself—an abyss across which stretches no mediating air, a blank and blind space. He felt her presence only as that of a being to be worshiped, to be heard with rapture, and yet addressed without fear.

Though not greatly fond of books, Lady Florimel had burrowed a little in the old library at Lossie House and had chanced upon the *Faerie Queene*. Turning over its pages, she came upon her own name. Her curiosity was roused and she resolved—no light undertaking—to read the poem through, and see who and what the lady, Forimel, was. The copy she had found was in small volumes, one of which she now carried about with her wherever she went. After making her first acquaintance with sea and the poem together, she soon came to fancy that she could not fix her attention on the book without the sound of the waves for an accompaniment to the verse.

It was a sultry afternoon and Forimel lay on the seaward side of the dune, buried in her book. The sky was foggy with heat, and the sea lay dull as if oppressed by the superincumbent air. The tide was rising slowly, with a muffled and sleepy murmur on the sand. As she read, Malcolm was walking toward her along the top of the dune, but not until he came almost above where she lay did she hear his step in soft sand.

She nodded kindly, and he descended, approaching her.

"Did you want me, my lady?" he asked.

"No," she answered.

"I wasn't sure whether you nodded because you wanted me or not," said Malcolm and turned to reascend the dune.

"Where are you going now?" she asked.

"Oh, nowhere in particular. I just came out to see how things were looking."

"What things?"

"Oh, just the sky and the sea in general."

"I won't detain you from such important business," said Lady Florimel, and dropped her eyes on her book.

"If you want my company, my lady, I can look about just as well here as anywhere else," said Malcolm.

And as he spoke he gently stretched himself on the dune about three yards aside and lower down. Florimel looked half amused and half annoyed, but she had brought it on herself and would punish him only by dropping her eyes again on her book and keeping silent.

Malcolm lay and looked at her for a few moments, pondering; then, fancying he had found the cause of her offense, rose, passed to the other side of her and lay down again, but at a still more respectful distance.

"Why did you move?" she asked without looking up.

"Because there's just the slightest breeze from the northeast."

"And you want me to shelter you from it?" asked Lady Florimel.

"No, no, my lady," returned Malcolm, laughing, "for as small as you are, you would be but little shelter."

"Why did you move then?" persisted the girl.

"Well, my lady, you see, it's hot. And I'm among the fish more or less all the time, and I didn't know I'd be meeting you when I set out. So I thought you might be smelling the fish on my clothes. It's healthy enough, but some folk don't like it. And for all I know you grand folks might be more sensitive to such things than we fishermen."

Simple as it was, the explanation served to restore her equanimity and she bowed her face once more to the book. After three stanzas she looked up and regarded the youth who lay watching her with the eyes of a servant.

"Well?" she finally said. "What are you waiting for?"

"I thought you wanted to say something to me, my lady. I beg your pardon," answered Malcolm, springing to his feet and turning to go.

"Do you ever read?" she asked, detaining him once again.

"Oh, yes," replied Malcolm, turning again and standing stock-still. "And I like best to read just as your ladyship's doing now, lying on a sandhill with the whole sea before me."

"And what do you read on such occasions?"

"Sometimes one thing, sometimes another—anything I can get hold of. I like travelbooks or history, if it's not too dry. I don't like to read sermons, though it seems there's more of them in Portlossie than anything else. Mr. Graham—that's the schoolmaster—has a fine library. But it's mostly Latin and Greek and though I like the Latin well enough, it's not what you read next to the sea, when you're always in need of a dictionary."

"Can you read Latin, then?"

"Yes. I can read Virgil some, and Horace. But ladies don't care about such things."

"You gentlemen give us no chance. You won't teach us."

"Now, my lady, don't begin to make sport of me, like my lord. I could hardly stand it from him and if you take to it as well, I'd just have to stay away from you. I'm no gentleman, and have too much respect for what becomes a gentleman to like being called one. But as for the Latin, I'd be proud to instruct your ladyship whenever you please."

"I'm afraid I've no great wish to learn," said Florimel. "Do you like novels?"

"I never saw a novel. There's not one of them among all Mr. Graham's books, and I imagine he has a full two hundred. I don't believe there's a single novel in all Portlossie."

"Don't be too sure. There are a good many in our library."

"I hadn't the presumption of counting the House in Portlossie. You have a whole lot of books up there, I imagine."

"Have you ever been in the library?" she asked.

"I've never set foot in the House—except in the kitchen and once or twice stepping across the hall from the one door to the other. That would really be something for me to see what kind of place great folks like you live in. It's not easy for the likes of us who have but a room or two to understand how you can fill such a huge place. But, oh, how I would like to see that library."

"Do you ever read poetry?"

"Sometimes," said Malcolm, "when it's old."

"One would think you're talking about wine! Does age improve poetry as well?"

"I don't know anything about wine, my lady. But I say old only because there's so little new poetry that I care about. Mr. Graham's very much taken with Mister Wordsworth—a good name for a poet. Do you know anything about him, my lady?"

"I never heard of him."

"For me I would rather have an old Scots ballad," said Malcolm. "I like Milton well. You can get a mouthful of his words. I don't like a verse that you can crumble between your lips and your teeth. I like verse that you must open your mouth to let out."

"I don't see how you can say that."

"Just listen, my lady. Here's a bit I came upon last night:
    'His volant touch,
    Instinct through all proportions, low and high,
    Fled and pursued transverse the resonant fugue.'

"Just listen to it! It's grand—even though you don't know what it all means."

"I do know what it means," said Florimel. "Let me see: 'volant' means—what does 'volant' mean?"

"It means 'fleeing,' I suppose," said Malcolm.

"Well, he means some musician or other."

"I know all the words but 'fugue.' "

"It's describing how the man's fingers, playing a fugue—on the organ, I suppose," said Florimel.

"A fugue'll be some sort of tune, then? That sheds a heap of light on it, my lady. I never saw an organ. What's it like?"

"Something like a piano."

"I never saw either one of them."

"Well, it's played with the fingers—like this," said Florimel as she demonstrated. "And the fugue is a kind of piece where one part pursues the other."

"That's it!" cried Malcolm eagerly. "That one turns and runs after the first; that'll be 'fled and pursued transverse.' I have it! I have it! See what it is, my lady, to have such schooling with music and all?"

Although the modesty of Malcolm led him to conclude the girl immeasurably his superior in learning because she could tell him what a fugue was, he soon found she could help him no more further, for she understood scarcely anything about grammar, and her vocabulary was limited enough. Nothing interfered, however, with her acceptance of the imputed superiority. For it is as easy for some to assume as it is for others to yield.

"I suppose you read Milton to your grandfather?"

"Yes, sometimes—in the long forenights."

"What do you mean by the 'forenights'?"

"I mean after it's dark but before you go to bed. He likes the battles of the angels best. As soon as it comes to any fighting, he gets up and starts marching around the floor. And sometimes he makes a sweep with his claymore. And once he almost whacked off my head, for he had made a mistake about where I was sitting!"

"What's a claymore?"

"A great big broadsword, my lady. As blind as my grandfather is you would swear he had fought with it in his day if you heard how he whirls it about his head as if it were a little piece of wood."

"But that's very dangerous," said Florimel, somewhat aghast at the recital.

"Ay it is!" assented Malcolm. "If you want to look in on us I would show you the claymore, and his knife, and his skene and all."

"I don't think I could venture it. He's too dreadful! I should be terrified at him."

"Dreadful! my lady? He's the quietest, kindliest old man. That is, provided you say nothing in favor of a Campbell or against any other Highland man. You see, he comes from Glenco, and the Campbells just fill him with hate—especially Campbell of Glenlyon, who was the worst of them all. You should hear him tell the story with his pipes, my lady. It's grand to hear him!"

In the midst of the conversation there came a blinding flash and a roar through the leaden air, followed by heavy drops of rain mixed with hailstones. At the flash, Florimel gave a cry and half rose to her feet, but at the thunder fell as if stunned by the noise. With a bound Malcolm was by her side, but when she perceived his terror for her, she smiled and, laying hold of his hand, sprang to her feet.

"Come, come," she cried; and, still holding his hand, hurried up the dune and down the other side of it. Malcolm accompanied her step for step, strongly tempted, however, to snatch her up and run for the bored craig whose cave would offer them the most ready protection from the sudden rainstorm. He could not think why she made for the road—high on an unscalable embankment, with the park wall on the other side. But she ran straight for a door in the embankment itself, dark between two buttresses, which having never seen it open, he had not thought of. For a moment she stood panting, while with trembling hand she put a key in the lock; then next she pushed open the creaking door and entered. As she turned to take out the key, she saw Malcolm yards away on the hedge of the dune in a cataract of rain. He stood with his hat in his hand, watching for a farewell glance.

"Why don't you come in?" she said impatiently.

He was beside her in a moment.

"I didn't know you wanted me in," he said.

"I wouldn't have you drowned," she returned, shutting the door.

"Drowned!" he repeated. "It would take a great deal to drown me. I stuck to the bottom of an overturned boat a whole night when I was but fifteen."

They stood in a tunnel which passed under the road, affording immediate communication between the park and the shore. The farther end of it was dark with trees.

"Don't you think, my lady," said Malcolm, "you had better make for the house? What with the wind and the wet together you'll get your death of cold. I'll go with you as far as you'll allow, just to keep it from blowing you away."

The wind suddenly fell and his last words echoed loud in the vaulted way. For a moment it grew darker in the silence and then a great flash carried the world away with it and left nothing but the blackness of the tunnel behind. The black storm clouds had brought the evening on much sooner than usual. A roar of thunder followed and even while it yet bellowed a white face flitted athwart the grating in the door and a voice of agony shrieked aloud:

"I dinna ken whaur it comes from!"

Florimel grasped Malcolm's arm; the face had passed so close to hers—only the grating between, and the cry cut through the thunder like a knife.

Instinctively, almost unconsciously, he threw his arm around her, to shield her from her own terror.

"Don't be afraid, my lady," he said. "It's nothing but the mad laird. He's a quiet enough creature, only he doesn't know where he comes from—he doesn't know where anything comes from—and he can't stand it. But the laird would never hurt a living creature."

"What a dreadful face!" said the girl, shuddering.

"It's not such a bad face," said Malcolm, "only the storm's frightened him something fierce, and it's more ghastly than usual now."

"Is there nothing to be done for him?" she said compassionately.

"Not on this side of the grave, I doubt, my lady," answered Malcolm.

Here coming to herself, the girl became aware of her support, and laid her hand on Malcolm's to remove his arm. He obeyed instantly and she said nothing.

"There was some talk," he went on hurriedly, with a quaver in his voice, "of putting him in the asylum at Aberdeen and not letting him roam the countryside the way he does. But it would have been sheer cruelty, for the creature likes nothing so well as running about and does no harm. He has just as good a right to the liberty God gave him as any man alive, and more than many."

"Is nothing known about him?"

"Everything's known about him, my lady, as is known about the rest of us. His father was the laird of Gersefel—and, for that matter, he's become the laird himself now. But they say he's taken such a disgust at his mother that he can't stand the very word of 'mother.' He just cries out when he hears it."

"It looks like the storm's clearing," said Florimel.

"I imagine it's only breaking for a moment," returned Malcolm, after surveying as much of the sky as was visible through the bars, "but I do think you should run for the House, my lady. I'll just follow you, a few yards behind, till I see you're safe. But don't worry—I'll take good care: I wouldn't have you seen in the company of a fisherman like me."

There was no doubting the perfect simplicity with which this was said, and the girl said nothing. They left the tunnel and, skirting the bottom of a little hill, were presently in the midst of a young wood through which a graveled path led toward the House. They had not gone far before a blast of wind more violent than any preceding it smote the wood and the trees, young larches and birches and sycamores, bent streaming before it. Lady Florimel turned to see where Malcolm was, and her hair went flying while her dress flew fluttering and straining, as if struggling to carry her off. She had never in her life been out in a storm and she found the battle joyously exciting. The roaring of the wind in the trees was grand; and the writhing, bowing, and struggling of the trees took such hold of her imagination that she flung out her arms and began to dance and whirl as if she were at the center of the storm. Malcolm, who had been some thirty paces behind, was with her in a moment.

"Isn't it splendid?" she cried.

"It does blow well—nearly as well as my daddy," said Malcolm, enjoying it quite as much as the girl.

"How dare you make game of such a grand uproar," said Florimel with superiority.

"Make game of the blast of the wind by comparing it with my grandfather!" exclaimed Malcolm. "Hoot, my lady! It's a compliment to the biggest blast that ever blew to be compared to an old man like him."

The blast of wind having abated, Florimel went on. Malcolm lingered, to place a proper distance between them.

"You needn't keep so far behind," said Florimel, looking back.

"As your ladyship pleases," answered Malcolm as he once again regained the distance between them. "I'll walk with you till you tell me to stop . . . Ah, my lady, so different you look from the other morning."

"What morning?"

"When you were sitting at the foot of the bored craig."

"Bored craig! What's that?"

"The rock on the beach with a hole through it. You know the rock well enough, my lady. You were sitting at the foot of it, reading your book, as white as if you had been made of snow. I thought of the angel at the sepulchre when I saw you then."

"And what do I look like today?" she asked.

"Oh, today you look like some creature of the storm, or maybe the storm itself taking human shape."

"Oh, dear," exclaimed Florimel interrupting, "I've lost my book!"

"I'll go back and look for it, my lady," said Malcolm. "I know every inch of the beach and if it's on the road we've come on, it'd be impossible that I wouldn't run across it. You'll soon be home now and the rain'll be coming down again if you don't hurry and get in," he added looking up at the clouds.

"But how am I to get it? I want it very much."

"I'll bring it up to the House and say that I found it wherever I find it. But I wish you would give me your pocket handkerchief to put it in, for I'm afraid I'd get it dirty before I get it back to you."

Florimel gave him her handkerchief and Malcolm took his leave, saying, "I'll be up in the course of half an hour, at the most."

The humble devotion and absolute service of the youth resembled that of a noble dog. Though it was unlikely to move admiration in Lady Florimel's heart, it could not fail to give her a quiet and welcome pleasure. He was an inferior who could be depended upon, and his worship was acceptable. Not a fear of his attentions becoming troublesome ever crossed her mind.

With eyes intent and keen as those of a gazehound, Malcolm retraced every step up to the grated door. But no volume was to be seen. Turning from the door of the tunnel, he climbed to the foot of the wall that crossed it above, and with a bound, a clutch at the top, and a pull and a scramble, was on the high road in a moment. From the road he dropped on the other side to the grass where, from the grated door, he retraced their path from the dune. Lady Florimel had dropped the book when she rose from the sand, and there Malcolm found it. He wrapped it in its owner's handkerchief and set out for the gate at the mouth of the river.

As he came to the gate onto the precincts of Lossie House, the keeper, a snarling fellow by the name of Bykes who was overly impressed with his mediocre authority, rushed out of his post and, just as Malcolm was entering the open way, shoved the gate in his face.

"You trying to come in without my leave?" he cried with a vengeful expression.

"What's that for?" said Malcolm, who had already interposed his great boot so that the spring bolt could not reach its catch.

"There's no land-lubbing rascals come in here," said Bykes setting his shoulder to the gate.

But the same instant he went staggering back to the wall of the gate-keeper's lodge, with the gate after him.

"Stick to the wall there," said Malcolm as he strode in.

The keeper pursued him with frantic abuse, but Malcolm never turned his head. Arriving at the House, he committed the volume to the cook, with a brief account of where he had picked it up, begging her to inquire whether it belonged to the House. The cook sent a maid with it to Lady Florimel, and Malcolm waited until she returned—with thanks and a half crown. He took the money, and returned by the upper gate through the town.

10

· · · · · · · · · · · · · · · · · · ·

The Accusation

The next morning, soon after their early breakfast, the gatekeeper stood in the door of Duncan MacPhail's cottage with a verbal summons for Malcolm to appear before his lordship.

"And I'm not to lose sight of you till you've put in your appearance," he added. "If you don't come peaceable, I'll have to make you."

"Where's your warrant?" asked Malcolm.

"You would have the impudence to demand my warrant?" cried Bykes indignantly. "Come your way, my man, or I'll make you smart for it."

"Keep a quiet tongue and go home for your warrant," said Malcolm. "It's there, doubtless—you wouldn't have dared to show your face on such an errand otherwise."

Duncan, who was dozing in his chair, awoke at the sound of heated words. His jealous affection perceived at once that Malcolm was being in-sulted. He sprang to his feet, stepped swifty to the wall, caught down his broadsword and rushed to the door.

"Where is ta rascal?" he shouted. "I'll cut him town! Show me ta lowlan' tief! I'll cut him town. Who'll pe insulting my Malcolm?"

But Bykes, at first sight of the weapon, had vanished in dismay.

"Hoot, toot, Daddy!" said Malcolm, taking him by the arm, "there's no-body here. The poor man couldn't stand the sight of the claymore. He fled like the autumn wind."

"Ta Lort pe praised!" cried Duncan. "But what would ta rascal pe want-ing, my son?"

Leading him back to his chair, Malcolm told him as much as he knew of the matter.

"Ton't you co for no warrant," said Duncan. "If my lord marquis will pe senting for you as one chentleman sents for another, *then* you co."

Within an hour Bykes reappeared, accompanied by one of the game-keepers—an Englishman. The moment he heard the door open, Duncan caught again at his broadsword.

"We want you, young man," said the gamekeeper, standing on the thresh-old with Bykes peeping over his shoulder.

"What for?"

"That's as may appear."

"Where's your warrant?"

"There."

"Lay it down on the table and go back to the door till I get a look at it," said Malcolm. He was afraid of the possible consequences of his grand-father's indignation.

The gamekeeper did at once as he was requested, evidently both amused with the bearing of the two men and admiring it. Having glanced at the paper, Malcolm put it in his pocket and, whispering a word to his grandfather, walked away with his captors.

As they went to the House, Bykes was full of threats; but Will told Malcolm as much as he knew of the matter—namely, that the head game-keeper, having lost some dozen of his sitting pheasants, had enjoined a strict watch along the wall; and that Bykes on his rounds the previous evening had caught sight of Malcolm in the very act of getting over it while looking for Florimel's book, and had gone to the marquis with the information against Malcolm.

No one about the premises except Bykes would have been capable of harboring suspicion of Malcolm, and the head gamekeeper had not the slightest. But knowing that his lordship found little enough to amuse him and anticipating some laughter from the confrontation of two such opposite characters, he had gone to the marquis with Bykes' report; and this was the result. Lord Lossie was not a magistrate, and the so-called warrant was merely a somewhat sternly worded expression of his desire that Malcolm should appear and answer to the charge.

The accused was led into a vaulted chamber opening from the hall. Lord

Lossie entered and took his seat in a great chair in one of the recesses.

"So, you young jackanapes!" he said half angry and half amused. "When I send for you, you decline to come without a magistrate's warrant, forsooth! It looks bad to begin with, I must say!"

"Your lordship would never have had me come at such a summons as that cantankerous toad Johnny Bykes brought me. If you'd but heard him! He spoke to me as if he had been sent to fetch me to your lordship by the scruff of my neck, and I didn't believe your lordship would do such a thing. Anyway, I wasn't going to stand for that. But it would have made you laugh, my lord, to see how he ran when my blind grandfather made at him with his broadsword!"

"You lying rascal!" cried Bykes; "Me afraid of such an old spider that doesn't even have the breath to fill the bag of his pipes!"

"Easy, Johnny Bykes. If you say an ill word about my grandfather, I'll give your neck a twist the very minute we're out of his lordship's presence."

"Threat! my lord," said the gatekeeper, appealing.

"And well merited," returned his lordship. "Well then," he went on, again addressing Malcolm, "what have you to say for yourself in regard to stealing my brood pheasants?"

"Mister MacPherson," said Malcolm with an inclination of his head toward the gamekeeper, "might have fun with such a tale. But, indeed, my lord, it's so ridiculous it hardly angers me. A man that can have all the fish in the whole ocean just for the taking to be such a contemptible wretch as would take your lordship's pretty creatures, not to mention the sin of it! It's beyond an honest man's even denying, my lord. And Mister MacPherson knows better, for look at him laughing in his own sleeve."

"Well, we've no proof of it," said the marquis; "but what do you say to the charge of trespassing?"

"The grounds have always been open to honest folk, my lord."

"Then where was the necessity of your getting in over the wall?"

"I beg your pardon, my lord; you have no proof against me of that either."

"Do you dare tell me," cried Bykes, recovering himself, "that I didn't see you with my own eyes leap the dyke—yes, and with something white, an awful lot like bird wings, fluttering in your hand?"

"Out or in, Johnny Bykes?"

"Oh, out."

"I *did* leap the dyke, my lord; but it was out, not in."

"How did you get in then?" asked the marquis.

"I got in, my lord," began Malcolm, then ceased.

"How did you get in?" repeated the marquis.

"Oh, there's many ways of getting in, my lord. The last time I came in, except for this time today, it was over the carcass of Johnny Bykes there, who would have kept me out."

"And you don't call that breaking in?" said Bykes.

"No, there was nothing to break, except it had been your bones, Johnny, and that would have been a pity, they're so good for running with."

"You had no right to enter against the will of my gatekeeper," said his lordship. "After all, what is a gatekeeper for?"

"I had a right, my lord, so long as I was upon my lady's business."

"And what was my lady's business, pray?" questioned the marquis.

"I found a book on the dunes, my lord, which looked to be hers, with the picture of the two beasts that stand at your lordship's door inside the cover of it. And so it turned out to be when I took it up to the House. There's the half crown she gave me."

Little did Malcolm think where the daintiest of ears were listening and the brightest of blue eyes looking down, part in merriment, part in anxiety, and part in interest. On a landing halfway up the stair stood Lady Florimel, peeping over the balusters, afraid to fix her eyes upon him lest she should make him look up.

"Yes, yes, I daresay," said the marquis, "but," he persisted, "what I want to know is how you got in the first time. You seem to have some reluctance to answer the question."

"Well, I have, my lord."

"Then I must insist on your doing so."

"Well, I just won't, my lord. It was a straightforward affair, and if your lordship were in my place, you wouldn't say more yourself."

"He's been after one of the girls about the place," whispered the marquis to the gamekeeper.

"Ask him, my lord, if it please your lordship, what it was he held in his hand when he lept the park wall," said Bykes.

"If it's all the same to his lordship," said Malcolm, without looking at Bykes, "it would be better not to ask, for it so goes against me to refuse him."

"I should like to know," said the marquis.

"You must trust me, my lord, that I was about no ill. I give you my word for that, my lord."

"But how am I to know what your word is worth?" returned Lord Lossie, well pleased with the dignity of the youth's behavior.

"To know what a man's word is worth, you must trust him first, my lord. It's not that much I'm asking of you. It comes but to this: that I have reasons, good to me and of no ill to you if you knew them, for not answering your lordship's questions. I'm not denying a word that Bykes has said. I never heard the man called a liar. But he is a cantankerous busybody that's not fit to be a gatekeeper, except it was on the backside where no one goes in or out."

"Would you have him let in all the tramps in the country?" asked the marquis.

"Of course not, my lord. But I would have him make no trouble for the likes of me that fetches the fish for your lordship's breakfast, such as is not likely to be about any mischief."

"There is a glimmer of sense in what you say," returned the marquis. "But, you know, it won't do to let anybody that pleases get over the park walls. Why didn't you get out at the gate?"

"The stream was between me and it, and it's a long way around."

"Well, I must lay some penalty on you, to deter others," said the marquis.

"Very well, my lord. So long as it's fair. I'll abide by it without complaining."

"It shan't be too hard. It's just this—to give John Bykes the thrashing he deserves the minute you're out of sight of the House."

"No, no, my lord. I can't do that," said Malcolm.

"So you're afraid of him after all!"

"Afraid of Johnny Bykes, my lord? Ha, ha!"

"You threatened him a minute ago, and now when I give you leave to thrash him you decline the honor."

"The disgrace, my lord. He's an older man and not half my size. But if he dares to say another word against my grandfather, then I *will* give him a little thrashing."

"Well, well be off with you both," said the marquis, rising.

No one heard the rustle of Lady Florimel's dress as she sped up the stairs, thinking to herself how very odd it was to have a secret with a fisherman. For her own sake as well as his, she was glad that he got off so well, for otherwise she would have felt bound to tell her father the whole story, and she was not so sure as Malcolm that he would have been satisfied with his "reasons." While she felt a touch of mingled admiration and gratitude when she found what a faithful squire he was, Lady Florimel also found herself somewhat irritated with Malcolm, having brought her into the awkward situation of sharing a secret with a youth of his position.

———

For a few days the weather was dull and unsettled, with cold flaws and an occasional sprinkle of rain. But then came a still gray morning, warm and hopeful, and before noon the sun broke out and the mists vanished. Malcolm had been to Scaurnose to see his friend, Joseph Mair, and was descending the steep path down the side of the promontory on his way home when his keen eye caught sight of a form on the slope of the dune which could hardly be other than that of Lady Florimel. She did not lift her eyes until he came quite near, and then only to drop them again with no more recognition than if he had been any other fisherman. Already more than half inclined to pick a quarrel with him, she fancied that, presuming upon their very commonplace adventure and its result, he approached her with an assurance he had never shown before. Her head was bent motionless over her book when he stood and addressed her.

"My lady," he began with his hat by his knee.

"Well?" she returned, without even lifting her eyes, for with the inherited privilege of her rank she could be insolent with coolness.

"I hope the little book wasn't too bad, my lady," he said.

"Tis of no consequence," she replied.

"If it were mine, I wouldn't think so," he returned, eyeing her anxiously. "Here's your ladyship's pocket handkerchief," he went on. "I've kept it nice and folded up ever since my daddy washed it out. It's pretty well done for a blind man, you'll see, and I ironed it myself as well as I could."

As he spoke he unfolded a piece of brown paper which he humbly offered her.

Taking it slowly from his hand, she laid it on the ground beside her with a stiff "Thank you," and a second dropping of her eyes that seemed meant to close the interview.

"I doubt my company's welcome today, my lady, and I'll soon be going," said Malcolm with trembling voice, "but there's one more thing I must mention. When I took your ladyship's book the other day, you sent me a half crown with your servant girl. In front of her I wasn't going to say a word against anything you wanted to do with regard to me; and I thought to myself that maybe it was necessary for your ladyship's dignity and the look of things—"

"How dare you hint at any understanding between you and me!" exclaimed the girl in cold anger.

"Lord, mem! what have I said to draw such fire from your eyes? I thought you did it only because you didn't want to look shabby before the lass—not giving anything to the lad that brought you your book."

He had taken the coin from his pocket and had been busy while he spoke, rubbing it in a handful of sand so that it was bright as new when he now offered it.

"You are quite mistaken," she rejoined ungraciously. "You insult me by supposing I meant you to return it."

"Do you think I could be paid for a turn to a neighbor, let alone taking a book to a lady?" said Malcolm with deep mortification. "That would be to despise myself. I like to be paid for my work, and I like to be paid well. But such as I did the other day can hardly be referred to as work. It can be no offense to give you back your half crown, my lady."

And again he offered the coin.

"I don't in the least see why you shouldn't take the money. You worked for it, I'm sure."

"Indeed, my lady, such a doctrine would take all the grace out of the world! What would life be worth if all was paid for? Take your half crown, my lady," he concluded in a tone of entreaty.

But the energetic outburst sufficed, in her present mood, only to disgust Lady Florimel.

"Do anything with the money you please; only go away, and don't plague me about it," she said icily.

"What can I do with what I won't let pass through my fingers?" said Malcolm with the patience of deep disappointment.

"Give it to some poor creature; you know someone who would be glad of it, I daresay."

"I'm not going to take credit for a liberality that isn't mine."

"You can tell how you earned it."

"And profess myself disgraced by taking a reward from a born lady for the same thing that I'd gladly do for any beggar in the land? No, no, my lady."

"Your words are certainly flattering when you put me on a level with any beggar in the country!"

"In regard to such service, my lady, you know well enough what I mean. Oblige me by taking back your money."

"How dare you ask me to take back what I once gave?"

"You couldn't have known what you were doing when you gave it, my lady. Take it back, and take a hundred weight off my heart."

He actually mentioned his heart!—Was that to be taken by a girl in Lady Florimel's mood?

"I beg you to annoy me no longer!" she said, muffling her anger as she once again sought her book.

Malcolm looked at her for a moment, then turned his face toward the sea, and for another moment stood silent. Lady Florimel glanced up but Malcolm was unaware of the movement. He lifted his hand, and looked at the half crown gleaming on his palm. Then with a sudden poise of his body and a sudden fierce action of his arm, he sent the coin swiftly across the sands into the tide. Before it had struck the water, he had turned and, with long stride and bent head, walked away.

A pang shot to Lady Florimel's heart.

"Malcolm!" she cried.

He turned instantly, came slowly back, and stood erect and silent before her.

She must say something. Her eye fell on the little parcel beside her, and she spoke the first thought that came.

"Will you take this?" she said, and offered him the handkerchief. In a dazed way he put out his hand and took it, staring at it as if he did not know what it was.

"It's some strange thing!" he said at length, with a motion of frustration with his hands. "You won't take even the washing of a pocket handkerchief from me and you would make me take a whole half crown from you! Mem, you're a grand and pretty lady. And you've got a way about you, even if it's but the set of your head, that would make an angel drop what he was carrying. But before I would affront someone who wanted nothing of me but goodwill, I would, I would—rather be the fisher-lad that I am."

A weak-kneed confession, truly. But Malcolm was unburdened at last. He laid the little parcel on the sand at her feet, almost reverentially, and again turned to go. But Lady Florimel spoke again.

"It is you who are affronting me now," she said gently. "When a lady gives her handkerchief to a gentleman, it is commonly received as a very great favor indeed."

"If I have made a mistake, my lady, I might well right it, not being a gentleman and not being used to the treatment of one. But I doubt a gentleman would have surmised what you were after with your handkerchief if you had offered him a half crown first."

"Oh, yes, he would—perfectly!" said Florimel with an air of offense.

"Then, my lady, for the first time in my life I wish I had been born a gentleman."

"In which case I certainly wouldn't have given it," said Florimel with perversity.

"Why not, my lady? I don't understand you again. There must be a great difference between us!"

"Because a gentleman would have presumed on such a favor."

"I'm gladder than ever I wasn't born one," said Malcolm, and slowly stooping, he lifted the handkerchief, "because if I had been I would have been looking down upon working men like myself as if they weren't made from the same flesh and blood. But I beg your ladyship's pardon for taking you wrong. And so long as I live I'll regard this as one of the feathers that the angel dropped as she sat by the bored craig. And when I'm dead I'll lay it upon my face so that maybe I'll get a sight of you as I pass. Good-day, my lady."

"Good-day," she returned kindly. "I wish my father would let me have a row in your boat."

"It's at your service when you please, my lady," said Malcolm.

Lady Florimel lay on the sand, and sought again to read. But for the last day or two she had been getting tired of it. Abandoning the page, her eyes rose and looked out upon the sea. Never, even from tropical shore, was richer-hued ocean beheld. Gorgeous in purple and green, in shadowy blue and flashing gold, it seemed to Malcolm. But Lady Florimel felt merely the loneliness. One deserted boat lay on the long sand. Without show of life the moveless cliffs lengthened far into the sea. Neither hope nor aspiration awoke in her heart at the sights before her. Was she beginning to be tired of her companionless liberty? Had even a quarrel with a fisher-lad been something of a pastime to her? And did she now wish she had detained him a little longer? Could she take any interest in him beyond such as she took in her father's dog or favorite horse?

Whatever might be her thoughts or feelings at this moment, it remained a fact that Florimel Colonsay, the daughter of a marquis, and Malcolm MacPhail, the grandson of a blind piper, were woman and man—and the man was the finer and deeper of the two this time.

Suddenly almost by Lady Florimel's side, as if he had risen from the sand, stood the form of the mad laird.

"I dinna ken whaur I come from," he said.

Lady Florimel started, half rose and, seeing the dwarf so near, sprang to her feet and fled straight for the door of the tunnel under the road and vanished. From thence she leisurely climbed the hill of the park where she looked down from a height of safety upon the shore. Seating herself she assayed her reading again, but was again startled—this time by a rough salute from Demon. Presently her father appeared, and Lady Florimel felt something like a pang of relief at being found there, and not on the farther side of the dune making it up with Malcolm.

11

· ·

The Pipes

A few days after these events a footman in the marquis' livery entered the Seaton, snuffing with emphasized discomposure the air of the village, and made his way to the cottage, asking directions, as he put it, "to a certain blind man who played on an instrument called the bagpipes." The style in which his message was delivered was probably modified by the fact that he found Malcolm seated with his grandfather at their evening meal; for he had been present when Malcolm was brought before the marquis by Bykes and had in some measure comprehended the nature of the youth. It was, therefore, in the politest phrase and thus entirely to Duncan's satisfaction when he requested Mr. Duncan MacPhail's attendance on the marquis the following evening at six o'clock to give his lordship and some distinguished visitors the pleasure of hearing him play on the bagpipes during dessert. To this summons the old man returned a stately and courteous reply, couched in the best English he could command, which, although considerably distorted by Gaelic pronunciation and idioms, was intelligible to the messenger who carried home the substance for the satisfaction of his master and what he could of the form for the amusement of his fellow servants.

Duncan, although he received it with perfect calmness, was yet overjoyed at the invitation. He had performed once or twice before the late marquis and, having ever since assumed the style of Piper to the Marquis of Lossie, now regarded the summons as confirmation in the office. The moment the sound of the messenger's departing footsteps died away, he caught up his pipes from the corner, filled the bag, and burst into such a triumphant onset of battle that all the children of the Seaton were in a few minutes crowded about the door. When he was thoroughly winded, he laid aside his instrument and, taking his broadsword from the wall, proceeded with the aid of brick dust and lamp oil to furbish hilt and blade with the utmost care, searching out spot after spot of rust, even to the smallest, with the delicate points of his great bony fingers. Satisfied at length with its brightness, he requested Malcolm to bring him the sheath which for fear of its coming to pieces, so old and crumbling was the leather, he kept laid up in the drawer with his sporran and his Sunday coat. His next business was to adorn the pipes with colorful streamers of ribbon. Asking the color of each and going by some principle of arrangement known only to himself, he affixed them, one after the other as he judged right, shaking and drawing out each to its full length with as much pride as if it had been a tone instead of a ribbon. This done, he resumed his playing, and continued it, notwithstanding the remonstrances of his grandson, until bedtime.

That night he slept but little, and as the day went on grew more and more excited. Scarcely had he swallowed his twelve o'clock dinner of sowens and oatcake, when he wanted to go and dress himself for his approaching visit. Malcolm, however, induced him to lie down a while and listen to him play. Malcolm succeeded, strange as it may seem with such an instrument, in lulling him to sleep. But he had not slept more than five minutes when he sprang from the bed wide awake, crying, "My poy, Malcolm! My son! You haf let me sleep in; and ta creat peoples will pe impatient for my music, and cursing me in teir hearts!"

Nothing would quiet him but the immediate commencement of the process of dressing, the result of which was even more pathetic from its intermixture of shabbiness and finery. The dangling brass-capped tails of his sporran in front, the silver-mounted dirk-knife on one side, with its hilt of black oak carved into an eagle's head, and the steel basket of his broadsword gleaming at the other; his great shoulder brooch of rudely chased brass; the pipes with their withered bag and gaudy streamers; the faded kilt, oiled and soiled; the stockings darned in twenty places; the brogues patched and patched until it would have been hard to tell a spot of the original leather; the round blue bonnet grown gray with the wind and weather; the belts that looked like an old harness ready to yield at a pull— all combined to form a picture ludicrous to a vulgar nature, but gently pitiful to the lover of his kind. He looked like a half-mouldered warrior awakened from the ancient past to walk in a world other than his own.

The whole Seaton turned out to see them start, Malcolm in his commonplace Sunday suit and Duncan in his colorful Highland attire. Men, women, and children lined the fronts and gables of the houses they passed on their way, for everybody knew where they were going and wished them good luck. Duncan strode along in front and Malcolm followed, carrying the pipes, regarding his grandfather with a mingled pride and compassion lovely to see. And thus they entered the nearest gate leading to the grounds. Bykes saw them and scoffed, but with discretion, and kept out of their way.

When they reached the House, they were taken to the servants' hall where refreshments were offered them. The old man ate sparingly, saying he wanted all the room for his breath, but swallowed a glass of ale with readiness. Besides anxious to do himself credit as a piper, he was on this occasion pleased to add a little fuel to the failing fires of old age, and the summons to the dining room being in his view long delayed, he had, before they left the hall, taken a second glass.

They were led along endless passages, up a winding stone stair, across a lobby and were requested at length to seat themselves in an anteroom which was filled with the sounds and smells of the neighboring feast. After another long wait they were at last conducted into the dining room. Duncan would, I fancy, even unprotected by his blindness, have strode unabashed into the very halls of heaven. As he entered there was a hush, for his poverty-stricken age and dignity told for one brief moment; then the buzz and laughter recommenced, an occasional oath emphasized itself in the confused noise of talk, the gurgle of wine, the ring of glass, the chink of china.

In Malcolm's vision, dazzled and bewildered at first, things gradually began to arrange themselves. His eyes soon found the lovely face of Lady Florimel, but after the first glance he dared hardly look again. She wore far too many jewels for one so young, for her father had given her all that had belonged to her mother, as well as some family diamonds; and her inexperience knew no reason why she should not wear them. The diamonds flashed and sparkled and glowed on her white neck which, being uncollared, dazzled Malcolm far more than the jewels. She was talking and laughing with a young man of weak military aspect whose eyes gazed unshrinking on her beauty.

The guests were not too numerous: a certain bold-faced countess, the fire in whose eyes had begun to tarnish; the soldier, her nephew, a wasted elegance; a long, lean man who dawdled with what he ate, and drank as if his bones thirsted; an elderly red-faced, bull-necked baron of the Hanoverian type; and two neighboring lairds and their wives, ordinary, and well pleased to be at the marquis' table.

Although the servants numbered as many as the dinner guests, Malcolm, who was keen-eyed and had a passion for service, soon spied an opportunity to make himself useful. Seeing one of the men, suddenly called away, set down a dish of fruit just as the countess was expecting it, he jumped up from where he sat next to Duncan, almost involuntarily, and handed it to her. Once in the current of things, he finished the round of the table with the dish while the marquis eyed him queerly.

While he was thus engaged, however, Duncan, either because his patience was now utterly exhausted or because he fancied a signal given, compressed all of a sudden his full-blown waiting bag and blasted forth such a wild howl of pilbroch that more than one of the ladies half started from their chairs. The marquis burst out laughing, but gave orders to him— a thing not to be effected in a moment, for Duncan was in full tornado. Understanding at length, he ceased with the air and almost the carriage of a suddenly checked horse, and slowly the strained muscles relaxed. He let the tube fall from his lips and the bag descended to his lap. He heard the ladies rise and leave the room, and not until the gentlemen sat down again to their wine was there any demand for the exercise of his art.

Now whether what followed had been prearranged or whether it was conceived on the spur of the moment, I cannot tell. While the old man was piping as bravely as his lingering mortification would permit, the marquis interrupted his music to make him drink a large glass of sherry, after which he requested him to play his loudest so they could hear what his pipes would do. At the same time he sent Malcolm with a message to the butler about some particular wine he wanted. Malcolm went more than willingly, but lost a good deal of time not knowing his way through the House. When he returned he found things frightfully changed.

As soon as he was out of the room and while the poor man was blowing his hardest, thinking to rejoice his hearers with the glorious music of the

Highland hills, one of their company—it was never known which, for each merrily accused the other—took a penknife and, going softly behind him, ran the sharp blade into the bag and made a great slit, so that the wind at once rushed out and the tune ceased in an instant. Not a laugh betrayed the cause of the catastrophe; in silent enjoyment the conspirators sat watching his movements. For one moment Duncan was so astounded that he could not think; the next he laid the instrument across his knees and began feeling for the cause of the sudden collapse. Tears had gathered in his eyes and were slowly dropping.

"I wass afraid, my lort and chentlemans," he said with a quavering voice, "tat my pag wass near her end, put I peliefed she would pe living beyond myself, my chentlemans."

He ceased abruptly, for his fingers had found the wound, and were prosecuting an inquiry: they ran along the smooth edges of the cut and detected treachery. He gave a cry like that of a wounded animal, flung his pipes from him and sprang to his feet. But, forgetting a step below him, he staggered forward and fell heavily. That instant Malcolm entered the room. He hurried to his assistance, helped him up, and seated him again on the steps.

"Malcolm, my son," he sobbed, "Tuncan is wronged in ta halls of ta stranger; tey haf stapped my pest friend to ta heart and I'm too plint to take fencheance. Malcolm, traw ta claymore of ta pard and fall upon ta traitors."

His quavering voice rose in a fierce though feeble chant and his hand flew to the hilt of his weapon. Malcolm, perceiving from the looks of the men that things were as his grandfather had divined, spoke indignantly: "You ought to be ashamed to call yourselves gentlefolk and play a poor blind man, who was doing his best to please you, such an ill-fared trick!"

As he spoke they made various signs to him not to interfere, but Malcolm paid them no heed and turned to his grandfather, eager to persuade him to go home. They had no intention of letting him off yet, however. Acquainted—probably through the gamekeeper—with the piper's peculiar antipathies, Lord Lossie now took up the game.

"It was too bad, of you, Campbell," he said, "to play the old man such a dog's trick."

At the word Campbell the piper shook off his grandson and sprang once more back to his feet in a trembling rage.

"I might haf known," he screamed, half choking, "that a cursed tog of a Cawmil was in it!"

He stood for a moment, swaying in every direction. For a moment silence filled the room.

"You needn't attempt to deny it; it really *was* bad of you, Glenlyon," said the marquis.

A howl of fury burst from Duncan's laboring bosom. His broadsword flashed from its sheath and, brokenly panting out the words, "Clenlyon! Ta creat defil! Haf I peen trinking with ta hellhount Clenlyon?" He would have run after everyone in the room with the great weapon, but he was already struggling in the arms of his grandson, who succeeded at length in forcing from his bony grasp the hilt of the terrible claymore. But as Duncan yielded his weapon, Malcolm lost his hold on him. He darted away, caught his dirk from its sheath, and shot in the direction of the last word he had heard. Malcolm dropped the sword and sprung after him; in mortal fear of what he would do with the long knife were he to manage to get near anyone.

"Gif me ta fillain by ta troat!" screamed the old man. "I'll stap his pag! I'll cut his chanter in two! Who put ta creat-cran' son of Inverriggen should pe cutting ta troat of ta tog Clenlyon?"

As he spoke he was running wildly about the room, brandishing his weapon, knocking over chairs, and sweeping bottles and dishes from the table. The clatter was tremendous and the smiles had faded from the faces of the men who had provoked the disturbance. The military youth looked scared; the Hanoverian's pig-cheeks were the color of lead; the long lean man was laughing like a skeleton; the marquis, though he retained his cool-ness, was yet looking a little anxious; the butler was peeping in at the door; while Malcolm was after his grandfather. The old man had just made a des-perate stab at nothing half across the table and was about to repeat it, when, spying danger to a fine dish, Malcolm reached forward to save it. But the dish flew in splinters and the dirk, passing through the thick of Malcolm's hand, pinned it to the table where Duncan, fancying he had at length stabbed Glenlyon, left it quivering.

"Tere, Clenlyon!" he said, and stood trembling in the ebb of passion, and murmuring to himself something in Gaelic.

Meantime, Malcolm had drawn the knife from the table and released his hand. The blood was streaming from it, and the marquis took his own hand-kerchief to bind it up; but the lad indignantly refused the attention and kept holding the wound tight with his left hand as he made his way once again to his grandfather.

"You must come home now, Daddy," said Malcolm.

"Is ta tog tead, then?" asked Duncan eagerly.

"No, he's breathing yet," answered Malcolm.

"I'll not co till ta tog will pe tead."

"What a horrible savage!" said one of the lairds, a justice of the peace. "He ought to be shut up in a madhouse."

"If you set about to do that," said Malcolm as he stooped to pick up the broadsword, "you'll have to start nearer home. And you'll please bear in mind that none here is an injured man except my grandfather himself."

"Hey!" said the marquis, "what do you make of all my dishes?"

"Indeed, my lord, you may comfort yourself that they weren't dishes with brains, for they seem to be quite scarce in the House of Lossie."

"You're a long-tongued rascal," said the marquis.

While this colloquy passed, Duncan had been feeling about for his pipes; having found them he clasped them to his bosom like a hurt child. "Come home, come home," he said, "your own pard has refenched you."

Malcolm took him by the arm and led him away. He went without a word, still clasping his wounded bagpipes to his bosom.

"You'll be hearing from me in the morning, my lad," said the marquis in a kindly tone, as they were leaving the room.

"I have no wish to hear anything more of your lordship. You have done enough tonight, my lord, to make you ashamed till your dying day—if you had any shame left in you."

The military youth muttered something about insolence and made a step toward him. Malcolm left his grandfather and stepped again into the room.

"No, no," interposed the marquis. "Don't you see the lad is hurt?"

The young gentleman turned reluctantly away and Malcolm led his grandfather from the house without further molestation. It was all he could do, however, to get him home. The old man's strength was utterly gone. Malcolm was glad indeed when at length he had him safe in bed by which time his hand had swollen to a great size and the suffering grown severe.

Thoroughly exhausted by his late fierce emotions, Duncan soon fell into a troubled sleep, whereupon Malcolm went to one of their neighbors, Meg Partan, and begged her to watch beside him until he should return. He left the house and made his way back up the hill.

To Malcolm's gentle knock, Miss Horn's door was opened by Jean. "What do you want at such an hour," she said, "when honest folk's in their night-caps?"

"I want to see Miss Horn, if you please," he answered.

"I'll warrant she's in her bed by now," said Jean. "But I'll go and see."

Before she went, however, Jean made sure that the kitchen door was closed. For whether she belonged to the class "honest folk" or not, Mrs. Catanach was in Miss Horn's kitchen, and neither were in their nightcaps.

Jean returned presently with an invitation for Malcolm to walk up to the parlor.

"I've gotten myself in a small mishap, Miss Horn," he said as he entered, "and I thought I couldn't do better than to come to you 'cause you can hold your tongue and that's more than money can buy around here."

The compliment was not thrown away on Miss Horn, to whom it was all the more pleasing that she could regard it as a just tribute. Malcolm told her all the story, rousing thereby a mighty indignation in her bosom and a succession of wild flashes in her eyes. Then he showed her his hand.

"Lord, Malcolm!" she cried; "it's a mercy I've no feeling or I couldn't stand the sight. My poor child!"

Then she rushed to the stair and shouted, "Jean, Jean! Fetch some hot water and linen cloths!"

"I have none of either," replied Jean from the bottom of the stair.

"Make up the fire and put on some water directly. I'll find some pieces of cloth," she added, turning to Malcolm, "if I have to rip the back from my best Sunday dress."

She returned with rags enough for a small hospital and, until the grumbling Jean brought the hot water, they sat and talked in the glimmering light of a tallow candle.

"It's a terrible house, yonder of Lossie," said Miss Horn, "and there's been terrible things done in it. The old marquis was a bad man. I don't dare say what he wouldn't do, even if half the tales they tell of him be true. The last one was a little better, and I thought this one wasn't going to be so bad. But it's clear he's tarred with the same stick as the others."

"I don't think he means anything too amiss," said Malcolm, whose wrath had by this time subsided a little through the quieting influences of Miss Horn's sympathy. "He's more thoughtless, I do believe, than deceitful—and all's done for fun. He spoke very kindly to me afterwards, but I couldn't accept it after the way he had humiliated my daddy. But you'd think he was old enough to know better by this time."

"An old fool's the worst fool of all," said Miss Horn. "But no prank of that kind, no matter how bad, is anything like the things that was said about his brother. Of course, no one ever came right out and said anything, mind you. They just hinted at it with downcast looks and a shake of the head as if the body itself would say, 'I could tell you . . . if I dared!' Frankly, I doubt myself if anything was actually *known*, though a whole lot was more than suspected. And where there's smoke, there must be fire."

As she spoke she was doing her best, with many expressions of pity, for his hand. When she had bathed and bound it up and laid it in a sling, he wished her good-night.

Arriving at home, Malcolm took over the watch at Duncan's troubled bedside, hearing him, at intervals, now lamenting over the murdered of Glenco, now exulting in a stab that had reached the heart of Glenlyon, and now bewailing his ruined bagpipes. At length toward morning he grew quieter, and Malcolm fell asleep in his chair.

12

· · · · · · · · · · · · · · · · · ·

The Offense

*W*hen he woke, Duncan still slept; and Malcolm, having got ready some tea, sat down again by the bedside and awaited the old man's waking.

The first sign of it that reached him was the feebly-uttered question: "Will ta tog pe tead, Malcolm?"

"As sure as you stabbed him," answered Malcolm.

"Then I'll be getting myself ready," said Duncan making a motion to rise.

"For what, Daddy?"

"For ta hanging, my son," answered Duncan coolly.

"Time enough for that, Daddy, when they send for you," returned Malcolm, cautious of revealing the facts of the case.

Duncan agreed and fell asleep again.

In a little while he awoke with a start.

"I'll pe hafing an efil tream, my son, Malcolm," he said; "or it was more than a tream. Cawmill of Clenlyon, God curse him, came to my pedside and said to me, 'MacDhonuill,' he said—for pein a tead man he would pe knowing my name—'MacDhonuill,' he said, 'what tid you mean py knifing my posterity?' And I answered and said to him, 'I pray it had peen yourself, you cursed Clenlyon.' And he said to me, 'It'll pe no coot wishing that; it would pe toing you no coot to turk me, for I'm a tead man. Put what troubles me,' he went on, 'is apout yourself.' 'Myself?' says I. 'Yourself' says he, 'for what's to pe tone with you who killed a man aal pecause he pore my name, and he wasn't efen a son of mine at aal!' And then I'll pe waking up, and beholt it was a tream!"

"And not such a bad dream after all, Daddy!" said Malcolm.

"Not an efil tream, my son, when it almost makes me wish I hadn't peen quite killing ta log!"

"Well, Daddy—maybe you'll be taking it for bad news, but you killed nobody."

"Tid I not trive my turk into ta tog?" cried Duncan fiercely. "Oh, no, oh, no! Then I'm ashamed of myself for efer, when I was so close to pe toing it. Put it'll haf to pe tone yet!"

He paused a few moments, and then resumed: "Put I tid kill something; what was it, Malcolm?"

"You sent a grand dish flying," answered Malcolm. "I'll warrant it cost a pound."

"I heart ta noise of preaking; put I tid stap something soft."

"You stuck your dirk into my lord's mahogany table," said Malcolm. "It needed a good pull to get it out again."

"Then my arm has not lost all its strength, Malcolm! I wish ta tabbe had peen ta ribs of Clenlyon!"

"You mustn't make such prayers, Daddy."

"Well, efen if I could forgif ta tead Cawmill, how will I pe forgifing him that ripped my poor pag? Oh, no! No more music for my tying tays, Malcolm! My pipes is tumb for efer and efer!"

"I'll soon set the bag right, Daddy. Or if I can't do that, we'll get a new one. Many a pilbroch'll come out of your pipes yet before you're done."

They were interrupted by the unceremonious entrance of the same footman who had brought the invitation. He carried a magnificent set of ebony pipes, with silver mountings.

"A present from my lord the marquis," he said bumptuously, almost rudely, and laid them on the table.

"It's a set of pipes," said Malcolm, "and a grand one at that, Daddy."

"Take tem away!" cried the old man in a voice too feeble to support the load of indignation it bore. "I'll pe taking no presents from the marquis tat would pe teceifing ole Tuncan, and making him trink with ta cursed Clenlyon. Tell tat to the marquis!"

Probably pleased to be the bearer of a message fraught with so much amusement, the man departed in silence with the pipes.

The marquis, although the joke had taken a serious turn, had yet been thoroughly satisfied with its success. The rage of the old man had been to his eyes ludicrous in the extreme, and the anger of the young one so manly as to be even picturesque. He had even made a resolve, half dreamy and of altogether improbable execution, to do something for the fisher fellow.

The pipes he had sent were a set that belonged to the House— ancient, and in the eyes of either connoisseur or antiquarian exceedingly valuable. But the marquis was neither the one or the other and did not in the least mind parting with them. As little as he doubt a propitiation through their means, he was utterly unprepared for a refusal of his gift and was nearly as much perplexed as annoyed with it.

For one thing he could not understand the offense taken by one in Duncan's lowly position; for although he had plenty of the Highland blood in his own veins, he understood nothing of the habits or intense feelings of the Gael. What was noble in him, however, did feel somewhat rebuked, and he was even a little sorry at having raised a barrier between himself and the manly young fisherman to whom he had taken a sort of liking from the first.

Of the ladies in the drawing room, to whom he had recounted the vastly amusing joke with all graphic delineation, although they had all laughed, none had appeared to enjoy the bad recital thoroughly, except the bold-faced countess. Lady Florimel regarded the affair as undignified at the best and was sorry for the old man, who must be mad, she thought, and was pleased only with the praises of her squire of low degree. The wound in his hand the marquis thought too trifling to mention or else serious enough to have clouded the clear sky of frolic under which he desired the whole trans-action to be viewed.

They were seated at their late breakfast when the lacky passed the win-dow on his return from his unsuccessful mission, and the marquis hap-pened to see him carrying the rejected pipes. He sent for him, heard his report, then with a quick nod dismissed him—his way, when angry—and sat silent.

"Wasn't it spirited—in such poor people too?" said Lady Florimel, the color rising in her face and her eyes sparkling.

"It was impudent," shouted the marquis with an oath.

"I think it was dignified," returned Lady Florimel with the same oath.

The marquis looked up, startled. The visitors, after a momentary silence, burst into a great laugh.

"I wanted to see," said Lady Florimel calmly, "whether I could swear if I tried. I don't think it tastes nice. I shan't take to it, I think."

"You'd better not in my presence, my lady," said the marquis, his eyes sparkling with fun.

"I shall certainly not do it out of your presence, my lord," she returned. "Now that I think of it," she went on, "I know what I will do: every time you say a bad word in *my* presence, I shall say it after you. I shan't mind who's there—parson or magistrate. Now you'll see."

"You will get into the habit of it."

"Except you get out of the habit first, Papa," said the girl, laughing mer-rily.

"You confounded little Amazon!" said her father.

"But what's to be done about those confounded pipes?" she resumed, watching the marquis from the corner of her eye.

"You can't allow such people to serve you so! Return your presents, indeed! Suppose I undertake the business?"

"By all means! But what will you do?" asked her father.

"Make them take them, of course. It would be quite horrible never to be quits with the old lunatic."

"As you please, Flory."

"Then you put yourself in my hands, Papa?"

"Yes, only you must mind what you're about, you know."

"That I will, and make them mind too," she answered, and the subject was dropped.

Lady Florimel counted on her influence with Malcolm and his, again, with his grandfather. But careful of her dignity, she would not make direct advances; she would wait an opportunity of speaking to him. But although she visited the sandhill almost every morning, an opportunity was not afforded her. Meanwhile, the state of Duncan's bag and of Malcolm's hand forbidding, neither pipes played nor gun was fired to arouse marquis or burgess. When a fortnight had thus passed, Lady Florimel grew anxious concerning the justification of her boast, and the more so that her father seemed to avoid all reference to it.

13

••••••••••••••••••••

The Reconciliation

At length it was clear to Lady Florimel that her father was expecting from her some able stroke of diplomacy and that it was high time something should be done to save her credit. Nor did she forget that the unpiped silence for the royal burgh was the memento of a practical joke of her father, so cruel that a piper would not accept the handsome propitiation offered on its account by a marquis.

On a lovely evening about sunset, therefore, Lady Florimel found herself for the first time walking from the lower gate toward the Seaton. Rounding the west end of the village, she came to the seafront where, encountering a group of children, she requested to be shown the blind piper's cottage. Ten of them started at once to lead the way, and she was presently knocking at the half-open door through which she could see the two at their supper of dry oatcake and dried skim-milk cheese, with a jug of cold water in marked contrast to the dinner just over at the House.

At the sound of her knock, Malcolm rose to answer. The moment he turned and saw her, the blood rose to his cheek. He opened the door wide and, in trembling tones, invited her to enter; then caught up a chair, dusted it with his cap, and placed it for her by the window where a red ray of the setting sun fell. Her quick eye caught sight of his bound-up hand.

"How have you hurt your hand?" she asked kindly.

Malcolm made signs that prayed for silence, and pointed to his grandfather. But it was too late.

"Hurt your hand, Malcolm, my son?" cried Duncan with surprise and anxiety mingled. "How will you pe toing tat?"

"Here's a bonny young lady come to see you, Daddy," said Malcolm, seeking to turn the question aside.

"I'm ferry clad to see ta ponny young laty, and I'm obliged for ta honor— put what'll pe hurting your hand, Malcolm?"

"I'll tell you everything, Daddy. This is my Lady Florimel, from the House."

"Hmm!" said Duncan, the pain of his insult keenly renewed by the mere mention of the scene of it. "Put," he went on, continuing aloud the reflections of a moment of silence, "she'll pe a laty and she's not to plame. Sit town, my laty, ta poor place is your own."

But Lady Florimel was already seated and busy in her mind as to how she could best enter on the object of her visit. The piper sat in silence, revolving a painful suspicion with regard to Malcolm's hurt.

"So you won't forgive my father, Mr. MacPhail?" said Lady Florimel.

"I'll forgive any man put two men," he answered: "Clenlyon, and ta man, whoefar he might pe, who would put upon me ta tiscrace of trinking in his company."

"But you're quite mistaken," said Lady Florimel in a pleading tone. "I don't believe my father knows the gentleman you speak of."

"Chentleman!" echoed Duncan. "He is a tog! No, he is no tog; togs is coot. He is a mongrel of a fox and a volf!"

"There was no Campbell at our table that evening," persisted Lady Florimel.

"Then who told Tuncan MacPhail a lie?"

"It was nothing but a joke, indeed!" said the girl, beginning to feel humiliated.

"It vass a paad choke, and might haf been ta hanging of poor Tuncan," said the piper.

Now Lady Florimel had heard a rumor of someone having been hurt in the affair of the joke, and her quick wits instantly brought that and Malcolm's hand together.

"It might have been," she said, risking a miss for the advantage. "It *was* well that you hurt nobody but your own grandson."

"Oh, my lady!" cried Malcolm with a despairing remonstrance—"and me holding it from him all this time! You should have considered an old man's feelings! He's as blind as a mole, my lady!"

"His feelings!" retorted the girl angrily. "He ought to know the mischief he does in his foolish rages."

Duncan had risen and was now feeling his way across the room. Having reached his grandson, he laid hold of his head and pressed it to his bosom.

"Malcolm!" he said in a broken and hollow voice. "Malcolm, my eagle of the crag, my hart of the heather! Was it yourself I stapped with my efil hand, my son? Tid I hurt my own poy? I'll nefer wear my turk again. Oh, no!"

He turned and, with bowed head seeking his chair, seated himself and wept.

Lady Florimel's anger vanished. She was by his side in a moment with her lovely young hand on the bony expanse of his, as it covered his face. On the other side Malcolm laid his lips to his ear and whispered, as if to a baby, "It's almost as well as ever, Daddy. It's none the worse. It was but a scratch, not even worth thinking twice about."

"Ta turk went through it, Malcolm! It went into ta table! I know now! Oh, Malcolm, Malcolm! Would to God I had killed myself pefore I know I hurt my poy!"

He made Malcolm sit down beside him and taking the wounded hand in both of his, sank into deep silence, utterly forgetful of the presence of Lady Florimel, who retired to her chair, kept silence also and waited.

"It was not a coot choke," he murmured at length, "upon an honest man. To put me in a rage is not a choke. And it was a ferry paad choke to make a pig hole in my poor pag. Put I'm clad Clenlyon was not tere, for I'm too plind to kill him."

"But surely you will forgive my father, when he wants to make it up. Those pipes have been in the family for hundreds of years," said Florimel.

"My own pipes haf peen in my own family for five or six chenerations at least," said Duncan, "and I was wondering why my poy tidn't pe menting my pag! My poor poy!"

"We'll get a new bag, Daddy," said Malcolm. "It's been needing mending for a long time, with old age."

"And then you will be able to play together," urged Lady Florimel.

Duncan's resolution was visibly shaken by the suggestion. He pondered for a while. At last he opened his mouth solemnly and said, with the air of one who has found a way out of a hitherto impassable jungle of difficulty, "If my lort marquis will come to Tuncan's house and say to Tuncan it was put a choke and he is sorry for it, then Tuncan will shake hands with ta marquis and take ta pipes."

A smile of pleasure lighted up Malcolm's face at the proud proposal. Lady Florimel smiled also, but with amusement.

"Will my laty take Tuncan's message to my lort ta marquis?" asked Duncan.

Now Lady Florimel had inherited her father's joy in teasing; and the thought of carrying him such an overture was irresistibly delightful.

"I will take it," she said as she rose to leave.

———

While they sat at dinner the next evening, she told her father all about her visit to the piper and ended with the announcement of the condition—word for word—on which the old man would consent to a reconciliation.

Had the proposal come from an equal whom he had insulted, the marquis would never have considered such a thing in the least; for to have done a wrong was nothing, to confess would be a disgrace. But here the offended party was of such a ludicrously low condition, and the proposal therefore so ridiculous, that it struck the marquis merely as a yet more amusing prolongation of the joke. Hence his reception of it was with uproarious laughter, in which all his visitors joined.

"The old windbag!" said the marquis.

When the merriment had somewhat subsided, the soldier youth who earlier had stepped aggressively toward Malcolm as if to engage him in battle, one Lord Meiklecham, proposed a whipping for the Highland beggar, whereupon Lady Florimel recommended that he try it on the young fisherman— a suggestion he met with spiteful silence.

A certain amount of admiration mingled itself with Lord Lossie's relish of an odd and amusing situation with the result that he was inclined to comply with the conditions of atonement partly for the sake of mollifying the wounded spirit of the Highlander. He turned to his daughter and said, "Did you fix an hour, Flory, for your poor father to make 'amende honorable'?"

"No, Papa; I did not go so far as that."

The marquis kept a few moments' grave silence.

"Your lordship is surely not meditating such a solecism!" said Mr. Morrison, the justice-laird.

"Indeed I am," said the marquis.

"It would be too great a condescension," said another, "and your lordship will permit me to doubt the wisdom of it. These fishermen form a class by themselves; they are a rough set of men, and only too ready to despise authority."

"The spirit moves me, and we are commanded not to quench the spirit," rejoined the marquis with a merry laugh. "Come, Flory, we'll go at once and have it over."

So they set out together for the Seaton, followed by the bagpipes, carried by the same servant as before, and were received by the overjoyed Malcolm and ushered into his grandfather's presence.

Whatever may have been the projected attitude of the marquis, the moment he stood on the piper's floor, the gentleman in him got the upper hand and his behavior to the old man was not only polite but respectful. At no period in the last twenty years had he been so nigh the kingdom of heaven as he was now when making his peace with the blind piper.

When Duncan heard his voice, he rose with dignity and made a stride or two toward the door, stretching forth his long arm to its full length, and spreading wide his great hand with the brown palm upward.

"I'm prout to see my lort ta marquis under my roof," he said. The visit had already sufficed to banish all resentment from his soul.

The marquis took the proffered hand kindly.

"I have come to apologize," he said.

"Not one vort more, my lort," interrupted Duncan. "My lort is come out of his own cootness, to pring me a creat kift, for he heart of ta sad accident which pefell my poor pipes. Tey was ferry old, my lort, and easily hurt."

"I am sorry—" said the marquis, but again Duncan interrupted him.

"It would pring me creat choy if my laty and your lordship will honor my poor house py sitting town and giffing me ta pleasure of offering tem a little music."

They sat down and at a sign from his lordship, the servant placed his charge in Duncan's hands and retired. The piper received the instrument with a proud gesture of gratification, felt it all over, and then filled the bag gloriously full. The next instant a scream invaded the astonished air and the piper was away on his legs as full of pleasure and pride as his bag of wind, strutting up and down the narrow chamber, turning this way and that with grand gestures and mighty sweeps.

Malcolm, erect behind their seated visitors, gazed with admiring eyes at every motion of his grandfather. To him there was nothing ridiculous in the display. And, indeed, on a hillside with valley beneath, the music would have been poetic; in a charging regiment, no one could have wished for more inspiring battle strains; even in a great hall it might have been welcome. But in a room of ten feet by twelve feet with wooden ceiling acting like a drumhead!—it was little below torture to the marquis and Lady Florimel. After some time they rose simultaneously to make their escape.

"My lord and lady must be going, Daddy," cried Malcolm over the pipes.

Absorbed in the sound which his lungs and fingers were creating, the piper had forgotten all about his visitors. But the moment his grandson's voice reached him, the tumult ceased.

"My lort," he said, "she'll pe ta craandest pipes I efer blew and I'm proud and tankful to my lort marquis and to ta Lort of Lorts for ta kift. Ta pipes shall co town from cheneration to cheneration to ta ent of time, until ta lout cry of ta trump of ta creat archangel when Clenlyon shall pe cast into ta lake of fire."

He ended with a low bow. They shook hands with him, thanked him for his music, wished him good-night and, with a kind nod to Malcolm, left the cottage.

Duncan resumed his playing the moment they were out of the house, and Malcolm, satisfied of his well-being for a couple of hours, went out in quest of solitude.

14

········•••••••••••••••·······

The Feast

*N*ot long afterward all classes in the neighborhood began to receive invitations to the entertainment which the marquis and Lady Florimel had resolved to give—shopkeepers and all socially above them individually by notes in the name of the marquis but in the handwriting of Mrs. Crathie, and the rest by the sound of the bagpipes and the proclamation from the lips of Duncan MacPhail. To the satisfaction of Johnny Bykes, the exclusion of improper persons was left in the hands of the gatekeepers.

For the sake of the fishermen, the first Saturday after the recently commenced home season of the herring fishing was appointed. When the day came it dawned propitious. As early as five o'clock, Mr. Crathie was abroad—now directing the workmen who were setting up tents and tables; now conferring with the house steward, butler, or cook; now mounting his horse and galloping off to the home farm or the distillery, or into town to Lossie Arms, where certain guests from a distance were to be accommodated. The neighboring nobility, professional guests and clergy were to eat with the marquis in the great hall. On the grass near the House tents were erected for the burgesses of the burgh and the tenants of the marquis' farms. Farther from the house, amongst the trees, were set long tables for the fishermen, mechanics and farm laborers. Here also was the place appointed for the piper.

As the hour drew near, the guests came trooping in at every entrance. By the sea gate came the fisher folk, many of the men in the blue jersey, the women mostly in short print gowns of large patterns. Each group that entered had a joke or jibe for Johnny Bykes, which he met in varying but always surly fashion. By the town gate came the people of Portlossie. By the new main entrance from the high road beyond the town came the lords and lairds, in yellow coaches, gigs and post-chaises. By another gate, far up the glen, came most of the country folk, some walking, some riding, all merry and with the best of intentions of enjoying themselves. As the common people approached the House, they were directed to their different tables by the sexton, for he knew everybody.

The marquis was early on the ground, going about amongst his guests and showing a friendly off-hand courtesy which influenced everyone favorably toward him. Lady Florimel soon joined him and straightway won all hearts present. She spoke to Duncan with cordiality: the moment he heard her voice he pulled off his hat, put it under his arm, and responded with a profuse dignity. Malcolm she favored with a smile which swelled his heart with pride. The bold-faced countess next appeared; she took the marquis' other arm, and nodded to his guests condescendingly and often. Then, to haunt the goings of Lady Florimel, came Lord Meikleham, receiving little encouragement but eager after such crumbs as he could gather. Suddenly the great bell under the highest of the gilded vanes rang a loud peal. The marquis led his chief guests to the hall and as soon as he was seated, the tables all began to be served simultaneously.

At that place where Malcolm sat with his grandfather grace was grievously foiled by Duncan for, unaware of what was going on, he burst out, at the request of a neighbor, with a tremendous blast on his pipes of which the company took immediate advantage and presently the clatter of knives and forks and spoons was the sole sound to be heard in that division of the feast. In the hall, ancient jokes soon began to flutter their moulded wings, and those more immediately around the marquis were soon laughing over the story of the trick he had played on the blind piper, and of the apology he had had to make in consequence. Perhaps something other than mere curiosity had to do with the wish of several of the guests to see the old man and his grandson. The marquis said the piper himself would take care they should not miss him, but he would send for the young fellow, who was equally fitted to amuse them, being quite as much a character in his way as the other.

He spoke to the man behind his chair and in a few minutes Malcolm made his appearance, following the messenger.

"Malcolm," said the marquis kindly, "I want you to keep your eyes open and see that no mischief is done about the place."

The marquis had no fear about the behavior of his guests, and had only wanted a color for his request of Malcolm's presence. "In the meantime," he added, "we are rather shorthanded here. Just give the butler a little assistance, will you?"

"Willingly, my lord," answered Malcolm, in the prospect of being useful and within sight of Lady Florimel, forgetting altogether that he had but halffinished his own dinner. The butler was glad enough to have his help, and after this day declared that in a single week he could make him a better servant than any of the men who waited at table.

It was desirable, however, that the sitting in the hall should not be prolonged; and so, after dinner and a few glasses of wine, the marquis rose and went to make the rounds of the other tables. Taking them in order, he came at last to those of the rustics, mechanics and fisher-folk. His appearance was greeted with shouts, and one of the oldest of the fishermen stood up and, in a voice accustomed to battle with windy uproars, called for silence. He then addressed their host.

"You'll make us proud by drinking a tumbler with us, your lordship," he said. "It's not every day we have the honor of your lordship's company."

"Or I of yours," returned the marquis with hearty courtesy. "I will do it with pleasure—or at least a glass; my head's not so well-seasoned as some of yours." As soon as he had filled his glass, he rose from the seat he had taken at the end of the table and drank to the fishermen of Portlossie, their wives and their sweethearts, wishing them a mighty conquest of herring, and plenty of children to keep up the breed and the war on the fish. His speech was received with hearty cheers, during which he sauntered away to rejoin his friends.

Having left the hall behind the marquis, Malcolm's attention soon thereafter had been drawn to two men of somewhat peculiar appearance, who applauded louder than any, only pretended to drink, and who occasionally interchanged knowing glances. He soon discovered that they had a comrade on the other side of the table who, apparently like themselves, had little or no acquaintance with anyone nearby. He did not like their countenances or their behavior and resolved to watch them. When the majority of the party forsook their drinks in favor of dancing to the sounds of Duncan's pipes and a small brass band, a harp, and two violins, provided by the marquis, the objects of Malcolm's suspicion remained at the table and by degrees drew together and began to confer. At length, when the dancers began to return in the quest of liquor, they rose and went away loiteringly through the trees. Malcolm kept them in sight and followed them through the gathering darkness, gliding after them from tree to tree. Presently he heard the sound of running feet and, in a moment more, spied the unmistakable form of the mad laird darting through the thickening dusk of the trees with gestures of wild horror. As he passed the spot where Malcolm stood, he cried in a voice like a suppressed shriek, "It's my mither! It's my mither! I dinna ken whaur I come from!"

His sudden appearance and outcry so startled Malcolm that for a moment he forgot his watch, and, when he looked again, the men had vanished. Not having any clue to their intent, he turned at once and made for it. As he approached the front, coming over the bridge, he fancied he saw a figure disappear through the entrance, and quickened his pace. Just as he reached it, he heard a door bang and, supposing it to be that which shut off the second hall whence rose the principal staircase, he followed this vaguest of hints and bounded to the top of the stair. Entering the first passage he came to, he found it nearly dark with a half-open door at the end, through which shone a gleam from some window beyond. Then this light was shut off for a moment as if by someone passing the window. He hurried on—noiselessly, for the floor was thickly carpeted—and came to the foot of a winding stone stair. He shot up the dark winding stairs, passed the landing of the second floor without even noticing it, and arrived in the attic regions under low, irregular ceilings which sloped away to hidden meetings with the floor in distant corners. His only light was the cold blue glimmer from an occasional storm window or skylight. He wandered about the vast area, trying in vain to recapture the trail but saw nothing.

Suddenly he caught sight of a gleam as from a candle at the end of a long, low passage on which he had come after much wandering. He crept toward it and, laying himself flat on the floor, peeped around a corner from which came the source of the light. His very heart stopped to listen. Seven or eight yards from him, with a small lantern in her hand, stood a short female figure he recognized immediately as bearing the soft, evil countenance of Mrs.

Catanach. Beside her stood a tall, graceful figure, draped in black from head to foot. Mrs. Catanach was speaking in a low tone, and what Malcolm was able to catch was evidently the close of a conversation.

"I'll do my best, you may be sure of that, my lady," she said. "There's something uncanny about the creature, and doubtless you was an ill-used woman and are in the right. But it's a fearsome venture, and might be investigated, you know. But you can trust me, and I'll not let you down."

As she ended speaking, she turned to the door just beyond her, tried to open it without success, drew from it a key and from a bunch she carried she made a choice of another, and began fumbling with it in the keyhole. Malcolm thought to himself that, whatever her further intent, he ought not to allow her to succeed in opening the door. He therefore rose to his feet, stepped softly out into the passage, sent his round blue hat spinning toward them at the same time as he began pounding on the floor and howling frightfully. Mrs. Catanach gave a cry of terror and dropped her lantern. It went out. Her companion had already fled, and Mrs. Catanach picked up her lantern and followed. But her hurried flight was soft-footed and gave sign only in the sound of her garments and a clank of keys.

Malcolm was able to find his way back to the hall without much difficulty and met no one on the way. When he stepped into the open air, a round moon was now visible through the trees. The merriment had grown louder and most of the ladies and gentlemen were dancing among the trees in the moonlight. A little removed from the rest, Lady Florimel was seated under a tree, with Lord Meikleham, probably her partner in the last dance. She was looking at the moon which shone upon her and there was a sparkle in her eyes and a luminousness upon her cheek which to Malcolm did not seem to come from the moon only. He passed on, with the first pang of jealousy in his heart, feeling now for the first time that the space between Lady Florimel and himself was indeed a gulf. But he cast the whole thing from him for the time being and hurried on from group to group to find the marquis.

Meeting with no trace of him there, he descended to the flower garden. But he searched through it with no better success, and at the farthest end was on the point of turning to leave it to look elsewhere when he heard a moan from the other side of a high wall which bounded the garden. Climbing up an espalier, he reached the top and looked down to the other side where, to his horror and rage, he saw the mad laird on the ground and the very men he had been following standing over him, brutally tormenting him apparently in order to make him get up and go along with them. One was kicking him, another pulling his head this way and that by the hair, and the third poking his hump.

Malcolm descended back into the garden, found a stake from a bed of sweetpeas; then, climbing up again, he dropped from the wall and rushed at the men with the stick poised in his hand.

"Don't be in such a rage, man!" cried one of the men, avoiding his blow, "we're not doing anything unlawful. It's only the mad laird. We're taking him to the asylum at Aberdeen—by the order of his own mother!"

At the word a choking scream came from the prostrate victim. Malcolm uttered a huge imprecation and struck at the fellow again, while another came up and fell upon Malcolm with vigor. But his stick proved too much for them, and at length one of them cried out, "It's the blind piper's son—I'll get him yet!" and took to his heels, followed by his companions.

More eager to rescue the laird than punish the men, Malcolm turned to help him and found the laird in utmost need—gagged, and with his hands tied mercilessly tight behind his back. His knife quickly released him, but the poor fellow was scarcely less helpless than before. He clung to Malcolm and moaned piteously, every moment glancing over his shoulder in terror of pursuit. After a few moments, he gave a shriek, and suddenly took to his heels. Anxious not to lose sight of him, Malcolm followed him up the steep side of the little valley.

They had not gone many steps from the top of the ascent, however, before the laird threw himself on the ground exhausted, and it was all Malcolm could do to get him to the town. At length Malcolm caught him up in his arms like a child, and hurried away with him to Miss Horn's.

"What's this!" exclaimed Miss Horn when she opened the door. "It's the laird—Mr. Stewart," returned Malcolm.

"Well, come in and set him down," said Miss Horn, turning and leading the way to her little parlor.

There Malcolm laid his burden on the sofa and gave a brief account of the rescue.

As soon as he had ended his tale, to which she had listened in silence with fierce eyes and threatening nose, she said, "He's in such an awful mess. I must wash his face and hands and put him to bed. Could you help me off with his clothes, Malcolm?" Then as if she had been his mother, she washed his face and hands, dried them tenderly, the laird submitting like a child. Then she took him by the hand and led him to the room where her cousin used to sleep. Malcolm put him to bed, where he lay perfectly still, whether awake or asleep they could not tell.

He then set out to go back to Lossie House, promising to return after he had taken his grandfather home and seen him also safe in bed.

15

The Laird

When Malcolm returned, Jean had retired for the night, and it was Miss Horn who admitted him and led him to her parlor. It was a low-ceilinged room, with lean spider-legged furniture and dingy curtains. Everything in it was suggestive of a comfort slowly vanishing. An odor of withered rose leaves pervaded the air.

Miss Horn had made a little fire in the old-fashioned grate, and a tea-kettle was singing on the hob. She made Malcolm sit down at the opposite end of the fire and began to question him about the day and how things had gone.

Miss Horn had the just repute of discretion, for, gladly hearing all the news, she had the rare virtue of not repeating things without some good reason. Malcolm, therefore, seated thus alone with her in the dead of night and bound to her by the bond of a common well-doing, had not hesitation in unfolding to her all his adventures of the evening. She sat with her big hands in her lap, making no remark, not even an exclamation, while he went on with the tale of the garret; but her listening eyes grew darker and fiercer as he spoke.

"There's some devilry there!" she said at length after he had finished. "Where two evil women come together, there must be the evil one himself between them."

"I don't doubt it," returned Malcolm, "and one of them is an evil woman, sure enough. But I know nothing about the other—only she must be a lady, by the way the midwife spoke to her."

"Just because you don't know about her," returned Miss Horn, "that's no reason not to think she's just as evil as the other." She paused. "I'll just have to tell you a story such as an old woman like me seldom tells to a young man like yourself."

"I'll watch my tongue, mem," said Malcolm.

"I'll trust your discretion," said Miss Horn, and straightway began: "Some years ago—and I'll warrant it's well over twenty—that same woman, Bobby Catanach, tried to make up to me in the way of a friendly acquaintance. She hadn't been around long and nobody knew where she came from—except maybe the marquis that then was. I could hardly endure her, except that I had reasons for allowing her to go on. She was cunning, the old wretch. She thought she would be able to get at something she thought I knew and so to entice me to open my mouth to her. She opened hers and told me story after story about this neighbor and that—and all kinds of things that she oughtn't to have let pass her lips. But she got nothing out of me— and she's hated me ever since."

Miss Horn paused and took a sip of her tea.

"One day I came upon her sittin' in my kitchen, holding a close conference with Jean. I had Jean then, and how I've kept her this long I hardly know. At that time, my cousin, Miss Grizel Campbell—my third cousin, she was—had come to live with me—as pretty a young thing as you'll ever see, but in poor health; and she couldn't stand to see the woman Catanach about the place either. She seemed just like a vulture; for whenever anyone was sick or had died, there was Bobby Catanach.

"So I was angered seeing her gossiping with Jean. The minute I walked in, up jumped Bobby and came after me and says to me, 'Eh, Miss Horn! there's terrible news: Lady Lossie's died! She's been dead three weeks!' 'Well,' said I, 'what's so terrible about that?' For I could never see anything terrible about a body dying in the ordinary natural way. 'We'll not miss her much down here,' said I, 'for I never heard of her being at the House since ever I can remember.' 'But that's not all,' said Bobby as she began to follow me up the stairs. She followed me up the stairs, right into my room, came in and closed the door behind her and turned to me and said: 'And do you know who else is dead?' she said. 'I've heard of nobody,' I answered. 'Who but the laird of Gersefell!' says she. 'I'm sorry to hear that, honest man,' said I, for everyone seemed to like Mr. Stewart. 'And what do you think of it?' said she. 'Think of it?' said I. 'What should I think of it, but that it's the will of Providence?' 'Well, that's just what it is not, Miss Horn!' Then she went on. 'Whose son is the hump-backed creature?' she asked. 'Whose but the poor dead man's?' said I. And then she came up close to me, and by this time I was sorry enough that I had let her follow me up the stairs, and she said, laying her hand upon my arm with a clasp, as if her and me was long friends, 'He's Lord Lossie's!' says she, and makes a face that might have turned a cat sick. 'And no sooner's my lady dead than *her* man, but not my lord, follows her! And what do you make of that?' she says. 'What do you make of it?' says I to her again. 'Oh, what do I know?' she said, with another evil look; and with a cunning laugh she turned away as if to go but turned back again. 'Maybe you didn't know that the dead man's wife was brought to bed herself about six weeks ago? And you know her condition!' 'Poor lady!' said I, thinking more of this evil gossip than of the pain of childbirth. 'Ay,' says she, with a devilish kind of laugh, 'for the baby's dead, they tell me—as pretty a young boy as you would ever see! And where do you think she had him? Not at her own place, but at Lossie House!' And with that she was out of the door, and down the stairs to Jean again. By this time I was angry enough myself to go after her and turn her out of the place, her and Jean together. I could hear her snickering to herself as she was going down the stairs. My very stomach turned. ·

"I can't say what was true or what was false in the scandal of her tale of the two couples, nor why she took the trouble to bring it to me; but it soon came to be said that the young laird was but half-witted as well as hump-backed, and that his mother couldn't stand him. And it was certain that the poor wee chap could as little stand his mother. If she came near him, he would give a great screech and run as fast as his wee little spider-legs would carry him—with her running after him with anything she could lay her hand on, they said—but I don't know. Anyway, the widow herself grew worse and worse in temper, and I don't doubt she was cruel to the poor little fellow—who knows but what it was because of her loss of the other child?—until he forsook the house altogether. And it seems to me that her first anger at her poor misformed child, who they say was hump-backed when he was born—her anger at him has been growing and growing till it's grown to downright hate."

"It's an awful thing you say, mem, and I don't doubt it's true. But how can a mother hate her own child?" said Malcolm.

"Well, in this case, Malcolm, he's perhaps the child of sin. For even a liar like Bobby Catanach may tell an evil truth; and he bears the marks of it, you see. So to her he's just a symbol of her sin running around the world, and that can't be pleasant to look at, and her heart is but looking for a grave for him to lay in out of her sight. She bore him, and she wants to bury him. And I'm thinking she bears the marquis—dead and gone as he is—a grudge yet, if it's true, for passing such an offspring upon her, and then not marrying her afterwards. It was said that the man that killed him in a duel so many years later was a friend of hers."

"But would folk do such awful things, mem—her a married woman and him a married man?"

"There's no saying what some men and women would do. I have much to be thankful for that I was such as no man would ever look twice at. But the point I had to come to was this: the woman you saw holding a secret conference with that Catanach woman was none other, I do believe, than Mistress Stewart, the poor laird's mother. And I have as little doubt that when you split them apart as you did, you brought to nought a plot of the two together against him. It looks good for nobody when there's a coming together of two such wandering stars of blackness as those two."

"His own mother!" exclaimed Malcolm.

The door opened, and the mad laird came in. His eyes were staring wide, but his look showed that he was only awake in some frightful dream. "Father o' lichts!" he murmured once and again, but making wild gestures, as if warding off blows. Miss Horn took him gently by the hand. The moment he felt her touch, his face grew calm, he submitted at once and was led back to bed.

"You may take your oath upon it, Malcolm," she said when she returned, "she means nothing but ill to that poor creature. But you and me—we'll defeat her yet, if it be the Lord's will. She wants her grip upon him for some evil reason or another—to lock him up in a madhouse, maybe, as the villains said, or, indeed, maybe to make away with him altogether."

A brief silence followed.

"Now," said Malcolm, "we come to the question of what the two of them could have wanted with that door."

"It's bound to be wrong—that's all a mortal can say, you can be sure of that. I've heard tell of some room or another in the House that there's a fearsome story about, and that's never opened for any reason. I've heard about it, but I can't remember it now, for I paid little attention at the time, and it's been many years. But it would be some devilish ploy of their own they would be after; it's little the likes of them would pay attention to such old wives' tales."

"Would you have me tell the marquis?" asked Malcolm.

"No, I would not; and yet you must do it. You have no business to know anything wrong in somebody's house and not tell them—besides, he put you in charge. But it'll do nothing for the laird; for what does the marquis care for anybody but himself?"

"He cares for his daughter," said Malcolm.

"Oh, yes!—as such folks can call caring. But there's not a blackguard in the whole country he would not sell her to, if he was from an old enough family, and had enough money."

"But what will we do with the laird?" said Malcolm.

"We must first see what we can do with him. I would try to keep him myself—that is, if he would stay—but then there's that Jean! She's gabbing and gossiping with the enemy, and I can't trust her. I think it would be better that you should take charge of him yourself, Malcolm. I would willingly bear any expense—for you wouldn't be able to look after him and keep up so well with your fishing, you know."

"I could take him in the boat with me to do my own line-fishing. But I don't know about the herring. Blue Peter wouldn't object, but it's rough work, and for a weak body like the laird to be out all night some nights, weather as we have to encounter, it might mean the death of him."

They came to no conclusion beyond this, that they would think it over and Malcolm would call in the morning. But before then, however, the laird had dismissed the question for them. When Miss Horn rose, after an all but sleepless night, she found that he had taken affairs into his own feeble hands and vanished.

16

•••••••••••••••••••

The Report

It being well known that Joseph Mair's cottage was one of the laird's resorts, Malcolm, as soon as he learned of his flight, set out to inquire whether they knew anything of him there. He had a little talk with Joseph, whom he found strolling along the cliffs toward the promontory, but he knew nothing of the laird. He pressed Phemy, but, if she knew anything she wasn't telling—more concerned, I suppose, with the laird's safety than she was to trust

Malcolm with whatever secrets she might have concerning the laird's places of refuge. He went by Lossie House on his return from Scaurnose, for he had not yet seen the marquis to whom he must report his adventures of the night before.

The marquis was not yet up, but Mrs. Courthope said she would send him word as soon as his lordship was to be seen. Malcolm, therefore, threw himself upon the grass and waited, his mind occupied with strange questions, most pressing among them how God could permit a creature to be born so distorted and helpless as the laird and then permit him to be so abused in consequence of his helplessness. The problems of life were beginning to bite. Everywhere things appeared uneven. He was not one to complain of mere external inequalities. If he was inclined to envy Lord Meikleham, it was not because of his social position; he was even now philosopher enough to know that the life of a fisherman was preferable to that of such a marquis as Lord Lossie—that the desirableness of a life is to be measured by the amount of interest and not the amount of ease in it, for the more ease the more unrest. Neither was he inclined to complain of the gulf that yawned so wide between him and Lady Florimel. The difficulty lay deeper: such a gulf existing, by a social law only less inexorable than a natural one, why should he feel the rent invading his individual being? In a word, though Malcolm put it in no such definite shape, why should a fisherlad find himself in danger of falling in love with the daughter of a marquis? Why should such a thing, seeing the very constitution of things rendered it an absurdity, be yet a possibility?

The church bell began, rang on, and ceased. The sound of the psalms came across the churchyard through the gray Sabbath air, and he found himself for the first time, a stray sheep from the fold. The service must have been half through before a lackey, to whom Mrs. Courthope had committed the matter when she went to church, brought him the message that the marquis would see him.

"Well, MacPhail, what do you want with me?" said his lordship as Malcolm entered.

"It's my duty to acquaint your lordship with certain proceedings that took place last night," answered Malcolm.

"Go on," said the marquis.

Thereupon Malcolm began at the beginning and told of the men he had watched, and how, in the fancy of following them, he had found himself in the garret, and what he saw and did there.

"Did you recognize either of the women?" asked Lord Lossie.

"One of them, my lord," answered Malcolm. "It was Mistress Catanach, the howdie."

"What sort of woman is she?"

"She's a midwife and some folk can't stand her, my lord. I know of no certain evil to lay to her charge, but I wouldn't trust her. My grandfather—and he's blind, you know—just trembles when she comes near him."

The marquis smiled. "What do you suppose she was about?" he asked.

"I know no more than the hat I flung in her face, my lord; but it could hardly be good she was after. At any rate, my lord, seeing you put me in charge, in a manner of speaking, I felt bound to keep her from entering the closed room—especially with her going creeping about your lordship's house like a worm."

"Quite right. Will you pull the bell there for me?"

He told the man who came to send Mrs. Courthope; but he said she had not yet come home from church.

"Could you take me to the room, MacPhail?" he asked.

"I'll try," answered Malcolm.

As far as the proper quarter of the attic, he went straight as a pigeon. Once there he had to retrace his steps once or twice but at length he stopped, and said confidently, "This is the door, my lord."

"Are you sure?"

"As sure as death, my lord."

The marquis tried the door and found it immovable.

"You say she had the key?"

"No, my lord. I said she had keys, but whether she had the key, I doubt if she knew herself. It may have been one of the bundle yet to try."

"You're a sharp fellow," said the marquis. "I wish I had such a servant about me."

"I would make a rough one, I have no doubt," returned Malcolm, laughing.

His lordship was of another mind, but pursued the subject no further.

"I have a vague recollection," he said, "of some room in the House having an old story or legend connected with it. I must find out. I dare say Mrs. Courthope knows. Meantime, you hold your tongue. We may get some amusement out of this yet."

"I will, my lord, like a man that's dead and buried."

"You are a rare one!" said the marquis.

Malcolm thought he was making game of him as before, but held his peace.

"You can go home now," said his lordship. "I will see to this affair."

"But just be careful meddling with Mrs. Catanach, my lord: she's no mouse."

"What! You're not afraid of an old woman?"

"Just a bit, my lord—that is, I'm not afraid of a dogfish or a rottan, but I would take them and grip them the right way, for they have teeth. Some folk think Mistress Catanach has more teeth than she shows."

"Well, if she's too much for me, I'll send for you," said the marquis good-humoredly.

"You cannot get me so easy, my lord; we're after the herring now."

"Well, well, we'll see."

"But I wanted to tell you one other thing, my lord," said Malcolm as he followed the marquis down the stairs.

"What is that?"

"I came upon another plot—a more serious one, being against a man that can't defend himself and could not cope with anything done against him—the poor mad laird."

"Who's he?"

"Everybody knows him, my lord. He's son of the lady of Kirkbyres."

"I remember her, an old flame of my brother's."

"I know nothing about that, my lord; but he's her son."

"What about him then?"

They had now reached the hall, and, seeing the marquis impatient, Malcolm confined himself to the principal facts.

"I don't think you had any business to interfere, MacPhail," said his lordship seriously. "His mother must know best."

"I'm not so sure of that, my lord! It would be a cruelty nothing short of devilish to lock up a poor harmless creature like that, as innocent as he is ill-shaped."

"He's as God made him," said the marquis.

"He's not as God will make him," returned Malcolm.

"What do you mean by that?" asked the marquis.

"It stands to reason, my lord," answered Malcolm, "that what's ill-made will be made over again. There's a day coming when all that's wrong will be set right, you know."

"And the crooked made straight," suggested the marquis, laughing.

"Doubtless, my lord. He'll be perfectly straightened out that day," said Malcolm with absolute seriousness.

"Bah! You don't think God cares about a misshapen lump of flesh like that!" exclaimed his lordship with contempt.

"As much as about yourself or my lady," said Malcolm. "If he didn't, he wouldn't be no God at all."

The marquis laughed again. He heard the words with his ears but his heart was deaf to the thought they clothed; hence he took Malcolm's earnestness for irreverence, and it amused him.

"You've got to set things right, anyhow," he said. "You mind your own business."

"I'll try, my lord; it's the business of every man, where he can, to loosen the chains of injustice and let the oppressed go free. Good-day to you, my lord."

So saying, the young fisherman turned and left the marquis laughing in the hall.

17

....

The Legend

When his housekeeper returned from church, Lord Lossie sent for her.

"Sit down, Mrs. Courthope," he said. "I want to ask you about a story I have a vague recollection of hearing when I spent a summer at this house some twenty years ago. It had to do with a room in the house that was never opened."

"There is such a story, my lord," answered the housekeeper. "The late marquis, I remember well, used to laugh at it and threaten now and then to dare the prophecy; but old Eppie persuaded him not to."

"Who is old Eppie?"

"She's gone now, my lord. She was over a hundred then. She was born and brought up in the House, lived all her days in it, and died in it; so she knew more about the place than anyone else—"

"Is ever likely to know," said the marquis, adding a close to her sentence. "And why wouldn't she have the room opened?" he asked.

"Because of the ancient prophecy, my lord."

"I can't recall a single point of the story."

"I wish old Eppie were alive to tell it," said Mrs. Courthope.

"Don't you know it then?"

"Yes, pretty well, but my English tongue can't tell it properly. It doesn't sound right out of my mouth. I've heard it a good many times, too, for I had often to take a visitor to her room to hear it, and the old woman liked nothing better than telling it. But I couldn't help remarking that it had grown a good bit even in my time. The story was like a tree: it got bigger every year."

"That's the way with a good many stories," said the marquis. "But tell me the prophecy at least."

"That is the only part I can give just as she gave it. It's in rhyme. I can hardly understand it, but I'm sure of the words."

"Let us have them, then, if you please."

Mrs. Courthope reflected for a moment, and then repeated the following lines:

> The lord quha wad sup on 3 throwmes o' cauld airn,
>   The ayr quha wad kythe a bastard and carena,
> The mayd quha wad tyne her man and her bairn,
>   Lift the sneck, and enter, and fearna

"That's it, my lord," she said in conclusion. "And there's one thing to be observed," she added, "that that door is the only one in all the passage that had a sneck, as they call it."

"What is a sneck?" asked his lordship, who was not much of a scholar in his country's tongue.

"What we call a latch in England, my lord. I took pains to learn the Scotch correctly, and I've repeated it to your lordship word for word."

"I don't doubt it," returned Lord Lossie, "but for the sense, I can make nothing of it. And you think my brother believed the story?"

"He always laughed at it, my lord, but pretended at least to give in to old Eppie's entreaties."

"You mean that he was more near believing it than he liked to confess?"

"That's not what I mean, my lord."

"Why do you say pretended, then?"

"Because when news of his death came, some people about the place would have it that he must have opened the door some time or other."

"How did they make that out?"

"From the first line of the prophecy."

"Repeat it again."

"The lord quha wad sup on 3 thowmes o' cauld airn," said Mrs. Courthope with emphasis, adding, "the three she always said was a figure 3."

"That implies it was written somewhere."

"She said it was legible on the floor in her day, as if burnt with a red-hot iron."

"And what does the line mean?"

"Eppie said it meant that the lord of the place who opened that door would die by a sword-wound. Three inches of cold iron it means, my lord."

The marquis grew thoughtful; his brother had died in a sword duel. For a few moments he was silent. "Tell me the whole story," he said at length.

Mrs. Courthope again reflected and began. The gist of the story she related went as follows:

In an ancient time there was a lord of Lossie who practiced unholy works. Although he lived almost entirely at the House of Lossie, he paid no attention to his affairs. A steward managed everything for him, and Lord Gernon trusted him for a great while without making the least inquiry into his accounts. There was no doubt in the minds of the people of the town—the old town, that is, that he had gained authority over the powers of nature; for he was able to rouse the winds, to bring down rain, to call forth the lightnings and set the thunders roaring over town and sea. This and many other deeds of dire note were laid to his charge in secret. The town cowered at the foot of the House in terror of what its lord might bring down upon it. Scarce one of them dared even to look from the door when the thunder was rolling over their heads, the lightnings flashing about the roofs and turrets of the House. And Lord Gernon himself was avoided in like fashion, although rarely had anyone the chance of seeing him, so seldom did he go out of doors. There was but one in the whole community—and that was a young girl, the daughter of his steward—who declared that she had no fear of him. She went so far as to uphold that Lord Gernon meant to harm nobody, and in consequence was regarded by the neighbors as unrighteously bold.

He worked in a certain lofty apartment on the ground floor, with cellars underneath. Strange to say, however, he always slept in the garret—as far removed from his laboratory as the limits of the House would permit; whence people said he dared not sleep in the neighborhood of his deeds, but sought shelter for unconscious hours in the spiritual shadow of the chapel, which was in the same wing as his chamber.

At length, by means of his enchantments, he discovered that the man whom he had trusted had been robbing him for many years. He summoned his steward and accused him of his dishonesty. The man denied it energetically, but a few mysterious waftures of the hand of his lord set him trembling, and after a few more his lips, moving by secret compulsion and finding no power in their owner to check their utterance, confessed all the truth, whereupon his master ordered him to go and bring his ledgers. He departed all but bereft of his senses, and staggered home as if in a dream. There he begged his daughter to go and plead for him with his lord, hoping she might be able to move him to mercy.

She obeyed, and from that hour disappeared. The people of the House maintained afterward that the next day, and for days following, they heard, at intervals, moans and cries from the wizard's chamber.

The steward's love for his daughter, though it could not embolden him to seek her in the tyrant's den, drove him, at length, to appeal to the justice of his country for what redress might yet be possible. He sought the court of the great Bruce and laid his complaint before him. That righteous monarch immediately dispatched a few of his trustiest men-at-arms, under the protection of a monk whom he believed a match for any wizard under the sun, to arrest Lord Gernon and release the girl. When they arrived at Lossie House they found it silent as the grave. The domestics had vanished; but by following the minute directions of the steward, whom no persuasion could bring to set foot across the threshold, they succeeded in finding their way to the parts of the House indicated by him. Having forced the laboratory and found it forsaken, they ascended, in the gathering dusk of a winter afternoon, to the upper regions of the House. Before they reached the top of the stairs that led to the wizard's chamber, they began to hear inexplicable sounds, which grew plainer, though not much louder, as they drew nearer to the door.

"If it weren't for the girl," said one of them in a scared whisper to his neighbor, "I would leave the wizard to the devil."

Scarcely had the words left his mouth when the door opened and out came a form whether phantom or living woman none could tell. Pale, forlorn, lost and purposeless, it came straight toward them, with wide unseeing eyes. They parted in terror from its path. It went on, looking to neither hand, and sank down the stairs. The moment it was beyond their sight, they came to themselves and rushed after it; but although they searched the whole House, they could find no creature in it, except a cat of questionable appearance and behavior, which they wisely let alone. Returning, they took up a position whence they could watch the door of the chamber day and night.

For three weeks they watched it, but neither cry nor other sound reached them. For three weeks more they watched it, and then an evil odor began to assail them, which grew and grew, until at length they were satisfied that the wizard was dead. They returned therefore to the king and made their report, whereupon Lord Gernon was decreed dead and his heir was invested. But for many years he was said to be still alive; and, indeed, whether he had ever died in the ordinary sense of the word was to old Eppie doubtful, for at various times there had arisen whispers of peculiar sounds, even strange cries, having been heard issuing from that room— whispers which had revived in the House in Mrs. Courthope's own time. It was said also that invariably, sooner or later after such cries were heard, some evil befell either the lord of Lossie or someone of his family.

"Show me the room, Mrs. Courthope," said the marquis, rising, as soon as she had ended.

The housekeeper looked at him with some dismay.

"What!" said his lordship. "You an Englishwoman and superstitious?"

"I am cautious, my lord, though not a Scotchwoman," returned Mrs. Courthope. "All I would presume to say is, don't do it without first taking time to think over it."

"I will not. But I want to know which room it is."

Mrs. Courthope led the way, and his lordship followed her to the very door, as he had expected, with which Malcolm had spied Mrs. Catanach tampering. He examined it well, and on the upper part of it found what might be the remnants of a sunk inscription, so far obliterated as to convey no assurance of what it was. He professed himself satisfied, and they went down the stairs together again.

18
· · · · · · · · · · · · · · · · · ·

The History

When the next Saturday came, many people of the village gathered for the wedding of Annie Mair and Charley Wilson. After a brief ceremony at the church, the wedding party issued—the bride walking between Blue Peter, her brother, and groomsman, each taking an arm of the bride, were followed by the rest of the company, mainly in trios. Thus arranged, they walked along the road to meet the bride's "first foot"—the first person met who would drink a toast to their good future and happy marriage.

They had gone about halfway to Portlossie from the Alton when a gentleman appeared, sauntering carelessly toward them. It was Lord Meikleham, lingering guest of the marquis and Lady Florimel. Malcolm was not the only one who knew him. Lizza Findlay, daughter of Meg Partan (Partan being but a nickname, the Scotch word for "crab," applied by certain of her neighbors as a lighthearted indication of her temper), and the prettiest girl in the company, blushed crimson. She had danced with him at Lossie House the previous week, and he had said things to her, by way of polite attention, which he would never have said had she been of his own rank. He would have lounged past with but a careless glance, but the procession halted by one consent, and the bride, taking a bottle and glass which her brother carried, proceeded to pour out a bumper of wine, while the groomsman addressed Lord Meikleham. "You're the bride's first foot, sir."

"What do you mean by that?" asked Lord Meikleham.

"It's for luck, sir," answered Joseph Mair. "A first foot who wouldn't bring bad luck upon a newly married couple must take a drink from the bride."

"Then by all means," said Lord Meikleham, lifting his hat and taking the drink, "allow me to congratulate you. I drink to the health of you both." And he drank down the glass.

"Is that the sole privilege connected with my good fortune?" said Lord Meikleham, after he had finished the drink. "If I take the bride's glass, I must join the bride's regiment. My good fellow," he went on, approaching Malcolm, "you have more than your share of the best things of this world."

For Malcolm had two partners, and the one on the side next to Lord Meikleham, who, as he spoke, offered her his arm, was Lizza Findlay.

"Not as shares go, my lord," returned Malcolm, tightening his arm on Lizza's hand. "Fisher-folk's ready enough to part with their wine, but not with their lasses!"

Lord Meikleham's face flushed, and Lizza looked down, very evidently disappointed; but the bride's father, with a more gentle bearing than most of them, interfered. "You see, my lord—we like to keep to ourselves for the present, for we're a rough set of folk for such as the likes of your lordship to speak with; but if it would please you to come over anytime in the evening and talk with us, you should be welcome, and we would count it a great honor from such as your lordship."

"I shall be most happy to," answered Lord Meikleham and, taking off his hat, he went his way.

The party returned to the home of the bride's parents, where a substantial meal of tea, bread and butter, cake and cheese was provided. Then followed another walk—some went toward the promontory, others down onto the beach—to allow the house to be made ready for the evening's amusements.

About seven Lord Meikleham made his appearance and had a hearty welcome. He had bought a showy brooch for the bride, which she accepted with the pleasure of a child. In their games, which had already commenced, he joined heartily, contriving ever through it all that Lizza Findlay should feel herself his favorite. In the general hilarity neither the heightened color of her cheek nor the vivid sparkle in her eyes attracted notice.

Meikleham was handsome and a lord; Lizza was pretty, even though a fisherman's daughter.

Supper followed, at which his lordship sat next to Lizza and partook of dried skate and mustard, bread and cheese and beer. Every man helped himself. Lord Meikleham and a few others were accommodated with knives and forks, but most were independent of such artificial aids.

After supper, more celebrations and ceremonies followed, and no one seemed to take the least notice that Meikleham and Lizza were absent.

———

In the course of a fortnight Lord Meikleham and his aunt had gone; and the marquis, probably finding it a little duller in consequence, began to pay visits in the neighborhood. Now and then he would be absent for a week or two, and although Lady Florimel had not had much of his society, she missed him at meals and felt the place grown dreary from his being no-where within its bounds.

On his return from one of his longer absences, he began to talk to her about a governess, but she rebelled utterly at the first mention of it. She had plenty of material for study, she said, in the library, and plenty of amusement in wandering about; and if he did force a governess upon her she would certainly murder the woman. Her easy-going father was amused, laughed, and said nothing more on the subject at the time.

Lady Florimel did not confess that she had begun to feel her life monot-onous, or mention that she had for some time been cultivating the acquain-tance of a few of her poor neighbors, finding their odd ways of life and thought and speech interesting. She had especially taken a liking to Duncan MacPhail. She found the old man so unlike anything she had ever heard or read of, so proud yet so overflowing with service, dusting a chair for her with his cap, yet drawing himself up offended if she declined to sit in it—more content to play the pipes while others dined, yet requiring a personal apology from the marquis himself for a practical joke—so full of kindness and yet of revenges. It was all so odd, so funny, so interesting. It nearly made her aware of human nature as an object of study. But Lady Florimel had never studied anything yet, had never even perceived that anything wanted studying—that is, demanded to be understood. What appeared to her most odd, most inconsistent, was his delight in what she regarded only as the menial and dirty occupation of cleaning lamps and candlesticks; the poetic side of it, rendered tenfold poetic by his blindness, she never saw.

Then he had such tales to tell her of mountain, stream, and lake; of love and revenge; such wild legends, haunting the dim emergent peaks of mist-swathed Celtic history; such songs, that sometimes she would sit and listen to him for hours on end.

It was no wonder, then, that in visiting him regularly in the absence of her father she should win the heart of the simple old man. And one evening, when in girlish merriment she took up his pipes, blew the bag full, and began to let a Highland air burst fitfully from the chanter, the jubilation of the old man broke all the bounds of reason. He jumped from his seat and capered about the room, calling her all the tenderest and most poetic names his English vocabulary would afford him.

Her visits were the greater comfort to Duncan now that Malcolm was absent almost every night and spent most days in a good many hours asleep; had it been otherwise, Florimel could hardly have made them so frequent. Before the fishing season was over, the piper had been twenty times on the verge of disclosing every secret in his life to the high-born maiden, so thoroughly did her youth and charm intoxicate him.

"It's a pity you haven't a wife to take care of you, Mr. MacPhail," she said one evening. "You must be so lonely without a woman to look after you."

A dark cloud came over Duncan's face, out of which his sightless eyes gleamed. "I'll haf my poy, and I'll pe wanting no wife."

"Surely you don't feel about women the way you feel about the Campbells," asked Florimel.

"Ton't efen mention ta wicket name!"

"But why do you hate the name so?" asked Florimel.

"Tidn't you know what ta tog would pe toing to my ancestors of Glenco!" cried the piper in a growl of hate and with the look of a maddened tiger.

"You quite terrify me!" said Florimel, rising as if to go.

The old man heard her rise. He fell on his knees and held out his arms in entreaty.

"I'm pegging your pardons, my laty. Sit town once more, anchel from hefen, and I'll say it no more. I'll tell you ta story, and then you'll know why ta name of ta cursed Cawmill makes my plood run hot."

He caught up his pipes and broke into a kind of chant, translating as he went; he related, in intermittent song and wail and dance, the legend of the Campbell from Glenlyon who slew the faithful in the vale of Glencoe:

Black rise the hills round the vale of Glencoe;
Hard rise its rocks up the sides of the sky;
Cold fall the streams from the snow on their summits;
Bitter are the winds that search for the wanderer.
Colder than ice borne down in the torrents.
Is the heart of the Campbell, the hell-hound Glenlyon.

To hunt the red-deer, is this a fit season?
Glenlyon, said Ian, the son of the chieftain,
What seek ye with cuns and with gillies so many?

Friends, a warm fire, good cheer, and a drink,
Said the liar of hell, with the death in his heart.

Come to my house—it is poor, but your own.
They gave them in plenty, they gave them with welcome.

Och hone for the chief! God's curse on the traitors!
Och hone for the chief, the father of his people!
He is struck through the brain, and not in the battle!
Nine men did Glenlyon slay, nine of the true hearts!
His own host he slew, the laird of Inverriggen.

Fifty they slew—the rest fled to the mountains.
In the deep snow the women and children
Fell down and slept, nor woke in the morning.

The bard of the glen, alone among strangers,
Allister, bard of the glen and the mountain,
Sing peace to the ghost of his father's father,
Slain by the curse of Glencoe, Glenlyon.

When he stopped, and gained some composure, he said, "You'll pe knowing now, my laty, why I'll pe hating ta fery name of Clenlyon."

"But it wasn't your grandfather that Glenlyon killed, Mr. MacPhail, was it?"

"And whose Cran'father would it pe then, my laty?" returned Duncan, drawing himself up.

"The Glencoe people weren't MacPhails. I've read the story of the massacre, and I know all about that."

"He might haf peen my mother's father, my laty."

"But you said it was your father's father in your song."

"I said Allister's father's father, my laty."

"I can't quite understand you, Mr. MacPhail. What has all this to do with your name? I declare, I don't know what to call you."

"Call me your old pard, Tuncan MacPhail, my sweet laty, and haf patience with me, and I'll be telling you all apout eferyting, only you must gif my old prains time to tink. My head crows fery stupid. After ta ploody massacre at Culloden[1] my father had to hide himself out of sight, and put upon himself a name that wasn't his at all. And my poor motter, who raised me, tidn't hear one wort from him for tree monts while he was away after ta pattle. And when he crept pack like a fox to see her one night when ta moon was not up, they made an acreement to co away togeter for a time, and to call temselves MacPhails. But py and py tey took teir own names back again."

"And why haven't you your own name now, if your parents took theirs back? I'm sure it's a much prettier name."

"Pecause I'm keeping the other, my tear laty."

"And why?"

"Pecause—pecause . . . I'll tell you anoter time. I'm too tired to talk more apout ta cursed Cawmills today."

"Then Malcolm's name is not MacPhail either?"

"No, it is not, my laty."

"Is he your son's son, or your daughter's son?"

"Perhaps not, my laty."

"I want to know what his real name is. Is it the same as yours? It doesn't seem respectable not to have your own names."[2]

"Oh yes, my laty, it is fery respectable. Many coot men haf had to porrow names from ter neighbors."

"I want to know what Malcolm's real name is," persisted Lady Florimel.

"Well, you see my laty," returned Duncan, "some people haf names and does not know tem. And some people hafn't names and does not know tem. And some people hafn't names and suppose tey do."

"You are talking riddles, Mr. MacPhail, and I don't like riddles!" said Lady Florimel with an offense which was not altogether pretended.

"Yes, surely—oh, yes! Call me Tuncan MacPhail, and neither more nor

---

[1]See Appendix 2, page 229.
[2]See Appendix 3, page 229.

less, my laty—not yet!" he returned most evasively.

"I see you won't trust me," said the girl, and rising quickly, she bade him good-night and left the cottage.

Duncan sat silent for a few minutes, then slowly his hand went out for his pipes, with which he consoled himself till bedtime.

Having made herself believe that she could influence the old man in any way she pleased, Lady Florimel was annoyed at failing to get from him any further hint sufficient to cast a glow of romance about the youth who had already interested her so much. Duncan also was displeased, but with himself for disappointing one he loved so much. He had for some time been desirous of opening his mind to her, and had indeed intended to lead up to a certain disclosure; but just at the last he clung to his secret and could not let it go. He had practiced reticence so long that he now recoiled from a breach of the habit which had become second nature to him.

A whole week passed, during which Lady Florimel did not come near him, and the old man was miserable. At length one evening, she once more entered the piper's cottage. She chose a time when Malcolm must be out to sea. Duncan knew her step the moment she turned the corner from the shore, and she had scarcely set her foot across the threshold before he broke out of the house to greet her. "Ach, my tear laty," began Duncan, and immediately launched into an explanation of his earlier refusal to speak openly about Malcolm's past, as if the conversation had just ended. "My laty must forgife me, for it is a long tale, not like anything you'll pe in ta way of peliefing; and it'll pe put ta tassel to another long tale which tears ta pag of my heart, and makes me feel a purning tevil in ta pocket of my posom. Put I'll tell you ta one half of it that pelongs to my poy Malcolm. He's a big poy now, put he wasn't so always. No, he was once a fery little small chilt, in my old plint arms. But they weren't old arms then. Why must people crow old, my laty?"

Lady Florimel answered with something commonplace, and, as if to fortify his powers of narration, Duncan slowly filled his bag. After a few strange notes, as of a spirit wandering in pain, he began his story. But he did not commence until he had secured a promise from Lady Florimel that she would not communicate his revelations to Malcolm, having, he said, very good reasons for desiring to make them himself so soon as a fitting time should arrive.

Avoiding all mention of his reasons either for assuming another name or for leaving his native glen, he told how he wandered forth with no companion but his bagpipes and nothing but the clothes he wore; he walked the shores of Inverness, Nairn, and Moray, offering at every house he came to on his road to play the pipes or clean the lamps and candlesticks, and receiving enough in return, mostly in food and shelter, but part in money, to bring him all the way from Glenco to Portlossie. Somewhere near the latter was a cave in which his father, after his flight from Culloden, had lain in hiding for six months, in hunger and cold and in constant peril of discovery; and having occasion, for reasons, as I have said, unexplained, in his turn to seek a place far from his beloved glen wherein to hide his head, he had set out to find the cave, which the memory of his father would render more of a home to him now than any other place on earth.

On his arrival at Portlossie, he put up at a small public house in the Seaton, from which he started the next morning to try to find the cave—a seemingly hopeless as well as perilous proceeding; but his father's description of its location and character had generated such a vivid imagination of it in the mind of the old man that he believed himself able to walk straight into the mouth of it. But he searched the whole of the east side of the promontory of Scaurnose, where it must lie, without finding such a cave as his father had depicted. Again and again he fancied he had come upon it, but was speedily convinced of his mistake.

From a desire of secrecy, day and night being otherwise much alike to him, Duncan generally chose the night for his wanderings amongst the rocks and probings of their hollows.

One night, or rather morning, for he believed it was considerably past twelve o'clock, he sat weary in a large open cave, listening to the rising tide, and fell fast asleep, his bagpipes across his knees. He came to himself with a violent start, for the bag seemed to be moving, and its last faint sound of wail was issuing from it. Heavens! There was a baby lying on it! For a time he sat perfectly bewildered but at length concluded that some wandering gypsy had made him a too-ready gift of the child she did not prize. Someone must be near. He called aloud, but there was no answer. The child began to cry. He sought to soothe it and it stopped. The moment that its welcome silence responded to his blandishments, the still small "Here am I" of the Eternal Love whispered its presence in the heart of the lonely man: something lay in his arms so helpless that to it, poor and blind and forsaken as he was, he was yet a tower of strength. He clasped the child to his bosom and, rising, set out, but with warier steps than before, over the rocks for the Seaton.

Already he would have much preferred concealing the child, lest he should be claimed—a thing in view of all the circumstances not very likely—but for the child's sake he took him to the boardinghouse where he had free entrance at any hour. Thither then he bore his prize, shielding him from the night air as well as he could with the bag of his pipes. He waked no one and, recently fed, the infant slept for several hours, then did his best to rouse the entire neighborhood.

Closely questioned, Duncan told the truth, but cunningly, in such a manner that some disbelieved him altogether. Others who had noticed his haunting of the rocks ever since his arrival in the area some weeks earlier concluded that he had brought the child with him and had kept him hidden until now. The popular conviction at length settled to this, that the child was the piper's grandson—but base-born, whom he was therefore ashamed to acknowledge, although heartily willing to minister to and bring up as a foundling. The latter part of this conclusion, however, was not alluded to by Duncan in his narrative to Florimel. It was enough to add that he took care to leave the former part undisturbed.

As to the baby, he was gloriously provided for; for he had at least a dozen foster-mothers at once—no woman in the Seaton who could enter a claim founded on the possession of the special faculty required, failing to enter that claim—with the result of an amount of jealousy almost incredible.

Meantime the town drummer fell sick and died. Miss Horn made known her favor of Duncan to supersede him. The opponents of this idea strove hard to get the drum recognized as an essential of the office, but Duncan declared that no noise of his making should be other than the noise of bagpipes. The more noble-minded of the authorities approved of the piper nonetheless for his independence, and in the end the bagpipes superseded the drum for a time.

It may be asked why Duncan should now be willing to give up his claim to any paternal property in Malcolm, confessing that they were not of the same blood.

One reason was doubtless the desire of confidence between himself and Lady Florimel. Another was the growing conviction that the youth had gentle blood in his veins. A third was that Duncan had now so thoroughly proved the heart of Malcolm as to have no fear of any change of fortune ever lessening his affection or causing him to behave other than as his real grandson.

It is not surprising that such a tale should have a considerable influence on Lady Florimel's imagination. Out of the scanty facts which formed a second volume, she began at once to construct both a first and a third. She dreamed of the young fisherman that night, and reflected in the morning on her interaction with him, recalling sufficient indications in him of superiority to his circumstances. For the first time now she found something on which to justify her dream: that he might well be the last scion of some noble family.

I do not intend the least hint that she began to fall in love with him. To balance his good looks and the nobility, to keener eyes yet more evident than to hers, in both moral and physical carriage, the equally undeniable clownishness of his dialect and tone had huge weight. And the peculiar straightforwardness of his behavior and address was not unfrequently to her plain rudeness. Besides these objectionable things, there was the persistent odor of fish about his garments—in itself sufficient to prevent the catastrophe of her loving him. The sole result of her thoughts was the resolve to get some amusement out of him by means of a knowledge of his history superior to his own.

19

. . . .

The Conspiracy

*O*ne warm August evening several days hence, Duncan was walking along the hard wet sand toward the Seaton, with Mr. Graham on one side of him and Malcolm on the other.

"I wish you had your sight but for a moment, Mr. MacPhail," said the schoolmaster. "How this sunset would make you leap for joy."

"Yes," said Malcolm, "it would make Daddy so happy he'd grab up his pipes and start playing!"

"And why woult I want my pipes ten?" asked Duncan.

"To praise God with," answered Malcolm.

"Ay, ay," murmured Duncan thoughtfully. "Tey are tat."

"What are they?" asked Mr. Graham solemnly.

"To praise God with," answered Duncan solemnly.

"I almost envy you," returned Mr. Graham, "when I think how you will praise God one day. What a glorious waking you will have!"

"Then it'll pe your opinion, Mr. Craham, that I'll pe sleeping soundly rather than pe lying wide awake in my coffin all ta time?"

"A good deal better than that, Mr. MacPhail!" returned the schoolmaster cheerily. "It's my opinion that you are, as it were, asleep now, and the moment you die, you will feel as if you had just woken up, and for the first time in your life. For one thing you will see far better than any of us do now."

But poor Duncan could not catch the idea; his mind was filled with a preventing fancy.

"Yes, I know—at ta tay of chutchment," he said. "Put what'll pe ta use of hafing my eyes opened pefore then. I won't pe able to see anything with all the earth above me—and ta cravestones tat my poy Malcolm will pe laying on ta top of his old crandfather to keep him warm, and to let people know tat ta plind piper is lying down pelow awake and fery uncomfortable."

"Excuse me, Mr. MacPhail, but that is all a mistake," said Mr. Graham positively. "The body is but a sort of shell that we cast off when we die, as the corn casts off its husk when it begins to grow. The life of the seed comes out of the earth in a new body, as St. Paul says—"

"Then," interrupted Duncan, "I'll pe crowing up out of my crave like a seed crowing up to pe corn or parley?"

The schoolmaster began to despair of ever conveying to the piper the idea that the living man is the seed sown and that when the body of this seed dies, then the new body, with the man in it, springs alive out of the old one—that the death of the one is the birth of the other.

"No, no," he said, almost impatiently, "*You* will never be in the grave: it is only your body that will go there, with nothing *like* life about it except the smile the glad soul has left on it. The poor body when thus forsaken is so dead that it can't even stop smiling. Get Malcolm to read to you out of the book of Revelation how there were multitudes even then standing before the throne. They had died in this world, yet there they were, well and happy."

They walked on but Mr. Graham could not convey the idea to Duncan's spiritual eyes any more than he could have conveyed the reality of the sunset to his physical ones.

Toward the opposite side of the bay, unknown to the trio, the mad laird sat inside a large cave with Joseph Mair's ten-year-old daughter, Phemy. She was one of those rare natures which have endless courage because they have no distrust; she therefore spent a good deal of time with the laird, and was not the least intimidated to follow him anywhere. On this warm evening she had followed him to the cave, which was as close to anything that the laird could call home. It was located at the water's edge on the opposite side of the promontory from Scaurnose, and was in fact the very cave in which Malcolm's grandfather had found refuge so many years before. There were many passageways and cavities going this way and that, as the cave opened away from the ocean and under the embankment behind it; and for the laird, for many years, it had offered a damp yet solitary refuge.

On this particular evening, Phemy had persuaded the laird to go home to her father's for the night. But just as they were about to leave the depths of the cave, the laird, with trembling hands, suddenly caught hold of Phemy and pulled her back into the darkness, and stammered in her ear, "There's somebody there! I dinna ken whaur I come from!"

Phemy went to the front of the passage and listened, but could hear nothing, and returned. "Stay where you are, laird," she said. "I'll go down, and if I hear or see nothing, I'll come back for you."

With careful descent, placing her feet on the well-known points unerringly, she crept to the end of the passageway they were in and peeped outside into the mouth of the cave which opened to the shore. The dusk was quickly descending, and the darkness of the cave offered her complete protection against being seen. She held her breath and listened, her heart beating so loudly that she feared it would deafen her to what would come next. A good many minutes, half an hour it seemed to her, passed, during which she heard nothing; but as she peeped out for the last time a figure glided into her field of vision by the cave's opening. It was that of a dumpy woman. She entered the opposite side of the cave, tumbled over an unseen form, and gave a loud cry, coupled with an imprecation. "The devil roast them that laid me such a trap!" she said.

"Hold your wicked tongue!" hissed a voice in return.

"Ow! You're there, are you, mem?" rejoined the other.

"Of course I'm here! Why are you so late?"

"I couldn't take the risk of being seen, mem. I had to take the back ways, if you know what I mean," said the late arrival.

"Woman, you'll drive me mad yet!" said the first.

"Well, mem," returned the other, suddenly changing her tone, "I'm more and more convinced that he's the very lad for your purpose. For one thing, you see, nobody knows where he came from, as the laird would say, and nobody can contradict a word—the old man less than anybody, for I can tell him what he knows to be the truth. Only I won't move till I know where he comes from."

"Wouldn't you prefer not knowing for certain? You could swear to it with better grace."

"It makes no difference to me which side of my teeth I chew on. But I won't swear until I know the truth. He's the man though, if we can get hold of him. He looks just right, you see, mem. He has a slight look of the marquis too—don't you think, mem?"

"Insolent wretch!"

"Take it easy! All things must be considered. It would but make the thing look the more likely. Folk even goes so far as to say that Humpy himself's not the son of the old laird, Mr. Stewart, honest man!"

"It's a wicked lie!" burst with indignation from the other.

"There may be worse things than a little lie. Anyway, one thing's easily proven: You lay very sick for a month or six weeks once upon a time at Lossie House. When they hear that at that time you gave birth to a boy child, which was stolen away and never heard of till now, 'It may well be,' folk'll say. It would give reasons, you see, and good ones, for the child being put out of sight, and would make the whole story more than likely in the judgment of them that heard it."

"You scandalous woman! That would be to confess to all the world that he was not the son of my late husband."

"They say that of him as it is, and how much worse off will you be? Let them say what they like, so long as we can show that he came from your body, and was born in wedlock? He's a good-looking lad—good enough to be your ladyship's and his lordship's—and so, as I was remarking, in the judgment of evil-minded folk, the more likely to be heir to old Stewart of Kirkbyres."

She laughed huskily.

"And," she went on, "I know well how to set such gossip going; I shouldn't be the first to ring the bell. No, no. I'd set Miss Horn's Jean to jabbering, and it'll be all over the town in a jiffy—at first in a kind of talk that nobody'll understand, but it'll grow louder and plainer, and finally it'll come to your ladyship's hearing; and then you can have me taken up before a justice of the peace to be questioned, that there may be no look of a compact between us. But, as I said before, I'll not move until I know all about the lad first, and then get leave from you."

"But what if we should be found out?"

"You can lay it all on me."

"And what will you do with it?"

"Take it with me," was the answer, accompanied by another husky laugh.

"Where to?"

"Ask no questions, and you'll be told no lies. Anyway, I will leave no tracks behind me. And for that matter, I must have my part in my hands the minute the thing's been sworn to. If you fail me, as agreed, you'll soon see me get more light on the subject, and confess to a great mistake. By the Mighty, but I'll swear the very opposite the next time I'm asked! Yes, and everyone will believe me. And where will you be then, my lady? For though I might mistake, you couldn't. They'll have you taken up for perjury."

"You're a dangerous accomplice," said the lady.

"I'm a tool you must take by the handle or you will scrape the edge," returned the other quietly.

"As soon, then, as I get a hold of that misbegotten elf—"

"Do you mean the young laird or the young marquis, mem?"

"You forget, Mrs. Catanach, that you are speaking to a lady."

"You must have been an awful lot like one one night, anyway, mem. But I'm done with my joking."

"As soon, I say, as I get my poor boy into proper hands, I shall be ready to take the next step."

"Why should you put it off till then? He wouldn't do much one way or the other."

"I will tell you. His uncle, Sir Joseph, prides himself on being an honest man, and if some busybody were to tell him that poor Stephen, as I am told people are saying, was no worse than harsh treatment had made him—for you know his father could not bear the sight of him to the day of his death— he would be the more determined to assert his guardianship and keep things out of my hands. But if I once had the poor fellow in an asylum, or in my own keeping, you see—"

"Well, mem," exclaimed the midwife with her gelatinous laugh, "if you and me was to fall out, there would really be a row! Ha, ha, ha!"

They rose and left the cave together and Phemy, trembling all over, rejoined the laird.

She understood little of what she had heard, and yet, enabled by her affection, retained a good deal of it in her mind. She rightly judged it better to repeat nothing of what she had overheard to the laird, to whom it would only redouble terror; and when he questioned her in his own way concerning it, she had little difficulty in satisfying him with a very small amount of information. When they reached her home, she told all she could to her father; whose opinion it was that the best they could do was to keep a yet more vigilant guard over the laird and his liberty.

20

·····················

The Move

One day toward the close of the fishing season, the marquis called upon Duncan and was received with a cordial, unembarrassed welcome.

"I want you, Mr. MacPhail," said the marquis, "to come and live in the little cottage on the banks of the creek which, they tell me, one of my game-keepers used to occupy. I'll have it put in order for you, and you shall live rent-free as my piper."

"I thank your lortship's crace," said Duncan, "and I would pe proud of ta honor, put it'll pe too far away from ta shore for my poy's fishing."

"I have a design on him too," returned the marquis. "They're building a little yacht for me—a pleasure boat, you understand—at Aberdeen, and I want Malcolm to be the skipper. But he is such a useful fellow, and so thoroughly to be depended upon, that I should prefer his having a room in the House. I should like to know he was within call any moment I might want him."

To Malcolm the proposal was full of attraction. True, Lord Lossie had once and again spoken to offend him, but the confidence he had shown in him had gone far to atone for that. And to be near Lady Florimel!—to be allowed books from the library, perhaps!—to have a nice room and all those lovely grounds all about him!—it was tempting!

The old man also, the more he reflected, liked the idea. The only thing he murmured at was being parted from his grandson at night. In vain Malcolm reminded him that, during the fishing season, he had to spend most nights alone; Duncan answered that he had but to go to the door and look out to sea, and there was nothing between him and his boy; but now he could not tell how many stone walls might be standing up to divide them. He was quite willing to make the trial, however, and see if they could bear it. Especially so since he sensed more importance in the marquis' statement, "You shall have all the lamps and candlesticks in the House to attend to and take charge of," than he had probably intended.

Nevertheless, he finally gave in; so Malcolm went to speak to the marquis. He did not altogether trust the marquis, but he had always taken a delight in doing anything for anybody. Still, as he pondered over the matter on his way, he shrank a good deal from placing himself at the beck and call of another: it threatened to interfere with that sense of personal freedom which is yet dearer perhaps to the poor than to the rich. But he argued with himself that he had found no infringement of it under Blue Peter when fishing, and that if the marquis were really as friendly as he professed to be, it was not likely to turn out otherwise with him.

Lady Florimel anticipated pleasure in Malcolm's probable consent to her father's plan, but certainly he would not have been greatly uplifted by a knowledge of the sort of pleasure she expected. For some time the girl had been suffering from too much liberty. It was amusement she hoped for from Malcolm's becoming, in a sense, one of the family at the House, to which she believed her knowledge of the extremely bare outlines of his history would largely contribute.

He was shown at once into the presence of his lordship, whom he found at breakfast with his daughter.

"Well, MacPhail," said the marquis, "have you made up your mind to be my skipper?"

"Willingly, my lord," answered Malcolm.

"Do you know how to manage a sailboat?"

"Certainly, my lord."

"Shall you want any help?"

"That depends on several things—her size, the will of the wind, and whether or not your lordship or my lady can handle the rudder."

"We can't settle about that, then, till she comes. I hear she'll soon be on her way now. But I cannot have you dressed like a farmer," said his lordship, looking sharply at the Sunday clothes which Malcolm had donned for the visit.

"What was I to do, my lord?" returned Malcolm apologetically. "The only other clothes I have are very fishy, and neither yourself nor my lady could abide them in the room with you."

"Certainly not," responded the marquis in a leisurely manner as he devoured his omelette. "I was thinking of your future position as skipper of my boat. What would you say to a kilt?"

"No, no, my lord," rejoined Malcolm. "A kilt's no seafaring clothes. A kilt wouldn't do at all, my lord."

"You cannot surely object to the dress of your own people?"

"The kilt's fine on a hill," said Malcolm, "I don't doubt; but faith!—seafaring, my lord?"

"Well, go to the best tailor in town and order a naval suit—white ducks and a blue jacket; two suits you'll want."

"One suit'll satisfy me fine to begin with, my lord. I'll just go to Jamie Sangster, who makes my clothes—not that they're many—and get him to measure me. He'll make them well enough for me. You're sure of the worth of your money from him."

"I tell you, go to the best tailor in town and order two suits."

"No, no, my lord, there's no need. I can't afford it, anyway. We're not made of money like your lordship."

"You booby! Do you suppose I would tell you to order clothes I did not mean to pay for?"

Lady Florimel found her expectation of amusement not likely to be disappointed!

"Hoots, my lord!" returned Malcolm, "that would never do. I must pay for my own clothes. I would be in constant fear of spoiling them if I didn't, and that would be enough to make anyone miserable."

"Well, well, please your pride and be off with you!" growled the marquis with a curse.

"Yes, let him please his pride and be off with him!" assented Lady Florimel, adding the same curse with perfect gravity.

Malcolm started and stared. Lady Florimel kept an absolute composure. The marquis burst into a loud laugh.

Malcolm stood for a moment. "I think I'm going daft!" he said at length, putting his hand to his head. "It's time I go. Good-morning, my lord."

The next morning Duncan called on Mrs. Findlay and begged her acceptance of his stock in trade. Having been his lordship's piper for some time, he said, he was now about to occupy his proper quarter within the House. She accepted graciously, expressing the hope that Duncan would not forget his old friends now that he was going amongst lords and ladies, to which Duncan returned as courteous an answer as if he had been addressing Lady Florimel herself.

Before the end of the week his few household goods were borne in a cart through the sea gate by Bykes, to whom Malcolm dropped a humorous, "Well, Johnny!" as he passed, receiving a nondescript kind of grin in return. The rest of the forenoon was spent in getting his place in order, and in the afternoon, arrayed in his new garments, Malcolm reported himself at the House. Admitted to his lordship's presence, he had a question to ask and a request as well.

"Have you done anything, my lord," he said, "about Mistress Catanach?"

"What do you mean?"

"About her cat-prowling about the house, my lord."

"No. You haven't discovered anything else, have you?"

"No, my lord. I haven't had a chance. But you may be sure she had no good design in it."

"I don't suspect her of any."

"Well, my lord, have you any objection to letting me sleep up yonder?"

"None at all—only you'd better see what Mrs. Courthope has to say about it. Perhaps you won't be so ready after you hear her story."

"But I have your lordship's leave to take any room I like?"

"Certainly. Go to Mrs. Courthope and tell her I wish you to choose your own quarters."

Having straightway delivered his lordship's message, Mrs. Courthope, wondering a little about it, proceeded to show him those portions of the House set apart for the servants. He followed her from floor to floor—last to the upper regions, and through all the confused rambling roofs of the old pile, now descending a sudden steep-yawning stair, now ascending another where none could have been supposed to exist.

Mrs. Courthope was more than kind, for she was greatly pleased at having Malcolm for an inmate. She led him from room to room, suggesting now and then a choice, and listening amusedly to his remarks of liking or disliking. At last he found himself following her along the passage in which was the mysterious door, but she never stayed her step, or seemed to intend showing one of the many rooms opening upon it.

"Such a lot of rooms!" said Malcolm, making a halt. "Who sleeps here?"

"Nobody has slept in one of these rooms for I dare not say how many years," replied Mrs. Courthope, without stopping; and as she spoke she passed the fearful door.

"I would like to see into this room," said Malcolm.

"That door is never opened," answered Mrs. Courthope, who had now reached the end of the passage and turned, lingering as she spoke to move on.

"And why not?" asked Malcolm, continuing to stand before it.

"I would rather not answer you just here. Come along. This is not a part of the House where you would like to be, I am sure."

"How do you know that, mem? And how can I say myself before you have shown me what the room's like? It may be the very place to take my fancy. Just open the door, mem, if you please, and let me have a look into it."

"I dare not open it. It's never opened, I tell you. It's against the rules of the House. Come to my room, and I'll tell you the story about it."

"Well, you'll let me see into the next, won't you? There's no law against opening it, is there?" said Malcolm, approaching the door next to the one in dispute.

"Certainly not; but I'm pretty sure, once you've heard the story I have to tell, you won't choose to sleep in this part of the House."

"Let's look, anyway."

So saying, Malcolm took upon himself to try the handle of the door. It was not locked. He peeped in, then entered. It was a small room, low-ceiled, with a deep dormer window in the high pediment of a roof, and a turret-recess on each side of the window. It seemed very light after the passage, and looked down upon the burn. It was comfortably furnished, and the curtains of its tent-bed were chequered in squares of blue and white.

"This is the very place for me, mem," said Malcolm as he came out. "That is," he added, "if you don't think it's too grand for the likes of me that's not been used to anything half so good."

"You're quite welcome to it," said Mrs. Courthope, all but confident he would not care to occupy it after hearing the tale of Lord Gernon.

She had not moved from the end of the passage while Malcolm was in the room. Somewhat hurriedly she now led the way to her own. It seemed half a mile off to the wondering Malcolm as he followed her down winding stairs, along endless passages and round innumerable corners. Arriving at last, she made him sit down and gave him a glass of homemade wine to drink, while she told him the story much as she had already told it to the marquis, adding a hope to the effect that if ever the marquis should express a wish to pry into the secret of the chamber, Malcolm would not encourage him in a fancy, the indulgence of which was certainly useless, and might be dangerous.

"Me!" exclaimed Malcolm with surprise. "As if he would heed a word I said!"

"Very little will sometimes turn a man either in one direction or the other," said Mrs. Courthope.

"But surely, mem, you don't believe in such fool old-world stories as that? It's well enough for a tale, but to think of somebody changing their behavior as a result of it baffles me."

"I don't say I believe it," returned Mrs. Courthope, a little pettishly, "but there's no good in mere foolhardiness."

"You surely don't think, mem, that God would let anything depend upon whether a man opened a door in his own house or not? It's against all reason," persisted Malcolm.

"There might be reasons we couldn't understand," she replied. "To do what we are warned against from any quarter, without good reason, must be foolhardy at best."

"Well, mem, I must have the room next to the old warlock's anyway, for that's the room I'm going to sleep in, and no other in this grand house."

Mrs. Courthope rose, full of uneasiness, and walked up and down the room.

"I'm taking upon me nothing beyond his lordship's own word," urged Malcolm.

"If you're to go by the very word," rejoined Mrs. Courthope, stopping to look him full in the face, "you might insist on sleeping in Lord Gernon's chamber itself."

"Well, and so I might," returned Malcolm.

The hinted possibility of having to change bad for worse appeared to quench further objection.

"I must get it ready myself, then," she said resignedly, "for the maids won't even go up that stair. And as to going into any of those rooms—"

"Indeed no, mem! You shan't do that," cried Malcolm. "Say not a word to one of them. I'd wager I'm as good as the old warlock himself at making a bed. Just give me the sheets and the blankets, and I'll do it as trim as any lass in the house."

"But the bed will want airing," objected the housekeeper.

"By all accounts, that's the last thing it's likely to want, lying next door to yon chamber. But many's the time I've slept upon the top of a boatload of herring, and if that never did me any harm, it's not likely a good bed will kill me even if it is a little rather full of moths."

Mrs. Courthope yielded and gave him all that was needed, and before night Malcolm had made his new quarters quite comfortable. He did not retire to them, however, until he had seen his grandfather laid down to sleep in his lonely cottage.

About noon the next day the old man made his appearance in the kitchen. How he had found his way to it neither he nor anyone else could tell. There happened to be no one there when he entered, and the cook when she returned stood for a moment in the door, watching him as he felt around, flitting about with huge bony hands whose touch was yet light as the poise of a butterfly. Not knowing the old man, she fancied at first he was feeling after something in the shape of food, but presently his hands fell upon a brass candlestick. He clutched it and commenced fingering it all over. Alas! it was clean, and with a look of disappointment he replaced it. Wondering yet more what his quest could be, she watched on. The next instant he had laid hold of a silver candlestick not yet passed through the hands of the scullery-maid, and for a moment she fancied him a thief for he rejected the brass and now took the silver. But he went no farther with it than the fireplace, where he sat down, and having spread his pocket hand-kerchief over his kilted knees, drew a similar rag from somewhere and commenced cleaning it.

By this time one of the maids who knew him had joined the cook, and also stood watching him with amusement. But when she saw the old knife drawn from his stocking, and about to be applied to the nozzle, to free it from adhering wax, it seemed more than time to break the silence. "That's a silver candlestick, Mister MacPhail," she cried, "and you mustn't take your knife to it or you'll scratch it dreadful."

An angry flush glowed in the withered cheeks of the piper; without the least start at the suddenness of her interference, he turned his face in the direction of the speaker. "You take old Tuncan's finkers for persons of no etchucation, mem. As if tey couldn't pe knowing ta silfer from ta prass! If tey wass so stupid, my nose would tell tem. Efen old Tuncan's knife'll pe knowing petter than to scratch ta silfer, or ta prass either. Old Tuncan's knife would pe scratching nothing petter than ta skin of a Cawmill."

Now the candlestick had no business in the kitchen, and if it were scratched the butler would be indignant; but the girl was a Campbell, and Duncan's words so frightened her that she did not dare interfere. She soon saw, however, that the piper had not over-vaunted his skill: the skene left not a mark upon the metal. In a few minutes he had melted away the wax he could not otherwise reach and had rubbed the candlestick perfectly bright, leaving behind no trace except an unpleasant odor of train-oil from the rag. From that hour he was cleaner of lamps and candlesticks, as well as blower of bagpipes, to the House of Lossie, and had everything provided necessary to the performance of his duties with comfort and success.

21

•••••••••••••••••••••

The Room

*M*alcolm's first night was rather troubled, not primarily from the fact that but a thin partition separated him from the wizard's chamber, but from the deadness of the silence around him; for he had been all his life accustomed to the near noise of the sea, and its absence had upon him the rousing effect of an unaccustomed sound. He kept hearing the dead silence—and it was no wonder that a succession of sleepless fits should at length have so shaken his mental frame as to lay it open to the assaults of nightly terrors, the position itself being sufficient to seduce his imagination and carry it over to the interests of his enemy.

But Malcolm had early learned that a man's will must, like a true monarch, rule down every rebellious movement of its subjects; and he was far from yielding to such inroads as now assailed him. Still, it was long before he fell asleep, and then only to dream without quite losing consciousness of his peculiar surroundings. He seemed to know that he lay in his own bed, and yet to be somehow aware of the presence of a pale woman in a white garment who sat on the side of the bed in the next room, still and silent, with her hands in her lap and her eyes on the ground. He thought he had seen her before; and he knew, notwithstanding her silence, that she was lamenting over a child she had lost. He knew also where her child was— that it lay crying in a cave down by the seashore but he could neither rise to go to her nor open his mouth to call. The vision kept coming and coming, like the same tune played over and over on a barrel-organ, and when he woke seemed to fill all the time he had slept.

About ten o'clock he was summoned to the marquis' presence, and found him at breakfast with Lady Florimel.

"Where did you sleep last night?" asked the marquis.

"Next door to the old warlock," answered Malcolm. Lady Florimel looked up with a glance of bright interest; her father had just been telling her the story.

"You did!" said the marquis. "Then Mrs. Courthope—did she tell you the legend about him?"

"Ay, she did, my lord."

"Well, how did you sleep?"

"Middling only."

"How was that?"

"I don't know, except that I was fool enough to find the place a little eerie."

"Ah!" said the marquis. "You've had enough of it! You won't try it again?"

"What's that you say, my lord?" rejoined Malcolm. "Would you have a man turn his back at the first little fear? No, my lord, that would never do!"

"Oh, then did you have a fright?"

"No, I can't say that either. Nothing worse came near me except a dream that plagued me; and it wasn't such a bad one after all."

"What was it?"

"I thought there was a pretty lady sitting on the bed in the next room, in her nightgown like, and she was very sorrowful in her heart, though she never let a tear fall down. She was crying about a little child she had lost, and I knew well enough where the child was—down in a cave near the shore, I thought—and I was just yearning to go to her and tell her to stop the grieving of her heart, but I couldn't move hand or foot; neither could I open my mouth to cry out to her. And I went on dreaming about the same thing over and over all the time I was asleep. But there was nothing so frightsome about that, my lord."

"No, indeed," said his lordship.

"Only it made me grieve too, my lord, because I couldn't do anything to help her."

His lordship laughed, but oddly, and changed the subject.

"There's no word of that boat yet," he said. "I must write again."

"May I show Malcolm the library?" asked Lady Florimel.

"I would like to see the books," added Malcolm.

"You don't know what a scholar he is, Papa."

"Little enough of that," said Malcolm.

"Oh, yes, I do," said the marquis, answering his daughter. "But he must keep the skipper from my books and the scholar from my boat."

"You mean a scholar who would skip your books, my lord. Faith! Such would be a skipper who would ill-scull your boat," said Malcolm, with a laugh at the poor attempt at humor.

"Bravo!" said the marquis, who certainly was not overcritical. "Can you write a good hand?"

"Not too bad, my lord."

"So much the better. I see you'll be worth your wages."

"That depends on the wages," returned Malcolm.

"And that reminds me, you've said nothing about them yet."

"Neither has your lordship."

"Well, what are they to be?"

"Whatever you think proper, my lord. Only don't make me go to Mister Crathie for them."

The marquis had sent away the man who was waiting when Malcolm entered, and during this conversation Malcolm had of his own accord been doing his best to supply his place. The meal ended; Lady Florimel desired him to wait a moment in the hall.

"He's so amusing, Papa!" she said. "I want to see him stare at the books. He thinks the schoolmaster's hundred volumes a grand library. He's such a goose! It's the greatest fun in the world watching him."

"Not such a goose," said the marquis, but he recognized himself in his child, and laughed.

Florimel ran off merrily, as bent on a joke, and joined Malcolm.

He followed her up two staircases, and through more than one long narrow passage. All the ducts of the house were long and narrow, causing him a sense of imprisonment, vanishing ever into freedom at the opening of some door into a great room. But never had he had a dream of such a room as that at which they now arrived. He started with a sort of marveling dismay when she threw open the door of the library and he beheld ten thousand volumes at a glance, all in solemn stillness. It was like a sepulchre of kings. But his astonishment took a strange form of expression, the thought in which was beyond the reach of his mistress.

"Eh, my lady!" he cried, after staring for a while in breathless bewilderment, "It just makes my head go round."

"It's a fine thing," said the girl, "to have such a library."

"Indeed it is, my lady! It's one of the privileges of rank," said Malcolm. "It takes a family that holds on through centuries in a house where things gather to make such an unaccountable gathering of books like that. It's a grand sight—worth living to see."

"Suppose you were to be a rich man some day," said Florimel in the condescending tone she generally adopted when addressing him, "it would be of the first things you would set about—wouldn't it—to get such a library together?"

"No, my lady. A library cannot be made all at once, any more than a house or a nation or a tree: they must all take time to grow, and so must a library. I wouldn't even know what books to go and ask for. I dare say, if I were to try, I couldn't at a moment's notice tell you the names of more than two score of books at the outside. Folk must make acquaintance among books as they would among living folk."

"But you could get somebody who knew more about them than yourself to buy them for you."

"I would as soon think of getting somebody to eat my dinner for me."

"That's not fair," said Florimel. "It would only be like getting somebody who knew more about cookery than yourself to order your dinner for you."

"You're right, my lady, but still I would as soon think of the one as the other. What would come of the likes of me, do you think, brought up on oatmeal and herring, if you was to set me down to such a dinner as my lord your father would eat every day and think nothing of it? But if someone else were in charge of buying my books, I imagine the first thing I would have to do would be to fling half of them into the stream."

"What good would that do?"

"Clear away the rubbish. You see, my lady, it's not the books, but what books. There must be many of the right sort here, though. I wonder if Mr. Graham ever saw them. He surely would have made mention of them if he had."

"What would be the first thing you would do, then, Malcolm, if you happened to turn out a great man after all?" said Florimel, sealing herself in a huge library chair, whence, having arranged her skirt, she looked up into the young fisherman's face.

"I imagine I would have to sit down and turn the change around in my mind a few times before I knew myself or what would become of me," he said.

"That's not answering my question," returned Florimel.

"Well, the second thing I would do," said Malcolm thoughtfully, and pausing a moment, "would be to get Mr. Graham to go with me to Aberdeen and take me through some classes there."

"But it's the first thing you would do that I want to know," persisted the girl.

"I tell you I would sit down and think about it."

"I don't count that as doing anything."

"Indeed, my lady, thinking's the hardest thing I know."

"Well, what is it you would think about first?" said Florimel, not to be diverted from her course.

"Well . . . the third thing I would do—"

"I want to know the first thing you would think about!"

"I cannot say yet what the third thing would be. Four years at the college would give me time to reflect upon a lot of things."

"I insist on knowing the first thing you would think about doing!" cried Florimel, with mock imperiousness but real tyranny.

"Well, my lady, if you will have it—but how great a man would you be making me?"

"Oh, let me see—yes, yes, the heir to an earldom. That's liberal enough, is it not?"

"That's as much as saying I would come to be an earl someday."

"Yes, that's what it means."

"And an earl's next to a marquis, isn't it?"

"Yes, he's in the next lower rank. But the difference is not so great as to prevent their meeting on a level of courtesy."

"I don't freely know what all that means, but if your ladyship's will is to make an earl of me, I'll not raise any objections."

He stood silent.

"Well?" said the girl.

"What's your will, my lady?" returned Malcolm as if roused from a reverie.

"Where's your answer?"

"I said I would be an earl to please your ladyship. I would be a flunky for the same reason, even if it was to wait upon yourself and no other."

"I ask you," said Florimel more imperiously than ever, "what is the first thing you would do if you found yourself no longer a fisherman but the son of an earl?"

"But I would always be a fisherman—to the end of creation, my lady."

"You refuse to answer my question!"

"By no means, my lady, if you will have an answer."

"I will have an answer."

"If you will have it, then, but—"

"No buts; but an answer."

"Well—it's your own fault, my lady!—I would just go down upon my knees, where I stood before you, and tell a heap of things that maybe by that time you would know well enough already."

"What would you tell me?"

"I would tell you that your eyes were like the very brightness of the light-ning itself, your cheeks like a white rose, your hair just the soft letting go of His hands when the Maker could do no more, your mouth just fashioned to drive folk daft that dare not come nearer, and for your shape, it were like nothing in nature but itself—You would have it, my lady!" he added apolo-getically—and well he might, for Lady Florimel's cheeks flushed long before he had reached the end of his celtic outpouring. Whether she was really angry or not, she had no difficulty in making Malcolm believe she was.

She rose from the chair—though not until he had ended—swept halfway to the door, then turned upon him with a flash.

"How dare you!" she said, her breed well obeying the call of the game, and she turned and left the room, leaving the poor fellow like a statue in the middle of it, with the books all turning their backs on him.

"Now," he said to himself, "she's off to tell her father and there'll be no end of his anger with me. But I'll just have to tell him the truth and he make of it what he likes."

With this resolution he stood his ground, every moment expecting the wrathful father to make his appearance and at least order him out of the house. But minute passed after minute and no wrathful father came. He grew calmer by degrees and by the time the great bell rang for lunch, he was buried in one of Milton's prose volumes.

———

My reader may well judge that Malcolm could not have been very far gone in love, seeing he was able to read. I remark in return that the force of his individuality and common sense, and his recognition of the great dis-tance between himself and Lady Florimel, allowed him to do so.

———

For some days Malcolm saw nothing more of Lady Florimel, but with his grandfather's new dwelling to see to, with the carpenter's shop and the blackship's forge open to him, and an eye to detect whatever he wanted setting right, the hours did not hang heavy on his hands. At length she thought she had punished him sufficiently for an offense for which she her-self was to blame, and began to indulge the interest she could not help feeling in him—an interest heightened by the mystery which hung over his birth, and by the fact that she knew that concerning him of which he was himself ignorant. She began again to seek his company under the guise of his help, half requesting, half commanding his services; and Malcolm found himself admitted afresh to the heaven of her favor. Young as he was, he read himself a lesson suitable to the occasion.

One afternoon the marquis sent for him to the library, but when he reached it his master was not there. He took down the volume of Milton in which he had been reading before, and was soon absorbed in it again.

He did not hear the marquis enter, and when he spoke Malcolm started, and almost dropped the volume. "I beg your lordship's pardon," he said, "I didn't hear you come in."

"I want you to do something for me," said the marquis.

Malcolm instantly replaced the book on its shelf and approached his master, saying, "Will your lordship let me read once in a while in this great place? I mean, when I'm not wanting other things to do and there's nobody here?"

"To be sure," answered the marquis, "only the scholar mustn't come with the skipper's hands."

"I'll take good care of that, my lord. I would as soon think of handling a book with work-like hands as I would of cooking a mackerel without cleaning it first."

"And when we have visitors, you'll be careful not to get in their way?"

"I will that, my lord."

"And now," said his lordship, rising, "I want you to take a letter to Mrs. Stewart of Kirkbyres. Can you ride?"

"I can ride bareback well enough for a fisherman," said Malcolm, "but I was never upon a saddle in my life."

"The sooner you get used to one, the better. Go and tell Stoat to saddle the bay mare. Wait in the yard; I will bring the letter to you myself."

"Very well, my lord," said Malcolm. He knew, from remarks he had heard about the stables, that the mare in question was a ticklish one to ride, but he would rather have his neck broken than object.

Hardly was she ready when the marquis appeared, accompanied by Lady Florimel, both expecting to enjoy a laugh at Malcolm's expense. But when the mare was brought out and he was going to mount her where she stood, something seemed to wake in the marquis' heart or conscience. He looked at Malcolm for a moment, then at the ears of the mare hugging her neck, and last at the stones of the paved yard.

"Lead her onto the grass, Stoat," he said.

The groom obeyed, all followed, and Malcolm mounted. The same instant he lay on his back on the grass amidst a general laugh, loud on the part of the marquis and lady, and subdued on that of the servants. But the next he was on his feet and, the groom still holding the mare, in the saddle again: a little anger is a fine spur for the side of even an honest intent. This time he sat for half a minute, and found himself once more on the grass. It was but once more: his mother earth had claimed him again only to complete his strength. A third time he mounted, and sat. As soon as she perceived it would be hard work to unseat him, the mare was quiet.

"Bravo!" cried the marquis, giving him the letter.

"Will there be an answer, my lord."

"Wait and see," he said.

Malcolm said a few words to the mare and rode off.

Both the marquis and Lady Florimel, whose laughter had altogether ceased in the interest of watching the struggle, stood looking after him with a pleased expression, which as he vanished up the glen changed to a mutual glance and smile.

"He's got good blood in him, however he came by it," said the marquis. "The country is more indebted to its nobility than is generally understood."

22
• • • • • • • • • • • • • • • • • • •

The Encounter

*M*alcolm felt considerably refreshed after his tussle with the mare and his victory over her, and much enjoyed his ride of ten miles. It was a cool autumn afternoon. A few of the fields were being reaped, one or two were crowded with stooks, while many crops of oats yet waved and rustled in various stages of vanishing green. On all sides cattle were lowing; overhead rooks were cawing; the sun was nearing the west, and in the hollows a thin mist came steaming up. Malcolm had never in his life been so far from the coast before. His road led him southward into the heart of the country.

The father of the late proprietor of Kirkbyres had married the heiress of Gersefell, an estate which bordered his own and was double its size, whence the lairdship was sometimes spoken of by the one name, sometimes by the other. The combined properties thus inherited by the late Mr. Stewart were of sufficient extent to justify him, although a plain man, in becoming a suitor for the hand of the beautiful daughter of a needy baronet in the neighborhood, with the already somewhat tarnished condition of whose reputation, having come into little contact with the world in which she moved, he was unacquainted. Quite unexpectedly she also, some years after their marriage, brought him a property of considerable extent—a fact which had doubtless had its share in the birth and nourishment of her consuming desire to get the estates into her own management.

Toward the end of his journey, Malcolm came upon a bare moorland waste on the long ascent of a low hill—very desolate, with not a tree or a house within sight for two miles. A ditch, half full of dark water, bordered on each side of the road, which went straight as a rod through a black peat moss lying cheerless and dreary on all sides—hardly less so where the sun gleamed from the surface of some stagnant pool filling a hole whence peats had been dug, or where a patch of cotton grass waved white and lonely in the midst of the waste expanse.

At length, when he reached the top of the ridge, he saw the house of Kirkbyres below him, with a small modern lodge nearby. He came to an old wall with an iron gate in the middle of it, within which the old house—a bare house—lifted its gray walls, pointed gables, and steep roof high into the pale blue air. He rode round the outer wall, seeking a back entrance, and arrived at a farmyard where a boy took his horse. Finding the kitchen door open, he entered and, having delivered his letter to the servant-girl, sat down to wait for the possible answer.

In a few minutes she returned and requested him to follow her. This was more than he had calculated upon, but he obeyed at once. The girl led him along a dark passage and up a winding stone stair, much worn, to a room richly furnished and older-fashioned, he thought, than any room he had seen in Lossie House.

On a settee, with her back to a window, sat Mrs. Stewart, a lady tall and slender, with well-poised, easy carriage, and a motion that might have suggested the lithe grace of a leopard. She greeted him with a bend of the head and a smile, which, even in the twilight and her own shadow, showed a gleam of ivory, and spoke to him in a hard sweet voice, wherein an ear more accustomed than Malcolm's might have detected an intent to please. He could not escape the contrast between the picture in his own mind of the mother of the mad laird and the woman before him.

"You have had a long ride, Mr. MacPhail," she said, "you must be tired."

"That didn't tire me, mem," returned Malcolm. "It was a fine afternoon and I had one of the marquis' best mares to carry me."

"You'll take a glass of wine, anyhow?" said Mrs. Stewart. "Will you oblige me by ringing the bell?"

"No, thank you, mem. The mare would be better with a mouthful of meal and water, but I needn't anything myself."

A shadow passed over the lady's face. She rose and rang the bell, then sat in silence until it was answered.

"Bring the wine and cake," she said; then turned to Malcolm. "Your master speaks very kindly of you. He seems to trust you thoroughly."

"I'm very glad to hear it, mem, but he has never had much cause to trust or distrust me."

"He seems to think that I might place equal confidence in you."

"I don't know. I wouldn't have you trust me too much," said Malcolm.

"You do not mean to contradict the good character your master gives you?" said the lady, with a smile and a look right into his eyes.

"I wouldn't have you trust me before you had my word," said Malcolm.

"I may use my own judgment about that," she replied with another winning smile. "But oblige me by taking a glass of wine."

She rose and approached the decanters.

"Indeed not, mem! I'm not used to it, and it might jumble my judgment," said Malcolm, who had placed himself on the defensive from the first, jealous of his own conduct as being the friend of the laird.

At his second refusal the cloud again crossed the lady's brow, but her smile did not vanish. Pressing her hospitality no more, she resumed her seat.

"My lord tells me," she said, folding her hands on her lap, "that you see my poor unhappy boy sometimes—"

"He's not so absolutely unhappy, mem," said Malcolm; but she went on without heeding the remark.

"—and that you rescued him not long ago from the hands of ruffians?" Malcolm made no reply.

"Everybody knows," she continued after a slight pause, "what an unhappy mother I am. It is many years since I lost the loveliest infant ever seen, while my poor Stephen was left to be the mockery of every urchin in the street."

She sighed deeply, and one of the fair hands took a handkerchief from a worktable near.

"Not in Portlossie, mem," said Malcolm. "There's very few of them so hardhearted or so ill-mannered. They're used to seeing him at the school, where he shows himself every once in a while; and he's a great favorite with them, for he's one of the best creatures of the living."

"A poor witless, unmanageable being. He's a dreadful grief to me," said the widowed mother with another deep sigh.

"A child could manage him," said Malcolm in strong contradiction.

"Oh, if only I could but convince him of my love! But he won't give me a chance. He has an unaccountable dread of me. It is a delusion which no argument can overcome. The more care and kindness he needs, the less he will accept from my hands. I long to devote my life to him, and he will not allow me. Ah, Mr. MacPhail, you little know a mother's heart. Even if my beautiful boy had not been taken from me, Stephen would still have been my idol, idiot as he is, and will be as long as he lives. And—"

"He's no idiot, mem," interposed Malcolm.

"—and just imagine," she went on, "what a misery it must be to a widowed mother, poor companion as he would be at best, to think of her boy roaming the country like a beggar! It's enough to break a mother's heart. If I could but persuade him to come home for a week, so as to have a chance with him. But it's no use trying; evil people have made mischief between us, telling wicked lies and terrifying the poor fellow. It is quite impossible except I get someone to help me; and there are so few who have influence with him."

Malcolm thought she must surely have had chances enough before he ran away from her, but he could not help feeling softened toward her.

"Supposing I was to tell him what you said?" he said.

"That would not be of the slightest use. He is so prejudiced against me, he would only shriek and go into one of those horrible fits."

"I don't see what's to be done then," said Malcolm.

"I must have him brought here: there is no other way."

"And what would be the good of that, mem? You just said he would run away if you did."

"I did not mean by force," returned Mrs. Stewart. "Someone he has confidence in must come with him. Nothing else will give me a chance. He would trust you now. Your presence would keep him from being terrified."

Her tone was so refined and her voice so pleading that the strength of his prejudices was swaying; and had it not been that he was already the partisan of her son, and therefore in honor bound to give him the benefit of every doubt, he would certainly have been gained over to work her will. He knew absolutely nothing against her—not even for certain that she was the person he had seen in Mrs. Catanach's company in the garret of Lossie House. But he steeled himself to distrust her, and held his peace.

"It is clear," she resumed after a pause, "that the intervention of some friend of both is the only thing that can be of the smallest use. I know you are a friend of his—a true one—and I do not see why you should not be a friend of mine as well. Will you be my friend too?"

She rose as she said the words and, approaching him, bent on him out of the shadow the full strength of her eyes, and held out a white hand. She knew only too well the power of a still fine woman of any age over a youth of twenty.

Malcolm, knowing nothing about it, yet felt hers, and was on his guard. He rose also, but did not take her hand.

"I have had only too much reason," she added, "to distrust some who, unlike you, professed themselves eager to serve me; but I know neither Lord Lossie nor you will play me false."

She took his great rough hand between her two soft palms, and for a moment Malcolm was tempted—not to betray his friend, but to simulate a yielding sympathy, in order to come at the heart of her intent and, should it prove false, to foil it the more easily. But the honest nature of him shrank from deception, even where the object of it was good. He was not at liberty to use falsehood for the discomfiture even of the false. A pretended friendship was of the vilest of despicable things.

"I can't help you, mem," he said. "I dare not. I have such a regard for your son that before I would do anything to harm him, I would have my own two hands chopped from the wrists."

"Surely, my dear Mr. MacPhail," returned the lady in her most persuasive tones and with her sweetest smile, "you cannot call it harming a poor idiot to restore him to the care of his own mother?"

"That would be as it turns out," rejoined Malcolm. "But I'm sure of one thing, mem, and that is, that he's not so much of an idiot as some folk would have him."

Mrs. Stewart's face fell. She turned from him, and going back to her seat hid her face in her handkerchief.

"I'm afraid," she said sadly, after a moment, "I must give up my last hope: you are not disposed to be friendly to me, Mr. MacPhail. You have been believing hard things of me."

"That's true, but not from hearsay alone," returned Malcolm. "The look of the poor fellow when he but hears the chance word 'mother' is a sight not to be forgotten. That couldn't come of nothing."

Mrs. Stewart hid her face on the cushioned arm of the settee and sobbed. A moment after she sat erect again, but languid and red-eyed, saying, as if with sudden resolve, "I will tell you all I know about it, and then you can judge for yourself. When he was a very small child I took him for advice to the best physicians in London and Paris: all advised a certain operation which had to be performed for consecutive months at intervals of a few days. Though painful, it was simple, yet of such a nature that no one was so fit to attend to it as his mother. Alas! instead of doing him any good, it has done me the worst injury in the world: my child hates me."

Again she hid her face on the settee.

The explanation was plausible enough, and the grief of the mother surely apparent. Malcolm could not but be touched. "It's not that I'm not willing to be your friend, mem, but I'm your son's friend already, and if he was to hear anything that made him mistrust me, it would go right to my heart."

"Then you can judge what I feel," said the lady.

"If it would heal your heart to hurt mine, I would think about it, mem, but if it hurt all three of us, and did good to none, it would be a misfit all together. I'll do nothing until I'm downright sure it's the part of a friend."

"That's what makes you the only fit person to help me that I know. If I were to employ other people in the affair, they might be rough with the poor fellow."

"Likely enough, mem," assented Malcolm, while the words put him afresh on his guard.

"But I might be driven to it," she added.

Malcolm responded with an unuttered vow.

"It might become necessary to use force, whereas you could lead him with a word."

"No, I'm not such a traitor."

"Where would be the treachery when you know it was for his own good?"

"That's just what I don't know, mem," retorted Malcolm. "See for yourself, mem," he continued, rousing himself to venture an appeal to the mother's heart: "here's a man it has pleased God to make not like other folk. His mind, though capable of more than people think who don't know him so well as I do, is certainly weak—though maybe the weakness lies more in the tongue than in the brain. But he's the gentlest of creatures—a downright gentleman, mem, if ever there was one—and kindly with any creature, both man and beast! A very child could guide him any way but one."

"Anywhere but to his own mother!" exclaimed Mrs. Stewart, pressing her handkerchief to her eyes and sobbing as she spoke. "There is a child he is very fond of I am told," she added, recovering herself.

"He likes all children," returned Malcolm, "and there's just one thing that makes his life endurable to him. And that's his liberty—just his liberty—to go where he likes, like the wind; to turn his face where he will in the morning, and back again at night if he likes; to wander—"

"Where?" interrupted his mother, a little too eagerly.

"Where he likes, mem; I wouldn't say exactly where with any certainty. But he likes to hear the sea moaning and watch the stars shining. It's my belief, if you took the liberty from the poor man, you would kill him."

"Then you won't help me?" she cried despairingly. "They tell me you are an orphan yourself and yet you will not take pity on a childless mother—

worse than the childless, for I had the loveliest boy once. He would be about your age now, and I have never had any comfort in life since I lost him. Give me my son, and I will bless you, love you."

As she spoke she rose and, approaching him gently, laid a hand on his shoulder. Malcolm trembled, but stood his mental ground.

"Indeed, mem, I can and I will promise you nothing," he said. "Are you to play a man false because he's less able to take care of himself than other folk? If I was sure that you could make it up, and that he would be happy with you afterward, it might be another thing; but except you forced him you couldn't get him to stay long enough for you to try; and even then he would die before you had convinced him. I don't doubt you have lost your chance with him, and must do your best to be content without him. I'll promise you this much, if you like: I shall tell him what you have said."

"Much good that will be!" replied the lady, with ill-concealed scorn.

"You think he wouldn't understand, but he understands fine."

"And you would come again, and tell me what he said?" she murmured, with the eager persuasiveness of reviving hope.

"Maybe, maybe not—I won't promise. Have you any answer to send back to my lord's letter, mem?"

"No, I cannot write; I cannot even think. You have made me so miserable."

Malcolm lingered.

"Go, go," said the lady dejectedly. "Tell your master I am not well. I will write tomorrow. If you hear anything of my poor boy, do take pity upon me and come and tell me."

The stiffer partisan Malcolm appeared the more desirable did it seem to Mrs. Stewart to gain him over to her side. She saw plainly enough that, if he were called on to give testimony as to the laird's capacity, his evidence would pull strongly against her plans; while if the interests of such a youth were wrapped up in them, that fact in itself would prejudice most people in favor of them.

23

The Blow

*W*ell, Malcolm," said his lordship when the youth reported himself. "How's Mrs. Stewart?"

"Not too well pleased, my lord," answered Malcolm.

"What! You haven't been refusing to—?"

"Indeed I have, my lord."

"Tut, tut! Have you brought me any message from her?" He spoke rather angrily.

"None but that she was not well, and would write in the morning."

The marquis thought for a few moments. "If I make a personal matter of it, MacPhail—I mean, you won't refuse me if I ask a personal favor of you?"

"I must know what it is before I say anything, my lord."

"You may trust me not to require anything you couldn't undertake."

"There might be two opinions, my lord."

"You young boor! What is the world coming to? By Jove!"

"As far as I can go with a clean conscience, I'll go—not one step farther," said Malcolm.

"You mean to say your judgment is a safer guide than mine?"

"No, my lord. I might well follow your lordship's judgment, but if there be a conscience in the affair, it's my own conscience I'm bound to follow, and not your lordship's or any other man's. Suppose the thing that seemed right to your lordship seemed wrong to me, what would you have me do then?"

"Do as I told you and lay the blame on me."

"No, my lord, that wouldn't work: I'm bound to do what I thought right, and lay the blame upon nobody, whatever came of it."

"You young hypocrite! Why didn't you tell me you meant to set up for a saint before I took you into my service?"

"Because I had no such intention, my lord. Surely a man might know himself not to be a saint and yet like to keep his hands clean."

"What did Mrs. Stewart tell you she wanted of you?" asked the marquis, almost fiercely, after a moment's silence.

"She wanted me to get the poor laird to go back to her; but I have my doubts, for all her fine words, what she would do to him, and I would sooner be hanged than have part in that."

"Why should you doubt what a lady tells you?"

"I wouldn't be that anxious to doubt her, except that I have heard things, you see, and am behoved to be on my guard."

"Well, I suppose, as you are a personal friend of the idiot—"

His lordship had thought to sting him, and paused for a moment, but Malcolm's manner revealed nothing except waiting watchfulness.

"—I must employ someone else to get hold of the fellow for her," he concluded.

"You wouldn't do that, my lord!" cried Malcolm in a tone of entreaty, but his master chose to misunderstand him.

"Who's to prevent me, I should like to know?" he said.

Malcolm accepted the misinterpretation involved, and answered, but calmly, "Me, my lord: I will. At any rate, I'll do my best."

"Upon my word!" exclaimed Lord Lossie; "you presume sufficiently on my good nature, young man!"

"Hear me one moment, my lord," returned Malcolm. "I've been turning it over in my mind, and I see, plain as the daylight, that I'm bound, being your lordship's servant and trusted by your lordship, to say that to you while

I was not similarly bound to say it to Mrs. Stewart. So, at the risk of angering you, I must tell your lordship, with all respect, that if I can help it there shall be no hand, gentle or not, laid upon the laird against his own will."

The marquis was getting tired of the contest. He was angry too, and nonetheless that he felt Malcolm in the right.

"Go to the devil, you booby!" he said, even more in impatience than in wrath.

"I'm thinking I needn't budge to do that," retorted Malcolm, angry also.

"What do you mean by that insolence?"

"I mean, my lord, that to go will be to go from him. He can't be far from your lordship's side this minute."

All the marquis' gathered annoyance broke out at last in rage. He started from his chair, made three strides to Malcolm and struck him in the face.

Malcolm staggered back till he was stopped by the door. "Hoot, my lord!" he exclaimed as he sought his blue cotton handkerchief, "you shouldn't have done that; you'll get blood on the carpet."

"You precious idiot!" cried his lordship, already repenting the deed, "why didn't you defend yourself?"

"The quarrel was my own, and I could do as I like, my lord."

"And why should you want to take such a blow? Not to raise a hand, even to defend yourself!" said the marquis, vexed both with Malcolm and himself.

"Because I saw I was in the wrong, my lord. The quarrel was of my own making: I had no right to lose my temper and be impudent. So I didn't dare defend myself. And I beg your lordship's pardon. But don't do me the wrong, my lord, of thinking that because I took a blow because I knew myself in the wrong that that's how I'd carry myself if someone was after the poor laird."

"Go along with you, and don't show yourself till you're fit to be seen. I hope it'll be a lesson to you."

"It will, my lord," said Malcolm. "But," he added, "there was no occasion to give me such a drubbing: a word would have put me more in the wrong."

So saying, he left the room with his handkerchief to his face.

The marquis was really sorry for the blow, chiefly because Malcolm, without a shadow of cowardliness, had taken it so quietly. Malcolm would, however, have had very much the worse of it had he defended himself, for his master had been a bruiser in his youth, and neither his left hand nor his right arm had yet forgot its cunning whatever its strength or agility.

For some time after he was gone, the marquis paced up and down the room, feeling strangely and unaccountably uncomfortable. "The great lout!" he kept saying to himself. "Why did he let me strike him?"

Malcolm went to his grandfather's cottage. In passing the window he peeped in. The old man was sitting with his bagpipes on his knees, looking troubled. When he entered, the old man held out his arms to him.

"Ter'll pe something wrong with you, Malcolm, my son!" he cried. "You'll pe hafing a hurt! I knows it, I has it within me, though I can't chust see it. Where is it?"

As he spoke he proceeded to feel his head and face.

"Pless my sowl! You are pleeding, Malcolm!" he cried the same moment.

"It's nothing to fret about, Daddy. It's hardly more than the flick of a salmon's tail."

"Put who'll haf tone it?" asked Duncan angrily.

"Oh, the master gave me a bit of a slap," answered Malcolm with indifference.

"Where is he?" cried the piper, rising in a wrath. "Take me to him, Malcolm. I'll slap him. I'll kill him. I will trive my turk into his wicked pody!"

"No, no, Daddy," said Malcolm. "We have had enough of knives already."

"Then you haf tone it yourself, Malcolm, my prave poy!"

"No, Daddy. I took my licks like a man, for I deserved them."

"Deserfed to pe peaten, Malcolm?—to pe peaten like a tog?"

"It wasn't that much, Daddy. I only told him that the devil was at his side."

"And no toubt it was true," cried Duncan, emerging from his despondency.

"Yes, so he was, only I had no right to say it."

"Put you striked him pack, Malcolm? Ton't say you tidn't give him pack his plow. Ton't tell me that, Malcolm."

"How could I hit my master, and myself in the wrong, Daddy?"

"Then I must pe toing it myself," said Duncan quietly, and with his lips compressed of calm decision turned toward the door to get his sword from the next room.

"Keep still, Daddy," implored Malcolm, laying hold of his arm, "and sit down until you hear all about it first."

Duncan yielded, for the sake of better instruction in the circumstances, over the whole of which Malcolm now went. But before he came to a close, he had skillfully introduced and enlarged upon the sorrows and sufferings and dangers of the laird, so as to lead the old man away from the quarrel, dwelling especially on the necessity of protecting Mr. Stewart from the machinations of his mother. Duncan listened to all he said with marked sympathy.

"And if the marquis dares to cross me in it," said Malcolm at last as he ended, "let him watch himself."

This assurance, indicative of a full courageous intent on the part of his grandson, for whose manliness he was jealous, greatly served to quiet Duncan; and he consented at last to postpone all quittance, in the hope of Malcolm's having the opportunity of a righteous quarrel for proving himself no coward. His wrath gradually died away, until at last he begged his boy to take his pipes, that he might give him a lesson. Malcolm made the attempt, but found it impossible to fill the bag with his swollen and cut lips, and had to beg his grandfather to play to him instead. He gladly consented, and played until bedtime, when, having tucked him up, Malcolm went quietly to his own room, avoiding supper and the eyes of Mrs. Courthope together. He fell asleep in a moment, and spent a night of perfect oblivion, dreamless of wizard lord or white lady.

Some days passed, during which Malcolm contrived that no one should see him: he stole down to his grandfather's early in the morning, and returned to his own room at night. Duncan told the people about that he was not very well, but would be all right in a day or two. It was a time of jubilation to the bard, and he cheered his grandson's retirement with music and with wild stories of highland locks and moors, chanted or told. Malcolm's face was now much better, though the signs of the blow were still plain enough upon it, when a messenger came one afternoon to summon him to the marquis' presence.

"Where have you been sulking all this time?" was his master's greeting.

"I haven't been sulking, my lord," answered Malcolm. "Your lordship told me to stay out of the way until I was fit to be seen, and not a soul's set an eye upon me until now."

"Where have you been then?"

"In my own room at night, and down at my grandfather's as long as folk was about—with a stroll or two up the stream."

"You couldn't encounter the shame of being seen with such a face, eh?"

"It might have been thought a disgrace to the one or the other of us, my lord—maybe to both."

"If you don't learn to curb that tongue of yours, it will bring you to worse."

"My lord, I confessed my fault and I put up with the blow. But if it hadn't been that I was in the wrong—well, things might have been different."

"Hold your tongue, I tell you! You're an honest, good fellow, and I'm sorry I struck you. There!"

"I thank your lordship."

"I sent for you because I've just heard from Aberdeen that the boat is on her way round. You must be ready to take charge of her the moment she arrives."

"I will be that, my lord. It doesn't suit me to be so long on the ground. I like to be out riding on the waves."

The next morning he got a telescope and, taking with him his dinner of bread and cheese and a book in his pocket, went out to the beach to look for the boat. Every few minutes he swept the horizon, but morning and afternoon passed and she did not appear.

He had just become aware of the first dusky breath of twilight when a tiny sloop appeared rounding the Deid Heid, as they called the promontory which closed in the bay on the east. The sun was setting, red and large, on the other side of the Scaurnose, and filled her white sails with a rosy sky as she came stealing round in a fair soft wind. The moon hung over her thin and pale and ghostly, with hardly shine enough to show that it was indeed she and not the forgotten scrap of a torn-up cloud. As she passed the point and turned the harbor, the warm hue suddenly vanished from her sails, and she looked white and cold, as if the sight of the Death's Head had scared the blood out of her.

"It's her!" cried Malcolm in delight. "About the size of a little herring boat, but no more like one than Lady Florimel's like Meg Partan. I had no idea she was going to be anything so bonny. But I'll not be fit to manage her in a squall, though. I'll have to get another hand. And I won't have a boy either. It must be a grown man. I'll have Blue Peter himself if I can get him."

He shut up the telescope, and in three or four minutes was waiting for her on the harbor wall.

Malcolm jumped on board, and the two men who had brought her round gave up their charge.

She was full-decked, with a dainty little cabin. Her planks were almost white. Everything was all so clean, her standing rigging so taut, everything so ship-shape that Malcolm was in raptures. If the burn had only been navigable, he would have towed the graceful creature home and laid her up under the very walls of the House! He made her snug for the night and went to report her arrival.

Great was Lady Florimel's jubilation. She would have set out on a "coasting voyage," as she called it, the very next day, but her father listened to Malcolm.

"You see, my lord," he said, "I must know all about her before I dare take you out in her. And I can't undertake to manage her all by myself. You must just give me another man to go with me."

"Get one," said the marquis.

Early in the morning, therefore, Malcolm went to Scaurnose and found Blue Peter among his nets. He could spare a day or two and would join him. They returned together, got the cutter into the offing and, with a westerly breeze, tried her every way. She answered her helm with readiness, rose as light as a bird, made a good board, and seemed in every way a safe boat.

"She's the bonniest craft ever launched!" said Malcolm, ending a description of her behavior and qualities rather too circumstantial for his master to follow.

They were to make their first trip the next morning, eastward, if the wind should hold, landing at a certain ancient ruin on the coast two or three miles from Portlossie.

24
· · · · · · · · · · · · · · · · · ·

The Sail

*L*ady Florimel's fancy was so full of the expected pleasure that she awoke soon after dawn. She rose and anxiously drew aside a curtain of her window. The day was one of God's odes written for men!

Below her window, under the tall bridge, the burn lay dark in a deep pool. Away to the north the great sea was merry with waves and spotted with their broken crests. Heaped against the horizon, it looked like a blue hill dotted all over with feeding sheep. But today she never thought why the waters were so busy. She dressed in haste, called her staghound, and set out the nearest way—that is, by the town gate for the harbor. She must make acquaintance with her new plaything.

Mrs. Catanach in her nightcap looked from her upper window as she passed, like a great spider from the heart of its web, and nodded significantly after her with a look and a smile such as might mean that for all her good looks she might have the heartache some day. But Mrs. Catanach was to have the first herself, for that moment her ugly dog, now and always with the look of being fresh from the ash-pit, rushed from somewhere and laid hold of Lady Florimel's dress, frightening her so that she gave a cry. Instantly her own dog, which had been loitering behind, came tearing up, five lengths at a bound, and descended like an angel of vengeance upon the offensive animal, which would have fled but found it too late. Opening his huge jaws, Demon took him across the flanks, much larger than his own, as if he had been a rabbit. His howls of agony brought Mrs. Catanach out in her petticoats. She flew at the hound, which Lady Florimel was in vain attempting to drag from the cur, and seized him by the throat.

"Take care! he is dangerous!" cried the girl.

Finding she had no power upon him, Mrs. Catanach forsook him, and in despairing fury rushed at his mistress. Demon saw it with one flaming eye, left the cur which, howling hideously, dragged his hindquarters after him into the house, and sprang at the woman. Then indeed was Lady Florimel terrified, for she knew the savage nature of the animal when roused. Truly, with his eyes on fire as now, his long fangs bared, the bristles on his back erect and his moustache sticking straight out, he might well be believed a wolf after all. His mistress threw herself between them and flung her arms tight round his neck.

"Run, woman! Run for your life!" she shrieked. "I can't hold him long."

Mrs. Catanach fled, cowed by terror. Her huge legs bore her huge body, a tragic-comic spectacle, across the street to her open door. She had hardly vanished, flinging it closed behind her, when Demon broke from his mistress and, going at the door as if launched from a catapult, burst it open and disappeared also.

Lady Florimel gave another shriek of horror and darted after him.

That same moment the sound of Duncan's pipes as he issued from the town gate reached her and, bethinking herself of her inability to control the hound, she darted again from the cottage and flew to meet him, crying aloud, "Mr. MacPhail! Duncan! Duncan! Stop your pipes and come here directly!"

"And who may pe calling me?" asked Duncan, who had not thoroughly distinguished the voice.

She laid her hand trembling with apprehension on his arm, and began pulling him along. "It's me—Lady Florimel," she said. "Come here directly. Demon has got into a house and is worrying a woman."

"God haf mercy!" cried Duncan. "Take my pipes, my laty, for fear anything paad should happen to tem."

She led him hurriedly to the door. But ere he had quite crossed the threshold, he shivered and drew back. "This is an efil house," he said. "I'll not co in."

A great floundering racket was going on above, mingled with growls and shrieks, but there was no howling.

"Call the dog, then. He will mind you, perhaps," she cried—knowing what a slow business an argument with Duncan was—and flew to the stairs.

"Temon! Temon!" cried Duncan with agitated voice.

Whether the dog thought his friend was in trouble next, I cannot tell, but down he came that instant, with a single bound from the top of the stair, right over his mistress's head as she was running up and, leaping out to Duncan, laid a paw upon each of his shoulders, panting with outlolled tongue.

But the piper staggered back, pushing the dog from him. "It is plood!" he cried—"ta efil woman's plood!"

"Keep him out, Duncan dear," said Lady Florimel. "I will go and see. There! he'll be up again if you don't mind."

Very reluctant, yet obedient, the bard laid hold of the growling animal by the collar; and Lady Florimel was just turning to finish her ascent of the stair and see what dread thing had come to pass when, to her great joy, she heard Malcolm's voice calling from the farther end of the street, "Hey, Daddy, what's happened that I didn't hear the pipes?"

She rushed out, the pipes dangling from her hand, so that the drone trailed on the ground behind her. "Malcolm! Malcolm!" she cried; and he was by her side in scarcely more time than Demon would have taken.

Rather incoherently, she quickly told him what had taken place. He sprang up the stair, and she followed.

In the front garret stood Mrs. Catanach facing the door, with such a malignant rage in her countenance that it looked demoniacal. Her dog lay at her feet with his throat torn out.

As soon as she saw Malcolm, she broke into a fury of vulgar imprecation.

"Hoots! for shame, Mistress Catanach!" he cried. "Here's my lady behind me, hearing every word."

"What but a curse would she have from me? I swear by God I'll make her pay for this, or my name's not—" She stopped suddenly.

"I thought as much," said Malcolm with a keen look.

"What are you to think? What should my name be but Bawby Catanach? You're even more upsetting since you turned my lady's flunky! Sorrow take you both! My poor Beauty killed by the hell-tyke of hers!"

"If you go on like that, the marquis'll have you drummed out of the town before two days are over," said Malcolm.

"Will he, then?" she returned with a confident sneer, showing all the teeth she had left.

"My lady, she's too ill-tongued for you to listen to," said Malcolm, turning to Florimel, who stood in the door white and trembling. "Just go down and tell my grandfather to send the dog up. There's surely some way of making her hold her tongue."

Mrs. Catanach threw a terrified glance toward Lady Florimel.

"Indeed I shall do nothing of the kind," replied Florimel. "For shame!"

"Hoots, my lady!" returned Malcolm. "I only said it to try the effect of it."

"You son of a devil!" cried the woman. "I'll make my amends for this if I have to roast my own heart to do it."

"Indeed, but you're doing that fine already! That foul brute of yours has gotten what he deserves too. I wonder what he thinks of salmon trout now, eh, mem?"

"Be done with it, Malcolm," said Florimel. "I am ashamed of you. If this woman is not hurt, we have no business in her house."

"Listen to her!" cried Mrs. Catanach contemptuously. "The woman!"

But Lady Florimel took no heed. She had already turned and was going down the stair. Malcolm followed in silence, nor did another word from Mrs. Catanach overtake them.

Arriving in the street, Florimel restored the pipes to Duncan—who, letting the dog go, at once proceeded to fill the bag—and, instead of continuing her way to the harbor, she turned back, accompanied by Malcolm and Demon.

"What a horrible woman that is!" she said with a shudder.

"Ay, she is. But I don't doubt that she would even be worse if she didn't break out that way once in a while," rejoined Malcolm.

"How do you mean?"

"It makes people frightened of her, and maybe sometimes puts it out of her power to do even worse. If ever she tries to make it up with you, my lady, I would have little to say to her if I was you."

"What could I say to a low creature like that?"

"You wouldn't know what she might be up to, or how she might set about it, my lady. I would have you mistrust her altogether. My daddy has a fine moral nose for vermin, and he can't abide her, though he never had a glimpse of her face, and in truth never even spoke to her."

"I will tell my father of her. A woman like that is not fit to live among civilized people."

"You're right there, my lady, but she would only go some other way about the same. Of course you must tell your father, but she's not fit for him to take any notice of."

As they sat at breakfast, Florimel did tell her father. His first emotion, however, at least the first he showed, was vexation with herself. "You must not be going out alone, and at such ridiculous hours," he said. "I shall be compelled to get you a governess."

"Really, Papa," she returned, "I don't see the good of having a marquis for a father if I can't go about as safe as one of the fisher-children. I might just as well be at school if I'm not to do as I like."

"What if the dog had turned on you?" he said.

"If he dared!" exclaimed the girl, and her eyes flashed.

Her father looked at her for a moment, then said to himself "There spoke a Colonsay!" and pursued the subject no further.

The day continued lovely, with a fine breeze. The whole sky and air and sea were alive with moving clouds, with wind, with waves flashing in the sun. Later, as they stepped on board the cutter amidst the little crowd gathered to see, Lady Florimel could hardly contain her delight. It was all she could do to restrain herself from dancing on the little deck halfswept by the tiller. The boat of a schooner which lay at the quay towed them out of the harbor. Then the creature spread her wings like a bird, leaned away to leeward, and seemed actually to bound over the waves. Malcolm sat at the tiller, and Blue Peter watched the canvas.

Lady Florimel turned out to be a good sailor, and her enjoyment was so contagious as even to tighten certain strings about her father's heart which had long been too slack to vibrate with any simple gladness. Her questions were incessant—first about the sails and rigging, then about the steering; but when Malcolm proceeded to explain how the water reacted on the rudder, she declined to trouble herself with that.

"Let me steer first," she said, "and then tell me how things work."

"That's always the best plan," said Malcolm. "Just put your hand on the tiller, my lady, and look out at yonder point they call the Deid Heid. You see, when I turn the tiller this way, her head falls off from the point; and when I turn it this other way, her head turns to it again. Hold her head just about two yards off it."

Florimel was more delighted then ever when she felt her own hand ruling the cutter—so overjoyed, indeed, that instead of steering straight she would keep playing tricks with the rudder. Every now and then Malcolm had to expostulate.

"Take it easy now, my lady. Don't steer quite so much. Hold her steady." Turning to her father, he said, "My lord, would you just say a word to my lady, or I'll be forced to take the tiller from her."

But by and by she grew weary of the attention required, and, giving up the helm, began to seek the explanation of its influence in a way that delighted Malcolm.

"You'll make a good skipper some day," he said, "you ask the right questions, and that's almost as good as knowing the right answers."

At length she threw herself on the cushions Malcolm had brought for her and, while her father smoked his cigar, gazed in silence at the shore. Here tow rocks, infinitely broken and jagged, filled all the tidal space. High cliffs of gray and brown rock, orange and green with lichen here and there rose behind—untouched by the ordinary tide, but at high water lashed by the waves of a storm. Beyond the headland which they were fast nearing, the cliffs and the sea met at half-tide.

The moment they rounded it—

"Look there, my lord," cried Malcolm, "there's Colonsay Castle, that your lordship gets your name from. It must be a hundred years since any Colonsay lived in it!"

Well he might say so, for they looked but saw nothing—only cliff rising from a white-fringed shore. Not a broken tower, not a ragged battlement invaded the horizon.

"There's nothing of the sort there!" said Lady Florimel.

"You mustn't look for a tower or pinnacle, my lady, for you won't see any; their time's long over. But just get the face of the cliffs in your eye, and travel along it until you come to a place that looks like mason work. It hardly rises above the cliff in most places, but here and there is a few feet of it."

Following his direction, Lady Florimel soon found the ruin. The front of a projecting portion of the cliff was faced with mason work; while on its side, the masonry rested upon jutting masses of the rock. Above, grass-grown heaps and mounds, and one isolated bit of wall pierced with a little window, like an empty eyesocket with no skull behind it, was all that was visible from the sea of the structure which had once risen lordly on the crest of the cliff.

"It is poor for a ruin even!" said Lord Lossie.

"But just consider how old the place is, my lord! It's as old as the time of the sea-roving Danes, they say. Maybe it's older than King Alfred! You must regard it only as a foundation; there're stones enough lying about to show that there must have been a great building on it once. I think it once must have been disconnected with the land and joined by a drawbridge. It's a wonderful old place, my lord."

"What would you do with it if it were yours, Malcolm?" asked Lady Florimel.

"I would spend my spare time patching it up, so it could stand up against the weather. It's pretty badly crumbled away."

"What would be the good of that? A rickle of old stones!" said the marquis.

"There surely aren't many more like it," returned Malcolm. "I wonder at your lordship!"

He was now steering for the foot of the cliff. As they approached, the ruin expanded and separated, and grew more detailed.

"Suppose you were Lord Lossie, Malcolm, what would you do with it?" asked Florimel, seriously, but with fun in her eyes.

"I would try to find the bottom of it first."

"What do you mean?"

"You'll see when we get into it. There's a lot of open places inside. Do you see that little square window? That lets the light into one of them. There may be vaults beneath vaults, too, for all I know, because those you can get into are half full of stones. I would have all that cleared out, and begin from the very foundation, building and patching and buttressing, until I got it as sound as a whale stone; and when I came to the top of the rock, there the castle would begin growing again; and grow it should, until there it stood as near what it was as the wit and the hand of man could make it."

"But all this is past rebuilding," said his lordship. "It would be barely possible to preserve the remains as they are."

"It would be hard to do, my lord. But just think what a grand place it would be to live in!"

The marquis burst out laughing.

"A grand place for gulls and kittiwakes and sea crows!" he said. "But where is it, pray, that a fisherman like you gets such extravagant notions? How do you come to think of such things?"

"Thoughts are free, my lord. If a thing be good to think, why shouldn't a fisher-lad think it? I've read a heap about old castles and such like in the history of Scotland, and there's many an old tale and ballad about them."

"Oh, look, Papa!" exclaimed Florimel, "we're almost to the shore."

"Slack the mainsheet, Peter. Don't rise, my lady; she'll be on the ground in another minute."

Almost immediately followed a slight grating noise, which grew loud, and before one could say her speed had slackened, the cutter rested on the pebbles, with the small waves of the just-turned tide flowing against her quarter. Malcolm was overboard in a moment.

"How the deuce are we to land here?" asked the marquis.

"Yes!" followed Florimel, "how the deuce are we to land here?"

"Hoots, my lady!" said Malcolm, "such words don't become your pretty mouth."

The marquis laughed.

"I ask you how are we to get ashore?" said Florimel with grave dignity, though an imp was laughing in the shadows of her eyes.

"I'll soon let you see that, my lady," answered Malcolm; and leaning over the low bulwark he had her in his arms almost before she could utter an objection. Carrying her ashore like a child—indeed, to steady herself she had to put her arm round his shoulder—he set her down on the gravel and left her as if she had been a burden of nets, then waded back to the boat.

"And how, pray, am I to go?" asked the marquis. "Do you fancy you can carry me in that style?"

"Oh, no, my lord! That wouldn't be dignified for a man. Just leap upon my back."

As he spoke he turned his broad shoulders, stooping.

The marquis accepted the invitation, and rode ashore like a schoolboy, laughing merrily.

They were in a little valley, open only to the sea, one boundary of which was the small promontory whereupon the castle stood. The side of it next to them rose perpendicular from the beach to a great height; whence, to gain the summit, they had to ascend by a winding path till they reached the approach to the castle from the landward side.

"Now wouldn't this be a great place to live, my lord?" asked Malcolm as they reached the summit—the marquis breathless, Florimel fresh as a lark. "Just look at this view! The very place for pirates like the old Danes! Nothing could escape the sight of them here. Just think, my lord, how grand would be the blustering blow of the wind about the turrets, as you stood at your window on a winter's day, looking out over the turbulent water, the air full of the smell of snow, the clouds a mile thick about your head, and no living creature but your family nearer than the farm town over yonder!"

"I don't see anything very attractive in your description," said his lordship. "And where," he added looking around him, "would be the garden?"

"What could you want with a garden, with the sea before you there? The sea's prettier than any garden!"

"And how would you get a carriage up here?" said the marquis.

"There's a road from the neck there that winds its way back inland. Oh, how nice it would be to clear away the loose stones, and let the natural grasses grow sweet and fine, and turn a lot of the highland sheep onto it. And if it were mine, I would gather all the little drains from all sides, till I had a pretty stream of water running down here where we stand, and over to the castle itself and through the court and kitchen, gurgling and running, and then out again, and down the face of the cliffs, splashing into the ocean. I would leave the rest to nature herself. It would be a grand place, my lord! And when you was tired of it, you could just run away to Lossie House, and hide there for a change. I would fine like to have the sorting out of it for your lordship."

"I dare say!" said the marquis.

"Let's find a nice place for our luncheon, Papa," urged Florimel.

"Shall I go back for the baskets then, my lord?" asked Malcolm.

"Yes, I think so. But you can take your time. We shan't want lunch for an hour yet."

"You must take care, my lord, how you go about among the ruins. There's awkward kind of holes about, and vaults just where you think there's none. I don't altogether like your going on ahead without me."

"Nonsense! Go along," said the marquis.

"But I'm not joking," persisted Malcolm.

"Yes, yes; we'll be careful," returned his master impatiently, and Malcolm ran down the hill, but not altogether satisfied with the assurance.

Amid such surroundings it was not so very difficult to wait for him to return with lunch. Florimel and the marquis continued along the path to have a peep at the ruins and choose a place for luncheon.

From the point where they stood, looking seaward, the ground sank to the narrow isthmus supposed by Malcolm to fill a cleft formerly crossed by a drawbridge and, beyond it, rose again to the grassy mounds in which lay so many of the old bones of the ruined carcass. Passing along the isthmus, where one side was the little bay in which they had landed, they clambered up a rude ascent of solid rock, and so reached what had been the center of the seaward portion of the castle. Here they came suddenly upon a small hole at their feet, going right down. Florimel knelt and, peeping in, saw the remains of a small spiral stair. The opening seemed large enough to let her through and, gathering her garments tight about her, she was halfway buried in the earth before her father, whose attention had been drawn elsewhere, saw what she was about. He thought she had fallen in, but her merry laugh reassured him, and before he could reach her she had screwed herself out of sight. He followed her in some anxiety but, after a short descent, rejoined her in a small vaulted chamber, where she stood looking from the little square window Malcolm had pointed out to them as they neared the shore. The bare walls around them were of brown stone, wet with the drip of rains. By breaches in the walls, where once might have been doors, Florimel passed from one chamber to another and another, each dark, brown, damp, and weather-beaten, while her father stood at the little window she had left, listlessly watching the two men on the beach far below landing the lunch from the cutter rising and falling with every wave of the flowing tide.

At length Florimel found herself on the upper end of a steep sloping ridge of hard, smooth earth, lying along the side of one chamber and leading across to yet another beyond, which, unlike the rest, was full of light. The passion of exploration being by this time thoroughly roused in her, she descended the slope, half sliding, half creeping. When she thus reached the hole into the bright chamber, she almost sickened with horror, for the slope went off steeper, till it rushed, as it were, out of a huge gap in the wall of the castle, laying bare the void of space and the gleam of the sea at a frightful depth below; if she had gone one foot farther, she could not have saved herself from sliding out of the gap. She gave a shriek of terror, and laid hold of the broken wall. To heighten her dismay she found at the very first effort, partly, no doubt, from the paralysis of fear, that it was impossible to re-ascend; and there she lay on the verge of the steeper slope, her head and shoulders in the inner of the two chambers, and the rest of her body in the outer, with the hideous vacancy staring at her. In a few moments it had fascinated her so that she dared not close her eyes lest it should leap upon her. The wonder was that she did not lose her consciousness and fall at once to the bottom of the cliff.

Her cry brought her father in terror to the top of the slope.

"Are you hurt, child?" he cried, not seeing the danger she was in.

"It's so steep, I can't get up again," she said faintly.

"I'll soon get you up," he returned cheerily, and began to descend.

"Oh, Papa!" she cried, "don't come a step nearer. If you should slip, we should go to the bottom of the rock together. Indeed, there is great danger! Do run for Malcolm!"

Thoroughly alarmed, yet mastering the signs of his fear, he enjoined her to keep perfectly still while he was gone, and hurried to the little window. Thence he shouted to the men below, but in vain, for the wind prevented his voice from reaching them. He rushed from the vaults, and began to descend at the first practicable spot he could find, shouting as he went.

The sound of his voice cheered Florimel a little, as she lay forsaken in her misery. Her whole effort now was to keep herself from fainting, and in this she was aided by a new shock, which, had her position been a less critical one, would itself have caused her a deadly dismay. A curious little sound came to her, apparently from somewhere in the dusky chamber in which her head lay. She fancied it made by some animal, and thought of the wildcats and otters of which Malcolm had spoken as haunting the caves; but, while the new fear mitigated the former, the greater fear subdued the less. It came a little louder, then again a little louder, growing like a hurried whisper, but without seeming to approach her. Louder still it grew, and yet was but an inarticulate whispering. Then it began to divide into some resemblance of articulate sounds. Presently, to her utter astonishment, she heard herself called by name.

"Lady Florimel! Lady Florimel!" said the sound plainly enough.

"Who's there?" she faltered, with her heart in her throat hardly knowing whether she spoke or not.

"There's nobody here," answered the voice. "I'm in my own bedroom at home where your dog killed mine."

It was the voice of Mrs. Catanach.

Anger, and the sense of a human presence, although an evil one, restored Lady Florimel's speech.

"How dare you talk such nonsense?" she said.

"Don't anger me again," returned the voice. "I tell you the truth. I'm sorry I spoke to your ladyship as I did this morning. It was the sight of my poor dog that drove me mad."

"I couldn't help it. I tried to keep mine off him, as you know."

"I do know it, my lady, that's why I beg your pardon."

"Then there's nothing more to be said."

"Yes, there is, my lady: I want to make you some amends. I know more than most people, and I know a secret that some would give their ears for. Will you trust me?"

"I will hear what you've got to say."

"Well, I don't care whether you believe me or not. I shall tell you nothing but the truth. What do you think of Malcolm MacPhail, my lady?"

"What do you mean by asking me such a question?"

"Only to tell you that by birth he is a gentleman, and comes of an old family."

"But why do you tell me?" asked Florimel. "What have I to do with it?"

"Nothing, my lady—or himself either. I hold the handle of the business. But you needn't think it's from any favor for him. I don't care what comes of him. There's no love lost between him and me. You heard yourself, this very day, how he abused both me and my poor dog, who is now lying dead on the bed beside me."

"You don't expect me to believe such nonsense as that!" said the girl.

There was no reply. The voice had departed; and the terrors of her position returned with gathered force in the desolation of redoubled silence that closes around an unanswered question. A trembling seized her, and she could hardly persuade herself that she was not slipping by slow inches down the incline.

Minutes that seemed hours passed. At length she heard feet and voices, and presently her father called her name, but she was too agitated to reply except with a moan. A voice she was glad to hear followed—the voice of Malcolm, confident and clear.

"Hold back, my lord," it said, "and let me come to her."

"You're not going down so!" said the marquis angrily. "You'll slip to a certainty and send her to the bottom."

"My lord," returned Malcolm, "I know what I'm about, and you don't. I beg you to stay out of the way and not upset the lassie."

His lordship obeyed, and Malcolm, who had been pulling off his boots as he spoke, now addressed Mair.

"Here, Peter!" he said, "hold on to the rope. I want to put it around her. But don't pull on it, for once we get the rope around her hold it taut and she'll be able to come up herself. Don't be afraid, my lady. There's no danger. I'm coming."

With the rope in his hand, he walked down the incline, and kneeling by Florimel, close to the broken wall, proceeded to pass the rope under and round her waist, talking to her, as he did so, in the tone of one encouraging a child.

"Now, now, my lady! My bonny lady. One minute and you're as safe as if you lay in your mother's lap!"

"I daren't get up, Malcolm! I daren't turn my back to it. I shall drop right down into it if I do!" she faltered, beginning to sob.

"No fear of that! There! You can't fall now, for Blue Peter has the other end, and Peter's as strong as two ponies. I'm going to take off your shoes next."

So saying, he towered himself a little through the breach, holding on by the broken wall with one hand, while he gently removed her sandals with the other. Drawing himself up again, he rose to his feet, and taking her by the hand, said, "Now, my lady, take a good grip of my hand, and as I lift you, give a scramble with your two feet, and as soon as you find them underneath you, just go up as if you were climbing a rather steep ascent. You couldn't fall even if you tried!"

At the grasp of his strong hand, the girl felt a great gush of confidence rise in her heart. She did exactly as he told her, scrambled to her feet and walked up the slippery way without one slide, holding fast to Malcolm's hand, while Joseph kept just feeling her waist with the loop of the rope as he drew it in. When she reached the top, she fell, almost fainting, into her father's arms, but was recalled to herself by an exclamation from Blue Peter. Just as Malcolm relinquished her hand, his foot slipped. But he slid down the side of the mound only—some six or seven feet to the bottom of the chamber, whence his voice came cheerily, saying he would be with them in a moment. When, however, ascending by another way, he rejoined them, they were shocked to see blood pouring from his foot; he had lighted amongst broken glass, and had felt a sting, but only now was aware that the cut was a serious one. He made little of it, however, bound it up and, as the marquis would not now hear of bringing the luncheon to the top, having, he said, had more than enough of the place, limped painfully after them down the shore.

Knowing whither they were bound and even better acquainted with the place than Malcolm himself, Mrs. Catanach, the moment she had drawn down her blinds in mourning for her dog, had put her breakfast in her pocket and set out from her back door, contriving mischief on her way. Arriving at the castle, she waited a long time before they made their appearance, but was rewarded for her patience, as she said to herself by the luck which had so wonderfully accompanied her cunning. From a broken loophole in the foundation of a round tower, she now watched them go down the hill. The moment they were out of sight, she crept like a fox from his earth, and having actually crawled beyond danger of discovery, hurried away inland, to reach Portlossie by footpaths and byways and there show herself on her own doorstep.

The woman's consuming ambition was to possess power over others. Hence she pounced upon a secret as one would a diamond in the dust—any fact, even, was precious, for it might be allied to some secret, might, in combination with other facts, become potent.

As to the mysterious communication she had made to her, Lady Florimel was not able to turn her mind to it, not indeed for some time was she able to think of anything.

Before they reached the bottom of the hill, however, Florimel had recovered her spirits a little, and had even attempted a laugh at the ridiculousness of her late situation. But she continued very pale. They sat down beside the baskets—on some great stones, fallen from the building above. Lady Florimel revived still more after she had had a morsel of partridge and a glass of wine, but every now and then she shuddered. As lunch progressed she recovered herself gradually and when it was over, his lordship rose, saying that it was time to re-embark—an operation less arduous than before, for in the present state of the tide, it was easy to bring the cutter so close to a tow rock that even Lady Florimel could step on board.

As they now had to beat to windward, Malcolm kept the tiller in his own hand. But indeed, Lady Florimel did not want to steer; she was so much occupied with her thoughts that her hands must remain idle.

Partly to turn them away from the more terrible portion of her adventure, she began to reflect upon her interview with Mrs. Catanach—if interview it could be called, where she had seen no one. At first she was sorry that she had not told her father of it and had the ruin searched; but when she thought of the communication the woman had made to her, she came to the conclusion that it was, for various reasons—not to mention the probability that he would have set it all down to the workings of an unavoidably excited nervous condition—better that she should mention it to no one but Duncan MacPhail.

When they arrived at the harbor-quay, they found the carriage waiting, but neither the marquis nor Lady Florimel thought of Malcolm's foot, and he was left to limp painfully home. As the carriage turned toward the town gate and hastened by, Florimel saw Mrs. Catanach, as she so often was, standing on her porch, shielding her eyes with her hand, and looking out to sea. However, as Malcolm passed some time later, the blinds were drawn down, the door was shut, and the place was silent as the grave. By the time he reached Lossie House, his foot was very much swollen. When Mrs. Courthope saw it, she sent him to bed at once and applied a poultice.

25

••••••••••••••••••

The Revelation

*T*he night long Malcolm kept dreaming of his fall; and his dreams were worse than the reality, inasmuch as they invariably sent him sliding out of the breach, to receive the cut on the rocks below. Very oddly this catastrophe was also occasioned by the grasp of a hand on his ankle. Invariably also, just as he slipped, the face of Mrs. Catanach appeared.

The next morning, Mrs. Courthope found him feverish and insisted on his remaining in bed—no small trial to one who had never been an hour ill in his life; but he was suffering so much that he made little resistance.

In the enforced quiescence and under the excitement of pain and fever, Malcolm first became aware of how much the idea of Lady Florimel had come to possess him. But even in his own thought, he never once came upon the phrase "in love" as representing his condition in regard of her; he only knew that he worshiped her and would be overjoyed to die for her. The rescue of Lady Florimel made him very happy: he had been of service to her. But so far was he from cherishing a shadow of presumption that as he lay there he felt it would be utter contentment to live serving her forever, even when he was old and wrinkled and gray like his grandfather. He never dreamed of her growing old and wrinkled and gray.

A single sudden thought sufficed to scatter his thoughts. Of course she would marry someday, and what then? He looked the inevitable in the face; but as he looked, he broke into a laugh—his soul had settled like a brooding cloud over the gulf that lay between a fisher-lad and the daughter of a marquis. But though the laugh was quite honestly laughed at himself, it was nevertheless a bitter one. For again came the question: why should an absurdity be a possibility? It was absurd, and yet it was possible. Had it been a purely logical question he was dealing with, he might not have been quite so puzzled. But to apply logic here, as he was attempting to do, was like attacking an eclipse with a broomstick.

His disjointed meditations were interrupted by the entrance of the man to whom alone of all men he could at such a time have given a hearty welcome. The schoolmaster seated himself by his bedside, and they had a long talk. When he rose to leave some time later, the sun was already dying in the west.

In the evening his grandfather came to see him, led through the maze of the House by Mrs. Courthope, and sat down full of tender anxiety which he was soon able to alleviate.

"Wounted in ta hand and ta foot!" said the seer. "What can it mean? It must mean something, Malcolm, my son."

"Well, Daddy, we must just wait and see," said Malcolm cheerfully.

A little talk followed, in the course of which it came into Malcolm's head to tell his grandfather the dream he had had so much of the first night he had slept in that room—but more for the sake of something to talk about that would interest one who believed in all kinds of prefigurations than for any other reason.

Duncan sat moodily silent for some time, and then, with a great heave of his broad chest, lifted his head, like one who had formed a resolution, and said: "The hour has come. I have long peen afrait to meet it; put it has come, and Allister will meet it. I'm not your cran'father, my son."

He spoke the words with perfect composure, but as soon as they were uttered, burst into a wail and sobbed like a child.

"You'll be my own father, then?" said Malcolm.

"No, no, my son. I'll not pe anything that's your own at all!" The tears flowed down his channeled cheeks.

For one moment Malcolm was silent, utterly bewildered. But he must comfort the old man first, and afterwards think about what he had said.

"You're my own daddy, whatever you are!" he said. "Tell me all about it, Daddy."

"I'll tell you all I'll pe knowing, my son, and I nefer told a lie, efen to a Cawmill."

He began his story in haste, as if anxious to have it over, but had to pause often from fresh outbursts of grief. It contained nothing more of the essential than I have already recorded, and Malcolm was perplexed to think why what he had known all the time should affect him so much in the telling. But when he ended with the bitter cry, "And now you'll pe loving me no more, my poy, my chilt, my Malcolm!" he understood it.

"Daddy, Daddy!" he cried, throwing his arms round his neck and kissing him, "I love you better than ever. And well I may!"

"But how can you, when you've cot none of ta plood in you, my son?" persisted Duncan.

"I have as much as I ever did, Daddy."

"Yes, put you tidn't know."

"But you did, Daddy."

"Yes, and inteet, I cannot tell why I'll pe loving you so much myself all ta time!"

"Well, Daddy, if you could love me so well, knowing I had no blood of your own—I can't help it: I must love you more than ever, now that I know it too. Daddy, Daddy, I had no claim upon you, and you have been father and grandfather and all to me!"

"What could I do, Malcolm, my poy? Ta chilt had no one, and I had no one, and so it was. You must pe my own poy after all!—and I'll not pe wondering put.—It might pe.—Yes, inteet not!"

His voice sank to the murmurs of a half-uttered soliloquy, and as he murmured he stroked Malcolm's cheek.

"What are you after now, Daddy?" asked Malcolm.

The only sign that Duncan heard the question was the complete silence that followed. When Malcolm repeated it, he said something in Gaelic, but finished the sentence thus, apparently unaware of the change of language:

"—only how else should I pe loving you so much, Malcolm, my son?"

"I know what Mister Graham would say, Daddy," rejoined Malcolm, at a half-guess.

"What would he say, my son? He's a coot man, your Mister Craham."

"He would say it was because we were all of one blood—because we all had one Father."

"Oh, yes, no toubt! We all come from ta same first parents; put tat will pe a fery long way off, before ta clans cot together. It'll not pe holding fery well now, my son. Tat was before ta Cawmills."

"That's not what he would mean, Daddy," said Malcolm. "He would mean that God was the Father of us all, and so we couldn't help loving one another."

"No; tat cannot pe right, Malcolm. For then we should haf to love efery-body. Now I love you, my son, and I hate Cawmill of Clenlyon. I love Mistress Partan when she'll not pe too rude to me, and I hate Mistress Catanach. She's a paad woman, tat I'll pe certain sure, though I nefer saw her to speak to her."

"Well, Daddy, there was nothing to make you love me. I was just a help-less human being, and so for that, and no other reason, you love me! And for myself I'm sure I couldn't love you better if you were twice my grand-father."

"He's my own poy!" cried the piper, much comforted; and his hand sought his head, and lighted upon it gently. "Put, maybe," he went on, "I might not haf loved you so much if I hadn't peen tinking sometimes—"

He checked himself. Malcolm's questions brought no conclusion to the sentence, and a long silence followed.

"Supposing I was to turn out a Campbell?" said Malcolm at length. The hand that was fondling his hair withdrew as if a serpent had bit it, and Duncan rose from his chair.

"Was it my own son to pe speaking such an efil thing!" he said in a tone of injured and sad expostulation.

"For anything you know, Daddy—you cannot tell but it might be."

"Ton't preathe it, my son!" cried Duncan in a voice of agony, as if he saw unfolding a fearful game the arch enemy had been playing for his soul. "Put it cannot pe," he resumed instantly, "for ten, how should I pe loving you, my son? I could not haf loved him if he had peen a Cawmill. My soul would haf shrunk back from him as from ta snake in ta tree. No, Malcolm! No, my son!"

"You wouldn't have me believe, Daddy, that if you had known by mark and hoof and horn that the creature they laid in your lap was a Campbell, you would have risen up, and let it die where it fell?"

"No, Malcolm; I would haf put my foot upon it, as I would on ta young fiper in ta heather."

"If I was to turn out one of that ill race, you would hate me, then, Daddy—after all! You would be well pleased to think how you stuck your knife through the ill hand of me, and wouldn't rest until you had it through the heart. I doubt I had better be up and away, Daddy, for who knows what you may do to me."

Malcolm made a movement to rise, and Duncan's quick ears understood it. He sat down again by his bedside and threw his arms over him.

"Lie town, lie town, my poy. If you ket up, tat will mean you are a Cawmill. No, no, my son! You are fery cruel to your old daddy. I would pe too sorry for my poy to hate him. It will pe so treadful to pe a Cawmill! No, no, my poy! I would take you to my posom, and tat would trive ta Cawmill out of you. Put ton't speak of it anymore, my son, for it cannot pe. I must co now, for my pipes will pe waiting for me."

Malcolm feared he had ventured too far, for never before had his grandfather left him except for work. But the possibility he had started might do something to soften the dire endurance of his hatred.

His thoughts turned to the new darkness let in upon his history and prospects. All at once the cry of the mad laird rang in his mind's ear: "I dinna ken whaur I come from!"

Duncan's revelation brought with it nothing to be done—merely room for shadowy conjecture. In merry mood he would henceforth be the son of some mighty man, in sad mood the son of some strolling gypsy, or worse, his very origin better forgotten.

Like a lurking phantom-shroud, the sad mood leaped from the field of his speculation and wrapped him in its folds: sure enough, he was but a beggar's brat! How henceforth was he to look Lady Florimel in the face? Humble as he had believed his origin, he had hitherto been proud of it; with such a high-minded sire as he deemed his own, how could he be other? But now! Nevermore could he look one of his old companions in the face! They were all honorable men; he a base-born foundling!

He would tell Mr. Graham, of course. But what could Mr. Graham say to it? The fact remained: he must leave Portlossie.

His mind went on brooding, speculating, devising. The evening sank into the night, but he never knew he was in the dark until the housekeeper brought him a light. After a cup of tea, his thoughts found pleasanter paths. One thing was certain—he must lay himself out, as he had never done before, to make Duncan MacPhail happy. With this one thing clear to both heart and mind, he fell fast asleep.

He woke in the dark, with that strange feeling of bewilderment which accompanies the consciousness of having been waked. But the dark into which he stared could tell nothing.

At length, something seemed doubtfully to touch the sense—the faintest suspicion of noise in the next room—the wizard's chamber; it was enough to set Malcolm on the floor. Forgetting his wounded foot and lighting upon it, the agony it caused dropped him at once on his hands and knees, and in this posture he crept into the passage. As soon as his head was outside his own door, he saw a faint gleam of light coming from beneath that of the next room. Advancing noiselessly, and softly feeling for the latch, his hands encountered a bunch of keys dangling from the lock but, happily did not set them to jingling. As softly, he lifted the latch, when, almost of itself the door opened a couple of inches, and with bated breath, he saw the back of a figure he could not mistake—that of Mrs. Catanach. She was stooping by the side of a tentbed much like his own, fumbling with the bottom hem of one of the check-curtains, which she was holding toward the light of the lantern on a chair. Suddenly she turned her face to the door, as if apprehending a presence; as suddenly he closed it, and turned the key in its lock. To do so he had to use considerable force, and concluded that its grating sound had been what waked him.

Having thus secured the prowler, he crept back to his room, considering what he should do next. The speedy result of his cogitations was that he dressed quickly, though with difficulty from the size of his foot, and set out on hands and knees for an awkward crawl to Lord Lossie's bedroom.

It was a painful journey, especially down the two spiral stone stairs, which led to the first floor where he lay. As he went, Malcolm resolved, in order to avoid rousing needless observers, to enter the room, if possible, before waking the marquis.

The door opened noiselessly. A night light, afloat in a crystal cup, revealed the bed and his master asleep, with one arm lying on the crimson quilt. He crept in, closed the door behind him, advanced halfway to the bed and in a low voice called the marquis.

Lord Lossie started up on his elbow, and without a moment's consideration seized one of a brace of pistols which lay on a table by his side, and fired. The ball went with a sharp thud into the thick mahogany door.

"My lord! My lord!" cried Malcolm. "It's only me!"

"And who the devil are you?" returned the marquis, snatching up the second pistol.

"Malcolm, your own henchman, my lord. It's a mercy I wasn't more like an honest man," said Malcolm, "or that bullet would have been right through my heart. Your lordship's a bit over rash."

"Rash! You rascal!" cried Lord Lossie; "when a fellow comes into my room on his hands and knees in the middle of the night? Get up, and tell me what you are after or, by Jove! I'll break every bone in your body."

A kick from his bare foot in Malcolm's ribs fitly closed the sentence. "You are over rash, my lord!" persisted Malcolm. "I can't get up. I have a foot the size of a small buoy!"

"Speak then, you rascal!" said his lordship, the pistol still cocked in his hand.

"Don't you think it would be better to lock the door, for fear the shot should bring any of the folk?" suggested Malcolm as he rose to his knees and leaned his hands on a chair.

"You're bent on murdering me—are you then?" said the marquis.

"If I had been that, my lord, I wouldn't have wakened you first."

"Well, what the devil is it all about? You needn't think any of the men will come. They're a pack of the greatest cowards ever breathed."

"Well, my lord, I have captured her at last, and I was bound to come and tell you. I have her under lock and key."

"Who?"

"Mistress Catanach, my lord."

"What's she to me that I should be waked out of a good sleep for her?"

"That's what I would have your lordship know; I don't."

"None of your riddles! Explain yourself and make haste. I want to go to bed again."

"Indeed, your lordship must just put on your clothes, and come with me."

"Where to?"

"To the warlock's chamber, my lord—where I locked that evil woman up."

Thus arrived at length, with a clear road before him, Malcolm told in a few words what had happened. As he went on the marquis grew interested, and by the time he had finished had got himself into dressing gown and slippers.

"Would you take your pistol?" suggested Malcolm slyly.

"What! to meet a woman?" said his lordship.

"Oh, no! but who knows there might be another murderer about? There might be two in one night!"

Impertinent as was Malcolm's humor, his master did not take it amiss; he lighted a candle, told him to lead the way, and took his revenge by making joke after joke upon him as he crawled along. With the upper regions of his house the marquis was as little acquainted as with those of his nature, and required a guide.

Arriving at length at the wizard's chamber, they listened at the door for a moment, but heard nothing; neither was there any light visible. Malcolm turned the key, and the marquis stood close behind, ready to enter. But the moment the door was unlocked, it was pulled open violently, and Mrs. Catanach, looking too high to see Malcolm who was on his knees, aimed a good blow at the face she did see, in the hope, no doubt, of thus making her escape. But it fell short, being countered by Malcolm's head in the softest part of her person, with the result of a clear entrance. The marquis burst out laughing, and stepped into the room with a rough joke. Malcolm remained in the doorway.

"My lord," said Mrs. Catanach, gathering herself together, and rising little the worse, save in temper, for the treatment he had commented upon, "I have a word for your lordship's own ear."

"Your right to be here does stand in need of explanation," said the marquis.

She walked up to him with confidence.

"You shall have an explanation, my lord," she said, "such as shall be my full quittance for intrusion even at this untimely hour of the night."

"Say on then," returned his lordship.

"Send that boy away then, my lord."

"I prefer having him stay," said the marquis.

"Not a word shall cross my lips till he's gone," persisted Mrs. Catanach. "I know him too well. Away with you!" she continued, turning to Malcolm.

"I know more about you than you know about yourself, but I'll make you laugh out of the wrong side of your mouth yet, my man!"

Malcolm, who had seated himself on the threshold, only laughed and looked to his master.

"Your lordship was never in the way of being frightened at a woman," said Mrs. Catanach, with an ugly expression of insinuation.

The marquis shrugged his shoulders.

"That depends," he said. Then turning to Malcolm, "Go along," he added; "only keep within call. I may want you."

"None of your listening at the keyhole, or I'll side-mark you. . . !" said Mrs. Catanach, finishing the sentence none the more mildly that she did it only in her heart.

"I wouldn't have you believe all that she says, my lord," said Malcolm with a significant smile as he turned to creep away.

He closed the door behind him and, lest Mrs. Catanach should repossess herself of the key, drew it from the lock; removing a few yards, he sat down in the passage by his own door. A good many minutes passed, during which he heard not a sound.

At length the door opened, and his lordship came out. Malcolm looked up and saw the light of the candle the marquis carried reflected from a face like that of a corpse. Different as they were, Malcolm could not help thinking of the only dead face he had even seen. It terrified him for the moment in which it passed without looking at him.

"My lord!" said Malcolm gently.

His master made no reply.

"My lord!" cried Malcolm, hurriedly pursuing him with his voice, "am I to leave the keys with her, and let her open what doors she likes?"

"Go to bed," said the marquis angrily, "and leave the woman alone"; with which words he turned into the adjoining passage and disappeared.

Mrs. Catanach had not come out of the wizard's chamber, and for a moment Malcolm felt strongly tempted to lock her in once more. But he reflected that he had no right to do so after what his lordship had said—else, he declared to himself he would have given her at least as good a fright as she seemed to have given his master, to whom he had no doubt she had been telling some horrible lies. He withdrew, therefore, into his room—to lie pondering again for a wakeful while.

This horrible woman claimed then to know more concerning him than his so-called grandfather, and from her profession it was likely enough; but information from her was hopeless—at least until her own evil time came; and then, how was anyone to believe what she might choose to say? So long, however, as she did not claim him for her own, she could, he thought, do him no hurt he would be afraid to meet.

But what could she be about in that room still? She might have gone, though, without the fall of her soft fat foot once betraying her!

Again he got out of bed, crept to the wizard's door and listened. But all was still. He tried to open it, but could not; Mrs. Catanach was doubtless spending the night there, and perhaps at that moment lay, evil conscience and all, fast asleep in the tent-bed. He withdrew once more, wondering whether she was aware that he occupied the next room; and having for the first time taken care to fasten his own door, he got into bed and fell asleep.

26

•••••••••••••••••••

The Rumor

Malcolm had flattered himself that he would at least be able to visit his grandfather the next day. But instead of that, he did not even make an attempt to rise—head as well as foot aching so much that he felt unfit for the least exertion—a phase of being he had never hitherto known. Mrs. Courthope insisted on advice, and the result was that a whole week passed before he was allowed to leave his room.

In the meantime a whisper awoke and passed from mouth to mouth in all directions through the little burgh—whence arising only one could tell, for even her mouthpiece, Miss Horn's Jean, was such a mere tool in the midwife's hands that she never doubted but Mrs. Catanach was, as she said, only telling the tale as it was told to her. Mrs. Catanach, therefore, kept herself artfully concealed as the author of the rumor.

The whisper, in its first germinal sprout, was merely that Malcolm was not a MacPhail; and even in its second stage it only amounted to this, that neither was he the grandson of Old Duncan. In the third stage of its development, it became the assertion that Malcolm was son of somebody of consequence; and the fourth that a certain person, not yet named, lay under shrewd suspicion. The fifth and final form it took was that Malcolm was the son of none other than Mrs. Stewart of Gersefell, who had been led to believe that he died within a few days of his birth, whereas he had in fact been carried off and committed to the care of Duncan MacPhail, who drew a secret annual stipend of no small amount in consequence.

Concerning this final form of the whisper, a few of the women of the burgh believed, or fancied they remembered, both the birth and the reported death of the child in question—also certain rumors afloat at the time which cast an air of probability over the new reading of his fate. In circles more remote from authentic sources, the general reports met with remarkable embellishments, but the framework of the rumor—what I may call the bones of it—remained undisputed.

From Mrs. Catanach's behavior, everyone believed that she knew all about the affair, but no one had a suspicion that she was the hidden fountain and prime mover of the report—so far to the contrary was it that people generally anticipated a frightful result for her when the truth came to be known, thinking that Mrs. Stewart would follow her with all the vengeance of a bereaved tigress. At length Mrs. Stewart herself began to figure more immediately in the affair, and it was witnessed that she had herself begun to search into the report. She had dashed into the town in a carriage—the horses covered with foam—and had hurried from house to house, prosecuting inquiries. It was said that, finding at length after much labor that she could arrive at no certainty even as to the first promulgator of the assertion, she had a terrible fit of crying. That she did not go near Duncan MacPhail was accounted for by the reflection that, on the supposition itself, he was of the opposite party, and the truth was not to be looked for from him.

At length it came to be known that, strongly urged and battling with a repugnance all but invincible, she had gone to see Mrs. Catanach, and had issued absolutely radiant with joy, declaring that she was now absolutely satisfied; as soon as she had communicated with the young man himself she would, without compromising anyone, take what legal steps might be necessary to his recognition as her son.

Although these things had been going on all the week that Malcolm was confined to his room, they had not reached this last point until after he was out again, and meantime not a whisper of them had come to his or Duncan's ears. Had they been still in the Seaton, one or other of the traveling ripples of talk must have found them. But Duncan had come and gone between his cottage and Malcolm's bedside without a single downy feather from the still widening flaps of the wings of fame ever dropping on him. And the only persons who visited Malcolm besides were the doctor—too discreet in his office to mix himself up with such gossip; Mr. Graham—to whom nobody, except it had been Miss Horn whom he had not seen for a fortnight, would have dreamed mentioning such a subject; and Mrs. Courthope—discreet like the doctor.

After a week he was sufficiently recovered to walk to his grandfather's cottage.

Duncan received him with delight, made him sit in his own chair, got him a cup of tea, and waited upon him with the tenderness of a woman. While he drank his tea, Malcolm recounted his last adventure in connection with the wizard's chamber.

"Tat will pe ta ped you saw in your feeshon," said Duncan, whose very eyes seemed to listen to the tale.

When Malcolm came to Mrs. Catanach's assertion that she knew more about him than he did himself, he said, "Then I peliefs ta voman toes, my poy. We are all poth of us in ta efil voman's power."

"Never a hair, Daddy!" cried Malcolm. "All power's in the hands of One that's not her master. She can know what she likes, but she can't part you and me, Daddy!"

"God forpid!" responded Duncan. "Put we must pe on our kard."

After a few moments more conversation, Malcolm left to walk alone out through the grounds. He was slowly wandering where never wind blew, between rows of stately hollyhocks, while his ears were filled with the sweet noises of a little fountain, when he suddenly came upon the marquis, who was, apparently, deep in thought, and startled by Malcolm's intrusion.

"Sorry, my lord," began Malcolm. I didn't mean to give you a fright."

"You didn't frighten me, you booby! It's just—"

"It's just what, my lord?" asked Malcolm.

"You had a look on your face, and it's enough to—but it's absurd!" and his voice trailed off.

Lord Lossie turned and left the arbor, with down-bent head, and hasty stride, obviously still in thought about whatever had upset him. Malcolm turned the other way.

Had the marquis been in London, he would have gone straight to his study, opened a certain cabinet, and drawn out a certain hidden drawer; being at Lossie, however, he walked up the glen to the bare hill overlooking the House, the royal burgh, the great sea, and his own lands lying far and wide around him. But all the time, all he could see was the low white forehead of his vision, a mouth of sweetness, and hazel eyes that looked into his very soul.

Malcolm walked back to the House, sought the lonely garret, flung himself upon his bed, and from his pillow gazed through the little dormer window on the pale blue skies above.

As he lay thus weighed upon rather than pondering, his eye fell on the bunch of keys which he had taken from the door of the wizard's chamber, and he wondered that Mrs. Courthope had not seen and taken them—apparently she had not missed them. And the chamber doomed to perpetual desertion lying all the time open to any stray foot! Once more at least he must go and turn the key in the lock.

As he went the desire awoke to look again into the chamber, for that night he had neither light nor time enough to gain other than the vaguest impression of it.

But for no lifting of the latch would the door open. How could the woman—witch she must be!—have locked it? He tried to unlock it. He placed one key, then another, in the lock. He went over the whole bunch. Mystery upon mystery! not one of them would turn. Thinking to himself, he began to try them the other way, and soon found one to throw the bolt *on*. He turned it in the other direction, and it threw the bolt *off*, still the door remained immovable! It must then—awful thought!—be fast on the inside. Was the woman's body lying there behind those check curtains? Would it lie there until it vanished, like that of the wizard—vanished utterly—bones and all, to a little dust, which one day a housemaid might sweep up in a pan?

On the other hand, if she had got shut in, would she not have made noise enough to be heard? He had been day and night in the next room! But it was not a spring-lock, and how could that have happened? Or would she not have been missed, and inquiry made after her? Only such an inquiry might well have never turned in the direction of Lossie House, and he might never have heard of it if it had.

Anyhow he must do something; and the first rational movement would clearly be to find out quietly for himself whether the woman was actually missing or not.

Tired as he was, he set out at once for the burgh, and the first person he saw was Mrs. Catanach standing on her doorstep shading her eyes with her hands, as she looked away out to the horizon over the roofs of the Seaton. He went no farther.

In the evening he found an opportunity of telling his master how the room was strangely closed; but his lordship pooh-poohed it, and said something must have gone wrong with the clumsy old lock.

With vague foresight, Malcolm took its key from the bunch, and, watching his opportunity, unseen hung the rest on their proper nail in the housekeeper's room. Then, having made sure that the door of the wizard's chamber was locked, he laid the key away in his own chest.

The next morning the marquis sent for Malcolm.

"Well, MacPhail," he said kindly as the youth entered, "how is that foot of yours getting on?"

"Just fine, my lord; there's nothing much the matter with it or me either, now that we're up. But I was nearing death being so long in bed."

"Hadn't you better come down out of that cockloft?" said the marquis, dropping his eyes.

"No, no, my lord; I don't care about parting with my neighbor just yet."

"What neighbor?"

"Oh, the old warlock, or whatever it is that holds such a tumult there."

"What! Is *he* troublesome now?"

"Oh, no! I'm not thinking that. But indeed I don't know, my lord!" said Malcolm.

"What do you mean, then?"

"If your lordship would allow me to force the door, I would be better able to tell you."

"Then the old man is not quiet."

"There's something not quiet."

"Nonsense! It's all your imagination—depend on it!"

"I don't think so."

"What *do* you think then? You're not afraid of ghosts, surely?"

"Not much. I have nothing on my conscience that I can't handle, even in the dead of night."

"Then you think ghosts come of a bad conscience? A kind of moral delirium tremens, eh?"

"I don't know, my lord. But that's the only kind of ghost I would be afraid of—at least that I would run from. I would a heap rather have a ghost in my house than an evil man, or woman—like Mistress Catanach, for instance, who's from the devil—"

"Nonsense!" said the marquis angrily; but Malcolm went on.

"—and must be just full of ghosts! And for anything I know, that'll be what makes ghosts of them after they're dead, setting them walking, as they call it. But in any case, I would have that door opened, my lord."

"Nonsense!" exclaimed the marquis once more, and shrugged his shoulders. "If I hear anything more about noises, or that sort of rubbish, I'll make you leave that room. I shall insist upon it!"

27

••••••••••••••••••••

The Discovery

The weather became unsettled with the approach of winter, and the marquis had a boathouse built at the west end of the Seaton. There the cutter was laid up, well wrapt in tarpaulins. A great part of his resulting leisure Malcolm spent with Mr. Graham, to whom he had, as a matter of course, unfolded the trouble caused him by Duncan's disclosure.

The more thoughtful a man is, and the more conscious of what is going on within himself, the more interest will he take in what he can know of his progenitors, to the remotest of generations. Malcolm had been as proud of the humble descent he supposed his own as Lord Lossie was of his mighty ancestry.

He reverenced Duncan both for his uprightness and for a certain grandeur of spirit; he looked up to him with admiration because of his gifts in poetry and music; and loved him endlessly for his unfailing goodness and tenderness to himself. At the same time he was the only human being to whom Malcolm's heart had gone forth as to his own; and now, with the knowledge of yet deeper cause for loving him, he had to part with the sense of filial relation to him! And this added a sting of mortification to Malcolm's sorrow, and the greatness of the legendary descent in which he had believed had been swept from him utterly. In losing these he had, as it were, to let go his hold, not only of his clan merely, but of his race; every link of kin that bound him to humanity had melted away from his grasp. He was alone in the world, a being without parents, without sister or brother, with none to whom he might look in confidence. He had waked into being, but all around him was dark, for there was no window by which the light of the world whence he had come, entering, might console him.

But a gulf of even greater blackness was about to open at his feet.

One afternoon, as he passed through the Seaton from the harbor, to have a look at the cutter, he heard the Partaness calling after him.

"Well, you're a sight for sore eyes—now that you've turned out to be somebody worth looking at!" she cried as he approached with his usual friendly smile.

"What do you mean by that, Mistress Findlay?" asked Malcolm, carelessly adding, "Is your man in?"

"Ay," she went on, without heeding either question, "you'll be set up grand now! You'll not be having a 'Fine day!' to fling at your old friends, the poor fisher-folk! Well, it's the way of the world!"

"What on earth's set you off like that, Mrs. Findlay?" said Malcolm. "It's not such a grand thing to be my lord's skipper—or henchman, as my daddy would have it—surely! It's a heap grander to be a free fisherman with a boat of your own. Like the Partan!"

"Hoots! You know well enough what I mean—as well as anyone else in Portlossie. And if you don't choose to let on about it to an old friend 'cause she's nothing but a fisher-wife, you're further down already than I thought you'd go, Malcolm—for it's by your own name I'll still call you, even if you were ten times a laird!—didn't I give you my breast when you could do nothing in the world but suck? And well you did, poor innocent that you was!"

"As sure's we're both alive," insisted Malcolm, "I know no more than a salted herring what you're driving at."

"Tell me that you don't know what all the country knows about your own self!" screamed the Partaness.

"I tell you, I know nothing; and if you don't tell me what you're after directly, I'll go to somebody else, and they'll tell me."

This was a threat sufficiently prevailing.

"It's not natural!" she cried. "Here's Mistress Stewart of the Gersefell been driving like mad about the place, in her carriage and how many horses I don't know, declaring—ay, swearing, they tell me—that one commonly called Malcolm MacPhail is neither more nor less than the son born of her own body in honest wedlock! And tell me you know nothing about it! What are you standing like that for, as gray-mouthed as a dying skate?"

For the first time in his life, Malcolm, young and strong as he was, felt sick. Sea and sky grew dim before him, and the earth seemed to reel under him.

"I don't believe it," he faltered, and turned away.

"You don't believe what I tell you!" screeched the wrathful Partaness. "You dare to say the word!"

But Malcolm did not care to reply. He wandered away, half unconscious of where he was, his head hanging, and his eyes creeping over the ground. The words of the woman kept ringing in his ears; but ever and anon, behind them as it were in the depth of his soul, he heard the voice of the mad laird, with its one lamentation: "I dinna ken whaur I come from." Finding himself at length at Mr. Graham's door, he wondered how he had got there.

It was Saturday afternoon, and the master was in the churchyard. Startled by Malcolm's look, he gazed at him in grave silent inquiry.

"Have you heard the evil news, sir?" said the youth.

"No; I'm sorry to hear there is any."

"They tell me Mistress Stewart's running about the town claiming me!"

"Claiming you! How do you mean?"

"For her own!"

"Not for her son?"

"Ay, sir. That's what they say. But you haven't heard of it?"

"Not a word."

"Then it must be gossip!" cried Malcolm energetically. "It was bad enough upon me already to know less of where I came from than the poor laird himself; but to come from where he came from was a thought even worse!"

"You surely don't despise the poor fellow so much as to scorn to have the same parents with him!" said Mr. Graham.

"The very opposite. But a woman who would so misguide the son of her own body, and for nothing but that he was born as he is—it's not lightly to be believed nor endured. I'll go to Miss Horn and see whether she's heard any such lying rumors."

But as Malcolm uttered her name, his heart sank within him, for their talk the night he had sought her hospitality for the laird came back to his memory, burning like an acrid poison.

"You can't do better," said Mr. Graham. "The report itself may be false— or true and the lady mistaken."

"She'll have to prove it well before I say true," rejoined Malcolm.

"And suppose she does?"

"In that case," said Malcolm, with a composure almost ghastly, "a man must take what mother it pleases God to give him. But faith! She won't do with me as with the poor laird. If she takes me up, she'll repent that she didn't let me lie. She'll be as little pleased with the one of her sons as the other, I can tell that for sure!"

"But think what you might do between mother and son," suggested the master, willing to reconcile him to the possible worst.

"It's too late for that," he answered. "The poor man's fiddle-strings are all hanging loose and there's not grip enough in the pegs to set them up again. He would think I had gone over to the enemy, and would stay out of my way as diligently as he stays out of hers. No, it would do nothing for him. If it weren't for what I see in him, I would have a great rebuttal to her claim; for how could any woman's own son have such a hatred of her as I have in my heart and very stomach? If she were my own mother, there would bound to be some natural drawings between us, you would think. But then there's the laird! The very name 'mother' makes him hold his sides and run."

"Still, if she be your mother, it's for better for worse, as much as if she had been your own choice."

"I don't know how it could be for worse," said Malcolm, who did not yet, even from his recollection of the things Miss Horn had said, comprehend what worst threatened him.

"It does seem strange," said the schoolmaster thoughtfully, after a pause, "that some women should be allowed to be mothers—that through them sons and daughters of God should come into the world!"

"I wonder what God thinks about it all. It makes a body wonder!" said Malcolm gloomily.

"I should not be surprised," said Mr. Graham, "that the day should come when men will refuse to believe in God simply on the ground of the apparent injustice of things. They would argue that there might be either an omnipotent being who did not care, or a good being who could not help, but that there could not be a being both all good and omnipotent or else he would never have suffered things to be as they are."

"What would people say if they heard you talk like that?" said Malcolm. "What would the clergy say?"

"Nothing very to the point, I fear. They would never face the question. They would probably try to burn me, as their spiritual ancestor Calvin would have done. Indeed, there are those about who would love nothing more than to ride me out of this place and this school, forever. They seem to be threatened by such questions, by facing them squarely as Jesus did in His day, by having a mind open wide enough to consider various possibilities. And they may have their will with me yet before they are done. But that's hardly my concern. We are told not to be anxious about the morrow, you know."

"How do you stand it, sir, being at the mercy of others' fears and doctrines?"

"Not now, my boy. You have got one thing to mind now, before all other things—namely, that you give this woman, whatever she be, fair play; if she is your mother, as such you must take her, that is as such you must treat her."

"You're right," returned Malcolm, and rose.

"Come back to me," said Mr. Graham, "with whatever news you gather."

"I will," answered Malcolm, and went to find Miss Horn.

He was shown into the little parlor, which, for all the grander things he had been amongst of late, had lost nothing of its first charm. There sat Miss Horn.

"Sit down, Malcolm," she said gruffly.

"Have you heard anything, mem?" asked Malcolm, standing.

"Ay, too much," answered Miss Horn, with all but a scowl. "You've been over to Gersefell, I reckon."

"Forbid it!" answered Malcolm. "Not till this hour—or at most two—did I hear the first cheep of it, and that was from Meg Partan. To no human soul have I made mention of it yet except Master Graham; to him I went right after I heard it."

"You couldn't have done better," said the grim woman, with relaxing visage.

"And here I am now, straight from him, to beg of you, Miss Horn, to tell me the truth of the matter."

"What do I know about it?" she returned angrily. "What should I know?"

"You might know whether the woman's been saying it or not."

"Who has any doubt about that?"

"Mistress Stewart's been saying she's my mother, then?"

"Ay, why not?" returned Miss Horn, with a piercing glower at the youth.

"God forbid!" exclaimed Malcolm.

"What did you say, laddie?" cried Miss Horn and, starting up, grasped his arm and stood gazing in his face.

"What else should I say?" rejoined Malcolm in surprise.

"God be praised!" exclaimed Miss Horn. "The mongrel may say what she likes now."

"You didn't believe it, mem?" cried Malcolm. "Tell me you didn't!"

"I didn't believe a word of it, laddie," answered Miss Horn eagerly. "How could I believe such a fine lad come of such a false mother."

"She might be anybody's mother, and false too," said Malcolm gloomily.

"That's true, laddie; and the more mother the falser! There's a world of witness right in the features of your own face that if she is indeed your mother, the marquis, and not poor honest hen-pecked John Stewart, was the father of you. The Lord forgive me! what am I saying?" adjected Miss Horn with a cry of self-accusation when she saw the pallor that overspread the countenance of the youth and his head drop on his chest: the last arrow had sunk to the feather. "It's only gossip anyway," she quickly resumed. "I don't believe you have a drop of her blood in the body of you. But," she hurried on, as if eager to obliterate the scoring impression of her last words, "that she's been saying it, there can be no manner of doubt. I saw her myself about the town, from one to another, with her long hair down the long back of her, and flying in the wind, like a body demented. The only question is, whether or not she believes it herself."

"What could make her say it if she didn't believe it?"

"Folks say she expects that way to get a grip of things out of the poor laird's trustees: you would be a son of her own capable of managing them. But she's never been to you about it?"

"Never a blink of the eye has passed between us since that day I went to Gersefell, as I told you, with a letter from the marquis. I thought I was too much for her then. I wonder she dared be at me again."

"She's dared her God, and now may well dare you. But what does your grandfather say about it?"

"He hasn't heard a chuckie's cheep of it."

"What are we talking about then? Can't he settle the matter offhand?"

Miss Horn eyed him keenly as she spoke.

"He knows no more about where I come from, mem, than your Jean, who's listening at the keyhole this very minute."

The quick ear of Malcolm had caught a slight sound of the handle, whose proximity to the keyhole was no doubt often troublesome to Jean.

Miss Horn seemed to reach the door with one spring. Jean was ascending the last step of the stair with a message on her lips concerning butter and eggs. Miss Horn received it and went back to Malcolm.

"No, Jean wouldn't do that," she said quietly.

But she was wrong, for, hearing Malcolm's words, Jean had retreated one step down the stair, and turned.

"But what's that you tell me about your grandfather, honest man?" Miss Horn continued.

"Duncan MacPhail's no blood of mine, and more's the pity!" said Malcolm sadly, and told her all he knew.

Miss Horn's visage went through wonderful changes as he spoke.

"Well, it's a mercy I have no feelings!" she said when he had done.

"Any woman can lay a claim to me that likes, you see," said Malcolm.

"She may lay what she likes, but it's not every egg laid has a chicken in it," answered Miss Horn. "Just you go home to old Duncan and tell him to turn the thing over in his mind till he's able to swear to the very night he found the child in his lap. But not a word must he say to a living soul about it before it's required of him."

"I would be the son of the purest fisher-wife in the Seaton rather than her," said Malcolm.

"And it shows you're better bred," said Miss Horn. "But she'll be at you before long, so watch what you say. Don't flee in her face; let her talk away, and mark her words. She may let a streak of light out of her dark lantern unawares."

Malcolm returned to Mr. Graham. They agreed there was nothing for it but to wait. He went next to his grandfather and gave him Miss Horn's message. The old man fell a-thinking, but could not be certain even of the year in which he had left his home. The clouds hung very black around Malcolm's horizon.

Lady Florimel had been on a visit in Morayshire for a couple of weeks, and so had heard nothing of the report until she returned.

"So you're a gentleman after all, Malcolm!" she said the next time she saw him.

The expression in her eyes appeared to him different from any he had encounterd there before. The blood rushed to his face; he dropped his head, saying merely, "It must be as it must be," and continued with the job he was doing.

But her words sent a new wind blowing into the fog. A gentleman she had said! Gentlemen married ladies! Could it be that a glory it was madness to dream of was yet a possibility? One moment, and his honest heart recoiled from the thought: not even for Lady Florimel could he consent to be the son of that woman! Yet the thought, especially in Lady Florimel's presence, would return, would linger, would whisper, would tempt.

In Florimel's mind also, a small demon of romance was at work. Uncorrupted as yet by social influences, it would not have seemed to her absurd that an heiress of rank should marry a poor country gentleman; but the thought of marriage never entered her head. She only felt that the discovery justified a nearer approach from both sides. She had nothing, not even a flirtation, in view. Flirt she might, likely enough, but she did not foremean it.

Had Malcolm been a schemer, he would have tried to make something of his position. But even the growth of his love for his young mistress was held in check by the fear of what that love tempted him to desire.

Within a day or two of her return, Mrs. Stewart called at Lossie House, and had a long talk with Lady Florimel, in the course of which she found no difficulty in gaining her to promise her influence with Malcolm. From his behavior on the occasion of their sole interview, she stood in a vague awe of him, and indeed could not recall it without a feeling of rebuke. Hence it came that she had not yet sought him; she would have the certainty first that he was kindly disposed toward her claim—a thing she would never have doubted but for the glimpse she had had of him.

28

••••••••••••••••••

The Lie

The relationship between Florimel and Malcolm grew gradually more familiar, until at length it was often hardly to be distinguished from such as takes place between equals, and Florimel was by degrees forgetting the present condition in the possible future of the young man. But Malcolm, on the other hand, as often as the thought of that possible future arose in her presence, flung it from him in horror, lest the wild dream of winning her should make him for a moment desire its realization.

The claim that hung over him haunted his very life, turning the currents of his thought into channels of speculation unknown before.

One day when these questions were fighting in his heart, all at once it seemed as if a soundless voice in the depth of his soul replied, "Thy soul, however it became known to itself, is from the pure heart of God."

And with the thought, the horizon of his life began to clear.

He had been rambling on the waste hill above Lossie House. It had a far outlook, but he had beheld neither sky nor ocean. The hills of Sutherland had invited his gaze, rising faint and clear over the darkened water at their base; the land of Caithness had lain lowly and afar; and east and west his own rugged shore had gone lengthening out, fringed with the white burst of the dark sea; but none of all these things had he noted.

Lady Florimel suddenly encountered him on his way home, and was startled by his look.

"Where have you been, Malcolm?" she exclaimed.

"I hardly know, my lady."

"What have you been about? Looking at things in general, I suppose?"

"No, they've been looking at me, I daresay; but I didn't heed them."

"You look so strangely bright," she said, "as if you had seen something both marvelous and beautiful!"

The words revealed a quality of insight not hitherto manifested by Florimel. In truth, Malcolm's whole being was irradiated by the flash of inward peace that had visited him. But Florimel's insight had reached its limit, and her judgment, vainly endeavoring to penetrate further, fell floundering in the mud.

"I know," she went on, "you've been to see your lady mother!"

Malcolm's face turned white as if blasted with leprosy. The same scourge that had maddened the poor laird fell hissing on his soul, and its knotted sting was the same word "mother." He turned and walked slowly away, fighting a tyrannous impulse to thrust his fingers in his ears and run and shriek.

"Where are your manners?" cried the girl after him, but he never stayed his slow foot or turned his bowed head, and Florimel wondered.

For the moment, his new-found peace had vanished. What could he do with a mother whom he could neither honor nor love? Love! If he could but cease to hate her! There was no question yet of loving.

But might she not repent? Ah, then, indeed! And might he not help her to repent? He would not avoid her. How was it that she had never yet sought him?

As he brooded thus, on his way to Duncan's cottage and, heedless of the sound of coming wheels, was crossing the road, he was nearly run over by a carriage coming round the corner at a fast trot. Catching one glimpse of the face of its occupant, as it passed within a yard of his own, he turned and fled back through the woods, with again a horrible impulse to howl to the winds the cry of the mad laird. When he came to himself he found his hands pressed hard on his ears, and for a moment felt a sickening certainty that he too was a son of the lady of Gersefell.

When he returned at length to the House, Mrs. Courthope informed him that Mrs. Stewart had called, and seen both the marquis and Lady Florimel.

Meantime he had grown again a little anxious about the laird, but as Phemy plainly avoided him, had concluded that he had found another concealment, and that the child preferred not being questioned concerning it.

With the library of Lossie House at his disposal, and almost nothing to do, it might now have been a grand time for Malcolm's studies; but alas! he too often found it all but impossible to keep his thoughts on the track through a single sentence of any length.

The autumn now hung over the verge of its grave. Hoarfrost lay thick on the fields. Summer was indeed gone, and winter was nigh with its storms and its fogs and its rotting rains and its drifting snows. Malcolm sorely missed the ministrations of compulsion: he lacked labor, the most helpful and most healing of all God's holy things.

All over the House big fires were glowing and blazing. Nothing pleased the marquis worse than the least appearance of stinting the consumption of coal. In the library two huge gratefuls were burning from dawn to midnight—well for the books anyhow, if their owner seldom showed his face amongst them. There were days during which, except the servant whose duty it was to attend to the fires, not a creature entered the room but Malcolm.

One morning he sat there alone at a window looking sea-wards. Lady Florimel entered in search of something to read. To her surprise, for she had heard of no arrival, in one of the windows sat a highland gentleman, looking out on the landscape. She was on the point of retiring again, when a slight movement revealed Malcolm.

The explanation was that the marquis, their sea-faring over, had at length persuaded Malcolm to don the Highland attire; it was an old custom of the House of Lossie that its lord's henchman should be thus distinguished, and the marquis himself wore the kilt when on his western estates in the summer, also as often as he went to court. He would not have succeeded with

Malcolm, however, but for the youth's love of Duncan.

It was no little trial to him to assume this dress in the changed aspect of his circumstances; for alas! he wore them in right of service only, not of birth, and the tartan of his lord's family was all he could claim.

He had not heard Lady Florimel enter. She went softly up behind him and laid her hand on his shoulder. He started at her touch.

"A penny for your thoughts," she said, retreating a step or two.

"I would give two to be rid of them," he returned, shaking his bushy head as if to scare the invisible ravens hovering about it.

"How fine you are!" Florimel went on, regarding him with an approbation too open to be altogether gratifying. "The dress suits you thoroughly. I didn't know you at first. I thought it must be some friend of Papa's. Now I remember he said once you must wear the proper dress for a henchman. How do you like it?"

"It's all one to me," said Malcolm. "I don't care what I wear if only I had a right to it!" he added with a sigh.

"It is too bad of you, Malcolm," rejoined Florimel in a tone of rebuke. "The moment fortune offers you a favor, you fall out with her—won't give her a single smile. You don't deserve your good luck."

Malcolm was silent.

"There's something on your mind," Florimel went on, partly from willingness to serve Mrs. Stewart, partly enticed by the romance of being Malcolm's comforter or perhaps confessor.

"Ay, there's is, my lady."

"What is it? Tell me. You can trust me."

"I could trust you, but I cannot tell you, I dare not—I must not!"

"I see you will not trust me," said Florimel, with a half-pretended, half-real offense.

"I would lay down my life—what there is of it—for you, my lady; but the very nature of my trouble won't be told. I must bear it alone."

It flashed across Lady Florimel's brain that the cause of his misery, the thing he dared not confess, was his love for her. Now, Malcolm standing before her in his present dress, and interpreted by the knowledge she believed she had of his history, was a very different person indeed from the former Malcolm in the guise of fisherman or sailor, and she felt as well as saw the difference; if she was the cause of his misery, why should she not comfort him a little? Why should she not be kind to him? Of course anything more was out of the question; but a little confession and consolation would hurt neither of them. Besides, Mrs. Stewart had begged her influence, and this would open a new channel for its exercise. Indeed, if he was unhappy through her, she ought to do what she might for him. A gentle word or two would cost her nothing, and might help to heal a broken heart! She was hardly aware, however, how little she wanted it healed—all at once.

"Can't you trust me, Malcolm?" she said, looking into his eyes very sweetly, and bending a little toward him; "can't you trust me?"

At the words and the look it seemed as if his frame melted. He dropped on his knees and, his heart half stifled in the confluence of the tides of love and misery, sighed out between the pulses in this throat: "There's nothing I could not tell you that ever I thought or did in my life, my lady; but it's other folk! It's like to burn a hole in my heart, and yet I dare not open my mouth."

There was a half angelic, half dog-like entreaty in his up-looking hazel eyes that seemed to draw hers down into his; she must put a stop to that.

"Get up, Malcolm," she said kindly. "What would my father or Mrs. Court-hope think?"

"I don't know, and I mostly don't care; between one thing and another, I'm almost totally distracted," answered Malcolm, rising slowly, but not taking his eyes from her face. "And there's my daddy!" he went on "—almost won over to the enemy—and I dare not tell even him that I can't abide it! You haven't been saying anything to him, have you, my lady?"

"I don't quite understand you," returned Florimel, rather guiltily, for she had been speaking with Duncan. "Saying anything to your grandfather? About what?"

"About—about—*her*, you know, my lady."

"What her?" asked Florimel.

"Her—the lady of Gersefell."

"And why—? What of her? What has that to do with—? Why, Malcolm! What can have possessed you? You actually seem to dislike her!"

"I can't stand her," said Malcolm, with the calm earnestness of one who is merely stating a fact, and for a moment his eyes, at once troubled and solemn, kept looking wistfully into hers, as if searching for a comfort too good to be found, then slowly sank and sought the floor at her feet.

"And why?"

"I can't tell you."

She supposed it to be unreasoned antipathy.

"But that is very wrong," she said, almost as if rebuking a child. "You ought to be ashamed of yourself. What! dislike your own mother?"

"Don't say the word, my lady!" cried Malcolm in a tone of agony, "or I'll turn and run like the mad laird. He's not a hair madder than I would be with such a mother."

He would have passed her to leave the room.

But Lady Florimel could not bear defeat. In any contest she must win or be shamed in her own eyes, and was she to gain absolutely nothing in such a passage with a fisher-lad? She would, she must, subdue him! Perhaps she did not know how much the sides of her intent were pricked by the nettling discovery that she was not the cause of his unhappiness.

"You're not going to leave me so!" she exclaimed, in a tone of injury.

"I'll go or stay as you will, my lady," answered Malcolm resignedly.

"Stay then," she returned. "I haven't half done with you yet."

"You must just tear my heart out," he rejoined wilh a sad half smile, and another of his dog-like looks.

"That's what you would do to your mother!" said Florimel severely.

"Say no ill of my mother!" cried Malcolm, suddenly changing almost to fierceness.

"Why, Malcolm!" said Florimel, bewildered, "what ill was I saying of her?"

"It's nothing less than an insult to my mother to call that woman—by her name," he replied with set teeth.

It was to him an offense against the idea of motherhood to call such a woman his mother.

"She's a very ladylike, handsome woman—handsome enough to be your mother even, Mr. Malcolm Stewart."

Florimel could not have dared the words but for the distance between them; but then neither would she have said them while the distance was greater. They were lost on Malcolm though, for never in his life having considered the question whether he was handsome or not, he merely supposed her making game of him and drew himself together in silence, with the air of one bracing himself to hear and endure the worst.

"Even if she should not be your mother," his tormentor resumed, "to show such a dislike to any woman is nothing less than cruelty."

"She must prove it," murmured Malcolm, not the less emphatically that the words were but just audible.

"Of course she will do that; she has an abundance of proof. She gave me a whole hour of proof."

"Long doesn't make it true," returned Malcolm; "there's comfort in that! Go on, my lady."

"Poor woman! It was hard enough to lose her son; but to find him again such as you seem likely to turn out, I should think ten times worse."

"No doubt, no doubt! But there's one thing worse."

"What is that?"

"To come upon a mother that—"

He stopped abruptly; his eyes went wandering about the room, and the muscles of his face worked convulsively.

Florimel saw that she had been driving against a stone wall. She paused a moment, and then resumed.

"Anyhow, if she is your mother," she said, "nothing you can do will alter it."

"She must prove it," was Malcolm's dogged reply.

"Just so; and if she can't," said Florimel, "you'll be no worse than you were before—and no better," she added with a sigh.

Malcolm lifted his questioning face to her searching eyes.

"Don't you see," she went on, very softly and lowering her look from the half-conscious shame of half-unconscious falseness, "I can't be all my life here at Lossie? We shall have to say good-bye to each other—never to meet again, most likely. But if you should turn out to be of good family, you know—"

Florimel saw neither the paling of his brown cheek nor the great surge of red that followed, but glancing up to spy the effect of her argument, did see the lightning that broke from the darkened hazel of his eyes, and again cast down her own.

"—then there might be some chance," she went on, "of our meeting somewhere—in London, or perhaps in Edinburgh and I could ask you to my house, after I was married, you know."

Heaven and earth seemed to close with a snap around his brain. The next moment they had receded an immeasurable distance, and in limitless wastes of exhausted being he stood alone. What time had passed when he came to himself he had not an idea; it might have been hours for anything his consciousness was able to tell him. But although he recalled nothing of what she had been urging, he grew aware that Lady Florimel's voice, which was now in his ears, had been sounding in them all the time. He was standing before her like a marble statue with a dumb thrill in its helpless heart of stone. He must end this! To know that measureless impassable leagues lay between them was unendurable. With such an effort as breaks the bonds of a nightmare dream, he turned from her and, heedless of her recall, went slowly, steadily out of the house.

While she was talking, his eyes had been resting with glassy gaze upon the far-off waters: The moment he stepped into the open air and felt the wind on his face, he knew that their turmoil was the travailing of sympathy, and that the ocean had been drawing him all the time. He walked straight to his little boat, lying dead on the sands of the harbor, launched it alive on the smooth water within the piers, stepped his mast, hoisted a few inches of sail, pulled beyond the sheltering seawalls, and was tossing amidst the torn waters whose jagged edges were twisted in the loose-flying threads of the northern gale. A moment more and he was sitting on the windward gunwale of his spoon of a boat, with the tiller in one hand and the sheet in the other, as she danced like a cork over the broken tops of the waves. For help in his sore need, instinct had led him to danger.

———

Leaving his boat again on the dry sand that sloped steep into the harbor an hour later, Malcolm took his way homeward along the shore. Presently he spied, at some distance in front of him, a woman sitting on the sand with her head bowed upon her knees. She had no shawl, though the wind was cold and strong, blowing her hair about wildly. Her attitude and whole appearance were the very picture of misery. He drew near and recognized her.

"What on earth's wrong with you, Lizzy?" he asked.

"Oh, nothing," she murmured, without lifting her head. The brief reply was broken by a sob.

"That can't be," persisted Malcolm, trouble of whose own had never yet rendered him indifferent to that of another. "Is it something I could help you with?"

Another sob was the only answer.

"I'm in a peck of troubles myself," said Malcolm. "I would sure help you if I could."

"Nobody can help me," returned the girl with an agonized burst, as if the words were driven from her by a convulsion of her inner world, and therewith she gave way, weeping and sobbing aloud. "I doubt I'll have to drown myself," she added with a wail, as he stood in compassionate silence, until the gust should blow over. Her eyes scarcely encountered his; again she buried her face in her hands and rocked herself to and fro, moaning in fresh agony.

"Your mother's been hard on you," he said. "But it'll blow over." As he spoke he set himself down on the sand beside her. But Lizza started to her feet crying.

"Don't come near me, Malcolm. I'm not fit for an honest man to come near. Stay away; I have the plague."

She laughed, but it was a pitiful laugh, and she looked wildly about, as if for some place to run to.

"I would be glad to take it myself, Lizzy. At any rate I'm too old a friend to be driven from you that way," said Malcolm, who could not bear the thought of leaving her on the border of the solitary sea, with the waves barking to her all the cold wintry night. Who could tell what she might do after the dark came down? He rose and would have taken her hand to draw it from her face; but she turned her back quickly, saying in a hard, forced voice:

"A man cannot help a woman, except it be to her grave." Then turning suddenly, she laid her hands on his shoulders, and cried: "For the love of God, Malcolm, leave me this moment! If I could only tell you what ailed me, I would. But I can't, I can't. Run, laddie; run and leave me!"

It was impossible to resist her anguished entreaty and agonized look. Sore at heart and puzzled in brain, Malcolm, yielding, turned from her and, with eyes on the ground, thoughtfully pursued his slow walk from the harbor toward the Seaton.

At the corner of the first house in the village stood three women, whom he saluted as he passed. The tone of their reply struck him a little, but not having observed how they watched him as he approached, he presently forgot it. The moment his back was turned to them, they turned to each other and interchanged looks.

"Fine feathers make fine birds," said one of them.

"Ay, but he looks bowed down," said another.

"And well he may! What'll his lady-mother say to such a thing? She'll not like being made a granny in such a way as that," said the third.

"Indeed, lass, there's few ought to think less of it," returned the first. Although they took little pains to lower their voices, Malcolm was far too much preoccupied to hear what they said. Perceiving plainly enough that the girl's trouble was much greater than a passing quarrel with her mother would account for, he resolved at length to take counsel with Blue Peter and his wife and, therefore, passing the sea gate, continued his walk along the shore and up the red path to the village of Scaurnose.

He found them sitting at their afternoon meal of tea and oatcake. A peat fire smouldered hot upon the hearth; a large kettle hung from a chain over it—a fountain of plenty whence the great china teapot, splendid in red flowers and green leaves, had been filled; the mantelpiece was crowded with the gayest of crockery. Phemy too was at the table. She rose as if to leave the room, but apparently changed her mind, for she sat down again instantly.

"Man, you're something to look at today—in your kilt and tartan hose!" remarked Mair as he welcomed him.

"I put them on to please my daddy and the marquis," said Malcolm, with a half-shamed-faced laugh.

"Aren't you cold about the knees?" asked the wife.

"Not that cold. I know they're there; but I get used to it."

"Well, sit down and have a cup of tea with us."

"I haven't much time to spare," said Malcolm; "but I'll take a cup of tea with you. If it weren't for little ears I would like your advice about one that wants a woman-friend, I'm thinking."

Phemy, who had been regarding him with compressed lips and suspended operations, deposited her bread and butter on the table and slipped from her chair.

"Where are you going, Phemy?" said her mother.

"Taking my ears away," returned Phemy.

"You creature!" exclaimed Malcolm. "You're too wise! Who'd have thought you to be so quick at the uptake!"

"When folk won't trust me—" said Phemy and ceased.

"What can you expect," returned Malcolm, while father and mother listened with amused faces, "when you won't trust other folk? Don't you know you can trust me, child? Phemy, where's the mad laird?"

A light flush rose to her cheeks, but whether from embarrassment or anger could not be told from her reply.

"I know of no one by that name," she said.

"Where's the laird of Kirkbyres, then?"

"Where you'll never lay a hand upon him!" returned the child, her cheeks now rose-red and her eyes flashing.

"Me lay a hand on him!" cried Malcolm, surprised at her behavior.

"Phemy! Phemy!" said her mother. "For shame!"

"There's no shame in it," protested the child indignantly.

"But there is shame in it," said Malcolm quietly, "for you wrong an honest man."

"Well, you can't deny it," persisted Phemy, in mood to brave the evil one himself, "that you was over at Kirkbyres on one of the marquis' mares, and held a long conversation with the laird's mother!"

"I went upon my master's errand," answered Malcolm.

"Oh, ay, I daresay! But who knows, with such a mother!"

She burst out crying and ran into the street.

Malcolm understood it now.

"She's like all the rest!" he said sadly, turning to her mother.

"I'm just affronted with the child!" she replied, with manifest annoyance in her flushed face.

"She's true to him," said Malcolm, "even if she can't be fair to me. Don't say a word to the lassie. She'll know me better after a while. And now for my story."

Mrs. Mair said nothing while he told how he had come upon Lizza, the state she was in, and what had passed between them. But he had scarcely finished when she rose, leaving a cup of tea untasted, and took her bonnet and shawl from a nail on the back of the door. Her husband rose also.

"I'll just go as far as the Boar's Craig with you myself, Annie," he said.

"I'm thinking you'll find the poor lassie where I left her," remarked Malcolm. "I imagine she dared not go home."

Arriving at the House, Malcolm read far into the night till his candle burned low in the socket. Suddenly he sat straight up in his chair, listening. He thought he heard a sound in the next room—it was impossible even to imagine of what; it was the mere abstraction of sound. He listened with every nerve, but heard nothing more; crept to the door of the wizard's chamber, and listened again—listened until he could no longer tell whether he heard or not, and felt like a deaf man imagining sounds. Finally he crept back to his own room and went to bed, all but satisfied that if it was anything it must have been some shaking window or door he had heard. But he could not get rid of the notion that he had smelt sulphur.

That night it was all over the town that Lizza Findlay was in a woman's worst trouble, and that Malcolm was the cause of it.

29
· · · · · · · · · · · · · · · · · ·

The Stairway

The winter was close at hand—indeed, in that northern region might already have claimed entire possession—but the trailing golden fringe of the skirts of autumn was yet visible behind him as he wandered away down the slope of the world. In the gentle sadness of the season, Malcolm could not help looking back with envy to the time when labor, adventure, danger, stormy winds and troubled waters would have helped him to bear the weight of the moral atmosphere which now from morning to night oppressed him. Of the new evil report abroad concerning him, nothing had as yet reached Malcolm. He went seldom into the Seaton, for the faces there were changed toward him. This he attributed to the reports concerning his parentage, and though he saw no reason why he should receive different treatment because of this, it yet explained to him the curious glances cast his way. He read and pondered and wrestled with difficulties of every kind; saw little of the marquis; and as the evenings grew longer, spent still larger portions of them with Duncan—now and then reading to him, but oftener listening to his music or taking a lesson in the piper's art. Since their last conversation, Lady Florimel's behavior to him was altered. She hardly ever sent for him now, and when she did, gave her orders so distantly that at length, but for his grandfather's sake, he could hardly have brought himself to remain in the House, even until the return of his master who was away from home. Malcolm contemplated proposing to him as soon as he came back that he should leave his service and resume his former occupation, at least until the return of summer should render it fit to launch the cutter again.

One day, a little after noon, Malcolm stepped from the House. The morning had broken gray and squally, with frequent sharp showers, and had grown into a gurly gusty day. Autumn was definitely past and winter fully arrived. He walked toward the down and straight to Miss Horn's. She received him with a cordiality such as she had never shown him before.

"Anything new, mem?" he asked, with the image of Mrs. Stewart standing ghastly on the slopes of his imagination.

"I wouldn't be fit to tell you, laddie, if it weren't, as you know, that the Almighty's very merciful to me in the matter of feelings. Your friends in the Seaton, and over at Scaurnose, have feelings, and that's why none of them has plucked up their heart to tell you of the wagging of slanderous tongues against you."

"What are they saying now?" asked Malcolm with considerable indifference.

"Nothing more or less than that you're the father of an unborn child," answered Miss Horn.

"I don't freely understand you," returned Malcolm, for the unexpectedness of the disclosure was scarcely to be mastered at once.

In plain and honest speech she made him at once comprehend the nature of the calumny. He started to his feet, and shouted, "Who dares say it?" so loud that the listening Jean almost fell down the stair.

"Who should say it but the lassie herself?" answered Miss Horn simply. "She must have the best right to say what's what."

"It would better become anybody but her," said Malcolm.

"What do you mean there, laddie?" asked Miss Horn.

"That none could know so well's herself it was a lie. Who is she?"

"Who but Meg Partan's Lizzy!"

"Poor lassie! is that it? Eh, but I'm sorry for her! She never said it was me. Whoever said it, surely you don't believe it of me, mem?"

"Me believe it! Malcolm MacPhail, will you dare insult a maiden woman that's stood clear of reproach until she's long past the age of it? It's not been all that difficult, I must allow, for I haven't been led into any temptations!"

"Eh, mem!" perceiving by the flash of her eyes and the sudden halt of her speech that she was really indignant. "I don't know what I have said to anger you!"

"Anger me! What—though I have no feelings! Will he dare imagine that he would be sitting there, and me holding him company if I believed him capable of turning out such a miserable, contemptible wretch! The Lord come between me and my wrath!"

"I beg your pardon, mem. A body can't put things together before he speaks. I'm obliged to you for taking my part."

"I take nobody's side but my own, laddie."

"Well, mem, what would you have me do? I can't send my old daddy

around the town with his pipes to proclaim that I'm not the man. I'm thinking I'll just have to leave the place."

"Would you send your daddy round with the pipes to say that you were
the man? You might as well do the one as the other. Many a better man has
been called worse, and folk soon forget that ever the lie was said. No, no;
never run from a lie. And never say, neither, that you didn't do the thing,
except it be laid straight to your face. Let a lie lay in the dirt. If you pick it
up, the dirt'll stick to you, even if you fling the lie over the dike at the end
of the world. No, no! Let a lie lay as you would the devil's tail!"

"Everything's going against me now!" sighed Malcolm.

"Old Job all over again!" retuned Miss Horn almost sarcastically. "The
devil had the worse of it though, and will have in the long run again. Meanwhile, you must face him!"

"What should I do then, mem?"

"Do? Who said you was to do anything? The best doing is to stand still.
Let the wave go over you without ducking."

"If I'm not to do anything, I almost wish I hadn't known," said Malcolm,
whose honorable nature writhed under the imputed vileness.

"It's better to know in what light you stand with other folk. It keeps you
from having to trust too much and so doing things or making remarks that
would be misread. You must keep an open road, so that the truth when it
comes out may have a free course. The one thing that spites me is that the
very folk that was the first to spread your ill report will be the first to wish
you well when the truth's known—ay, and they'll persuade themselves that
they stuck up for you all along."

"There must be some judgment on lying."

"The worst wish I have for any backbiter is that he may live to be affronted with himself. After that he'll be good enough company for me. Go
your way, laddie; say your prayers, and hold up your head. Who wouldn't
rather be accused of all the sins of the Commandments than to be guilty of
one of them?"

Malcolm did hold up his head as he walked away.

Not a single person was in the street. Far below, the sea was chafing and
tossing—gray-green broken into white. The roar of the wind was increasing
rapidly. It was growing into a hurricane, and even for his practiced foot, it
was not easy to walk up the hill with steady footing. But he was hardly
conscious of it; his thoughts kept him well occupied.

He must face the lies out, and he must accept any mother God had given
him. But how was he to endure the altered looks of his old friends? Faces
indifferent before had grown suddenly dear to him, and opinions he would
have thought valueless once had become golden in his eyes. Had he been
such as to deserve their reproaches, he would doubtless have steeled himself to despise them. But his innocence bound him to the very people who
judged him guilty. And there was that awful certainty slowly, but steadily
drawing nearer—that period of vacant anguish in which Lady Florimel must
vanish from his sight and the splendor of his life go with her, to return no
more.

But not even yet did he cherish any fancy of coming nearer to her than the idea of absolute service authorized. As often as the fancy had, compelled by the lady herself, crossed the horizon of his thoughts, a repellent influence from the same source had been at hand to sweep it afar into its antenatal chaos. But his love rose ever from the earth to which the blow had hurled it, purified again, once more all devotion and no desire, careless of recognition beyond the acceptance of its offered service, and content that the be-all should be the end-all.

The night descended as rapidly as the storm increased. As he approached the House, it had already grown so dark and the winds so violent that he began to fear it might be closed for the night ere he reached it.

When he came within sight of it, however, he perceived, by the hurried movement of lights that, instead of being folded in silence, the House was in unwonted commotion. As he hastened to the north door, so fiercely did the wind dispute every step he made toward it that when at length he reached and opened it, a blast burst wide the opposite one, and roared through the hall like a torrent. Lady Florimel, flitting across it at the moment, was almost blown down, and shrieked aloud for help. Malcolm was already at the south door, exerting all his strength to close it, when she saw him and, bounding to him, with white face and dilated eyes, exclaimed—

"Oh, Malcolm! what a time you have been getting back!"

"What's wrong, my lady?" cried Malcolm with respondent terror.

"Don't you hear it?" she answered. "The wind is blowing the house down. There's just been a terrible fall, and every moment I hear it going. If my father would only come! We shall all be blown into the burn!"

"No fear of that, my lady!" returned Malcolm. "The walls of the old place are as strong as live rock, and will stand the worst wind that ever blew—this side of the tropics anyway. I'll just go and see what's the mischief."

He was moving away, but Lady Florimel stopped him.

"No, no, Malcolm!" she said. "It's very silly of me, I daresay, but I've been so frightened. They're such a set of geese—Mrs. Courthope, and the butler, and all of them! Don't leave me, please!"

"I must go and see what's amiss, my lady," answered Malcolm. "But you can come with me if you like. What's fallen, do you think?"

"Nobody knows. It fell with a noise like thunder, and shook the whole house."

"It's far too dark to see anything from the outside," rejoined Malcolm—at least before the moon's up. But I can soon satisfy myself whether the devil's in the house or not."

He took a candle from the hall table and went up the square staircase, followed by Florimel.

"Why is it, my lady, that the house isn't locked up and everybody in their beds?" he asked.

"My father is coming home tonight. Didn't you know? But I should have thought a storm like this enough to account for people not being in bed!"

"It's a fearful night for him to be so far from his! Where's he coming from? You never speak to me now, my lady, and nobody told me."

"He was to come from Fochabers tonight. Stoat took the bay mare to meet him yesterday."

"He would never start in such a wind! It's fit to blow the saddle off the mare's back!"

"He may have started before it came to blow like this," said Florimel.

Malcolm liked the suggestion the less because of its probability, believing, in that case, he should have arrived long ago. But he took care not to increase Florimel's alarm.

By this time Malcolm knew well the whole of the accessible inside of the roof—better far than anyone else about the House. From one part to another, over the whole of it, he now led Lady Florimel. To Florimel it looked a dread waste, a region deserted and forgotten, mysterious with far-reaching nooks of darkness, and now awful with the wind raving and howling over slates and leads so close to them on all sides.

At length they approached Malcolm's own quarters, where they would have to pass the very door of the wizard's chamber to reach a short ladder-like stair that led up into the midst of naked rafters, when, coming upon a small storm window near the end of a long passage, Lady Florimel stopped and peeped out.

"The moon is rising," she said and stood looking.

Malcolm glanced over his shoulder. Eastward a dim light shone up from behind the crest of a low hill. A great part of the sky was clear, but huge masses of broken cloud went sweeping across the heavens. The wind had moderated.

"Aren't we somewhere near your friend the wizard?" said Lady Florimel, with a slight tremble in the tone of mockery with which she spoke.

Malcolm answered as if he were not quite certain.

"Isn't your own room somewhere hereabouts?" asked the girl sharply.

"We'll just go to one other queer place," observed Malcolm, pretending not to have heard her, "and if the roof be all right there, I'll not bother my head about it until the morning. It's but a few steps farther, and then up a little stairway."

A fit of her not unusual obstinacy had, however, seized Lady Florimel.

"I won't move a step," she said, "until you have told me where the wizard's chamber is."

"Behind you, my lady, if you will have it," answered Malcolm, not unwilling to punish her a little; "just at the far end of the hall there."

Even as he spoke, there sounded somewhere as it were the slam of a heavy iron door, the echoes of which seemed to go searching into every cranny of the multitudinous garrets. Florimel gave a shriek and, laying hold of Malcolm, clung to him in terror. A sympathetic tremor, set in motion by her cry, went vibrating through the fisherman's powerful frame, and almost involuntarily he clasped her close. With wide eyes they stood staring down the long passage, of which, by the poor light they carried, they could not see a quarter of the length. Presently they heard a soft foot-fall along its floor, drawing slowly nearer through the darkness; and slowly out of the darkness grew the figure of a man, huge and dim, clad in a long flowing garment and coming straight on to where they stood. They clung yet closer together. The apparition came within three yards of them, and then they recognized Lord Lossie in his dressing gown.

They started, and broke apart. Florimel flew to her father, and Malcolm stood, expecting the last stroke of his evil fortune. The marquis looked pale, stern and agitated. Instead of kissing his daughter on the forehead as was his custom, he put her from him with one expanded palm, but the next moment drew her to his side. Then approaching Malcolm, he lighted the candle he carried, which a draught had extinguished on the way.

"Go to your room, MacPhail," he said, and turned from him, his arm still around Lady Florimel.

They walked away together down the long passage, vaguely visible in flickering fits. All at once their light vanished, and with it Malcolm's eyes seemed to have left him. But a merry laugh, the silvery thread in which was certainly Florimel's, reached his ears, and brought him to himself.

For two or three dismal hours he lay with eyes closed but sleepless. At length he opened them wide and looked out into the room. It was a bright moonlit night; the wind had sunk to rest; all the world slept in the exhaustion of the storm. He only was awake; he could lie no longer. He would go out and discover, if possible, the mischief the tempest had done.

He crept down the little spiral stair used only by the servants and was presently in the open air. First, he sought a view of the building against the sky, but could not see that any portion was missing. He then proceeded to walk around the House in order to find what had fallen.

There was a certain neglected spot nearly under his own window, far in the back where no one ever went, where he saw a heap of blackened stones and mortar. Here was the avalanche whose fall had so terrified the household! The formless mass had yesterday been a fair-proportioned and ornate stack of chimneys.

He sat down and fell once again to thinking. The marquis must dismiss him in the morning; would it not be better to go away now and spare old Duncan a terrible fit of rage? He would suppose he had fled from the pseudo-maternal net of Mrs. Stewart. But his nature recoiled both from the unmanliness of such a flight and from the appearance of conscious wrong it must involve, and he dismissed the notion. Scheme after scheme for the future passed through his head as his eyes went listlessly straying about him. Suddenly he found them occupied with a low iron-studded door in the wall of the House, which he had never seen before. He descended and found it hardly closed, for there was no notch to receive the heavy latch. Pushing it open on great rusty hinges, he saw within what in the shadow appeared a precipitous descent. His curiosity was roused. He stole back to his room and fetched his candle; and having, by the aid of his tinderbox, lighted it in the shelter of the heap, peeped again through the doorway and saw what seemed a narrow cylindrical pit, only, far from showing a great yawning depth, it was filled with stones and rubbish to nearly the bottom of the door. The top of the door reached almost to the valuted roof one part of which, close to the inner side of the circular wall, was broken. Below this breach, fragments of stone projected from the wall, suggesting the remnants of a stair.

One foot on the end of a long stone sticking vertically from the rubbish, and another on one of the stones projecting from the wall, and his head was already through the break in the roof and in a minute more he was climbing a small, broken, but quite passable spiral staircase, almost a counterpart of that already described as going like a huge augerbore through the house from top to bottom—that indeed by which he had just descended.

Not until he reached the top of the stair did he find a door. It was iron-studded and heavily hinged, like that below. It opened outward—noiselessly he found, as if its hinges had been recently oiled, and admitted him to a small closet, the second door of which he opened hurriedly, with a beating heart. Yes! there was the check-curtained bed! It must be the wizard's chamber! Crossing to another door, he found it both locked and further secured by a large iron bolt in a strong staple. This latter he drew back, but there was no key in the lock. With scarce a doubt remaining, he shot down the one stair and flew up the other to try the key that lay in his chest. One moment more and he stood in the same room, admitted by the door next his own.

Some exposure was surely not far off! Anyhow, here was room for counter-plot on the chance of baffling something underhand—villainy most likely where Mrs. Catanach was concerned! And yet with the control of it thus apparently given into his hands, he must depart, leaving the House at the mercy of a low woman, for the lock of the wizard's door would not exclude her long if she wished to enter the building! He would not go, however, without revealing all to the marquis, and would at once make some provision toward her discomfiture.

Going to the forge and bringing thence a long bar of iron to use as a lever, he carefully drew from the door frame the staple of the bolt, and then replaced it so that while it looked just as before, a good push would now send it into the middle of the room. Lastly, he slid the bolt into it, and having carefully removed all traces of disturbance, left the mysterious chamber by its own stair. Once more he ascended the passage through the House, locked the door, and retired to his room with the key.

He had now plenty to think about beyond himself! Here certainly was some small support to the legend of the wizard earl. The stair which he had discovered had been in common use at one time; its connection with other parts of the House had been cut off and by degrees it had come to be forgotten altogether. Mrs. Catanach must have discovered it the same night on which he found her there, had gone away by it then, and had certainly been making use of it since. When he smelt the sulphur, she must have been lighting a match.

It was now getting toward morning and at last he was tired. He went to bed and fell asleep. When he woke, it was late, and as he dressed he heard the noise of hoofs and wheels in the stable yard. He was sitting at breakfast in Mrs. Courthope's room when she came in full of surprise at the sudden departure of her lord and lady. The marquis had rung for his man, and Lady

Florimel for her maid, as soon as it was light; orders were sent at once to the stable; four horses were put to the traveling carriage; and they were gone, Mrs. Courthope could not tell whither.

Dreary as was the House without Florimel, things had turned out a shade or two better than Malcolm had expected, and he braced himself to endure his loss.

30

●●●●●●●●●●●●●●●●●●●●

The Abduction

*T*hings were going pretty well for the laird. Phemy and he drew yet closer to each other and he became yet more peaceful in her company, secure in the knowledge that his places of hiding were known but to the two of them. For some time life for the laird had gone on much as before. He spent a good deal of time with Phemy, especially at night—in the fields, along the shore; and when he had need of a roof over his head, Phemy's little garret was his second home, his first being the cave. Though they did not become aware of his proximity (his custom, with Phemy's assistance, often being to creep in late at night for a few scant hours of sleep and then to make his silent exit before the rising of the sun in the morning) until after Malcolm's most recent visit, his secret was well kept with Joseph and Annie Mair. They knew Malcolm would do nothing in any way to harm him or to reveal him, yet they nevertheless thought it best to keep him from the added burden of knowing too much concerning the laird. Though he had little interaction with them, the laird had learned to trust them almost as much as he did their daughter, and came to even spend days there.

Little were the laird and Phemy aware how tight the net of capture was slowly drawing around them, for though they had seen or heard nothing of their would-be assailants, the plottings of Mrs. Catanach and Mrs. Stewart and her hirelings were unknowingly closing in on them.

One night the laird and Phemy were out on the shore. The laird was searching the horizon for any spot in heaven or earth where the Father of Lights might show foot or hand or face and thereby grant him a brief interview, that he might question him concerning where he came from. He had at length seated himself on a lichen-covered stone, with his head buried in his hands, as if, wearied with vain search for him outside, he would now look within, and see if God might not be there. Suddenly a sharp exclamation from Phemy reached him from where she played some distance away. He listened—

"Run! Run! Run!" she cried—the last word prolonged into a scream.

While it yet rang in his ears, the laird was halfway down the shore toward the promontory. In the open country he had not a chance. But knowing every cranny in the rocks large enough to hide him, with anything like a good head start for his short-lived speed, he was all but certain to evade his pursuers, especially in such a dark night as this.

He was not in the least anxious about Phemy, never imagining she might be less sacred in other eyes than in his, and knowing neither that her last cry of loving solicitude had gathered intensity from a cruel grasp, nor that while he fled in safety, she remained a captive.

Trembling and panting like a hare just escaped from the hounds, he squeezed himself into a cleft, where he sat half covered with water until the morning began to break. Then he drew himself out and crept along the shore, from point to point, with keen circumspection, until he was to the village. But having reached his burrow in Phemy's garret and pulled down his rope ladder and ascended, he found, with dismay, that the loft had been invaded during the night. He knew he was no longer safe, even there.

He threw himself on the ground outside for a moment, then started to his feet, caught up his cloak, and fled from Scaurnose as if a visible pestilence had been behind him.

When her parents discovered that Phemy did not come down for breakfast, it occasioned them no anxiety. But when they had heard nothing of either Phemy or the laird by the noon meal, they went outside and up the ladder at the back of their small house into the loft. Seeing its condition they were naturally seized with the dread that something evil had befallen them. They supposed that Phemy was either with him or had herself set out to look for him. As the day wore on they began to show signs of growing uneasiness. Still the two might be together, and the explanation of their absence a very simple and satisfactory one. But before night, anxiety had insinuated itself through their whole being—nor theirs alone, but had so mastered and possessed the whole village that at length all employment was deserted and every person capable joined in a search along the coast, fearing to find their bodies at the foot of some cliff. The report spread to the neighboring villages. In Portlossie Duncan went round with his pipes, arousing attention by a brief blast, and then crying the loss at every corner. As soon as Malcolm heard of it, he hurried to find Joseph, but the only explanation of their absence he was prepared to suggest was one that had already occurred to almost everybody—that the laird had been captured by the emissaries of his mother, and that, to provide against a rescue, they had carried off his companion with him. On which supposition there was every probability that, within a few days at the most, Phemy would be restored unhurt.

"There can be little doubt they have gotten a hand on him at last, poor fellow!" said Joseph. "But whatever's come to them, we can't sit down and wait without knowing how Phemy's faring, poor little lamb! You must go over to Kirkbyres, Malcolm, and get a word from your mother, and see if anything can be made out about her."

The proposal fell on Malcolm like a great billow.

"Blue Peter," he said, looking him in the face, "I took it as a mark of your friendship that you never spoke the word to me. What right has any man to call that woman my mother? I have never allowed it!"

"I'm thinking," returned Joseph, the more easily nettled that his horizon also was full of trouble, "that your word on the matter won't go so far as hers. You'll not be subpoenaed for your witness on the point."

"I would as soon go a mile into the mouth of hell as to go to Kirkbyres!" said Malcolm.

"I have my answer then," said Peter, and turned away.

"But I'll go," Malcolm went on. "The thing that must be must be. Only I'll tell you this, Peter," he added, "if ever you say such a word in my hearing again, that is, before the woman has proven herself in what she says, I'll go by you afterward without speaking."

Joseph, who had been standing with his back to his friend, turned and held out his hand. Malcolm took it.

"One question before I go, Peter," he said. "Why didn't you tell me what folk was saying about me and Lizzy Findlay?"

"Because I didn't believe a word of it, and I wasn't going to add to your troubles."

"Lizzy never said such a thing?"

"Never!"

"I was sure of that! Now I'll be off to Kirkbyres, God help me! I would rather face Satan. But don't expect any news. If she knows, she's all the more certain not to tell. Only you can't say I didn't do my best for you."

It was the hardest trial of the will Malcolm had yet had to encounter. He walked determinedly home. Stoat saddled a horse for him while he changed his dress, and once more set out for Kirkbyres.

Had Malcolm been at the time capable of attempting an analysis of his feeling toward Mrs. Stewart, he would have found it very difficult to effect. Satisfied as he was of the untruthful nature of the woman who claimed him, and conscious of a strong repugnance to any nearer approach between them, he was yet aware of a certain indescribable fascination in her. This, however, only caused him to recoil from her all the more.

He was shown into a room where the fire had not been many minutes lit. It had long narrow windows, over which the ivy had grown so thick that he was in it some moments before he saw through the dusk that it was a library.

A few minutes passed, then the door softly opened and Mrs. Stewart glided swiftly across the floor with outstretched arms.

"At last!" she said, and would have clasped him to her bosom. But Malcolm stepped back.

"No, no, mem!" he said. "It takes two to do that."

"Malcolm!" she exclaimed, her voice trembling with emotion—of some kind.

"You may call me your son, mem, but I know no ground yet for calling you my—"

He could not say the word.

"That is very true, Malcolm," she returned gently; "but this interview is not of my seeking. I wish to precipitate nothing. So long as there is a single link, or half a link even, missing from the chain of which one end hangs at my heart—"

She paused, with her hand on her bosom, apparently to suppress rising emotion. Had she had the sentence ready for use?

"—I will not subject myself," she went on, "to such treatment as it seems I must look for from you. It is hard to lose a son, but it is harder yet to find him again after he has utterly ceased to be one."

Here she put her handkerchief to her eyes.

"Till the matter is settled, however," she resumed, "let us be friends—or at least not enemies. What did you come for now? Not to insult me surely. Is there anything I can do for you?"

Malcolm felt the dignity of her behavior, but nonetheless, after his own straightforward manner, answered her question to the point: "I came about nothing concerning myself, mem. I came to see whether you know anything about Phemy Mair."

"Is it a wo—? I don't even know who she is. You don't mean the young woman that—? Why do you come to me about her? Who is she?"

Malcolm hesitated a moment. If she really did not know what he meant, was there any risk in telling her? But he saw none.

"Who is she, mem?" he returned. "I think she must be the laird's good angel, though in shape she's but a wee lassie. She makes up for a heap to the laird. Him and her, mem, they've disappeared together, nobody knows where."

Mrs. Stewart laughed a low unpleasant laugh, but made no other reply. Malcolm went on.

"And it's not to be wondered at if folk will have it that you must know something about it, mem."

"I know nothing whatever," she returned emphatically. "Believe me or not, as you please," she added, with heightened color. "If I did know anything," she went on, with apparent truthfulness, "I don't know that I should feel bound to tell it. As it is, however, I can only say I know nothing of either of them. That I do say most solemnly."

Malcolm turned, satisfied at least that he could learn no more.

"You're not going to leave me so?" the lady said, and her face grew sad.

"There's nothing more between us, mem," answered Malcolm, without even turning his face.

"You will be sorry for treating me so someday."

"Well then, mem, I will be; but that day's not today."

"Think what you could do for your poor witless brother if—"

"Mem," interrupted Malcolm, turning right round and drawing himself up in anger, "prove that I am your son, and that minute I'll ask you who was my father."

Mrs. Stewart changed color—neither with the blush of innocence nor with the paltor of guilt, but with the gray of mingled rage and hatred. She took a step forward with the quick movement of a snake about to strike, but stopped midway, and stood looking at him with glittering eyes, teeth clenched, and lips half open.

Malcolm returned her gaze for a moment or two.

"You never was the mother, whoever was the father of me!" he said, and walked out of the room.

He had scarcely reached the door when he heard a heavy fall, and looking around saw the lady lying motionless on the floor. Thoroughly on his guard, however, and fearful both of her hatred and her blandishments, he only made the more haste downstairs. In a minute he was mounted and trotting fast home, considerably happier than before, inasmuch as he was now almost beyond doubt convinced that Mrs. Stewart was not his mother.

31

The Letters

*E*ver since the visit of condolence with which the narrative of these events opened, there had been a coolness between Mrs. Mellis and Miss Horn. Mr. Mellis's shop was directly opposite Miss Horn's house, and his wife's parlor was over the shop, looking into the street. Hence the two neighbors could not but see each other pretty often; beyond a stiff nod, however, no sign of smoldering friendship had as yet broken out. Miss Horn was consequently a good deal surprised when, having gone into the shop to buy some trifle, Mr. Mellis informed her, in all but a whisper, that his wife was very anxious to see her alone for a moment, and begged her to have the goodness to step up to the parlor. His customer gave a small snort, betraying her first impulse to resentment, but her nobler nature, which was never far from the surface, constrained her compliance.

Mrs. Mellis rose hurriedly when the plumb-line figure of her neighbor appeared, ushered in by her husband, and received her somewhat embarrassed.

"Sit down, Miss Horn," she said. "It's been a long time since we had news together."

Miss Horn seated herself with a begrudged acquiescence.

"Were you at home last night, mem, between the hours of eight and nine?"

"Who am I to be asked such a question?" shot back Miss Horn as the whole battery of her indignation awoke. "Who but yourself would have dared it, Mistress Mellis?"

"Softly, softly, Miss Horn!" expostulated her questioner. "I have no wish to pry into any secrets of yours, or—"

"Secrets!" shouted Miss Horn.

But her consciousness of good intent and all but assurance of final victory upheld Mrs. Mellis's determination not to yield to a like manner.

"—or Jean's either," she went on apparently regardless; "but I would want to be sure you knew all about your own house that a body might chance to see from the middle of the street."

"The parlor blind's gone up crooked ever since that thumb-fingered Watty Witherspail made a new roller for it. If that be what you mean, Mistress Mellis—"

"Hoots!" returned the other. "How far can you trust to that Jean of yours, mem?"

"No farther than the length of my nose, or the width of my two eyes," was the scornful answer.

"In that case, I may speak out," said Mrs. Mellis.

"Use your freedom."

"Well, I will. You was hardly out of the house last night, before—"

"You saw me go out?"

"Ay, I did."

"Why did you ask me then?"

"Well, I needn't have asked. But that's not the point. You hadn't been gone, as I was saying, five minutes, when a light came into the bedroom next to your parlor, and Jean appeared with a candle in her hand. There was no light in this room but the light of the fire, and not much of that, for it was mostly peat, so I saw her well enough without being seen myself. She came straight to the window and drew down the blind, but lost herself a bit or she would never have set down her candle where it cast a shadow on herself and her doings upon the blind."

"And what was she after?" cried Miss Horn, without any attempt to conceal her growing interest.

"She made nothing of it, whatever it was, for down the street came the schoolmaster, and knocked at the door, and went in and waited until you came home."

"Well?" said Miss Horn.

But Mrs. Mellis held her peace.

"Well!?" repeated Miss Horn.

"Well?" returned Mrs. Mellis with curious deference, "all that I take it upon me to say is, think twice before you trust that Jean of yours."

"I trust nothing to her! What did you see, Mistress Mellis?"

"You needn't speak like that," returned Mrs. Mellis, for Miss Horn's tone was threatening. "I'm not Jean!"

"What did you see?" repeated Miss Horn, more gently, but not less eagerly.

"Whose is that chest of mahogany drawers in that bedroom, if I may presume to ask?"

"Whose but mine?"

"They're not Jean's?"

"Jean's!"

"You might be letting her keep a few things in them, for all I know."

"Jean's things in my Grizel's drawers! A likely thing!"

"Hmm! They were poor Miss Campbell's, were they?"

"They were Grizel Campbell's drawers as long as she had use for any; but why should you say poor, I don't know, except it be that she's gone where they haven't much that needs laying in drawers. That's neither here nor there. Do you mean to tell me that Jean was fiddling with those drawers? They're all locked, every one of them. And they're good locks."

"Not too good to have keys to them, are they?"

"The keys are in my pocket," said Miss Horn, clapping her hand to the skirt of her dress. "They're in my pocket, though I haven't had the feelings to make use of them since she left me."

"Are you sure they were there last night, mem?"

Miss Horn seemed struck.

"I had on my black silk last night!" she answered vaguely, and was then silent, pondering doubtfully.

"Well, mem, just put on your black silk again tonight and come over about eight o'clock; and you'll be able to judge by her doings when you're not in the house, if there be anything amiss with Jean. There can't be much ill done yet, that's a comfort."

"What ill, beyond meddling with what doesn't concern her, could the woman do?" said Miss Horn with attempted confidence.

"That you should know best yourself, mem. But Jean's an awful gossip, and a lady like your cousin might have left documents behind her that she would not just like to hear proclaimed from the housetops. Not that she'll ever hear anything more, poor thing!"

"What do you mean?" cried Miss Horn, half frightened, half angry.

"Just what I say, no more and no less," returned Mrs. Mellis. "Miss Campbell may well have left letters, for instance, and how would they fare in Jean's hands?"

"When I never had the heart to open her drawers!" exclaimed Miss Horn, enraged at the very notion of the crime. "I have no feelings, thank God."

"I doubt Jean has her full share of feelings belonging to fallen human nature," said Mrs. Mellis. "But you just come and see with your own eyes and judge for yourself; it's no business of mine."

"I'll come tonight, Mrs. Mellis. Only let it be between the two of us."

"I can hold my tongue, mem, that is from all but one. So long as married folk sleeps in one bed, it's ill to hold anything between them."

"Mr. Mellis is a good man, and I don't care what he knows," answered Miss Horn.

She descended to the shop, and having bought enough to account to Jean for her lengthened stay, for she had beyond a doubt been watching the door of the shop, she crossed the street, went up to her parlor, and rang the bell. The same moment Jean's head was popping in at the door: she had her reasons for always answering the bell like a bullet.

That night, Miss Horn descended the stairway into the kitchen, and called out as she crossed the threshold at eight o'clock, "I'm going out now, Jean."

She turned toward the head of the street, in the direction of the church, but out of the range of Jean's vision, made a circuit back and entered Mr. Mellis's house by the garden in the rear.

In the parlor she found a supper prepared to celebrate the renewal of old goodwill. The clear crystal on the table; the new loaf so brown; the rich, clear-complexioned butter; the self-satisfied hum of the kettle; the bright fire; and the dish of boiled potatoes, the pink eggs, the yellow haddock, and the crimson strawberry jam all combined their influences. From below came the sound of the shutters which Mr. Mellis was putting up a few minutes earlier than usual; and presently they sat down to the table, and, after prologue judged suitable, proceeded to enjoy the good things before them.

But Miss Horn was uneasy. The thought of what Jean might have already discovered had haunted her all day long; for her reluctance to open her cousin's drawers had arisen mainly from the dread of finding justified a certain painful suspicion which had haunted the whole of her relationship with Griselda Campbell—namely, that the worm of a secret had been lying at the root of her life, the cause of all her illness, and of her death at last. She had fought with the suspicion a thousand times. Never was there a greater contrast between manner and nature than existed in Margaret Horn; the shell was rough, the kernel absolute delicacy. Not for a moment had her suspicion altered her behavior to the gentle suffering creature toward whom she had adopted the relation of an elder and stronger sister. To herself she steadily excused her cousin's withholdment of confidence. And now the thought of eyes like Jean's exploring Grizel's forsaken treasures made her so indignant and restless that she could hardly even pretend to enjoy her friend's hospitality.

Mrs. Mellis had so arranged the table and their places that she and her guest had only to lift their eyes to see the window of their watch. Their plan was to extinguish their own the moment Jean's light should appear, and so watch without the risk of counter discovery.

"There she comes!" cried Mrs. Mellis; and her husband and Miss Horn made such haste to blow out the candle that they knocked heads, blew in each other's faces, and the first time missed it. Jean approached the window with hers in her hand, and pulled down the blind. But alas, beyond the form of a close-bent elbow moving now and then across a corner of the white field, no shadow appeared on it.

Miss Horn rose.

"Sit down, mem. Sit down. You have nothing to go on yet," exclaimed Mr. Mellis.

"I can sit no longer," returned Miss Horn. "I have enough to go on: the woman has no business there. I'll just slip across and go in, as quiet as I can. But I'll warrant I'll make a racket before I come out again!"

With a grim diagonal nod she left the room.

Although it was now quite dark, she yet deemed it prudent to go by the garden gate into the back lane, and so cross the street lower down. Opening her own door noiselessly, thanks to Jean, who kept the lock well oiled for reasons of Mrs. Catanach's, she closed it silently, and, long-boned as she was, crept up the stairs like a cat. The light was shining from the room; the door was ajar. She listened at it for a moment, and could distinguish nothing. Then fancying she heard the rustle of paper, could bear it no longer, pushed the door open and entered. There stood Jean, staring at her with fear-blanched face, a deep top-drawer open before her, and her hands full of things she was in the act of replacing. Her terror culminated, and its spell broke in a shriek, when her mistress sprang upon her like a tigress.

The watchers in the opposite house heard no cry and only saw a heave of two intermingled black shadows across the blind, after which they neither heard nor saw anything more. The light went on burning until its final struggle with the darkness began, when it died with many a flickering throb. Unable at last to endure the suspense, now growing to fear, any longer, they stole across the street, opened the door, and went in. Over the kitchen-fore, like an evil spirit of the squabby order, crouched Mrs. Catanach, waiting for Jean; no one else was to be found.

About ten o'clock the same evening Mr. Graham sat by his peat fire when he heard someone lift the latch of the outer door and then knock at his inner. His invitation to enter was answered by the appearance of Miss Horn, gaunt and grim as usual, but with more than the usual fire gleaming from the shadowy cavern of her bonnet. She made no apology for the lateness of her visit, but seated herself at the other side of the table, and laid upon it a paper parcel, which she proceeded to open with much deliberation. Having at length untied the string with the long fingers of a hand which trembled so as almost to defeat the attempt, she took from the parcel a packet of old letters sealed with spangled wax, and pushed it across the table to the schoolmaster, saying, "Here, Sandy Graham! Nobody but yourself has a right to say what's to be done with them!"

He put out his hand and took them gently, with a look of sadness, but no surprise.

"Don't think I've been reading them. No, no! I would not read an honest man's letters, be they written to whom they might."

Mr. Graham was silent.

"You're a good man, Sandy Graham," Miss Horn resumed, "if God ever took pains to make one. Don't think anything between you and her would have brought me at this time of night to disturb you in your own chamber. No, no! Whatever was between the two of you had an honest man in it, and I would have taken my time to give you back your letters. But there's some of another signature here!"

As she spoke she drew from the parcel a small cardboard box, broken at the sides, and tied up with a bit of tape. This she undid, and, turning the box upside down, tumbled its contents out on the table before him. "What do you make of these?" she said.

"Do you want me to—?" asked the schoolmaster with trembling voice.

"I do," she answered.

There were a number of little notes—some but a word or two, and signed with initials; others longer and signed in full. Mr. Graham took up one of them reluctantly and unfolded it softly. He had hardly looked at it when he started and exclaimed, "God have mercy! What can be the date of this?"

There was no date to it. He held it in his hands for a minute, his eyes fixed on the fire, and his features almost convulsed with his efforts at composure; then laid it gently on the table, and said without turning his eyes to Miss Horn,

"I cannot read this. You must not ask me. It refers doubtless to the time when Miss Campbell was governess to Lady Annabel. I see no end to be answered by my reading one of these letters."

"I daresay. Whoever saw that wouldn't look?" returned Miss Horn, with a glance keen as an eagle's into the thoughtful eyes of her friend.

"Why not do by the writer of these as you have done by me? Why not take them to him?" suggested Mr. Graham.

"That would be but thumb-fingered work," exclaimed Miss Horn, "to let go of the only piece of thread we've got into this matter."

"I don't understand you."

"Well, Sandy Graham, there's things that's not easy to talk about. Man that you are, you're the only human being I would open my mouth to about this, and that's because you love the memory of my poor lassie, Grizel Campbell."

"It's not her memory, it is herself I love," said the schoolmaster with trembling voice. "Tell me what you please; you may trust me."

"If I needed you to tell me that, I would trust you as I would a big black dog with butter. Hearken, Sandy Graham!"

The result of her communication and their following conference was that she returned about midnight with a journey before her, the object of which was to place the letters in the safekeeping of a lawyer friend in the neighboring county town.

Long before she reached home, Mrs. Catanach had left—not without communication with her ally. In spite of a certain precaution adopted by her mistress, the first thing the latter did when she entered being to take the key of the cellar stairs from her pocket, and release Jean, who issued crestfallen and miserable, and was sternly dismissed to bed. The next day, however, for reasons of her own, Miss Horn permitted her to resume her duties about the house without further remark, as if nothing had happened serious enough to render further measures necessary.

32

• • • • • • • • • • • • • • • • • • •

The Investigation

*A*bandoning all her remaining effects to Jean's curiosity—if indeed it were no worse demon that possessed her—Miss Horn, carrying a large parcel, betook herself to the Lossie Arms, to await the arrival of the mail coach from the west, on which she was pretty sure of a vacant seat.

Although the journey was but of a few miles, it seemed long and wearisome to her active spirit. At length the coach drove into the town, and stopped at the Duff Arms. Miss Horn descended, straightened her long back with some difficulty, shook her feet, loosened her knees, and marched off with the stride of a grenadier to find her lawyer.

Their interview did not take much time, and when it was over, Miss Horn commenced a round of visits to the friends she had in the place before her return trip. Though her thoughts were busy as she walked through the town, she gradually became aware that she was being watched and followed wherever she went. Now from behind a tree, now from a corner of the mausoleum, now from behind a rock, now over the parapet of the bridge, the mad laird had been observing her. Again and again he had made a sudden movement as if to run and accost her, but he had always drawn back again and concealed himself more carefully than before.

Since he lost Phemy, fear had been slaying him. No one knew where he slept; but in the daytime he haunted the streets, judging them safer than the fields or woods. The moment anyone accosted him, however, he fled like the wind. The vision of Miss Horn was like the dayspring from on high to him; a familiar face. Though he could not approach her, he knew her to be his friend.

There was indeed a change upon him! His clothes hung about him—not from their ragged condition only, but also from the state of skin and bone to which he was reduced, his hump showing like a great peg over which they had been carelessly cast. Half the round of his eyes stood out from his face. He had always been ready to run, now he looked as if nothing but weakness and weariness kept him from running always. Though she could not seem to get closer to him, Miss Horn was able to mark the sad alteration.

As Miss Horn rode home later in the day, she reproached herself not a little for not making a greater effort to speak to the laird, and ask him about Phemy. It was, therefore, with a certain shame, that she set out immediately on her arrival to tell Malcolm that she had seen him. No one at the House being able to inform her where he was at the moment, she went to Duncan's cottage. There she found the piper, who could not tell her where his boy was, but gave her a hearty welcome and offered her a cup of tea, which, as it was now late in the afternoon, Miss Horn gladly accepted. As he bustled about to prepare it, refusing all assistance from his guest, he began to open his mind to her on a subject much in his thoughts—namely, Malcolm's inexplicable aversion to Mrs. Stewart.

"Ta name of Stewart will pe a nople name, mem," he said.

"It's good enough to know a body by," answered Miss Horn.

"If ta poy will pe a Stewart," he went on, heedless of the indifference of her remark, "who'll pe knowing put he'll may pe of ta royal plood!"

"There didn't look to be much royalty about old John, honest man, who couldn't rule a wife, though he had but one!" returned Miss Horn.

"If you please, mem, ton't pe too sharp on ta poor man whose wife will not pe a coot wife. If ta wife pe ta pad wife, she will pe ta pad wife however; and ta poor man will pe hafing ta pad wife and ta plame of it too; and tat will pe more as'll be fair, mem."

"Indeed, you never said a truer word, Master MacPhail!" assented Miss Horn. "It's a mercy that a lone woman like me, who has a masterful temper and no feelings, was never put to the temptation of occupying such a perilous position."

The old man was silent and Miss Horn resumed the main subject of their conversation.

"But though he might object to a father that wasn't honorable," she said, "you can't help wondering at the young lad not caring to have such a mother."

"And what would pe ta harm with ta motter? Is she not a coot woman, and a coot leddy?"

"You know what folk say about her goodness to her son!"

"Yes, put tat will pe ta lies of people. People is always telling lies."

"Well, that's true. It's a pity, supposing him to be hers, how small folk makes the chance of his being a Stewart for all that!"

"I'll not pe comprestanding you," said Duncan, bewildered.

"He's a wise son that knows his own father!" remarked Miss Horn, with more point than originality. "The lady never bore the best of characters, as far as my memory takes me, and that's back before John and her was married anyway. No, no; I doubt that John Stewart is the father of Malcolm MacPhail."

Duncan leaped up with a Gaelic explosion of concentrated force, and cried, "Ta woman is not pe no mother to Tuncan's poy!"

"Huly, huly, Mr. MacPhail!" interposed Miss Horn, with good-natured revenge; "it may be nothing but folk's lies, you know. Besides, there's still no proof one way or the other."

"It will pe enough to kill my poy to haf a woman like tat to pe ta motter of him. Why tidn't ta poy pe telling me why he wouldn't pe hafing her?"

"It would be nearly as bad as having her for a wife," assented Miss Horn, "but not quite."

The old man sought the door, as if for a breath of air; but as he went he blundered, and felt about as if he had just been struck blind. Ordinarily he walked in his house, at least, as if he saw every inch of the way. Presently he turned and resumed his seat.

"Was the child laid mother-naked into your hands, Master MacPhail?" asked Miss Horn, who had been meditating.

"Och, no! He had his clo'es on," answered Duncan.

"Have you any of them left?" she asked again.

"Inteet not," answered Duncan.

"You were staying at the Inn, weren't you?"

"Yes, mem, and they was coot to me."

"Who dressed the child for you?"

"Och, I trest him myself," said Duncan, still jealous of the women who had nursed the child.

"But no one?" suggested Miss Horn.

"Mistress Partan will pe toing a coot teal of tressing him, sometimes. Mistress Partan is a coot woman when she'll pe coot."

Here Malcolm entered and Miss Horn told him what she had seen of the laird and gathered concerning him.

"That looks bad for Phemy," remarked Malcolm, when she had described his forlorn condition. "She can't be with him, or he wouldn't be like that. Have you anything by way of counsel, mem?"

"I would counsel a word with the laird himself if it could be gotten. He may not know what's happened to her, but he may tell you the last he saw of her, and that may be more than you know now."

"He's taken such a doubting of me that I'm afraid it'll be hard to get to him, and still harder to talk to him, for when he's frightened he can hardly move his jawbone, not to say speak. I must try though and do my best. You think he's lurking around Fife House, do you then, mem?"

"He's been seen there—off and on."

"Well, I'll just go and put on my fisher-clothes, and set out at once. I must go over to Scaurnose first though, to let them know that he's been seen. It'll be but small comfort I imagine."

"Malcolm, my son," interjected Duncan, who had been watching for the conversation to afford him an opening, "if you'll pe meeting anyone will call you ta son of tat woman, gif him a coot plow in ta face, for you'll pe no son of a loose woman like tat, efen if she proof it. If you'll pe her son, old Tuncan will pe tisowning you for efer and efer."

"What's brought you to this, Daddy?" asked Malcolm, who could not help feeling curious, and indeed almost amused, as much as he disliked any allusion to the matter.

"Nefer you mind. Miss Horn will pe hafing coot reasons tat Mistress Stewart'll not can pe your mother."

Malcolm turned to Miss Horn.

"I've said nothing to Master MacPhail but what I've said more than once to you, laddie," she replied to the eager questioning of his eyes. "Go your way. The truth must win out over the lie in the long run. Off with you to Blue Peter!"

When Malcolm reached Scaurnose he found Phemy's parents in a sad state. Joseph asked to accompany him in the search and Malcolm agreed.

The sun was down, and a bone-piercing chill assailed them as they left the cottage. Almost in silence they walked together to the county town, put up at a little inn near the river, and at once began to make inquiries. Not a few persons had seen the laird at different times, but none knew where he slept or chiefly haunted. There was nothing for it but to set out in the morning, and stray hither and thither, on the chance of somewhere finding him.

Even as Malcolm and Blue Peter were straying about the town aimlessly in search of the laird the following morning, one whose designs were not so wholesome set out in similiar aimless fashion for the Seaton to see what glimmer of gossip she might uncover that would suit her devious purposes. The first person she encountered was the Partaness, standing at her door looking angry at the world.

"I heard a queer tale about Meg Horn at Duff Harbor the other day," said the midwife, speaking disrespectfully both to ease her own heart and to call forth the feelings of the other, who also, she knew, disliked Miss Horn.

"Ay, and what might that be?"

"But she might be a friend of yours, Mistress Findlay? Some folks like her, though I can't say I'm one of them."

"Friend of mine!" exclaimed the Partaness. "She was over here last night, sure enough. She was bulliraggin' at me, but I sent her on her way!"

"What bone had she to pick with you?"

"Oh, you would have taken her for a thief-catcher, and me for the thief! She insisted that I kept some duds of the baby Malcolm MacPhail, the reprobate, when he first came to the Seaton—a poor scratching brat as red as a lobster! It just drives me daft to think he ever got the breast of me that he should grow up to serve me so. But I'll soon get the grip of him yet, or my name's not—what they call me!"

"It's the way of the world, Mistress Findlay. What could you expect of one born in sin and brought forth in iniquity?"—a stock phrase of Mrs. Catanach's, glancing at her profession and embracing nearly the whole of her belief.

"The more's the pity he should have had the milk of an honest woman!"

"But what could the old lady be after? What was her business with it? She never did anything for the child?"

"Na, not her! Doubtless it was for the identifying of him to the lady of Gersefell. She had sent her, I don't wonder. She might have chosen a more welcome messenger."

"But you had nothing of the kind, I'll warrant."

"Never a thread. There was a long nightgown upon the child, wound round and round him, like graveclothes—if it had but been the Lord's will! It made me wonder at the time, for that's not how a baby that had been cared for should have been clad."

"Was there name or mark upon it?" asked Mrs. Catanach.

"None; there was but the place where part of the red dye of the thing had been torn out."

"And what became of the garment?"

"Oh, I cut it down later for some play clothes for the child when he was running about. That ever I should have taken a needle to cloth for such a devil's youngster! To me that was mother to him! The Lord keep me from going mad when I think of it!"

"And how's Lizzy—" began Mrs. Catanach, prefacing a fresh remark.

But at her name the mother flew into such a rage that, fearful of scandal, her companion would have exerted all her powers of oiliest persuasion to appease her. But if there was one thing Mrs. Catanach did not understand, it was the heart of a mother.

"Hoots, Mistress Findlay! Folk'll hear you. Hold your tongue! I'll never put my hand to the saving of her if you wish, or her child either," said the midwife, thinking thus to pacify her.

Then, like the eruption following mere volcanic unrest, out broke the sore-hearted woman's wrath. She raved and scolded and abused Mrs. Catanach, till at last she was driven to that final resource—the airs of an injured woman. She turned and walked back to the upper town with the Partaness, true to her name, snapping her pincers after her.

Notwithstanding the quarrel, Mrs. Catanach did not return without having gained something; she had learned that Miss Horn had been foiled in which she had no doubt was an attempt to obtain proof that Malcolm was not the son of Mrs. Stewart. That discovery was a grateful one; for who could have told but there might be something in existence to connect him with another origin than she and Mrs. Stewart would assign him?

33

· · · · · · · · · · · · · · · · · · ·

The Handwriting

The next day the marquis returned. Almost his first word was the desire that Malcolm should be sent to him. But nobody knew more than that he was missing; whereupon he sent for Duncan. The old man explained his boy's absence and as soon as he was dismissed took his way to the town, and called upon Miss Horn. In half an hour, the good lady started on foot for Duff Harbor. It was already growing dark; but there was one feeling Miss Horn had certainly been created without, and that was fear.

As she approached her destination, tramping eagerly along in a half-cloudy, half-star-lit night with a damp east wind blowing cold from the German Ocean, she was startled by the swift rush of something dark across the road before her. It came out of a small wood on the left toward the sea and bolted through a hedge on the right.

"Is that you, laird?" she cried; but there came no answer.

She walked straight to the house of her lawyer friend, and, after an hour's rest, the same night set out again for Portlossie, which she reached in safety by her bedtime.

Lord Lossie was very accessible. Since his retirement from the more indolent life of the metropolis to the quieter and more active pursuits of the country, his character had bettered a little—the hard soil had in a few places cracked a hair's-breadth. To this betterment the company of his daughter had chiefly contributed; for if she was little more developed in the right direction than himself, she was far less developed in the wrong, but certain circumstances of late occurrence had had a share in it as well, occasioning a revival of old memories which had a considerable sobering effect upon him.

As he sat at breakfast, about eleven o'clock on the morning after his return, one of his English servants entered with the message that a person, calling herself Miss Horn and refusing to explain her business, desired to see his lordship for a few minutes.

"Who is she?" asked the marquis.

The man did not know.

"What is she like?"

"An odd-looking lady, my lord, and very oddly dressed."

"Show her into the next room. I shall be with her directly."

Finishing his cup of coffee and pea-fowl's egg with deliberation, while he tried his best to recall in what connection he could have heard the name before, the marquis at length sauntered into the morning room in his dressing gown. There stood his visitor waiting for him, black and gaunt and grim, in a bay window, whose light almost surrounded her, so that there was scarcely a shadow about her.

"To what am I indebted—" began his lordship.

But Miss Horn speedily interrupted, "You're not indebted at all, my lord, until you know what it's for."

"Good!" returned his lordship and waited with a smile. She promised amusement, and he was ready for it. But it hardly came.

"Do you know this handwriting, my lord?" she inquired, sternly advancing a step and holding out a scrap of paper at arm's length. The marquis took it, glanced at it, and a shadow swept over his face, but vanished instantly—the mask of nonexpression which a man of his breeding always knows how to assume.

"Where did you get this?" he said quietly, with just the slightest catch in his voice.

"I got it, my lord, where there's more like it."

"Show me them."

"I've shown you plenty for you to get the idea," she answered.

"You refuse? If they are not my property, then why did you bring me this?"

"Are they your property, my lord?"

"This is my handwriting."

"You admit that?"

"Certainly, my good woman. You did not expect me to deny it?"

"God forbid, my lord! But will you admit that you're the lawful husband of the deceased? It will stay just between your lordship and me in the meantime."

He sat down holding the scrap of paper between his finger and thumb. "I will buy them of you," he said coolly after a moment's thought.

The form of reply which first arose in Miss Horn's indignant soul never reached her lips. "It's no trade," she answered with the coldness of suppressed wrath. "I don't deal in such wares."

"What do you deal in then?" asked the marquis.

"In truth and fair play, my lord," she answered, and was again silent.

So was the marquis for some moments, but was the first to resume.

"If you think the papers to which you refer of the least value, allow me to tell you it is an entire mistake."

"There was one who thought them of value," replied Miss Horn, "but who can tell? Scots law may put life into them yet, and give them a value to somebody besides me."

"What I mean, my good woman, is that if you think the possession of those papers gives you any hold over me which you can turn to your advantage, you are mistaken."

"God forgive you, my lord! My advantage! I thought your lordship was more of a gentleman by this time, or I would have sent a lawyer to you in place of coming myself."

"I trust you have discovered nothing in those letters to afford ground for such harsh judgment," said the marquis seriously.

"No, not a word in them, but more out of them. You won't try to tell me that a man who leaves a woman, let alone his wife—or one that he calls his wife—to all the pains of a mother and the penalties of the unmarried, without ever asking how she was making out, keeps his right to be considered a gentleman? In any case, a woman like myself won't allow him the title. God forbid it!"

"You are very frank and plain spoken," said the marquis.

"I'm plain made. I know good from bad, and a little besides. Now either those letters of your lordship's are every one a lie, or else you deserted your wife and child—"

"Alas!" interrupted the marquis with some emotion, "she deserted me and took the child with her."

"Who ever dared such a lie about my Grizel!" shouted Miss Horn. "It was but a fortnight or three weeks, as near as I can judge, after the birth of your child that Grizel Campbell—"

"Were you with her then?" again interrupted the marquis in a tone of sorrowful interest.

"No, my lord, I was not. If I had been I wouldn't be upon such an errand as this today. For nearly twenty years she and I've been keeping house together, till she died in my arms, and in that time never a day was she out of my sight, or once—"

The marquis leaped to his feet exclaiming, "What in the name of God do you mean, woman?"

"I don't know what you mean, my lord. I am but telling you that Grizel Campbell, up till that day—and that's been a little over six months now—"

"Good God!" cried the marquis, "and here have I—Woman, are you speaking the truth? If—"

The marquis strode several times up and down the floor. "I'll give you a thousand pounds for those letters," he said suddenly.

"They're not worth that, my lord. But I will not part with them except to him that proves himself the rightful heir to them."

"A husband inherits from his wife."

"Or maybe a son might claim them first, I don't know. But there's lawyers, my lord, to settle the doubt."

"Her son? You don't mean—"

"I do, my lord. I mean Malcolm MacPhail."

"God in heaven!"

"His name's more in your mouth than in your heart I think, my lord."

Lord Lossie was striding up and down the room, his hands clenched. "Can you prove what you say?"

"No, my lord," answered Miss Horn.

"Then what the devil," roared the marquis, "do you mean coming to me with such a cock-and-bull story?"

"There's neither cock-crow nor bull-roar to it, my lord. I come to you in the hopes that you'll help clear it up, for I don't know what we could do without you. There's but one other that knows the truth, and she's the worst liar out of purgatory—not that I believe in purgatory, but it's a lighter word to make use of."

"Who is she?"

"By name she's Bawby Catanach, and by nature she's what I tell you."

"It can't be MacPhail. Mrs. Stewart says he's her son, and the woman Catanach is her chief witness in support of the claim."

"The devil's in it, my lord. Don't you believe a word Mistress Stewart or Bawby Catanach would say to you. If he is Mistress Stewart's, who was his father?"

"You think he resembles my late brother: he has the look of him, I must confess."

"He has, my lord. But anybody that knew his mother, as you and I knew her, my lord, would see another likeness as well."

"I grant nothing."

"You granted that Grizel Campbell was your wife, my lord, when you admitted to that handwriting. Even if it were nothing but a written promise, with a child to follow, it would be marriage enough in this country, even without a ceremony."

"But all that means nothing as far as the child's concerned. Why do you fix on this young fellow? You say you can't prove it."

"But you could, my lord, if you were as set upon justice as I am. If you won't help in the matter, I'll go on ahead with it myself with the Lord's help."

The marquis, who had all this time continued his walk up and down the floor, stood still finally, looking out the window. "This is a very serious matter," he said.

"It is that, my lord," replied Miss Horn.

"You must give me a little time to turn it over in my head."

"Isn't twenty years enough time, my lord?" rejoined Miss Horn.

"I swear to you that till this moment I believed her twenty years in the grave. My brother sent me word that she died in childbed, and the child with her. I was in Brussels with the duke."

Miss Horn made three great strides, caught the marquis' hand in both hers and said, "I praise God you're an honest man, my lord."

"I hope so," said the marquis, and seized the advantage. "You'll hold your tongue about this?" he added, half inquiring, half requesting.

"As long as I see reason to, my lord—no longer," answered Miss Horn. "Right must be done."

"Yes, if you can tell what right is."

"Right's right, my lord," persisted Miss Horn. "I'll have no qualifications."

His lordship once again began to walk up and down the room, every now and then taking a stolen glance at Miss Horn—a glance of uneasy anxious questioning. She stood rigid, her eyes on the ground, waiting what he would say next.

At length he broke the silence, "Can I trust you, woman? I want to be certain you will do nothing with those papers until you hear from me."

"I'll do nothing before tomorrow. Farther than that I will not pledge," answered Miss Horn, and with the words moved toward the door.

The marquis went to his own room. The tears that should have long since been wept rose to his eyes. Genuine had been his affection for the girl who had risked and lost so much for him. It was with no evil intent that he persuaded himself that for both their sakes it would be best for the time being to keep their marriage secret. But then he had been suddenly called away by the prince on a private mission soon after their marriage. He had hoped for a speedy return, had therefore left her without arrangement for correspondence, but was delayed by the difficulties of the case. All he ever heard more of her was from his brother, then the marquis, who gave him a cynical account of the discovery of her condition, followed almost immediately by one of her death and that of her infant. He was deeply stung for a time.

But time passed, he returned, and saw no need to make public what was over. At length he married Florimel's mother. His love for her was not as great as had been his for his first wife, but he endeavored to conduct himself in some measure like a gentleman. For this he had been rewarded by a decrease in the rate of his spiritual submergence. In time she died, leaving him with only Florimel, whom he loved and made his whole life.

And now what was he to do?

Certainly the youth was one to be proud of—one in a million. But there were other and terrible considerations. Convenient half-measures, he feared, would find no favor with Miss Horn. But she declared herself unable to prove Malcolm his son without the testimony of Mrs. Catanach who was even now representing him as the son of Mrs. Stewart. But Mrs. Catanach could certainly not be ignorant of what had happened. For that night when Malcolm and he found her in the wizard's chamber had she not proved her strange story—of having been carried to that very room blindfolded, and after attendance on the birth of a child, whose mother's features she had not once seen, in like manner been carried away again? Had she not proved the story true by handing him the ring she had drawn from the lady's finger and sewn, for the sake of future identification, into the lower edge of one of the bed curtains?—which was the very diamond he had given his wife from his own finger when they parted. She probably believed the lady to have been Mrs. Stewart, and the late marquis the father of the child. Should he see Mrs. Catanach? And what then?

He had no difficulty thinking through the reasons why his brother would have provided for the secret delivery of the child and his abduction from the wizard's chamber. The elder marquis had judged his younger brother unlikely to live long and had therefore expected his own daughter, Annabel, to succeed himself. But now the younger might any day publicly acknowledge his marriage to the governess and legalize the child, a male. He had therefore secured the disappearance of the child, and the belief of his brother in the death of both.

Lord Lossie was roused from his reverie by a tap at the door, which he knew for Malcolm's, and answered with admission.

When he entered, his master saw that a change had passed upon him already, and for a moment believed that Miss Horn had broken faith with him and told Malcolm. He was soon satisfied to the contrary, however, but would have found it hard to understand had he been told that the elevation of the youth's countenance had its source in the conviction that he was not the son of Mrs. Stewart.

"So here you are at last!" said the marquis.

"Ay, my lord."

"Did you find Stewart?"

"Yes, my lord; but it did us little good, for he knew nothing about the lassie, and almost lost his wits at the news."

"No great loss!" said the marquis. "Go and send Stoat here; I bought a horse while I was away—a great black mare, a bit wild perhaps. She should be here inside a week. I want him to make a place for her."

"Could I have a word with your lordship first?"

"Make haste then."

"I've been thinking about going back to the fishing, my lord," said Malcolm. "This is too easy a life for me. And besides, a life without danger or work in it is too dull. But that's neither here nor there, I know, so long's you want me out of the house, my lord."

"Who told you I wanted you out of the house? By Jove! I should have made shorter work of it if I had. What put that idea into your head? Why should I?"

"If your lordship knows no reason, then who am I to give you one. I thought—but the thought itself's an impudence."

"You young fool! You thought because I came upon you as I did in the garret the other night—Bah! As if I could not trust—!"

For the moment Malcolm forgot how angry his master had certainly been. Everything seemed about to come right again. But his master remained silent.

"I hope my lady's well," ventured Malcolm at length.

"Quite well. She's with Lady Bellair in Edinburgh."

"I don't like her," said Malcolm.

"Who asked you to like her?" said the marquis. But he laughed as he said it.

"I beg your lordship's pardon," returned Malcolm. "It was none of my business who my lady was with."

"Certainly not. But I don't mind confessing that Lady Bellair is not one I should choose to give authority over Lady Florimel. You have quite a regard for your young mistress, I know, Malcolm."

"I would die for her, my lord."

"That's a common enough assertion," said the marquis.

"Not with fisher-folk. I don't know how it may be with your people, my lord."

"Well, even with us it means something. It implies at least that you would risk your life for someone. But perhaps it may mean more than that in the mouth of a fisherman? Do you fancy there is such a thing as devotion—real devotion, I mean, self-sacrifice, you know?"

"I don't doubt it, my lord."

"Without fee or hope of reward?"

"There must be some capable of it, my lord, or what would the world be like?"

"You certainly have pretty high notions of things, MacPhail. For my part, I can easily enough imagine a man risking his life; but devoting it! That's another thing altogether. What, for instance, would you do for Lady Florimel now? You say you would die for her. What does dying mean on a fisherman's tongue?"

"It means everything, my lord—short of evil. I would starve for her, but I wouldn't steal. I would fetch for her, but I wouldn't lie."

"Would you be her servant all your days? Come now!"

"More than willingly, my lord—if she would only have me, and keep me."

"But supposing you came to inherit the Kirkbyres property?"

"My lord," said Malcolm solemnly, "that's a hard test to put me to, and it means nothing. I would rather clean my lady's boots from morning to evening than be the son of that woman, even if she were born a duchess. Try me with something more worth your while, your lordship."

But the marquis seemed to think he had gone far enough for the present. With gleaming eyes he rose, took his withered love letter from the table, put it in his waistcoat pocket; he turned from the door, ordered him to bring his riding coat and boots, and, ringing the bell, sent a message by another to Stoat to saddle the bay mare.

34

•••••••••••••••••••••

The Homegoing

When Malcolm and Joseph set out from Duff Harbor to find the laird, they could hardly be said to have gone in search of him. All in their power was to seek the parts where he was occasionally seen in the hope of chancing upon him; and they wandered in vain about the woods of Fife House all that week, returning disconsolate every evening to the little inn. Sunday came and went without yielding a trace of him. Monday passed like the days that had preceded it, and they were returning dejectedly when suddenly they caught sight of a head peering over the parapet of the bridge. They dared not run for fear of terrifying him, if it should be the laird, and hurried quietly to the spot. But when they reached the end of the bridge, its round back was bare from end to end. On the other side of the river, the trees came close up, and pursuit was hopeless in the gathering darkness.

"Laird, laird! They've taken away Phemy, and we don't know where to look for her," cried the poor father aloud.

Almost the same instant, and as if he had issued from the ground, the laird stood before them. The men started back with astonishment—soon changed into pity, for there was light enough to see how miserable the poor fellow looked. Neither exposure nor privation had thus wrought upon him: he was simply dying of fear. Having greeted Joseph with embarrassment, he kept glancing doubtfully at Malcolm, as if ready to run at his least movement. In a few words Joseph explained their quest, with trembling voice and tears that would not be denied enforcing the tale. Before he had done, the laird's jaw had fallen, and further speech was impossible to him. But by gestures sad and plain enough, he indicated that he knew nothing of her, and had supposed her safe at home with her parents. In vain they tried to persuade him to go back with them, promising every protection. For sole answer he shook his head mournfully.

There came a sudden gust of wind among the branches. Joseph, little used to trees and their ways with the wind, turned toward the sound and Malcolm unconsciously followed his movement. When they turned again, the laird had vanished, and they took their way homeward in sadness.

Mrs. Stewart was sitting in her drawing room alone: she seldom had visitors at Kirkbyres. What she meditated over her knitting by the firelight it would be hard to say.

She looked up, gave a cry, and started to her feet: Stephen stood before her, halfway between her and the door. Revealed in a flicker of flame from the fire, he vanished in the following shade, and for a moment she stood in doubt of her seeing sense. But when the coal flashed again, there was her son, regarding her out of great eyes that looked as if they had seen death. A ghastly air hung about him as if he had just come back from Hades, but in his silent bearing there was a sanity, even dignity, which strangely impressed her. He came forward a pace or two, stopped, and said, "Dinna be frichtit, mem. I'm come. Sen' the lassie home an' du wi' me as ye like. But I think I'm deein', an' ye needna misguide me."

His voice, although it trembled a little, was clear and unimpeded, and though weak, in its modulation, manly.

Something in the woman's heart responded.

"I don't know what you mean, Stephen," she said, more gently than he had ever heard her speak. Was it motherhood or simple pity? Or was it that sickness gave her hope and she could afford to be kind, now?

Was it an agony of mind or of body, or was it but a flickering of the shadows upon his face? A moment, and he gave a half-choked shriek, and fell on the floor. His mother turned from him with disgust an rang the bell. "Send Tom here," she said.

An elderly, hard-featured man came.

"Stephen is in one of his fits," she said.

The man looked about him. He could see no one in the room but his mistress.

"There he is," she continued, pointing to the floor. "Take him away. Get him up to the loft and lay him in the hay."

The man lifted his master like an unwieldy log and carried him, convulsed, from the room.

Stephen's mother sat down again by the fire and resumed her knitting.

Malcolm had just seen his master set out for his solitary ride when one of the maids informed him that a man from Kirkbyres wanted him. Hiding his reluctance, he went with her and found Tom, who was Mrs. Stewart's servant and had been about the place all his days.

"Mr. Stephen's come home, sir," he said, touching his cap.

"It's not possible!" returned Malcolm. "I saw him last night."

"He came about ten o'clock, sir, and had a turn of the fainting sickness on the spot. He's very ill now, and the mistress sent me over to ask if you would oblige her by going to see him."

"Has he taken to his bed?" asked Malcolm.

"We put him in it, sir. He's raving mad, and I'm thinking he's not far from his last days."

"I'll go with you directly," said Malcolm.

In a few minutes they were riding fast along the road to Kirkbyres, neither with much to say to the other, for Malcolm distrusted everyone about the place, and Tom was by nature taciturn.

"What made them send for me, do you know?" asked Malcolm at length, when they had gone about halfway.

"He cried out about you in the night," answered Tom.

When they arrived, Malcolm was shown into the drawing room, where Mrs. Stewart met him with red eyes.

"Will you come and see my poor boy?" she said.

"I will do that, mem. Is he very ill?"

"Very. I'm afraid he's in a bad way."

She led him to a dark old-fashioned chamber, rich and gloomy. There, sunk in the down of a huge bed with carved ebony posts, lay the laird, far too ill to notice the luxury to which he was unaccustomed. His head kept tossing from side to side, and his eyes seemed searching in vacancy.

"Has the doctor been to see him, mem?" asked Malcolm.

"Yes, but he says he can't do anything for him."

"Who waits upon him, mem?"

"One of the maids and myself."

"I'll just stay with him."

"That will be very kind of you."

"I'll stay with him till I see him out of this, one way or another," added Malcolm, and sat down by the bedside of his poor distrustful friend. There Mrs. Stewart left him.

The laird's eyes would now and then meet those of Malcolm, as they gazed tenderly upon him, but the living thing that looked out of the windows was darkened, and saw him not. Occasionally a word would fall from him, or a murmur of half-articulation.

"I dinna ken whaur I come from! I dinna ken whaur I'm gaein to!—If He would but come oot an' show himsel'—O Lord! take the devil off my puir back—O Father of Lichts! make him tak the hump wi' him. I don't like it, though it's been my constant companion this mony a lang year!"

But in general he only moaned.

All the waning afternoon Malcolm sat by his side, and neither mother, maid, nor doctor came in.

"Will I ever ken whaur I came from? The wine's guid. Gie me a drap mair, if ye please, Lady Horn. I thought the grave was a better place. I hae lain softer afore I dee'd—Phemy! Phemy! Rin, Phemy! Rin! I'll bide wi' them this time. Ye run, Phemy!"

As it grew dark the air turned very chill, and snow began to fall thick and fast. Malcolm laid a few sticks on the smouldering peat fire, but they were damp and did not catch. All at once the laird gave a shriek, and crying out, "Mither, mither!" fell into a fit so violent that the heavy bed shook with his convulsions. Malcolm held his wrists and called aloud. No one came, and thinking that no one could help, he waited in silence for what would follow.

The fit passed quickly, and he lay quiet. The sticks had meantime dried, and suddenly they caught fire and blazed up. The laird turned his face toward the flame; a smile came over it; and his eyes opened wide and with such an expression of seeing gazed beyond Malcolm.

"Eh, the bonny Man! The bonny Man!" murmured the laird.

Malcolm turned but saw nothing, and turned again to the laird: his jaw had fallen, and light was fading out of his face like the last of a sunset. He was dead.

Malcolm rang the bell, told the woman who answered it what had taken place, and hurried from the house, glad at heart that his friend was at rest.

He had ridden but a short distance when he was overtaken by a boy on a fast pony, who pulled up as he neared him.

"Where are you going?" asked Malcolm.

"I'm going for Mistress Catanach," answered the boy.

"Go your way then, and don't hold the dead waiting," said Malcolm with a shudder.

The boy cast a look of dismay behind him and galloped off.

The snow still fell, and the night was dark. Malcolm spent nearly two hours on his way, and met the boy returning, who told him that Mrs. Catanach was not to be found.

His road lay down the glen, past Duncan's cottage, at whose door he dismounted, but he did not find him. Taking the bridle on his arm, he walked by his horse the rest of the way. It was about nine o'clock, and the night very dark. As he neared the House, he heard Duncan's voice.

"Malcolm, my son! Will it pe your own self?" it said.

"It is, Daddy," answered Malcolm.

The piper was sitting on a fallen tree, with the snow settling softly upon him.

"But it's too cold for you to be sitting there in the snow, and the dark too!" said Malcolm.

"Ta darkness doesn't ket inside me," returned the seer. "Ah, my poy! I peen fery uneasy till you'll pe coming home."

"What's the matter, Daddy?" asked Malcolm. "Anything wrong at the House?"

"Something will pe wrong, yes, put I cannot tell where. No, my pody will not pe full of light!"

"The poor laird's gone home," said Malcolm. "I wonder if he knows yet, or if he goes asking everyone he meets if he can tell him where he comes from. He's mad no more, anyway."

"How? Will he pe tead? Ta poor lairt! Ta poor maad lairt!"

"Yes, he's dead. Maybe that'll be troubling your sight, Daddy."

"No, my son. Ta maad lairt was not fery maad, and if he was maad, he was not paad, and it was not ta plame of him; he was coot always."

"He was that, Daddy."

"Put it will pe something fery paad, and it will be troubling my spirit. All is not well, my son."

"Well, don't distress yourself, Daddy. Let come what will come. Just come in with me and sit down by the fire in your cottage, and I'll come to you as soon as I've been to see the master doesn't want me for anything. But maybe you'd better come with me to my room first," he went on, "for the master doesn't like to see me in anything but the kilts."

"And why will you not pe in ta kilts now?"

"I've been riding, Daddy, and the trousers fit the saddle better than the kilts."

"I'll not pe knowing tat. Old Allister, your creat—my own crandfather was ta pest horseman ta worlt efer saw, and he nefer haf trousers on his lecks nor ta saddle on his horse's pack."

Thus chatting they went to the stable, and from the stable to the House, where they met no one, and went straight up to Malcolm's room—the old man making as little of the long ascent as Malcolm himself.

35
● ● ● ● ● ● ● ● ● ● ● ● ● ● ● ● ● ●

The Rescue

*B*rooding over the sad history of his young wife and the prospects of his daughter, the marquis rode over fields and through gales till the darkness began to fall, and the bearings of his perplexed position came plainly before him.

If Malcolm were acknowledged and the date of his mother's death known, what would Florimel be in the eyes of the world? Where was the future he had marked out for her? He had no money to leave her, and she must be helplessly dependent on her brother.

Malcolm, on the other, might make a good match, or, with the advantages he could secure him, in the army, better still in the navy, could well push his way into the world.

Miss Horn could produce no testimony, and Mrs. Catanach had asserted him to be the son of Mrs. Stewart. He had seen enough, however, to make him dread certain possible results if Malcolm were acknowledged as the laird of Kirkbyres. No, there was but one hopeful measure, one which he had even already approached in a tentative way—an appeal, namely, to Malcolm himself, in which, while acknowledging his probable rights, but representing in the strongest possible manner the difficulty of proving them, he would set forth in their full dismay the consequences to Florimel of their public recognition and offer, upon the pledge of his word to a certain line of conduct, to start him in any path he chose to follow.

Having thought the thing out pretty thoroughly, as he fancied, and resolved at the same time to feel his way toward negotiations with Mrs. Catanach, he turned and rode home.

After a tolerable dinner, he was sitting over a bottle of port when the door of the dining room opened suddenly, and the butler appeared, pale with terror. "My lord, my lord!" he stammered as he closed the door behind him.

"Well? What the devil's the matter now?"

"Your lordship didn't hear it then?" faltered the butler.

"You've been drinking," said the marquis, lifting his seventh glass of port.

"I didn't say I heard it, my lord."

"Heard what, in the name of Beelzebub?"

"The ghost, my lord."

"The what!" shouted the marquis.

"That's what they call it, my lord. It's what comes of having that wizard's chamber in the house, my lord."

"You're a set of fools," said the marquis, "—the whole kit of you!"

"That's what I say, my lord. I don't know what to do with them, screaming in hysterics. Mrs. Courthope is trying her best with them; but it's my belief she's about as bad herself."

The marquis finished his glass of wine, poured out and drank another, then walked to the door. When the butler opened it, a strange sight met his eyes. All the servants in the House, men and women—Duncan and Malcolm alone excepted—had crowded after the butler, everyone being afraid of being left behind; and there gleamed the crowd of ghastly faces in the light of the great hall-fire. Such was the silence that the marquis heard the low howl of the waking wind, and the snow like the patting of soft hands against the windows. He stood for a moment, more than half-enjoying their terror, when from somewhere in the building a far-off shriek, shrill and piercing, rang in every ear. Some of the men drew in their breath with a gasp, but most of the women screamed outright, and that set the marquis cursing.

Duncan and Malcolm had but just entered the bedroom of the latter, when the shriek rent the air close beside them, and for a moment deafened their senses. So agonized, so shrill, so full of dismal terror was it that Malcolm stood aghast, and Duncan started to his feet with responsive out-cry. But Malcolm at once recovered himself.

"Stay here till I come back," he whispered and hurried noiselessly out.

In a few minutes he returned, during which all had been still. "Now, Daddy," he said, "I'm going to drive in the door of the next room. There's some devilry at work there. You stand in the door, and if ghost or devil would run by you, grip it, and hold on like Demon the dog."

"I will, I will!" muttered Duncan in a strange tone. "Ochone! that I'll not pe hafing my turk with me!"

Malcolm took the key of the wizard's chamber from his chest, and his candle from the table, which he set down in the passage. In a moment he had unlocked the door, put his shoulder to it and burst it open. A light was extinguished, and a shapeless figure went gliding away through the gloom. It was no shadow, however, for dashing itself against the door at the other side of the chamber, it staggered back with an imprecation of fury and fear, pressed two hands to its head, and, turning at bay, revealed the face of Mrs. Catanach.

In the door stood the blind piper, with outstretched arms, and hands ready to clutch, the fingers curved like claws, his knees and haunches bent, leaning forward like a rampant beast prepared to spring. In his face was wrath, hatred, vengeance, disgust—an enmity of all mingled kinds.

Malcolm was busied with something in the bed, and when she turned Mrs. Catanach saw only the white face of hatred gleaming through the darkness.

"You old devil!" she cried, with an addition too coarse to set down, and threw herself upon him.

The old man never said a word, but with indrawn breath hissing through his clenched teeth, clutched her and down they went together in the passage, the piper undermost. He had her by the throat, it is true, but she had her fingers in his eyes, and kneeling on his chest, kept him down with a vigor of hostile effort that drew the very picture of murder. It lasted but a moment, however, for the old man, spurred by torture as well as hate, gathered what survived of a most sinewy strength into one huge heave, threw her back into the room, and rose, with the blood streaming from his eyes, just as the marquis came round the near end of the passage, followed by Mrs. Courthope, the butler, Stoat, and two of the footmen. Heartily enjoying a row, he stopped instantly and, signing a halt to his followers, stood listening to the mud-geyser that now burst forth from Mrs. Catanach's throat.

"You blind son of Satan!" she cried, "didn't I take you to do with you what I liked? And that son you call your grandson—Ha, ha! Him your grandson! He's nothing, he's nothing but one of your hated Campbells!"

"A teanga a' diabhuil mhoir, tha thu ag denamh breug (O tongue of the great devil! thou art making a lie!)," screamed Duncan, speaking for the first time.

"God lay me dead in my sins if he be anything but a bastard Campbell!" she asserted with a laugh of demoniacal scorn. "Your precious Malcolm's nothing but the dyke-side brat of the late Grizel Campbell, that folk took for a saint 'cause she said nothing! I laid the Campbell pup in your scarecrow arms with my own hands, upon the top of your cursed screeching bagpipes that so often drove sleep from my eyes! No, you would have none of me! But I gave you a Campbell child to your heart for all that, you old hungry, spider-legged, worm-eaten idiot!"

A torrent of Gaelic broke from Duncan, into the midst of which rushed another from Mrs. Catanach, similiar, but coarse in vowel and harsh in consonant sounds.

The marquis stepped into the room. "What is the meaning of this?" he said with dignity.

The tumult of Celtic altercation ceased. The piper drew himself up to his full height and stood silent. Mrs. Catanach, red as fire with exertion and wrath, turned ashy pale. The marquis cast on her a searching and significant look.

"See here, my lord," said Malcolm.

Candle in hand, his lordship approached the bed. The same moment Mrs. Catanach glided out with her usual downy step, gave a wink as of mutual intelligence to the group at the door, and vanished.

On Malcolm's arm lay the head of a young girl. Her thin, worn countenance was stained with tears and livid with suffocation. She was recovering, but her eyes rolled stupid and visionless.

"It's Phemy, my lord—Blue Peter's lassie that was taken," said Malcolm.

"It begins to look serious," said the marquis. "Mrs. Catanach! Mrs. Courthope!"

He turned toward the door. Mrs. Courthope entered, and a head or two peeped in after her. Duncan stood as before, drawn up and stately, his visage working, but his body motionless as the statue of a sentinel.

"Where is the Catanach woman gone?" cried the marquis.

"Cone!" shouted the piper. "Cone! and her huspant will pe waiting to kill her? Och nan ochan!"

"Her husband!" echoed the marquis.

"Ach! I can't pe helping it, my lort—no more till one will pe tead, and tat should pe ta woman, for she'll pe a paad woman—ta worstest woman efer was married, my lort!"

"That's saying a good deal," returned the marquis.

"Not one wort more as enough, my lort," said Duncan, "Ochone! Ochone! Why did I marry her? You would haf stapt her long aco, my lort, if she had peen your wife, and you was knowing the tamned fox and padger she was. Ochone! And I tidn't haf my turk at my side or my knife in my boot!"

He shook his hands like a despairing child, then stamped and wept in the agony of frustrated rage.

Mrs. Courthope took Phemy in her arms, and carried her to her own room, where she opened the window and let the snowy wind blow full upon her. As soon as she came quite to herself, Malcolm set out to bear the good tidings to her father and mother.

Only a few nights before, Phemy had been taken to the room where they found her. She had been carried from place to place, and had been some of the time, she believed, in Mrs. Catanach's own house. They had always kept her in the dark and removed her at night, blindfolded. When asked if she had never cried out before, she said she had been too frightened; and when questioned as to what had made her do so then, she knew nothing of it. She remembered only that a horrible creature appeared by the bedside, after which all was blank. On the floor they found a hideous death-mask, doubtless the cause of the screams which Mrs. Catanach had sought to stifle with the pillows and bedclothes.

When Malcolm returned, he went at once to the piper's cottage, where he found him in bed, utterly exhausted, and as utterly restless.

"Well, Daddy," he said, "I don't doubt I dare not come near you now."

"Come to my arms, my poor poy!" faltered Duncan. "I'm sorry in my heart for my poy! Nefer you mind, my son; you couldn't help ta Cawmill mother, and you'll pe my own poy anyway. Ochone! It will pe a plot upon you all your tays, my son, and I can't help you, and it'll pe preaking my old heart!"

"If God thought the Campbells worth making, Daddy, I don't see that I have any right to complain that I came from them."

"I hope you'll pe forgifing ta plind old man, howefer. I couldn't see or I would haf known petter at once."

"I don't know what you mean, Daddy."

"That I'll do you a creat wrong, and I'll pe fery sorry for it, my son."

"What wrong did you do me, Daddy?"

"That I was to let you crow up a Cawmill, my poy. If I tid put know ta paad plood was in you, I wouldn't haf tone you so wrong as to pring you up."

"That's a wrong not hard to forgive, Daddy. But it's a pity you didn't let me lie, for then maybe Mistress Catanach would have brought me up herself. There! See what you have saved me from."

"Yes, put I couldn't save you from ta Cawmill plood, my son. Malcolm, my poy," he added after a pause, and with the solemnity of a mighty hate, "ta efil woman herself will pe a Cawmill—ta woman Catanach will pe a Cawmill, and I tidn't know it pefore I was in ta ped with ta worsest Cawmill tat efer God made; and I peck His pardon, for I'll not pelief He wass making ta Cawmills."

"Don't you think God made me, Daddy?" asked Malcolm. The old man thought for a little while.

"Tat will tepent on who was your father, my son," he replied. "If he too will pe a Cawmill—Ochone! Ochone! Put tere may pe some coot plood in you, which is enough to say God will pe making you, my son. Put ton't pe asking, Malcolm. Ton't pe asking!"

"What am I not to ask, Daddy?"

"Ton't pe asking who made you, who was ta father of you, my poy. I would rather not pe knowing, for ta man might pe a Cawmill too. And if I couldn't pe lofing you no more, my son, I would tie pefore my time, and my tays would pe long in ta land under ta crass, my son."

But the memory of the sweet face whose cold loveliness he had once kissed was enough to outweigh with Malcolm all Duncan's prejudices, and he was proud to take up even her shame. To pass from Mrs. Stewart to her was to escape from the clutches of a vampire to the arms of a sweet mother-angel.

Deeply concerned for the newly-discovered misfortunes of the old man to whom he was indebted for this world's life at least, he anxiously sought to soothe him; but he had far more and far worse to torment him than Malcolm even yet knew, and with burning cheeks and bloodshot eyes, he lay tossing from side to side, now uttering terrible curses in Gaelic, now weeping bitterly. Malcolm took his loved pipes and with the gentlest notes he could draw from them tried to charm to rest the ruffled waters of his spirit. But his efforts were all in vain, and believing at length that he would be quieter without him, he went to the House and to his own room.

The door of the adjoining chamber stood open, and the long forbidden room lay exposed to any eye. Little did Malcolm think as he gazed around it that it was the room in which he had first breathed the air of the world; in which his mother had wept over her false position and his reported death; and from which he had been carried, by Duncan's wicked wife, down the ruinous stair, and away to the lip of the sea, to find a home in the arms of the man whom he had just left on his lonely couch, torn between the conflicting emotions of a gracious love for him and a frightful hate of her.

36

. . . .

The Accident

*T*he next day, Miss Horn, punctual as fate, presented herself at Lossie House and was shown at once into the marquis' study, as it was called. When his lordship entered, she took the lead the moment the door was shut.

"By this time, my lord, you'll doubtless have made up your mind to do what's right," she said.

"That's what I have always wanted to do," returned the marquis.

"Hmm!" remarked Miss Horn as plainly as inarticulately.

"In the affair," he supplimented, adding, "it's not always so easy to tell what is right. This woman Catanach—we must get her to give credible testimony. Whatever the fact may be, we must have strong evidence. And there comes the difficulty that she has already made an altogether different statement."

"It means nothing, my lord. It was never made before a justice of the peace."

"I wish you would go to her and see how she is inclined."

"Me go to Bawby Catanach!" exclaimed Miss Horn.

"You would have no objection, however, to my seeing her, I presume— just to let her know that we have an inkling of the truth?" asked the marquis.

Now all this was the merest talk, for of course Miss Horn could not long remain in ignorance of the declaration fury had, the night previous, forced from Mrs. Catanach. But he must, he thought, put her off and keep her quiet, if possible, until he had come to an understanding with Malcolm, after which he would no doubt have his trouble with her.

"You can do as your lordship likes," answered Miss Horn, "but I wouldn't have it said of me that I had any dealings with her. Who knows but what she might say you tried to bribe her? There's nothing she wouldn't do if she thought it worth her while. Not that I'm afraid of her. Let her be! Only don't trust a word she says!"

The marquis meditated.

"I wonder whether the real source of my perplexity occurs to you, Miss Horn," he said at length. "You know I have a daughter?"

"Well enough, my lord."

"By my second marriage."

"No marriage at all, my lord."

"True—if I confess to the first."

"All the same whether you confess it or not, my lord."

"Then you see," the marquis went on, refusing offense, "what the admission of your story would make of my daughter?"

"That's plain enough, my lord."

"Now, if I have read Malcolm right, he has too much regard for his—mistress—to put her in such a false position."

"That is, my lord, you would have your lawful son bear his improper name."

"No, no, it need never come out what he is. I will provide for him—as a gentleman, of course."

"It can't be, my lord. You could do nothing for him with that face of his but that out it would come that you are the father. And it wouldn't be long before the tale was out about the name of his mother—Mistress Catanach would see to that. And I won't have my poor Grizel called what she isn't!"

"What does it matter, now that she's dead and gone?" said the marquis, false to the dead in his love for the living.

"Dead and gone, my lord! What do you call dead and gone? It's a mercy I have no feelings," she added, arresting her handkerchief on its way to her eyes and refusing to acknowledge the single tear that ran down her cheek.

Plainly she was not the kind of woman whose character the marquis had grown to think typical of womankind.

"Then you won't leave the matter to husband and son?" he said reproachfully.

"I tell you, my lord, I would do nothing but what I saw to be right. Let this affair out of my hands—I dare not. That lad you might get to work anything against himself. He's just like his poor mother like that."

"If Miss Campbell was his mother," said the marquis.

"Miss Campbell!" cried Miss Horn. "I'll thank your lordship to call her by her rightful name, and that's Lady Lossie!"

The heart of the marquis was only occupied by his daughter, and had not accommodation at present for either his dead wife or his living son. Once more he sat thinking in silence for a while.

"I'll make Malcolm a post captain in the navy and give you a thousand pounds," he said at length, hardly knowing that he spoke.

Miss Horn rose to her full height and stood, like an angel of rebuke, before him. Not a word did she speak, only looked at him for a moment, and turned to leave the room. The marquis saw his danger, and striding to the door, stood with his back against it.

"Do you think you can scare me, my lord?" she asked with a scornful laugh. "Get out of the way and let me go!"

"Not until I know what you are going to do," said the marquis seriously.

"I have nothing more to transact with your lordship. You and I are strangers, my lord."

"Tut, tut! I was but trying you."

"And if I had taken the disgrace you offered me, you would have drawn back?"

"No, certainly."

"You weren't trying me then. You were doing your best to corrupt me."

"I'm no splitter of hairs. I beg you to give me another day to think about this."

"What's the use? All the thinking in the world can't alter a single fact. You must do right by my laddie or I must make you."

"You would find a lawsuit heavy, Miss Horn."

"And you would find the scandal of it hard to bear, my lord. It would be sad for Miss—, I don't know what name she has a right to, my lord."

The marquis uttered a frightful imprecation, and sitting down, hid his face in his hands.

Miss Horn stirred, but instead of securing her retreat, approached him gently and stood by his side. "My lord," she said, "I can't stand to see a man in trouble. Women are born to it and they take it and are thankful. But a man never gives in to it, and so it comes harder upon him. Hear me, my lord: if there is a man on this earth who would shield a woman, that man is Malcolm Colonsay."

"If only she weren't his sister," murmured the marquis.

"But just think about it, my lord, would it be any worse to let another man marry her without telling him that she was illegitimate?"

"You insolent old woman!" cried the marquis, losing his temper, discretion and manners altogether. "Go and do your worst!"

So saying he left the room, and Miss Horn found her way out of the House in a temper quite as fierce as his—in character, however, entirely different inasmuch as it was righteous.

At that very moment Malcolm was in search of his master; and seeing the back of him disappear in the library, to which he had gone in a half-blind rage, he followed him.

"My lord," he said.

"What do you want?" returned his master in a rage.

"I thought your lordship would like to see the old stairway I came upon the other day that goes down from the wizard's chamber—"

"Curse you with all your tomfoolery!" said the marquis. "If you ever mention that cursed hole again, I'll kick you out of the House."

Malcolm turned and left the room.

Lord Lossie paced up and down the library for a whole hour—a long time to be in one mood, and by degrees his wrath assuaged. But at the end of it he knew no more what he was going to do than when he left Miss Horn in the study. Then came the gnawing of restlessness: he must find something to do.

The thing he always thought of first was a ride, but the mare was lamed and his new prize—but she would be too violent anyway!—was not yet arrived. He would go and see what the rascal had come bothering about—alone though, for he could not at present endure the sight of the fisher-fellow.

In a few moments he stood in the wizard's chamber and glanced round it with a feeling of discomfort rather than sorrow—of annoyance at the trouble of which it had been for him, rather than regret for the agony and contempt which his selfishness had brought upon the woman he loved. Then spying the door in the farthest corner, he made for it and in a moment more, his curiosity now thoroughly roused, was slowly gyrating down the steps of the old screw-stair.

Malcolm, meanwhile, had gone to his room. Now, hearing someone next door, he half suspected who it was and went in. Seeing the closet door open, he hurried to the stair and shouted down, "My lord, my lord! or whoever you are. Be careful! Take care how you go or you'll get a terrible fall. The stairs at the bottom are broken!"

Down a few feet the stairs were quite dark, and he dared not follow too fast for fear of falling and causing the accident he feared. As he descended he kept repeating his warnings, but either his master did not hear or heeded too little, for presently Malcolm heard a rush, a dull fall, and a groan. Hurrying as fast as he dared with the risk of falling on him, he found the marquis lying amongst the stones in the ground entrance, apparently unable to move and white with pain. Presently, however, he got up, swore a good deal, and limped painfully into the House.

The doctor who was sent for immediately pronounced the kneecap seriously injured and applied leeches. Inflammation set in, and another doctor and surgeon were sent for from Aberdeen. They came, applied poultices, and again leeches, and enjoined the strictest repose. The pain was severe, but to one of the marquis' temperament the enforced quiet was worse.

37

The Promise

The marquis was loved by his domestics, and the accident cast a gloom over Lossie House. Outside, the course of events waited upon his recovery. Miss Horn was too generous not to delay proceedings while her adversary was ill.

Malcolm had of course hastened to the schoolmaster with the joy of his deliverance from Mrs. Stewart, but Mr. Graham had not acquainted him with the discovery Miss Horn had made, to which Malcolm's report of the wrath-born declaration of Mrs. Catanach had now supplied the only testimony wanting. As Malcolm left, Mr. Graham pondered the strange, even ironic, fact that for the past twenty years he had been calmly devoted to one he could never marry, who had all along been herself a wife and indeed mother of his favorite pupil! And yet this very knowledge only elevated Griselda even further in his mind. With something like pride he viewed her determination to endure shame rather than break the promise of secrecy she had given her husband, never dreaming that her son was in fact alive and nearby every day.

To Miss Horn he now carried Malcolm's narrative of late events, tenfold strengthening her position; but she was anxious in her turn that the revelation concerning his birth should come to him from his father. Hence Malcolm continued in ignorance of the strange dawn that had begun to break on the darkness of his origin.

The hours went by, the days lengthened into weeks and the marquis' condition did not improve. More and more he desired the attendance of Malcolm who was consequently a great deal about him serving with a love which was certainly more than the instinct of the relation between them would have produced. The marquis had soon satisfied himself that the relation was as yet unknown to him, and was all the better pleased with his devotion and tenderness.

The inflammation continued, increased and spread. They began to talk of amputation, but the marquis refused to listen and would not consent to it.

"We fear gangrene, my lord," said the physician calmly.

"So do I. Keep it off," returned the marquis.

"We fear we cannot, my lord."

It had, in fact, already commenced.

"Let it mortify then, but let me keep my leg," said his lordship.

"I trust, my lord, you will reconsider it," said the surgeon. "We should not have dreamed of suggesting a measure of such severity had we not reason to dread that gentler means would but lessen your lordship's chance of recovery."

"You mean then that my life is in danger!"

"We fear," said the physician, "that the amputation proposed is the only thing that can save it."

"What a brace of blasted bunglers you are!" cried the marquis, and turning away his face, lay silent.

The two doctors looked at each other, and said nothing.

Malcolm was in the room, and a keen pang shot to his heart at the verdict. The men retired to consult. Malcolm approached the bed.

"My lord," he said gently.

No reply came.

"Don't leave us, my lord—not yet," Malcolm persisted. "What's to come of my lady?"

The marquis gave a gasp. Still he made no reply.

"She has nobody, you know, my lord, that you would like to trust her with."

"You must take care of her when I am gone, Malcolm," murmured the marquis, and his voice was now gentle with sadness and broken with misery.

"Me! my lord?" returned Malcolm. "Who would pay any attention to me? And what could I do with her? Her lady-maids could do more with her, though I would lay down my life for her, as I told you, my lord; and she knows it well enough."

Silence followed. Both men were thinking.

"Give me a right, my lord, and I'll do my best," said Malcolm at length breaking the silence.

"What do you mean?" growled the marquis, whose mood had altered.

"Give me a legal right, my lord, and see if I don't."

"See what?"

"See if I don't look after my lady."

"How am I to see? I shall be dead."

"Please, God, my lord, you'll be alive and well—in a better place, if not here to look after my lady yourself."

"Oh, I dare say," muttered the marquis.

"But you'll listen to the doctors, my lord," Malcolm went on, "and not die without time to consider it."

"Yes, yes; tomorrow I'll have another talk with them. We'll see about it. There's time enough yet. They're all bunglers, every one of them. They never give a patient the least credit for common sense."

After a few minutes' silence, during which Malcolm thought he had fallen asleep, the marquis resumed abruptly. "What do you mean by giving you a legal right?" he said.

"There's some way of making one person guardian over another so that the law'll uphold him, isn't there, my lord?"

"Yes, surely. Well! Rather—odd wouldn't it be?—a young fisher-lad guardian to a marchioness! Eh? They say there's nothing new under the sun; but that sounds rather like it I think."

Malcolm was overjoyed to hear him speak with something like his old manner. He felt he could stand any amount of chaff from him now, and so the proposition he had made in seriousness, he went on to defend in the hope of giving amusement, yet with a secret wild delight in the dream of such full devotion to the service of Lady Florimel.

"It would seem queer enough, my lord, no doubt; but folk mustn't mind the appearance of a thing if it is straight and fair. They couldn't laugh me out of my rights—lady Bellair or any of them—or talk me out of them either."

"But there would be lawyers and expenses, Malcolm?"

"You could leave so much to be spent upon the carrying out of your lordship's will."

"And who would see that you applied it properly?"

"My own conscience, my lord, or Mr. Graham if you liked."

"And how would you live yourself?"

"Oh, leave that to me, my lord. Only don't imagine I would expect you to give me anything. I hope I have more pride than that. Every pound note or shilling would be laid out for her, or else saved for her."

"By Jove, it's a daring proposal!" said the marquis, and, which seemed strange to Malcolm, not a single thread of ridicule ran through the tone in which he made the remark.

The next day came but brought with it neither strength of body nor of mind. Again his professional attendants besought him, and he heard them more quietly, but rejected their proposition as positively as before. In a day or two he ceased to oppose it, but would not hear of preparation. Hour passed into hour, and days passed into a week, when they finally assailed him with a solemn and last appeal.

"Nonsense!" answered the marquis. "My leg is getting better. I feel no pain at all—in fact nothing but a little faintness. Your ridiculous medicines, I don't doubt!"

"You are in the gravest danger, my lord. It is all but too late even now."

"Tomorrow, then, if it must be. Today I could not endure to have my hair cut; and as to having my leg off—pooh! the thing's preposterous!"

He turned white and shuddered, for all the nonchalance of his speech.

When the next day came, there was not a surgeon in the land who would have taken his leg off. He looked in their faces, and seemed for the first time convinced of the necessity of the measure.

"You may do as you please," he said. "I am ready."

"Not today, my lord," replied the doctor. "Your lordship is not equal to it today."

"I understand," said the marquis, and paled frightfully and turned his head aside.

When Mrs. Courthope suggested that Lady Florimel should be sent for, he flew into a frightful rage and spoke as it is to be hoped he had never spoken to a woman before. She took it with perfect gentleness, but could not repress a tear. The marquis saw it, and his heart was touched.

"You must not mind a dying man's temper," he said.

"It's not for myself my lord," she answered.

"I know; you think I'm not fit to die. And you are right. Never was one less fit for heaven, or less willing to go to hell."

"Wouldn't you like to see a clergyman, my lord?" she suggested sobbing.

"A clergyman!" he cried. "I would as soon see the undertaker. What could he do but tell me I was to be damned—a fact I know better than he does. That is, if it's not all an invention of the cloth, as in my soul I believe it is. I've said so many times these forty years."

"Oh, my lord, do not fling away your last hope!"

"You don't imagine me to have a chance then? Good soul! you don't know any better."

"The Lord is merciful."

The marquis laughed—that is, he tried, failed, and grinned.

"Mr. Cairns would be only too happy to come see you, my lord."

"Bah! A low pettifogger of a minister, with the soul of a bullock. I've been bad enough, God knows. But I haven't sunk to the level of his help yet. If he's God Almighty's factor—well, I would rather have nothing to do with either."

"That is if you had a choice, my lord," said Mrs. Courthope, her temper yielding a little, though in truth his speech was not half so irreverent as it seemed to her.

In the middle of the night, as Malcolm sat by his bed thinking him asleep, the marquis spoke suddenly. "You must go to Aberdeen, tomorrow, Malcolm," he said.

"Very well, my lord."

"And bring Mr. Glennie the lawyer back with you."

"Yes, my lord."

"Go to bed then."

"I would rather stay, my lord. I wouldn't be able to sleep a wink for wanting to be back beside you."

The marquis yielded and Malcolm sat by him all the night through. He tossed about, would doze off and murmur strangely, and then wake up and ask for brandy and water, yet be content with the lemonade Malcolm gave him.

The next day he quarreled with every word Mrs. Courthope uttered, kept forgetting he had sent Malcolm away and was continually wanting him. His fits of pain were more severe, alternated with drowsiness, which deepened at times into stupor. It was late before Malcolm returned.

"Is Mr. Glennie with you?" asked his master feebly.

"Yes, my lord."

"Tell him to come here at once."

When Malcolm returned with the lawyer, the marquis directed him to set a table and chair beside the bedside, light four candles, and get everything ready that would be necessary for writing, and then go to bed.

38
••••••••••••••••••

The Witness

*B*efore Malcolm was awake, his lordship had sent for him. When he reentered the sick chamber, Mr. Glennie had vanished, the table had been removed, and instead of the radiance of the wax lights, the cold gleam of an early morning sun filled the room. The marquis looked ghastly, but was sipping chocolate with a spoon.

"Well, how are you today, my lord?" asked Malcolm.

"Nearly well," he answered, "but curse these carrion-crow doctors. I think they're the ones that are killing me. Curse them!"

"You'll have Lady Florimel swearing something awful if you go on that way, my lord," said Malcolm.

The marquis laughed feebly.

"And what's more," Malcolm continued, "I don't doubt they're a little particular about the way you talk up yonder, my lord."

The marquis eyed him keenly.

"You don't anticipate that inconvenience for me?" he said. "I'm pretty sure to have my bed down where they're not so precise."

"Don't break my heart, my lord!" cried Malcolm, the tears rushing to his eyes.

"I should be sorry to hurt you, Malcolm," rejoined the marquis gently, almost tenderly. "I won't go there if I can help it. I shouldn't like to break any more hearts. But how the devil am I to keep out of it? The fact is, I'm not fit for the other place, and I don't know if I believe there even is such a place. But if there be, I trust in God there isn't any other, or it will go badly with your poor master, Malcolm. Such a multitude of things I thought I had done with forever keep coming up and grinning at me. It nearly drives me mad, Malcolm; and I wanted to die like a gentleman, with a cool bow and a sharp face-about."

"Won't you have a word with someone who knows about dying and death?" said Malcolm, scarcely able to reply.

"No," answered the marquis, "that Cairns is a fool."

"I didn't mean him, my lord."

"Who the devil did you mean then?"

"No devil, but an honest man that's been his worst enemy so long as I've known him. Master Graham, the schoolmaster."

"Pooh!" said the marquis. "I'm too old to go to school."

"I'm not talking about Latin and Greek, but righteousness and truth. In what is and what is to be."

"What? Has the schoolmaster the second sight?"

"Yes, but one that goes a sight further than most."

"He could tell me what's going to become of me?"

"As well as any man, my lord."

"Well, take him my compliments and tell him I should like to see him," said the marquis after a pause.

"He'll come directly, my lord."

"Of course he will!" said the marquis.

"Just as readily, my lord, as he would go to any tramp that sent for him at such a time as this," returned Malcolm, who did not relish either the remark or its tone.

"What do you mean by that? You don't think it such a serious affair, do you?"

"My lord—" Malcolm paused. "—my lord, you haven't a chance."

The marquis was dumb. He had actually begun once more to buoy himself up with earthly hopes.

Dreading a recall of his commission, Malcolm slipped from the room and sped to the schoolmaster's. The moment Mr. Graham heard the marquis' message he rose without a word and led the way from the cottage. Hardly a sentence passed between them as they went, for they were on a solemn errand.

"Mr. Graham's here, my lord," said Malcolm.

"Where? Not in the room?" returned the marquis.

"Waiting at the door, my lord."

"Bah! You needn't have been so ready. Have you told the sexton to get a new spade? But you may let him in. And leave me alone with him."

Mr. Graham walked gently up to the bedside.

"Sit down, sir," said the marquis courteously, pleased with the calm and unobtrusive bearing of the man. "They tell me I'm dying, Mr. Graham."

"I'm sorry it seems to trouble you, my lord."

"What! Wouldn't it trouble you then?"

"I don't think so, my lord."

"Ah! You're one of the elect, no doubt?"

"That's a thing I never did think about, my lord."

"What do you think about then?"

"About God."

"And when you die you'll go straight to heaven, of course."

"I don't know, my lord. That's another thing I never trouble my head about."

"Ah, you're like me then. I don't care much about going to heaven. What do you care about?"

"The will of God. I hope your lordship will say the same."

"No, I won't. I want my own will."

"Well, that is to be had, my lord."

"How?"

"By taking His will for yours as the better of the two, which it must be in every way."

"That's all moonshine!"

"It is light, my lord."

"Well, I don't mind confessing, if I am to die, I should prefer heaven to the other place, but I trust I have no chance of either. Do you now honestly believe there are two such places?"

"I don't know, my lord."

"You don't know! And you come here to comfort a dying man?"

"Your lordship must first tell me what you mean by 'two such places.' And as to comfort, going by my notions, I cannot tell which you would be more or less comfortable in; and that, I presume, would be the main point with your lordship."

"And what, pray sir, would be the main point with you?"

"To get nearer to God."

"Well, I can't say I want to get nearer to God. It's little He's ever done for me."

"It's a good deal He has tried to do for you, my lord."

"Who interfered? What stood in His way, then?"

"Yourself, my lord."

"I wasn't aware of it. When did He ever try to do anything for me and I stood in His way?"

"When He gave you one of the loveliest of women, my lord," said Mr. Graham with solemn, faltering voice, "and you left her to die in neglect and her child to be brought up by strangers."

The marquis gave a cry. The unexpected answer bit deep.

"What have you to do with my affairs!" he almost screamed. Then after a pause, he sighed, "God knows I loved her."

"You loved her, my lord?"

"I did, by God!"

"Love a woman like that and come to this?"

"Come to this? We must all come to this sooner or later, I fancy. Come to what, in the name of Beelzebub?"

"That having loved her you are content to lose her. In the name of God, have you no desire to see her again?"

"It would be an awkward meeting," said the marquis.

"Because you wronged her?" suggested the schoolmaster.

"Because they lied to me, by George!"

"Which they dared not have done, had you not lied to them first."

"Sir!" shouted the marquis, with all the voice he had left.—"O God, have mercy! I cannot punish the scoundrel."

"The scoundrel is the man who lies, my lord."

"Were I anywhere else—You are a blasted coward to speak so to a man who cannot even turn on his side to curse you. You would not dare it but that you know I cannot defend myself."

"You are right, my lord; your conduct is indefensible."

"By heaven! if I could but get this cursed leg under me, I would throw you out of the window!"

"I shall go out by the door, my lord. While you hold by your sins, your sins will hold by you. If you should want me again, I shall be at your lordship's command."

He rose and left the room, but had not reached his cottage before Malcolm overtook him with a second message from his master. He turned around at once.

"Mr. Graham," said the marquis a few moments later, "you must have patience with me. I was very rude to you, but I was in horrible pain."

"Don't mention it, my lord."

"Then you really and positively believe in the place they call heaven?"

"My lord, I believe that those who open their hearts to the truth shall see the light on their friends' faces again, and be able to set right what was wrong between them."

"It's a week too late to talk of setting right."

"It's never too late. Go and tell her you are sorry, my lord. That will be enough for her."

"Ah! But there's more than her concerned."

"You are right, my lord. There is another—one who cannot be satisfied that one of His children should be treated as you treated women."

"But the Deity you talk of—"

"I beg your pardon, my lord: I spoke of no deity. I talked of a living Love that gave us birth and calls us His children. Your deity I know nothing of."

"Call him what you please: He won't be put off so easily."

"He won't be put off at all. Not one jot or tittle. He will forgive you anything, but He will pass nothing. Will your wife forgive you?"

"She will, when I explain."

"Then why should you think the forgiveness of God, which created her forgiveness, should be less?"

Whether the marquis could grasp the reasoning may be doubtful.

"Do you really suppose God cares whether a man comes to good or ill?"

"If He did not, He could not be good himself."

"Then you don't think a good God would want to punish poor wretches like us?"

"Your lordship has not been in the habit of regarding himself as a poor wretch. And remember, you can't call a child a poor wretch without insulting the father of it."

"That's quite another thing."

"But on the wrong side for your argument, seeing the relation between God and the poorest creature is infinitely closer than that between any father and his child."

"Then He can't be so hard on us as the parsons say, even in the afterlife?"

"He will give absolute justice, which is the only good thing. He will spare nothing to bring His children back to himself, their sole well-being, whether He achieve it here—or there."

It was Mr. Graham who broke the silence that followed.

"Are you satisfied with yourself, my lord."

"No, by George!"

"You would like to be better?"

"I would."

"Then you are of the same mind with God."

"Yes, but I'm not a fool. It won't do to say I should like to be, I must be, and that's not so easy. It's too hard to be good. I would have to fight for it, but there's no time. How is a poor devil to get out of such an infernal scrape?"

"Keep the Commandments."

"That's it, of course. But there's not time, I tell you—no time! At least that's what those cursed doctors will keep telling me."

"If there were but time to draw another breath, there would be time to begin."

"How am I to begin? Which am I to begin with?"

"There is one commandment that includes all the rest."

"Which is that?"

"To believe in the Lord Jesus Christ."

"That's cant!"

"After thirty years' trial of it, it is to me the essence of wisdom. It has given me a peace which makes life or death all but indifferent to me."

"What am I to believe about Him, then?"

"You are to believe in Him, not about Him."

"I don't understand."

"He is our Lord and Master, Elder Brother, King, Saviour, the Divine Man, the human God. To believe in Him is to give ourselves up to Him in obedience—to search out His will and do it."

"But there's no time, I tell you!" the marquis almost shrieked.

"And I tell you there is all eternity to do it in. Take Him for your Master, and He will demand nothing of you which you are not able to perform. This is the open door to bliss. With your last breath you can cry to Him, and He will hear you as He heard the thief on the cross. It makes my heart swell to think about it. No cross-questioning of the poor fellow, no preaching to him. He just took him with Him where He was going, to make a man of him."

"Well, you know something of my history: what would you have me do now, at once I mean. What would the Person you are speaking of have me do?"

"That is not for me to say, my lord."

"You could give me a hint."

"No. God himself is telling you. For me to presume to tell you would be to interfere with Him. What He would have a man do He lets him know in his mind."

"But what if I had not made up my mind before the last came?"

"Then I fear He would say to you, 'Depart from me, you worker of iniquity.'"

"That would be hard when another minute might have done it."

"If another minute would have done it, you would have had it."

A paroxysm of pain followed, during which Mr. Graham silently left him.

39

·····················

The Farewell

*W*hen the fit was over and he found Mr. Graham gone, he asked Malcolm, who had resumed his watch, how long it would take Lady Florimel to come from Edinburgh.

"Mr. Crathie left with four horses last night," said Malcolm, "but the roads are bad. She won't be here before sometime tomorrow."

The marquis stared aghast: they had sent for her without his orders!

"Malcolm," he said after a moment.

"Yes, my lord."

"Is there a lawyer in Portlossie?"

"Yes, my lord, there's old Mr. Carmichael."

"He won't do. He was my brother's rascal. Is there no one besides?"

"Not in Portlossie, my lord. There'd be none nearer than Duff Harbor."

"Take the buggy and bring him here directly. What's his name?"

"Soutar, my lord."

"Well, be back here in an hour."

In a hour and a quarter, Miss Horn's friend stood by the marquis' bedside. Malcolm was dismissed but was presently summoned again to receive more orders. Fresh horses were put on the buggy and he was sent out once more, this time to fetch a justice of the peace, a Mr. Morrison. The distance was greater than to Duff Harbor and the roads were worse. The rising north wind was against them as they returned. It had grown to a gale by the time they reached Lossie House, and it was late.

When Malcolm entered the marquis' room, he found him alone. "Is Morrison here? What the devil took you so long?"

"The roads were heavy, my lord, and you can hear the wind."

"Well, if you had known what depended on it, you would have driven faster. Go and tell Mrs. Courthope I want Soutar. You'll find her crying somewhere—the old chicken!—because I swore at her. What harm could that do the old goose?"

"It'll be more for love of your lordship than anything else."

"You think so? Why should she care? Go and tell her I'm sorry. But really, she ought to be used to me by this time! Tell her to send Soutar directly."

Mr. Soutar came.

"Fetch Morrison," said the marquis, "and go to bed."

When Malcolm awoke about midnight, he quietly went back to the marquis' room. No one was there but Mrs. Courthope. The shadow had crept far along the dial. His face had grown ghastly, the skin had sunk to the bones, and his eyes stood out.

"Is she come yet?" he murmured.

"No, my lord."

The lids fell again, softly.

"Be good to her, Malcolm."

"I will, my lord," he said solemnly.

The night slowly waned. He woke sometimes, but soon dozed off again. The two watched by him till the dawn. The marquis appeared a little revived, but was hardly able to speak. Mostly by signs he made Malcolm understand that he wanted Mr. Graham, but that someone else must go for him. Mrs. Courthope went.

As soon as she was out of the room, he lifted his hand with effort, laid feeble hold on Malcolm's jacket, and drawing him down, kissed him on the forehead. Malcolm burst into tears and sank weeping by the bedside.

Mr. Graham entered a little after, and seeing Malcolm on his knees, knelt also and broke into prayer.

"O blessed Father," he said, "who knows this strange thing we call death, breathe more life into the heart of your dying son, that in the power of life he may face death. O Lord Christ, who died yourself, heal this man in his sore need—heal him with strength to die."

A faint "Amen" came from the marquis.

"You sent him into the world, help him out of it. O God, we belong to you utterly. We hold our hearts up to you, make them what they must be. Give your dying child hope and courage and peace—the peace of Him who overcame all the terrors of humanity and even death itself and lives forevermore. Amen."

"Amen," murmured the marquis and slowly lifting his hand from the coverlid, he laid it on the head of Malcolm who did not know it was the hand of his father blessing him ere he died.

"Be good to her," said the marquis once more.

"I will, I will," burst from Malcolm in sobs; and he wailed aloud.

The day wore on and the afternoon came. Still Lady Florimel had not arrived, and still the marquis lingered.

As the gloom of the twilight was deepening into the early darkness, Malcolm became aware of the sound of wheels, which came rapidly nearer till at last the carriage swung up in front of the House. A moment later and Florimel was running across the room.

"Papa! Papa!" she cried, and throwing her arm over him, laid her cheek to his.

The marquis could not even return her embrace: he could only receive her into the depths of his shining, tearful eyes.

"Flory!" he murmured, "I'm going away. I'm going—I've got—to make an apology. Malcolm, be good—"

The sentence remained unfinished. The light faded from his face. He had to carry it with him. He was dead.

Lady Florimel gave a loud cry, and fainted. Malcolm lifted her and bore her tenderly to her own room. He left her to the care of the women and returned to the chamber of death.

Meantime Mr. Graham and Mr. Soutar had come. When Malcolm re-entered, the schoolmaster took him kindly by the arm and said, "Malcolm, there can be neither place nor moment fitter for the solemn communication I am commissioned to make to you: I have, in the presence of your dead father, to inform you that you are the late marquis' son, by his first wife, Griselda Campbell. You are now the marquis of Lossie. And God forbid that you should be less worthy as marquis than you have been as fisherman!"

Malcolm stood stupefied.

For a while he seemed to be turning over in his mind something he had heard read from a book. Presently he came to himself, walked over to the dead body and kissed it. Then he fell on his knees and wept.

After a few moments he recovered himself, rose, turned to the two men, and asked, "Gentlemen, how many know of this turn of things?"

"None but Mr. Morrison, Mrs. Catanach, and ourselves so far as I know," answered Mr. Soutar.

"And Miss Horn," added Mr. Graham. "She first brought out the truth of it, and ought to be the first to know of your recognition by your father."

"I'll tell her myself," returned Malcolm. "And, gentleman, I beg of you, until I know what I'm about and what I'm going to do, to keep this quiet and don't open your mouth about it to anyone."

"Until you give us leave, we are silent," they said.

The door opened, and, in all the conscious dignity conferred by the immunities and prerogatives of her calling, Mrs. Catanach walked into the room.

"A word with you, Mistress Catanach," said Malcolm.

"Certainly, my lord," answered the howdy with mingled presumption and respect, and followed him into the dining room. "Well, my lord—" she began before he had turned from shutting the door behind them.

"Mistress Catanach," interrupted Malcolm, turning and facing her, "if I be under any obligation to you, it is from another tongue I must hear it. But I have an offer to make you: So long as it doesn't come out that I'm anything better than a fisherman, I'll give you twenty pounds a year—paid quarterly. But the moment folk says who I am, you'll not touch a pound more, and I'll count myself free to pursue anything I can prove against you."

Mrs. Catanach attempted a laugh of scorn, but her face was gray as putty.

"Yes or no?" said Malcolm.

"Yes, my lord," said the howdy, reassuming at least outward composure and with it held out her hand.

"No, no!" said Malcolm, "no payments ahead of time! Three months of holding your tongue, and you'll have five pounds; and Mister Soutar of Duff Harbor will pay it into your hand. But break truth with me, and you'll hear of it; for if you were hanged the world would be but the cleaner. Now get out of the House, and never let me see you about the place again. But before you go, I give you fair warning, I mean to find out about everything you've done."

The blood of red wrath was seething in Mrs. Catanach's face.

"Get out of the House," said Malcolm, "or I'll set the hounds on you to show you the way."

Her face turned the color of ashes, and with hanging cheeks and wicked eyes, she hurried from the room. Malcolm watched her out of the House, then following her into the town, brought Miss Horn back with him to aid in the last of earthy services, and hastened to Duncan's cottage.

But to his amazement and distress, it was forsaken and the hearth cold. In his attendance on his father, he had not seen the piper—he could not remember for how many days; and on inquiry he found that, although he had not been missed, no one could recall having seen him later than three or four days ago. The last he could hear of him in the neighborhood was that, about a week before, a boy had spied him sitting on a rock in the old cave, with his pipes in his lap. Searching the cottage, he found that his broadsword and dirk, with all his poor finery, were gone.

That same night Mrs. Catanach also disappeared.

A week later Lord Lossie was buried. Malcolm followed the hearse with the household. Miss Horn walked immediately behind him on the arm of the schoolmaster.

Lady Florimel wept incessantly for three days; on the fourth she looked out on the sea and thought it very dreary; on the fifth she found a certain gratification in hearing herself called the marchioness; on the sixth she tried on the mourning dress and was pleased; on the seventh she went with the funeral and wept again; on the eighth came Lady Bellair, who on the ninth carried her away.

To Malcolm she had not once spoken.

Mr. Crathie set up his office in the House itself, took upon himself the function of steward as well as factor, and was for a time the master of the place.

Malcolm helped Stoat with the horses and did odd jobs for Mr. Crathie. From his likeness to the old marquis, the factor had a favor for him, firmly believing Malcolm's father to be the late marquis' brother and Mrs. Stewart his mother. Hence he allowed him a key to the library, of which Malcolm made good use.

Appendix 1

Ed. Note: In 1685, Charles II, the King of England, died after a reasonably popular and progressive reign. He was succeeded by his brother, James II, who demonstrated bad judgment and who, therefore, became increasingly unpopular throughout the country. Thus it was that in 1688 certain prominent English leaders sent an invitation to William of Orange in the Netherlands and his wife, Mary, daughter of James, to come over to England to assume the crown. William seized upon the opportunity and soon sailed for England with a large army behind him. The support of James was so badly eroded that the revolution took place nearly without bloodshed. James abdicated to the Continent, and Parliament quickly elected William and Mary to the British throne.

However, William was not as popular or easily acknowledged in Scotland and Ireland as he was in England. Therefore, as James began to gather some support in an attempt to regain the crown, he found willing followers in the north. Though James never did mount a serious threat and though William's position became gradually more solid, there remained fervent support for James in the Scottish highlands among many of the highly emotional and sometimes violent clans. A party was formed there in opposition to the English and Scottish governments, backing the old king instead.

William sent an army to Scotland to put down this uprising against him, but the Highlanders surprised it in the narrow gorge of Killiecrankie and almost completely annihilated the troops. However, the leader of the Scottish rebels was killed and without him the resistance was soon disbanded and William's position in Scotland was secured.

Among a few of the Highland clans, however, there yet remained extreme opposition to William. Of them the MacDonald clan was one of the most reluctant to accept what had now become inevitable. In 1691 William issued to the clan chieftains an order to take an oath of allegiance before January 1, 1692, or else be treated as rebels in arms against the government. This would then be met with force. By taking the oath they were offered pardon for their part of the massacre of the army at Killiecrankie. By this time most of the clans willingly agreed.

However, the head of a small branch of the Macdonald clan, MacIan Macdonald of Glencoe, postponed making his submission till the very last day as a statement of defiance, so as to be known as the very last man to submit. But a series of unfortunate circumstances brought disaster upon him. He traveled the relatively short distance to Fort William to take the oath but was astonished and alarmed to discover that there was no magistrate there with power to receive his oath. He was therefore forced to travel on to Inverary, the next nearest point of civil administration. The weather turned against him and a snowstorm held up his journey; he did not arrive until January 2. Then to his further dismay he found that the sheriff-deputy had temporarily left his headquarters and thus Macdonald's oath of submission did not take place until January 6.

The somewhat-belated submission might certainly have been pardoned under the circumstances. But certain hereditary enemies of the Macdonalds seized upon the moment as a chance to wipe out old grievances (the Macdonalds had indeed been a lawless, marauding lot, more than once having killed members of rival clans indiscriminately). A warrant was therefore signed (whether knowingly or not has never been fully discovered) by William, authorizing the complete annihilation of the Glencoe Macdonalds. The enemies of the clan simply reported that by January 1, they had not subscribed to the oath, omitting the information that compliance had been willingly intended and attempted and had, in fact, been made within five days.

Soon afterward a regiment of soldiers under the command of the leader of a rival clan, Campbell of Glenlyon, was sent to Glencoe to carry out the edict, but ostensibly to collect taxes. Since they acted friendly in every way and since Campbell was related to Macdonald's wife, they were received unsuspectingly by the clansmen, who entertained them hospitably for twelve days. Then at five o'clock on the morning of February 13, they turned upon their hosts, and the soldiers, in obedience to the orders of their officers, fell suddenly upon the sleeping Macdonalds. Tradition tells tales of many Campbells evading the horrible task, warning people up and down the exposed mountain glen to escape before the day came. But when it did finally arrive, men, women and children were killed indiscriminately. In the bloody massacre, some forty persons were killed outright before another 110 escaped in the darkness. However, the majority of these also lost their lives from exposure and starvation in the desolate, snowbound mountains where they tried to hide. Very few escaped altogether. Their houses were then plundered and burned and their livestock driven off.

The scandalous affair created angry public reaction throughout the entire country. There had been earlier attempts to liquidate unruly clans, but no crime had so infuriated or disgusted people before. And the betrayal was unforgivable to a Highland people where hospitality was traditionally matched with the highest respect for a man's host. Especially, public opinion could not overlook the fact that the Macdonalds had indeed taken their oath so that there was no possible justification for the massacre. The immediate responsibility must certainly be laid on Sir John Dalrymple, the king's principal minister in Scotland, who had long been hostile to the Macdonald clan and took this opportunity for revenge. Yet William himself signed the order and thereby made himself accountable as well. The whole story of treachery and cold-blooded atrocity is a sad testimony to the barbarity of the times and blackened the reputation of William's government in Scotland for many years.

Appendix 2

Ed. Note: In the 1690s, supporters of the Stuart family monarchy (James II) rose against the claim to the throne of William of Orange. In Scotland these rebels were known as Jacobites and their efforts eventually resulted in the Glencoe massacre, as previously noted. Some fifty years later another Jacobite rebellion was mounted in support of Charles Edward, the Stuart prince. A major battle was fought at Cultoden Moor (near Nairn), which turned out to be the last stand made by the Stuarts, in 1745. The insurrectionary forces (which included many Macdonalds once again fighting against Campbells) were completely defeated by the Earl of Cumberland, and many Scotsmen lost their lives.

Appendix 3

Ed. Note: George MacDonald included himself into his own fiction in many ways, which frequently can be as stimulating and intriguing to ferret out of the story for the MacDonald enthusiast as unraveling the plot itself. The ancestry of Duncan MacPhail provides a case in point concerning the often-autobiographical nature of MacDonald's novels. Though MacDonald's son Greville, in his biography of his father, assures us that Duncan was not an actual portrait of MacDonald's grandfather or any ancestor, there are nevertheless some fascinating clues in *The Fisherman's Lady* that suggest that MacDonald, in gradually revealing Duncan's past, was actually revealing to us his own lineage.

The clues are as follow: We know that Duncan's real name is not MacPhail, and in chapter 12 he sheds light on that fact by telling Malcolm that Campbell of Glenlyon called him "MacDhonuill" in a dream—much closer to MacDonald. Now we find him revealing to Lady Florimel, by bits, that indeed, though he clouds it by saying, "I said Allister's father's father . . . ," we are to deduce that it was his own ancestors—possibly grandfather or great-grandfather—that were at Glencoe, whether killed or escaped, we cannot really tell from the narrative. In other words, Duncan is a MacDonald, a descendant from the Glencoe Macdonalds, who has, for reasons we do not know, kept the pseudonym MacPhail. Then by talking about his actual parents in relation to the battle of Culloden, he brings the genealogy much closer to himself. Duncan's being a MacDonald himself explains his aversion to the Campbell name—the mortal enemy of all descendants of Glencoe.

Now, what do we know about the actual ancestors of George MacDonald? From *George MacDonald and His Wife* (Greville MacDonald) and *George MacDonald* (Joseph Johnson, Haskell House Publishers, New York), we can glean the following facts. George MacDonald's great-great-great-grandfather escaped from Glencoe; Alastir—half-brother of the chief—was away from home, had some warning of the treachery, and so left the valley altogether with his family and some livestock. His son, name unknown, who would have been George MacDonald's great-great-grandfather eventually settled in a small town on the north Banff coast by the name of Portsoy where he became a quarryman and polisher of marble. His son William became the town Piper of Portsoy and went to fight for Prince Charles. Apparently many of George MacDonald's ancestors fought at Culloden and lost their lives, but his great-grandfather William (Piper of Portsoy) escaped. He did, however, probably lose his eyesight. So strong were his loyalties that he named his son Charles Edward, after the Prince. Young Charles Edward (MacDonald's grandfather) was but three months old when the Culloden disaster took place and his mother, William's wife, died upon hearing the news of it. Following Culloden, Cumberland ruthlessly stalked every fugitive of the battle he could find. Tradition says that William made his escape with his eldest son through Nairn and Moray and eventually returned to Portsoy. But his home was closely watched by his enemies so he hid for months among the caves nearby. (Caves in this region have long been associated with pipers.) Eventually, perhaps because the loss of his eyesight was considered sufficient penalty, the old piper was forgotten. The timing is somewhat vague in the accounts, so we cannot be sure at what point his wife died and when he began to care for his younger son, Charles Edward, still just a baby. Tradition has it that he did raise a large family after Culloden; however, only the two sons mentioned were later able to be accounted for.

George MacDonald's grandfather, Charles Edward MacDonald, later moved south from Portsoy to Huntly where he was a successful businessman in weaving and bleaching. He had nine children, one of whom was named George who would later be known as George MacDonald, Sr. The family remained in Huntly and it was there, in 1824, that George MacDonald (Jr.) was born.

Certainly the parallels between MacDonald's heritage and Duncan's cannot be drawn exactly. For Duncan most closely resembles MacDonald's great-grandfather William rather than his grandfather. And Duncan describes the flight of his father from Culloden which would suggest that his parallel is in fact Charles Edward. So while no positive identities are consistent at all points, nevertheless MacDonald is assuredly giving us many intriguing glimpses into his own background through the lips of Duncan, blind piper of Portlossie.

One final interesting point. Duncan's reference to Allister is a bit of a mystery. For he talks about Allister's grandfather being slain at Glencoe, which would place Allister in the approximate generation of MacDonald's great-grandfather William. However, Greville MacDonald identifies Ian's half-brother "Alastir" as the ancestor who in fact escaped from Glencoe. He also identifies yet another "Alastair" MacDonald, the leader in the Battle of Inverlochy against the Campbells who was extolled in song by one of the most notorious of the MacDonald bards, Iain Tom (John Brown). Further light is shed on this in chapter 25 by Duncan where he finally identifies himself as the "Allister" of his song—named presumably after his earlier ancestors—and once again confirms his parallel with MacDonald's great-grandfather William whose "father's father" was indeed at Glencoe (although not slain). Here then is George MacDonald's ancestry and how it ties in with the facts of the story.

George MacDonald	born—Huntly, 1824
George MacDonald, Sr.	Huntly
Charles Edward MacDonald	born three months after Culloden, raised by William, moved to Huntly to start business
William MacDonald	town piper of Portsoy, fought at Culloden, lost eyesight, hid in caves, raised sons
(great-great-grandfather) MacDonald	first MacDonald to settle at Portsoy, became a quarryman
"Alastir" MacDonald	half-brother of Ian at Glencoe, escaped massacre with his family (1692)
. . .	
"Alastair"/Iain Lom (John Brown)	fought Campbells at Inverlochy (1614)

George MacDonald's grandmother, Mrs. Charles Edward, was a strict Calvinist whose passion and zeal for saving souls from eternal burning knew few limits. She is accurately characterized in the novel *Robert Falconer* as she cruelly burned her son's violin, one of his most prized and joyous possessions (a scene witnessed by her young grandson George). Possibly from some similiar passion for truth (who can tell?), she destroyed all the documents in the family chanter-chest and thus forever eliminated positive proof that the grandfather of the Portsoy town-piper was indeed one of the few of his clan to have escaped Glencoe with his wife. However, in the absence of such documentation, MacDonald's son Greville attests to the family outline as I have given it here.

By way of interest, *MacDonald* wrote *Malcolm*, here entitled *The Fisherman's Lady*, in 1873–74 and used as the setting the very familiar coast of Banffshire with which his family had so long been associated. A map of the region, at the beginning of this book, will reveal from whence MacDonald derived many of the names used in the novel. MacDonald spent several summers in the little fishing town of Cullen, approximately ten miles west of Portsoy, and it is this town which forms the basis for Portlossie. Much of the geography of the novel corresponds closely with this rocky section of the coastline.

The
Marquis'
Secret

Contents

Characters—*The Marquis' Secret*

Malcolm Colonsay—The Marquis of Lossie
Hector Crathie—The factor of Lossie House
Mr. Stoat—Lossie House groom
Kelpie—Malcolm's mare
Mrs. Courthope—Lossie House housekeeper
Miss Horn—Malcolm's friend
Lizza Findlay—Seaton village girl
Joseph Mair (Blue Peter)—Malcolm's best friend
Annie Mair—Blue Peter's wife
Mr. Soutar—Duff Harbor lawyer
Davy—Young cabinboy
Lady Florimel Gordon (Colonsay)—Malcolm's half sister
Lord Liftore (formerly Lord Meikleham)—Lady Bellair's nephew
Mr. Wallis—London servant of Florimel's
Arnold Lenorme—London painter
John Findlay (Partan)—Lizza's father
Meg Findlay (Partan)—Lizza's mother
Alexander Graham—Malcolm's friend, a schoolmaster
Lady Clementina Thornicroft—Friend of Florimel's
Travers—Yacht's mate
Caley—Florimel's maid
Mrs. Catanach—Portlossie midwife
Griffith—Florimel's groom
Mr. & Mrs. Merton—Portland Place servants
Rose—Portland Place servant girl
Duncan MacPhail—Malcolm's adopted grandfather
Johnny Bykes—Lossie House gatekeeper
Mrs. Crathie—Hector Crathie's wife
Phemy Mair—Blue Peter's daughter
Mr. Morrison—Local magistrate

1

· · · · · · · · · · · · · · · · · · · ·

The Stable Yard

$\mathcal{I}$t was one of those exquisite days that come in every winter and seem like the beautiful ghost of summer. The loveliness of the morning, however, was but partially visible from the spot where Malcolm Colonsay stood in the stable yard of Lossie House, ancient and roughly paved. He stood on the unleveled stones grooming the coat of a powerful and fidgety black mare. Nothing about him indicated he was anything but an ordinary stable-hand.

The mare looked dangerous. Every now and then she cast back a white glance of the one visible eye; but the youth was on his guard and as wary as fearless in his handling of her. When at length he had finished with her coat, he took from his pocket a lump of sugar and held it for her to bite at with angry-looking teeth. It was a cold, crisp morning, bright with the morning's sun. But for all the cold, there was keen life in the air.

As they stood thus, a man who looked half farmer, half lawyer appeared on the opposite side of the court in the shadow.

"You are spoiling that mare, MacPhail!" he cried.

"I could hardly do that, sir; she couldn't be much worse," returned Malcolm.

"It's whip and spur she needs, not sugar."

"She has had, and shall have both in turn, and I hope they'll do something for her when the time comes, sir."

"Her time shall be short here, anyway. She's not worth the sugar you give her."

"Eh, Mr. Crathie—just look at her," said Malcolm in a tone of expostulation as he stepped back a few paces and regarded her with admiring eye. "Have you ever seen such legs, and such a neck, and such a head, and such hindquarters? She's beautiful in every way except for her temper, and she can't help that like you and I can. She's such a beauty; it's little wonder the marquis bought her the moment he laid eyes on her."

"She'll be the death of somebody someday. The sooner we get rid of her the better. Just look at that!" he added as the mare laid back her ears and made a vicious snap at nothing in particular.

"She was bound to be a favorite of my—master, the marquis," returned Malcolm. "It's only too bad he didn't live long enough to tame and ride her himself. I know he was looking forward to it. Knowing that, sir, I would not want to part with her."

"I'll take any offer within reason for her," said the factor. "You'll just ride her to Forres market next week and see what you can get for her. I do think she's quieter, though, since you took her in hand."

"I'm sure she is, but it won't last a day if she's sold. The moment I leave her she'll be just as bad as ever. She has a kind of liking to me because I give her sugar and she can't throw me, but she's no better in her heart yet. She's an unsanctified brute. I couldn't think of selling her like this."

"Let whoever buys beware," said the factor.

"Oh, yes, let them! I don't object as long as they know what she's like before they buy her," rejoined Malcolm.

The factor burst out laughing. To his judgment, the youth had spoken like an idiot. "We'll not send you to sell," he said. "Stoat shall go with you, and you shall have nothing to do but hold the mare and your own tongue."

"Sir," said Malcolm seriously, "you don't mean what you say? You said yourself she'd be the death of somebody, and to sell her without telling what she's like would be to break the sixth commandment clean to shivers."

"That may be good doctrine in church, my lad, but it's pure heresy in the horse market. No, no! You buy a horse as you take a wife—for better or worse, as the case may be. A woman's not bound to tell her faults when a man wants to marry her."

"Hoot, sir! There's no comparison. Mistress Kelpie here's plenty ready to confess her faults by giving anyone who wants to know a taste of them— she won't even wait to be asked. And if you expect me to hold my tongue about them, Mr. Crathie, I'd as soon think of selling Blue Peter a rotten boat. And, besides, there's the eighth commandment as well as the sixth. There's no exceptions about horseflesh. We must be as honest with that as anything else."

"There's one commandment, my lad," said Mr. Crathie with the dignity of intended rebuke, "you seem to find hard to learn, and that is to mind your own business."

"If you mean catching herring, maybe you're right," said Malcolm. "I know more about that than horse-selling, and it's a mite cleaner."

"None of your impudence," returned the factor. "The marquis isn't here to uphold you in your follies. That they amused him is no reason why I should put up with them. So keep your tongue between your teeth or you'll find it the worse for you."

Malcolm smiled a little oddly, and held his peace.

"You're here to do what I tell you, and make no remarks," added the factor.

"I'm aware of that, sir—within certain limits," returned Malcolm.

"What do you mean by that?"

"I mean within the limits of doing by your neighbor as you would have your neighbor do by you; that's what I mean, sir."

"I've told you already that doesn't apply in horse-dealing. Every man has to take care of himself in the horse market. That's understood. If you had been brought up amongst horses instead of herring, you would have known that as well as any other man."

"I don't doubt I'll go back to the herring, then, for they're likely to prove the more honest of the two. But there's no hypocrisy in Kelpie, and she must have her day's feed whatever comes of it."

At the word "hypocrisy" Mr. Crathie's face grew red. He was an elder in the church and had family worship every night as regularly as his toddy. The word was offensive and insolent to him. He would have turned Malcolm adrift on the spot had he not remembered the favor of the late marquis for the lad, as well as the favor of the present marchioness, as well as his own instructions to deal kindly with him. Choking down, therefore, his rage and indignation, he said sternly, "Malcolm, you have two enemies—a long tongue and a strong conceit. You have little enough to be proud of. I advise you to mind what you're about and show suitable respect to your superiors, or as sure as judgment you'll be back to your fish guts."

While he spoke, Malcolm had been smoothing Kelpie all over with his palm; the moment the factor ceased talking he ceased stroking and with one arm thrown over the mare's back looked him full in the face. "If you imagine, Mr. Crathie," he said, "that I count it any worldly promotion that brings me under the orders of a man less honest than he might be, you're mistaken. I don't think it's pride this time. I'll lay out Blue Peter's long nets for him, but I won't lie for any factor between here and Davy Jones' locker."

It was too much for him. Mr. Crathie's feelings overcame him, and he was a wrathful man to see as he strode up to the youth with clenched fist.

"Keep away from the mare, for Heaven's sake, Mr. Crathie!" cried Malcolm.

But even as he spoke, the gleaming iron of Kelpie's horseshoes opened on the terror-struck factor with a lightning kick. He started back, white with dismay, having by a bare inch of space and a bare moment of time escaped what he called eternity. Dazed with fear, he turned and staggered halfway across the yard before he recovered himself. Then he turned again and with what dignity he could scrape together said, "MacPhail, you go about your business. You are dismissed!"

In his foolish heart he believed Malcolm had made the brute strike out.

"I can't go until Stoat comes home," answered Malcolm.

"If I see you about the place after sunset, I'll horsewhip you," said the factor and walked away.

Malcolm again smiled oddly, but made no reply. He undid the mare's halter and led her into the stable. There he fed her, standing by her while she ate, not once taking his eye off her. Ever since her arrival, just several days after the marquis' death, Malcolm had taken her in hand in the hope of taming her a little. The factor, who still regarded Malcolm as something even lower than a servant under his charge, allowed both him and the horse to remain in the hopes of by-and-by selling her for a greater price than the marquis had paid.

When the mare had finished her oats, Malcolm left her busy with her hay, for she was a huge eater, and went into the house, passing through the kitchen and ascending the spiral stone stairs to the library. As he went along the narrow passage on the second floor, Mrs. Courthope peeped after him from one of the bedrooms and watched him as he went, nodding her head two or three times with decision. He reminded her so strongly, not of his father the late marquis, but of his brother who had preceded him, that she felt all but certain, whoever might be his mother, that he had as much of the Colonsay blood in his veins as any marquis of them all.

Malcolm went straight to a certain corner and from amongst a dingy set of old classics took down a small volume, sat down and began to read. But he could not keep his mind on the words, for he was occupied with other things. He recalled how the late marquis, about three months before, had on his deathbed secretly acknowledged him his son and committed to his trust the welfare of his sister. The memory of this charge was never absent from his heart. His had been an agonizing perplexity these recent months. For to appear as the marquis of Lossie was not merely to take from Florimel the title she supposed her own but to declare her illegitimate, seeing that the marquis' first wife—Malcolm's mother—was still alive when she was born, a fact rendering void his marriage to Florimel's mother. How was he to act so that as little scandal might befall her whom he loved so much?

Despite his own rough education his thoughts were not troubled about his own prospects. Mysteriously committed to the care of a poor blind Highland piper settled amongst the local fishing people of the Seaton, he had, as he grew up, naturally fallen into their ways of life and labor. He had but lately abandoned the calling of a fisherman to take charge of the marquis' yacht, whence by degrees he had, in his helpfulness, become indispensable to him and his daughter and had come to live in the House of Lossie as a privileged servant. He owed his book education mainly to the friendship of the parish schoolmaster.

If he could content himself with Florimel's future and at the same time, in good conscience, remain faithful to the people who were his charge as marquis, it is doubtful Malcolm would ever have seen the need to identify himself as the marquis. He was perfectly content as fisherman, stable-hand, or servant insofar as he could be sure he was in fact serving Florimel's best interests.

But events over which Malcolm exercised no control now seemed to be making such an option impossible. For not only was Florimel gone from Portlossie and therefore out of reach of his ministrations; she was being swept into a circle of acquaintances judged by Malcolm, at the very least, to be more concerned for their own welfare than hers. The marchioness of Lossie, as she was now called—for the family was one of two or three in Scotland in which the title descends to an heiress—had been, since her father's death, under the guardianship of a certain dowager countess. Lady Bellair had taken her first to Edinburgh and then to London. It was with Florimel's potential suitor, Lady Bellair's nephew Lord Meikleham, that Malcolm was most concerned. Malcolm received tidings of her through Mr. Soutar, the late marquis' lawyer of Duff Harbor. The last amounted to this— that as rapidly as the proprieties of mourning would permit, she was circling the vortex of London society. Malcolm found himself almost in despair of ever being the least service to her as a brother. If he might but once more be her skipper, her groom, her attendant, he might at least learn how to reveal to her the bond between them without breaking it in the very act and so ruining the hope of serving her and his charge to their father.

The door to the library opened and in walked Miss Horn. She looked stern, gaunt, hard-featured—almost fierce. She shook Malcolm's hand with a sort of loose dissatisfaction, and dropped into one of the easy chairs with which the library abounded.

"Do you call yourself an honest man, Malcolm?"

"I call myself nothing," he answered, "but I would hope to be what you say, Miss Horn."

"Oh, I don't doubt you wouldn't steal or tell lies about a horse; I've just come from some wagging of tongues about you. Mistress Crathie tells me her man's steaming angry with you that you won't tell a wordless lie about the black mare. But a gentleman mustn't lie, not even by saying nothing. And yet what's your life right now but a lie, Malcolm? You that's the honest marquis of Lossie to waste your time and the strength of your body wrestling with that devil of a horse, when that half sister of yours is going to the very devil of perdition himself among the godless gentry of London! Aren't you letting her live believing a lie? Aren't you allowing her to go on as if she was someone more than mortal when you know she's no more the marchioness of Lossie than you're the son of old Duncan MacPhail? Faith, man! You've lost the truth just like your father, even if you've gained the world in exchange."

"Say nothing against the dead, mem. He's made up with my mother before now I imagine. And anyway, he confessed her his wife and me her son before he died, and what more did he have time to do?"

"It's a fact," returned Miss Horn, "and now look at you. What your father confessed to with the very death throws of his laboring spirit—that same confession you place back in a cloud of secrecy rather than removing the blot from the memory of one who, I believe, I loved more as my third cousin than you do as your own mother."

"There's no blot on her memory, mem," returned Malcolm, "or I would be marquis tomorrow. There's not a soul who knows she was a mother but knows she was wife and whose wife, too."

Miss Horn had neither wish nor power to reply and so changed her front of attack. "And so, Malcolm Colonsay," she said, "you have no less than made up your mind to spend your days in your own stable, neither better or worse than a servant at Lossie Arms? And after all I have done to make a gentleman of you, coming to your father like a very lion in his den and making him confess the thing against every hair upon his stiff neck? Losh, laddie, it was a picture to see him standing with his back to the door like an obstinate bull!"

"Hold your tongue, mem. I can't stand to hear my father spoken of like that. For, you see, I loved him before I knew there was a drop of his blood in me."

"Well, that's very well, but father and mother's man and wife. You didn't come from father alone."

"That's true, mem. And it can't be that I should ever forget the face you showed me in the coffin—the prettiest, saddest face I ever saw," returned

Malcolm with a quaver in his voice. "And don't you think, mem, that I'm going to forget the dead because I'm more concerned about the living. I tell you I just don't know what to do. With my father's dying words committing her to my charge and the more than regard I have for Lady Florimel herself, how can I take the very sunshine out of her life? How can I get near enough to her to do any good turn worth doing? And here I am, her own half brother, with nothing in my power but to scar her heart or else lie! Even supposing she was well married first, how would she stand with her husband when he came to know she was no marchioness and had no lawful right to any name but her mother's? And before that, what right could I have to allow any man to marry her without knowing the truth about her? Poor thing! She looks down on me from the top of her pretty head as from the heights of heaven. But I'll let her know yet, if only I can find the right way to do it." He gave a sigh with the words, and a pause followed.

"The truth's the truth," resumed Miss Horn, "not more, not less."

"Yes," responded Malcolm, "but there's a right and a wrong time for the telling of it. It's not as if I had a hand in any long lie. It was nothing of my doing, as you know, mem. To myself I was never anything but a fisherman."

"And what about your own folk? How on earth are you to do your duty by them if you don't take your power and reign? You have the power and the money to do whatever you like for them that's been settled on your land all around for many a generation. They're honest folk. If a man's a king he's bound to reign over them."

"Ay, mem. I've thought how much I would like to build a big harbor at Scaurnose for the fisher-folk that're my own flesh and blood. But the foundation must be laid in righteousness first, mem. And I'll not set out to do anything until I can do it without ruining my sister."

"Well, one thing's clear: you'll never know what to do so long as you hang about a stable full of four-footed animals with no sense and some two-footed ones with less."

"I don't doubt you're right there, mem, and if I could but take poor Kelpie away with me. For I'm thinking I must go," said Malcolm.

"Where to, then?" asked Miss Horn.

"Oh, to London; where else?"

"And what will your lordship do there?"

"Don't say lordship to me, mem, I beg you. I'm not used to it just yet. I doubt I ever will be."

"I know nothing but that you're bound to be a lord and not a stableman. And I won't let you rest until you rise up and say, 'What next?' "

"I've been asking myself that very question for the last three months," said Malcolm.

"I daresay," said Miss Horn. "But you've been saying it inside and I would have you up and *say* it!"

"If I but knew what to do!" said Malcolm for the thousandth time.

2

·····················

The Trouble

When Miss Horn left him—with a farewell kindlier than her greeting—
Malcolm went back to the stable, saddled Kelpie, and took her out for an
airing. As he passed the factor's house, Mrs. Crathie saw him from the window. She rose and looked after him from the door—a proud woman jealous
of her husband's dignity, still more jealous of her own. "The very image of
the old marquis!" she said to herself as he passed. "If the brute would but
break a bone or two of his! The impudence of the fellow!"

The mare was fresh and the roads hard from the frost. He turned, therefore, toward the Seaton. To its westward side the sand lay smooth, flat, and
wet along the edge of the receding tide. He gave Kelpie the rein, and she
sprang into a wild gallop. But finding, as they approached the stony part
from which rose the Bored Craig, that he could not pull her up in time, he
turned her head toward the long dune of sand which, a little beyond the
tide, ran parallel with the shore. It was dry and loose and the ascent steep.
Kelpie's hoofs sank at every step, and when she reached the top, with side-
spread struggling haunches and flared pulsating nostrils, he had her in
hand. She stood panting, yet pawing and dancing, making the sand fly in
all directions.

Suddenly a young woman with a child in her arms rose, as it seemed to
Malcolm, from nearly under Kelpie's head. She wheeled and reared and
seemed, whether in wrath or terror, to strain every nerve to unseat her rider.

"Stand back, Lizzy!" cried Malcolm. "She's a mad brute and I might not
be able to hold her."

Lizza seemed to pay his words no heed but simply stood with a sad look
and gazed at Kelpie as she went on plunging and kicking about on the top
of the dune.

"I reckon you wouldn't care if the she-devil knocked out your brains, but
you have the child, Lizzy. Have mercy on the child and run to the bottom!"

"I want to talk to you, Malcolm MacPhail," she said in a tone which
revealed a depth of trouble.

"I don't think I can listen very well right now," said Malcolm. "But wait a
minute." He swung himself from Kelpie's back and, hanging hard on the bit
with one hand, searched with the other in the pocket of his coat, saying as
he did so, "Sugar, Kelpie, sugar!"

The animal gave an eager snort, settled on her feet, and began sniffing
about him. He made haste, for if her eagerness should turn to impatience,
she would do her best to bite him. After crunching three or four lumps, she

stood rather quiet. Malcolm would have to make the best of it he could.

"Now, Lizzy," he said hurriedly, "speak while you can."

"Malcolm," said the girl—and looked him full in the face for a moment, for agony had overcome shame—"Malcolm, he's going to marry Lady Florimel."

Malcolm was silent—stunned.

Could Lizza have learned more concerning his sister than he yet had?

Lizza had never uttered the name of the father of her child, and all her people knew was that he could not have been a fisherman, for then he would have married her before the child was born. But Malcolm had had a suspicion from the first, and now her words but confirmed it. And was that fellow going to marry his sister? He turned white with dismay, then red with anger and stood speechless.

But he was quickly brought to himself by a sharp pinch under the shoulder blade from Kelpie's long teeth. He had forgotten her, and she had taken the advantage.

"Who told you that, Lizzy?"

"I'm not at liberty to say, Malcolm. But I'm sure it's true and my heart's about to break."

"I'm sorry," said Malcolm. "But is it anybody that knows what he says?"

"Well, I don't really know if she *knows*, but I think she must have good reason or she wouldn't have said it. Oh, me! Malcolm, you're about the only one who doesn't look down on me now. So when I saw you coming up the dune, I just felt I had to tell you."

"I wouldn't want you to tell me anything you promised not to tell," said Malcolm, "but I'll gladly listen to anything you want to tell me."

"I have nothing much to tell, Malcolm, except that my Lady Florimel's going to be married to Lord Meikleham—Lord Liftore, they call him now. Oh, me!"

"Heaven forbid she should be married to any such blackguard!" cried Malcolm.

"Don't call him names, Malcolm. I can't stand it, though I have no right to defend him."

"I won't say a word that'll hurt your sad heart," he returned, "but if you knew all, you'd know I have a fair-sized bone to pick with his lordship myself."

The girl gave a low cry. "You wouldn't hurt him, Malcolm?" she said in terror at the thought of the elegant youth in the clutches of an angry fisherman, even if he were the generous Malcolm MacPhail himself.

"I would rather not," he replied, "but we'll have to see how he carries himself."

"Don't do anything to him for my sake, Malcolm. You can have nothing against him yourself."

The descending darkness made it too dark for Malcolm to see the keen look of wistful regret with which Lizza tried to pierce the gloom and read his face. For a moment the poor girl thought he meant he had loved her himself. But far other thoughts were in Malcolm's mind—one was that she whom he had loved before he knew her of his own blood he would rather see married to any honest fisherman in the Seaton of Portlossie than to such a lord as Meikleham. He had seen enough of him at Lossie House to know what he was. And puritanical, fish-catching Malcolm had ideas above most lords of his day. The thought of the alliance was horrible to him. It was yet possible to be avoided, however; only what could he do and at the same time avoid grievous hurt? "I don't think he'll every marry my lady," he said.

"What makes you say that, Malcolm?" returned Lizza with eagerness.

"I can't tell you just now—" Malcolm was interrupted by Kelpie's sudden lurch to get free of him.

"—the madness is coming back to her, Lizzy. I've got to get her home," he said as he once more jumped on Kelpie's back. "I'll talk to you later, and don't you worry."

Back at the stable, Malcolm heard the factor striding across the stones toward him as he was settling Kelpie into her stall. As the door opened he cried out in exultant wrath, "MacPhail! Come out of there! What right do you have to be on the premises? Didn't I turn you out this morning?"

"Ay, sir, but you didn't pay me my wages," said Malcolm.

"No matter. You're nothing better than a housebreaker if you enter any building about the place."

"I break no lock," returned Malcolm. "I have the key my lord gave me."

"Give it to me; I'm master here now!"

Mr. Crathie was a man who did well under authority, but in wielding it himself was overbearing and far more exacting than the marquis had been. Full of presumed importance and yet doubtful of its adequate recognition by those under him, he had grown imperious and resented with indignation the slightest breach of his orders. Hence, he was in no great favor with the fisher-folk. Now all the day he had been fuming over Malcolm's behavior to him in the morning; and when he went home and learned that his wife had seen him upon Kelpie as if nothing had happened, he became furious and had been wandering about the grounds brooding on the words Malcolm had spoken, waiting for some further opportunity to put the impudent lad in his place. He could not rid himself of the acrid burning of Malcolm's words, for they had contained truth, which stings greater than any poison.

"Indeed, I'll do no such thing, sir. What he gave me I'll keep."

"Give up that key or I'll go at once and get a warrant against you for theft!"

"We'll refer it to Mr. Soutar."

The factor cursed, "What has he to do with my affairs, you lowbred rascal? Come out of there or I'll horsewhip you for a dirty blackguard!"

"Whip away," said Malcolm.

"Get out of my sight," the factor cried, "or I'll shoot you like a dog!"

"Go and fetch your gun," said Malcolm, "and if you find me waiting here for you, you can have me."

The factor uttered a horrible imprecation.

"Hoots, sir! Be ashamed of yourself. Go home to your mistress and I'll be up in the morning for my wages."

"If you set foot on the ground again, I'll set every dog in the place on you."

Malcolm laughed. "If I was to turn the order the other way, Mr. Crathie, who do you think they'd mind, me or you?"

"Give me that key and go about your business."

"No, no, sir. What my lord gave me I'll keep for all the factors in the world," returned Malcolm. "And as for leaving the place, if I'm not in your service, Mr. Crathie, I'm not under your orders. I'll go when it suits me."

Having finished with Kelpie, he walked past the threatening factor with confident stride toward the sea gate, and thence toward Scaurnose. The door of Blue Peter's cottage was opened by his wife. Malcolm, instead of going in, called to his friend, whom he saw by the fire with Phemy on his knee, to come out and speak to him.

Blue Peter at once obeyed the summons. "There's nothing wrong, I hope, Malcolm," he said as he closed the door behind him.

"Mr. Graham would say," returned Malcolm, "nothing was ever wrong but what you did wrong yourself or wouldn't put right when you had the chance. But I've come to ask your counsel, Peter. Come with me down by the shore and I'll tell you about it."

"You don't want the mistress knowing it?" asked his friend. "I don't like to keep secrets from her."

"You shall judge for yourself and tell her or not tell her as you like. Only she'll have to hold her tongue."

"She can hold her tongue like a gravestone," said Peter.

As they spoke, they reached the cliff that hung over the shattered shore. It was a cold, clear night. Scattered bits of snow lay all about them. The sky was clear and full of stars, for the wind that blew cold from the northwest had dispelled the snowy clouds. Then Malcolm turned to his friend and, laying his hand on his arm, said, "Blue Peter, did I ever tell you a lie?"

"No, never. What makes you ask such a thing?"

"Because I want you to believe me now, and it won't be easy."

"I'll believe anything you tell me—that can be believed," said Joseph.

"Well, I have come to the knowledge that my name's not MacPhail—it's Colonsay, man!—I'm the marquis of Lossie!"

Without a moment's hesitation, Blue Peter pulled off his cap.

"Peter," cried Malcolm, "don't break my heart! Put on your hat."

"The Lord be thanked, my lord," said Blue Peter. "And what'll be your lordship's will."

"First and foremost, Peter, that my best friend after my old daddy and the schoolmaster won't turn against me because I had a marquis instead of a piper or a fisherman for my father."

"That's not likely, my lord," returned Blue Peter, "when the first thing I say is, 'What would you have me do?' Here I am, asking no questions."

"Well, I'd like you to hear the story of it."

"Say on, my lord," said Peter.

Malcolm was silent for a few moments. "I'm thinking, Peter," he said, "that I'd be obliged to you to only say 'my lord' to me when we're alone, and even then I'd prefer you not. I don't want to grow used to it and, between you and me, I don't like it. And now I'll tell you all I know."

When he had ended the tale of what had come to his knowledge and how it had come, Peter said, "Give me the grip of your hand, my lord. May God keep you long in life and honor to rule over us! Now, if you please, what are you going to do?"

"Tell me, Peter, what do you think I ought to do?"

"That would take a heap of thinking," returned the fisherman. "But one thing seems plain: you can't let your sister remain exposed to any temptation you could keep from her. That would not be as you promised your father. I do not think he would like my Lady Florimel to be under the influence of such a one as Lady Bellair—where he is now at least. You must go to her. You have no choice, my lord."

"But what am I to do when I go?"

"That's what you have to go and see."

"And that's what I've been telling myself, and what Miss Horn's been telling me too. But it's another thing to get my own thoughts straight. You see, I'm afraid for hurting her in pride, to bring her down to put myself up."

"My lord," said Peter solemnly, "you know the life of poor fisherfolk. You know these people. Do you count as nothing the providence which has now set you over them? Why would God have given you such an upbringing as no marquis' son ever had, or maybe ever will have, if it isn't that you should take these people in hand and do your best for them? If you forget them, you'll be forgetting Him that made them and you and the sea and the herring."

"You speak the truth, as I have felt in my heart, Peter. But I so badly don't want to hurt her."

A silence followed.

"Now listen," Malcolm said with resolve in his voice, "will you sail with me to London . . . tonight?"

The fisherman was silent a moment, then answered, "I will, my lord, but I must tell my wife."

"Run and fetch her here."

"I'll have her here in a minute," said Joseph as he ran back toward the house.

For a few minutes Malcolm stood alone in the dim starlight of winter, looking out on the dusky sea, dark as his own future. He anticipated its difficulties but never thought of its perils. It was seldom anything oppressed him more than the doubt of what he ought to do. But the first step toward action is the beginning of the death of doubt, and so the tide of Malcolm's feeling ran higher than night as he stood thus alone under the stars waiting to embark for he knew not where.

His thoughts were interrupted by the return of Blue Peter with his wife. She threw her arms around Malcolm's neck and burst into tears.

"Hoots, my woman," said her husband, "what are you crying about?"

"Peter," she answered, "it's just like a death. He's going to leave us and go home to his own. And I can't stand that he should grow strange to us that have known him so long."

"That'll be an evil day," returned Malcolm, "when I grow strange to any friend. I'll have to be long down the low road before that would be possible. I may not be able to do what you would like. But trust me, I'll be fair to you. And now I want Blue Peter to go with me and help me do what I have to do, if you have no objection."

"No, I've none. I would go myself if I could be of any use," answered Mrs. Mair. "But women are usually in the way."

"Thank you. Now, Peter, we must be off."

"Not tonight, surely?" said Mrs. Mair, a little taken by surprise.

"The sooner the better, Annie," replied her husband, "and we couldn't have a better wind. Just run home and get some food together for us and then come after us to Portlossie."

Malcolm and Blue Peter set off for the Seaton to launch the marquis' cutter while Annie Mair went home to get some oatcakes, dried fish, and other provisions for the voyage. When the two men reached the Seaton, they found plenty of hands ready to help them with the little sloop. Malcolm said he was going to take her to Peterhead and they asked few questions. Once afloat there was very little to be done, for she had been laid up in perfect condition; and as soon as Mrs. Mair appeared with her basket and they had put a keg of water, some fishing line, and a pan of mussels for bait on board, they were ready to sail and bade their friends a good-bye, leaving them to imagine they were gone but for a day or two, probably on some business of Mr. Crathie's.

With the wind from the northwest, they soon reached Duff Harbor where Malcolm went on shore and saw Mr. Soutar. With a landsman's prejudice he made strenuous objection to such a mad prank as sailing to London at that time of year, but in vain. Malcolm saw nothing mad in it, and the lawyer had to admit he ought to know best. He brought on board with him a lad of Peter's acquaintance and, now fully manned, they set sail again and by the time the sun appeared were not far from Peterhead.

Malcolm's spirits kept rising as they bowled over the bright, cold water. He never felt so capable as when at sea. His energies had first been called out in combat with the elements, and hence he always felt strongest, most at home, and surest of himself on the water. His spirits were also buoyed with the prospect of once more seeing his spiritual guide, Mr. Graham, the late schoolmaster of Portlossie, whom the charge of questionable teaching had ultimately driven from the place shortly after the marquis' death and who was now residing in London.

They put in at Peterhead, purchased a few provisions, and again set sail. Malcolm became increasingly aware that he must soon come to a conclusion as to the steps he must take when he reached London. But think as he would, he could plan nothing beyond finding out where his sister lived and going to look at the house and then getting into it if he might.

They knew all the coast as far as the Firth of Forth; after that they had to be more careful. They had no charts on board, nor could they have made much use of any. But the winds continued favorable and the weather cold, bright, and full of life. Off the Nore they had rough weather and had to stand off and on for a day and a night till it moderated. They spoke to someone on a fishing boat, received directions, and found themselves in smooth water more and more as the channel narrowed. They ended their voyage at length below London Bridge in a very jungle of masts.

3
●●●●●●●●●●●●●●●●●●●●

The City

*L*eaving Davy to keep the sloop, the two fishermen went on shore. Passing from the narrow precincts of the river, they found themselves at once in the roar of London city. Stunned at first, then excited, then bewildered, then dazed, without any plan to guide their steps, they wandered about until, unused to the hard stones, their feet ached. It was a dull day in March. A keen wind blew round the corners of the streets. They wished themselves at sea again.

"Such a lot of people!" said Blue Peter.

"It's hard to imagine," rejoined Malcolm, "that God can look after them in such a tumult."

The two raw Scotchmen looked very out of place on the London streets. At length a policeman directed them to a Scotch eating house where they fared well and from the landlady gathered directions by which they could guide themselves toward Curzon Street, a certain number in which Mr. Soutar had given Malcolm as Lady Bellair's address.

Having found it, the door was opened to Malcolm's knock by a slatternly charwoman who informed him that Lady Bellair had removed her establishment to Lady Lossie's house in Portland Place. After many curious perplexities, odd blunders, and vain endeavors to understand shop signs and window notices and with the help of many policemen, at length they found their way to the stately region of Portland Place.

The house he sought was one of the largest in the area. He would not, however, yield to the temptation to have a good look at it for fear of attracting some attention from its windows and being recognized. They turned, therefore, into some of the smaller streets lying between Portland Place and Great Portland Street where, searching about, they came upon a decent-looking public house and inquired about lodgings. They were directed to a woman in the neighborhood who kept a dingy little curiosity shop. On payment of a week's rent in advance, she allowed them to occupy a small bedroom. But Malcolm did not want Peter with him that night. He wished to feel perfectly free, and besides, it was more than desirable that Peter should go and look after the boat and the boy.

Left alone, he once more fell to his hitherto futile scheming: how was he to get near his sister? He would not lie, and if he appeared before her with no reason to give, would she not be far too offended with his presumption to retain him in her services? And except he could be near her as a servant, he did not see a chance of doing anything for her without disclosing facts which might make all further service impossible. Plan after plan rose and then passed from his mind. Finally the only resolution he could come to was to write Mr. Soutar, to whom he had committed the protection of Kelpie, to send her up by the first smack from Aberdeen. He did so and also wrote Miss Horn, telling her where he was. Then he went out and made his way back to Portland Place.

Night had closed in, and presently it began to snow. Through the night and the snow went carriages in all directions. The hoofs of the horses echoed from the hard road. Could that house really belong to him? It did, yet he dared not enter. He walked up and down the opposite side of the street some fifty times but saw no sign of vitality about the house. At length a coach stopped at the door and a man got out and knocked. The door opened and he entered. The coach waited. After about a quarter of an hour he came out again, accompanied by two ladies, one of whom Malcolm judged by her figure to be Florimel. They all got into the carriage and Malcolm braced himself for a difficult run. But because of the snow, the coachman drove carefully and he found no difficulty in keeping near them.

They stopped at the doors of a large, dark-looking building which Malcolm judged, but wondered, to be a church of some kind. They went up a great flight of stairs, and still he went after them. When he reached the top, they were just vanishing round a curve, when his advance was checked. A man came up to him, said he could not come there, and gruffly requested him to show his ticket.

"I haven't got one. What is this place?" said Malcolm.

The man gave a look of contemptuous surprise and, turning to another who lounged behind him, said, "Tom, here's a gentleman who wants to know where he is. Can you tell him?"

The man laughed and then said, "You go down there and pay for a pit-ticket, and you'll soon know where you are, mate."

Malcolm went and after a few inquiries and the outlay of two shillings found himself in the pit of one of the largest of the London theaters.

The play was begun and to the lit stage Malcolm's eyes were instantly drawn. He was all but unaware of the multitude of faces about him. However, by degrees he accustomed himself to his surroundings, the strange new place he was in and the silent crowd all about him, and then began a systematic search for his sister amongst the ladies in the boxes. But when he found her he dared not fix his eyes upon her lest his gaze should make her look at him and she should recognize him. Alas! her eyes might have rested on him twenty times without his face once rousing in her mind the thought of the fisher-lad of Portlossie. All that had passed between them in the days already old was virtually forgotten.

As he gathered courage and began to look more closely, he felt that some sort of change had already passed upon her. It was Florimel, yet not the very Florimel he had known. She was more beautiful, but not so lovely in his eyes—much of what had charmed him had vanished. She was more stately, but the stateliness had a little hardness mingled with it. Surely she was not so happy as she had been at Lossie House. She was dressed in black, with a white flower in her hair. Beside her sat the bold-faced Lady Bellair, and behind them was her nephew Lord Meikleham, now Lord Liftore.

A fierce indignation seized the heart of Malcolm at the sight. Behind the form of the earl, his mind's eye saw that of Lizzy Findlay out in the wind on the Boar's Tail dune, her old shawl wrapped about herself and the child of the man who sat there so composed and comfortable. His features were fine and clear-cut, his shoulders broad, and his head well-set; he had much improved in looks since Malcolm offered to fight him with one hand in the dining room of Lossie House. Every now and then he leaned forward between his aunt and Florimel and spoke to the latter. To Malcolm's eyes she seemed to listen with some haughtiness. Now and then she cast him an indifferent glance. Malcolm was pleased. Lord Liftore had apparently not swept her off her feet—not yet, anyway. But he was annoyed to see once or twice a look between them that indicated some sort of intimacy at least.

During the last scene of the play as Malcolm turned to glance at his sister and her companions, his eyes fell on a face near him in the pit which was apparently absorbed in someone in the same direction. It was that of a young man a few years older than himself—a large man with prominent eyebrows and dark penetrating eyes. To Malcolm it seemed that his gaze was also on his sister, but as they were a long way from the boxes he could not be certain. Once he thought he saw her look at him. But of that also he could not tell positively.

The moment the play was over Malcolm rose and made his way through the crowd to the foot of the stairs which Florimel and her companions had gone up earlier. He had stood but a little while when he saw in front of him the same man he had observed in the pit, apparently waiting also. After some time his sister, Lady Bellair, and Liftore came slowly down the stairs in the descending crowd. Her eyes seemed searching the multitude that filled the lobby. Presently an imperceptible glance of recognition passed between the two of them and the young man placed himself so that she would have to pass next to him in the crowd. Malcolm thought they had grasped hands for a second as she passed. She turned her head slightly and seemed to put to him a question, with her lips only. He replied in the same manner. But not a feature had moved nor a word been spoken. Neither of her companions had seen the young man, and he remained where he was until they had left the house. Malcolm stood also, much inclined to follow him. But when his attention was diverted in another direction for a moment, the man had disappeared.

He therefore walked home, but before he had reached his lodging he had resolved on making trial of a plan which had previously occurred to him but which till now had seemed too risky. His plan was to watch the

house until he saw some entertainment going on, then present himself as if
he had but just arrived from her ladyship's country seat. At such a time no
one would acquaint her with his appearance and he would, as if it were but
a matter of course, at once take his share in waiting on the guests. By this
means he might perhaps get her a little accustomed to his presence before
she could be at leisure to challenge it.

The next day Malcolm spent with Blue Peter, sight-seeing mostly and in
learning their way about London. Peter was already anxious to get out of
the city but agreed to stay at least until Malcolm's way became clear. As
soon as Peter was gone to return to the boat late in the afternoon, Malcolm
dressed himself in his kilt which he had brought with him to London and,
when it was dusk, took his bagpipes under his arm and set out for Portland
Place. Since the highland dress was that in which Florimel had been most
used to seeing him recently, he felt it might prove his best opportunity to
gain entrance into the house. He did not know what purpose the pipes
might serve but wanted to be ready for any opportunity. He had hopes for a
speedy success of his plan since he fancied he had read on his sister's lips,
in the silent communication that passed between her and her friend in the
crowd, the words *come* and *tomorrow*. It might have been his imagination,
yet it was something.

Up and down the street he walked without seeing a sign of life about the
house. But at length the hall light was lit. Then the door opened and a servant rolled out a carpet over the wide pavement which the snow had left
wet and miry. The first carriage arrived a few minutes later and was followed
by others. It proved to be but a modest dinner party and after some time
had elapsed and no more carriages appeared since the last, Malcolm
judged the dinner must now be in full swing and therefore rang the bell of
the front door.

It was opened by a huge footman. Malcolm would have stepped in at
once and told his tale at his leisure, but the servant, who had never seen
the dress Malcolm wore except on street beggars, quickly closed the door.
Before it reached the post, however, it found Malcolm's foot barring its way.

"Go along, Scotchy! You're not wanted here," said the man pushing the
door hard. "Police is just round the corner!"

One of the weaknesses Malcolm owed his Celtic blood was an utter impatience of rudeness. "Open the door and let me in," he said.

"What's your business?" asked the man on whom Malcolm's fierce tone
had its effect.

"My business is with Lady Lossie," said Malcolm.

"You can't see her; she's at dinner."

"Let me in and I'll wait. I've come from Lossie House."

"Take away your foot and I'll go see," said the man.

"No, you open the door," returned Malcolm.

The man's answer was an attempt to kick his foot out of the doorway. If
he were to let in a tramp, what would the butler say?

But thereupon Malcolm set his port-vent to his mouth, rapidly filled his
bag, and then sent from the instrument such a shriek that involuntarily his

adversary pressed both hands to his ears. With a sudden application of his knee, Malcom sent the door wide and entered the hall with his pipes in full cry, but only for a moment. For down the stairs bounded Demon, Florimel's huge Irish staghound, and springing on Malcolm put and instant end to his music. The footman laughed, expecting to see him torn to pieces. But when he saw instead the fierce animal, a foot on each of Malcolm's shoulders licking his face with a long tongue, he began to doubt.

"The dog knows you," he said sulkily.

"So shall you before long," returned Malcolm. "Was it my fault I made the mistake of looking for civility from you?"

"I'll go and fetch Wallis," said the man and, closing the door, left the hall.

Now this Wallis had been a fellow servant of Malcolm's at Lossie House, but he did not know that he had gone with Lady Bellair when she took Florimel away; almost everyone had left at the same time. He was now glad indeed to learn there was one amongst the servants who knew him.

Wallis presently made his appearance, with a dish in his hands, on his way to the dining room, from which came the confused noises of the feast.

"You'll be come to wait on Lady Lossie," he said. "I haven't a moment to speak to you now, for we're serving dinner, and there's a party."

"Never mind me. Give me that dish. I'll take it in; you can go for another," said Malcolm, laying his pipes in a safe spot.

"You can't go into the dining room like that!" said Wallis.

"This is how I waited on my lord," returned Malcolm, "and this is how I'll wait on my lady."

Wallis hesitated. But there was something about the fisher-fellow that was too much for him. As he spoke, Malcolm took the dish from his hands and with it walked into the dining room.

Once there, one reconnoitring glance was sufficient. The butler was at the sideboard opening a champagne bottle. He had his hand on the cork as Malcolm walked up to him.

"I'm Lady Lossie's man from Lossie House. I'll help you to wait," said Malcolm.

To the eyes of the butler he looked a savage. But there he was in the room, with a dish in his hands and speaking intelligibly. He peeped into Malcolm's dish. "Take it round, then," he said.

So Malcolm settled into the business of the hour.

It was some time after he knew where she was before he ventured to look at his sister—he would have her already familiarized with his presence before their eyes met. That crisis did not arrive during dinner.

Lord Liftore was one of the company, and so—to Malcolm's pleasure, for he felt in him an ally against the earl—was Florimel's mysterious friend.

Scarcely had the ladies gone to the drawing room when Florimel's maid, who knew Malcolm, came in quest of him. Lady Lossie desired to see him.

"What is the meaning of this, MacPhail?" she said, when he entered the room where she sat alone. "I did not send for you. Indeed, I thought you had been dismissed with the rest of the servants."

How differently she spoke! And she used to call him Malcolm! The girl

Florimel was gone. She had forgotten the half friendship that had been between them, that much was certain. And it appeared to Malcolm she had even forgotten his service that had once been such a part of her daily life.

But Florimel had not so entirely forgotten the past as Malcolm thought—not so entirely at least, but that his appearance, and certain difficulties in which she had begun to find herself, brought something of it again to her mind.

"I thought," said Malcolm, "your ladyship might not choose to part with an old servant at the will of a factor and so took upon me to appeal to your ladyship to decide the question."

"But how is that? Did you not return to your fishing when the household was broken up?"

"No, my lady. Mr. Crathie kept me to help Stoat and do odd jobs about the place."

"And now he wants to discharge you?"

Then Malcolm told her the whole story, in which he gave such a description of Kelpie that Florimel expressed a strong wish to see her, for she was almost passionately fond of horses.

"You may soon do that, my lady," said Malcolm. "Mr. Soutar is not of the same mind as Mr. Crathie and is going to send her here. It will be but the cost of the passage from Aberdeen, and she will fetch a better price here if your ladyship should revolve to part with her. She won't fetch a third of her value anywhere, though, on account of her bad temper and ugly tricks."

"But as to yourself, MacPhail, what are you going to do?" said Florimel. "I don't like to have to part with you, but if I keep you I don't know what to do with you. No doubt you could serve in the house, but that is not at all suitable to your education and previous life."

"If your ladyship should wish to keep Kelpie, you will have to keep me too, for she will let no one else near her."

"And pray tell me what use, then, can I make of such an animal?"

"Your ladyship, I should imagine, will want a groom to attend you when you are out on horseback, and the groom will need a horse. So here we are, Kelpie and me!" answered Malcolm.

Florimel laughed. "I see," she said. "You contrive I shall have a horse nobody can manage but yourself." She rather liked the idea of a groom mounted on such a fine animal and had too much well-justified faith in Malcolm to anticipate dangerous results.

"My lady," said Malcolm, appealing to her knowledge of his character for his last means of persuasion, "my lady, did I ever tell you a lie?"

"Certainly not, Malcolm, so far as I know."

"Then," continued Malcolm, "I'll tell your ladyship something that you may find hard to believe, and yet is as true as that I loved your ladyship's father. Your ladyship knows he had a kindness for me?"

"I do know it," answered Florimel, gently, moved by the tone of Malcolm's voice and expression.

"Then I make bold to tell your ladyship that on his deathbed, your father desired me to do my best for you—took my word that I would be your lady-ship's true servant."

"Is it so, indeed, Malcolm?" returned Florimel with a serious wonder in her gaze. She had loved her father, and it sounded in her ears almost like a message from the tomb.

"It's as true as I stand here, my lady," said Malcolm.

Florimel was silent for a moment. Then she said, "How is it that only now you come to tell me?"

"Your father never desired me to tell you, my lady; only he never imag-ined you would want to part with me, I suppose. But when you did not care to keep me and never said a word to me when you went away, I could not tell how to do as I had promised him. It wasn't that one hour I forgot his wish, but that I feared to presume; for if I should displease your ladyship, my chance was gone. So I kept about Lossie House as long as I could, hop-ing to see my way to some plan or another. But when at length Mr. Crathie turned me away, what was I to do but come to your ladyship? And if your ladyship will let things be as before—in the way of service, I mean—I can't doubt, my lady, but that it'll be pleasant in the sight of your father whenever he may come to know of it."

Florimel gave a strange, half-startled look. Hardly more than once since her father's funeral had she heard him alluded to, and now this fisher-lad spoke of him as if he were still at Lossie House.

Malcolm understood the look. "I know what you're thinking, my lady. But I can't help it. To love anything is to know it immortal. He's living to me, my lady. And why not? Didn't he turn his face to the light before he died? And Him that rose from the dead said that whoever believed in Him should never die."

Florimel continued a moment looking at him fixedly in the face. She remembered how strange he had always been, yet at the same time she caught the glimmering idea that in this young man's simplicity was an in-corruptible treasure.

Malcolm seldom made the mistake of stamping down on any seeds of truth which might have been planted. He knew when to say no more, and for a time neither spoke. For all the coolness of her upper crust, Lady Florimel's heart was warmed with the possession of such a strong, devoted, disinterested squire.

"I wish you to understand," she said at length, "that I am not at present mistress of this house, although it belongs to me. I am but the guest of Lady Bellair, who has rented it of my guardians. I cannot, therefore, arrange for you to be here. But you can find accommodations in the neighborhood and come for me at one o'clock every day for orders. Let me know when your mare arrives; I shall not want you till then. You will find room for her in the stables. You had better consult the butler about your groom's livery."

Malcolm was astonished at the womanly sufficiency with which she gave orders, yet he left her with the gladness of one whose righteous desire had been fulfilled. He spoke with the butler and went home to his lodging. There he sat down and meditated.

A yearning pity arose in his heart. He feared his sister's stately composure was built mainly on her imagined position in society rather than her character. Would it be cruel to destroy that false foundation? At present, however, he need not attempt to answer the question. Familiarity with her surroundings, even as a groom, would probably reveal much. Meantime, it was enough that he would now be so near her that no important change could take place without his knowledge and without his being able to interfere if necessary.

4

· · · · · · · · · · · · · · · · · · · ·

The Painter

The next day Wallis came to see Malcolm and take him to the tailor's. They talked about the guests of the previous evening.

"There's a great change in Lord Meikleham," said Malcolm.

"There is that," said Wallis. "I consider him much improved. But he's succeeded to the title. He's the earl now, and Lord Liftore. And a big, strong man he's become."

"Is there no news of his marriage?" asked Malcolm. "They say he has great property."

"But she's just a lassie yet," said Wallis, "though she's changed quite as much as he."

"Who are you speaking of?" asked Malcolm, anxious to hear the talk of the household on the matter.

"Why, Lady Lossie, of course. Anybody with half an eye can see as much as that."

"It's settled, then?"

"That would be hard to say. Her ladyship is too much like her father. No one can tell what may be in her mind to do the next minute. But he's ever hovering about her. And I think my lady, too, has set her mind on it. And I can't see how she could do better. I can see no possible objection to the match."

"We used to think he drank too much," suggested Malcolm. "And besides, he's not worthy of her."

"Well, I confess, his family won't compare with hers. There's a grandfather in it somewhere that was a banker or brewer or soap boiler, or something of the sort, and she and her people have been earls and marquises ever since they walked arm-in-arm out of the ark. But that doesn't seem to matter as much as it used to. Mrs. Tredger, that's our ladyship's maid—only this is secret—says it's all settled. She knows it for certain fact, only there's nothing to be said about it yet. She's so young, you know."

"Who was that man that sat nearly opposite my lady, on the other side of the table?" asked Malcolm.

"I know who you mean. Didn't look like the rest of them, did he? Odd-and-end sort of people, like he is, never do. He's some fellow that's painting Lady Lossie's portrait. Why he should be asked to dinner because of that, I don't know. But London's a strange place! There's no such thing as respect of persons here. I declare to you, Malcolm MacPhail, it makes me quite uncomfortable at times to think who I may have been waiting on without knowing it. That painter-fellow—Lenorme they call him—makes me down-right angry. To see him stare at Lady Lossie as he does!"

"A painter must want to get a right good hold of the face he's got to paint," said Malcolm. "Is he here often?"

"He's been here five or six times already," answered Wallis. "I'm sure there's been time to finish the picture by now! And if she's been once in his studio, she's been twenty times—to give him sittings, as they call it. He's making a pretty penny of it, I'll be bound."

Wallis liked the sound of his own voice, and a great deal more talk of similar character followed before they got back from the tailor's. Malcolm was tired enough of him by the time he set out for a walk with Blue Peter, whom he found waiting at his lodgings.

That night, Florimel's thoughts were full. Already life was not what it had been to her, and the feeling of a difference is often what sets one thinking. While her father lived she had been supplied with a more than sufficient sense of well-being. Since his death, too, there had been times when she fancied an enlargement of life in the sense of freedom and power which came with the consciousness of being a great lady with an ancient title. But she had soon found she had less the feeling of freedom within as before. She was very lonely, too. Lady Bellair had always been kind, but there was nothing about her to make a home for the girl's heart. She felt in her no superiority, and for a spiritual home that is essential. She was not one in whom she could place genuine confidence. The innocent nature of the girl had begun to recoil from what she saw in the woman of the world. And yet she had in herself worldliness enough to render her freely susceptible of her influences.

On the morning after she had taken Malcolm into her services, Florimel awoke between three and four and lay awake, weary yet sleepless. It was not, however, the general sense of unfitness in the conditions of her life that kept her mind occupied and thus awake. Nor was it dissatisfaction with Lady Bellair or the loneliness in the sterile waste of fashionable life or its weariness with the same shows and people and parties. But instead her thoughts rested on the young painter Malcolm had twice seen near her.

Some few weeks ago she had accompanied a friend to his study for which she was sitting for her portrait. The moment she entered, the appearance of the man and his surroundings laid hold of her imagination. Although on the verge of popularity, he was young, not more than twenty-five. His movements were graceful, his address manly, and he displayed confident modesty and unobtrusive humility. Pictures stood on easels, leaned against chairbacks, glowed from the wall—each contributing to the atmosphere of the place. Lenorme was seated, not at his easel, but at a piano half hidden in a corner. They had walked straight in with no announcement and thus came upon him in the midst of a bar of a song in a fine tenor voice. He stopped immediately and came to meet them from the farther end of the study. He shook hands with Florimel's friend and turned with a bow to her. As their eyes met the blood rose to Florimel's face.

While Mrs. Barnardiston sat, Florimel flitted about the room like a butterfly, looking at one thing after another and asking now the most ignorant, now the most penetrating question—disturbing the work, but sweetening the temper of the painter. For the girl had bewitched him at first sight. Sooner than usual he professed himself content with the sitting and then proceeded to show the ladies some of his sketches and pictures. As he did so, Florimel happened to ask to see one standing in disgrace with its front to the wall. He put it, half reluctantly, on an easel and disclosed what was to be the painting of the goddess of nature being gazed upon enraptured by a youth below with outstretched arms. But on the great pedestal where should have sat the goddess there was no form visible. Florimel asked why he had left it so long unfinished, for the dust was thick on the back of the canvas.

"Because I have never seen the face or figure," the painter answered, "that claimed the position."

As he spoke his eyes seemed to Florimel to lighten strangely, and then as if by common consent they turned away and looked at something else. Presently Mrs. Barnardiston, who could sing a little and cared more for sound than form or color, began to glance over some music on the piano, curious to find what the young man had been singing, whereupon Lenorme said to Florimel hurriedly, almost in a whisper with a sort of hesitating assurance, "If *you* would give me a sitting or two—I know I am presumptuous— but if you would, I . . . I would have the picture finished in a week."

"I will," said Florimel, flushing and looking up in his face. "It would have been selfish," she said to herself as they drove away, "to refuse him."

The first interview followed and all the interviews that followed now passed through her mind as she lay awake in the darkness preceding the dawn. One of the feelings now of concern to her was the sense of lowered dignity she felt because of the relation in which she stood to the painter. Her rank had already grown to seem to her so identified with herself that she was hardly capable of the analysis that should show it distinct from her being. Yet even though in the circle in which she now moved she repeatedly heard, on all sides, professions, arts and trades alluded to with implied contempt, she nevertheless never entered the painter's study but with trembling heart, uncertain foot, and fluttering breath. It was at once an enchanted paradise and a forbidden garden. Though the woman in her was drawn to Lenorme, the marchioness in her could not overcome his lowly station. She was excited to be with him, yet afraid of being seen at the same time. And by this time things had gone far enough between them to add greatly to Florimel's inward strife.

She knew Lady Bellair was set upon her marriage with her nephew. Now she recoiled from the idea of marriage and dismissed it into the indefinite future. She had no special desire to please Lady Bellair from the point of gratitude, for she was perfectly aware that the relation between them was not without its advantage to that lady's position. Neither could she persuade herself that Lord Liftore was at all the sort of man she could become genuinely proud of as a husband. Yet, she felt destined to be his wife. On the other hand, she had no great dislike of him. He was handsome, well-informed, capable—a gentleman, she thought, of good regard in the circles in which they moved. To be sure, he was her inferior in rank, and she would rather have married a duke. But she was by no means indifferent to the advantages of having a husband with money enough to restore the somewhat tarnished prestige of her family to its former brilliancy. She had never said a word to encourage the scheming of Lady Bellair; neither had she ever said a word to discourage her hopes or give her ground for doubt. Hence, Lady Bellair had naturally come to regard the two as nearly engaged. But Florimel's aversion to the idea of marriage grew as did her horror at the thought of the slightest whisper of what was between her and Lenorme.

There were times when she asked herself whether she had been altogether above reproach in the encouragement she was giving the painter. She never once had visited him without a companion, though that companion was sometimes only her maid; but her real object was covered by the pretext of sitting for a portrait, which Lady Bellair pleased herself to imagine would one day be presented to Lord Liftore. But she could not fail to occasionally doubt whether the visits she paid and the liberties she allowed him could be justified on any ground other than that she was prepared to give him all and become his wife. All, however, she was not prepared to give him.

With such causes for uneasiness in her young heart and brain, it is no wonder that to such an unexperienced and troubled heart the assurance of one absolutely devoted friend should come with healing and hope. Even if that friend should be but a groom altogether incapable of understanding her position. A clumsy, ridiculous fellow, she said to herself, from whom she could never disassociate the smell of fish, and who could not be prevented from uttering unpalatable truths at uncomfortable moments, yet whose thoughts were as chivalrous as his person was powerful. She actually felt stronger and safer to know he was near and at her beck and call.

5

The Factor

*M*r. Crathie, seeing nothing more of Malcolm, believed himself at last well rid of him; but it was days before his wrath ceased to flame, and then it went on smoldering. Nothing occurred to take him to the Seaton, and no business brought any of the fisher-people to his office during that time. Hence, for some time he heard nothing of the mode of Malcolm's departure. When at length, in the course of ordinary talk the news reached him that Malcolm had taken the yacht with him, he was enraged beyond measure at the impudence of the theft, as he called it, and rushed to the Seaton in a fury. He had this consolation, however: the man who accused him of dishonesty and hypocrisy had proved but a thief.

He found the boathouse indeed empty and went storming from cottage to cottage, but came upon no one from whom his anger could draw nourishment. At length he reached the Partan's and commenced abusing him as an aider and abettor of the felony. But Meg Partan was at home also, as Mr. Crathie soon learned to his cost. She returned his tongue-lashing as only she was capable of.

"Hold your tongue, woman," said the factor. "I have nothing to say to you."

"Ah, it's a pity you wasn't foreordained to be marquis yourself! It must be a sore vex to you that you're nothing but a lowly factor!"

"If you don't mind your manners, Mistress Findlay," said Mr. Crathie in glowing indignation, "perhaps you'll find that the factor is as much as the marquis when he's all there is for one."

"Lord save us, listen to the man!" cried the Partaness. "Who would have thought it of him? His father, honest man, would never have spoken like that to Meg Partan, but then he was an honest man."

"I've a great mind to take out a warrant against you, John Findlay," resumed the factor, doing the best his wrath would allow to ignore the outbursts from the wife present, "for your part in stealing the marchioness of Lossie's pleasure boat. And as for you, Mistress Findlay, I would have you remember that this house—as far, at least, as you are concerned—is mine, although I am but the factor and not the marquis; and if you don't keep that unruly tongue of yours a little quieter in your head, I'll turn you right out on the street. For there's not a house in all the Seaton that belongs to another than her ladyship. And I run her affairs around here now!"

"Indeed, Mr. Crathie," returned Meg Partan, a little sobered by the threat, "you would have more sense than to run the risk of an uprising of the fisher-folk. They would hardly stand to see me and my man mistreated like that, not to say that her ladyship herself would never allow any of her own folk to be turned out for doing nothing wrong!"

"Her ladyship would give herself small concern over it," returned the factor. "And as for the town, the folk would like the quiet too much to lament the loss of you!"

"The devil's in the man!" cried Meg in high scorn.

"You see, sir," interposed the mild Partan, "we didn't know there was anything out of the ordinary in it. If we had but known that he was out of your good graces—"

"Hold your tongue before you lie, man," interrupted his wife. "You know well enough that you would have done whatever Malcolm MacPhail asked of you for any factor in Scotland!"

"You *must* have known," said the factor, apparently heedless of the last outbreak of evil temper and laying a cunning trap for the information he sorely wanted, "else why was it that not a soul went with him? He could hardly manage the boat alone."

"What put such a thing into your head?" rejoined Meg, defiant of the hints her husband sought to convey to her. "There's many that would have been only too ready to go; only who should have gone but him that went with him and his lordship from the first?"

"And who was that?" asked Mr. Crathie.

"Who but Blue Peter!" answered Meg.

"Hmm!" said the factor in a tone that, for almost the first time in her life, made the woman regret that she had spoken, and therewith he rose and left the cottage.

"Oh, mother!" cried Lizza, appearing from the back of the cottage. "You've brought ruin on the earth. He'll have Peter and Annie out of their house by midsummer now!"

"I *dare* him!" cried her mother in the impotence and self-despite of a mortifying blunder. "I'll raise the town upon him!"

The factor ran half the way home, flung himself trembling in anger on his horse, vouchsafing his anxious wife scarce any answer to her inquiries and galloped to Duff Harbor to Mr. Soutar. I will not occupy my tale with their interview. Suffice it to say that the lawyer succeeded at last in convincing the demented factor that it would be prudent to delay measures for the recovery of the yacht and the arrest and punishment of its abductors until he knew what Lady Lossie would say to the affair. She had always had a liking for the lad, Mr. Soutar said, and he would not be in the least surprised to hear that Malcolm had gone straight to her ladyship and put himself under her protection. No doubt by this time the boat was at its owner's disposal; it would be just like the fellow. He always went the nearest road anywhere, and to prosecute him for a thief would, in any case, but bring down the ridicule of the whole coast upon the factor and breed him endless annoyance in the getting of his rents, especially amongst the fishermen. The result was that Mr. Crathie went home—not indeed a humbler or wiser man than he had gone, but a thwarted man and therefore the more dangerous in the channels left open to the outrush of his angry power.

The result of his submerged anger made itself known to Blue Peter's wife within the week: they had till midsummer to leave the premises. Annie asked that, with her husband away, couldn't this wait until he could discuss it with the factor personally? Mr. Crathie replied coolly, however, that it was his very absence which made him guilty in the matter, and he hoped, therefore, that Peter would be home soon to make their arrangements for new quarters. Annie replied that she had no way of knowing when he would be home but expected him within a week or two. And with that the factor bid her good-day.

6

....

The Suitor

The chief cause of Malcolm's anxiety had been, and still was, Lord Liftore. Knowing what he knew of his character, Malcolm's whole nature revolted against the thought of him marrying his sister. At Lossie he had made himself agreeable to her, and now, if not actually living in the same house, he was there at all hours of the day.

It took nothing from his anxiety to see that his lordship was even more fine looking than before. His admiration of Florimel had been growing as well, and if he had said nothing definite, it was only because his aunt represented the importunity declaring of himself just yet; she was too young. Still, all the time she had been under his aunt's care, he had had abundant opportunity for paying her all sorts of attention and compliments and for recommending himself, and he had made use of the privilege. For one thing, assured that he looked well in the saddle, he had constantly encouraged Florimel's love of riding and desire to become a thorough horsewoman, and they had ridden a good deal together.

For a long time Lady Bellair had had her mind set on a match between the daughter of her old friend, the marquis of Lossie, and her nephew. And it was with this in view that, when invited to Lossie House, she had begged leave to bring Lord Meikleham with her. The young man was from the first sufficiently taken with the beautiful girl to satisfy his aunt and would, even then, have shown greater attention to her had he not met Lizza Findlay and found her more than pleasing. He had not purposed to do her wrong from the beginning. But even when he had seen plainly to what their mutual attraction was tending, he had given himself no trouble to resist it. And through the whole unhappy affair he had not had one small struggle with himself for the girl's sake. To himself he was all in all. What was the shame and humiliation of the girl herself compared to the honor of having been

shone upon for a brief period by his honorable countenance? Since he left
her at last with many promises, not one of which he had had any intention
of fulfilling, he had never taken the least further notice of her either by gift
or letter. He had taken care also that it should not be in her power to write
to him, and now he did not even know that he was a father.

Lizza was a good girl and had promised to keep the matter secret until
she heard from him, whatever might be the consequences, and surely there
was fascination enough in the holding of a secret with such as he to enable
her to keep her promise. He would requite her when he was lord of Lossie.
Meantime, although it was even now in his power to make rich amends, he
would prudently leave things as they were and not run the risk that must lie
in opening communications.

And so the young earl held his head high, looked as innocent as may be
desirable for a gentleman and had many a fair, clean hand laid in his, while
Lizza flitted about half an alien amongst her own, with his child wound in
her old shawl of Lossie tartan—wandering frequently at dusk over the dunes
with the wind blowing keen upon her from the regions of eternal ice. There
were many who made Lizza keenly aware of her disgrace, but there was one
man who showed her even greater kindness than before. That man, strange
to say, was the factor. With all his faults he had some chivalry, and he
showed it to the fisher-girl. This was all the more remarkable in that since
Malcolm's departure he had grown all the more bitter against his friends and
against the fisher-folk in general. It was sore proof to Mr. Crathie that his
discharged servant was in favor with the marchioness when the order came
from Mr. Soutar to send Kelpie to London. She had written to him herself
for her own horse; now she sent for this brute through her lawyer. It was
plain Malcolm had been speaking against him.

Since Malcolm's departure the factor had twice been on the point of
poisoning the mare. It was with difficulty he found two men to take her to
Aberdeen. But it had been done, and Malcolm was waiting for her at the
wharf in the gray of a gurly dawn when at length the smack arrived in London. They had had a rough passage and the mare was considerably subdued by sickness. But after pacing for a little while in relative quietness, the
evil spirit in her began to awake, and before he reached the mews Malcolm
was very near wishing he had never seen her. But when he led her into the
stable, he was encouraged to find that she had not forgotten Florimel's horse
and they greeted each other with an affectionate neigh. This, along with all
the feed she could devour, quieted her considerably.

Before noon Lord Liftore came round to the mews: his riding horses
were there. Malcolm was not at the moment in the stable.

"What animal is that?" he asked of his own groom, catching sight of
Kelpie in her loose box.

"One just in from Scotland for Lady Lossie, my lord," answered the man.

"Lead her out and let me see her."

"She's not in a good temper, my lord, the groom that brought her says.
He told me not to go near her till she's got used to the sight of me."

"Oh, you are afraid, are you?" said Liftore, whose breeding had not taught him courtesy to his inferiors.

At such a challenge, the man proceeded to walk into her box. He was careful, but it was in vain. In a moment she had wheeled, jammed him against the wall, and taken his shoulder in her teeth. He gave a yell of pain. His lordship caught up a stable broom and attacked the mare with it over the door but she still kept hold of her man. Luckily Malcolm was not far off and, hearing the noise, rushed in just in time to save the groom's life. He jumped the partition and seized the mare with a mighty grasp and soon compelled her to open her mouth. The groom staggered and just managed to open the door before he fell on the stones. Lord Liftore called for help and they carried him into the saddle room while one ran for a doctor.

Meantime Malcolm was putting a muzzle on Kelpie, and while he was thus occupied his lordship came from the saddle room and approached the box. "Who are you?" he asked. "I think I've seen you before."

"I was servant to the late marquis of Lossie, my lord, and am now groom to her ladyship."

"What a fury you've brought here. She'll never do for London!"

"I told the man not to go near her, my lord."

"What's the use of her if no one can go near her?"

"I can, my lord. She'll do for me to ride after my lady well enough. If only I had room to exercise her a bit."

"Take her into the park early in the morning and gallop her round. Only mind she doesn't break your neck. What can have made Lady Lossie send for such a creature?"

Malcolm held his peace.

"I'll try her myself some morning," his lordship went on, who thought himself a better horseman than he was.

"I wouldn't advise that, my lord."

"Who the devil asked your advice?"

"Ten to one she'd kill you, my lord."

"That's for me to watch out for then," said Liftore, noticeably perturbed at Malcolm's insolence, and went into the house.

As soon as Malcom had finished with Kelpie, he went to tell his mistress of her arrival. She told him to bring the mare around in half an hour. He went back, took off her muzzle, fed her, and while she ate her corn put on the spurs he had prepared expressly for use with her. Then he saddled her and rode her around.

Having had her fit of temper she was to all appearance going to be fairly good for the rest of the day. And she looked splendid! She was a large mare, an animal most men would have been pleased to possess and proud to ride. Florimel came to the door to see her, accompanied by Liftore, and was so delighted with the very sight of her that she sent at once to the stable for her own horse that she might ride out attended by Malcolm. His lordship also ordered his horse.

They went straight to the park for a little gallop, and Kelpie was behaving very well.

"What did you have two such savages, horse and groom, brought here from Scotland for, Florimel?" asked his lordship as they cantered gently along.

Florimel looked back and cast an admiring glance on the two. "Do you know I am rather proud of them," she said.

"He's a clumsy fellow, the groom; and, for the mare, she's downright wicked," said Liftore.

"At least neither is a hypocrite," returned Florimel, with Malcolm's account of his quarrel with the factor in her mind. "The mare is just as wicked as she looks, and the man is good. That man you call a savage, my lord, never told a lie in his life."

"I know what you mean," he said. "You don't believe my professions." As he spoke he edged his horse close up to hers. "But," he went on, "if I know that I speak the truth when I swear that I love—confound the fellow! What's he about now with his horse-devil?"

For at that moment his lordship's horse, a high-spirited but timid animal, had sprung away from the side of Florimel's, and as he did, suddenly there stood Kelpie on her hind legs pawing the air to keep him from bolting. Florimel, whose old confidence in Malcolm was now more than revived, was laughing merrily at the discomfiture of his lordship's attempt at love-making. Her behavior and his own frustration put him in such a rage that, wheeling quickly around, he struck Kelpie with his whip across the haunches. She plunged and kicked violently, came within an inch of breaking his horse's leg, and flew across the rail into the park. Nothing could have suited Malcolm better. He did not punish her as he would have done had she been to blame but took her a great round at racing speed, while his mistress and companion looked on. Finally, he hopped her over the rail again and brought her up, dripping and foaming, to his mistress. Florimel's eyes were flashing and Liftore looked still angry. "Don't do that again, my lord," said Malcolm. "You're not my master, and if you were, you would have no right to break my neck."

"No fear of that. That's not how your neck will be broken, my man," said his lordship with an attempted laugh; for, though he was all the angrier than he was ashamed of what he had done, he dared not further wrong the servant before his mistress.

A policeman came up and laid his hand on Kelpie's bridle.

"Take care what you're about," said Malcolm; "the mare's not safe. There's my mistress, the marchioness of Lossie."

The man saw an ugly look in Kelpie's eye, withdrew his hand, and turned to Florimel.

"My groom is not to blame," she said. "Lord Liftore struck his mare."

The man gave a look at Liftore, seemed to take his likeness, touched his hat, and withdrew.

"You'd better ride the jade home," said Liftore.

Malcolm only looked at his mistress. She moved on and he followed.

Malcolm was not so innocent in the affair as he had seemed. The expression on Liftore's face as he drew nearer to Florimel was to him so hateful that he interfered in a very literal fashion. Kelpie had been doing no more than he made her until the earl struck her.

"Let us ride to Richmond tomorrow," said Florimel, "and have a good gallop in the park. Did you ever see a finer sight than that animal on the grass?"

"The fellow's too heavy for her," said Liftore. "I should very much like to try her myself."

Florimel pulled up and turned to Malcolm. "MacPhail," she said, "have that mare of yours ready whenever Lord Liftore chooses to ride her."

"I beg your pardon, my lady," returned Malcolm, "but would your ladyship make a condition that he not mount her anywhere on the stones?"

"By Jove!" said Liftore scornfully, "you fancy yourself the only man that can ride!"

"It's nothing to me, my lord, if you break your neck, but I am bound to tell you I do not think your lordship will sit my mare. Stoat can't, and I can only because I know her as well as my own palm."

The young earl made no answer and they rode on, Malcolm nearer than his lordship liked.

"I can't think, Florimel," he said, "why you should want that fellow about you again. He is not only awkward, but insolent as well."

"I should call it straightforward," returned Florimel.

"My dear Lady Lossie! See how close he is riding to us now."

"He is anxious, I daresay, as to your lordship's behavior. He is like some dogs that are a little too careful of their mistresses—touchy as to how they are addressed: not a bad fault in a dog—or groom either. He saved my life once, and he was a great favorite with my father. I won't hear anything against him."

"But for your own sake, just consider. What will people say if you show any preference for a man like that?" said Liftore, who had already become jealous of the man who he feared could ride better than himself.

"My lord!" exclaimed Florimel, with a mingling of surprise and indignation in her voice and, suddenly quickening her pace, dropped him behind.

Malcolm was after her so instantly that it brought him abreast of Liftore. "Keep your own place," said his lordship with stern rebuke.

"I keep pace to my mistress," returned Malcolm.

Liftore looked at him as if he would strike him. But he thought better of it, apparently, and rode after Florimel.

———

By the time Malcolm had put Kelpie up after the ride, he had to hurry to the wharf. Since he was again in Florimel's service, and it appeared his stay in London would be a lengthy one, Blue Peter had made preparations to return home on the same smack which had brought Kelpie from Aberdeen and was scheduled to depart that same afternoon. On the way, Malcolm reflected on what had just passed and was not altogether pleased with himself. He had nearly lost his temper with Liftore. And to attract attention to himself was almost to insure frustration to his plan.

When he reached the wharf, he found they had nearly got her freight on board the smack. Blue Peter stood on the deck.

"I hardly know you in those riding clothes," he said.

"Nobody in London would look twice at me now," returned Malcolm. "But you remember how we were stared at when we first came!"

That same moment came the command for all but passengers to go ashore. The men grasped hands, looked each other in the eyes, and parted—Blue Peter down the river and to Scaurnose and Annie, and Malcolm to the yacht lying still in the Upper Pool. He saw it taken properly in charge and arranged for having it towed up the river and anchored in the Chelsea Reach.

When Malcolm at length reached his lodging, he found there a letter from Miss Horn containing information where the schoolmaster was to be found in the London wilderness. It was now getting rather late, and the dusk of a spring night had begun to gather; but little more than the breadth of the Regent's Park lay between him and his only friend in London, and he set out immediately for Camden Town.

The relation between him and his late schoolmaster was indeed of the strongest and closest. Long before Malcolm was born and ever since had Alexander Graham loved Malcolm's mother, but not until within the last few months had he learned that Malcolm was the son of Griselda Campbell. The discovery was to the schoolmaster like the bursting out of a known flower on an unknown plant. He knew then, not why he had loved the boy—for he loved every one of his pupils—but why he had loved him with such a peculiar affection.

An occasional preacher in his younger days, he had accepted the vacant position of schoolmaster at Portlossie where he made the acquaintance of Griselda Campbell who was governess to Lady Annabel, the only child of the late marquis' elder brother, at that time himself marquis. A love for her began to consume him, though it was hopeless from the first. Silence was the sole armor of his privilege. So long as he was silent he might love on, nor be grudged the bliss of his visions. And Miss Campbell thought of him more kindly than he knew. But before long the late marquis fell in love with her and persuaded her to a secret marriage. She became Malcolm's mother at a time when her husband was away. But the marquis of the time, jealous for the succession of his daughter and fearing his brother might yet make public his marriage, contrived, with the assistance of the midwife, to remove the infant and persuade the mother that he was dead and also to persuade his brother of the death of both mother and child. After this time, imagining herself willfully deserted by her husband, yet determined to endure shame rather than break the promise of secrecy she had given him, the poor young woman accepted the hospitality of her distant relative, Miss Horn, and continued with her till she died. Though Mr. Graham lived for twenty years in friendly relations with Miss Horn and Miss Campbell, neither suspected his innermost feelings, and it was not until Miss Campbell's death that he came to know the strange fact that the object of his calm, unalterable devotion had been a wife all those years and the mother of his favorite pupil. About the same time he was dismissed from the school on the charge of heretical teaching, founded on certain religious conversations he had had with some of the fisher-people who sought his advice, and thereupon he had left the place and gone to London. He hoped there to earn a meager income through tutoring and with the assistance of what occasional preaching opportunities might come his way.

It was a lovely evening. There had been rain in the afternoon, but before the sun had set it had cleared up and the ethereal, sweet scents of buds and grass and ever-pure earth moistened with the waters of heaven was all about Malcolm as he walked through the park.

After not a few inquires, he found himself at a stationer's shop, a poor little place, and learned that Mr. Graham lodged over it and was then at home. He was shown up into a shabby room with an iron bedstead, a chest of drawers, a table, a few bookshelves in a recess over the washstand, and two chairs. On one of these, by the side of a small fire in a neglected grate, sat the schoolmaster reading his Plato.

He looked up as the door opened and, notwithstanding his strange dress, recognized at once his friend and pupil, rose hastily, and welcomed him with hand and eyes and countenance, but without a word spoken. For a few moments the two stood silent, holding the other's hand and gazing in the other's eyes, then sat down on each side of the fire.

They looked at each other again; then the schoolmaster rose, rang the bell and, when it was answered by a rather careworn young woman, requested her to bring tea.

"I'm sorry I cannot give you cakes or fresh butter, my lord," he said with a smile. "The former are not to be had, and the latter is beyond my means."

He was a man of middle height, but so thin that notwithstanding a slight stoop in the shoulders he looked rather tall—on the young side of fifty but apparently a good way on the other, partly since the little hair he had was gray. About Portlossie he had been greatly respected in certain circles and much loved by his students; and when the presbytery dismissed him, there had been many tears on the part of his pupils.

"You look fine, my friend," said Malcolm.

"Thank you," returned Mr. Graham. "The Lord provides for my every need. I have students to keep me busy and midweek preaching at Hope Chapel."

After their tea followed a long talk, Malcolm first explaining his present position and then answering many questions of the master as to how things had gone since he had left. Next followed anxious questions on Malcolm's side as to how his friend found himself in London.

It was late before Malcolm left.

7

•••••••••••••••••••••

The Park

*T*he next day at noon, mounted on Kelpie, Malcolm was in attendance upon his mistress, who was eager for a gallop in Richmond Park. Lord Liftore, who had intended to accompany her, had not made his appearance yet, but Florimel did not seem any less desirous of setting out at the time she had appointed Malcolm. The fact was that she had said one o'clock to Liftore, intending twelve, that she might get away without him. Kelpie seemed on her good behavior, and they started quietly enough. By the time they got out of the park upon the Kensington road, however, the evil spirit had begun to wake in her. Still, whatever her escapades, they caused Florimel nothing but amusement, for her confidence in Malcolm—that he could do whatever he believed he could—was unbounded. They were hardly into the park when Lord Liftore, followed by his groom, came suddenly up behind them at such a rate as quite destroyed the small stock of equanimity Kelpie had to go on. She bolted.

Florimel was a good rider and knew herself quite mistress of her horse, and if she now followed, it was at her own will. She wanted to make the horses behind her bolt also, if she could. His lordship came flying after her and his groom after him, but she kept increasing her pace until they were all at full stretch, thundering over the grass, upon which Malcolm had at once turned Kelpie, giving her little rein and plenty of spur. Gradually, Florimel slackened speed and at last pulled up suddenly. Liftore and his groom went past her like the wind. She turned at right angles and galloped back to the road. There on a gaunt thoroughbred sat Lenorme, whom she had already passed and signaled to remain thereabout. They drew alongside each other. The three riders were now far away over the park, and still Kelpie held on and the other horses after her.

"I little expected such a pleasure," said Lenorme.

"I meant to give it to you, though," said Florimel with a merry laugh. "Bravo, Kelpie! take them with you!" she cried, looking after the still-retreating horses. "I have got a groom since I saw you last, Arnold," she went on. "See if I don't get some good for us out of him. I want to tell you all about it. I did not mean Liftore to be here when I sent you word, but he has been too much for me."

Lenorme replied with a look of gratitude, and as they walked their horses along she told him all concerning Malcolm and Kelpie.

"Liftore hates him already," she said, "and I can hardly wonder; but you must not, for you will find him useful. He is one I can depend on. You should have seen the look Liftore gave him when he told him he could not sit his mare! It would have been worth gold to you.

"He thinks no end of his riding," Florimel continued; "but if it were not so improper to have secrets with another gentleman, I would tell you that he rides just average. He wants to ride Kelpie, and I have told my groom to let him have her. Perhaps he'll break his neck."

Lenorme smiled grimly.

"You wouldn't mind, would you, Arnold?" added Florimel with a roguish look.

"Would you mind telling me, Florimel, what you mean by the impropriety of having secrets with another gentleman? Am I the other gentleman?"

"Why, of course. You know Liftore imagines he has only to name the day."

"And you allow an idiot like that to cherish such a degrading idea of you?"

"Why, Arnold! What does it matter what a fool like him thinks?"

"If you don't mind it, I do. I feel it an insult that he should dare think of you like that."

"I don't know. I suppose I shall have to marry him someday."

"Lady Lossie, do you want to make me hate you?"

"Don't be foolish. It won't be tomorrow nor the next day."

"Oh, Florimel! What is to come of this? Do you want to break my heart? I hate to talk rubbish. You won't kill me; you will only ruin my work and possibly drive me mad."

Florimel drew close to his side, laid her hand on his arm, and looked in his face with a witching entreaty. "We have the present, Arnold," she said.

"So has the butterfly," answered Lenorme, "but I had rather be the caterpillar with a future. Why don't you put a stop to the man's lovemaking? He can't love you or any woman. He doesn't know what love means. It makes me ill to hear him when he thinks he is paying you irresistible compliments. They are so silly! So mawkish! I want to help you grow as beautiful as God meant you to be when He first thought of you."

"Stop, stop, Arnold! I'm not worthy of such love," said Florimel, again laying her hand on his arm. "I do wish for your sake I had been born a village girl."

"If you had been, then I might have wished for your sake that I had been born a marquis. As it is, I would rather be a painter than any nobleman in Europe; that is, with you to love me."

"This won't do at all," said Florimel with the authority that should belong only to one in the right. "You will spoil everything! I dare not come to your studio if you are going to behave like this. It would be very wrong of me. And if I am never to come and see you, I shall die. I know I shall!"

The girl was so full of the delight of the secret love between them that she cared only to live in the present as if there were no future beyond. Lenorme wanted to make the future better than the present. The word "marriage" put Florimel in a rage. She thought herself superior to Lenorme because he, in the dread of losing her, would have her marry him at once, while she was more than content with the bliss of seeing him now and then. Often her foolish talk stung him with bitter pain—worst of all when it compelled him to doubt whether there was that in her to be loved as he was capable of loving. At one moment she would reveal herself in such a sudden rush of tenderness as seemed possible only to one ready to become his altogether and forever; the next, she would start away as if she had never meant anything.

They rode in silence for some hundred yards. At length he spoke. "What, then, can you gain, my lady marchioness," he said with soft seriousness and a sad smile, "by marrying one of your own rank? I should lay new honor and consideration at your feet. I am young; I have done fairly well already. And you know, too, that the names of great painters go down with honor from generation to generation when my lord this or my lord that is remembered only as a label to the picture that makes the painter famous. I am not a great painter yet, but I will be one if you will be good to me. And men shall say, when they look on your portrait in ages to come, 'No wonder he was such a painter when he had such a woman to paint!' "

"When shall the woman sit for you again, painter?" said Florimel—sole reply to his rhapsody.

The painter thought a little. Then he said, "I don't like that servant woman of yours. She has two evil eyes—one for each of us. I have again and again caught their expression when they were upon us and she thought none were upon her. I can see without lifting my head when I am painting, and my art has made me quick at catching expressions and, I hope, interpreting them."

"I don't altogether like her myself," said Florimel. "Of late I am not so sure of her as I used to be. But what can I do? I must have somebody with me, you know. And Caley is the most available. A thought strikes me, but— yes! You shall see what I will dare for you, faithless man."

She set off at a canter, turned onto the grass, and rode to meet Liftore, whom she saw in the distance returning, followed by the two grooms. "Come on!" she cried, looking back; "I must account for you. He sees I have not been alone."

Lenorme joined her, and they rode along side by side.

The earl and the painter knew each other; as they drew near, the painter lifted his hat and the earl nodded.

"You owe Mr. Lenorme some acknowledgment, my lord, for taking charge of me after your sudden desertion," said Florimel. "Why did you gallop off in such a mad fashion?"

"I am sorry," began Liftore, a little embarrassed.

"Oh, don't trouble yourself to apologize," said Florimel. "I have always understood that great horsemen find a horse more interesting than a lady. It is a mark of their breed, I am told."

She knew Liftore would not be ready to confess he could not hold his hack.

"If it hadn't been for Mr. Lenorme," she added, "I should have been left without a squire, subject to any whim of my four-footed servant here."

As she spoke she patted the neck of her horse. The earl, on his side, had been looking the painter's horse up and down with a would-be humorous expression of criticism. "I beg your pardon, marchioness," he replied, "but you pulled up so quickly that we shot past you. I thought you were close behind, and preferred following.—Seen his best days, eh, Lenorme?" he said, turning to the painter, willing to change the subject.

"I fancy he doesn't think so," returned the painter. "I bought him out of a butterman's cart three months ago. He's been coming to himself ever since. Look at his eye, my lord."

"Are you knowing in horses, then?"

"I can't say I am, beyond knowing how to treat them something like human beings."

Malcolm was just near enough, on the pawing and foaming Kelpie, to catch what was passing. "The fellow will do," he thought to himself. "He's worth a score of such earls!"

"Ha, ha!" said his lordship. "I don't know about that. He's not the best of tempers, I can see. But look at that demon of Lady Lossie's—that black mare there! I wish you could teach her some of your humanity. By the way, Florimel, I think now we are upon the grass," he said loftily, as if submitting to injustice, "I will presume to mount the reprobate."

The gallop had communicated itself to Liftore's blood, and besides, he thought after such a run Kelpie would be less extravagant in her behavior.

"She is at your service," said Florimel.

He dismounted, his groom rode up, he threw him the reins, and called Malcolm, "Bring your mare here, my man."

Malcolm rode her up halfway and dismounted. "If your lordship is going to ride her," he said, "will you please get on her here? I would rather not take her near the other horses."

"Well, you know her better than I do. You and I must ride about the same length, I think."

So saying, his lordship carelessly measured the stirrup leather against his arm and took the reins.

"Stand well forward, my lord. Don't mind turning your back to her head. I'll look after her teeth; you mind her hind hoof," said Malcolm, with her head in one hand and the stirrup in the other.

Kelpie stood rigid as a rock, and the earl swung himself up cleverly enough. But hardly was he in the saddle, and Malcolm had just let her go, when she plunged and lashed out. Then, having failed to unseat her rider, she stood straight up on her hind legs.

"Give her her head, my lord!" cried Malcolm.

She stood swaying in the air, Liftore's now-frightened face half hidden in her mane, and his spurs stuck in her flanks.

"Come off her, my lord, for heaven's sake! Off with you!" cried Malcolm as he leaped at her head. "She'll be on her back in a moment!"

Liftore only clung the harder. Malcolm caught her head just in time; she was already falling backward.

"Let all go, my lord. Throw yourself off!"

Malcolm swung her toward him with all his strength, and just as his lordship fell off behind her, she fell sideways to Malcolm and clear of Liftore.

As Malcolm was on the side away from the little group, and their own horses were excited, those who had looked breathlessly on at the struggle could not tell how he had managed it; but when they expected to see the groom writhing under the weight of the demoness, there he was with his knee upon her head while Liftore was gathering himself up from the ground, only just beyond the reach of her iron-shod hoofs.

"Thank God," said Florimel, "there is no harm done! Well, have you had enough of her yet, Liftore?"

"Pretty nearly, I think," said his lordship, with an attempt at a laugh as he walked rather feebly and foolishly toward his horse. He mounted with some difficulty and looked very pale.

"I hope you're not much hurt," said Florimel kindly as she moved toward him.

"Not in the least—only disgraced," he answered almost angrily. "The brute's a perfect Satan. You must part with her. With such a horse and such a groom you'll get yourself talked of all over London. I believe the fellow himself was at the bottom of it. You really must sell her."

"I would, my lord, if you were my groom," answered Florimel, whom his accusation of Malcolm had filled with angry contempt.

Malcolm was seated quietly on her head. She had ceased sprawling, and lay nearly motionless but for the heaving of her sides with her huge inhalations. She knew from experience that struggling was useless.

"I beg your pardon, my lady," said Malcolm, "but I daren't get up."

"How long do you mean to sit there?" she asked.

"If your ladyship wouldn't mind riding home without me, I would give her a good half hour of it. I always do when she throws herself over like that."

"Do as you please," said his mistress. "Let me see you when you get home. I should like to know you are safe."

Florimel returned to the gentlemen, and they rode homeward.

In about two hours Malcolm reported himself. Lord Liftore had gone home, they told him. The painter-fellow, as Wallis called him, had stayed to lunch but was gone also, and Lady Lossie was alone in the drawing room.

She sent for him. "I am glad to see you are safe, MacPhail," she said. "It is clear your Kelpie—don't be alarmed; I am not going to make you part with her—but it is clear she won't always do for you to attend me upon. Suppose now I wanted to dismount and make a call or go into a shop?"

"There is a sort of friendship between your Abbot and her, my lady. She would stand all the better if I had him to hold as well."

"Well, but how would you put me up again?"

"I never thought of that, my lady. Of course I daren't let you come near Kelpie."

"Could you trust yourself to buy another horse to ride after me about town?" asked Florimel.

"No, my lady, not without a ten days' trial. But there's Mr. Lenorme. If he would go with me, I fancy between us we could do pretty well."

"Ah! a good idea!" returned his mistress. "But what makes you think of him?" she added, willing enough to talk about him.

"The look of the gentleman and his horse together and what I heard him say," answered Malcolm.

"What did you hear him say?"

"That he knew he had to treat horses something like human beings. I've often fancied, within the last few months, that God does with some people something like as I do with Kelpie."

"I know nothing about theology," she said, and went to write a note to the painter.

"Maybe not, my lady, but this concerns biography rather than theology. No one could tell what I meant except he had watched his own history and that of people he knew."

"And horses too?"

"It's hard to get at their insides, my lady, but I suspect it must be so. I'll ask Mr. Graham."

"What Mr. Graham?"

"The schoolmaster of Portlossie."

"Is he in London, then?"

"Yes, my lady. He believed too much to please the presbytery and they turned him out."

"I should like to see him. He was very attentive to my father on his death-bed. Next time you see him give him my compliments, and ask if I can be of any service to him."

"I'll do that, my lady. I'm sure he will take it very kindly."

Florimel sat down at her writing table and wrote a note. "There," she said, "take that note to Mr. Lenorme. I have asked him to help you in the choice of a horse."

"What price would you be willing to go, my lady?"

"I leave that to Mr. Lenorme's judgment—and your own," she added.

"Thank you, my lady," said Malcolm, and went to find the painter.

8

. . . .

The Request

The address on the note Malcolm had to deliver took him to a house in Chelsea—one of a row of beautiful old houses fronting the Thames, within sight of the spot where Malcolm had put up the cutter, with little gardens between them and the road. The servant who took the note returned immediately and showed him up to the study, a large back room looking over a good-sized garden, with stables on one side. There sat Lenorme at his easel. "Ah!" he said, "I'm glad to see that wild animal has not quite torn you to pieces. Take a chair. What on earth made you bring such an incarnate fury to London?"

"I see well enough now, sir, she's not exactly the one for London use, but if you had once ridden her, you would never quite enjoy another between your knees."

"Here your mistress tells me you want my assistance in choosing another horse."

"Yes, sir—to attend upon her in London."

"I don't profess to know horses. What made you think of me?"

"I saw how you sat your own horse, and I heard you say you bought him out of a butterman's cart and treated him like a human being. That was enough for me. 'That gentleman and I would understand one another,' I said to myself."

"I'm glad you think so," said Lenorme, with entire courtesy. Although so much more a man of the world, he was able in a measure to look into Malcolm and appreciate him, both as a result of his nature and his art.

"You see, sir," Malcolm went on, encouraged by the simplicity of Lenorme's manner, "if they were nothing like us, how should we be able to get on with them at all, teach them anything, or come a hair nearer them, do what we might? For all her wickedness, I firmly believe Kelpie has a sort of regard for me: I won't call it affection, but perhaps it comes as near that as may be possible to one of her temper."

"Now I hope you will permit me, Mr. MacPhail," said Lenorme, who had been paying more attention to Malcolm than to his words, "to give a violent wrench to the conversation, and turn it upon yourself. You can't be surprised, and I hope you will not be offended, if I say you strike one as not altogether like your calling. No London groom I have ever spoken to in the least resembles you. How is it?"

"I hope you don't mean to imply, sir, that I don't know my business?" returned Malcolm.

"Anything but that. Come now," said Lenorme, growing more and more interested in his new acquaintance, "tell me something about your life. Account for yourself. If you will make a friendship of it, you must do that."

"I will, sir," said Malcolm, and with the word began to tell him most things he could think of as bearing upon his mental history up to and after the time also when his birth was disclosed to him. In omitting that disclosure he believed he had without it quite accounted for himself.

"Well, I must admit," said Lenorme when he had ended, "that you are no longer unintelligible, not to say incredible. You have had a splendid education, in which I hope you give the herring and Kelpie their due share, as well as Mr. Graham, of whom you speak so fondly." He sat silently regarding him for a few moments. Then he said, "I'll tell you what, now; if I help you buy a horse, you must help me paint a picture."

"I don't know how I'm to do that," said Malcolm; "but if you do, that's enough. I shall be only too happy to do what I can."

"Then I'll tell you. But you're not to tell anybody: it's a secret. I have discovered there is no suitable portrait of Lady Lossie's father. It is a great pity. His brother and his father and grandfather are all in Portland Place, in Highland costume, as chiefs of their clan; only his place is vacant. Lady Lossie, however, has in her possession one or two miniatures of him which, although badly painted, I should think may give the outlines of his face and head with tolerable correctness. From the portraits of his predecessors and from Lady Lossie herself, I have gained some knowledge of what is common to the family; and from all together I hope to gather and paint what will be recognizable by her as a likeness of her father, which afterward I hope to better by her first remarks. These remarks I hope to get first from her feelings unadulterated by criticism, through the surprise of coming upon the picture suddenly; afterward from her judgment at its leisure. Now, I remember seeing you wait at table—the first time I saw you—in the Highland dress. Will you come to me so dressed, and let me paint from you?"

"I'll do better than that, sir!" cried Malcolm eagerly. "I'll get up from Lossie House my lord's very dress that he wore when he went to court—his jeweled dirk and broadsword with the hilt of real silver. That'll greatly help your design upon my lady, for he dressed up in them all more than once just to please her."

"Thank you," said Lenorme very heartily; "that will be of immense advantage. Write at once!"

"I will. Only I'm bigger than my late master, and you must mind that."

"I'll see to it. You get the clothes and all the rest of the accouterments."

"I'll go write to Mrs. Courthope, the housekeeper, tonight, to send the things at once. When would it be convenient for you to go look at some horses with me, Mr. Lenorme?" he said.

"I shall be at home all tomorrow," answered the painter, "and ready to go with you any time you'd like to come for me."

As he spoke he held out his hand and they parted like old friends.

The next morning Malcolm took Kelpie into the park and gave her a good breathing. He was turning home with her again when one of her evil fits began to come upon her, beginning as always with the straightening of her muscles and the flaming of her eyes. He well knew it would soon end in a wild paroxysm of rearing and plunging. He had more than once tried the exorcism of patience, sitting sedately upon her back; but on these occasions the tempest that followed had been of the very worse description, so that he concluded it better to confront her attacks head-on by using his spiked heels with vigor. And since he had adopted this procedure they had become, if no less violent, certainly fewer.

Upon this occasion he had a stiff tussle with her but as usual had gained the victory and was riding slowly along, Kelpie tossing up now her head, then her heels in indignant protest against obedience in general. Suddenly a lady on horseback came galloping up with her groom behind her; she had seen something of what had been going on. As she pulled up, Malcolm reined in. But Kelpie was now as unwilling to stop as she had been before to proceed and the fight began again, the spurs once more playing a free part.

"Man! Man!" cried the lady in reproof, "do you know what you are about?"

"It would be a bad job for her and me if I did not, my lady," said Malcolm, and as he spoke he smiled in the midst of the struggle. He seldom got angry with Kelpie.

But the smile only made his conduct appear in the lady's eyes more cruel. "How is it possible you can treat the poor animal so unkindly? Why, her poor sides are actually..." A shudder and look of distress completed the sentence.

"You don't know what she is, my lady, or you would not think it necessary to intercede for her."

"But if she is naughty, is that any reason why you should be cruel?"

"No, my lady; but it is the best reason why I should try to make her good."

"You will never make her good that way!"

"Improvement gives ground for hope," said Malcolm.

"But you must not treat a poor dumb animal as you would a responsible human being."

"She's not so very poor, my lady. She has all she wants and does nothing to earn it—nothing at all with goodwill. For her dumbness, that's a mercy. If she could speak she wouldn't be fit to live amongst decent people. But for that matter, if someone hadn't taken her in hand, dumb as she is, she would have been shot long ago."

"Better that than live with such usage."

"I don't think she would agree with you, my lady. My fear is that, for as cruel as it looks to your ladyship, she enjoys the fight. In any case, I am certain she has more regard for me than any other being in the universe."

"Who *can* have any regard for you," said the lady very gently, in utter mistake of his meaning, "if you have no command of your temper? You must learn to rule yourself first."

"That's true, my lady; and so long as my mare is not able to be a law to herself, I must be a law to her too."

"But have you never heard of the law of kindness? Surely you could do so much more without the severity."

"With some natures I grant you, my lady, but not with such as she. Horse or man—they never know kindness till they have learned to fear. Kelpie would have torn me to pieces before now if I had taken your way with her. But unless I can do a good deal more with her yet, she will be nothing better than a natural brute beast made to be taken and destroyed."

All this time Kelpie was trying hard to get at the lady's horse to bite him; but she did not see that. She was too much distressed and was growing more and more so. "I wish you would let my groom try her," she said. "He's an older and more experienced man than you. He has two children. He would show you what can de done by gentleness."

"It would be a great satisfaction to my old Adam to let him try her," said

Malcolm. "But it would be murder, not knowing myself what experience he has had."

"I see," said the lady to herself, but loud enough for Malcolm to hear, for her tenderheartedness had made her both angry and unjust, "his self-conceit is equal to his cruelty—just what I might have expected."

With those words she turned her horse's head and rode away, leaving a lump in Malcolm's throat. It added hugely to the bitterness of being thus rebuked that he had never seen such a beautiful face in his life. She was young—not more than twenty—tall and with a stately grace. It tried Malcolm sorely that such gentleness and beauty should be so unreasonable. Was he never to have the chance of convincing her how mistaken she was concerning his treatment of Kelpie?

Malcolm gazed after her long and earnestly. "It's an awful thing to have a woman like that angered at you," he said to himself, "—as pretty as she is angry. It's a painful thing to be misjudged. But it's no more than God puts up with every hour of the day. But He's patient. So long as He knows He's in the right, He lets folk think what they like—till He has time to make them know better. Lord, make my heart clean within me, and then I'll care little for any judgment but yours!"

For the lady, she rode away, sadly strengthened in her notion that Malcolm was, in fact, the beast and Kelpie the higher creature of the two.

Malcolm rode home and put the demoness in her stall.

9

· · · · · · · · · · · · · · · · · · · ·

The Boy

It was a lovely day, but Florimel would not ride; she would not go out again until she could have a choice of horses to follow her. Malcolm must go at once to Mr. Lenorme, "Your Kelpie is all very well in Richmond Park—and I wish I were able to ride her myself, Malcolm—but she will never do in London."

His name sounded sweet on her lips. "Who knows, my lady," he answered his mistress, "but you may ride her someday? Give her a bit of sugar every time you see her—on your hand so that she may take it with her lips and not catch your fingers."

"You shall show me how," said Florimel. "But in the meantime here is a note for Mr. Lenorme. I do so want to ride again."

Malcolm left immediately. The moment his arrival was announced to Lenorme, he came down and went with him, and in an hour or two they had found very much the sort of horse they wanted. Malcolm took him home for trial, and Florimel was pleased with him. The earl's opinion was not to be had, for he had hurt his shoulder when he fell from the rearing Kelpie the day before and was confined to his room in Curzon Street.

In the evening, Malcolm put on his yachter's uniform and set out again for Chelsea. There he took a boat and crossed the river to the yacht, which lay near the other side in the charge of an old salt whose acquaintance Blue Peter had made when lying below the bridges. On board he found all tidy and shipshape. He dived into the cabin, lighted a candle, and made some measurements: all the little luxuries of the next—carpets, cushions, curtains, and other things—were at Lossie House, having been removed when the *Psyche* was laid up for winter. He was going to replace them, and he was anxious to see whether he could not fulfill a desire he had once heard Florimel express to her father—that she had a bed on board and could sleep there. He found it possible and had soon contrived a berth: even a tiny stateroom was within the limits of construction.

Returning to the deck, he was consulting Travers about a carpenter when, to his astonishment, he saw young Davy, the boy they had brought from Duff Harbor and whom he understood to have gone back with Blue Peter, gazing at him from before the mast.

"How do you come to be here?" said Malcolm. "Peter was to take you home with him."

"If you please, Mister MacPhail," said Davy, "I made him think I was going."

"I gave him your wages," said Malcolm.

"Ay, he told me that, but I let them go and gave him the slip and returned ashore, close behind you yourself, sir. I couldn't go without a word with you to see whether you wouldn't let me stay, sir. I'm not too smart, they tell me, but I could do what you'd tell me and keep from doing anything you told me not to do."

The words of the boy pleased Malcolm, more than he judged it wise to show. He looked hard at Davy. There was little to be seen in his face except the best and only thing—truth.

"But," said Malcolm, almost satisfied, "how is this, Travers? I never gave you any instructions about the boy."

"I seed the boy aboard before," answered the old man, "and when he come aboard again, just after you left, I never as much as said to mysel', 'Is it all right?' I axed him no questions and he told me no lies."

"Look here, Davy," said Malcolm, turning to him, "can you swim?"

"Ay, I can, sir," answered Davy.

"Jump overboard, then, and swim ashore," said Malcolm, pointing to the Chelsea bank.

The boy made two strides to the side of the larboard gunwale and would have been over the next instant, but Malcolm caught him by the shoulder. "That'll do, Davy; I'll give you a chance."

"Thank you, sir," said Davy. "I'll do what I can to please you, sir."

"Well, I'll write to your mother and see what she says," said Malcolm. "Now I want to tell you, both of you, that this yacht belongs to the marchioness of Lossie, and I have command of her, and I must have everything on board shipshape and clean. If there's the head of a nail visible, it must be as bright as silver."

He then arranged that Travers was to go home that night and bring with him the next morning an old carpenter friend of his. He would himself be down by seven o'clock to set him to work.

The result was that before a fortnight was over, he had the cabin thoroughly fitted up with all the luxuries it had formerly possessed and as many more as he could think of to compensate for the loss of the space occupied by the daintiest little stateroom—a very jewel box for softness and richness and comfort. In the cabin, amongst the rest of his additions, he had fixed in a corner a set of tiny bookshelves and filled them with what books he knew his sister liked and some that he liked for her. By that time also he had arranged with Travers and Davy a code of signals.

The day after Malcolm had his new hack, he rode him behind his mistress in the park. When they left the park Florimel went down Constitution Hill, and, turning westward, she stopped and said to Malcolm, "I am going to run in and thank Mr. Lenorme for the trouble he has been about the horse. Which is the house?"

She pulled up at the gate. Malcolm dismounted, but before he could get near to assist her she was already halfway up the walk, flying, and he was but in time to catch the rein of Abbot, already moving off, curious to know whether he was actually trusted alone. In about five minutes she came out again, glancing about her all ways but behind—with a scared look, Malcolm thought. But she walked more slowly and stately than usual down the path. In a moment Malcolm had her in the saddle, and she cantered away past the hospital into Sloan Street and across the park home. "She knows the way," he thought.

Florimel had found her daring visit to Lenorme stranger and more fearful than she had expected; her courage was not quite so masterful as she had thought. The next day she got Mrs. Barnardiston to meet her at the studio. But she contrived to be there first by some minutes, and her friend found her seated and the painter looking as if he had fairly begun his morning's work. When she apologized for being late, Florimel said she supposed her groom had brought round the horses before his time; being ready, she had not looked at her watch. She was sharp on other people for telling stories, but of late had ceased to see any great harm in telling one to protect herself.

Malcolm found it dreary waiting in the street while she sat for the painter. He would not have minded it on Kelpie, for she was occupation enough, but with only a couple of quiet horses to hold, it was dreary. One thing he had by it, however, and that was a good lesson in waiting—a grand thing for any man, and most of all for those in whom the active is strong.

The next day Florimel did not ride until after lunch but took her maid with her to the studio, and Malcolm had a long morning with Kelpie.

At length the parcel he had sent for from Lossie House arrived. He had explained to Mrs. Courthope what he wanted the things for, and she had made no difficulty of sending them to the address he gave her. Lenorme had already begun the portrait, had indeed been working at it very busily and was now quite ready for him to sit. The early morning being the only time a groom could contrive to spare—and that involved yet earlier attention to his horses—they arranged that Malcolm should be at the study every day by seven o'clock until the painter's object was gained. So he mounted Kelpie at half-past six of a fine breezy spring morning, rode across Hyde Park and down Grosvenor Place and so reached Chelsea, where he put up his mare in Lenorme's stable.

As soon as he arrived he was shown into the painter's bedroom, where lay the portmanteau he had carried thither himself the night before. Out of it, with a strange mingling of pleasure and sadness, he now took the garments of his father's vanished state. He handled each with the reverence of a son. Having dressed in them, he drew himself up with not a little of the Celt's pleasure in fine clothes and walked into the painting room. Lenorme started with admiration of his figure and wonder at the dignity of his carriage. He almost sprang at his palette and brushes: whether or not he succeeded with the likeness of the late marquis, it would be his own fault if he did not make a good picture. He painted eagerly and they talked little, and only about trivialities.

"Confound it!" he cried suddenly, and sprang to his feet, but without taking his eyes from his picture. "What have I been doing all this time but making a portrait of you, MacPhail, and forgetting what you were there for! And yet," he went on, hesitating and catching up the miniature for a closer look, "I have got a certain likeness! Yes, it must be so, for I seen in it also a certain look for Lady Lossie. Well, I suppose a man can't altogether help what he paints anymore than what he dreams.—That will do for this morning, anyhow, I think, MacPhail. Make haste and put on your own clothes, and come into the next room to breakfast. You must be tired with standing so long."

"It is about the hardest work I ever tried," answered Malcolm, "but I doubt if I am as tired as Kelpie. I've been listening for the last half hour to hear the stalls flying."

10

• • • • • • • • • • • • • • • • • • •

The Eavesdropper

Florimel was beginning to understand that the shield of the portrait was not large enough to cover many more visits to Lenorme's studio. Still, she must and would venture, and should anything be said, there, at least, was the portrait. For some weeks it had been all but finished, was never off its easel, and always showed wet paint somewhere. He kept the last of it lingering, ready to prove itself almost, yet not altogether, finished. What was to follow its absolute completion neither of them could tell. The worst of it was that their thoughts about it differed. It must be remembered that Florimel had had no mother since her childhood, that she was now but a girl, and that of genuine love she had little more than enough to serve as salt to the passion. In Florimel's case, there was much of the childish in it. Definitely separated from Lenorme, she would have been merry again in a fortnight; and yet, though she half knew this herself and at the same time was more than half ashamed of the whole affair, she did not give it up—would not—only intended by and by to let it go. It was no wonder, then, that Lenorme, believing, hoping she loved him, should find her hard to understand.

The painter was not merely in love with Florimel; he loved her. I will not say that he was in no degree dazzled by her rank, but such thoughts were only changing hues on the feathers of his love.

A day or two passed before Florimel went again to the studio, accompanied, notwithstanding Lenorme's warning and her own doubt, yet again by her maid, a woman, unhappily, of Lady Bellair's finding. At Lossie House, Malcolm had felt a repugnance to her, both moral and physical. When first he heard her name, one of the servants speaking of her as Miss Caley, he took it for Scaley; and if that was not her name, yet it was her nature.

This time Florimel rode to Chelsea with Malcolm, having directed Caley to meet her there. And, the one designing to be a little early and the other to be a little late, two results naturally followed—first, that the lovers had a few minutes alone; and second, that when Caley crept in, noiseless and unannounced as a cat, she had her desire and saw the painter's arm round Florimel's waist and her head on his chest. She crept out again as quietly as she had entered. Through the success of her trick it came about that Malcolm, chancing to look up from his horses to the room where he always breakfasted with his new friend, saw in one of the windows a face radiant with the expression of evil discovery.

Caley was of the common class of servants in this, that she considered service servitude and took her amends in selfishness. Her one thought was to make the most of her position. She was clever, greedy, cunning. She rather liked her mistress, but watched her in the interests of Lady Bellair. She had a fancy for the earl, a natural dislike to Malcolm, which she concealed in distant politeness, and for all the rest of the house, indifference.

The look on Caley's face gave Malcolm something to think about. Clearly she had a triumph. What could it be? The nature of the woman had by this time become clear to him as a result of his interaction with her in the house; it was clear the triumph was not in good. It was plain, too, that it was in something which had that very moment occurred, and could hardly have to do with anyone but her mistress. She had gone into the house but a moment before, a minute or two behind her mistress, and he knew with what a catlike step she went about. She had undoubtedly surprised them—discovered how matters stood between her mistress and the painter. He pieced together everything almost as it had taken place. She had seen without being seen and had retreated with her prize! Florimel was then in the woman's power. What was he to do? He must clearly tell her somehow.

Once arrived at a resolve, Malcolm never lost time. They had turned but one corner on their way home when he rode up to her. "Please, my lady," he began, "I must tell you something I happened to see while I waited with the horses," he said.

The earnestness of his tone struck Florimel. She looked at him with eyes a little wider and waited to hear.

"I happened to look up at the drawing-room windows, my lady, and Caley came to one of them with such a look on her face! I can't exactly describe it to you, my lady, but—"

"Why do you tell me?" interrupted his mistress with absolute composure and hard, questioning eyes. Then, before he could reply, a flash of thoughts seemed to cross her face with a quick single motion of her eyebrows, and it was instantly altered and thoughtful. She seemed to have suddenly perceived some cause for taking a mild interest in his communication. "But it cannot be, Malcolm," she said in quite a changed tone. "You must have taken someone else for her. She never left the studio all the time I was there."

"It was immediately after her arrival, my lady. She went in about two minutes after your ladyship, and could not have had much more than time to go upstairs when I saw her come to the window. I felt bound to tell you."

"Thank you, Malcolm," returned Florimel kindly. "You did right to tell me, but it's of no consequence. Mr. Lenorme's housekeeper and she must have been talking about something."

But her eyebrows were now thoughtfully contracted over her eyes.

"There had been no time for that, I think, my lady," said Malcolm.

Florimel turned again and rode on. Malcolm saw that he had succeeded in warning her and was glad. But had he foreseen to what it would lead, he would hardly have done it.

Florimel was indeed very uneasy. She could not help strongly suspecting that she had betrayed herself to one who, if not an intentional spy, would yet be ready enough to make a spy's use of anything she might have picked up. What was to be done? It was now too late to think of getting rid of her: that would be but her signal to disclose whatever she had seen and so not merely enjoy a sweet revenge, but account with clear satisfactoriness for her dismissal. What would not Florimel have now given for someone who could sympathize with her and yet counsel her! She was afraid to venture another meeting with Lenorme. Besides, she was not a little shy of the advantage the discovery would give him in pressing her to marry him. And now first she began to feel as if her sins were going to find her out.

A day or two passed. She watched her maid, but discovered no change in her manner or behavior. Weary of observation, she was gradually settling into her former security when Caley began to drop hints that alarmed her. Might it not be the safest thing to take her into confidence? It would be such a relief, she thought, to have a woman she could talk to! The result was that she began to lift a corner of the veil that hid her trouble. The woman encouraged her, and at length the silly girl threw her arms round the scaly one's neck, much to that person's satisfaction, and told her she loved Mr. Lenorme. She said she knew, of course, that she could not marry him. She was only waiting a fit opportunity to free herself from a connection which, however delightful, she was unable to justify. Could Lenorme have known her capable of unbosoming herself to such a woman, it would almost have slain the love he bore her.

Caley first comforted the weeping girl and then began to insinuate encouragement. She must indeed give him up—there was no help for that— but neither was there any necessity for doing so all at once. Mr. Lenorme was a beautiful man, and any woman might be proud to be loved by him. She must take her time to it. She could trust her.

The first result was that, on the pretext of bidding him farewell and convincing him that he and she must meet no more, Florimel arranged with her woman one evening to go the next morning to the studio. She knew the painter to be an early riser and always at his work before eight o'clock. But although she tried to imagine she had persuaded herself to say farewell, certainly she had not yet brought her mind to any resolve in the matter. At seven o'clock in the morning the marchioness, habited like a housemaid, slipped out by the front door, turned the corners of two streets, found a hackney-coach waiting for them and arrived in due time at the painter's abode.

When the door opened and Florimel glided in, the painter sprang to his feet to welcome her, and she flew softly into his arms; for, the study being large and full of things, she was not aware of the presence of Malcolm who was there for an early morning sitting. From behind a picture of an easel he saw them meet, but shrinking from being an open witness to their secret, and also from being discovered in his father's clothes by the sister who knew him only as a servant, he instantly sought escape. Nor was it hard to find, for near where he stood was a door opening into a small intermediate chamber next to the drawing room, and by it he fled, intending to pass through to Lenorme's bedroom and change his clothes. With noiseless stride he hurried away but could not help hearing a few passionate words that escaped his sister's lips before Lenorme could warn her they were not alone—words which, it seemed to him, come only from a heart whose very pulse was devotion.

"How can I live without you, Arnold?" said the girl as she clung to him.

Lenorme gave an uneasy glance behind him, saw Malcolm disappear, and answered, "I hope you will not try, my darling."

"Oh, but you know this can't last," she returned with playfully affected authority. "It must come to an end. They will interfere."

"Who can? Who will dare?" said the painter with confidence.

"People will. We had better stop it ourselves—before it all comes out and we are shamed," said Florimel, with perfect seriousness.

"Shamed!" cried Lenorme. "Well, if you can't help being ashamed of me—and perhaps, as you have been brought up you can't—do you not then love me enough to encounter a little shame for my sake? I should welcome worlds of such for yours."

Florimel was silent. She kept her face hidden on his shoulder, but was already halfway to a quarrel.

"You don't love me, Florimel," he said after a pause.

"Well, suppose I don't!" she cried, half defiantly. Drawing herself from him, she stepped back two paces and looked at him with saucy eyes, in which burned two little flames of displeasure that seemed to shoot up from the red spots glowing upon her cheeks. Lenorme looked at her. He had often seen her like this before and knew that the shell was charged and the fuse lighted. But within lay a mixture even more explosive than he had suspected, for she was conscious of having now been false to him. That rendered her temper dangerous. Lenorme had already suffered severely from the fluctuations of her moods. They had almost been too much for him. He could endure them, he thought, to all eternity if he had her to himself, safe and sure; but this confidence often failed him. If, after all, she should forsake him, he knew he would survive it; but he knew also that life could never be the same again, that for a season work would be impossible. It was no wonder, then, if her behavior sometimes angered him. And now a black fire in his eyes answered the blue flash in hers. A word of indignant expostulation rose to her lips, but a thought came that repressed it. He took her hand and led her—her hand lying dead in his. It was but to the other end of the room he led her, to the picture of her father, now all but finished.

Malcolm stepped into the drawing room, where the table was laid as usual for breakfast. There stood Caley helping herself to a spoonful of honey. At his entrance she started violently, and her sallow face grew earthy. For some seconds she stood motionless, unable to take her eyes off the apparition, as it seemed to her, of the late marquis, in wrath at her encouragement of his daughter in disgraceful courses. Malcolm, supposing she was ashamed of herself, took no further notice of her and walked deliberately toward the other door. Before he reached it she knew him. Burning with the combined ires of fright and shame, conscious also that by the one little contemptible act of greed in which he had surprised her she had justified the aversion which her woman instinct had from the first recognized in him, she darted to the door, stood with her back against it, and faced him flaming. "So!" she cried, "this is how my lady's kindness is abused! The insolence! Her groom goes and sits for his portrait in her father's court dress! My lady shall know this," she concluded, with a vicious clenching of her teeth and two or three small nods of her neat head.

Malcolm stood regarding her with a coolness that yet inflamed her wrath. He could not help smiling at the reaction of shame and indignation. Had her anger been but a passing flame, that smile would have turned it into enduring hate. She hissed in his face.

"Go and have the first word," he said, "but leave that door and let me pass."

"Let you pass, indeed! What would you pass for—the son of old Lord James and a married woman? I don't care *that* for you," and she snapped her fingers in his face.

Malcolm turned from her and went to the window, taking a newspaper from the breakfast table as he passed and there sat down to read until the way should be clear. Carried beyond herself by his utter indifference, Caley darted from the room and went straight into the study.

Lenorme led Florimel in front of the picture. She gave a great start and turned and stared pallid at the painter. The effect upon her was such as he had not foreseen, and the words she uttered were not such as he could have hoped to hear. "What would he think of me if he knew?" she cried, clasping her hands.

That moment Caley burst into the room, her eyes like a cat's. "My lady!" she shrieked, "there's MacPhail the groom, my lady, dressed up in your honored father's bee-utiful clothes as he always wore when he went to dine with the prince! And please, my lady, he's so rude, I could hardly keep my hands off him."

Florimel flashed a dagger of question in Lenorme's eyes. The painter drew himself up. "It was at my request, Lady Lossie," he said.

"Indeed!" returned Florimel, in high scorn, and glanced again at the picture. "I see," she went on. "How could I be such an idiot! It was my groom's, not my father's likeness you meant to surprise me with!" Her eyes flashed as if she would annihilate him.

"I have worked hard in the hope of giving you pleasure, Lady Lossie," said the painter with wounded dignity.

"And you have failed," she adjoined cruelly.

The painter took the miniature after which he had been working from a table near, handed it to her with a proud obeisance, and the same moment dashed a brushful of dark paint across the face of the picture.

Florimel turned away and walked from the study. The door of the drawing room was open, and Caley stood by the side of it. Florimel, too angry to consider what she was about, walked in. There sat Malcolm in the window in her father's clothes and his very attitude, reading the newspaper. He did not hear her enter. He had been waiting till he could reach the bedroom unseen by her, for he knew from the sound of the voices that the study room was open. Her anger rose yet higher at the sight. "Leave the room," she said.

He started to his feet, and now perceived that his sister was in the dress of a servant.

"Take those clothes off instantly," said Florimel slowly, replacing wrath with haughtiness as well as she might.

Malcolm turned to the door without a word. He saw that things had gone wrong where most he would have wished them to go right.

"I'll see that they're well aired, my lady," said Caley, with sibilant indignation.

Malcolm went to the study. The painter sat before the picture of the marquis, with his elbows on his knees and his head between his hands. "Mr. Lenorme," said Malcolm, approaching him gently.

"Oh, go away," said Lenorme without raising his head. "I can't bear the sight of you just yet."

Malcolm obeyed. He was in his own clothes, booted and belted, in two minutes. Three sufficed to replace his father's garments in the portmanteau, and in three more he and Kelpie went plunging past his mistress and her maid as they drove home in their lumbering vehicle.

"The insolence of the fellow!" said Caley, loud enough for her mistress to hear notwithstanding the noise of the rattling windows. "A pretty pass we are come to!"

But already Florimel's mood had begun to change. She felt that she had done her best to alienate men on whom she could depend, and that she had chosen for a confidante one whom she had no ground for trusting.

She got safe and unseen to her room, and Caley believed she had only to improve the advantage she had now gained.

Things had taken a turn that was not to Malcolm's satisfaction, and his thoughts were as busy all the way home as Kelpie would allow. He had ardently desired that his sister should be thoroughly in love with Lenorme, for that seemed to open a clear path out of his worst difficulties. Now they had quarreled and were both angry with him. The main fear was that Liftore would now make some progress with her. Things looked dangerous. Even his warning against Caley had led to a result the very opposite of his intent and desire. And now it recurred to him that he had once come upon Liftore talking to Caley and giving her something that shone like a sovereign.

When Florimel returned from her unhappy visit and had sent her attendant to get her some tea, she threw herself upon her bed. She was yet tossing in her own disharmony when Malcolm came for orders. To get rid of herself and Caley both, she desired him to bring the horses round at once.

It was more than Malcolm had expected. He ran: he might yet have a chance of trying to turn her in the right direction. He knew that Liftore was neither in the house nor at the stable. With the help of the earl's groom he was round in ten minutes. Florimel was all but ready. She sprang from Malcolm's hand to the saddle and led as straight northward as she could go, never looking behind her till she drew rein on the top of Hampstead Heath. When he rode up to her, Florimel said, half ashamed, "Malcolm, I don't think my father would have minded you wearing his clothes."

"Thank you, my lady," said Malcolm. "At least he would have forgiven anything meant for your pleasure."

"I was too hasty," she said. "But the fact was, Mr. Lenorme had irritated me, and I foolishly mixed you up with him."

"When I went into the studio after you left it this morning, my lady," Malcolm ventured, "he had his head between his hands and would not even look at me."

Florimel turned her face aside, and Malcolm thought she was sorry; but she was only hiding a smile. She had not yet gotten beyond the kitten stage of love and was pleased to find she gave pain.

"If your ladyship never had another true friend, Mr. Lenorme is one," added Malcolm.

"What opportunity can you have had for knowing?" said Florimel.

"I have been sitting for him every morning for a good many days," answered Malcolm. "He is something like a man!"

Florimel's face flushed with pleasure. She liked to hear him praised, for he loved her.

"You should have seen, my lady, the pains he took with that portrait. He would stare at the little picture you lent him of my lord for minutes, as if he were looking through it at something behind it; then he would go and gaze at your ladyship on the pedestal, as if you were the goddess herself, about to tell him everything about your father; and then he would hurry back to his easel and give a touch or two to the face, looking at it all the time as if he loved it. It must have been a cruel pain that drove him to smear it as he did."

Florimel began to feel a little motion of shame somewhere in the mystery of her being. But to show that to her servant would be to betray herself—all the more that he seemed the painter's friend.

"I will ask Lord Liftore to go and see the portrait, and if he thinks it good I will buy it," she said. "Mr. Lenorme is certainly very clever with his brush."

Malcolm saw that she said this not to insult Lenorme but to blind her groom, and made no answer.

"I will ride there with you tomorrow morning," she added in conclusion and moved on.

Malcolm touched his hat and dropped behind. But the next moment he was by her side again. "I beg your pardon, my lady, but would you allow me to say one word more?"

She bowed her head.

"That woman Caley, I am certain, is not to be trusted. She does not love you, my lady."

"How do you know that?" asked Florimel, speaking steadily but writhing inwardly with the knowledge that the warning was too late.

"I have tried her spirit," answered Malcolm, "and know that it is of the devil. She loves herself too much to be true."

After a little pause Florimel said, "I know you mean well, Malcolm, but it is nothing to me whether she loves me or not. We don't look for that nowadays from servants."

"It is because I love you, my lady," said Malcolm, "that I know Caley does not. If she should get hold of anything your ladyship would not wished talked about—"

"That she cannot," said Florimel, but with an inward shudder. "She may tell the whole world all she can discover."

She would have cantered on as the words left her lips, but something in Malcolm's look held her. She turned pale, she trembled. Her father was looking at her as only once had she seen him—in doubt whether his child lied. The illusion was terrible. She shook in her saddle. The next moment she was galloping along the grassy border of the heath in wild flight from her worst enemy, whom yet she could never by the wildest of flights escape; it was the self which had just told a lie to the servant of whom she had so lately boasted that he never told one in his life. Then she grew angry. What had she done to be thus tormented? She, a marchioness, thus pestered by her own menials—pulled opposing directions by a groom and a maid! She would turn them both away and have nobody about her either to trust or suspect.

She turned and rode back, looking the other way as she passed Malcolm.

When they reached the top of the heath, riding along to meet them came Liftore—this time to Florimel's consolation and comfort; she did not like riding unprotected with a good angel at her heels. So glad was she that she did not even take the trouble to wonder how he had discovered the road she went. She never suspected that Caley had sent his lordship's groom to follow her until the direction of her ride should be evident, but took his appearance without question as a lover-like attention and rode home with him, talking the whole way and cherishing a feeling of triumph over both Malcolm and Lenorme. Had she not a protector of her own kind? Could she not, when they troubled her, pass from their sphere into one beyond their ken? For the moment the poor, weak lord who rode beside her seemed to her foolish heart a tower of refuge. She was particularly gracious and encouraging as they rode, and fancied again and again that perhaps the best way out of her troubles would be to encourage and at last accept him.

Malcolm followed, sick at heart that she should prove herself so shallow.

When she went to her room, there was Caley taking from a portmanteau that had been delivered the Highland dress which had occasioned so much. A note fell, and she handed it to her mistress. Florimel opened it, grew pale as she read it and asked Caley to bring her a glass of water. No sooner had her maid left the room than she sprang to the door and bolted it. Then the tears burst from her eyes; she sobbed despairingly and but for the help of her handkerchief would have wailed aloud. When Caley returned she answered to her knock that she was lying down and wanted to sleep. She was, however, trying to force further communication from the note. In it the painter told her that he was going to set out the next morning for Italy, and that her portrait was at the shop of certain carvers and gilders, being fitted with a frame for which he had made drawings. Three times she read it, searching for some hidden message to her heart. She held it up between her and the light, then before the fire till it crackled like a bit of old parchment; but all was in vain. By no device, intellectual or physical, could she coax the shadow of a meaning out of it beyond what lay plain on the surface. She must—she would—see him again.

That night she was merrier than usual at dinner, and after it, sang ballad upon ballad to please Liftore; then went to her room and told Caley to arrange for yet another visit to Mr. Lenorme's studio. She positively must, she said, secure her father's portrait ere the ill-tempered painter—all men of genius were hasty and unreasonable—should have it destroyed utterly, as he was certain to do before leaving, and with that she showed her Lenorme's letter. Caley was all service, only saying that this time she thought they had better go openly. She would see Lady Bellair as soon as Lady Lossie was in bed and explain the thing to her.

11

●●●●●●●●●●●●●●●●●●●

The Confrontation

The next morning the two drove to Chelsea in the carriage. When the door opened Florimel walked straight up to the study. There she saw no one, and her heart, which had been fluttering strangely, sank and was painfully still, while her gaze went wandering about the room. Again the tears gushed from the heart of Florimel. As she choked down a cry, suddenly arms were around her. Never doubting whose the embrace, she leaned her head against his bosom, and slowly opening her tearful eyes, lifted them to the face that bent over hers.

It was Liftore's!

She was dumb with disappointment and dismay. It was a hateful moment. He kissed her forehead and eyes and sought her mouth. She shrieked aloud. In her very agony at the loss of one to be kissed by another! And there! It was too degrading, too horrid!

At the sound of her cry someone started up at the other end of the room. An easel with a large canvas on it fell, and a man came forward with great strides. Liftore let her go, with a muttered curse on the intruder, and she darted from the room into the arms of Caley, who had had her ear against the other side of the door. That same instant Malcolm received from his lordship a well-planted blow between the eyes, which filled them with flashes and darkness. The next the earl was on the floor. The ancient fury of the Celt had burst up into the nineteenth century and mastered a noble spirit. All Malcolm could afterward remember was that he came to himself dealing Liftore, still on the floor, repeated blows. His lordship, struggling to rise, turned up a face white with hate and impotent fury. "You flunkie!" he cursed. "I'll have you shot like a mangy dog!"

"Meantime I will chastise you like an insolent nobleman," said Malcolm, who had already almost recovered his self-possession. "You dare to touch my mistress!" Liftore sprang to his feet and rushed at him. Malcolm caught him by the wrist with a fisherman's grasp. "My lord, I don't want to hurt you. Take a warning and let it be, for fear of worse," he said and threw his hand from him with a swing that nearly dislocated his shoulder.

The warning sufficed. His lordship cast him one scowl of concentrated hate and revenge, and hurried from the house.

At the usual morning hour Malcolm had ridden to Chelsea, hoping to find his friend in a less despairing and more companionable mood than when he left him. To his surprise and disappointment he learned that Lenorme had sailed by the packet for Ostende the night before. He asked leave to go into the study. There on its easel stood the portrait of his father as he had last seen it—disfigured with a great smear of brown paint across the face. He knew that the face was dry, and he saw that the smear was wet. He would see whether he could, with turpentine and a soft brush, remove the insult. In this endeavor he was so absorbed, and by the picture itself was so divided from the rest of the room that he neither saw nor heard anything until Florimel cried out.

Naturally, those events made him yet more dissatisfied with his sister's position. Evil influences and dangers were on all sides of her, the worst possible outcome being that loving one man, she could marry another—and him such a man as Liftore! Whatever he heard in the servant's hall, both tone and substance, only confirmed the unfavorable impression he had of the bold-faced countess from the first. The oldest of her servants had, he found, the least respect for their mistress, although all had a certain liking for her, which gave their disrespect the heavier import. He must get Florimel away somehow. While all was right between her and the painter, he had been less anxious about her immediate surroundings, trusting that Lenorme would before long deliver her. But now she had driven him from the very country, and he had left no clue to follow him by. His housekeeper could tell nothing of his purposes. The gardener and she were left in charge as a matter of course. He might be back in a week or a year; she could not even conjecture.

Seeming possibilities, in varied mingling with rank absurdities, kept passing through Malcolm's mind as, after Liftore's punishment, he lifted the portrait, set it again upon its easel and went on trying to clean the face of it with no small promise of success. But as he made progress, he grew anxious lest with the defilement he should remove some of the color as well. The painter alone, he concluded at length, could be trusted to restore the work he had ruined.

He left the house, walked across the road to the riverbank, and gave a short, sharp whistle. In an instant Davy was in the dinghy, pulling for shore. Malcolm went on board the yacht, saw that all was right, gave some orders, went ashore again, and mounted Kelpie.

In pain, wrath, and mortification Liftore rode home. What would the men at his club say if they knew he had been thrashed by a scoundrel of a groom for kissing his mistress? The fact would soon be out. He must do his best to have it taken for what it ought to be—fiction. It was the harder upon him that he knew himself no coward. He must punish the rascal somehow—he owed it to society to punish him—but at present he did not see how, and the first thing was to have the first word with Florimel. He must see her before she saw the ruffian.

Mistress and maid road home together in silence. The moment Florimel heard Malcolm's voice she had left the house. Caley, following, had heard enough to know that there was a scuffle at least going on in the study, and her eye witnessed against her heart that Liftore could have no chance with the detested groom. Would MacPhail thrash his lordship? If he did, it would be well she should know it.

As to Florimel, she was enraged at the liberties Liftore had taken with her. But alas, was she not in some degree in his power? He had found her there and in tears! How did he come to be there? If Malcolm's judgment of her was correct, Caley might have told him. Was she already false? She pondered within herself and cast no look upon her maid until she had concluded how best to carry herself toward the earl. Then glancing at the hooded cobra beside her, she said, "What an awkward thing that Lord Liftore, of all moments, should appear just then! How could it be?"

"I'm sure I haven't an idea, my lady," returned Caley. "My lord has always been kind to Mr. Lenorme, and I suppose he has been in the way of going to see him at work. Who would have thought my lord was such an early riser? There are not many gentlemen like him nowadays, my lady. Did your ladyship hear the noise in the studio after you left it?"

"I heard high words," answered her mistress, "nothing more. How on earth did MacPhail come to be there as well? From you, Caley, I will not conceal that his lordship behaved indiscreetly; in fact, he was rude. And I can quite imagine that MacPhail thought it his duty to defend me. It is all very awkward for me. Who could have imagined him there and sitting behind amongst the pictures! It almost makes me doubt whether Mr. Lenorme be really gone."

"It seems to me, my lady," returned Caley, "that the man is always just where he ought not to be, always meddling with something he had no business with. I beg your pardon, my lady," she went on, "but wouldn't it be better to get some staid elderly man for a groom—one who has been properly bred up to his duties and taught his manners in a gentlemen's stable? It is so odd to have a groom from a rough seafaring set—one who behaves like the rude fisherman he is, never having had to obey orders of lord or lady! The want of it is, your ladyship will soon be the town's talk if you have such a groom on such a horse after you everywhere."

Florimel's face flushed. Caley saw she was angry and held her peace.

Breakfast was hardly over when Liftore walked in slowly, looking pale. Florimel threw herself back in her chair and held out her left hand to him in an expansive, benevolent sort of way. "How dare you come into my presence looking so well pleased with yourself, my lord, after giving me such a fright this morning?" she said. "You might at least have made sure that there was—that we were—" She could not bring herself to complete the sentence.

"My dearest girl," said his lordship, not only delighted to get off so pleasantly, but profoundly flattered by the implied understanding, "I found you in tears. How could I think of anything else? It may have been stupid, but I trust you will think it pardonable."

Caley had not fully betrayed her mistress to his lordship, and he had, entirely to his own satisfaction, explained the liking of Florimel for the society of the painter as mere fancy.

"It was no wonder I was crying," said Florimel. "Anyone would have cried to see the state my father's portrait was in."

"You father's portrait?"

"Yes. Didn't you know? Mr. Lenorme has been painting one from a miniature I lent him—under my supervision of course; and just because I let fall a word that showed I was not altogether satisfied with the likeness, what should the wretched man do but catch up a brush full of filthy black paint and smudge the face all over!"

"Oh, Lenorme will soon set it to rights again. He's not a bad fellow. I will go about it this very day."

"You'll not find him, I'm sorry to say. There's a note I had from him yesterday. And the picture's quite unfit to be seen—utterly ruined. But I can't think how you could miss seeing it."

"To tell you the truth, Florimel, I had a bit of a scrimmage after you left me in the studio." Here his lordship did his best to imitate a laugh. "Who should come rushing upon me out of the back regions of paint and canvas but that mad groom of yours! I don't suppose you knew he was there?"

"No. I saw a man's feet, that was all."

"Well, there he was, for what reason the devil knows, and when he heard your little startled cry—what should he fancy but that you were frightened and he must rush to the rescue! And so he did with a vengeance. I don't know when I shall quite forget the blow he gave me." And again Liftore laughed, or thought he did.

"He struck you!" exclaimed Florimel, rather astonished, but hardly able for inward satisfaction to put enough indignation into her tone.

"He did, the fellow! But don't say a word about it, for I thrashed him so unmercifully that, to tell the truth, I had to stop because I grew sorry for him. I am sorry now. So I hope you will take no notice of it. In fact, I had begun to like the rascal. You know I was never favorably impressed with him. By Jove! it's not every mistress that can have such a devoted attendant. But he is hardly, with all his virtues, the proper servant for a young lady to have about her. He has had no proper training at all, you see. But you must let the villain nurse himself for a day or two anyhow. It would be torture to make him ride after what I gave him."

Florimel knew that her father had on one occasion struck Malcolm and that he had taken it with the utmost gentleness, confessing himself in the wrong. The blow Malcolm struck Liftore was for her, not himself. Therefore, while her confidence in Malcolm's courage remained unshaken, she was yet able to believe that Liftore had done as he said and supposed that Malcolm had submitted. In her heart she pitied without despising him.

Caley herself took him the message that he would not be wanted. As she delivered it, she smiled an evil smile and dropped a mocking curtsey, with her gaze fixed on his two black eyes and the great bruise between them.

When Caley returned to her mistress and reported the condition of his face, Florimel informed her of the chastisement he had received from Liftore and desired her to find out for his condition, whether he had any broken ribs or the like, for she was anxious about him. But preferably from someone else, possibly the wife of his lordship's groom to whom he would undoubtedly have gone with anything like a serious injury. Florimel felt sorrier for him than she could well understand, seeing he was but a groom—a great lumbering fellow, all his life used to hard knocks, which probably never hurt him.

That her mistress should care so much about him added yet an acrid touch to Caley's spite, but she put on her bonnet and went to the mews. She had begun to fear Malcolm a little as well as hate him. And indeed he was rather a dangerous person to have about when it came to her own schemes.

"Merton's wife knows nothing, my lady," she said on her return. "I saw the fellow in the yard going about much as usual. He will stand a good deal of punishment I fancy, my lady, like that brute of a horse he makes such a fuss with. I can't help wishing, for my lady's sake, we had never set eyes upon him. He'll do us all mischief yet before we're rid of him."

But Florimel was not one to be talked into an opinion she did not choose. Neither would she render to her maid her reasons for not choosing. She had repaired her fortifications, strengthened herself with Liftore, and was confident.

"The fact is, Caley," she said, "I have fallen in love with Kelpie and never mean to part with her—at least till I can ride her—or she kills me. So I can't do without MacPhail. The man must go with the mare. Besides, he is such a strange fellow; if I turned him away, I should quite expect him to poison her before he left."

The maid's face grew darker. That her mistress had the slightest intention of ever mounting that mare she did not find herself fool enough to believe, but of other reasons she could think plenty. And such there certainly were, though none of the sort which Caley's low imagination now supplied. Caley had no faculty for understanding the kind of confidence she reposed in her groom and was the last sort of person to whom her mistress could ever impart the fact of her father's leaving her in charge to his young henchman. And to the memory of her father she faithfully clung, so that no matter how unpleasant Malcolm from time to time became, she yet regarded him not the less confidently.

When later that afternoon Liftore mounted to accompany Lady Lossie, it took all the pluck that belonged to his high breed to enable him to smile, with twenty counselors in different parts of his body persuading him that he was at least a liar. As they rode, Florimel asked how he came to be at the studio that morning. He told her that he had wanted very much to see her portrait before the final touches were given to it. He could have made certain suggestions, he believed, that no one else could. He had indeed, he confessed, heard from his aunt that Florimel was to be there that morning for the last time. It was, therefore, his only chance. But he had expected to be there hours before she was out of bed. For the rest he hoped he had been punished enough, since her rascally groom—and here once more his lordship laughed peculiarly—had but just failed of breaking his arm. It was, in fact, all he could do to hold the reins.

12

••••••••••••••••••••

The Daydream

*A*s the days passed and Florimel heard nothing of Lenorme, the uneasiness that came with her thoughts of him gradually diminished. Her imagination began to work on her concerning the person and gifts and devotion of the painter. When lost in her blissful reveries she often imagined herself—while not exactly marrying Lenorme in the flushed face of an outraged London society—fleeing with him from the judgment of all to some blessed isle of the southern seas. But this mere fancy, as lacking in courage as it was in realism, she was far from capable of carrying into effect. But even the poorest dreaming has its influences, and the result of hers was that the attentions of Liftore became again distasteful to her. And no wonder, for indeed his lordship's presence made a poor show beside that of the painter in the ideal world of the woman who, though she could not in truth be said to love him, certainly had a strong fancy for him.

The pleasure of her castle-building was but seldom interrupted by any thought of the shamefulness of her behavior to him. That did not matter much. Her selfishness closed her eyes to her own falsehood. Meantime, as the past with its trembling joys glided away, widening the space between her and her false fears and shames, she gathered courage to resist Liftore's attentions, and his lordship began to find her as uncertain and variable as ever. Assuredly, as his aunt said, she was yet a girl incapable of knowing even her own mind, and he must not press his suit. Nor was there any jealousy or fear to urge him on, for society regarded her as his.

There was one good process, unknown to her, going on in Florimel. Despite the discomfort often occasioned her by Malcolm, her confidence in him was increasing. And now that the kind of danger threatening her seemed altered, she leaned upon him by degrees more and more, even more than she could have accounted for on the ground that he was a loyal attendant authorized by her father. In a matter of imagined duty, he might make presumptions, but that was a small thing beside the sense of safety his very presence brought with it.

If only Lenorme would come back and allow her to be his friend—his only young lady friend—leaving her at perfect liberty to do just as she liked, then all would be well, perfectly comfortable! In the meantime, life was endurable without him and would be, provided Liftore did not make himself disagreeable. If he did, there were other gentlemen who might be induced to keep him in check. She would punish him; she knew how. She liked him better, however, than any of those.

It was out of pure kindness to Malcolm, upon Liftore's representation of how he had punished him, that for the rest of the week she dispensed with his attendance. But he, unaware of the lies Liftore had told her and supposing she resented the liberty he had taken in warning her against Caley, feared the breach would go on widening. Everything seemed to be going counter to his desires. A whole world of work lay before him—a harbor to build, a numerous fisher-clan to house as they ought to be housed, justice to do on all sides, righteous servants to appoint in place of oppressors, mortgages, and debts to pay off. He had Miss Horn to thank, he wanted to see the schoolmaster again, and he especially had his first friend and father, Old Duncan, to find and minister to. Not a day passed without these and many other concerns pressing upon him. Yet to set his sister free from the dangers he felt threatened her was his first business, and that business as yet refused to be done. He was hemmed in, shut up, in stubborn circumstances from a long-reaching range of duties which called aloud upon his conscience. What made it all the more disheartening was that having discovered, as he hoped, how to gain his first end, his sister's behavior to and the consequent disappearance of Lenorme had swept the whole possibility from him, leaving him more resourceless than ever.

When Sunday evening came he made his way to Hope Chapel, as was his occasional practice, not a long walk from his lodgings, where many Scots gathered for prayer and worship services and the site of Mr. Graham's intermittent preaching. Walking in, he was shown to his seat by a grimy-faced pew-opener. It was with a mind full of varied thoughts that he sat there thinking of the past and what would become of his future. But his thoughts would have been stranger still had he seen who sat several pews behind him watching him like a cat watching a mouse, or rather like a half-grown kitten watching a rat, for she was a little frightened of him, even while resolving to have him. And how could she doubt her final success when her plans were already affording her so much more than she had expected and so soon? He was large game, however, not to be stalked without care and due foresight.

She had been seeking some means for drawing her net around him without his knowledge for some time and had been frequenting the little chapel regularly since stumbling into a service conducted by Sandy Graham some weeks before. "The old heretical schoolteacher become a preacher!" she said to herself as she sat in the shadows of the last row. "Bless me! Will wonders never cease? Who knows what birds may come to gather around the scarecrow Sandy Graham?" And she laughed an oily, contemptuous laugh in the depths of her profane person.

Since then her incognito attendance had in mind the hope of crossing Malcolm's path to subtly gain some advantage over him. She was one to whom intrigue, founded on the knowledge of private history, was as the very breath of her being. Her one passion was to exercise wherever she could whatever measure of control she could gain over those in high places. Her calling as a midwife had at various times in the past led her into certain relationships which afforded her this very sort of grip on unwilling lords and ladies who unknowingly sought her assistance, and the scope of influence of her profession was even now the foundation for her hoped-for advantage over Malcom and, possibly, Lady Florimel as well.

Mrs. Catanach had followed Florimel from Portlossie to Edinburgh and then to London, but not yet had seen how to approach her with probable advantage. In the meantime she had renewed old relations with a certain herb doctor in Kentish Town, at whose house she was now accommodated. Through him she had been able to acquire certain poison weeds of occult power but had, as yet, discovered no possibility of making use of them. But she bade her time, depended on the fortuitous falling of circumstances as one thread was knotted to another until all together had made a clue to guide her straight through the labyrinth to the center, to lay her hand on the collar of the demon of the House of Lossie. It was the biggest game of her life and had been its game for many long, patient years of waiting. Now, however, she sensed the time of her fulfillment drawing nigh.

When the congregation was dismissed, Malcolm saw no trace of the watchful eyes that had been glued to his back. She had slipped out noiselessly some moments before. And as he walked home, he was followed by a little boy far too young to excite suspicion, who had come with Mrs. Catanach to watch her horse. He was the grandson of her friend the herb doctor. When she learned that he was lodged so near Portland Place, she concluded that he was watching his sister and chuckled over the idea of his being watched in turn by herself.

Every day for weeks after her declaration concerning the birth of Malcolm, her evil mind had exercised itself to the utmost to invent some way of undoing her own testimony. She would have had no moral scruples in eating her words, but a magistrate and a lawyer had been present and she feared the risk. Malcolm's behavior to her after his father's death had embittered the unfriendly feelings she had cherished toward him for years. While she had believed him baseborn, and was even ignorant as to his father, she had long tried to secure power over him for the annoyance of the old blind man to whom she had committed him and whom she hated with the hatred of a wife with whom for the best of reasons he had refused to live. But she had found in the boy Malcolm a rectitude over which she could gain no influence. And it even added to her vile indignation that she regarded him as owing her gratitude for not having murdered him at the instigation of his uncle. When at length, to her endless chagrin, she had herself unwittingly supplied the only lacking link in the testimony that should raise him to rank and wealth, she imagined that she had enlarged the obligation infinitely and might henceforth hold him in her hand as a tool for her further operations. When, therefore, he banished her from Lossie House and bound her in silence, she hated him with her whole huge power of hating.

And now she must make speed. For his incognito person in a great city whose ways would still be largely unfamiliar to him afforded a thousandfold facility for doing him mischief. And first she saw that she must draw closer a certain loose tie she had already placed between herself and the household of Lady Bellair. This tie was an influence with the credulous confidence of a certain ignorant and utterly romantic scullery maid, whom she had spied coming and going from the house and had by degrees managed to make acquaintance. She gradually secured a power over her through her imagination by revealing some of the most secretive of disclosures. Among her other favors she had promised to compound for her a mixture—some of whose disgusting ingredients, as potent as hard to procure, she named in her awe-stricken hearing—which when administered under certain conditions and with certain precautions would infallibly secure for her the affections of any man she desired.

This same girl the cat lady now sought and from her learned all she knew about Malcolm, for which Mrs. Catanach supplied a new portion of the love potion—only slightly altered—with some further instructions on its use. Pursuing her inquiries into the composition of the household, however, Mrs. Catanach soon discovered a far more capable and indeed less-scrupulous associate and instrument in Caley. I will not introduce my reader to any of their evil counsels except to say that Mrs. Catanach assumed and retained the upper hand and gathered from Caley much valuable information for her schemes. Doubtless she saw that the very similarity of their designs must cause an eventual rupture between herself and Caley. For neither could expect the other to endure such a rival near her hidden throne of influence. For the aim of both was power in a great family, with consequent money and consideration and midnight counsels and the wielding of all the weapons of hint and threat and insinuation. There was one difference, indeed, since in Caley's eye money was the chief thing, while raw power itself was the midwife's bliss.

13

•••••••••••••••••••

The Lady

*F*lorimel and Lady Clementina Thornicroft—the same who in the park rebuked Malcolm for his treatment of Kelpie—had met several times during the spring and had been mutually attracted. Left an orphan like Florimel, but at yet an earlier age, Lady Clementina had been brought up with a care that had gone over into severity, against which her nature had revolted with an energy that gathered strength from her own repression of its signs. The lack of discipline in her goodness came out at times amusingly; she would always side at first with the lower or weaker or worse. If a dog had torn a child and was going to be killed in consequence, she would not only intercede for the dog, but absolutely side with him, mentioning that and that provocation which the naughty child must have given him ere he could have been goaded to the deed. Once, when the schoolmaster in her village was going to cane a boy for cruelty to a cripple, she pleaded for his pardon on the ground that it was worse to be cruel than to be a cripple and therefore more to be pitied. Everything painful was, to her, cruel.

Lady Clementina was drawn to the young marchioness, over whom was cast the shadow of a tree that gave but baneful shelter. She liked her frankness, her activity, her daring, and fancied that, like herself, she was at noble feud with that infernal parody of the kingdom of heaven called Society. She did not well understand her relation to Lady Bellair, concerning whom she was in doubt whether or not she was her legal guardian, but she saw plainly enough that the countess wanted to secure her for her nephew. She saw too that, being a mere girl and having no scope of choice in the limited circle of their visitors, she was in great danger of yielding without a struggle. She longed to take Florimel in charge like a poor little persecuted kitten, for the possession of which each of a family of children was contending. What if her father had belonged to a rowdy set, was that any reason why his innocent daughter should be devoured, body and soul and possessions, by those of the same set who had not yet perished in their sins?

With her passion for redemption, therefore, she seized every chance of improving her acquaintance with Florimel; and it was her anxiety to gain such a standing in her favor as might further her coveted ministration that had prevented her from bringing her charge of brutality against Malcolm as soon as she discovered whose groom he was. When she had secured her footing on the peak of her friendship, she would unburden her soul, and meantime the horse must suffer for her mistress.

Happily for Florimel, she had by this time made progress enough to venture a proposal that Florimel should accompany her to a small estate she had on the south coast, with a little ancient house upon it—a strange place altogether, she said—to spend a week or two in absolute quiet. Only she must come alone, without even a maid; she would take none herself. This she said because, with the instinct, if not quite insight, of a true nature, she could not endure the woman Caley.

"Will you come with me there for a fortnight?" concluded Clementina.

"I shall be delighted," returned Florimel without a moment's hesitation. "I am getting quite sick of London. There's no room in it. And there's the spring all outside, and it can't get in here. I shall be only too glad to go with you!"

"And on those hard terms—no maid, you know?" insisted Clementina.

"The only thing wanted to make the pleasure complete. I shall be happy to be rid of her."

"I am glad to see you so independent."

"You don't imagine me such a baby as not to be able to get on without a maid! You should have seen me in Scotland! I hated having a woman about me then. And indeed, I don't like it a bit better now. Only everybody has one, and your clothes need looking after," added Florimel, thinking what a weight it would be off her if she could get rid of Caley altogether. "But I *should* like to take my horse," she said. "I don't know what I should do in the country without Abbot."

"Of course, we must have our horses," returned Clementina. "And, yes, you had better bring your groom."

"Oh, you will find him very useful. He can do anything and everything and is so kind and helpful."

"Except to his horse," Clementina was on the point of saying, but thought again. She would first secure the mistress and bide her time to attack the man.

Before they had parted, the two ladies had talked themselves into ecstasies over the anticipated enjoyments of their scheme. It must be carried out at once.

"Let us tell nobody," said Lady Clementina, "and set off tomorrow."

"Enchanting!" cried Florimel in full response.

Then her brow clouded. "There is one difficulty, though," she said. "No man could ride Kelpie with a led horse, and if we had to employ another, Liftore would be sure to hear where we had gone."

"That would spoil all," said Clementina. "But how much better it would be to give that poor creature a rest and bring the other I see him on sometimes."

"And by the time we came back there would not be a living creature, horse or man, anything bigger than a rat, about the stable. Kelpie herself would de dead of hunger, if she hadn't been shot. No, no. Where Malcolm goes Kelpie must go. Besides, she's such fun—you can't think."

"Then I'll tell you what," said Clementina after a moment's pause of perplexity: "we'll *ride* down. It's not a hundred miles, and we can take as many days on the road as we please."

"Better and better!" cried Florimel. "We'll run away with each other. But what will dear old Bellair say?"

"Never mind her," rejoined Clementina. "She will have nothing to say. You can write and tell her as much as will keep her from being really alarmed. Order your man to get everything ready, and I will instruct mine. He is such a staid old fellow, you know, he will be quite enough for protection. Tomorrow morning we will set out together for a ride in Richmond Park, that lying in our way. You can leave a letter on the breakfast table, saying you are gone with me for a while."

So the thing was arranged. They would start quite early the next morning and, that there might be no trouble in the streets, Malcolm should go before with Kelpie and await them in the park.

Malcolm was overjoyed at the prospect of an escape to the country, and yet more to find that his mistress wanted to have him with her—more still to understand that the journey was to be kept a secret. Perhaps now, far from both Caley and Liftore, he might say something to open her eyes; yet how should he avoid the appearance of a talebearer?

It was a sweet, fresh morning late in the spring. He had set out an hour before the rest and now a little way within the park, was coaxing Kelpie to stand, that he might taste the morning in peace. As he thought, he realized how sorely he missed the adventure of the herring fishing. Kelpie, however, was as good as a stiff gale. If only all were well with his sister! Then he would go back to Portlossie and have fishing enough. But he must be patient and follow as he was led. By the time the two ladies with their attendant appeared, he felt such a masterdom over Kelpie as he had never felt before. They rode twenty miles that day with ease, putting up at the first town. The next day they rode about the same distance. The next they rode nearly thirty miles. On the fourth, with an early start and a good rest in the middle, they accomplished a yet greater distance, and at night arrived at Wastbeach.

Florimel scarcely cast a glance around the dark old-fashioned room into which she was shown, but went at once to bed, and when the old housekeeper carried her something from the supper table at which she had been expected, she found her already fast asleep. By the time Malcolm had put Kelpie to rest, he also was a little tired and lay awake no moment longer than his sister.

14
•••••••••••••••••••

The Horse

With rats and mice, cats and owls and creaks and cracks, there was no quiet about the place from night to morning; and with swallows and rooks, cocks and kine, horses and foals, dogs and pigeons, turkeys and geese, and every farm creature but pigs—which, with all her zootrophy, Clementina did not like—no quiet from morning to night. But if there was no quiet, there was plenty of calm, and the sleep of neither brother nor sister was disturbed.

When Florimel awoke, the sun was shining into the room by a window far off at the farther end. It must have been shining for hours, so bright and steady did it shine. She sprang out of bed refreshed and strong. A few aching remnants of stiffness was all that was left of the old fatigue. It was a heavenly joy to think that no Caley would come knocking at her door. She glided down the long room to the sunny window, drew aside the rich old faded curtain, and peeped out. Nothing but pines and Scotch firs all about and everywhere. They came within a few yards of the window. She threw it open. The air was still, the morning sun shone hot upon them and the resinous odor exhaled from their bark and their needles and their fresh buds filled the room—sweet and clean. There was nothing, not even a fence, between this wing of the house and the wood.

All through his deep sleep Malcolm heard the sound of the sea—whether of the phantom sea in his soul or of the world sea to whose murmurs he had listened with such soft delight as he fell asleep, matters little. The sea was with him in his dreams. But when he awoke, it was to no musical crushing of waterdrops, no half-articulated tones of animal speech, but to tumult and outcry from the stables. It was but too plain that he was wanted. Either Kelpie had waked too soon, or he had overslept himself; she was kicking furiously. Hurriedly induing a portion of his clothing, he rushed down and across the yard, shouting to her as he ran, like a nurse as she runs up the stairs to a screaming child. She stopped once to give an eager whinny and then fell to again. Griffith, the groom, and the few other men about the place were looking on appalled. He darted to the cornbin, got a great pottleful of oats, and shot into her stall. She buried her nose in them like the very demon of hunger, and he left her for the few moments of peace that would follow. He must finish dressing as fast as he could. Already, after four days of travel, which with her meant anything but a straightforward jogtrot struggle with space, she needed a good gallop. When he returned he found her just finishing her oats and beginning to grow angry with her own nose for getting so near the bottom of the manager. While there was yet no worse sign, however, than the fidgeting of her hindquarters, and she was still busy, he made haste to saddle her. But her unusually obstinate refusal of the bit and his difficulty in making her open her unwilling jaws gave unmistakable indication of coming difficulty. Anxiously he asked the bystanders about some open place where he might let her go—fields or tolerably smooth heath or sandy beach. He dared not take her through the trees, he said, while she was in such a humor: she would dash herself to pieces. They told him there was a road straight from the stables to the shore and there miles of pure sand without a pebble. Nothing could be better. He mounted and rode away.

Florimel was yet but half dressed when the door of her room opened suddenly and Lady Clementina darted in. With a glide like the swoop of an avenging angel, she pounced upon Florimel, caught her by the wrist, and pulled her toward the door. Florimel was startled, but made no resistance. She half led, half dragged her up a stair that rose from a corner of the hall gallery to the battlements of a little square tower, whence a few yards of the beach, through a chain of slight openings amongst the pines, was visible. Upon that spot of beach a strange thing was going on, at which afresh Clementina gazed with indignant horror.

There was Kelpie rearing on end, striking out at Malcolm with her forehoofs, and snapping with angry teeth, then upon those teeth receiving such a blow from his fist that she swerved and, wheeling, flung her hind hoofs at his head. But Malcolm was too quick for her; she spent her heels in the air and he had her by the bit. Again she reared, and would have struck at him, but he kept well by her side and with the powerful bit forced her to rear to her full height. Just as she was falling backward, he pushed her head from him and, bearing her down sideways, seated himself on it the moment it touched the ground. Then first the two women turned to each other. An arch of victory bowed Florimel's lip. Her eyebrows were uplifted; the blood flushed her cheek and darkened the blue in her wide-opened eyes. Lady Clementina's forehead was gathered in vertical wrinkles over her nose, her eyes were contracted, while her teeth and lips were firmly closed. When Clementina's gaze fell upon her visitor, the fire in her eyes burned more angry still. Her soul was stirred by the presence of wrong and cruelty, and here, her guest, and looking her straight in the eyes, was a young woman—one word from whom would stop it all—actually enjoying the sight!

"Lady Lossie, I am ashamed of you!" she said with reproof, and turning from her, she ran down the stairs.

Florimel turned again toward the sea. Presently she caught sight of Clementina as she sped swiftly to the shore and after a few short minutes of disappearance saw her emerge upon the space of sand where sat Malcolm on the head of the demoness.

"MacPhail, are you a man?" cried Clementina, startling him so that in another instant the floundering mare would have been on her feet.

"I hope so, and a bold one," was on Malcolm's lips for reply, but he bethought himself in time. "I am sorry that what I am compelled to do should annoy your ladyship," he said.

With indignation and breathlessness—she had run so fast—Clementina had exhausted herself in that one exclamation and stood panting and staring. The black bulk of Kelpie lay outstretched on the yellow sand, giving now and then a sprawling kick.

As Malcolm spoke he cautiously shifted his position and, half rising, knelt with one knee where he had sat before, looking observantly at Lady Clementina.

The champion of oppressed animality soon recovered speech. "Get off the poor creature's head instantly," she said with dignified command. "I will permit no such usage of a living thing on my ground."

"I am very sorry to seem rude, my lady," answered Malcolm, "but to obey you might be to ruin my mistress' property. If the mare were to break away, she would dash herself to pieces in the wood."

"You have goaded her to madness."

"I am the more bound to take care of her, then," said Malcolm. "But indeed it is only temper—such temper, however, that I almost believe she is at times possessed of a demon."

"The demon is in yourself. There is none in her but what your cruelty has put there. Let her up, I command you."

"I dare not, my lady. If she were to get loose, she would tear your ladyship to pieces."

"I will take my chance."

"But I will not, my lady. I know the danger and have to take care of you who do not. There is no occasion to be uneasy about the mare. She is tolerably comfortable. I am not hurting her—not much. Your ladyship does not reflect how strong a horse's skull is. And you see what great powerful breaths she draws."

"She is in agony!" cried Clementina.

"Not in the least, my lady. She is only balked of her own way and does not like it."

"And what right have you to balk her of her own way? Has she no right to a mind of her own?"

"She may of course have her mind, but she can't have her way. She has got a master."

"And what right have you to be her master?"

"That my master, my Lord Lossie, gave me charge of her."

"I don't mean that sort of right. That goes for nothing. What right in the nature of things can you have to tyrannize over any creature?"

"None, my lady. But the higher nature has the right to rule the lower in righteousness. Even you can't have your own way always, my lady."

"I certainly cannot now, so long as you keep in that position. Pray, is it in virtue of your being the higher nature that you keep *my* way from *me*?"

"No, my lady. But it is in virtue of right. If I wanted to take your ladyship's property, your dogs would be justified in refusing me my way. I do not think I exaggerate when I say that if my mare here had *her* way, there would not be a living creature about your house by this day next week."

Lady Clementina had never yet felt upon her the power of a stronger nature than her own. She had had to yield to authority, but never to superiority. Hence her self-will had been abnormally developed. Her very compassion was self-willed. Now for the first time, she continuing altogether unaware of it, the presence of such a nature began to operate upon her. The calmness of Malcolm's speech and the immovable decision of his behavior told.

"But," she said, more calmly, "your mare has had four long journeys, and she should have rested today."

"Rest is just the one thing beyond her, my lady. There is a volcano of life and strength in her you have no conception of. I could not have dreamed of a horse like her. She has never in her life had enough to do. I believe that is the chief trouble with her. What we all want, my lady, is a master—a real, right master. I've got one myself, and—"

"You mean you want one yourself," said Lady Clementina. "You've only got a mistress, and she spoils you."

"That is not what I meant, my lady," returned Malcolm. "But one thing I know is that Kelpie would soon come to grief without me. I shall keep her here till her half hour is out and then let her take another gallop."

Lady Clementina turned away. She was defeated. Malcolm knelt there on one knee, with a hand on the mare's shoulder, so calm, so imperturbable, so ridiculously full of argument, that there was nothing more for her to do or say. Indignation, expostulation, were powerless upon him as mist upon a rock. He was the oddest, most incomprehensible of grooms.

Going back to the house, she met Florimel and turned again with her to the scene of discipline. Ere they reached it Florimel's delight with all around her had done something to restore Clementina's composure. The place was precious to her, for there she had passed nearly the whole of her childhood. After a moment Clementina interrupted Florimel's ecstasies by breaking out in fresh accusation of Malcolm, not untempered, however, with a touch of dawning respect. At the same time, her report of his words was anything but accurate, for, as no one can be just without love, so no one can truly report without understanding. But there was no time to discuss him now, as

Clementina insisted on Florimel's putting an immediate stop to his cruelty.

When they reached the spot, there was the groom again seated on his animal's head. "Malcolm," said his mistress, "let the mare get up. You must let her off the rest of her punishment this time."

Malcolm rose again to his knee. "Yes, my lady," he said. "But perhaps your ladyship wouldn't mind helping me to unbuckle her girths before she gets to her feet. I want to give her a bath. Come to this side," he went on, as Florimel advanced to do his request, "round here by her head. If your lady-ship would kneel upon it, that would be best. But you mustn't move till I tell you."

"I will do anything you bid me, exactly as you say, Malcolm," responded Florimel.

"There's the Colonsay blood! I can trust that!" cried Malcolm, with a par-donable outbreak of pride in his family.

Clementina was shocked at the insolent familiarity of her poor little friend's groom, but Florimel saw none and kneeled, as if she had been in church, on the head of the mare, with the fierce crater of her fiery brain blazing at her knee. Then Malcolm lifted the flap of the saddle, undid the buckles of the girths and, drawing them a little from under her, laid the saddle on the sand, talking all the time to Florimel lest a sudden word might seem a direction and she should rise before the right moment had come.

"Please, my Lady Clementina, will you go to the edge of the wood? I can't tell what she may do when she gets up. And please, my Lady Florimel, will you run there, too, the moment you get off her head?"

When he had gotten rid of the saddle, he gathered the reins together in his bridle-hand, took his whip in the other, and softly and carefully straddled across her huge barrel without touching her.

"Now, my lady," he said, "run for the wood."

Florimel rose and fled, heard a great scrambling behind her and, turning at the first tree which was only a few yards off, saw Malcolm, whom the mare had lifted with her, sticking by his knees on her bare back. The mo-ment her forefeet touched the ground he gave her the spur severely and after one plunging kick, off they went westward over the sands, away from the sun, nor did they turn before they had dwindled to such a speck that the ladies could not have told by their eyes whether it was moving or not. At length they saw it swerve a little. By and by it began to grow larger, and after another moment or two they could distinguish what it was, tearing along toward them like a whirlwind, the lumps of wet sand flying behind like an upward storm of clods. What a picture it was!

As he came in front of them, Malcolm suddenly wheeled Kelpie and dashed her straight into the sea. The two ladies gave a cry—Florimel of delight, Clementina of dismay, for she knew the coast, and that there it shelved suddenly into deep water. But that was only the better to Malcolm; it was the deep water he sought, though he got it with a little pitch sooner than he expected. He had often ridden Kelpie into the sea at Portlossie, even in the cold autumn weather when first she came into his charge, and noth-ing pleased her better or quieted her more. He was a heavy weight to swim with, but she displaced much water. She carried her head bravely, he balanced sideways, and they swam splendidly. To the eyes of Clementina the mare seemed to be laboring for her life.

When Malcolm thought she had had enough of it, he turned her head to the shore. But then came the difficulty. So steeply did the shore shelve that Kelpie could not get a hold with her hind hoofs to scramble up into the shallow water. The ladies saw the struggle, and Clementina, understanding it, was running in an agony right into the water with the vain idea of helping them. Malcolm threw himself off, drawing the reins over Kelpie's head as he fell and, swimming but the length of them shoreward, felt the ground with his feet and stood. Kelpie, relieved of his weight, floated a little farther on to the shelf, got a better hold with her forefeet, some hold with her hind ones, and was beside him in a moment. The same moment Malcolm was on her back again, and they were tearing off eastward at full stretch. So far did the lessening point recede in the narrowing distance that the two ladies sat down on the sand and started talking about Florimel's more uncategorical groom, as Clementina, herself the most uncategorical of women, to use her own scarcely justifiable epithet, called him. She asked if such persons abounded in Scotland. Florimel could but answer that this was the only one she had met with.

"It's a pity he is such a savage. He might be quite an interesting character. Can he read?"

"He reads Greek," said Florimel.

"Ah, but I meant English," returned Clementina, whose thoughts were a little astray. Then laughing at herself, she explained: "I mean, can he read aloud? I put the last of the Waverly novels in the box I had sent here. We shall have it tomorrow, or the next day at the latest. I was wondering whether he could read the Scotch as it ought to be read. I have never heard it spoken, and I don't know how to imagine it."

"We can try him," said Florimel. "It will be great fun anyhow. He is *such* a character! You will be *so* amused with the remarks he will make!"

"But can you venture to let him talk to you?"

"If you ask him to read, how will you prevent him? Unfortunately, he has his thoughts, and they *will* come out."

"Is there no danger of his being rude?"

"If speaking his mind about anything in the book be rudeness, he will most likely be rude. Any other kind of rudeness is as impossible to Malcolm as to any gentleman in the land."

"How can you be so sure of him?" said Clementina, a little anxious as to the way in which her friend regarded the young man.

"My father was—yes, I may say so—attached to him; so much so that he—I can't quite say what—but something like made him promise never to leave my service. And this I know for myself that not once, ever since that man came to us, has he done a selfish thing or one to be ashamed of. I could give you proof after proof of his devotion."

Florimel's warmth did not reassure Clementina. She was never quite so generous toward human beings as toward animals. "I would not have you place too much confidence in him, Florimel," she said. "There is something about him I cannot get at the bottom of. Depend upon it, a man who can be cruel would betray on the least provocation."

Florimel smiled, as she had good reason to, but Clementina did not understand the smile and therefore did not like it. She feared the young fellow had already gained too much influence over his mistress. "Florimel, my love," she said, "listen to me. Your experience is not so ripe as mine. That man is not what you think him. One day or other he will, I fear, make himself worse than disagreeable. How *can* a cruel man be unselfish?"

"I don't think him cruel at all. But then I haven't such a soft heart for animals as you. We should think it silly in Scotland. You wouldn't teach a dog manners at the expense of a howl. You would let him be a nuisance rather than give him a cut with a whip. What a nice mother of children you will make, Clementina! That's how the children of good people are so often a disgrace to them."

"You are like all the rest of the Scotch I ever knew," said Lady Clementina. "The Scotch are always preaching. I believe it is in their blood. You are a nation of parsons. Thank goodness my morals go no further than doing as I would be done by! I want to see creatures happy about me."

Malcolm was pulling up his mare some hundred yards off. Even now she was unwilling to stop, but it was at last only from pure objection to whatever was wanted of her. When she did stand she stood stock-still, breathing hard. "I have actually succeeded in taking a little out of her at last, my lady," said Malcolm as he dismounted. "Have you got a bit of sugar in your pocket, my lady? She would take it quite gently now."

Florimel had none, but Clementina had, for she always carried sugar for her horse. Malcolm held the demoness very watchfully, but she took the sugar from Florimel's palm as neatly as an elephant and let her stroke her nose over her wide red nostrils without showing the least of her usual inclination to punish a liberty with death. Then Malcolm rode her home, and she was at peace till evening, when he took her out again.

15

· · · · · · · · · · · · · · · · · ·

The Reading

*A*nd now followed a pleasant time. Wastbeach was the quietest of neighborhoods. It was the loveliest of spring-summer weather, and the variety of scenery on moor, in woodland and on the coast within easy reach of such good horsewomen was wonderful. The first day they rested the horses that would rest, but the next they were in the saddle immediately after an early breakfast. They took the forest way. In many directions were tolerably smooth rides. Malcolm, so far as human companionship went, found it dull, for Lady Clementina's groom regarded him with the contempt of superior age—the most contemptible contempt of all, since years are not the wisdom they ought to bring, and the first sign of that is modesty. Again and again his remarks tempted Malcolm to incite him to ride Kelpie. But conscience, the thought of the man's family, and the remembrance that Kelpie required all his youthful strength, schooled him to the endurance of middle-aged arrogance.

When his mistress mentioned the proposal of her friend with regard to the new novel, he at once expressed his willingness to attempt compliance, fearing only, he said, that his English would prove offensive and his Scotch unintelligible. The task was nowise alarming to him, for he had read aloud much to the schoolmaster, who had insisted that he should read aloud when alone, especially verse, in order that he might get all the good of its outside as well as inside—its sound as well as its thought. On the whole they were so much pleased with his first day's reading, which took place the very day the box arrived, that they concluded to have him read to them daily while they busied their fingers with their embroidery.

There was not much of a garden about the place, but there was a little lawn amongst the pines, in the midst of which stood a huge old patriarch with red stem and grotesquely contorted branches. Beneath it was a bench, and there, after their return from their two hours' ride, the ladies sat, while the sun was at its warmest, on the mornings of their first and second readings. Malcolm sat on a wheelbarrow. On the second day they resolved to send for their reader again as soon as they had tea. But when they sent, he was nowhere to be found, and they concluded on a stroll.

Anticipating no further requirement of his service that day, Malcolm had gone out. Drawn by the sea, he took his way through the dim, solemn, boughless wood, as if to keep a moonlight tryst with his early love. As dusk fell he wandered along the sand, far down the shore and back, and then began to sing an old Scotch ballad.

Ever as he halted for a word the moonlight and the low waves on the sand filled up the pauses. He looked up to the sky, at the moon and rose-diamond stars, his thought half dissolved in feeling and his feeling half crystallized to thought.

Out of the dim wood came two lovely forms into the moonlight and softly approached him—so softly that he knew nothing of their nearness until Florimel spoke. "Is that you, MacPhail?" she said.

"Yes, my lady," answered Malcolm.

"What were you singing?"

"You could hardly call it singing, my lady. We should call it crooning in Scotland."

"Croon it again, then."

"I couldn't, my lady. It's gone."

"You don't mean to pretend that you were extemporizing?"

"I was crooning what came like the birds, my lady. I couldn't have done it if I had thought anyone was near." Then, half ashamed, and anxious to turn the talk from the threshold of his secret chamber, he said, "Did you ever see a lovelier night, ladies?"

"Not often, certainly," answered Clementina.

She was not quite pleased and not altogether offended at his addressing them dually. A curious sense of impropriety in the state of things bewildered her—she and her friend talking thus in the moonlight on the seashore, doing nothing, with her groom—and such a groom!—she asking him to sing again and he addressing them both with a remark on the beauty of the night. Yet all the time she had a doubt whether this young man, whom it would certainly be improper to encourage by addressing from any level but one of lofty superiority, did not belong to a higher sphere than theirs; while certainly no man could be more unpresuming or less forward, even when opposing this opinion to theirs.

"This is just the sort of night," Malcolm resumed, "when I could almost persuade myself I was not quite sure I wasn't dreaming. It makes a kind of borderland between waking and sleeping, knowing and dreaming. In a night like this I fancy we feel something like the color of what God feels when He is making the lovely chaos of a new world—a new kind of world such as has never been before."

"I think we had better go in," said Clementina to Florimel and turned away.

Florimel made no objection, and they walked toward the wood.

"You really must get rid of him as soon as you can," said Clementina when again the moonless night of the pines had received them. "He is certainly more than half a lunatic. It is almost full moon now," she added, looking up. "I have never seen him so bad."

Florimel's clear laugh rang through the wood. "Don't be alarmed, Clementina," she said. "He has talked like that ever since I knew him; and if he is mad, at least he is no worse than he has always been. It is nothing but poetry—yeast on the brain, my father used to say. We should have a fish-poet of him—a new thing in the world, he said. He would never be cured till he broke out in a book of poetry. I should be afraid my father would break the catechism and not rest in his grave till the resurrection if I were to send Malcolm away."

For Malcolm, he was at first not a little amazed at the utter blankness of the wall against which his words had dashed themselves. Then he smiled queerly to himself and said, "I used to think every pretty lady was bound to be a poetess, for how else would she be pretty except for the harmony within her being? And what's that but the poetry of *the* Poet. But I know better than that now. For there go two of the prettiest I've ever seen, but there's more poetry in old man-faced Miss Horn than a dozen like them. Has anybody ever seen a sight so grand as my Lady Clementina? But to hear the nonsense that comes out of her. And all because she won't let her heart rest long enough to let it grow bigger but has always got to be setting things right before their time and before she's even fit for the job!"

Florimel succeeded so far in reassuring her friend as to the safety if not the sanity of her groom that she made no objection to yet another reading from the novel, upon which occasion an incident occurred that did far more to reassure her than all the attestations of his mistress.

Clementina, in consenting, had proposed it being a warm, sunny afternoon, that they should go down to the lake and sit with their work on the bank while Malcolm read. More than a mile in length, but quite narrow, it lay on the seashore—a lake of deep, fresh water, with nothing between it and the sea but a bank of sand. Clementina was describing to Florimel the peculiarities of the place: how there was no outlet to the lake, how the water went filtering through the sand into the sea, how in some parts it was very deep and what large pike there was in it. Malcolm sat a little aside, as usual, with his face toward the ladies and the book open in his hand, waiting a sign to begin. He was looking at the lake, which here was some fifty yards broad, reedy at the edge, dark and deep in the center.

All at once he sprang to his feet, dropped the book, ran down to the brink of the water undoing his buckled belt and pulling off his coat as he ran, threw himself over the bordering reeds into the pool, and disappeared with a great splash. Clementina gave a scream. She had no doubt that in the sudden ripeness of his insanity, he had committed suicide. But Florimel, though startled by her friend's cry, laughed and cried out assurances that Malcolm knew well enough what he was about. It was longer, however, than even she found pleasant before a black head appeared—yards away, for he had risen at great slope, swimming toward the other side. What *could* he be after? Near the middle he swam more softly and almost stopped. Then first they spied a small dark object on the surface. Almost at the same moment it rose into the air. They thought Malcolm had flung it up. Instantly they perceived that it was a bird, a swift. Somehow it had dropped into the water, but a lift from Malcolm's hand had restored it to the air of its bliss.

But instead of turning and swimming back, Malcolm held on and, getting out on the farther side, ran down the beach and rushed into the sea, rousing once more the apprehensions of Clementina. The shore sloped rapidly, and in a moment he was in deep water. He swam a few yards out, swam ashore again, ran round the end of the lake, found his coat and got from it his pocket handkerchief. Having therewith dried his hands and face, he wrung out the sleeves of his shirt a little, put on his coat, returned to his place, and said as he took up the book and sat down, "I beg your pardon, my ladies, but just as I heard my Lady Clementina say '*pikes*,' I saw the little swift in the water. There was no time to lose; Swiftie had but a poor chance." As he spoke he proceeded to find the place in the book.

"You don't imagine we are going to have you read in such a plight as that? cried Clementina.

"I will take good care, my lady. I have books of my own, and I handle them like babies."

"You foolish man! It is of you in your wet clothes, not of the book, I am thinking," said Clementina indignantly.

"I'm much obliged to you, my lady, but there's no fear of me. You saw me wash the fresh water out. Salt water never hurts.

"You must go and change, nevertheless," said Clementina.

Malcolm looked to his mistress. She gave him a sign to obey and he rose. He had taken three steps toward the house when Clementina recalled him. "One word, if you please," she said. "How is it that a man who risks his life for that of a little bird can be so heartless to a great noble creature like that horse of yours? I cannot understand it."

"My lady," returned Malcolm with a smile, "I was no more risking my life than you would be in taking a fly out of the milk jug. And for your question, if your ladyship will only think you cannot fail to see the difference. Indeed, I explained my treatment of Kelpie to your ladyship that first morning in the park, when you so kindly rebuked me for it, but I don't think your ladyship listened to a word I said."

Clementina's face flushed, and she turned to her friend with a "Well!" in her eyes. But Florimel kept her head bent over her embroidery, and Malcolm, no further notice being taken of him, walked away.

16

The Discussion

The next day the reading was resumed and for several days was regularly continued. Each day, as their interest grew, longer and longer time was devoted to it. A question of morals began to arise in Malcolm's mind and finally he paused a moment and said, "Do you think it was right, my ladies, for the hero here to lay down his wealth on behalf of the lady?"

"It was most generous of him," said Clementina.

"Splendidly generous," replied Malcolm, "but I so well remember when Mr. Graham first made me see that the question of duty does not always lie between a good thing and a bad thing. A man has very often to decide between one good thing and another."

"What are the two good things here to choose between?" asked Clementina.

"That is the right question and logically put, my lady," rejoined Malcolm. "The two things are—let me see—on one hand the protection of my lady, and on the other what he owed to his tenants and perhaps society in general. There is generosity on the one side and dry duty on the other." Naturally, by this point, Malcolm's personal interest in the story and discussion was excited—here were elements strangely correspondent with the circumstances of his present position.

"But," said Lady Clementina, "is not generosity something more than duty—something higher, something beyond it?"

"Yes," answered Malcolm, "so long as it does not go against duty, but keeps in the same direction—is in harmony with it. I imagine as we grow we shall come to see that generosity is but our duty. The man who chooses generosity at the expense of justice, even if he gives up everything of his own, is nothing beside the man who for the sake of right will even appear selfish in the eyes of men and may even, at times, go against his own heart. How two men may look—from the outside—is nothing."

Florimel made a neat little yawn over her work. Clementina's hands rested a moment in her lap, and she looked thoughtful. "Then you are taking the side of duty against generosity?" she said after a moment.

"Think, my lady," said Malcolm. "The essence of wrong is injustice. To help another by wrong is to do injustice to somebody else. What honest man could think of that twice?"

"Might not what he did be wrong in the abstract, without having reference to any person?"

"There is no wrong man can do but against the living Right. Surely you believe, my lady, that there is a living Power of right, who *will* have right done?"

"In plain language, I suppose you mean, do I believe in a God?"

"That is what I mean, if by a God you mean a being who cares about us and loves justice—that is, fair play—one whom, therefore, we wrong to the very heart when we do a thing that is not just."

"I would gladly believe in such a being if things were so that I could. As they are, I confess it seems to be the best thing to doubt it. How can I help doubting it when I see so much suffering, oppression, and cruelty in the world?"

"I used to find that a difficulty. Indeed, it troubled me sorely until Mr. Graham helped me see that ease and prosperity and comfort—indeed, the absence of those things you mentioned—are far from what God intends us to have. What if these things, or the lack of them, should be but the means of our gaining something in its very nature so much better that—"

"But why should a being have to suffer for that 'something better' you speak of? What kind of a God would make that 'the means' for our betterment? Your theory is so frightful!"

"But suppose He knows that the barest beginnings of the good He intends would reconcile us to those difficult means and even cause us to choose His will at any expense of suffering?"

Clementina said nothing for a moment. Religious people, she found, could think as boldly as she.

"I tell you, Lady Clementina," said Malcolm, rising and approaching her a step or two, "if I had not the hope of one day being good like God himself, if I thought there was no escape out of the wrong and badness I feel within me, not all the wealth and honors of the world could reconcile me to life."

"I have read of saints," said Clementina with yet a cool dissatisfaction in her tone, "uttering such sentiments, and I do not doubt such were imagined by them. But I fail to understand how, even supposing these things true, a young man like yourself should, in the midst of a busy world and with an occupation which, to say the least . . ."

Here she paused. After a moment Malcolm ventured to help her: "Is so far from an ideal one, would you say, my lady?"

"Something like that," answered Clementina and concluded, "I wonder how *you* can have arrived at such ideas."

"There is nothing so unusual about it, my lady," returned Malcolm. "Why should not a youth, a boy, a child desire with all his might that his heart and mind should be clean, his will strong, his thoughts just, his head clear, his soul dwelling in the place of life? Why should I not desire that my life should be a complete thing and an outgoing of life to my neighbor?"

"Still, how did you come to begin so much earlier than others?"

"All I know, my lady, is that I had the best man in the world to teach me."

"And why did not I have such a man to teach me? I could have learned of such, too."

"If you are able now, my lady, it does not follow that it would have been the best thing for you sooner. Some learn far better for not having begun early and will get on faster than others who have been at it for years. As you grow ready for it, somewhere or other you will find what is needful for you in a book or a friend, or best of all, in your own thoughts."

"But I still want you to explain to me how the God in whom you profess to believe can make use of such cruelties?"

"My lady," remonstrated Malcolm, "I never pretended to explain. All I say is that if I had reasons for hoping there was a God and I found from my observations of life that suffering often was able to lead to a valued good, then there would be nothing unreasonable about His using suffering for the highest, purest, and kindest of motives. If a man would lay claim to being a lover of truth, he ought to give the idea—the mere idea—of God fair play, lest there should be a good God after all and he all his life doing Him the injustice of refusing Him his trust and obedience."

"And how are we to give the mere idea of Him fair play?" asked Clementina, by this time fighting with her emotions, confused and troublesome.

"By looking at the heart of whatever claims to be a revelation of Him."

"It would take a lifetime to read the half of such."

All this time Florimel was working away at her embroidery, a little smile of satisfaction flickering on her face. She was pleased to hear her clever friend talking so with her strange vassal. As to what they were saying, she had no idea. Probably it was all right, but to her it was not interesting. She was mildly debating with herself whether she should tell her friend about Lenorme.

Clementina's work now lay on her lap and her hands on her work, while her eyes at one time gazed on the grass at her feet, at another searching Malcolm's face with a troubled look. The light of Malcolm's candle was beginning to penetrate into her dusky room, the power of his faith to tell upon the weakness of her unbelief. For there is no strength in unbelief.

But whatever the nature of Malcolm's influence upon Lady Clementina, she resented it. Something in her did not like him, or was it his confidence. She knew he did not approve of her, and she did not like being disapproved of. Neither did she approve of him. He was far too good for an honest and brave youth. Not that she could say she had seen dishonesty or cowardice in him, or that she could have told which vice she would prefer to season his goodness and thus bring him to the level of her ideal. And then, for all her theories of equality, he was a groom! Therefore, to a lady, he ought to be repulsive, at least when she found him intruding into the chamber of her thoughts!

For a time her eyes had been fixed on her work, and there had been silence in the little group.

"My lady," said Malcolm, and drew a step nearer to Clementina.

She looked up. How lovely she was with the trouble in her eyes! "If only she were what she might be!" he thought. "If the form were but filled with the Spirit, the body with life!"

"My lady," he repeated, a little embarrassed, "I fear you will never arrive at an understanding of God so long as you cannot bring yourself to see the good that often comes as a result of pain. For there is nothing, from the lowest, weakest tone of suffering to the loftiest acme of pain, to which God does not respond. There is nothing in all the universe which does not in some way vibrate within the heart of God. No creature suffers alone; He suffers with His creatures and through it is in the process of bringing His sons and daughters through the cleansing and glorifying fires, without which the created cannot be made the very children of God, partakers of the divine nature and peace."

"I cannot bring myself to see the right of it."

"Nor will you, my lady, so long as you cannot bring yourself to the good they get by it. My lady, when I was trying my best with poor Kelpie, you would not listen to me."

"You are ungenerous," said Clementina, flushing.

"My lady," persisted Malcolm, "you would not understand me. You denied me a heart because of what seemed in your eyes cruelty. I knew I was saving her from death at the least, probably from a life of torture. There is but one way God cares to govern—the way of the Father-King. Poor parable though it be, my relation to Kelpie must somehow parallel God's dealing with us. The temporary suffering is for a greater good."

After a few moments of silence, Clementina took up her work. Malcolm walked slowly away.

After his departure, Clementina attempted to find what Florimel thought of the things her strange groom had been saying. But she had not thought about them nor had a single notion concerning the matter of their conversation. Seeking to interest her in it and failing, she found, however, that she had greatly deepened its impression upon herself.

Florimel had not yet quite made up her mind whether or not she should open her heart to Clementina, but she approached the door of it in requesting her opinion upon the matter of marriage between persons of social conditions widely parted. Now Clementina was a radical of her day, a reformer, one who complained bitterly that some should be so rich and some so poor. But it is one thing to have opinions and another to be called upon to show them beliefs. It is one thing to declare all men equal and another to tell the girl who looks up to you for advice that she ought to feel at perfect liberty to marry—say, a groom. And when Florimel proposed the general question, Clementina might well have hesitated, and indeed she did hesitate, but in vain she tried to persuade herself that it was solely for the sake of her young and inexperienced friend that she did so. Had Florimel been open with her and told her what sort of man was in her thoughts—had she told her that he was a gentleman, a man of genius, noble, and indeed better bred than any man she knew—the fact of his profession as an artist would only have clenched Lady Clementina's decision in his favor. But Florimel putting the question as she did, how should Clementina imagine anything other than that it referred to Malcolm? A strange confusion of feeling was the consequence. Her thoughts heaved in her like the half-shaped monsters of a spiritual chaos, and amongst them was one she could not at all identify. A direct answer she found impossible. She therefore declined giving an answer of any sort—was not prepared with one, she said. Much was to be considered; no two cases were just alike.

They were summoned to tea, after which she retired to her room, shut the door, and began to think—an operation which, seldom easy if worth anything, was in the present case peculiarly difficult, both because Clementina was not used to it and the subject of it was herself.

Lady Clementina's attempt was as honest as she dared make it. It went something after this fashion: "How is it possible I should counsel a young creature like that, with all her gifts and privileges, to marry a groom? Yes, I know how different he is from any other groom that ever rode behind a lady. But does she understand him? Is she capable of such a regard for him as could outlast a week of closer intimacy? At her age it is impossible she should know what she was doing in daring such a thing. And how could I advise her to do what I could not do myself? But, then, is she in love with him?"

She rose and paced the room, then threw herself on the couch, burying her face in the pillow. Presently, however, she rose again and walked up and down the room—almost swiftly now. I can but indicate the course of her thoughts: "If what he says be true, it opens another and higher life. What a man he is, and so young! Has he not convicted me of feebleness and folly and made me ashamed of myself? What better thing could man or woman do for another than give the chance of becoming such as she had but dreamed the shadow of? He is a gentleman—every inch! Hear him talk! Scotch, no doubt and, well, a *little* long-winded—a bad fault at his age! But see him ride! See him swim—and to save a bird! But then he is hard—severe at best! All religious people are so severe! They think they are safe themselves and so can afford to be hard on others! He would serve his wife the same as his mare if he thought she required it! And I *have* known women for whom it might be the best thing. I am a fool, a soft-hearted idiot! He told me I would give a baby a lighted candle if it cried for it. Or didn't he? I believe he never uttered a word of the sort; he only thought it."

She stood still in the middle of the room. For a minute she stood without definite thought in her brain. Then came something like this: "Then Florimel *does* love him and wants help to decide whether she should marry him or not. Poor, weak thing! But if I were in love with him, I would marry him. Would I? It is well, perhaps, that I am not! But she! He is ten times too good for her! But I am *her* counsel, not his. And what better could come to her than to have such a man for a husband instead of that contemptible Liftore, with his grand earldom ways and proud nose? But this groom is a man—all a man, grand from the center out, as the great God that made him! Yes, it must be a great God that made such a man as that—that is, if he *is* the same as he looks—the same all through. But am I bound to give her advice? Surely not, I may refuse. And rightly so! A woman that marries from advice instead of from a mighty love is wrong. I need not speak. I shall just tell her to consult her own heart and conscience and follow them. But gracious me! Am I then going to fall in love with the fellow—this stableman who pretends to know his Maker? Certainly not! There is *nothing* of the kind in my thoughts. Besides, how should I know what falling in love means? I was never in love in my life and don't mean to be. If I were so foolish as to imagine myself in any danger, would I be such a fool as be caught in it? I should think not, indeed!"

Here came a pause. Then she started once more walking up and down the room, now hurriedly. "I will *not* have it!" she cried aloud, and checked herself, alarmed at the sound of her own voice. But her soul went on loud enough for the thought-universe to hear: "There *can't* be a God, or He would never subject His women to what they don't choose. If a God had made them, He would have them be queens over themselves at least. A slave to things inside myself—thoughts and feelings I refuse, and which I *ought* to have control over! I don't want this in me, yet I can't drive it out! I *will* drive it out. It is not me. But it will not go!"

Again she threw herself on her couch, but only to rise again and yet once more pace the room: "Nonsense! it is *not* love. It is merely that nobody could help thinking about one who had been so much before her mind for so long—one, too, who had made her think. Ah, there, I do believe, lies the real secret of it all! There's the main cause of my trouble and nothing worse! I must not be foolhardy, though, and remain in danger, especially as, for anything I can tell, he may be in love with that foolish child. People, they say, like people that are not at all like themselves. Then I am sure he might like me! She *seems* to be in love with him! I know she cannot be half in real love with him; it's not in her."

She did not rejoin Florimel that evening; it was part of the understanding between the ladies that each should be at absolute liberty. She slept little during the night, started awake as often as she began to slumber, and before morning came was a good deal humbled. When she appeared at breakfast her countenance bore traces of her suffering, but a headache—real enough—gave answer to the not very sympathetic solicitude of Florimel. Happily, the day of their return was near at hand. She must put an end to the interaction she was compelled to admit was, at least, in danger of becoming dangerous. This much she had with certainty discovered concerning her own feelings, that her head grew hot and her heart cold at the thought of the young man belonging more to the mistress who could not understand him than to herself who imagined she could, and it wanted no experiences in love to see it was therefore time to be on guard against herself.

17

•••••••••••••••••••

The Pictures

The next was the last day of the reading. They must finish the tale that morning and on the following set out to return home, traveling as they had come.

" 'It is the opinion of many that he has entered into a Moravian mission, for the use of which he had previously drawn considerable sums . . . ,' " read Malcolm, and paused with the book half closed.

"Is that all?" asked Florimel.

"Not quite, my lady," he answered. "There isn't much more, but I was just thinking whether we hadn't come upon something worth a little reflection—whether we haven't here a window into the mind of the author."

"And you think you can find him out?" said Clementina dryly.

"I believe he's just around a single corner. One thing I think I can say for certain—he believes in a God."

"How do you make that out?"

"Because the author makes his noble-hearted hero—whom he certainly had no intention of disgracing—turn Moravian. My conclusion from it is that, in his judgment, nobleness leads in the direction of religion, that he considers it natural for a noble mind to seek comfort there for its deepest sorrows."

"Well, it may be so. But what is religion without consistency in action?" said Clementina.

"Nothing," answered Malcolm.

"Then how can you, professing to believe as you do, cherish such feelings of anger as you confessed you sometimes had?"

"I don't cherish them, my lady. But I succeed in avoiding hate better than in suppressing contempt, which perhaps is the worse of the two."

Here he paused, for here was a chance that was not likely to recur. He might say before two ladies what he could not say before one. If he could but rouse Florimel's indignation! Clementina's eyes continued fixed upon him. At length he spoke: "I will try to make two pictures in your mind, my lady, if you will help me to paint them: a long seacoast, my lady, and a stormy night. On the margin of the sea a long dune or sandbank and on top of it, her head bare and her thin cotton dress nearly torn from her by the wind, a young woman, worn and white, with an old, faded tartan shawl tight about her shoulders, and the shape of a baby inside it upon her arm."

"Oh, she doesn't mind the cold," said Florimel. "When I was there I didn't mind it a bit."

"She does not mind the cold," answered Malcolm; "she is far too miserable for that."

"But she has no business to take the baby out on such a night," continued Florimel, carelessly critical. "You ought to have painted her by the fireside. They all have fires to sit at. I have seen them through the windows many a time."

"Shame had driven her from it," said Malcolm, "and there she was."

"Do you mean you saw her yourself wandering about?" asked Clementina.

"Twenty times, my lady."

Clementina was silent.

"Well, what comes next?" said Florimel.

"Next comes a young gentleman—but this is a picture in another frame, although of the same night—a young gentleman in evening dress, sipping his wine warm and comfortable, in the bland temper that should follow the best of dinners, his face beaming with satisfaction after some boast concerning himself, or with silent success in the concoction of one or two compliments to have at hand when he joins the ladies in the drawing room."

"Nobody can help such differences," said Florimel. "If there were nobody rich, who would there be to do anything for the poor? It's not the young gentleman's fault that he is better born and has more money than the poor girl."

"No," said Malcolm, "but what if the poor girl has the young gentleman's child to carry about from morning to night?"

"Oh, well, I suppose she's paid for it," said Florimel, whose innocence must have been supplemented by some stupidity born of her flippancy.

"Do be quiet, Florimel," said Clementina; "you don't know what you are talking about."

Her face was in a glow, and one glance at it set Florimel's in a flame. She rose without a word, but with a look of mingled confusion and offence, and walked away. Clementina gathered her work together. But ere she followed her she turned to Malcolm, looked him calmly in the face and said, "No one can blame you for being angry—even for hating—such a man."

"Indeed, my lady, but someone would—the only One for whose praise or blame we ought to care more than a straw for. He tells us we are neither to judge nor to hate. But—"

"I cannot stay and talk with you," said Clementina. "You must pardon me if I follow your mistress."

Another moment and he would have told her all, in the hope of her warning Florimel. But she was gone.

Florimel was offended with Malcolm; he had put her confidence in him to shame. But Clementina was not only older than Florimel, but in her loving endeavors had heard many a pitiful story and was now saddened by the

tale rather than shocked at the teller. Indeed, Malcolm's mode of acquaint-
ing her with the grounds of the feeling she had challenged pleased both her
heart and her sense of what was becoming; while as a partisan of women,
finding a man also of their part, she was ready to offer him the gratitude of
womankind. "What a rough diamond is here!" she thought. "Yet, what fault
could the most fastidious find with his manners? True, he speaks as a servant. But where would be his manners if he did not? But in no way of thinking is he in the smallest degree servile. He is like a great pearl, clean out of
the sea—bred, it is true, in the midst of strange surroundings, but pure as
the moonlight; and if a man, so environed, yet has grown so grand, what
might he not become with such privileges as—"

Good Clementina! what did she mean? Did she imagine that such mere
gifts as she might give him could do for him more than the great sea, with
the torment and conquest of its winds and tempests, more than his own
ministrations of love and victories over passion and pride?

Not for a moment did she imagine him in love with her. Possibly she
admired him too much to attribute to him such an intolerable and insolent
presumption as that would have appeared to her own inferior self. In one
resolve she was confident that her behavior toward him should be such as
to keep him just where he was, affording him no smallest excuse for taking
one step nearer, and they would soon be in London, where she would see
nothing—or next to nothing—more of him. But should she ever cease to
thank God—that is, if ever she came to find Him—that in this room He had
shown her what He could do in the way of making a man? Heartily she
wished she knew a nobleman or two like him. In the meantime, she meant
to enjoy with carefulness the ride to London, after which things should be
as before they left.

The morning arrived; they finished breakfast; the horses came round, all
but Kelpie. The ladies mounted. Ah, what a morning to leave the country
and go back to London! The sun shone clear on the dark pine woods; the
birds were radiant in song; all under the trees the ferns were unrolling each
its mystery of ever-generating life.

They started without Malcolm, for he must always put his mistress up
and then go back to the stable for Kelpie. In a moment they were in the
wood, crossing its shadows. It was like swimming their horses through a sea
of shadows. Then came a little stream and the horses splashed it about like
children. Half a mile more and there was a sawmill with a mossy wheel, a
pond behind dappled with sun and shade, a dark rush of water along a
brown trough, and the air full of the sweet smell of sawn wood. Clementina
had not once looked behind and did not know whether Malcolm had yet
joined them or not. All at once the wild vitality of Kelpie filled the space
beside her, and the voice of Malcolm was in her ears. She turned her head.
He was looking very solemn. "Will you let me tell you, my lady, what this
always makes me think of?" he said.

"What in particular do you mean?" returned Clementina coolly.

"This smell of new-sawn wood that fills the air, my lady."

She bowed her head in consent.

"It makes me think of Jesus in His father's workshop," said Malcolm—"how He must have smelled the same sweet scent of the trees of the world, broken for the uses of men; that is so sweet to me. Oh, my lady, it makes the earth very holy and very lovely to think that as we are in the world, so was He in the world. Oh, my lady, think! If God should be so nearly one with us that it was nothing strange to Him thus to visit His people, then He is so entirely our Father that He cares even to death that we should understand and love Him!"

He reined Kelpie back, and as she passed on his eyes caught a glimmer of emotion in Clementina's. He fell behind and all that day did not come near her again.

Florimel asked her what he had been saying, and she compelled herself to repeat a part of it.

"He is always saying such odd, out-of-the-way things," remarked Florimel. "I used to, like you, fancy him a little astray, but I soon found I was wrong. I wish you could have heard him tell a story he once told my father and me. It was one of the wildest you ever heard. I can't tell to this day whether or not he himself believed it. He told it quite as if he did."

"Could you not make him tell it again as we ride along? It would shorten the way."

"Do you want the way shortened? I don't. But indeed it would not do to tell it here. It ought to be heard just where I heard it. You must come and see me at Lossie House in autumn, and then he shall tell it to you. Besides, it ought to be told in Scotch, and there you will soon learn enough to follow it. Half the charm depends on that."

Although Malcolm did not again approach Clementina that day, he watched almost her every motion as she rode. Her lithe, graceful back and shoulders, the noble poise of her head, and the motions of her arms, easy yet decided, were ever present to him, though sometimes he could not have told whether to his sight or his mind—now in the radiance of the sun, now in the shadow of the wood, now against the green of the meadow, now against the blue of the sky, and now in the faint moonlight.

Day glided after day. Soft and lovely as a dream the morning dawned, the noon flowed past, the evening came. Through it all, daydream and nightly trance, before him glowed the shape of Clementina, its every motion a charm. After that shape he could have been content—oh, how content—to ride on and on. Occasionally his mistress would call him to her, and then he would have one glance at the dayside of the wondrous world he had been following. Little he thought that all the time she was thinking more of him than of her surroundings. That he was the object of her thoughts, not a suspicion crossed the mind of the simple youth. How could he imagine a lady like her taking a fancy to what, for all his marquisate, he still was in his own eyes—a raw young fisherman, only just learning how to behave himself? Even the intellectual phantom, nay, even the very phrase, of being in love with her, had never risen upon the dimmest verge of his consciousness; and that although her being had now become to him of all but absorbing interest. Malcolm's main thought was: what a grand thing it would be to rouse a woman like Clementina to lift her head into the higher regions into which a knowledge of God would bring her! All the journey Malcolm was thinking how to urge the beautiful lady into finding for herself whether she had a Father in heaven or no.

On the second day of the journey he rode up to his mistress and told her, taking care that Lady Clementina should hear, that Mr. Graham was now preaching in London, adding that for his part he had never before heard anything fit to call preaching. Florimel did not show much interest, but asked where, and Malcolm fancied he could see Lady Clementina make a mental note of the place.

"If only," he thought, "she would let the power of that man's faith have a chance of influencing her."

The ladies talked a good deal, but Florimel was not in earnest about anything. Besides, Clementina's thoughts could not have passed into Flori-mel and become her thoughts. Their hearts, their natures, would have to come nearer first. Advise Florimel to disregard rank and marry the man she loved! As well counsel the child to give away the cake he would cry for with intensified selfishness the moment he had parted with it! Still, there was that in her feeling for Malcolm which rendered her doubtful in Florimel's presence.

Between the grooms little passed. Griffith's contempt for Malcom found its least offensive expression in silence, its most offensive in the shape of his countenance. He could not make him the simplest reply without a sneer. Malcolm was driven to keep mostly behind. If by any chance he got in front of his fellow groom, Griffith would instantly cross his direction and ride between him and the ladies. His look seemed to say he had to protect them.

18

The Return

The latter part of the journey was not so pleasant; it rained. It was not cold, however, and the ladies did not mind it much. It accorded with Clementina's mood; and as to Florimel, but for the thought of meeting Caley, her fine spirits would have laughed the weather to scorn. Malcolm was merry. Griffith was the only miserable one of the party. He was tired, and did not relish the thought of the work to be done before getting home. They entered London in a wet fog, streaked with rain and dyed with smoke. Florimel went with Clementina for the night, and Malcolm carried a note from her to Lady Bellair, after which, having made Kelpie comfortable, he went to his lodgings.

When he entered the curiosity shop below his room, the woman received him with evident surprise, and when he would have passed through to the stairs, stopped him with the unwelcome information that, finding he did not return and knowing nothing about himself or his occupation, she had, as soon as the week for which he had paid in advance was out, let the room to an old lady from the country.

"It's no great matter to me," said Malcolm; "only I am sorry you could not trust me a little."

"It's all you know, young man," she returned. "People as lives in London must take care of themselves, not wait for other people to do it. I took your things and laid them all together, and the sooner you find another place for them the better.

In ten minutes he had gathered his belongings in his carpetbag and a paper parcel; then carrying them he reentered the shop. "Would you oblige me by allowing these to stay here till I can come for them?"

The woman was silent for a moment. "I'd rather see the last of them," she answered. "You'll find plenty who'll take you in. No, I can't do it. Take 'em with you."

Malcolm turned and, with his bag in one hand and the parcel under the other, stepped from the shop into the dreary night. There he stood in the drizzle. He concluded after a moment to leave the things with Merton while he went to find a lodging.

Merton was a decent sort of fellow, and Malcolm found him quite as sympathetic as the small occasion demanded. "It ain't no sort of night," he said, "to go lookin' for a bed. Let's go speak to my old woman."

He lived over the stable and they had but to go up the stairs. Mrs. Merton sat by the fire. A cradle with a baby was in front of it. On the other side sat Caley whose exultation she suppressed as they entered—for here came what she had been waiting for—the firstfruits of certain arrangements between her and Mrs. Catanach. She greeted Malcolm distantly, but not spitefully. "I didn't know you lodged with Mrs. Merton, MacPhail," she said with a look at the luggage he had placed on the floor.

"Lawks, miss!" cried the woman, "wherever should we put him?"

"You'll have to find that out, Mother," said Merton. "Surely you've enough room for him someplace, with a truss of straw to help. You'll manage somehow, I'll be bound." And with that he told of Malcolm's condition.

"Well, I suppose we must manage somehow," answered his wife, "but I'm afraid we couldn't make him over-comfortable."

"I don't know, but I suppose we *could* take him at the house," said Caley reflectively. "There is a small room empty in the garret, I know. It ain't much more than a closet, to be sure, but if he could put up with it for a night or two, just till he found better. I could run across and see what they say."

Malcolm wondered at the change in her, but could not hesitate. The least chance of getting settled into the house was not to be thrown away. He thanked her heartily. She rose and went, and they sat and talked till her return. She had been delayed, she said, by the housekeeper—"the cross old patch" had objected to taking in anyone from the stables.

"I'm sure," she went on, "there ain't a ghost of a reason why you shouldn't have the room. Nobody else wants it, or is likely to. But it's all right now, and if you'll come across in about an hour, you'll find it ready for you. One of the girls in the kitchen—I forget her name—offered to make it tidy for you. Only take care—I give you warning. She's a great admirer of you, Mr. MacPhail."

Therewith she took her departure, and at the appointed time Malcolm followed her. The door was opened to him by one of the maids whom he knew by sight and she led him to that part of the house he liked best, immediately under the roof. The room was indeed little more than a closet in the slope of the roof, with only a skylight. But just outside the door was a storm window from which he had a glimpse of the mews-yard. The place smelt rather badly of mice, but in other respects looked clean, and his education had not tended to fastidiousness. He took a book from his bag and read a good while, then went to bed and fell fast asleep.

In the morning he woke early as was his habit, sprung at once on the floor, dressed, and went quietly down. The household was yet motionless. He had begun to descend the last stair when all at once he turned deadly sick and had to sit down, grasping the balusters. In a few minutes he recovered and made the best speed he could to the stable where Kelpie was now beginning to demand her breakfast.

Malcolm had never in his life felt a sickness like that, and it seemed awful to him. He found himself trembling. Just as he reached the stable, where he heard Kelpie clamoring with hoofs and teeth in her usual manner when she judged herself neglected, the sickness returned and with it such a fear of the animal he heard thundering and clashing on the other side of the door as amounted to nothing less than horror. She was a man-eating horse, and was now crying out for her groom, that she might devour him! He gathered, with agonizing effort, every power within him: "How can I quail in the face of such a creature?" he said to himself. "Doesn't God demand of me action according to what I *know*, not what I may chance to *feel*? Well, God is my strength, and I will lay hold of my strength—Kelpie, here I am!"

Therewith the sickness abated so far that he was able to open the stable door. Having brought himself at once into the presence of his terror, his will arose and lorded it over his shrinking, quivering nerves and like slaves they obeyed him. Malcolm tottered to the cornbin, staggered up to Kelpie, fell against her hindquarters as they dropped from a great kick, but got into the stall beside her. She turned eagerly, darted at her food, swallowed it greedily, and was quiet as a lamb while he dressed her.

———

Meantime, things were going rather badly at Portlossie and Scaurnose, and the factor was the cause of it. Some said he had indeed come under the influence of the devil; others said he took more counsel with his bottle than was good for him. Almost all the fishers found him surly, and upon some he broke out in violent rage, while to certain whom he regarded as Malcolm's special friends he carried himself with even more cruel oppression. Ever since Malcolm's departure to London, Mr. Crathie's bitterness had grown extreme, not only toward him but against Blue Peter for his hand in the affair.

The notice to leave at midsummer clouded the destiny of Joseph Mair and his family, and every householder in the two villages believed that to take them in would be to call down the same fate upon himself. But Meg Partan at least was not to be intimidated. Let the factor rage as he would, Meg was absolute in her determination that if the cruel sentence were carried out—which she hardly expected—her house would be shelter for the Mairs. That would leave her own family and theirs three months more to look for another abode. Certain of Blue Peter's friends ventured a visit of intercession to the factor, and were received with composure until their object appeared, and his wrath burst forth once more.

Only the day before he had learned from Miss Horn that Malcolm was still in the service of the marchioness and in constant attendance upon her when she rode. It almost maddened him. He had, for some time, taken to drinking more toddy after his dinner, and it was fast ruining his temper. To complete the troubles of the fisher-folk the harbor at the Seaton had, by a severe storm, been so filled with sand as to be now inaccessible at lower than half tide, nobody as yet having made it his business to see it attended to.

But in the midst of his anxieties about Florimel, Malcolm had not been forgetting his people. As soon as he was a little settled in London, he had written to Mr. Soutar, and to architects and contractors, on the subject of a harbor at Scaurnose. But there were difficulties, and the matter had been making slow progress. Malcolm, however, insisted, and in consequence of his determination to have the possibilities of the thing thoroughly understood, three men appeared one morning on the rocks at the bottom of the cliff on the west side of the Nose. The children of the village discovered them and carried their news. The men being all out in the bay, the women left their work and went to see what the strangers were about. Since they could make nothing of their proceedings, they naturally became suspicious. To whom the fancy first occurred nobody ever knew, but such was the unhealthiness of the moral atmosphere of the place caused by the injustice of Mr. Crathie that it quickly became universally received that they were sent by the factor, and for some purpose only too consistent with the treatment Scaurnose had invariably received ever since it was first the dwelling of fishers. For what rents they had to pay! And how poor was the shelter for which they paid so much—without a foot of land to grow a potato in! To crown all, the factor was now about to drive them in a body from the place—Blue Peter first, one of the best and most considerate men among them. His notice to quit was but the beginning of a clearance.

It was, therefore, easy to see what these villains were about on the precious rock which was their only friend, that did its best to give them the sole shadow of a harbor they had cutting off the wind from the northeast a little. What could they be about but marking the spots where to bore the holes for the blasting powder that should scatter it to the winds and allow the wild sea howling in upon Scaurnose. It would be seen what their husbands and fathers would say to it when they came home! In the meantime, they must themselves do what they could. What were they men's wives for if not to act for their husbands when they happened to be away?

The result was a shower of stones upon the unsuspecting surveyors, who immediately fled and carried the report of their reception to Mr. Soutar at Duff Harbor. He wrote to Mr. Crathie who, till then, had heard nothing of the business, and the news increased both his discontent with his superiors and his wrath with those whom he had come to regard as his rebellious subjects.

19

The Attack

*C*hough unable to eat any breakfast, Malcolm persuaded himself that he felt nearly as well as usual when he went to receive his mistress' orders. Florimel would not ride today, so he saddled Kelpie and rode the Chelsea to look in on the progress of the boat once more. To get rid of the mare, he rang the stable bell at Mr. Lenorme's and the gardener let him in. As he was putting her up, the man told him that the housekeeper had heard from his master. Malcolm went to the house to learn what he might and found, to his surprise, that if Lenorme had gone to the Continent, he was there no longer. That the letter, which contained only directions concerning some of his pictures, was dated from Newcastle and bore the Durham postmark of a week ago. Malcom remembered he had heard Lenorme speak of Durham cathedral, and in the hope that he might be spending some time there, begged the housekeeper to allow him to go to the study to write to her master. When he entered, however, he saw something that made him change his plan, and, having written, instead of sending the letter as he had intended to the postmaster at Durham, he left it upon an easel. It contained merely an earnest entreaty to be made and kept acquainted with his movements, that he might at once let him know if anything should occur that he ought to be informed of.

He found all on board the yacht in shipshape, only Davy was absent. Travers explained that he sent him on shore for a few hours every day. He was a sharp boy, he said, and the more he saw the more useful he would be.

"When do you expect him?" asked Malcolm.

"At one o'clock," answered Travers.

"It is one now," said Malcolm.

A shrill whistle came from the Chelsea shore.

"And there's Davy," said Travers.

Malcolm got into the dinghy and rowed ashore.

"Davy," he said, "I don't want you to be all day on board, but I can't have you be longer away than an hour at a time. Now listen well."

"Ay, ay, sir," said Davy.

"Do you know Lady Lossie's house?"

"No, sir; but I know what she looks like."

"How is that?"

"I've seen her two or three times, riding with yourself to the house over there."

"Would you know her again?"

"I would."

"It's a good way to see a lady across the Thames and know her again."

"Ow! but I used the spyglass," answered Davy.

"You are sure of her, then?"

"I am that, sir."

"Then come with me and I will show you where she lives. I will not ride faster than you can run. But mind you don't look as if you belonged to me."

"Okay, sir, but there's someone taking notice of me already."

"What do you mean?" asked Malcolm.

"There's a wee laddie been after myself several times."

"Did you do anything?"

"He wasn't big enough to lick."

To see what the boy could do, Malcolm let Kelpie go at a good trot. Davy kept up without effort, now shooting ahead, now falling behind, now stopping to look in at a window, and now to cast a glance at a game of pitch-and-toss. No mere passerby could have suspected that the sailor boy belonged to the horseman. He dropped him not far from Portland Place, telling him to go and look at the number but not stare at the house.

All the time he had had no return of the sickness, but, although thus occupied, he had felt greatly depressed. Having some business in the afternoon at the other end of Regent's Park, he was returning through the park on foot when, sunk in thought and suspecting no evil, he was struck down from behind and lost his consciousness. When he came to himself he was lying in a nearby public house, with his head bound up, and a doctor standing over him who asked him if he had been robbed. He searched his pockets and found that his old watch was gone, but his money left.

One of the men standing about said he would see him home. He half thought he had seen him before and did not like the look of him, but accepted the offer, hoping to get on the track of something thereby. As soon as they entered the comparative solitude of the park once more, he begged his companion, who had scarcely spoken all the way, to give him his arm and leaned upon it as if still suffering, but watched him closely.

About the middle of the park, where not a creature was in sight, he felt him begin to fumble in his coat pocket and draw something from it. But when Malcom snatched away his other arm, his fist followed it and the man fell. He made no resistance while Malcolm took from him a short stick, loaded with lead, and his own watch, which he found in his waistcoat pocket. Then the fellow rose with apparent difficulty, but the moment he was on his legs, ran like a hare, and Malcolm let him go, for he felt unable to follow.

As soon as he reached home he went to bed for the rest of the day, for his head ached severely! Before he came to himself, Malcolm had a dream, which, although very confused, was in parts more vivid than any he had ever had. His surroundings in it were those in which he actually lay, and he was ill, but he thought it the one illness he had had just recently. His head ached, and he could rest in no position he tried. Suddenly he heard a step he knew better than any other approaching the door of his chamber. It opened, and his grandfather in great agitation entered, not following his hands, however, in the fashion usual to blindness, but carrying himself like any man. He went straight to the washstand, took up the water bottle and, with a look of mingled wrath and horror, dashed it on the floor. That same instant a cold shiver ran through the dreamer, and his dream vanished. But instead of waking in his bed, he found himself standing in the middle of the floor, his feet wet, the bottle in shivers about them, and the neck of the bottle in his hand. He lay down, grew delirious, and tossed about.

It was evening, and someone was near his bed. He saw the glitter of two great black eyes watching him and recognized the young woman who had admitted him to the house the night of his return and whom he had since met once or twice as he came and went. It was his secret admirer, the scullery maid, who, the moment she perceived he was aware of her presence, threw herself on her knees at his bedside, hid her face, and began to weep. The sympathy of his nature rendered yet more sensitive by weakness and suffering, Malcolm laid his hand on her head and sought to comfort her.

"Don't be alarmed about me," he said, "I shall soon be all right again."

"I can't bear it," she sobbed. "I can't bear to see you like that and all my fault."

"Your fault! What can you mean?" said Malcolm.

"But I did go for the doctor, for all it may be the hanging of me," she sobbed. "Miss Caley said I wasn't to, but I would and I did. They can't say I meant it—can they?"

"I don't understand," said Malcolm feebly.

"The doctor says somebody's been poisoning you," said the girl, with a cry that sounded like a mingled sob and howl; "and he's been apokin' all sort of things down your poor throat."

And again she cried aloud in her agony.

"Well, never mind. I'm not dead you see, and I'll take better care of myself after this. Thank you for being so good to me; you've saved my life."

"Oh, you won't be so kind to me when you know all, Mr. MacPhail," sobbed the girl. "It was me that gave you the horrid stuff, but God knows I didn't mean to do you no harm no more than your own mother."

"What made you do it, then?" asked Malcolm.

"The witch-woman told me to. She said that if I gave it to you, you would—you would—"

She buried her face in the bed and so stifled a fresh howl of pain and shame.

"And it was all lies—lies!" she resumed, lifting her face again which now flashed with rage, "for I know you'll hate me worse than ever now."

"My poor girl, I never hated you," said Malcolm.

"No, but you did as bad; you never looked at me. And now you'll hate me out and out. And the doctor says if you die, he'll have it all searched into, and Miss Caley looks at me as if she suspects me of a hand in it. They won't let alone till they've got me hanged for it, and it's all of love for you."

"Well, you see I'm not going to die just yet," he said, "and if I find myself going, I shall take care the blame falls on the right person. What was the witch-woman like? Sit down on the chair there and tell me about her."

She obeyed with a sigh and gave him such a description as he could not mistake. He asked where she lived, but the girl had never met her anywhere but in the street, she said.

Questioning her very carefully as to Caley's behavior to her, Malcolm was convinced that she had a hand in the affair. Indeed, she had happily more to do with it than even Mrs. Catanach knew, for she had traversed her treatment to the advantage of Malcolm. The midwife had meant the potion to work slowly, but the lady's maid had added to the pretended philtre a certain ingredient, and the combination, while it wrought more rapidly, had yet apparently set up a counteraction favorable to the efforts of his struggling vitality.

But Malcolm's strength was now exhausted. He turned faint, and the girl had the sense to run to the kitchen and get him some soup. As he took it, her demeanor made him uncomfortable. It is to any true man a hateful thing to repel a woman's affections—it is such a reflection upon her.

"I've told you everything, Mr. MacPhail, and it's gospel truth I've told you," said the girl, after a long pause. It was a relief when she first spoke, but the comfort vanished as she went on and with slow, perhaps unconscious movements approached him. "I would have died for you, and here that devil of a woman has been making me kill you! Oh, how I hate her! Now you will never love me a bit—not one tiny little bit forever!"

There was a tone of despairing entreaty in her words that touched Malcolm deeply.

"I am more indebted to you than I can speak or you imagine," he said. "You have saved me from my worst enemy. Do not tell any other what you have told me, or let anyone know that we have talked together. The day will come when I shall be able to show my gratitude."

Something in his tone struck her, even through the folds of her passion. She looked at him a little amazed and for a moment the tide ebbed. Then came a rush that overmastered her. She flung her hands above her head and cried, "That means you will do anything but love me!"

"I cannot love you as you mean," said Malcolm. "I promise to be your friend, but more is out of my power."

A fierce light came into the girl's eyes. But that instant a terrible cry such as Malcolm had never heard, but which he knew must be Kelpie's, rang through the air, followed by shouts of men, the tones of fierce execration, and the clash and clang of hoofs. In Malcolm's absence for most of the afternoon and evening, Kelpie had become so wildly uproarious that Merton could hardly manage the other horses. Forgetting everything else, Malcolm sprang from the bed and ran to the window outside his door.

The light of their lanterns dimly showed a confused crowd in the yard of the mews, and amidst the hellish uproar of their coarse voices, he could hear Kelpie plunging and kicking. Again she uttered the same ringing scream. He threw the window door open and cried to her that he was coming, but the noise was far too great for his enfeebled voice. Hurriedly he added a garment or two to his half dress, rushed to the stairs, hardly seeing his new friend who watched anxiously at the head of it, and shot from the house.

When he reached the yard the uproar had not abated. But when he cried out to Kelpie, through it all came a whinny of appeal, instantly followed by a scream. When he got up to the lanterns, he found a group of wrathful men with stable forks surrounding the poor animal, from whom the blood was streaming before and behind. Fierce as she was she dared not move, but stood trembling, with the sweat of terror pouring from her. Yet her eye showed that not even terror had cowed her. She was but biding her time.

Her master's first impulse was to scatter the men right and left, but on second thought, of which he was even then capable, he saw that they might have been driven to apparent brutality in defence of their lives, and besides he could not tell what Kelpie might do if suddenly released. So he caught her by the broken halter and told them to fall back. They did so carefully— it seemed unwillingly. But the mare had eyes and ears only for her master. What she had never done before, she nosed him over face and shoulders, trembling all the time. Suddenly one of her tormentors darted forward and gave her a terrible prod in the off hindquarter. But he paid dearly for it. Before he could draw back, she lashed out, and shot him half across the yard with his knee joint broken. The whole set of them rushed at her.

"Leaver her alone!" shouted Malcolm, "or I will take her part. Between us we'll do for a dozen of you."

"The devil's in her," said one of them.

"You'll find more of him in that rascal groaning yonder. You had better see to him. He'll never do such a thing again, I fancy. Where is Merton?"

They drew off and went to help their comrade, who lay senseless. When Malcolm led Kelpie in, she stopped suddenly at the stable door and started back shuddering, as if the memory of what she had endured there overcame her. Every fibre of her trembled. He saw that she must have been pitifully used before she broke loose and got out. But she yielded to his coaxing, and he led her to the stall without difficulty.

Kelpie had many enemies amongst the men of the mews. Merton had gone out for the evening, and they had taken the opportunity of getting into her stable and tormenting her. At length she broke her fastenings; they fled, and she rushed out after them.

Malcolm washed and dried his poor animal, handling her as gently as possible, for she was in a sad plight. It was plain he must not have her here any longer; worse to her, at least, was sure to follow. He went up, trembling himself now, to Mrs. Merton. She told him she was just running to fetch him when he arrived; she had no idea how ill he was. But he felt all the better for the excitement, and after he had taken a cup of strong tea, wrote to Mr. Soutar to provide men on whom he could depend, if possible the same who had taken her there before, to await Kelpie's arrival at Aberdeen. There he must also find suitable housing and attention for her at any expense until further direction, or until, more probably, he should claim her himself. He added many instructions to be given as to her treatment.

Until Merton returned he kept watch, then went back to the chamber of his torture which, like Kelpie, he shuddered to enter. The cook let him in and gave him his candle, but hardly had he closed his door when a tap came on it and there stood Rose, his preserver. He could not help feeling embarrassed when he saw her.

"I see you don't trust me," she said.

"I do trust you," he answered. "Will you bring me some water. I dare not drink anything that has been standing."

She looked at him with inquiring eyes, nodded her head, and went. When she returned, he drank the water.

"There! you see I trust you," he said with a laugh. "But there are people about who, for certain reasons, want to get rid of me. Will you be on my side?"

"That I will," she answered eagerly.

"I have not got my plans laid yet, but will you meet me somewhere near this time tomorrow night? I shall not be home, perhaps, all day."

She stared at him with great eyes, but agreed at once, and they appointed time and place. He then bade her good-night, and the moment she left him he lay down on the bed to think. But he did not trouble himself yet to unravel the plot against him, or to determine whether the violence he had suffered had the same origin with the poisoning. Nor was the question merely how to continue to serve his sister without danger to his life; for he had just learned what rendered it absolutely imperative that she should be removed from her present position. Mrs. Merton had told him that Lady Lossie was about to accompany Lady Bellair and Lord Liftore to the Continent. That must not be, whatever means might be necessary to prevent it. Before he went to sleep, things had cleared themselves up considerably.

20

The Abduction

*M*alcolm awoke much better and rose at his usual hour. His head felt clear, his body refreshed, and his determination as strong as ever. Kelpie rejoiced him by affording little other sign of the cruelty she had suffered than the angry twitching of her skin when hand or brush approached a wound. Having urgently committed her to Merton's care, he mounted Honor and rode to Aberdeen wharf. There to his relief, for time was growing precious, he learned that a smack was due to sail the next morning for Aberdeen. He arranged at once for Kelpie's passage and, before he left, saw to every contrivance he could think of for her safety and comfort. He then rode to the Chelsea Reach.

At his whistle Davy tumbled into the dinghy and was rowing for the shore almost before his whistle had ceased ringing in Malcolm's own ears. He left him with his horse, went on board, and gave various directions to Travers. Then he took Davy with him and bought many things at different shops, which he ordered to be delivered to Davy when he should call for them. Having next instructed him to get everything on board as soon as possible and appointed to meet him at the same place and hour he had arranged with Rose, he went home.

A little anxious lest Florimel might have wanted him, for it was now past the hour at which he usually waited her orders, he learned to his relief that she had gone shopping with Lady Bellair. Malcolm set out for the hospital where they had carried the man Kelpie had so terribly mauled. He went, not merely led by sympathy, but urged by a suspicion also which he desired to verify or remove. On the plea of identification, he was permitted to look at him for a moment but not to speak to him. It was enough. He recognized him at once as the same whose second attack he had foiled in Regent's Park. He remembered having seen him about the stable, but had never spoken to him. Returning, he gave Merton a hint to keep his eye on the man and some money to spend for him as he judged best. He then took Kelpie for an airing. To his surprise she fatigued him so much that when he had put her up again, he was glad to go and lie down.

When it came near the time of meeting Rose and Davy, he got his things together in the old carpetbag, which held all he cared for, and carried it with him. As he drew near the spot, he saw Davy already there, keeping a sharp lookout on all sides. Presently Rose appeared, but drew back when she saw Davy. Malcolm went to her.

"Rose," he said, "I am going to ask you to do me a great favor. But you cannot except you are able to trust me."

"I do trust you," she answered.

"All I can tell you now is that you must go with that boy tomorrow. Before night you shall know more. Will you do it?"

"I will."

"Be at this very spot, then, tomorrow morning at six o'clock. Come here, Davy. This boy will take you where I shall tell him."

She looked from the one to the other.

"I'll risk it," she said.

"Put on a clean frock, and take a change of linen with you and your dressing things. No harm shall come to you."

"I'm not afraid," she answered, but looked as if she would cry.

"Of course you will not tell anyone."

"I will not, Mr. MacPhail."

"You are trusting me a great deal, Rose; but I am trusting you too—more than you think. Be off with that bag, Davy, and be here at six tomorrow morning to carry this young woman's for her." Davy vanished.

"Now, Rose," continued Malcolm, "you had better go and make your preparations."

"Is that all, sir?" she said.

"Yes. I shall see you tomorrow. Be brave."

Something in Malcolm's tone and manner seemed to work strangely on the girl. She gazed up at him half frightened, but submissive, and went at once, looking, however, somewhat disappointed.

Malcolm rose early the next morning and, having fed and dressed Kelpie, strapped her blanket behind her saddle and rode her to the wharf. He had no great difficulty with her on the way, though it was rather nervous work at times. But of late her submission to her master had been decidedly growing. When he reached the wharf, he rode her straight along the gangway onto the deck of the smack, as the easiest if not perhaps the safest way of getting her on board. As soon as she was properly secured, and he had satisfied himself as to the provision they had made for her, impressed upon them the necessity of being bountiful to her and brought a loaf of sugar on board for her use, he left her with a lighter heart than he had had ever since he fetched her from a similar deck.

It was a long way to walk home, but he felt much better and thought nothing of it. And all the way, to his delight, the wind met him in the face; a steady westerly breeze was blowing. He reached Portland Place in time to present himself for orders at the usual hour. On these occasions his mistress not infrequently saw him herself, but to make sure, he sent up the request that she would speak with him.

"I am sorry to hear you have been ill, Malcolm," she said kindly, as he entered the room where he happily found her home.

"I am quite well now, thank you, my lady," he returned. "I thought your ladyship would like to hear something I happened to come to the knowledge of the other day."

"Yes, what was that?"

"I called at Mr. Lenorme's to learn what news there might be of him. The housekeeper let me go up to his painting room, and what should I see there, my lady, but the portrait of my lord marquis more beautiful than ever, the brown smear all gone and the likeness, to my mind, greater than before."

"Then Mr. Lenorme is come home!" cried Florimel, scarce attempting to conceal the pleasure his report gave her.

"That I cannot say," said Malcolm. "His housekeeper had a letter from him a few days ago from Newcastle. If he is come back, I do not think she knows it. It seems strange, for who should touch one of his pictures but himself except, indeed, he got some friend to set it to right for your ladyship? Anyhow, I thought you would like to see it again."

"I will go at once," Florimel said, rising hastily. "Get the horses, Malcolm, as fast as you can."

"If my lord Liftore should come before we start?" he suggested.

"Make haste," returned his mistress impatiently.

Malcolm did make haste and so did Florimel. What precisely was in her thoughts who shall say, when she could not have told herself? But doubtless the chance of seeing Lenorme urged her more than the desire to see her father's portrait. Within twenty minutes they were riding down Grosvenor Place and happily heard no following hoofbeats.

When they came near the river, Malcolm rode up to her and said, "Would your ladyship allow me to put up the horses in Mr. Lenorme's stable? I think I could show your ladyship a point or two about the portrait that may have escaped you."

Florimel thought for a moment and concluded it would be less awkward, would indeed tend rather to her advantage with Lenorme, should he really be there, to have Malcolm with her.

"Very well," she answered. "I see no objection. I will ride round with you to the stable, and we can go in the back way."

They did so. The gardener took the horses, and they went up to the study. Lenorme was not there, and everything was just as when Malcolm was last in the room. Florimel was much disappointed, but Malcolm talked to her about the portrait and did all he could to bring back vivid the memory of her father. At length with a little sigh she made a movement to go.

"Has your ladyship ever seen the river from the next room?" said Malcolm, and as he spoke, threw open the door near which they stood.

Florimel, who was always ready to see, walked straight into the drawing room and went to the window.

"There is that yacht lying there still," remarked Malcolm. "Does she not remind you of the *Psyche*, my lady?"

"Every boat does that," answered his mistress. "I dream about her. But I couldn't tell her from many another."

"People used to boats learn to know them like the faces of their friends, my lady. What a day for a sail!"

"Do you suppose there is one for hire?" said Florimel.

"We can ask," replied Malcolm, and with that went to another window, raised the sash, put his head out, and whistled. Over tumbled Davy into the dinghy at *Psyche*'s stern and was rowing for the shore ere the minute was out.

"Why, they're answering your whistle already!" said Florimel.

"A whistle goes farther and perhaps is more imperative than any other call," returned Malcolm evasively. "Will your ladyship come down and hear what they say?"

A wave from her girlhood came washing over her, and Florimel flew merrily down the stairs and across the hall and garden and road to the riverbank, where was a little wooden landing, with a few steps, at which the dinghy was landing.

"Will you take us on board and show us your boat?" asked Malcolm.

"Ay, ay, sir," answered Davy.

Without a moment's hesitation, Florimel took Malcolm's offered hand and stepped into the boat. Malcolm took the oars and shot the little tub across the river. When they got alongside the cutter, Travers reached down both his hands for hers, and Malcolm held one of his for her foot, and Florimel sprang on deck.

"Young woman on board, Davy?" whispered Malcolm.

"Ay, sir—down below," answered Davy, and Malcolm jumped up and stood by his mistress.

"She is like the *Psyche*," said Florimel, turning to him, "only the mast is not so tall."

"Her topmast is struck, you see, my lady—to make sure of her passing clear under the bridges."

"Ask them if we couldn't go down the river a little way," said Florimel. "I should so like to see the houses from it."

Malcolm conferred a moment with Travers and returned.

"They are quite willing, my lady," he said.

"What fun!" cried Florimel, her girlish spirit all at the surface. "How I should like to run away from horrid London altogether and never hear of it again! Dear old Lossie House and the boats and the fishermen!" she added meditatively.

The anchor was already up and the yacht drifting with the falling tide. A moment more and she spread a low treble-reefed mainsail behind, a little jib before and the western breeze filled and swelled and made them alive. With wind and tide she went swiftly down the smooth stream. Florimel clapped her hands with delight. The shores and all their houses fled up the river. They slid past rowboats and great heavy barges loaded to the lip, with huge red sails and yellow, glowing and gleaming in the sun.

"This is the life!" cried Florimel, as the river bore them nearer and nearer to the vortex—deeper and deeper into the tumult of London. They darted through under Westminster Bridge, and boats and barges more and more numerous covered the stream. Waterloo Bridge, Blackfriar's Bridge they passed; Southwark Bridge—and only London Bridge lay between them and the open river, still widening as it flowed to the ocean. London and the parks looked unendurable from this more varied life, more plentiful air and, above all, more abundant space. The very spirit of freedom seemed to wave his wings about the yacht, fanning full her sails. Florimel breathed as if she never could have enough of the sweet wind. For minutes she would be silent, her parted lips revealing her absorbed delight; then she would break out in a volley of questions, now addressing Malcolm, now Travers. She tried Davy too, but Davy knew nothing except his duty there. Not indeed until Gravesend appeared did it occur to Florimel that perhaps it might be well to think by-and-by of returning. But she trusted everything to Malcolm, who, of course, would see that everything was as it ought to be.

Her excitement began to flag a little. She was getting tired. The bottle had been strained by the ferment of the wine. She turned to Malcolm. "Had we not better be putting about?" she said. "I should like to go on forever, but we must come another day, better provided. We shall hardly be in time for lunch." It was nearly four o'clock, but she rarely looked at her watch and indeed wound it up only now and then.

"Will you not go below and have some lunch, my lady?" said Malcolm.

"There can't be anything on board!" she answered.

"Come and see, my lady," rejoined Malcolm, and led the way.

When she saw the little cabin, she gave a cry of delight.

"Why, it is just like our own cabin in the *Psyche*," she said, "only smaller, isn't it, Malcolm?"

"It is smaller, my lady," returned Malcolm, "but then there is a little stateroom beyond."

On the table was a nice meal—cold, but not the less agreeable in the summer weather. Everything looked charming. There were flowers; the linen was snowy, and the bread was the very sort Florimel liked best.

"It is a perfect fairy tale!" she cried. "And I declare, here is our crest on the forks and spoons! What does it all mean, Malcolm?"

But Malcolm had slipped away and gone on deck again, leaving her to food and conjecture, while he went to bring Rose up from the forecabin for a little air. Finding her fast asleep, however, he left her undisturbed.

Florimel finished her meal and set about examining the cabin more closely. The result was bewilderment. How could a yacht, fitted with such completeness, such luxury, be lying for hire in the Thames? As for the crest on the plate, that was a curious coincidence; many people had the same crest. But both materials and colors were like those of the *Psyche*! Then the pretty bindings on the bookshelves attracted her. Every book was either one she knew or one of which Malcolm had spoken to her! He must have had a hand in the business! Next she opened the door of the stateroom. But when she saw the lovely little white berth and the indications of every comfort belonging to a lady's chamber, she could keep her pleasure to herself no longer. She hastened to the companionway, and called Malcolm.

"What does it all mean?" she said, her eyes and cheeks glowing with delight.

"It means, my lady, that you are on board your own yacht, the *Psyche*. I brought her with me from Portlossie and have had her fitted up according to the wish you once expressed to my lord, your father, that you could sleep on board. Now you might make a voyage of many days in her."

"Oh, Malcolm!" was all Florimel could answer. She was too pleased to think as yet of any of the thousand questions that might naturally have followed.

"Why, you've got the *Arabian Nights* and all my favorite books there!" she said at length. "How long shall we have before we get among the ships again?"

She fancied she had given orders to return and that the boat had been put about.

"A good many hours, my lady," answered Malcolm.

"Ah, of course!" she returned; "it takes much longer against the wind and tide. But my time is my own," she added, rather in the manner of one asserting a freedom she did not feel, "and I don't see why I should trouble myself. It will make some to-do, I daresay, if I don't appear at dinner; but it won't do anybody any harm. They wouldn't break their hearts if they never saw me again."

"Not one of them, my lady," said Malcolm.

She lifted her head sharply, but took no further notice of his remark.

"I won't be plagued anymore," she said, holding counsel with herself, but intending Malcolm to hear. "I will break with them rather. Why shouldn't I be free?"

"Why indeed?" said Malcolm. A pause followed, during which Florimel stood apparently thinking, but in reality growing sleepy.

"I will lie down a little," she said, "with one of these lovely books."

The excitement, the air, and the pleasure generally had wearied her. Nothing could have suited Malcolm better. He left her. She went to her berth and fell fast asleep.

21

· · · · · · · · · · · · · · · · ·

The Disclosure

*W*hen Florimel awoke, it was some time before she could think where she was. A strange, ghostly light was about her, in which she could see nothing plain; but the motion helped her to understand. She rose and crept to the companion ladder and up on deck. Wonder upon wonder! A clear, full moon reigned high in the heavens, and below there was nothing but water, rushing past the boat. Here and there a vessel, a snow cloud of sails, would glide between them and the moon and turn black. The mast of the *Psyche* had shot up to its full height; the reef points of the mainsail were loose, and the gaff was crowned with its topsail; foresail and jib were full, and she was flying as if her soul thirsted within her after infinite spaces. Yet what more could she want? All around her was wave rushing upon wave and above her blue heaven and regnant moon. Florimel gave a great sigh of delight.

But what did it mean? What was Malcolm about? Where was he taking her? What would London say to such an extraordinary escapade? Lady Bellair would be the first to believe she had run away with her groom—she knew so many instances of that sort of thing—and Lord Liftore would be the next. It was too bad of Malcolm! But she did not feel very angry with him, notwithstanding, for had he not done it to give her pleasure? And assuredly he had not failed. He knew better than anyone how to please her—better even than Lenorme.

She looked around her. No one was to be seen but Davy, who was steering. The mainsail hid the men, and Rose, having been on deck for two or three hours, was again below. Florimel turned to Davy, but the boy had been schooled and only answered, "I mustn't talk so long's I'm steering, mem."

She called Malcolm. He was beside her in a moment. The boy's reply had irritated her and, coming upon this sudden and utter change in her circumstances, made her feel as one no longer lady of herself and her people, but a prisoner.

"Once more, what does this mean, Malcolm?" she said, in high displeasure. "You have deceived me shamefully! You led me to believe we were on our way back to London, and here we are out to sea! Am I no longer your mistress? Am I a child, to be taken where you please? And what, pray, is to become of the horses you left at Mr. Lenorme's?"

Malcolm was glad of a question he was prepared to answer.

"They are in their own stalls by this time, my lady. I took care of that."

"Then it was all a trick to carry me off against my will!" she cried, with growing indignation.

"Hardly against your will, my lady," said Malcolm, embarrassed and thoughtful, in a tone apologetic.

"Utterly against my will!" insisted Florimel. "Could I ever have consented to go to sea with a boatful of men and not a woman on board? You have disgraced me, Malcolm."

Between anger and annoyance she was on the point of crying.

"It's not so bad as that, my lady. Here, Rose!"

At his word Rose appeared.

"I've brought one of Lady Bellair's maids for your service, my lady," Malcolm went on. "She will do the best she can to wait on you."

Florimel gave her a look. "I don't remember you," she said.

"No, my lady. I was in the kitchen."

"Then you can't be of much use to me."

"A willing heart goes a long way, my lady," said Rose prettily.

"That is true," returned Florimel, rather pleased. "Can you get me some tea?"

"Yes, my lady."

Florimel turned and, much to Malcolm's content, vouchsafing him not a word more, went below.

Presently a little silver lamp appeared in the roof of the cabin, and in a few minutes Davy came, carrying the tea tray and followed by Rose with the teapot. As soon as they were alone, Florimel began to question Rose; but the girl soon satisfied her that she knew little or nothing. When Florimel pressed her how she could go she knew not where at the desire of a fellow servant, she gave such confused and apparently contradictory answers that Florimel began to think ill of both her and Malcolm and to feel more uncomfortable and indignant. The more she dwelt upon Malcolm's presumption and speculated as to his possible design in it, the angrier she grew.

She went again on deck. By this time she was in a passion, little mollified by the sense of her helplessness.

"MacPhail," she said, laying the restraint of dignified utterance upon her word, "I desire you to give me a good reason for your most unaccountable behavior. Where are you taking me?"

"To Lossie House, my lady."

"Indeed!" she returned with scornful and contemptuous surprise. "Then I order you to change your course at once and return to London!"

"I cannot, my lady."

"Cannot! Whose orders but mine are you under, pray?"

"Your father's, my lady."

"I have heard more than enough of that unfortunate statement and the measureless assumptions founded upon it. I shall heed it no longer!"

"I am only doing my best to take care of you, my lady, as I promised him. You will know it one day if you will but trust me."

"I have trusted you ten times too much and have gained nothing in return but reasons for repenting it. Like all other servants made too much of, you have grown insolent. But I shall put a stop to it. I cannot possibly keep you in my service after this. Am I to pay a master where I want a servant?"

Malcolm was silent.

"You must have some reason for this strange conduct," she went on. "How can your supposed duty to my father justify you in treating me with such disrespect? Let me know your reasons. I have a right to know them."

"I will answer you, my lady," said Malcolm. "Davy, go forward; I will take the helm. Rose, bring my lady a fur cloak you will find in the cabin.—Now, my lady, if you will speak low that neither Davy nor Rose shall hear us—Travers is nearly deaf—I will answer you."

"I ask you," said Florimel, "why you have dared to bring me away like this. Nothing but some danger threatening me could justify it."

"There you say it, my lady."

"And what is the danger, pray?"

"You were going on the Continent with Lady Bellair and Lord Liftore and without me to do as I had promised."

"You insult me!" cried Florimel. "Are my movements to be subject to the approbation of my groom? Is it possible my father could give his henchman such authority over his daughter? I ask you again, where was the danger?"

"In your company, my lady."

"So!" exclaimed Florimel, attempting to rise in sarcasm as she rose in wrath, lest she should fall into undignified rage. "And what may be your objection to my companions?"

"That Lady Bellair is not respected in any circle where her history is known and that her nephew is a scoundrel."

"It but adds to the wrong you heap on me that you compel me to hear such wicked abuse of my father's friends," said Florimel, struggling with tears of anger. But for regard to her dignity she would have broken out in fierce and voluble rage.

"If your father knew Lord Liftore as I do, he would be the last man my lord marquis would see in your company."

"Because he gave you a beating, you have no right to slander him," said Florimel spitefully.

Malcolm laughed.

"May I ask how your ladyship came to hear of that?"

"He told me himself," she answered.

"Then, my lady, he is a liar, as well as worse. It was I who gave him the drubbing he deserved for his insolence to my—mistress. I am sorry to mention the disagreeable fact, but it is absolutely necessary you should know what sort of man he is."

"And if there be a lie, which of the two is more likely to tell it?"

"That question is for you, my lady, to answer."

"I never knew a servant who would not tell a lie," said Florimel.

"I was brought up a fisherman," said Malcolm.

"And," Florimel went on, "I have heard my father say no gentleman ever told a lie."

"The Lord Liftore is no gentleman," said Malcolm. "But I am not going to plead my own cause even to you, my lady. If you can doubt me, do. I will let his lordship's character and actions speak for themselves."

"And what, pray tell, am I to take that to mean?"

"Just this, my lady, that there is even now a poor fisher-girl at Portlossie who knows more as to his true nature than you do yourself."

"What am I to care for some girl I don't even know?"

"If you would be a marchioness, she would be your subject, and it would therefore be your duty to care. And for her child as well, brought into this world through the evil and selfish whim of a man not worthy to marry a single poor fisher-girl in the whole village."

"How dare you drag me into such talk! Even you ought to know there are things a lady cannot hear. You affront me so, after I made the mistake of thinking you had good breeding! Can I not escape your low talk?"

"My lady, I am sorrier than you think; but which is worse, that you should hear such a thing spoken of, or make a friend of the man who did it—Lord Liftore."

Florimel turned away, and gave her seeming attention to the moonlit waters, sweeping past the swift-sailing cutter. Malcolm's heart ached for her; he thought she was deeply troubled. But she was not half so shocked as he imagined. Infinitely worse would have been the shock to him could he have seen how little the charge against Liftore had touched her. Alas! evil communications had already in no small degree corrupted her good manners. But had she spoken out what was in her thoughts as she looked over the great wallowing water, she would merely have said that for all that, Liftore was no worse than other men. They were all the same. It was very unpleasant, but how could a lady help it? What need Lady Lossie care about the fisher-girl, or any other concerned with his past, so long as he behaved like a gentleman to her? Malcolm was a foolish, meddling fellow, whose interference was the more troublesome than it was honest.

She stood thus gazing on the waters that heaved and swept astern, but without knowing that she saw them, her mind full. And still and even the waters rolled and tossed away behind in the moonlight.

"Oh, my lady!" exclaimed Malcolm at last, "what it would be to have a soul as big and clean as all this—the water, the sky, the stars!"

She made no reply, did not turn her head or acknowledge that she heard him. A few minutes more she stood, then went below in silence, and Malcolm saw no more of her that night.

22

• • • • • • • • • • • • • • • • • • •

The Preacher

$\mathcal{I}$t was on the Sunday during which Malcolm lay at the point of death from the poisoning that while he was at the worst, Florimel was talking to Clementina, who had called to see whether she would not go and hear the preacher of whom he had spoken with such fervor.

Florimel laughed. "You seem to take everything for gospel Malcolm says, Clementina."

"Certainly not," returned Clementina, rather annoyed. "But I do heed what Malcolm says and intend to find out, if I *can*, whether there is any reality in it. I thought you had a high opinion of your groom."

"I would take his word for anything a man's word can be taken for," said Florimel.

"But you don't set much store by his judgment?"

"Oh, I daresay he's right. But I don't care for the things you like so much to talk to him about. He's a sort of poet, anyhow, and poets must be absurd. They are always either dreaming or talking about their dreams; they care nothing for the realities of life. No, if you want advice you must go to your lawyer or clergyman, or some man of common sense, neither groom nor poet."

"Then, Florimel, it comes to this—that this groom of yours is one of the truest of men and one who possessed your father's confidence, but you are so much his superior that you are incapable of judging him and justified in despising his judgment."

"Only in practical matters, Clementina."

"A duty toward God is with you such a practical matter that you cannot listen to anything he has got to say about it?"

Florimel shrugged her shoulders.

"For my part, I would give all I have to know there was a God worth believing in."

"Clementina!"

"What?"

"Of course there's a God. It is very horrible to deny it."

"Which is worse—to deny *it* or to deny *Him*? Now, I confess to doubting *it*—that is, the very fact of a God. But you seem to me to deny God himself, for you admit there is a God—think it very wicked to deny that—and yet you don't take interest enough in Him to wish to learn anything about Him. You won't *think*, Florimel. I don't fancy you every really *think*."

Florimel again laughed. "I am glad," she said, "that you don't judge me *incapable* of that high art. But it is not so very long since Malcolm used to hint something much the same about yourself, my lady."

"Then he was quite right," returned Clementina. "I am only just beginning to think, and if I can find a teacher, here am I, his pupil."

"Well, I suppose I can spare my groom quite enough to teach you all he knows," Florimel said.

Clementina reddened. "I was thinking of his friend Mr. Graham, not himself," she said.

"You cannot tell whether he has got anything to teach you."

"Your groom's testimony gives likelihood enough to make it my duty to go and see. I intend to find the place this evening."

"It must be some little ranting Methodist conventicle. He would not be allowed to preach in a church, you know, removed from the parish on charges of heresy."

"Of course not. The Church of England is like the apostle that forbade the man casting out devils and got forbid himself for it. She is the most arrant respecter of persons I know, and her Christianity is worse than a farce. It was that first of all that drove me to doubt."

Once more Florimel laughed aloud. "Another revolution, Clementina, and we shall have you heading the riffraff to destroy Westminster Abbey."

"I would follow any leader to destroy falsehood," said Clementina.

"Really, Clementina," said Florimel, "my groom is quite an aristocrat beside you!"

"Well, will you or will you not go with me to hear this schoolmaster?"

"I will go with you anywhere if only it were to be seen with such a beauty," said Florimel, and the thing was settled.

Later that day, when they arrived at Hope Chapel, the ladies were ushered in and Clementina sat waiting her hoped-for instructor. When Mr. Graham rose to read the psalm, great was Clementina's disappointment. He looked altogether, as she thought, of a sort with the place—dreary—and she did not believe it could be the man of whom Malcolm had spoken.

But she soon began to alter her involuntary judgment of him when she found herself listening to an utterance beside which her most voluble indignation would have been but as the babble of a child. Sweeping, incisive denunciation, logic and poetry combining in one torrent of genuine eloquence, poured confusion and dismay upon head and heart of all those who set themselves up for pillars of the Church without practicing the first principles of the doctrine of Christ. Clementina listened with her very soul. All doubt as to whether this was Malcolm's friend vanished within two minutes of his commencement. If she rejoiced a little more in finding that such a man thought as she thought, she gained this good notwithstanding— the presence and power of a man who believed the doctrine he taught. She saw that if what this man said was true, then the gospel was represented by men who knew nothing of its real nature, and by such she had been led into a false judgment.

During the week that followed, Clementina reflected with growing delight on what she had heard and looked forward to hearing more of a kind correspondent on the approaching Sunday. Nor did the shock of the disappearance of Florimel with Malcolm abate her desire to be taught by Malcolm's friend.

Lady Bellair was astounded, mortified, enraged. Liftore turned gray with passion, then livid with mortification at the news. Not one of all their circle, as Florimel had herself foreseen, doubted for a moment that she had run away with that groom of hers. Indeed, upon examination it became evident that the scheme had gone for some time in hand. The yacht they had been on board had been lying there for months, and although she was her own mistress and might marry whom she pleased, it was no wonder she had run away. For how could she have held her face to it, or up, after it?

The latter part of that week was the sorest time Clementina had ever passed. But, like a true woman, she fought her own misery and sense of loss, as well as her annoyance and anxiety, constantly saying to herself that, be the thing as it might, she could never cease to be glad that she had known Malcolm MacPhail.

Whatever may have been the influence of the schoolmaster upon the congregation gathered in Hope Chapel, there were those whose foundations were seriously undermined by his forthrightness. He shortly thereafter received a cool letter of thanks for his services, written by the ironmonger in the name of the deacons, enclosing a check in acknowledgment of them. The check Mr. Graham returned saying that, as he was not a preacher by profession, he had no right to take fees.

When the end of her troubled week came, Clementina walked across the Regent's Park to Hope Chapel but found no Mr. Graham in the pulpit. A strange sense of loneliness and desolation seized her, yet she lingered on the porch. Now that Malcolm was gone, how was she to learn when Mr. Graham would be preaching?

"If you please, ma'am," said a humble and dejected voice.

She turned and saw the tired and smoky face of the pew-opener, who had been watching her from the lobby and had crept out after her. She dropped a curtsey and went on. But he spoke up, detaining her: "Oh, ma'am, we shan't see *him* no more. Our people here—they're good people, but they don't like to be told the truth. It seems to me as if they knowed it so well, they thought as how there was no need for them to mind it."

"You don't mean that Mr. Graham has given up preaching here?"

"They've given up astin' of 'im to preach, lady. But if ever there was a good man in that pulpit, Mr. Graham he do be that man."

"Do you know where he lives?"

"Yes, ma'am, but it would be hard to direct you."

"I should be greatly obliged to you," said Clementina; "only I am sorry to cause you the trouble."

"To tell the truth, I'm only too glad to get away," he returned, "for the place do look like a cemetery, now *he's* out of it."

It was a good half-hour's walk, and during it Clementina held what conversation she might with her companion. When they reached the place, the Sunday-sealed door of the stationer's shop—for there was no private entrance to the house—was opened by a sad-faced woman. She led her through the counter into his dingy little room above, looking out on a yard but a few feet square. There sat the schoolmaster in conversation with a lady, one of the leaders in the church, trying in vain to set some of Mr. Graham's dangerous ideas straight in his mind.

"I hope you will pardon me," said Clementina, "for venturing to call upon you and, as I have had the misfortune to find you occupied, allow me to call another day."

"Stay now if you will, madam," returned the schoolmaster with an old-fashioned bow of courtesy. "This lady has done laying her commands upon me, I believe."

"As you think proper to call them commands, Mr. Graham, I conclude you intend to obey them," said Mrs. Marshall with a forced smile and an attempt at pleasantry.

"Not for the world, madam," he answered.

The lady made no answer beyond a facial flush as she turned to Clementina, "Good evening, ma'am," she said, and walked out.

"I beg your pardon," said the schoolmaster when she was gone. "But indeed the poor woman can hardly help her rudeness, for she is very worldly and believes herself very pious. It is the old story—hard for the rich."

Clementina was struck. "I, too, am rich and worldly," she said. "But I know that I am not pious, and if you would but satisfy me that religion is common sense, I would try to be religious with all my heart and soul."

"I willingly undertake the task. But let us know each other a little first. And lest I should afterward seem to have taken an advantage of you, I hope you have no wish to be nameless to me, for my friend Malcolm MacPhail had so described you that I recognized your ladyship at once."

"Indeed, it is because of what Malcolm said of you that I ventured to come to you."

"Have you seen Malcolm lately?" he asked, his brow clouding a little. "It is more than a week since he has been to me."

Thereupon, with embarrassment such as she would never have felt except in the presence of pure simplicity, she told of his disappearance with his mistress.

"And you think they have run away together?" said the schoolmaster, his face beaming with what, to Clementina's surprise, looked almost like merriment.

"Yes, I think so," she answered. "Why not, if they choose?"

"I will say this for my friend Malcolm," returned Mr. Graham composedly, "that whatever he did I should expect to find not only all right in intention but prudent and well devised also. The present may well seem a rash, ill-considered affair for both of them, but—"

"I see no necessity either for explanation or excuse," said Clementina, too eager to mark that she interrupted Mr. Graham. "In making up her mind to marry him Lady Lossie has shown greater wisdom and courage that, I confess, I had given her credit for."

"And Malcolm?" rejoined the schoolmaster softly. "Should you say of him that he showed equal wisdom?"

"I decline to give an opinion upon the gentleman's part in the business," answered Clementina laughing, but glad there was so little light in the room, for she was painfully conscious of the burning of her cheeks. "Besides, I have no measure to apply to Malcolm," she went on a little hurriedly. "He is like no one I have ever talked with, and I confess there is something about him I cannot understand. Indeed, he is beyond me altogether."

"Perhaps, having known him from infancy, I might be able to explain him," returned Mr. Graham in a tone that invited questioning.

"Perhaps, then," said Clementina, "I may be permitted, in jealousy for the teaching I have received of him, to confess my bewilderment that one so young should be capable of dealing with such things as he delights in. The youth of the prophet makes me doubt his prophecy."

"At least," rejoined Mr. Graham, "the phenomenon coincides with what the Master of these things said of them—that they were revealed to babes and not to the wise and prudent. As to Malcolm's wonderful facility in giving them form and utterance, that depends so immediately on the clear sight of them that, granted a little of the poetic gift developed through reading and talk, we need not wonder much at it."

"You consider your friend a genius?" asked Clementina.

"I consider him possessed of a kind of heavenly common sense. A thing not understood lies in his mind like a fretting foreign body. But there is a far more important factor concerned than this exceptional degree of insight. Understanding is the reward of obedience. Obedience is the key to every door. I am perplexed at the stupidity of the ordinary religious being. In the most practical of all matters he will talk and speculate and try to feel, but he will not set himself to *do*. It is different with Malcolm. From the first he has been trying to obey. Nor do I see why it should be strange that even a child should understand these things. If a man may not understand the things of God whence he came, what shall he understand?"

"How, then, is it that so few understand?"

"Because where they know, so few obey. This boy, I say, did. If you had seen, as I have, the almost superhuman struggles of his will to master the fierce temper his ancestors gave him, you would marvel less at what he has so early become. I have seen him, white with passion, cast himself on his face on the shore and cling with his hands to the earth as if in a paroxysm of bodily suffering, then after a few moments rise and do a service to the man who had wronged him. Is it any wonder that the light should so soon spring forth in a soul like that? When I was a younger man, I used to go out with the fishing boats now and then, drawn chiefly by my love for the boy who earned his own bread that way before he was in his teens. One night we were caught in a terrible storm and had to stand out to sea in the pitch dark. He was not then fourteen. 'Can you let a boy like that steer?' I said to the captain. 'Yes, a boy like that's just the right kind,' he answered. 'Malcolm'll steer as straight as a porpoise because there's no fear of the sea in him.' When the boy was relieved, he crept over to where I sat. 'You're not afraid, Malcolm?' I asked. 'Afraid?' he rejoined with some surprise. 'I wouldn't want to hear the Lord say, "*O you of little faith!*" 'But,' I persisted, 'God may mean to drown you.' 'And why not?' he returned. 'If you were to tell me I might be drowned without His meaning it, then I should be frightened enough.' Believe me, my lady, the right way is simple to find, though only they that seek it can find it. But I have allowed myself," concluded the schoolmaster, "to be carried adrift in my laudation of Malcolm. You did not come to hear praises of him, my lady."

"I owe him much," said Clementina. "But tell me, Mr. Graham, how is it that you know there is a God and one fit to be trusted as you trust Him?"

"In no way that I can bring to bear on the reason of another so as to produce conviction."

"Then what is to become of me?"

"I can do for you what is far better. I can persuade you to look for yourself to see whether or not there lies a gate, a pathway, into belief right before you. Entering by that gate, walking on that path, you shall yourself arrive at the conviction which no man could give you. The man who seeks the truth in any other manner will never find it. Listen to me a moment, my lady. I loved that boy's mother. Because she could not love me, I was very unhappy. Then I sought comfort from the unknown Source of my life. He gave me to understand His Son, and so I understood himself, came to know Him, and was comforted."

"But how do you know it was not all a delusion, the product of your own fervid imagination? Do not mistake me; I want to find it true."

"It is a right and honest question, my lady. I will tell you. First of all, I have found all my difficulties and confusions clearing themselves up ever since I set out to walk in that way. Not life's difficulties, but difficulties of belief. My consciousness of life is threefold what it was: my perception of what is lovely around me, and my delight in it; my power of understanding things and of ordering my way; the same with my hope and courage, my love to my kind, my power of forgiveness. In short, I cannot but believe that my whole being and its whole world are in the process of rectification for me. And if I thus find my whole being enlightened and redeemed and know, therefore, that I fare according to the word of the Man of whom the old story tells; if I find that His word and the resulting action founded on that word correspond and agree and open a heaven in and beyond me; if the Lord of the ancient tale, I say, has thus held word with me, am I likely to doubt much or long whether there be such a Lord or no?"

"What, then, is the way that lies before me for my own door? Help me to see it."

"It is just the old way—that of obedience. If you have ever seen the Lord, if only from afar—if you have any vaguest suspicion that the Jew Jesus, who professed to have come from God, was a better man, a different man, than other men—one of your first duties must be to open your ears to His words and see whether they seem to you to be true. Then, if they do, to obey them with your whole strength and might. This is the way of life, which will lead a man out of its miseries into life indeed."

There followed a little pause and then a long talk about what the schoolmaster had called the old story, in which he spoke with such fervid delight of this and that point in the tale, removing this and that stumbling block by giving the true reading or right interpretation, showing the what and why and how, that, for the first time in her life, Clementina began to feel as if such a man must really have lived, that His feet must really have walked over the acres of Palestine, that His human heart must indeed have thought and felt, worshiped and borne, with complete humanity. Even in the presence of her new teacher and with his words in her ears, she began to desire her own chamber that she might sit down with the neglected story and read her herself.

23

· · · · · · · · · · · · · · · · · · · ·

The Crisis

When Mr. Crathie heard of the outrage the people of Scaurnose had committed upon the surveyors, he vowed he would empty every house in the place. His wife warned him that such a wholesale proceeding would put him in the wrong in the eyes of the whole country since they could not *all* have been guilty. He replied that it would be impossible—the rascals hung together so—to find out the ringleaders. She returned that even if his discrimination was not altogether correct, he should nevertheless make a difference. The factor was persuaded and made out a list of those who were to leave, in which he took care to include all the principal men of the place.

Scaurnose, on the receipt of the papers all at the same time, was like a hive about to swarm. Endless and complicated were the comings and goings between the houses the dialogues and consultations. In the middle of it, in front of the little public house, stood all that day and the next a group of men and women, never the same in its composition for five minutes at a time, but like a cloud ever dissolving and continuously reforming. The result was a conclusion to make common cause with the first victim of the factor's tyranny—namely, Blue Peter, whose expulsion would arrive three months before theirs.

Three of them, therefore, repaired to Joseph's house, commissioned with the following proposal and condition—that Joseph should defy the notice given him to quit, they pledging themselves that he should not be expelled. Whether he agreed or not, they were equally determined, they said, when their turn came, to defend the village. But if he would cast his lot with them, they would, in defending him, gain the advantage of having the question settled three months sooner for themselves. Blue Peter sought to dissuade them, specially insisted on the danger of bloodshed. They had anticipated the objection, but being of the youngest and roughest in the place, the idea of a scrimmage was not at all repulsive to them. They answered that a little bloodletting would do nobody any harm, neither would there be much of that, for they scorned the use of any weapon sharper than their fists. Nobody would be killed but every meddlesome authority taught to let Scaurnose and the fishers alone.

It was a lovely summer evening a few days later, and the sun going down just beyond the point of the Scaurnose shone straight upon the Partan's door. That it was closed in such weather had a significance. Doors were oftener closed in the Seaton now. The spiritual atmosphere of the place was less clear and open than before. The behavior of the factor and the troubles of their neighbors had brought a cloud over the feelings and prospects of its inhabitants.

A shadow darkened the door of the Findlay's cottage. An aged man in highland dress stood and knocked. The many-colored ribbons adorning the bagpipes which hung at his sides somehow enhanced the look of desolation in his appearance. He was bent over his staff. His knock was tentative and doubtful, as if unsure of a welcoming response. He was broken and sad.

A moment passed. The door was unlatched and within stood the Partaness, wiping her hands in her apron. "Preserve us all! You're a sight for sore eyes, Master MacPhail," she cried, holding out her hand which the blind man took as if he saw as well as she. And so he was, for Duncan looked older and feebler and certainly shabbier than before in his worn-out dress. "Well, come into the house—you're as welcome as ever!"

"Thanks to yourself, Mistress Partan," said Duncan as he followed her in, "and my heart thanks you for ta coot welcome. It will pe a long time since I saw you."

Meg stopped in the middle of the kitchen to get a chair for the old man. "Sit ye down there by the fire till I make ye a cup of tea. Or maybe you would prefer a bowl of porridge and milk. It's not that much I have to offer you, but you couldn't be more welcome!"

The old man sat down with a grateful, placid look, and while the tea was steeping, Mrs. Findlay, by judicious questions, gathered from him the history of his recent adventures.

Unable to rise above the terrible schism in his being occasioned by the conflict between horror at the Campbell blood and affection for the youth in whose veins it ran, he had concluded to rid himself of all the associations of place and people and event now grown so painful to him and to make his way back to his native Glencoe—there to endure his humiliation as best he might. But he had not gone many day's journey before a farmer found him on the road insensible and took him home. As he recovered he found his longing for his boy Malcolm growing. He had been a good boy, he said to himself; there was not a least fault to find in him. He was as brave as he was kind, as sincere as clever, as strong as he was gentle, and he could play on the bagpipes. But his mother was a Campbell, and for that there was no help. He had lived as a man of honor, and he would have to die a man of honor as well, hating the Campbells to their last generation. Hard fate for him! How bitter to actually love a Campbell! Mrs. Catanach had indeed won her revenge. But though he could not tear the youth from his heart, at least he could go farther and farther from him.

As soon as he was able, he resumed his journey westward and southward, and at length reached his native glen, the wildest spot for miles. There he found the call of the winds unchanged, yet when his soul cried out in its agonies, they held no soothing response for the heart of the suffering man. Days passed before he came upon a creature who remembered him; for more than twenty years were gone and a new generation had come up since he left the glen. Worst of all, the clan spirit was dying out. The hour of the Celt was gone. There was not even a cottage where he could hide his head. The one he had forsaken had fallen to ruins, and now there was nothing left but its foundations. The people of the inn at the mouth of the valley did their best for him, but he learned by accident that they had had Campbell connections, and rising that instant, he left it forever.

He wandered about for a time, playing his pipes, and everywhere was hospitably treated. But at length his heart could endure its hunger no more; he *must* see his boy, or die. He gathered himself, therefore, to return from whence he had come and walked as straight as possible, for one in his condition, to the cottage of his quarrelsome but true friend Meg Partan—to learn that his benefactor, the marquis, was dead and Malcolm gone.

But here alone could he hope ever to see him again, and so that same night he sought his cottage on the grounds of Lossie House, never doubting his right to reoccupy it. But the door was locked and he could find no entrance. He went to the House and there was referred to the factor. But when he knocked at his door and requested the key of the cottage, Mr. Crathie came raging out of his dining room, cursed him for an old highland goat, and heaped insults on him and his grandson. It was well for him he kept his distance from the old man, for thenceforth the door of the factor's cottage carried in it the marks of every weapon that Duncan bore.

He returned to Mistress Partan white and trembling in a mountainous rage with "ta low-pred hount of a factor!" Her sympathy was enthusiastic, for they shared a common wrath. Then she divulged to him the tale of the factor's cruelty to the fishers, his hatred of Malcolm, and his general wildness of behavior.

Duncan remained where he was, and the general heart of the Seaton was a little revived by the return of one whose presence reminded them of a better time. The factor was foolish enough to attempt to induce Meg to send her guest away.

"We want no such knaves, old or young, about Lossie," he said. "If the place is not kept decent, we'll never get the young marchioness to come near it again."

"Indeed, factor," returned Meg, enhancing the force of her statement by a marvelously rare composure, "the first thing that'll make the place as decent as it's been for the last ten years would be to send factors back where they came from."

"And where might that be?" asked Mr. Crathie.

"That's more than I can rightly say," answered Mrs. Findlay, "but wise old folk say it's somewhere within the swing of Satan's tail."

The reply on the factor's lips as he left the house tended to justify the rude sarcasm.

24

* * * * * * * * * * * * * * * * * * *

The Truth

There came a breath of something in the east. It was neither wind nor warmth. It was light before it is light to the eyes of men. Slowly and slowly it grew until, like the dawning soul in the face on one who lies in faint, the life of light came back to the world. Florimel woke, rose, went on deck, and for a moment was fresh born. The sun peered up like a mother waking and looking out on her frolicking children. Black shadows fell from sail to sail, slipping and shifting, and one long shadow of the *Psyche* herself shot over the world to the very gates of the west. The joy of bare life swelled in Florimel's bosom. She looked up, she looked around, she breathed deep. She turned and saw Malcolm at the tiller, and the cloudy wrath sprang upon her. He stood composed and clear and cool as the morning, now glancing at the sunny sails, where swayed across and back the dark shadows of the rigging, as the cutter leaned and rose, like a child running and staggering over the multitudinous and unstable hillocks. She turned from him.

"Good-morning, my lady! What a morning it is!"

Florimel cast on him a scornful look. For he had the impertinence to speak as if he had done nothing amiss, and she had no ground for being offended with him. She made him no answer. A cloud came over Malcolm's face, and until she went again below, he gave his attention to his steering.

In the meantime, Rose, who happily had turned out as good a sailor as her new mistress, had tidied the little cabin; and Florimel found, if not quite such a sumptuous breakfast laid as at Portland Place, yet a far better appetite than usual to meet what there was. When she had finished, her temper was better, and she was inclined to think less indignantly of Malcolm's share in causing her so great a pleasure. At this moment she could have imagined no better thing than thus to go tearing through the water to her home. For although she had spent little of her life at Lossie House, she could not but prefer it unspeakably to the schools in which she had passed almost the whole of the preceding portion of it. There was little in the affair she could have wished otherwise except its origin. She was mischievous enough to enjoy even the thought of the consternation it would cause at Portland Place. She did not realize all its awkwardness. A letter to Lady Bellair when she reached home, she said to herself, would set everything right; and if Malcolm had now repented and put about, she would instantly have ordered him to hold on for Lossie. But is was mortifying that she should have come at the will of Malcolm and not by her own—worse than mortifying that perhaps she would have to say so. If she were going to say so, she must turn him away as soon as she arrived. She dared not keep him after that in the face of society. But she might take flight as altogether her own madcap idea. Her thoughts went floundering until she was tired.

The dawning out of the dreamland of her past appeared the image of Lenorme. Her behavior to him had not yet roused in her shame or sorrow or sense of wrong. She had driven him from her; she was ashamed of her relation to him; she had caused him bitter suffering; she had all but promised to marry another man. Yet, she had not the slightest wish for that man's company there and then; with no one of her acquaintance but Lenorme could she have shared this conscious splendor of life. "Would to God he had been born a gentleman instead of a painter!" she said to herself.

The day passed on. Florimel grew tired and went to sleep, woke and had her dinner, took a volume of the *Arabian Nights* and read herself again to sleep; woke again, went on deck, saw the sun growing weary in the west. And still the unwearied wind blew, and still the *Psyche* danced on as unwearied as the wind.

Not a word all day had been uttered between Malcolm and his mistress. When the moon appeared, with the waves sweeping up against her face, he approached Florimel where she sat in the stern. Davy was steering.

"Will your ladyship come forward and see how the *Psyche* goes?" he said. "At the stern you can see only the passive part of her motion. It is quite another thing to see the will of her at work in the bows."

At first she was going to refuse, but changed her mind. She said nothing, but rose and permitted Malcolm to help her forward.

It was the moon's turn now to be level with the water, and as Florimel stood on the starboard side, leaning over and gazing down, she saw her shine through the little feather of spray the cutwater sent curling up before it and turn it into pearls and semiopals.

"My lady," said Malcolm breaking the silence, "I can't bear to have you angry with me."

"Then you ought not to have deserved it," returned Florimel.

"My lady, if you knew all, you would not say I deserved it."

"Tell me all, then, and let me judge."

"I cannot tell you all yet, but I tell you something which may perhaps incline you to feel merciful. Did your ladyship ever think what could make me so much attached to your father?"

"No, indeed. I never saw anything peculiar in it. Even nowadays there are servants to be found who love their masters. It seems to me natural enough. Besides, he was very kind to you."

"It was natural indeed, my lady—more natural than you think. Kind to me he was, and that was natural too."

"Natural to him, no doubt, for he was kind to everybody."

"My grandfather told you something of my early history, did he not, my lady?"

"Yes—at least I think I remember his doing so."

"Will you recall it, and see whether it suggests something?"

But Florimel could remember nothing in particular, she said. She had, in truth, forgotten almost everything of the story, as much as she was interested at the time.

"I cannot think what you mean," she added. "If you are going to be mysterious, I shall resume my place by the tiller."

"My lady," said Malcolm, "your father knew my mother and persuaded her that he loved her."

Florimel drew herself up and would have looked him to ashes if wrath could burn. Malcolm saw he must come to the point at once or the parley would cease.

"My lady," he said, "your father was my father too. I am the son of the marquis of Lossie and your brother—your ladyship's half brother, that is."

She looked a little stunned. The gleam died out of her eyes and the glow out of her cheek. She turned and leaned over the bulwark. He said no more, but stood watching her.

She raised herself suddenly, looked at him and said, "Do I understand you?"

"I am your brother," Malcolm repeated.

She made a step forward and held out her hand. He tenderly took the little thing in his great gasp. Her lip trembled. She gazed at him for an instant, full in the face, with a womanly, believing expression.

"My poor Malcolm," she said, "I am sorry for you."

For a moment her heart was softened and it almost seemed as though some wrong had been done. Why should one be a marchioness and the other but a groom? Yet it also explained so much—every peculiarity of the young man, every gift of mind and body, his strength and courage and nobleness.

As usual her thoughts were confused. The one moment the poor fellow seemed to exist only on sufferance, the next she thought how immeasurably he was indebted to the family of Colonsays. Then arose the remembrance of his arrogance and presumption in assuming on such low ground her guardianship—absolute tyranny over her. Was she to be dictated to by a low-born, low-bred fellow like that? Especially when he presumed to have a right to such power? Such a right ought to exclude him forever from her presence! She turned to him again.

"How long have you known this—painful you must find it—this awkward and embarrassing fact? I presume you do know it?" she said coldly and searchingly.

"My father confessed it on his deathbed."

"Confessed!" echoed Florimel's pride, but she restrained her tongue. "It explains much," she continued. "There has been a great change in you since then. Mind you, I only say explains. It could never justify such behavior as yours—no, not if you had been my true brother. There is some excuse, I daresay, to be made for your ignorance and inexperience. No doubt the discovery turned your head. Still I am at loss to understand how you could imagine that sort of—that sort of thing gave you any right over me."

"Love has its rights, my lady," said Malcolm.

Again her eyes flashed and her cheek flushed. "I cannot permit you to talk so to me. You must not flatter yourself that you can be allowed to cherish the same feelings toward me as if you were really my brother. I am sorry for you, Malcolm, as I said already; but you have altogether missed your mark if you think this can alter facts, or shelter you from the consequences of presumption."

Again she turned away. Malcolm's heart was sore for her. How grievously she had sunk from the Lady Florimel of the old days! Had he been able to see such a rapid declension, he would have taken her away long ago and let come of her feelings what might. He had been too careful over them.

"Indeed," Florimel resumed, but this time without turning toward him, "I do not see how things can possibly, after what you have told me, remain as they are. I should not feel at all comfortable in having one about me who would be constantly supposing he had rights. It is very awkward indeed, Malcolm, very awkward! But it is your own fault you are so changed, and I must say I should not have expected it. I should have thought you had more good sense. If I kept you and tried to tell people why I wanted to have you about me, they would tell me to get rid of you. And if I said nothing, there would always be something coming up that required explanation. Besides, you would forever be trying to convert me to one or another of your foolish notions. I hardly know what to do. If you had been my real brother, it would have been different."

"I am your real brother, my lady, and have tried to behave like one since I knew it."

"Yes, you have been troublesome. But if you had been a real brother, of course, I should have treated you differently."

"I don't doubt it, my lady, for everything would have been different then. I should have been the marquis of Lossie, and you would have been Lady Florimel Colonsay. But it would have made little difference in one thing—I could not have loved you better than I do now."

The emotion in Malcolm's voice seemed to touch her a little.

"I believe it, my poor Malcolm. But then you are so rude! Take things into your own hands and do things for me I don't want done. Don't you see the absurdity of it all? It would be very awkward indeed for me to keep you now, forever having to explain about you. Perhaps when I am married it might be arranged, I don't know. Possibly a gamekeeper's place—how would that suit you? That is a half-gentlemanly kind of post. I will speak to the factor and see what can be done. But now, on the whole, Malcolm, I think it would be better for you to go. I am very sorry. I wish you had not told me."

"What will you do with Kelpie, my lady?" asked Malcolm quietly.

"There it is, you see!" she returned. "So awkward! If you had not told me, things could have gone on as before, and for your sake I could have pretended I came on this voyage of my own will and pleasure. Now, I don't know what I can do—except, indeed, you—let me see—I don't know, but you might be able to stay till you got her so far trained that another man could manage her. I might even be able to ride her myself. Will you promise?"

"I will promise not to let the fact come out so long as I am in your service, my lady."

"After all that has passed, I think you might promise me a little more! But I will not press it."

"May I ask what that might be, my lady?"

"I am not going to press it, for I do not choose to make a favor of it. Still, I do not see that it would be such a mighty favor to ask—of one who owes respect at least to the House of Lossie. But I will not ask. I will only suggest, Malcolm, that you should leave this part of the country—say this country altogether—and go to America, or South Wales, or the Cape of Good Hope. If you will take the hint and promise never to speak a word of this unfortunate—yes, I must be honest and allow there is a sort of relationship between us—but if you will keep it secret, I will take care that something is done for you, something more than you could have any right to expect. And mind, I am not asking you to conceal anything that could reflect honor upon you or dishonor upon us."

"I cannot, my lady."

"I scarcely thought you would. Only you hold such grand ideas about God and self-denial that I thought it might be agreeable to you to have an opportunity of exercising the virtue at a small expense and a great advantage."

Malcolm was miserable. Who could have dreamed to find her such a woman of the world! He must break off the hopeless interview.

"Then, my lady," he said, "I suppose I am to give my chief attention to Kelpie, and things are to be as they have been?"

"For the present. And as to this last piece of presumption—concerning this voyage—I will so far forgive you as to take the proceeding on myself—mainly because it would have been my very choice had you submitted it to me. There is nothing I should have preferred to a sea voyage and returning to Lossie House at this time of the year. But you also must be silent on your insufferable share in the business. And for the other matter, the least arrogance or assumption I shall consider to absolve me at once from all obligation toward you of any sort. Such relationships are never acknowledged."

"Thank you—sister," said Malcolm—a last forlorn experiment. And as he said the word he looked lovingly in her eyes.

"If I once hear that word on your lips again as between you and me, Malcolm, I shall that very moment discharge you from my service! You have no claim upon me, and the world will not blame me."

"Certainly not, my lady. I beg your pardon. But there is one perhaps who will blame you a little."

"I know what you mean, but I don't pretend to any of your religious motives. When I do, then you may bring them to bear upon me."

"I was not so foolish as you think me, my lady. I merely imagined you might be as far on as a Chinaman," said Malcolm, with a poor attempt at a smile.

"What insolence do you intend now?"

"The Chinese, my lady, pay highest respect to their departed parents. When I said there was one who would blame you a little, I meant your father."

He touched his cap and withdrew.

"Send Rose to me," Florimel called after him and presently, with her, went down to the cabin.

And still the *Psyche* flew.

During the voyage no further allusion was made by either to what had passed. By the next morning Florimel had yet again recovered her temper, and, nothing fresh occurring to irritate her, kept it and was kind.

By the time their flight was over, Florimel almost felt as if it had indeed been undertaken at her own desire and notion and was quite prepared to assert that such was in fact the case.

25

······················

The Piper

It was two days after the longest day of the year, when there is no night in those regions, only a long twilight. There had been a week of variable weather, with sudden changes of wind to east and north and round again by south to west, and then there had been a calm for several days. All Portlossie, more or less, the Seaton especially, was in a state of excitement, and its little neighbor Scaurnose was more excited still. There the man most threatened, and with the greatest injustice, was the only one calm amongst the men, and amongst the women his wife was the only one that was calmer than he. Blue Peter was resolved to abide the stroke of wrong and not resist the powers of the factor. He had a dim perception that it was better that one should suffer than that order should be destroyed and law defied. Suffering, he might still in patience possess his soul and all be well with him. But what would become of the country if everyone wronged were to take the law into his own hands? He had not found a new home. Indeed, he had not heartily set about searching for one; in part because he was buoyed up by the hope he read so clearly in the face of his more trusting wife—that Malcolm would come to deliver them.

Miss Horn was growing more and more uncomfortable concerning events and dissatisfied with Malcolm for allowing them to progress unimpeded. She had not for some time heard from him, and here was his most important duty unattended to—she would not yet say neglected—the wellbeing of his tenantry, left in the hands of an unsympathetic, self-important underling, who was fast losing all the good sense he had once possessed! Was the life and history of all these brave fishermen and their wives and children to be postponed to the pampered feelings of one girl? said Miss Horn to herself. She had written to him within the last month a very hot letter indeed, which had afforded no end of amusement to Mrs. Catanach, as she sat in his old lodging over the curiosity shop, but, I need hardly say, had not reached Malcolm.

The blind piper had been restless all day. Questioned again and again by Meg Partan as to what was amiss with him, he always returned her odd and evasive answers. Every few minutes he got up from cleaning her lamp to go to the shore. He had but to cross the threshold and take a few steps through the yard to reach the road that ran along the seafront of the village. On the one side were the cottages; on the other, the shore and ocean wide outstretched. He would walk straight across this road until he felt the sand under his feet and there stand for a few moments facing the sea and, with nostrils distended, breathing deep breaths of the air from the northeast, then turn and walk back to Meg Partan's kitchen to resume his ministration of light.

Thus it went on the whole day, and as the evening approached he grew still more agitated. The sun went down and the twilight began and, as the twilight deepened, still his excitement grew. Straightaway it seemed as if the whole Seaton had come to share in it. Men and women were all out-of-doors; and, late as it was when the sun set, there could hardly have been one older that a baby yet in bed. The men with their hands in their trouser pockets were lazily smoking pigtail in short clay pipes, and some of the women, in short blue petticoats, doing the same. Some stood in their doors talking with neighbors, but these were mostly the elder women; the younger ones—all but Lizza Findlay—were out in the road. One man half leaned on the windowsill of Duncan's former abode, and round him were two or three more and some women, talking about Scaurnose and the factor and what the lads would do tomorrow, while the hush of the sea on the pebbles mingled with their talk.

Once more there was Duncan, standing as if looking out to sea and shading his brows with his hand as if to protect his eyes from the glare of the sun and thus enable his sight.

"There's the old piper again!" said one of the group, a young woman. "He looks foolish enough standing there like that, as if he couldn't see for the sun in his eyes."

"Hold your tongue, lass," rejoined an elderly woman beside her. "There's more things than you know, as the Book says. There's eyes that can see and there's eyes that can't and some eyes—"

"Ta poat! Ta poat of my chief!" cried the seer suddenly. "She is coming like a dream in ta night, put one tat will not pe cone with ta morning!"

He spoke as one suppressing a wild joy.

"What'll that be, Grandfather?" the woman who had last spoke, respectfully inquired, while those within hearing hushed each other and stood in silence.

"And who will it pe put my own son?" answered the piper. "Who should it pe put my own Malcolm! I see his poat coming rount ta Tead Head. She flits over ta water like a pale ghost over Morven. Put it's ta young and ta strong she is pringing home to Tuncan."

Involuntarily all eyes turned toward the point called Death's Head, which bounded the bay on the east.

"It's too dark to see anything," said the man on the windowsill. "There's a bit of a fog come up."

"Yes," said Duncan, "it'll pe too tark for you who have no eyes put to speak of. Put you'll wait a few, and you'll pe seeing as well as me. Oh, my poy! My poy! Ta Lord pe praised! I'll die in peace, for he'll pe only the one half of him a Cawmill, and he'll pe safe at last, as sure as tere's a heaven to come to and a hell to come from. For the half tat's not a Cawmill must pe ta strong half, and it will trag ta other half into heaven—where it will not pe welcome, howefer."

As if to get rid of the unpleasant thought that his Malcolm could not enter heaven without taking half a Campbell with him, he turned from the sea and hurried into the house but to catch up his pipes and hasten out again, filling the bag as he went. Arriving once more on the verge of the sand, he stood facing the northeast, and began blowing a pilbroch loud and clear.

Meantime Meg Partan had joined the same group.

"Hech, sirs!" she cried, "if the old man's right, it'll be the marchioness herself that's heard of the ill doings of her factor and now's coming to see after her fold. And it'll be Malcolm's doing. But the fine lad won't know the state of the harbor and he'll be making for the mouth of it and he'll run that bonny boat aground between the two piers. And that'll not be a proper homecoming for the lady of the land. And what's more, Malcolm'll get the blame. So some of you must get down to the pierhead to look out and give him warning!"

Her own husband was the first to start, proud of the foresight of his wife.

"Faith, Meg!" he cried, "you're just as good at seeing in the distance as the piper himself!"

By the time the Partan and his companions reached the pierhead, something was dawning in the vague of sea and sky that might be a sloop standing for the harbor. In a moment they were in a boat and making for the open bay.

The wind had now fallen to the softest breath, and the little vessel came on slowly. The men rowed hard, shouting and waving a white shirt, and soon they heard a hail which none could mistake for other than Malcolm's. In a few minutes they were on board, greeting their old friend with jubilation. Briefly the Partan communicated the state of the harbor and recommended running the Fisky ashore about opposite the brass swivel.

"All the men and women in the Seaton," he said, "will be there to haul her up."

Malcolm took the helm, gave his orders, and steered further westward. By this time the people on shore had caught sight of the cutter. They saw her come stealing out of the thick dark and go gliding along the shore like a sea ghost over the dusky water—faint, uncertain, noiseless, glimmering. It could be no other than the Fisky! Both their lady and their friend Malcolm must be on board. They were certain, for how could the one of them come without the other? And doubtless the marchioness, whom they all remembered as a good-humored, handsome young lady, never shy of speaking to anybody, had come to deliver them from the hateful red-nosed ogre, her factor! Out at once they all set along the shore to greet her arrival, each running regardless of the rest, so that from the Seaton to the middle of the Boar's Tail dune there was a long, straggling broken string of hurrying fisherfolk, men and women, old and young, followed by all the children. The piper, too asthmatic to run, but not too asthmatic to walk and play his bagpipes, delighted the heart of Malcolm, who could not mistake the style, believed he brought up the rear, but he was wrong. The very last came Mrs. Findlay and Lizza, carrying between them their little deal kitchen table for her ladyship to step out of the boat upon, and Lizza's child fast asleep on the top of it.

The foremost ran and ran until they saw that the Fisky had chosen her couch and was turning her head to the shore, when they stopped and stood ready with greased planks and ropes to draw her up. In a few moments the whole population was gathered in the June midnight, darkening the yellow sands between tide and dune. The *Psyche* was well manned now with a crew of six. On she came under full sail till within a few yards of the beach, when in one and the same moment every sheet was let go, and she swept softly up like a summer wave and lay still on the shore. The butterfly was asleep. But before she came to rest, the instant indeed that her canvas went fluttering away, thirty strong men had rushed into the water and laid hold of the now broken-winged thing. In a few minutes she was high and dry.

Malcolm leaped on the sand just as the Partaness came bustling up with her kitchen table between her two hands like a tray. She set it down and across it shook hands with him violently, then caught it up and deposited it firmly on its legs beneath the cutter's waist.

"Now, my lady," said Meg, looking up at the marchioness, "set your little foot on my table and we'll think of it ever after when we eat our dinner from it."

Florimel thanked her, stepped lightly upon it, and sprang to the sand, where she was received with words of welcome from many and shouts which rendered them inaudible from the rest. The men, their hats in their hands, and the women, curtseying, made a lane for her to pass through.

Followed by Malcolm, she led the way over the dune, nor would she accept any help in climbing it, straight for the tunnel. Malcolm had never laid aside the key to the private doors his father had given him while he was yet a servant. They crossed by the embrasure of the brass swivel. That implement had now long been silent, but they had not gone many paces from the bottom of the dune when it went off with a roar. The shouts of the people drowned out the startled cry with which Florimel, involuntarily mindful of old and, for her, better times, turned toward Malcolm. For a brief moment the spirit of her girlhood came back. She had not looked for such a reception and was both flattered and touched by it. Possibly, had she then understood her position and her duty toward them.

Malcolm unlocked the door of the tunnel, and she entered, followed by Rose, who felt as if she were walking in a dream. As he stepped in after them, he was seized from behind and clasped in an embrace he knew at once.

"Daddy, Daddy!" he said, and turning, threw his arms round the piper.

"My poy, my poy! My own son Malcolm!" cried the old man in a whisper of intense satisfaction and suppression. "You must pe forgifing me for coming pack to you. Put I cannot help lofing you, and you must forget that you are a Cawmill."

Malcolm kissed his cheek and said, also in a whisper, "My own daddy! I've a heap to tell you, but I must see my lady home first!"

"Co! Co!" cried the old man, pushing him away. "Do your duties to my ladyship first, and then come to your old daddy."

"I'll be with you in half an hour or less."

"Coot poy! Coot poy! Come to Mistress Partan's."

"Ay, ay, Daddy!" said Malcolm, and hurried through the tunnel.

As Florimel approached the ancient dwelling of her race, now her own to do with as she would, her pleasure grew. Whether it was the time that had passed or the twilight, everything looked strange—the grounds wider, the trees larger, the house grander and more anciently venerable. And all the way the birds sang in the hollow. The spirit of her father seemed to hover about the place and, while the thought that her father's voice would not greet her when she entered the hall cast a solemn, funereal state over her simple return, her heart yet swelled with satisfaction and pride. All this was hers to work her pleasure with, to confer as she pleased! No thought of her tenants, fishers, or farmers, who did their strong part in supporting the ancient dignity of her house, had even an associated share in the bliss of the moment. She had forgotten her reception already, or regarded it only as the natural homage to such a position and power as hers.

The drawing room and hall were lighted. Mrs. Courthope was at the door, as if she expected her, and greeted her warmly, but Florimel was careful to take everything as a matter of course.

"When will your ladyship please to want me?" asked Malcolm.

"At the usual hour, Malcolm," she answered.

He turned and ran to the Seaton.

His first business was the accommodation of Travers and Davy, but he found them already housed at the Salmon Inn, with Jamie Ladle teaching Travers to drink toddy. They had left the *Psyche* snug: she was high above the highwater mark, and there were no tramps about. They had furled her sails, locked the companion door, and left her.

Mrs. Findlay rejoiced over Malcolm as if he had been her own son from a far country; but the poor piper between politeness and gratitude on the one hand and the urging of his heart on the other was sorely tried by her talkativeness. He could hardly get in a word. Malcolm perceived his suffering and, as soon as seemed prudent, proposed that he should walk with him to Miss Horn's, where he was going to sleep, he said, that night.

As soon as they were out of the house, Malcolm assured Duncan, to the old man's great satisfaction, that had he not found him there, he would within another month have set out to roam Scotland in search of him.

Miss Horn had heard of their arrival and was wandering about the house, unable even to sit down until she saw the marquis. To herself she always called him the marquis; to his face he was always Malcolm. If he had not come, she declared, she could not have gone to bed—yet she received him with an edge to her welcome. He had to answer for his behavior. They sat down, and Duncan told a long, sad story; which finished with the toddy that had sustained him during the telling. The old man thought it better, for fear of annoying his Mistress Partan, to go home. As it was past one o'clock, they both agreed.

And then, at last, Malcolm poured forth his whole story, and his heart with it, to Miss Horn, who heard and received it with understanding and a sympathy which grew ever as she listened. At length she declared herself perfectly satisfied, for not only had he done his best, but she did not see what else he could have done. She hoped, however, that now he would contrive to get this part over as quickly as possible, for which, in the morning, she said she would show him good reasons.

26

· · · · · · · · · · · · · · · · · · · ·

The Homecoming

*M*alcolm had not yet, after all the health-giving of the voyage, entirely recovered from the effects of the ill-compounded potion. Indeed, sometimes the fear crossed his mind that never would he be the same man again. Hence, it came that he was weary and overslept himself the next day—but it was no great matter; he had yet time enough. He swallowed his breakfast as a working man alone can and set out for Duff Harbor. At Leith, where they had put in for provisions, he had posted a letter to Mr. Soutar, directing him to have Kelpie brought on to his own town, whence he would fetch her himself. The distance was several miles, the hour nine, and he was a good enough walker. It was the loveliest of mornings to be abroad.

When he reached the Duff Arms, he walked straight into the yard where the first thing he saw was a stableboy in the air, hanging on to a twitch on the nose of the rearing Kelpie. In another instant he would have been killed or maimed for life and Kelpie loose, scouring the streets of Duff Harbor. When she heard Malcolm's voice and the sound of his running feet, she stopped as if to listen. He flung the boy aside and caught her halter. Once or twice more she reared, in the vain hope of so ridding herself of the pain that clung to her lip and nose, nor did she, through the mist of her anger and suffering, quite recognize her master in his yacht uniform. But the torture decreasing, she grew able to scent his presence, welcomed him with her usual glad whinny and allowed him to do with her as he would.

Having fed her, found Mr. Soutar and arranged several matters with him, he set out for him.

That was a ride! Kelpie was mad with life! He jumped her into every available field, and she tore its element of space at least to shreds with her spurning hoofs. He would have entered at the grand gate, but found no one at the lodge, for the factor, to save a little, had dismissed the old keeper. He had, therefore, to go through the town, where, to the awestricken eyes of the population peeping from doors and windows, it seemed as if the terrible horse would carry him right over the roofs of the fisher-cottages below and out to sea. "Eh, but he's a terrible creature that Malcolm MacPhail!" said the old wives to each other, for they felt there must be something wicked in him to ride like that. But he turned her aside from the steep hill and passed along the street that led to the town gate of the House.

Whom should he see, as he turned into it, but Mrs. Catanach, standing on her own doorstep, shading her eyes with her hand and looking far out over the water through the green smoke of the village below. As long as he could remember her, it had been her wont to gaze thus; though what she could at such times be looking for, except it were the devil in person, he found it hard to conjecture.

The keeper of the town gate greeted Malcolm, as he let him in, with a pleased old face and words of welcome; but added instantly, as if it were no time for the indulgence of friendship, that it was a terrible business going on at the Nose.

"What is it?" asked Malcolm, in alarm.

"You've been so long away," answered the man, "that I doubt you'll even know the factor—But the Lord save me! If he knew I had said such a thing, he would turn me out of my house in a minute."

"But you've said nothing yet," rejoined Malcolm.

"I said factor and that's almost enough, for he's like a roaring lion and raging bear among the people ever since you left."

"But you haven't told me what is the matter at Scaurnose!" said Malcolm impatiently.

"Oh, just this—that on this same midsummer's day, Blue Peter, honest fellow, is to quit his house. He's been under notice for three months. You see—"

"To quit!" exclaimed Malcolm. "What for? Such a thing's never been heard of."

"Faith, it's heard of now," returned the gatekeeper. "Quitting's as plentiful as crabgrass. Indeed, there's nothing else heard of around here *but* quitting, for the full half of Scaurnose is under the same notice for Michaelmas, and the Lord knows when it will all end."

"But what's it for? Blue Peter's not the man to misbehave himself."

"Well, you know more yourself than anyone else as to what it's all about; for they say—that is, *some* say, that it's all your fault, Malcolm."

"What do you mean, man? Speak out," said Malcolm.

"They say it's all because of your abducting the marquis' boat and because you and Peter went off together."

"That'll hardly hold, seeing the marchioness herself came home in her last night."

"Ay, but you see the decree's already gone out, and what the factor says is like the laws of the Medes and the Persians, that they says is not to be altered. I don't know myself."

"Oh, well, if that be all, I'll see to it with the marchioness."

"Ay, but you see there's a lot of lads there, I'm told, that has vowed that neither the factor, or factor's man, shall ever set foot in Scaurnose from this day on. Go down to the Seaton yourself and see how many of your old friends you'll find there. Man, they're all over at Scaurnose to see what's going to happen. The factor's there I know and some constables with him— to see that his order's carried out. And the lads, they've been fortifying the place—as they call it—for the last time. They've dug a trench, they tell me, that no one but a hunter on his horse could jump over, and they're posted along the town side of it with sticks and stones and boat oars and guns and pistols. And if there's not a man or two killed already—"

Before he finished his sentence Kelpie was levelling herself for the sea gate.

Johnny Bykes was locking it on the other side, in haste to secure his eye-share of what was going on, when he caught sight of Malcolm tearing up. Mindful of the old grudge, also that there was no marquis now to favor his foe, he finished the arrested act of turning the key, drew it from the lock, and to Malcolm's orders, threats, and appeals, returned for all answer that he had no time to attend to him, and so left him looking through the bars. Malcolm dashed across the turn and round the base of the hill, dismounted, unlocked the door in the wall, got Kelpie through, and was in the saddle again before Johnny was halfway from the gate. When he saw him, he trembled, turned, and ran for its shelter again in terror and did not perceive until he reached it that the insulted groom had gone off like the wind in the opposite direction.

Malcolm soon left the high road and cut across the fields over which the wind bore cries and shouts, mingled with laughter and the animal sounds of coarse jeering. When he came nigh the cart-road which led into the village, he saw at the entrance of the street a crowd and rising from it the well-known shape of the factor on his horse. Nearer the sea, where was another entrance through the backyards of some cottages, was a smaller crowd. Both were now pretty silent, for the attention of all was fixed on Malcolm's approach. As he drew Kelpie up, foaming and prancing, and the group made way for her, he saw a deep, wide ditch across the road, on whose opposite side was ranged irregularly the flower of Scaurnose's younger manhood, calmly, even merrily prepared to defend their entrenchment. They had been chafing the factor and loudly challenging the constables to come on, when they recognized Malcolm in the distance, and expectancy stayed the rush of their bruising wit. For they regarded him as beyond a doubt come from the marchioness with messages of goodwill. When he rode up, therefore, they raised a great shout, everyone welcoming him by name. But the factor, who, to judge by appearances had had his forenoon dram ere he left home, burning with wrath, moved his horse in between Malcolm and the assembled Scaurnoseans on the other side of the ditch. He had self-command enough left, however, to make an attempt at the lofty superior. "Pray, what is your business?" he said, as if he had never seen Malcolm in his life before. "I presume you come with a message?"

"I come to beg you, sir, not to go further with this business. Surely the punishment is already enough!" said Malcolm respectfully.

"Who sends me this message?" asked the factor, his teeth clenched, and his eyes flaming.

"One," answered Malcolm, "who has some influence for justice and will use it, upon whichever side the justice may lie."

The factor cursed, losing utterly his slender self-command and raising his whip.

Malcolm took no heed of the gesture, for he was at the moment beyond his reach.

"Mr. Crathie," he said calmly, "you are banishing the best man in the place."

"No doubt! No doubt, seeing he's a crony of yours," laughed the factor in mighty scorn. "A canting, prayer-meeting rascal!" he added.

"Is that any worse than a drunken elder of the church?" cried Dubs from the other side of the ditch, raising a roar of laughter.

The very purple forsook the factor's face and left it a corpselike gray in the fire of his fury.

"Come, come, my men! that's going too far!" said Malcolm.

"And who are you for a truant fisherman to be giving counsel without our asking for it?" shouted Dubs, altogether disappointed in the poor part Malcolm seemed to be taking. "Give the factor there your counsel."

"Out of my way," said Mr. Crathie, still speaking through clenched teeth. He came straight upon Malcolm. "Home with you! or-r-r—"

Again he raised his whip, this time plainly with intent.

"For heaven's sake, factor, mind the mare!" cried Malcolm. "Ribs and legs and bones will start breaking all round if you anger her with your whip."

As he spoke, he drew a little aside that the factor might pass if he pleased. A noise arose in the smaller crowd, and Malcolm turned to see what it meant. Off his guard, he received a stinging cut over the head from the factor's whip. Simultaneously Kelpie stood up on end, and Malcolm tore the weapon from the treacherous hand.

"If I gave you what you deserve, Mr. Crathie, I should knock you and your horse together into that ditch. A touch of the spur would do it. I am not quite sure that I oughtn't to. A nature like yours takes forbearance for fear."

While he spoke, his mare was ramping and kicking, making a clean sweep all around her. Mr. Crathie's horse turned restive from sympathy, and it was all his rider could do to keep his seat. As soon as he got Kelpie a little quieter, Malcolm drew near and returned him his whip. He snatched it from his outstretched hand and essayed a second cut at him, which Malcolm rendered powerless by pushing Kelpie close up to him. Then suddenly wheeling, he left him.

On the other side of the trench the fellows were shouting and roaring with laughter.

"Men!" cried Malcolm, "you have no right to stop up this road. I want to go and see Blue Peter."

"Come on, then!" cried one of the young men, emulous of Dubs' humor, and spread out his arms as if to receive Kelpie to his bosom.

"Stand out of the way," said Malcolm, "I am coming." As he spoke he took Kelpie a little around, keeping out of the way of the factor who sat trembling with rage on his still excited animal, and sent her at the trench. The men scampered right and left and Malcolm, rather disgusted, took no notice of them, flew over the trench, and sent Kelpie at a full gallop toward Blue Peter's.

A cart, loaded with their little all, the horse in the shafts, was standing at Peter's door, but nobody was near it. Hardly was Malcolm well into the yard, however, when out rushed Annie and, heedless of Kelpie's demonstrative repellance, reached up her hands like a child, caught him by the arm while he was busied with his troublesome charge, drew him toward her, and held him till, in spite of Kelpie, she had kissed him again and again.

"Oh, Malcolm! Oh, my lord!' she said, "you have saved my faith. I knew you would come!"

"Hold your tongue, Annie. I mustn't be known," said Malcolm.

Out next came Blue Peter, his youngest child in his arms.

"Eh, Peter! I'm happy to see you!" cried Malcolm. "Give me a grip of your honest hand!"

The two friends shook hands heartily.

"Peter," said Malcolm, "you were right not to resist the factor. But I'm glad they wouldn't let you go."

"I would have been halfway to Port Gordon by now," said Peter.

"But you'll not be going to Port Gordon by now," said Malcolm. "Just go to the Salmon Inn for a few days till we see how things turn out."

"I'll do anything you like, Malcolm," said Peter and went into the house to get his hat.

In the street arose the cry of a woman, and into the yard rushed one of the fisher-wives, followed by the factor. He had found a place on the eastern side of the village, where, jumping a low earth wall, he got into a little back-yard. When the woman to whose cottage it belonged caught sight of him through the window, she ran out and fell to abusing him in no measured language. He rode at her in his rage, and she fled shrieking her vituperation. Beside himself with the rage of murdered dignity, he rode up and struck at her over the corner of the cart, whereupon, from the top of it, Annie Mair ventured to expostulate.

"Hoot, sir! Have you forgotten yourself altogether to hit at a woman like that!"

He turned upon her and gave her a cut on the arm and hand, so stinging that she cried out and nearly fell from the cart. Out rushed Peter and flew at the factor, who from his seat of vantage began to ply his whip about his head. But Malcolm, who, when the factor appeared, had moved aside to keep Kelpie out of mischief and saw only the second of the two assaults, came forward with a scramble and a bound.

"Stand back, Peter," he cried. "This belongs to me. I gave him back his whip so I'm accountable.—Mr. Crathie!" and as he spoke he edged his mare up to the panting factor, "the man who strikes a woman must be taught that he is a scoundrel, and that job I take. I would do the same if you were the lord of Lossie instead of his factor."

Mr. Crathie, knowing himself now in the wrong, was a little frightened at the speech and began to bluster and stammer, but the swift descent of Malcolm's heavy riding whip on his shoulders and back made him voluble in curses. Then began a battle that could not last long with such odds on the side of justice. In less than a minute the factor turned to flee and, spurring out of the court, galloped up the street at full stretch.

While Malcolm was thus occupied, his sister was writing to Lady Bellair. She told her that having gone out for a sail in her yacht, which she had sent for from Scotland, the desire to see her home had overpowered her to such a degree that of the intended sail she had made a voyage, and here she was, longing just as much now to see Lady Bellair; and if she thought proper to bring a gentleman to take care of her, he also should be welcomed for her sake. It was a long way for her to come, she said, and Lady Bellair knew what sort of place it was; but there was nobody in London now, and if she had nothing more enticing on her schedule, etc. She ended with begging her, if she was mercifully inclined to make her happy with her presence, to bring her Caley and her hound Demon. She had hardly finished when Malcolm presented himself.

She received him very coldly and declined to listen to anything about the fishers. She insisted that, being one of their party, he was prejudiced in their favor; and that, of course, a man of Mr. Crathie's experience must know better than he what ought to be done with such people, in view of protecting her rights and keeping them in order. She declared that she was not going to disturb the old way of things to please him, and said that he had now done her all the mischief he could, except, indeed, he were to head the fishers and sack Lossie House. Malcolm found that by making himself known to her as her brother, he had but given her confidence in speaking her mind when she desired to humiliate him. She was still, however, so far afraid of her brother that she sat in some dread lest he might chance to see the address of the letter she had been writing.

I may mention here that Lady Bellair accepted the invitation with pleasure for herself and Liftore, promised to bring Caley, but utterly declined to take charge of the dog. Thereupon, Florimel, who was fond of the animal, wrote to Clementina, urging her to visit her and begging her, if she could find it within herself to comply, to allow the deerhound to accompany her. Clementina was the only one of her friends, she said, for whom the animal had shown a preference.

Malcolm retired from his sister's presence much depressed, saw Mrs. Courthope, who was kind as ever, and betook himself to his own room, next to that in which his strange history began. There he sat down and wrote urgently to Lenorme, stating that he had an important communication to make and begging him to start for the north the moment he received the letter. A messenger from Duff Harbor well mounted, he said, would insure his presence within a couple of hours.

He found the behavior of his old acquaintances and friends in the Seaton much what he had expected: the few were as cordial as ever, while the many still resented, with a mingling of the jealousy of affection, his forsaking of the old life for a calling they regarded as unworthy of one bred, at least, if not born a fisherman. The women were all cordial.

27

·····················

The Preparation

The heroes of Scaurnose expected a renewal of the attack, and in greater force, the next day. They made their preparations accordingly, strengthening every weak point around the village. They were put in great heart by Malcolm's espousal of their cause, as they considered his punishment of the factor. But when he prevailed upon them to allow Blue Peter to depart, arguing that they had less right to prevent than the factor had to compel him, they once more turned upon him. What right had he to dictate to them? He did not belong to Scaurnose! He reasoned with them that the factor, although he had not justice, had the law on his side and could turn out whom he pleased. They said, "Let him try!" He told them that they had given great provocation, for he knew that the men they had assaulted came surveying for a harbor, and that they ought at least to make some apology for having mistreated them. It was all useless. That was the women's doing, they said; besides, they did not believe him. If what he said was true, what was the thing to them, seeing they were all under notice to leave? Malcolm said that perhaps an apology would be accepted. They told him if he did not take himself off, they would serve him as he had served the factor. Finding expostulation a failure, therefore, he begged Joseph and Annie to settle themselves again as comfortably as they could and left them.

Contrary to the expectation of all, however, and considerably to the disappointment of the party of hotheads, the next day was as peaceful as if Scaurnose had been a halcyon nest floating on the summer waves; and it was soon reported that, in consequence of the punishment he had received from Malcolm, the factor was far too ill to be troublesome to any but his wife. This was true, but, severe as his chastisement was, it was not severe enough to have had any such consequences but for his late growing habit of drinking whiskey. Malcolm, on his part, was greatly concerned to hear the result of his severity. He refrained, however, from calling to inquire, knowing it would be interpreted as an insult, not accepted as a sign of sympathy. He went to the doctor instead, who, to his consternation, looked very serious at first. But when he learned all about the affair, he changed his view considerably and condescended to give good hopes of his coming through, even adding that it would lengthen his life by twenty years if it broke him of his habits of whiskey drinking and rage.

And now Malcolm had a little time of leisure, which he put to the best possible use in strengthening his relations with the fishers. He had nothing to do about the House except look after Kelpie; and Florimel, as if determined to make him feel that he was less to her than before, much as she used to enjoy seeing him sit his mare, never took him out with her—always Stoat. He resolved, therefore, seeing he must yet delay action a while in the hope of the appearance of Lenorme, to go out as in the old days after the herring, both for the sake of splicing, if possible, what strands had been broken between him and the fishers and of renewing for himself the delights of elemental conflict. With these views, he hired himself to the Partan, whose boat's crew was shorthanded. And now, night after night, he revelled in the old pleasure, enhanced by so many months of deprivation. Joy itself seemed embodied in the wind blowing on him. When it came on to blow hard, instead of making him feel small and weak in the midst of the storming forces, it gave him a glorious sense of power and unconquerable life.

It answered also all his hopes in regard to his companions and the fisherfolk generally. Those who had really known him found the same old Malcolm, and those who had doubted him soon began to see that at least he had lost nothing in courage or skill or goodwill. Before long he was even a greater favorite than before.

Duncan's former dwelling happened to be then occupied by a lonely woman. Malcolm made arrangements with her to take them both in; so that in relation to his grandfather, too, something very much like the old life returned for a time.

The factor continued very ill. He had sunk into a low state, in which his former indulgence was greatly against him. Every night the fever returned, and at length his wife was worn out with watching and waiting upon him.

And every morning Lizza Findlay, without fail, called to inquire how Mr. Crathie spent the night. To the last, while quarreling with every one of her neighbors with whom he had anything to do, he had continued kind to her, and she was more grateful than one in other trouble than hers could have understood. But she did not know that an element in the origination of his kindness was the belief that it was by Malcolm she had been wronged and forsaken.

Again and again she had offered, in the humblest manner, to ease his wife's burden by sitting with him at night; and at last, finding she could hold up no longer, Mrs. Crathie consented. But even after a week she found herself still unable to resume the watching. So, night after night, resting at home during a part of the day, Lizza sat by the sleeping factor, and when he woke ministered to him like a daughter. Nor did even her mother object, for sickness is a wondrous reconciler. Little did the factor suspect, however, that it was partly for Malcolm's sake she nursed him, anxious to shield the youth from any possible consequences of his righteous vengeance.

"I'm a poor creature, Lizzy," he said, turning his heavy face one midnight toward the girl, as she sat half dozing, ready to start awake.

"God comfort ye, sir!" said the girl.

"He'll take good care of that!" returned the factor. "What did I ever do to deserve it? There's that MacPhail, now—to think of him! Didn't I do what man could for him? Didn't I keep him about the place when all the rest were dismissed? Didn't I give him the key of the library that he might read and improve his mind? And look what comes of it!"

"Ya mean, sir," said Lizza, quite innocently, "that that's the way you've done toward God, so He won't heed you?"

The factor had meant nothing in the least like it. He had merely been talking as the imps of suggestion tossed up. His logic was as sick and helpless as himself. So that he held his peace—stung in his pride, at least, perhaps in his conscience too—only he was not prepared to be rebuked by a girl like her, who had—well, he must let it pass. How much better was he himself?

But Lizza was loyal. She could not hear him speak so of Malcolm and hold her peace as if she agreed in his condemnation.

"You'll know Malcolm better some day, sir," she said.

"Well, Lizzy," returned the sick man, in a tone that but for feebleness would have been indignant, "I have heard a good deal of the way women will stand up for men that have treated them cruelly, but for you to stand up for *him*, well that passes—"

"He's the best friend I ever had," said Lizza.

"Girl! How can you sit there and tell me so to my face?" cried the factor, his voice strengthened by the righteousness of the reproof it bore. "If it were not the dead of the night—"

"I tell you nothing but the truth, sir," said Lizza, as the threat died away. "But you must lie still or I will go for your wife. If you are worse in the morning, it will be my fault, because I couldn't stand to hear such things said about Malcolm."

"Do you mean to tell me," persisted her charge, heedless of her expostulation, "that the fellow who brought you to disgrace and left you with a child you could ill provide for—and I well know never sent you a penny all the time he was away, whatever he may have done now—is the best friend you ever had!"

"Now, God forgive you, Mr. Crathie, for thinking such a thing!" cried Lizza, rising as if she would leave him. "Malcolm MacPhail is as innocent of any sin like mine as my little child itself."

"You mean to tell me he's not the father?"

"No, nor never will be the father of any child whose mother isn't his wife!" said Lizza, with burning cheeks and resolute voice.

The factor, who had risen on his elbow to look her in the face, fell back in silence. Neither of them spoke for what seemed to the watcher a long time, and when she ventured to look at him, he was asleep.

He lay in one of those troubled slumbers into which weakness and exhaustion will sometimes pass very suddenly. When he awoke, there was Lizza looking down on him anxiously.

"What are you looking like that for?" he asked crossly.

She did not like to tell him that she had been alarmed by his dropping asleep. In her confusion she fell back on the last subject.

"There must be some mistake, Mr. Crathie," she said. "I wish you would tell me what makes you hate Malcolm MacPhail as you do."

The factor, although he seemed to himself to know well enough, was yet a little puzzled how to reply. Therewith, a process began that presently turned into something with which never in his life before had his inward parts been acquainted—a sort of self-examination. He said to himself, partly in the desire to justify his present dislike—he would not call it "hate," as Lizza did—that he used to get on with the lad well enough and had never taken offense at his freedoms, making no doubt his manner came of his blood, and he could not help it, being a chip off the old block. But when he ran away with the marquis' boat and went to the marchioness and told her lies against him, then what could he do but dislike him?

Arriving at this point, he opened his mouth and gave the substance of what preceded it for answer to Lizza's question. But she replied at once, "Nobody'll ever make me believe that Malcolm MacPhail ever told a lie against you or anybody. I don't believe he ever told a lie in his life. And about the boat, sir, you know that he was the master of it. It was under his charge, and besides, you yourself don't know that much about boats or sailing."

"But it was me that engaged him again after all the servants at the House had been dismissed. He was *my* servant!"

"That does make it look a little bad, no doubt," allowed Lizza, with something almost of cunning. "How was it, then, that he came to do it at all?"

"I discharged him."

"And what for, if I may be so bold as to ask?" she went on.

"For insolence!"

"Would you tell me how he answered you? Don't think me meddling, sir. But I'm sure there's been some mistake. You couldn't be so good to me and so mean to him without there being some misunderstanding."

It was consoling to the conscience of the factor, in regard of his behavior to the two women, to hear his own praise for kindness from a woman's lips. He took no offense, therefore, at her persistent questioning, but told her as well and as truly as he could remember, with no more than the all-but-unavoidable exaggeration with which feeling will color fact, the whole passage between Malcolm and himself concerning the sale of Kelpie. He closed with an appeal to the judgment of his listener, in which he confidently anticipated her verdict.

"A most ridiculous thing, as you can see yourself as well as anybody, Lizzy! To call an honest man like myself a hypocrite. There's not a child alive that doesn't know that the seller of a horse is bound to extol him and the buyer to take care of himself. I'm not saying it allowable to tell a downright lie, but you may come nearer it in horse-dealing without sinning than in any other kind of business. It's like love and war, in both of which it's well known that all things are fair. The law should read, 'Love and war and horse-dealing'—don't you see, Lizzy?"

But Lizza did not answer. The factor, hearing a stifled sob, lifted himself to his elbow.

"Lie still, sir," said Lizza. "It's nothing. I was only just thinking that that would be the way the father of my child reasoned with himself when he lied to me."

The astonished factor opened his mouth as if to speak, but then held his peace and settled back down on his bed, trying to think.

Now Lizza, for the last few months, had been going to school, the same school with Malcolm, open to all comers—the only school where one is sure to be led in the direction of wisdom. There she had been learning to some purpose—as plainly appeared before she had done with the factor.

"Which church are you an elder in, Mr. Crathie?" she asked presently.

"Why, the Church of Scotland, of course!" answered the patient in some surprise at her ignorance.

"Yes, I know," returned Lizza, "but whose property is it?"

"Whose but the Redeemer's."

"And do you think, Mr. Crathie, that if Jesus Christ had had a horse to sell that He would have hidden from the buyer one hair of a fault the beast had? Would He not have done to his neighbor as He would have his neighbor do to him?"

"Lassie, lassie! You can't compare the likes of Him to such as us. What would He have had to do with horseflesh anyway?"

Lizza held her peace. Here was no room for argument. He had flung the door of his conscience in the face of her who woke it. But it was too late, for the word was already in. God never gave man a thing to do concerning which it were irreverent to ponder how the Son of God would have done it.

The factor fell to thinking, and thinking more honestly than he had thought for many a day. Presently it was revealed to him, that, if he were in the horse market wanting to buy, and a man there who had to sell said to him—"He wouldn't do for you, sir; you would be tired of him in a week," he would never remark, "What a fool the fellow is!" but—"Well now, I call that neighborly!" He did not get quite so far, just then, as to see that every man to whom he might want to sell a horse was as much his neighbor as his own brother. But at least the warped glass of a bad maxim had been cracked in his window.

———

Days and days passed and still Malcolm had no word from Lenorme. He was getting hopeless in respect of that quarter of possible aid. But so long as Florimel could content herself with the quiet of Lossie House, there was time to wait, he said to himself. She was not idle, and that was promising. Every day she rode out with Stoat. Now and then she would make a call in the neighborhood and, apparently to trouble Malcolm, took care to let him know that on one of these occasions her call had been upon Mrs. Stewart. One thing he did feel was that she had made no renewal of her friendship with his grandfather. She had, alas, outgrown the girlish fancy. Poor Duncan took it much to heart. Though Malcolm knew not of it, Florimel was expecting the arrival of Lady Bellair and Lord Liftore with the utmost impatience. They, for their part, were making the journey by the easiest possible stages, tacking and veering and visiting everyone of their friends that lay between London and Lossie. They thought to give Florimel the little lesson that, though they accepted her invitation, they had plenty of friends in the world besides her ladyship and were not dying to see her.

One evening Malcolm, as he left the grounds of Mr. Morrison on whom he had been calling, saw a traveling carriage pass toward Portlossie. Something like fear laid hold of his heart, more than he had ever felt except when Florimel and he, on the night of the storm, took her father for Lord Gernon the wizard. As soon as he reached certain available fields, he sent Kelpie tearing across them, dodged through a firwood, and came out on the road half a mile in front of the carriage. As again it passed him, he saw that his fears were facts, for in it sat the bold-faced countess and the mean-hearted lord. Something must be done at last, and until it was done good, watch must be kept.

I must here note that, during this time of hoping and waiting, Malcolm had attended to another matter of importance. Over every element influencing his life, his family, his dependents, his property, he desired to possess a lawful, honest command. Where he had to render account, he would be head. Therefore, through Mr. Soutar's London agent, to whom he sent Davy and who he brought acquainted with Merton, and his former landlady at the curiosity shop, he had discovered a good deal about Mrs. Catanach from her London associates, among them the herb doctor and his little boy who had watched Davy. He had now almost completed an outline of evidence, which, grounded on that of Rose, might be used against Mrs. Catanach at any moment. He had also set inquiries on foot in the track of Caley's antecedents and had discovered more than the acquaintance between her and Mrs. Catanach. He was determined to crush the evil powers which had been ravaging his little world.

28

• • • • • • • • • • • • • • • • • • • •

The Visit

*C*lementina was always ready to accord any reasonable request Florimel could make of her, but her letter lifted such a weight from her heart and life that she would now have done whatever she desired, reasonable or unreasonable. She had no difficulty in accepting Florimel's explanation that her sudden disappearance was but a breaking of the social jail, the flight of the weary bird from its foreign cage back to the country of its nest. That same morning she called upon Demon. The hound, feared and neglected, was rejoiced to see her and there was no ground for dreading his company. It was a long journey, but if it had been across a desert instead of through her own country, the hope that lay at the end of it would have made it more than pleasant.

The letter would have found her at Wastbeach instead of London had not the society and instructions of the schoolmaster detained her a willing prisoner to its heat and glare and dust. Him only in all London she must see to bid good-bye. To Camden Town therefore she went that same evening, when his work would be over for the day. As usual she was shown into his room, and as usual she found him poring over his Greek New Testament.

"Ah!" he said, and rose as she entered, "this, then, is the angel of my deliverance! You see," he went on, "old man as I am and peaceful, the summer does lay hold upon me and sets me longing after the green fields and living air."

"I wish I could be more a comfort to you," answered Clementina, "but I have come to tell you I am going to leave you, though for a little while only, I trust."

"You do not take me by surprise, my lady. I have, of course, been looking forward for some time to my loss and your gain. The world is full of little deaths—deaths of all sorts and sizes, rather let me say. For this one I was prepared. The good summer land calls you to its bosom, and you must go."

"Come with me!" cried Clementina.

"A man must not leave his work—however irksome—for the most peaceful pleasure," answered the schoolmaster.

"But you do not know where I want you to come."

"What difference can that make, my lady. I must be with the children whom I have been engaged to teach, and whose parents pay me for my labor—not with those who can do well without me."

"But I cannot do without you—not for long at least."

"What! Not with Malcolm to supply my place?"

Clementina blushed. "Ah! do not be unkind, master," she said.

"Unkind!" he repeated. "You could not yet imagine the half of what I hope for and from you."

"I *am* going to see Malcolm," she said with a little sigh. "That is, I am going to visit Lady Lossie at her place in Scotland—your old home, where so many must love you. Can't you come? I shall be traveling alone, except my servants."

A shadow came over the schoolmaster's face: "I never do anything of myself. I go not where I wish, but where I seem to be called or sent. I used to build many castles, not without a certain beauty of their own—that is, when I was less understanding. Now I leave them to God to build for me: He does it better and they last longer. But I do not think He will keep me here for long, for I find I cannot do much for these children. This ministration I take to be more for my good than theirs—a little trail of faith and patience for me. True, I *might* be happier where I could hear the larks, but I do not know anywhere that I have been more peaceful than in this little room."

"It is not at all a fit place for *you*," said Clementina.

"Gently, my lady. It is a greater than thou that sets the bounds of my habitation. Perhaps He may give me a palace one day. But the Father has decreed for His children that they shall know the thing that is neither their ideal nor His. All in His time, my lady. He has much to teach us. When do you go?"

"Tomorrow morning."

"Then God be with you. He *is* with you; only my prayer is that you may know it."

"Tell me one thing before I go," said Clementina. "Are we not commanded to bear each other's burdens and so fulfill the law of Christ? I read it today."

"Then why ask me?"

"For another question: does not that involve the command to those who have burdens that they should allow others to bear them?"

"Surely, my lady. But I have no burden to let you bear."

"Why should I have so much and you so little?"

"My lady, I have millions more than you. I have been gathering the crumbs under my Master's table for thirty years."

"I believe you are just as poor as the apostle Paul when he sat down to make a tent or as our Lord himself after He gave up carpentry."

"You are wrong there, my lady. I am not so poor as they must often have been."

"But I don't know how long I may be away, and you may fall ill, or—or—see—some book you may want very much."

"I have my Testament, my Plato, my Shakespeare, and one or two besides whose wisdom I have not yet quite exhausted."

"I can't bear it!" cried Clementina almost on the point of weeping. "Let me be your servant." As she spoke she rose, and walking softly up to him where he sat, knelt at his knees and held out suppliantly a little bag of silk. "Take it—Father," she said, hesitating and with effort, "take your daughter's offering—a poor thing to show her love, but something to ease her heart."

He took it, and weighted it up and down in his hand with an amused smile, but his eyes full of tears. It was heavy. He opened it and emptied it on a chair within his reach and laughed with delight as its contents came tumbling out. "I never saw so much gold in my life if it were all taken together," he said. "What beautiful stuff it is! But I don't want it, my dear. It would but trouble me. Besides, you will want it for your journey."

"That is a mere nothing. I am afraid I am very rich. It is such a shame! But I can't well help it. You must teach me how to become poor."

Clementina had been struggling with herself; now she burst into tears.

"Because I won't take a bagful of gold from you when I don't want it," he said, "do you think I should let myself starve without coming to you? I promise you I will let you know—come to you if I can—the moment I get too hungry to do my work well and have no money left. My sole reason for refusing it now is that I do not need it."

But for all his loving words and assurances, Clementina could not stay her tears.

"See then, for your tears are hard to bear, my daughter," he said, "I will take one of these golden ministers, and if it has flown from me before you return, I will ask for another."

A moment of silence followed, broken only by Clementina's failures in quieting herself.

He opened the bag and slowly, reverentially, drew from it one of the new sovereigns with which it was filled. She took his hand, pressed it to her lips, and walked slowly from the room.

He took the bag of gold from the chair and followed her down the stairs. Her carriage was awaiting her at the door. He handed her in, and laid the bag on the little seat in front.

The coachman took the queer, shabby, un-London-like man for a fortune-teller his lady was in the habit of consulting and paid homage to his power with the handle of his whip as he drove away. The schoolmaster returned to his room—not to his Plato or Shakespeare, not even to Saul of Tarsus, but to the Lord himself.

29

The Awakening

*W*hen Malcolm took Kelpie to her stall the night of the arrival of Lady Bellair and her nephew, he was rushed upon by Demon. The hound had arrived a couple of hours before, while Malcolm was out. He wondered he had not seen him with the carriage he had passed, never suspecting he had had another conductress.

I have not said much concerning Malcolm's feelings with regard to Lady Clementina, but all this time the sense of her existence had been like an atmosphere pervading his thoughts. He saw in her the promise of all he could desire to see in a woman. His love was not of the blind little-boy sort, but of a deeper, more exciting, keen-eyed kind, that sees faults where even a true mother will not, so jealous is it of the perfection of the beloved.

If I say, then, that Malcolm was always thinking about Lady Clementina when he was not thinking about something he *had* to think about, have I not said nearly enough? Should I ever dream of attempting to set forth what love is in such a man for such a woman? There are comparatively few that have more than the glimmer of a notion of what love means. God only knows how grandly, how passionately, yet how calmly the man and the woman He has made might love each other. Malcolm's lowly idea of himself did not at all interfere with his loving Clementina, for at first his love was entirely dissociated from any thought of hers. When the idea, the mere idea, of her loving him presented itself, he turned from it. The thought was in its own nature too unfit. From a social point of view there was, of course, little presumption in it. The marquis of Lossie bore a name that might pair itself with any in the land, but Malcolm did not yet feel that the title made much difference to the fisherman. He was what he was, and that was something very lowly indeed.

Yet the thought would at times dawn up from somewhere in the infinite matrix of thought that perhaps if he went to college and graduated and dressed like a gentleman and did everything as gentlemen do—in short, claimed his rank and lived as a marquis should—then was it not, might it not be, within the bounds of possibility—just within them—that the great-hearted, generous, liberty-loving Lady Clementina might not be disgusted if he dared feel toward her as he had never felt and never could feel toward any other? At length, such thoughts rising again and again—gradually more frequently—and ever accompanied by such reflections, he felt as if he must run to her, calling aloud that he was the marquis of Lossie, and throw himself at her feet.

But feeling thus, where was his faith in her principles? How, now, was he treating the truth of her nature? Where, now, were his convictions of the genuineness of her profession? Where were those principles, that truth, those professions if after all she would listen to a marquis and would not listen to a groom? To herald his suit with his rank would be to insult her. And would he not deprive her of the chance to prove her truth if, as he approached her, he called on the marquis to supplement the man!

But what, then, was the man, fisherman or marquis, to dare to such a glory as the Lady Clementina! And in the end he knew that he could not condescend to be accepted as Malcolm, marquis of Lossie, knowing he would have been rejected as Malcolm MacPhail, fisherman and groom. Accepted as marquis, he would forever be haunted with the question whether she would have accepted him as groom. No, he would choose the greater risk of losing her for the chance of winning her the greater.

So far Malcolm got with his theories; but the moment he began to think in the least practically, he recoiled altogether from the presumption. Under no circumstances could he ever have the courage to approach Lady Clementina with a thought of himself in his mind. She had never shown him personal favor. He could not tell whether she had listened to what he had tried to lay before her. He did not know that she had gone to hear his master. His surprise would have equaled his delight at the news that she had already become as a daughter to the schoolmaster.

And what had been Clementina's thoughts since learning that Florimel had not run away with her groom? Her first feeling was an utterly in-articulate, undefined pleasure that Malcolm was free to be thought about. The second was something like relief that the truest man she had ever met, except his master, was not going to marry such an unreality as Florimel. Clementina, with all her generosity, could not help being doubtful of a woman who could make a companion of such a man as Liftore.

Then she began to grow more and more curious about Malcolm. She had already gathered much real knowledge of him, both from himself and Mr. Graham. And she was curious as to whether he might not already be engaged to some young woman in his own station of life. In the lower ranks of society, men married younger. And yet, on the other hand, was it possible that in a fishing village there would be any choice of girls who could understand him when he talked about Plato and the New Testament? But of course, what did she know about the fishers, men and women? There were none at Wastbeach. For anything she knew to the contrary, they might all be philosophers, and a fitting match for Malcolm might be far easier to find amongst them than in the society to which she herself belonged, where in truth the philosophical element was rare enough.

Then arose in her mind the half-pictorial vision of a whole family of brave, believing, daring, saving fisher-folk sacrificing to the rest and all devoted to their neighbors. Their very toils and dangers were but additional means to press their souls together. Why had she been born an earl's daughter, never to look a danger in the face, never to have the chance of a true life—that is, a grand, simple, and noble one?

But had she no power to order her own steps, to determine her own being? Was she nailed to her rank? Was she not a free woman, without even a guardian to trouble her? She had no excuse to act ignobly. Would it then be—would it be a *very* unmaidenly thing if . . . The rest of the sentence did not even take the shape of words. But she answered it nevertheless, "Not so unmaidenly as presumptuous." And besides, there was little hope that *he* would ever presume to. . . . He was such a modest youth, with all his directness and fearlessness. If he had no respect for rank—and that was—yes, she would say the word, *hopeful*—he had, on the other hand, the profoundest respect for the human, and she could not tell how that might come to bear in this case.

Then she fell to thinking of the difference between Malcolm and any other servant she had ever known. She knew that most servants, while they spoke with the appearance of respect in presence, altered their tone entirely when beyond the circle of the eye: theirs was eye-service. But here was a man who touched no imaginary hat while he stood in the presence of his mistress, neither swore at her in the stable yard. He looked her straight in the face and would upon occasion speak, not his mind, but the truth to her. The conviction was clear that if one dared in his presence but utter the name of his mistress lightly, whoever he were, he would have to answer to him for it. What a lovely thing was true service!

Ah, but for her to take the initiative would provoke the conclusion, as revolting to her as unavoidable to him, that she judged herself his superior—so much so as to be absolved from the necessity of behaving to him on the ordinary footing of man and woman. What a ground to start from with a husband! Especially since he was so immeasurably her superior that the poor little advantage of rank on her side vanished like a candle in the sunlight. No, she would have to let it all go—let him go, rather. For if she did approach him, what if he should be tempted by rank and wealth and accept her? That would be worse still—far worse—for then he would be shorn of his glory and prove to be of the ordinary human type after all. No, he could be nothing to her nearer than a bright star blazing unreachable above her.

Thus went the thoughts to and fro in the minds of each. Neither could see the way. Both feared the risk of loss; neither could hope greatly for gain.

30

•••••••••••••••••••

The Petition

*H*aving put Kelpie up and fed and bedded her, Malcolm took his way to the Seaton, full of busily anxious thought. Things had taken a bad turn. The enemy was in the House with his sister, and he had no longer any chance of judging how matters were going, as now he never rode with her. But at least he could haunt the House. He would run, therefore, to his grandfather and tell him that he was going to occupy his old quarters at the House that night.

Returning directly and passing through the kitchen to ascend the small corkscrew stairs the servants generally used, he encountered Mrs. Courthope, who told him that her ladyship had given orders that her maid, who had come with Lady Bellair, should have his room. He was at once convinced that Florimel had done so with the intention of banishing him from the House, for there were dozens of rooms vacant and many of them more suitable.

It was a hard blow! How he wished for Mr. Graham to consult! And yet Mr. Graham was not of much use where any sort of plotting was wanted. He asked Mrs. Courthope to let him have another room, but she looked so doubtful that he withdrew his request and went back to his grandfather. It was Saturday and not many of the boats would go fishing. But he could not rest and would go line fishing with the *Psyche*'s dinghy.

In an hour the sun was down, the moon was up, and he had caught more fish than he wanted. The fountain of his anxious thoughts was flowing more rapidly once again. He must go ashore. He must go up to the House. Who could tell what might be going on there? He drew in his line, purposing to take the best of the fist to Miss Horn and some to Mrs. Courthope, as in the old days.

The *Psyche* still lay on the sands, and he was rowing the dinghy toward her, when, looking shoreward, he thought he caught a glimpse of someone seated on the slope of the dune. Yes, there was someone there, sure enough. The old times rushed back on his memory. Could it be Florimel? Alas, it was not likely she would now be wandering about alone. But if it were! Then for one attempt more to rouse her slumbering conscience to break with Liftore!

He rowed swiftly to the *Psyche*, beached, and drew up the dinghy, and climbed the dune. Plainly enough, it was a lady who sat there. It might be one from the upper town enjoying the lovely night. It might be Florimel, but how could she have gotten away, or wished to get away, from her newly arrived guests? There was no other figure to be seen all along the sands. He drew nearer. The lady did not move. If it were Florimel, would she not know him as he came, and would she wait for him?

He drew nearer still. His heart gave a great throb. Could it be, or was the moon weaving some hallucination in his troubled brain? If it was a phantom, it was that of Lady Clementina. His spirit seemed to soar aloft and hang hovering over her while his body stood rooted to the spot. She sat motionless, gazing at the sea. Malcolm thought that she could not know him in his fisher-clothes and would take him for some rude fisherman staring at her. He must address her at once. He came forward and said, "My lady!"

She did not start; neither did she speak. She did not even turn her face. She rose first, then turned and held out her hand. Three steps more and he had it in his, and his eyes looked straight into hers. Neither spoke. The moon shone full on Clementina's face. A moment she stood, then slowly sank again upon the sand and drew her skirts about her with a silent show of invitation. The place where she sat was a little terraced hollow in the slope, forming a convenient seat. Malcolm saw, but could not believe she actually made room for him to sit beside her—alone with her in the universe. It was too much; he dared not believe it. Again she made a movement. This time he could not doubt her invitation. It was as if her soul made room in her unseen world for him to enter and sit beside her. But who could enter heaven in his workday garments?

Seeing his hesitation, she said, at last, "Won't you sit by me, Malcolm?"

"I have been catching fish, my lady," he answered, "and my clothes must be unpleasant. I will sit here."

He went a little lower on the slope and laid himself down, leaning on his elbow.

"Do freshwater fishes smell the same as sea fishes, Malcolm?" she asked.

"Indeed, I am not certain, my lady. Why?"

"Because if they do, do you remember what you said to me as we passed the sawmill in the wood?"

It was by silence Malcolm showed he did remember.

"Does not this night remind you of that one at Wastbeach when we came upon you singing?" said Clementina.

"It *is* like it, my lady—now. But, a little ago, before I saw you, I was thinking of that night and thinking how different this was."

Again a moon-filled silence fell, and once more it was the lady who broke it. "Do you know who is at the House?" she asked.

"I do, my lady," he replied.

"I had not been there more than an hour or two," she went on, "when they arrived. I suppose Florimel—Lady Lossie—thought I would not come if she told me she expected them."

"And would you have come, my lady?"

"I cannot endure the earl."

"Neither can I. But then I know more about him than your ladyship does, and I am miserable for my mistress."

It stung Clementina as if her heart had taken a beat backward. But her voice was steadier than it had yet been as she returned. "Why should you be miserable for Lady Lossie?"

"I would die rather than see her marry that man," he answered.

Again her blood stung her in the left side. "You do not want her to marry, then?" she said.

"I do," answered Malcolm, emphatically, "but not that fellow."

"Whom, then, if I may ask?" ventured Clementina trembling.

But Malcolm was silent. He did not feel it right to say.

Clementina turned sick at heart. "I have heard there is something dangerous about the moonlight," she said. "I think it does not suit me tonight. I will go home."

Malcolm sprang to his feet and offered his hand. She did not take it, but rose more lightly, though more slowly, than he. "How did you come from the park on the House grounds, my lady?" he asked.

"By a gate over there," she answered, pointing. "I wandered out after dinner and the sea drew me."

"If your ladyship will allow me, I will take you a much nearer way back," he said.

"Do then," she returned.

He thought she spoke a little sadly and set it down to her having to go back to her fellow guests. What if she should leave tomorrow morning? he thought. Could he ever be sure she had been with him this night? Or would he think it a dream?

They walked across the grassy sand toward the tunnel in silence, he pondering what he could say that might keep her from going so soon.

"My lady never takes me out with her now," he said at length. He was going to add that, if she liked, he and Kelpie could show her the country. But then he saw that if she were not with Florimel, his sister would be riding everywhere alone with Liftore. Therefore he stopped short.

"And you feel forsaken—deserted?" returned Clementina, sadly still.

"Rather, my lady."

They had reached the tunnel. It looked very black when he opened the door, but there was just a glimmer through the trees at the other end.

"Do I walk straight through?" she asked.

"Yes, my lady. You will soon come out in the light again," he said.

"Are there no steps to fall down?"

"None, my lady. But I will go first if you wish."

"No, that would but cut off the little light I have," she said. "Come beside me."

They passed through in silence, except for the rustle of her dress and the dull echo that haunted their steps. In a few moments they came out among the trees, but both continued silent. The still, thoughtful moonlight seemed to press them close together, but neither knew that the other felt the same.

They reached a point in the road where another step would bring them in sight of the House.

"You cannot go wrong now, my lady," said Malcolm. "If you please, I will go no farther."

"Do you not live in the House?" she asked.

"I used to do as I like, and could be there or with my grandfather. I did mean to be at the House tonight, but my lady has given my room to her maid."

"What! That woman Caley?"

"I suppose so, my lady. I must sleep tonight in the village. If you could, my lady—" he added, after a pause and faltering, hesitating. "If you could— if you would not be displeased at my asking you," he resumed—"if you *could* keep my lady from going farther with that—I shall call him names if I go on."

"It is a strange request," Clementina replied after a moment's reflection. "I hardly know, as the guest of Lady Lossie, what answer I ought to make to it. One thing I will say, however, though you may know more of the man than I, you can hardly dislike him more. Whether I can interfere is another matter. Honestly, I do not think it would be of any use. But I do not say I will not. Good-night."

She hurried away and did not again offer her hand.

Malcolm walked back through the tunnel, his heart singing and making melody. Oh, how lovely—how more than lovely, how divinely beautiful she was! And so kind and friendly! But something seemed to trouble her too, he said to himself. He little thought that he, and no one else, had spoiled the moonlight for her. He went home to glorious dreams—she to a troubled, half-wakeful night. Not until she had made up her mind to do her utmost to rescue Florimel from Liftore, even if it gave her to Malcolm, did she find a moment's quiet. It was morning then, but she fell fast asleep, slept late and woke refreshed.

31

The Reconciliation

*M*r. Crathie was slowly recovering, but still very weak. He did not, after having turned the corner, get well as fast as the doctor judged he ought, and the reason was plain to Lizza, dimly perceptible to his wife—he was ill at ease.

A man may have more on his mind and a more sensitive conscience than his neighbors give him credit for. They may know and understand him up to a certain point in his life, but then a crisis, by them unperceived, arrives after which the man, to all eternity, could never be the same as they had known him. The fact that a man has never up to any point yet been aware of anything outside himself cannot shut Him out who is beyond and who is able to sting even the most inactive of consciences.

The sources of restlessness deep in the soul of hard, commonplace, business-worshiping Hector Crathie were now two: the first, that he had lifted his hand to a woman; the second, the old ground of his quarrel with Malcolm brought up by Lizza.

All his life, Mr. Crathie had prided himself on his honesty in business and was therefore in one of the most dangerous moral positions a man can occupy. Asleep in the mud, he dreamed himself awake on a pedestal. The honesty in which a man can pride himself must be a small one, for mere honesty will never think of itself at all. The limited honesty of the factor clung to the interests of his employers, and he let the rights of those he encountered take care of themselves. Those he dealt with were to him rather as enemies than friends—not enemies to be prayed for, but to be spoiled. Malcolm's doctrine of honesty in horse-dealing was to him ludicrously new. His notion of honesty in that kind was to cheat the buyer for his master if he could, proud to write in his book a large sum against the name of the animal. He would have scorned the idea of making a farthing by it himself through any business quirk whatever, but he would not have been the least ashamed if, having sold Kelpie, he had heard—say, after a week of her possession—that she had dashed out her purchaser's brains. He would have been a little shocked, a little sorry perhaps, but not at all ashamed. "By this time," he would have said, "the man ought to have been up to her and either taken care of himself or sold her again." —to dash out another man's brains instead!

That Malcolm or the fallen fisher-girl should judge differently in no way troubled him. What could they know about the rights and wrongs of business? The fact, which Lizza brought to bear upon him, that our Lord would not have done such a thing was to him no argument at all. He said to himself that no one could be expected to do like Him, that He was divine and didn't have to fight for a living and was only intended to show us what sinners we were, not to be imitated. After all, religion was one thing, but business was another. And a very proper thing too, with customs and, indeed, laws of its own far more definite than those of religion. To mingle the one with the other was not merely absurd; it was irreverent and wrong, certainly never intended in the Bible. It was always "the Bible" with him—never the will of Christ.

But though he could dispose of the questions thus satisfactorily, yet as he lay ill, without any distractions, the thing haunted him. A night came during which he was troubled and feverish. He had a dream in which he saw the face of Jesus looking at him, full of sorrowful displeasure. And in his heart he knew it was because of a certain transaction in horse-dealing for which he had lauded his own cunning—adroitness, he considered it— and success. One word only he heard from the Man in the dream: "Worker of iniquity!" and he woke with a great start.

From that moment truths began to be facts to him. The beginning of the change was indeed very small. Every beginning is small, but every beginning is a creation. His dull and unimaginative nature had received a gift in a dream, and the seed began to sprout. Henceforth, the claims of his neighbor began to reveal themselves and his mind to breed conscientious doubts and scruples with which, struggle as he might against it, a certain respect for Malcolm would keep coming and mingling.

Lizza's nightly ministrations had not been resumed, but she called often and was a good deal with him; for Mrs. Crathie had learned to like the humble, helpful girl. One day, when Malcolm was seated, mending a net among the thin grass and great red daisies of the links by the banks of the stream where it crossed the sands from the Lossie grounds to the sea, Lizza came up to him and said, "The factor would like to see you, Malcolm, as soon as you could go to him." She waited for no reply. Malcolm rose and went.

At the factor's, the door was opened by Mrs. Crathie herself who led him into the dining room where she plunged at once into business, doing her best to keep down all manifestation of the profound resentment she had against him. "You see, Malcolm," she said, as if persuing instead of beginning a conversation, "he's pretty sore over the little fracas between you and him. Just make your apologies to him and tell him you're sorry for misbehaving to him. Tell him that, Malcolm, and here's a half crown for you."

"But, mem," said Malcolm, taking no notice for either the coin or the words that accompanied the offer, "I can't lie. I wasn't drunk and I'm not sorry."

"Hoot!" returned Mrs. Crathie, "I'll warrant you can lie well enough if you had the occasion. Take your money and do what I tell you!"

"If Mr. Crathie wishes to see me, mem," rejoined Malcolm, "I am ready. If not, please allow me to go."

The same moment the bell whose rope was at the head of the factor's bed rang. "Come this way," she said and, turning, led him up the stairs to the room where her husband lay.

Entering, Malcolm stood astonished at the change he saw upon the strong man, and his heart was filled with compassion. The factor was sitting up in bed, looking very white and worn and troubled. Even his nose had grown thin and white. He held out his hand to him and said to his wife, "Take the door to you, Mistress Crathie," indicating which side he wished it closed from.

"You were some hard on me, Malcolm," he went on grasping the youth's hand.

"I doubt it was too hard," said Malcolm who could hardly speak for the lump in this throat.

"Well, I deserved it. But eh, Malcolm. I can't believe it was me; it had to have been the drink."

"It *was* the drink," rejoined Malcolm, "so before you rise from that bed, sir, why don't you swear to our great God that you'll never again take more than one small glass at one sitting."

"I swear it, Malcolm," said the factor.

"It's easy to swear now, but when you're up again it'll be hard to keep your oath.—Oh, Lord," spoke the youth, breaking out into an almost involuntary prayer, "help this man to keep truth with you.—And now, Mr. Crathie," he resumed, "I'm your servant, ready to do anything I can. Forgive me, sir, for laying it onto you over-hard."

"I forgive you," said the factor, delighted to have something to forgive.

"I thank you from my heart," answered Malcolm, and again they shook hands.

"But, Malcolm," he added, "how will I ever show my face again?"

"Oh, folks are terrible good-natured," returned Malcolm eagerly, "when you allow that you're in the wrong. I do believe that when a man confesses to his neighbor and says he's sorry, he thinks more of him than he did before. You see, we all know we have done wrong, but we haven't usually confessed it. And it's a funny thing, but a man will think it grand of someone else to confess, but when the time comes when there's something he needs to repent of himself, he hesitates for fear of the shame of having to confess it. To me the shame lies in *not* confessing after you know you're in the wrong. You'll see, sir, the fisherfolk will mind what you say to them a heap better now."

"Do you really think so?" sighed the factor.

"I do, sir. Only when you grow better you mustn't let Satan tempt you into thinking that this repenting was but a weakness of the flesh instead of an enlightenment of the Spirit."

"I'll bind myself to it!" cried the factor eagerly. "Go and tell them all in my name that I take back every notice I gave. Do you think it would be good to take a pound note apiece to the two women?"

"I wouldn't do that, sir," answered Malcolm. "For your own sake, I wouldn't to Mistress Mair, for nothing would make her take it; it would only affront her. You'll have many a chance of making it up to them both, ten times over, before you and them part ways."

"I must leave the country, Malcolm."

"Indeed, sir, you'll do nothing of the kind! The fishers themselves would rise up to prevent you from doing that, as they did with Blue Peter. As soon as you're able to be out and about again, you'll see plain enough that there's no occasion for anything like that. Portlossie wouldn't know itself without you. Just give me a commission to say to the two honest women that you're sorry for what you did, and that's all that need be said between you and them, or their men either."

The result showed that Malcolm was right, for the very next day, instead of looking for gifts from him, the two injured women came to the factor's door with the offering of a few fresh eggs and a great lobster.

32

•••••••••••••••••••••

The Understanding

*M*alcolm's custom was, immediately after breakfast, to give Kelpie her airing—and a tremendous amount of air she wanted for the huge animal furnace of her frame and the fiery spirit that kept it alight. Then, returning to the Seaton, to change the dress of a groom, in which he always appeared about the House lest by chance his mistress should want him, for that of a fisherman so that he could help with the nets or boats or with whatever else was going on. As often as he might he went also to the long shed where the women prepared the fish for salting, took a knife and wrought as deftly as any of them, throwing a rapid succession of cleaned herrings into the preserving brine. It was no wonder he was a favorite with the women. Although the place was malodorous and the work dirty, Malcolm had been accustomed to the sight and smell from earliest childhood. Still it was work most men would not do. He had such a chivalrous humanity that it could not bear to see man or woman at anything scorned except that he bore a hand in it himself. He did it half in love, half in terror of being unjust.

He had gone to Mr. Crathie in his fisher-clothes and the nearest way led him past a corner of the House overlooked by one of the drawing-room windows. Clementina saw him pass and, judging by his garb that he would probably return presently, went out in hope of meeting him. As he was going back to his net by the sea gate, he caught sight of her on the opposite side of the burn, accompanied only by a book. He walked through it, climbed the bank, and approached her.

It was a hot summer afternoon. The burn ran dark and brown and cool in the deep shade, but the sea beyond was glowing in light. No breath of air was stirring; no bird sang. The sun was burning high in the west.

Clementina stood awaiting him. "Malcolm," she said, "I have been watching all day, but have not found a single opportunity of speaking to your mistress as you wished. But to tell the truth, I am not sorry, for the more I think about it the less I see what to say. That another does not like a person can have little weight with one who does, and I *know* nothing against him. I wish you would release me from your request. It is such an ugly thing to speak to one's hostess to the disadvantage of a fellow guest!"

"I understand," said Malcolm. "It was not a right thing to ask of you."

"Thank you. Had it been before you left London! Lady Lossie is very kind, but does not seem to put the same confidence in me as before. She and Lady Bellair and that man make a trio, and I am left outside. I almost think I ought to go. Even Caley is more of a friend than I am. I cannot get rid of the suspicion that something not right is going on. There seems a bad air about the place. Those two are playing their game with the inexperience of that poor child, your mistress."

"I know that very well, may lady, but I hope yet they will not succeed," said Malcolm.

By this time they were near the tunnel.

"Could you let me through the other way—to the shore?" asked Clementina.

"Certainly, my lady. I wish you could see the boats go out. They will all be starting together as soon as the tide turns."

"Could I not go with you—for one night—just for once, Malcolm?"

"My lady, it would hardly do, I am afraid. If you knew the discomforts to one unaccustomed, I doubt you would want to go. You would need to be a fisherman's sister—or wife—I fear, my lady, to get through it."

Clementina smiled gravely, but did not reply. Malcolm, too, was silent, thinking. "Yes," he said at last, "I see how we could manage it. You shall have a boat for your own use, my lady, and—"

"But I want to see just what you see and feel what you feel. I don't want a rose-leaf notion of the thing. I want to understand what you fishermen encounter and experience."

"But look what clothes, what boots, we fishers must wear to be fit for our work! But I suppose you could have a true idea—as far as it reaches. All right, you shall go in a real fishing boat with a full crew and all the nets, and you shall catch real herrings. Only you shall not be out any longer than you please. But there is hardly time to arrange it for tonight, my lady."

"Tomorrow, then?"

"Yes, I have no doubt I can manage it by then."

"Oh, thank you!" said Clementina. "It will be a great delight."

"And now," suggested Malcolm, "would you like to go through the village and see some of the cottages, and how the fishers live?"

"If they would not think me intrusive," answered Clementina.

"There is no danger of that," rejoined Malcolm. "If it were someone such as Lady Bellair who would patronize them and then blame what she might call their poverty on sin and childishness as if she were their spiritual and social superior, they might very likely think it rude. The whole question reminds me of what Mr. Graham said: that in the kingdom of heaven to rule is to raise; a man's rank is in his power to uplift."

"I would I were in the kingdom of heaven if it be as you and Mr. Graham take it for!" said Clementina.

"You must be in it, my lady, or you couldn't wish it to be such as it is."

"Can one be in it and yet seem to himself to be out of it, Malcolm?"

"So many are out of it that seem to be in it, my lady, that one might well imagine it the other way around with some."

"That seems an uncharitable thing to say, Malcolm."

"Our Lord speaks of many coming up to His door confident of admission, whom He yet sends away. Faith is obedience, not confidence."

"Then I do well to fear."

"Yes, my lady, so long as your fear makes you knock the louder."

"But if I be in, as you say, how can I go on knocking?"

"There are a thousand more doors to knock at after you are in, my lady. No one content to stand just inside the gate will be inside it long. It is one thing to be in and another to be satisfied that we are in. Such a satisfying as comes from our own feelings may, you see from what our Lord says, be a false one. He who does what the Lord tells him *is* in the kingdom, even if every feeling of heart and brain told him otherwise."

During their talk they reached the Seaton, and Malcolm took her to see his grandfather.

"Tall and faer, chentle and coot!" murmured the old man as he held her hand for a moment in his. "She'll not pe a Cawmill, Malcolm?"

"No, no, Daddy—far from that," answered Malcolm.

"Then my laty will pe right welcome to Tuncan's heart," he replied and, taking her hand, led her to a chair.

When they left they visited the Partaness. Clementina's heart was drawn to the young woman who sat in a corner rocking her child in its wooden cradle, never lifting her eyes from her needlework. She knew her for the fisher-girl of Malcolm's picture.

From house to house he took her, and wherever they went they were welcomed. The fishers and their wives did the honors of their poor houses in a homely and dignified fashion. "What would you do now if you were lord of the place?" asked Clementina as they left and walked toward the sea gate. "What would be the first thing you would do?"

"As it would be my business to know my tenants that I might rule them," he answered, "I should be in no hurry to make changes, but would talk openly with them, understand them, and try to be worthy of their confidence. Of course I would see a little better to their houses and improve their harbor; and I would build a boat for myself to show them a better kind. But I would spend my best efforts to make them follow Him whose first servants were the fishermen of Galilee."

A pause followed.

"Don't you sometimes find it hard to remember God all through your work?" asked Clementina.

"I don't try to consciously remember Him every moment. For He is in everything, whether I am thinking of it or not. When I go fishing, I go to catch God's fish. When I take Kelpie out, I am teaching one of God's wild creatures. When I read the Bible or Shakespeare, I am listening to the word of God, uttered in each after its own kind. When the wind blows on my face, it is God's wind."

After a little pause, "And when you are talking to a rich, ignorant, proud lady?" said Clementina, "what do you feel then?"

"That I would it were my Lady Clementina instead," answered Malcolm with a smile.

She held her peace.

When he left her, Malcolm hurried to Scaurnose and arranged with Blue Peter for his boat and crew the next night. Returning to his grandfather, he found a note waiting him from Mrs. Courthope to the effect that, as Miss Caley had preferred another room, there was no reason why, if he pleased, he should not reoccupy his own.

33

. . . .

The Sail

*T*he next morning the sun dawned crisp and warm as the boats slipped slowly back with a light wind to the harbor of Portlossie. Malcolm did not wait to land the fish, but having changed his clothes and taken his breakfast with Duncan, who was always up early, went up to the House to look after Kelpie. When he had done with her, finding some of the household already in motion, he went through the kitchen and up the old corkscrew stairs to his room, to have the sleep he generally had before breakfast. Presently came a knock at his door, and there was Rose. She had either been watching for him or had learned from Mrs. Courthope that he might be returning to the House.

The girl's behavior to Malcolm was changed. The conviction had been growing in her that he was not what he seemed, and she regarded him now with a vague awe. But there was a fear in her eyes now. She looked this way and that and timidly followed him to the door to tell him, once out of sight of the other servants, that she had seen the woman who gave her the poisonous philtre talking to Caley the night before at the foot of the bridge, after everybody else was in bed. She had been miserable until she could warn him. He thanked her heartily and said he would be on his guard. She crept softly away. He secured his door, lay down and, trying to think, fell asleep.

When he awoke, his brain was clear. The very next day, whether Lenorme came or not, he would declare himself. That night he would go fishing with Lady Clementina, but not one day longer would he allow those people to be about his sister. Who could tell what might not be brewing, or into what abyss, with the help of her friends, the woman Catanach might plunge Florimel?

He rose, took Kelpie out, and had a good gallop. On his way back he saw, in the distance, Florimel riding with Liftore. The earl was on his father's bay mare. He could not endure the sight and dashed home at full speed.

Learning from Rose that Lady Clementina was in the flower garden, he found her at the swan basin feeding the goldfish.

"My lady," he said, "I have got everything arranged for tonight."

"And when shall we go?" she asked eagerly.

"At the turn of the tide, about half-past seven. But seven is your dinner hour."

"It is of no consequence. But could you not make it half an hour later, and then I should not seem rude?"

"Make it any hour you please, my lady, so long as the tide is falling."

"Let it be eight, then, and dinner will be almost over. Shall I tell them where I am going?"

"Yes, my lady. It will be better. They will look amazed, for all their breeding."

"Whose boat is it, that I may be able to tell them if they should ask me?"

"Joseph Mair's. He and his wife will come and fetch you. Annie Mair will go with us—if I may say us. Will you allow me to go in your boat, my lady?"

"I couldn't go without you, Malcolm."

"Thank you, my lady. Indeed, I don't know how I could let you go without me. Not that there is anything to fear, or that I could make it the least safer, but somehow it seems my business to take care of you."

"Like Kelpie?" said Clementina, with a merrier smile than he had ever seen on her face before.

"Yes, my lady," answered Malcolm, "if to do for you all and the best you will permit me to do is to take care of you like Kelpie."

Clementina gave a little sigh.

"Mind you don't scruple, my lady, to give what orders you please. It will be *your* fishing boat for tonight."

Clementina bowed her head in acknowledgment.

The evening came, and the company at Lossie House was still seated at the table, Clementina heartily weary of the vapid talk that had been going on all through the dinner, when she was informed that a fisherman of the name of Mair was at the door, accompanied by his wife, saying they had an appointment with her. She had already acquainted her hostess with her arrangements for going fishing that night; now she rose and excused herself. Clementina hurriedly changed her dress, hastened to join Malcolm's messengers, and almost in a moment had made the two childlike people at home with her by the simplicity and truth of her manner. They had not been with her five minutes before thy said in their hearts that here was the wife for the marquis if he could get her.

They took the nearest way to the harbor—through the town. All in the streets and at the windows stared to see the grand lady from the House walking between a Scaurnose fisherman and his wife, chatting away with them as if they were all fishers together.

"I'm glad to see the young woman—and a pretty lass she is—in such good company," said Miss Horn to herself. "I'm thinking the hands of the marquis must be in this!"

The boat and crew were all ready to receive her. On the shore stood Malcolm with a young woman whom Clementina recognized at once as the girl she had seen at the Findlays.

"My lady," he said, approaching, "would you do me the favor to let Lizzy go with you. She would like to attend to your ladyship, because, being a fisherman's daughter, she is used to the sea, and Mrs. Mair is not so much at home upon it, being a farmer's daughter from inland."

Receiving Clementina's thankful assent, he turned to Lizza and said, "Mind you, tell my lady what reason you know why my mistress at the House shouldn't be married to Lord Liftore—he that was Lord Meikleham. You can speak to my lady there as you would to myself."

Lizza blushed a deep red and glanced at Clementina, but there was no annoyance in her face. Malcolm hoped that if she heard, or guessed, Lizza's story, Clementina might yet find some way of bringing her influence to bear on his sister even at the last hour of her chance; from which, for her sake, he shrank the more the nearer it drew. Clementina held out her hand to Lizza and again accepted her offered service with kindly thanks. Peter took his wife in his arms and, walking through the few yards of water between, lifted her into the boat. Malcolm and Clementina turned to each other. He was about to ask leave to do her the same service, but she spoke before him. "Put Lizzy on board first," she said.

He obeyed and when, returning, he again approached her, "Are you able, Malcolm?" she asked. "I am very heavy."

He smiled, took her in his arms like a child, and had placed her on the cushions before she had time to contest the mode of her transference. Then taking a stride deeper into the water, he scrambled on board. The same instant the men gave way and away glided the boat out into the measureless north with the tide, where the horizon was now dotted with the sails that had preceded it.

No sooner were they afloat than a kind of enchantment enwrapped and possessed the soul of Clementina. Everything seemed all at once changed utterly. The cliffs, the rocks, the sands, the dune, the town, the very clouds that hung over the hill above Lossie House were all transfigured. Out they rowed and drifted till the coast began to open up beyond the headlands on either side. There a light breeze was waiting them. Up went three short masts, and three darkbrown sails shown red in the sun. Malcolm came aft, over the great heap of brown nets, and got down in a little well, there to sit and steer the boat. For now, obedient to the wind in its sails, it went frolicking over the sea.

The slow twilight settled into night. The nets were thrown out and sunk straight into the deep, stretched between leads below and floats and buoys above, and the sails were brought down. The boat was still, anchored, as it were, by hanging acres of curtain, and all was silent. Most of the men were asleep in the bows of the boat; all were lying down but one. That one was Malcolm. The boat rose and sank a little, just enough to rock the sleeping children a little deeper into their sleep. Malcolm thought all slept. He did not see how Clementina's eyes shone as she gazed at the vault of stars in the heavens. She knew that Malcolm was near her, but she would not speak, she would not break the peace. Then softly woke a murmur of sound that strengthened and grew and swelled at last into a song. She feared to stir lest she should interrupt its flow.

There was an auld fisher—he sat by the wa',
    An' luikit oot ower the sea:
The bairnies war playin'; he smilit on them a',
    But the tear stude in his e'e.
        An' it's oh to win awa', awa'!

Refrain:
    An' it's oh to win awa'
Whaur the bairns come home, an' the
    wives they bide,
An' God is the Father o' a'!

Jocky an' Jeamy an' Tammy oot there,
    A'i' the boatie gaed doon;
An' I'm ower auld to fish ony mair,
    An' I hinna the chance to droon.
        An' it's oh to win awa', awa'! (Repeat refrain)

An' Jeanie she grat to ease her hert,
    An' she easit hersel' awa';
But I'm ower auld for the tear to stert,
    An' sae the sighs maun blaw.
        An' it's oh to win awa', awa'! (Repeat refrain)

Lord, steer me hame whaur my Lord has steerit,
    For I'm tired o' life's rockin' sea;
An' dinna be lang, for I'm nearhan' fearit
    'At I'm maist ower auld to dee.
        An' it's oh to win awa', awa'! (Repeat refrain)

Again the stars and sky were everything, and there was no sound but the slight lapping of the water against the edge of the boat. Then Clementina said, "Did you make that song, Malcolm?"

"Yes, my lady."

"I didn't know you could enter like that into the feelings of an old man."

"And why not, my lady? I never can see a living thing without asking how it feels. I've often, when out like this, tried to fancy myself a herring caught by the gills in the net down below, instead of the fisherman in the boat above going to haul him out."

"And did you succeed?"

"Well, I fancy I came to understand as much of him as he does himself. But would you not like to sleep, my lady?"

"No, Malcolm. I would much rather hear you talk. Could you not tell me a story now. Lady Lossie mentioned one you told her once about an old castle not far from here."

"Eh, my lady," broke in Annie Mair, who had waked up while they were speaking. "I wish you would make him tell you that story, for my man's heard him tell it and he says it is terrible gruesome. I would sure like to hear it— Wake up, Lizzy," she went on, in her eagerness waiting for no answer, "Malcolm's going to tell the tale of the old Colonsay castle."

Malcolm could see no reason not to tell the strange and wild story requested of him and thereupon commenced it, but modified the Scotch considerably for the sake of unaccustomed ears.

When it was ended, Clementina said nothing. All was silent for a time.

When the time was right, up sprang the men and went each to his place. As they pulled in the nets a torrent of gleaming fish poured in over the gunwale of the boat. Such a take it was! A light westerly wind was blowing and all the boats were now ready to seek the harbor. Heavy-laden, they crept slowly to the land. As she lay snug and warm, with the cool breath of the sea on her face, a half sleep came over Clementina. No word passed between her and Malcolm all their homeward way. Each was brooding over the night and its joy that enclosed them together. Clementina also had in her mind a scheme for attempting what Malcolm had requested of her. The next day she must try it, thinking that, if she failed, she must leave at once for England.

They glided once more through the harbor. When Clementina's foot touched the shore, she felt like one waked out of a dream. She turned away from the boat and its crew and with Malcolm and Lizza passed along the front of the Seaton. Arriving at the entrance of her home, Lizza bade them good-night, and Clementina and Malcolm were left. Now drew near the full power, the culmination of the mounting enchantment of the night, for Malcolm. When the Scaurnose people should have passed them, they would be alone. There would not be a living soul on the shore for hours. From the harbor, the nearest way to the House was by the sea gate, but where was the haste with the lovely night around them, private as a dream shared only by two? Instead, therefore, of turning up by the side of the stream where it crossed the shore, he took Clementina once again in his arms unforbidden and carried her over. Then the long sands lay open to their feet.

Presently they heard the Scaurnose party behind them. As by common resolve they turned to the left and, crossing the end of the dune, resumed their former direction. The voices passed on the other side, and they heard them slowly fade into the distance. At length Malcolm knew his friends were winding the red path to the top of this cliff. And now the shore was bare of any presence, bare of sound except the rush of the rising tide. But behind the long sandhill, for all they could see of the sea, they might have been in the heart of a continent.

"Who could imagine the ocean so near us, my lady?" said Malcolm after they had walked for some time without word spoken.

"Who can tell what may be near us?" she returned.

"True, my lady. Our future is near us, holding thousands of things unknown."

As they spoke they came opposite the tunnel, but Malcolm turned from it and they ascended the dune. Far in the east lurked a suspicion of dawn. They descended a few paces and halted again.

"Did your ladyship ever see the sunrise?" asked Malcolm.

"Never in open country," she answered.

"Then stay and see it now, my lady. He'll rise just over yonder. A more glorious chance you could not have."

Clementina slowly sank on the sand of the slope. Malcolm took his place a little below, leaning on his elbow and looking at her. Thus they waited the sunrise.

Was it minutes or only moments passed in that silence, whose speech was only the soft ripple of the sea on the sand? Neither could have answered the question. At length said Malcolm, "I am thinking of changing my service, my lady."

"Indeed, Malcolm?"

"Yes, my lady. My—mistress does not want to turn me away, but she is tired of me and does not want me any longer."

"But you would never think of forever forsaking a fisherman's life for that of a servant, surely, Malcolm?"

"What would become of Kelpie, my lady?" rejoined Malcolm, smiling to himself.

"Ah!" said Clementina. "I had not thought of her. But you cannot take her with you," she added.

"There is nobody about the place who could, or rather who would, do anything with her. They would sell her. I have enough to buy her, and perhaps somebody might not object to the encumbrance, but hire me and her together . . . *your* groom wants to find a coachman's place, my lady."

"Oh, Malcolm! Do you mean you would be *my* groom?" cried Clementina, pressing her palms together.

"If you would have me, my lady; but I have heard you say you would have none but a married man."

"But, Malcolm, don't you know anybody that would . . . Could you not find someone—some lady that . . . I mean, why shouldn't you be a married man?"

"For a very good and, to me, rather sad reason, my lady. The only woman I could marry or should ever be able to marry would not have me. She is very kind and very noble, but . . . it is preposterous, the thing is too preposterous. I dare not have the presumption to ask her."

Malcolm's voice trembled as he spoke and a few moments' pause followed, during which he could not lift his eyes. The whole heaven seemed pressing down upon him.

But his words had raised a storm in Clementina's bosom. A cry broke from her, but she called up all the energy of her nature and stilled it that she might speak. The voice that came was little more than a sob-scattered whisper, but to her it seemed as if all the world must hear. "Oh, Malcolm," she panted, "I *will* try to be good and wise. Don't marry anybody else— *anybody*, I mean; but come with Kelpie and be my groom, and wait and see if I don't grow better."

Malcolm leaped to his feet and threw himself at hers. He had heard but in part and he *must* know all. "My lady," he said with intense quiet, "take me for fisherman, groom, or what you will. I offer the whole sum of service that is in me."

Slowly, gently, Clementina knelt before him. In clear, unshaken tones, for she feared nothing now, she said, "Malcolm, I am not worthy of you. But take me—take my very soul if you will, for it is yours."

The two entranced souls looked at each other. Clementina rose, and they stood hand in hand, speechless.

"Ah, my lady," said Malcolm at length, "what is to become of this delicate smoothness in my great rough hand? Will it not be hurt?"

"You don't know how strong it is, Malcolm. There!" she said and squeezed his hand tightly.

"I can scarcely feel it with my hand, my lady; it goes through to my heart. It shall lie in mine as the diamond in the rock."

"No, no, Malcolm! Now that I am going to be a fisherman's wife, it must be a strong hand—it must work. What will you have me do to rise a little nearer your level? Shall I give away my lands and money? Shall I live with you in the Seaton or will you come and fish at Wastbeach?"

"Forgive me, my lady. I can't think of those things now—even with you in them. Let us not now, when your love makes me happier than ever I was, talk of times and places."

A silence fell. But he resumed: "My lady, I know I shall never love you aright until you have made me better. When the face of the least lovely of my neighbors needs but to appear to rouse in my heart a divine tenderness, then it must be that I shall love you better than now. Now, alas! I am so swayed toward wrong, so fertile of resentments and indignation! You must help cure me, my divine Clemency. But am I a poor lover to talk, this first glorious hour, of anything but my lady and my love?"

"Alas! I am beside you but a block of marble," said Clementina. "You are so eloquent, my—"

"New groom," suggested Malcolm, gently.

Clementina smiled. "But my heart is so full," she went on, "that I cannot think the smallest thought. I hardly know that I feel. I only know that I want to weep."

All at once they became aware that an eye was upon them. It was the sun. He was ten degrees up the slope of the sky, and they had never seen him rise. And with the sun came a troubled thought. It suddenly occurred to Clementina that she would rather not walk up to the door of Lossie House with Malcolm at this hour of the morning. Yet neither could she well appear alone.

Before she had spoken her anxiety, Malcolm rose. "You won't mind being left, my lady," he said, "for a quarter of an hour or so, will you? I want to bring Lizzy to walk home with you."

He went, and Clementina sat alone on the dune. She watched the great strides of her fisherman as he walked along the sands. She was a little weary, laid her head own upon her arm, and slept. In a moment, it seemed, she opened her eyes, calm as a child, and there stood her fisherman.

"I have been explaining to Lizzy, my lady," he said, "that your ladyship would rather have her company up to the door than mine. Lizzy is to be trusted, my lady."

Clementina rose and they went straight to the door in the bank, through the tunnel and young wood and along the lovely path—the three together. When they drew near the House, Malcolm left them. After they had rung a good many times, the door was opened by the housekeeper, looking just a little scandalized.

"Please, Mrs. Courthope," said Lady Clementina, "will you give orders that when this young woman comes to see me today, she shall be shown up to my room?"

Then she turned to Lizza and thanked her for her kindness, and they parted—Lizza to her baby, and Clementina to yet a dream or two. Long before her dreams were sleeping ones, however, Malcolm was out in the bay in the *Psyche*'s dinghy catching mackerel—some should be for his grandfather, some for Miss Horn, some for Mrs. Courthope, and some for Mrs. Crathie.

34

The Announcement

When Malcolm had caught as many fish as he wanted, he rowed to the other side of Scaurnose. There he landed, left the dinghy in the shelter of the rocks, climbed the steep cliff, and sought Blue Peter at his home. Though the sun was up, the brown village was yet quiet as a churchyard. Some of the men had not yet returned from the night's fishing, others were asleep. But he was the only one awake; on the threshold of Peter's cottage sat little Phemy.

"Are you already up, Phemy?" asked Malcolm, smiling as he approached.

"Ay, for some time," she said.

"Would you tell your father I would like to see him?"

In a few minutes Blue Peter appeared, rubbing his eyes.

"I'm sorry to have to wake you, friend Peter," began Malcolm, "but I had to talk to you. I'm going to speak out today, declare myself."

"Well, I am glad of that, Malcolm!—I beg your pardon, my lord, I should say—Annie!"

"Keep it quiet though, man. I don't want it out in Scaurnose first. I've come to ask you to stand by me when the time comes."

"I will do that, my lord."

"Well, go and gather your boat crew and fetch them down to the cove. I'll tell them, and maybe they'll stand by me too."

"There's little fear of them letting you down, if I know my men," answered Peter and went off, nearly only half dressed, while Malcolm went back down the path and waited by his boat.

At length six men appeared coming down the winding path. All but Peter were no doubt wondering why they were called so soon from their beds on such a peaceful morning after being out the night before.

Malcolm went to meet them. "Friends," he said, "I'm in need of your help."

"Anything you like, Malcolm, except it be to ride your mare," answered one.

"It's not that," returned Malcolm. "It's nothing so fearsome or hard. The hard part will be to believe what I'm going to tell you. But first you must promise to hold your tongues for half a day."

"Ay, we'll not tell," said one. "We'll hold our tongues," said another; "you can depend on us!"

"Well," said Malcolm, "my name's not Malcolm MacPhail, but—"

"We all know that," said one, rather sarcastically.

"And what more do you know?" asked Blue Peter with some anger at his interruption.

"Well, nothing much," the man answered.

"Then you know little!" said Peter, and the others laughed.

"My name's Malcolm Colonsay," resumed Malcolm quietly, "and I'm the next marquis of Lossie."

A dead silence followed, and in doubt and astonishment two or three of them had to suppress a strong inclination to laugh. But after a few moments first one, then another, looked at Blue Peter and, perceiving that the matter was to him not only serious but evidently no news, each began slowly to come to his senses.

"You mustn't take it hard, my lord," said Peter, "if the lads be a bit taken aback with the news. It is a sudden shift in the wind for them."

"I wish your lordship well," thereupon said one and held out his hand.

"Long life to your lordship!" said another, and the rest followed. Each spoke a hearty word and shook hands with him after which followed a good deal of laughter and many questions from all around.

"Time enough later to clear it all up," said Malcolm laughing. "It is enough for now that you believe me and trust me. And that I am able to trust you. For serious matters must be attended to today, and I need you to stand with me should things go difficult with certain things I must do."

"We are with you, my lord," they seemed to answer in unison. "We are at your service."

With the understanding that they were to be ready at his call and that they should hear from him in the course of the day, Malcolm left them and rowed back to the Seaton. There he took his basket of fish on his arm which he went and distributed according to his purpose, ending with Mrs. Courthope at the House. Leaving there he spent thirty minutes with Miss Horn.

Then he fed and dressed Kelpie, saddled her, and galloped to Duff Harbor where he found Mr. Soutar at breakfast and arranged with him to be at Lossie House at two o'clock. On his way back he called on Mr. Morrison and requested his presence at the same hour. Skirting the back of the House and riding as fast as he could, he then made straight for Scaurnose and appointed his friends to be near the House at noon, so placed as not to attract attention and yet within hearing of his whistle from door or window in the front. Returning to the House, he put up Kelpie, rubbed her down, and fed her. Then, finding there was yet some time to spare, paid a visit to the factor. He was cordial and, to Malcolm's great satisfaction, much recovered. He had a better than pleasant talk with him.

While they were out in the fishing boat together, Lizza had told Clementina her story, and Clementina, in turn, had persuaded Lizza to tell Lady Lossie her secret. It was in the hope of an interview with her false lover that the poor girl had consented so easily. A great longing had risen within her to have the father of her child acknowledge him—even if only to her—taking him just once in his arms. That was all. She had no hope for herself. With trembling hands, and heart beating wildly, she dressed her baby and herself as well as she could and about one o'clock went to the House.

Nothing could have better pleased Lady Clementina than that Liftore and Lizza should meet in Florimel's presence, but she recoiled altogether from the small stratagems, not to mention the lies necessary, to bring about such a confrontation. So she had to content herself with bringing the two girls together. After Lizza's arrival, they sat together for a few moments while Lizza calmed herself and then Clementina went to look for Florimel. She found her in a little room adjoining the library where she often went. Liftore had, if not quite complete freedom of the spot, yet privileges there; but at that moment Florimel was alone. Clementina informed her that a fisher-girl with a sad story which she wanted to tell her had come to the House. Florimel, who was not only kindhearted, but relished the position she imagined herself to occupy as lady of the place, at once assented to her proposal to bring the young woman to her there.

When Clementina entered with Lizza carrying her child, Florimel instantly suspected the truth, both as to who she was and as to the design of her appearance. Her face flushed and her heart filled with anger, chiefly against Malcolm, but against the two women as well, who, she did not doubt, had lent themselves to his designs, whatever they might be. She rose, drew herself up, and stood prepared to act both for Liftore and herself.

Scarcely, however, had the poor girl opened her mouth to speak when Lord Liftore, daring an entrance without warning, opened the door and walked into the room. Looking about, he stopped and began an apology almost at once. But Lizza, hearing his voice, turned with a cry and fell at his feet and held up her child imploringly. Taken altogether by surprise, the earl stared for a moment and then fell back on the pretense of knowing nothing about her.

"Well, young woman," he said, "what do you want with me? I didn't advertise for a baby. Pretty child, though."

Lizza turned white as death, and her whole body seemed to give a heave of agony. Clementina had just taken the child from her arms when she sank motionless at his feet. Florimel went to the bell.

But Clementina prevented her from ringing. "I will take her away," she said; "do not expose her to your servants." Then gathering her courage, she went on: "Lady Lossie, Lord Liftore is the father of this child. If you can marry him after the way you have seen him use its mother, you are not too good for him, and no one will trouble themselves about you any longer!"

"I know the author of this false accusation!" cried Florimel. "You have been listening to the inventions of an ungrateful dependent. You slander my guest. What right do you have—"

"Is it a false accusation, my lord? Do I slander you?" said Clementina, turning sharply upon the earl. He made her a cool, obeisant bow, but said nothing.

Clementina ran into the library, laid the child in a big chair, and returned for the mother. She led her from the room, but from the doorway turned and said, "Good-bye, Lady Lossie. I thank you for your hospitality, but I can, of course, remain as your guest no longer."

"Of course not!" Florimel responded with the air of a woman of forty.

"Florimel, you will curse the day you marry that man!" she cried and closed the door.

As they left the House, they immediately came upon Malcolm walking toward it from the factor's. He immediately surmised the scope of Clementina's plot.

"Malcolm," groaned the poor girl, holding out the baby, "he won't admit to it. He won't allow that he knows anything about me or the child."

"He's a rascal, Lizzy! But don't worry, we'll take care of your child," he said, and bent over to kiss it tenderly.

At that very moment he lifted his eyes to the House where, leaning from the window above them, he saw Florimel and Liftore. Liftore turned to Florimel with a smile that seemed to say, "There! I told you so; he's the father himself!"

Malcolm strode toward the House.

Lizza ran after him, "Malcolm, Malcolm!" she cried, "don't hurt him. For my sake. He's the father of my child!"

"I won't lay a hand on him, Lizzy."

When the earl saw Malcolm coming, although he was no coward, for the next few seconds his heart doubled its beats. But of all things he must not show fear before Florimel. "What can the fellow be after now?" he said. "I'll go down to him."

"No, no! Don't go near him. He may be violent," objected Florimel. "He is a dangerous man!"

Malcolm reached the top of the flight of stairs just as Liftore was emerging from the drawing room, followed closely by Florimel, fearful of what was about to happen.

"MacPhail," she said like an indignant goddess as she hastened toward them, "I discharge you from my service. Leave this house instantly!"

Malcolm turned immediately, flew down the stairs and outside for a brief parley with Peter who had all the time been close by. Returning through the hall he saw Rose, who had been waiting anxiously in the kitchen. "Come with me," he said without stopping and again approached the stairs.

He entered the drawing room. The earl had Florimel's hand in his and their tone was quiet as he burst suddenly through the door.

"For heaven's sake, my lady!" cried Malcolm, "hear me one word before you promise that man anything."

The earl retreated from Florimel and turned upon Malcolm in a fury. But now he did not have the advantage of the stairs as a moment ago and hesitated. Florimel's eyes filled with wrath.

"I tell you for the last time, my lady," said Malcolm, "if you marry that man, you will marry a liar and a scoundrel."

Liftore laughed, and his imitation of scorn was wonderfully successful, for he felt sure of Florimel, now that she had thus taken his part. "Shall I ring for the servants, Lady Lossie, to put the fellow out?" he said. "That man is as mad as a March hare."

Clementina and Lizza, having reentered the house after Malcolm, followed Rose up the stairs after him, and the three of them listened, from the landing, in fear and anticipation of the proceedings inside the drawing room. Lizza, fearing what might happen, suddenly opened the door and reentered the room.

"So," cried Florimel, "this is the way you keep your promise to my father?"

"It is, my lady. To associate the name of Liftore with his would be a blot on his memory. My lady, I beg a word with you in private."

"You insult me!"

"I beg of you, my lady, for your own dear sake."

"Once more I order you to leave my house, and never set foot in it again!" she said and rang the bell for the servants.

"You hear her ladyship!" cried Liftore; "Get out!" He approached threateningly.

"Stand back," said Malcolm. "If it were not that I promised the poor girl carrying your baby, I would soon—"

It was unwisely said, for the earl came on all the bolder, and it was all Malcolm could do to parry, evade, or stop his blows. He had already taken several severe ones when the voice of Lizza came in agony from next to the door, "Defend yourself, Malcolm! I can't stand it, I give you back your promise."

"We'll manage yet, Lizzy," said Malcolm and kept warily retreating toward a window. He continued holding off Liftore as best he could. Suddenly he dashed his elbow through a pane of glass and gave a loud shrill whistle and at the same moment received a blow over his eye. Blood followed. But already Clementina and Rose had darted between them, and full of rage as he was, Liftore was compelled to restrain himself.

The few menservants now came hurrying all together into the room.

"Take that rascal there and put him under the pump," said Liftore. "He is mad."

"My fellow servants know better than to touch me," said Malcolm.

The men looked to their mistress. "Do as my lord tells you," she said, "and instantly!"

"Men," said Malcolm, "I have spared that foolish lord there for the sake of this fisher-girl and his child, but don't one of you touch me."

Stoat was a brave enough man and not a little jealous of Malcolm, but he dared not obey his mistress.

And now came the tramp of many feet along the landing and six fishermen entered.

Forimel started forward. "My brave fishermen!" she cried. "Take that mad man, MacPhail, and put him out of my grounds."

"I can't do that, my lady," answered their leader.

"Take Lord Liftore," Malcolm said to them, "and hold him while I make him acquainted with a fact or two which he may judge of consequence to him."

The men walked straight up to the earl. He struck right and left, but was overpowered and in a moment held fast.

Then Malcolm stepped into the middle of the room, approaching his sister.

"I tell you to leave this House!" Florimel shrieked, beside herself with fury.

"Florimel!" said Malcolm solemnly, calling his sister by her real name for the first time.

"You insolent wretch!" she cried. "What right have you, if you be, as you say, my baseborn brother, to call me by my name?"

"Florimel!" repeated Malcolm—and the voice was like the voice of her father—"I have done what I could to serve you."

"And I want no more such service," she returned, beginning to tremble.

"But you have driven me almost to extremities," he went on, heedless of her interruption.

"Will nobody take pity on me?" said Florimel imploringly, looking about the room. Then finding herself ready to burst into tears, she gathered all her pride, stepped up to Malcolm, looked him in the face, and said:

"Pray, sir, is this House yours or mine?"

"Mine," answered Malcolm. "I am the marquis of Lossie, and while I am your elder brother and the head of the family, you shall never with my consent marry that man."

Liftore uttered a fierce imprecation.

"If you dare give breath to another such word, I will have you gagged," said Malcolm. "If my sister marries that man," he continued and then turned again to Florimel, "not one shilling shall she take with her beyond what she may happen to have in her purse at that moment. She is in my power and I will use it to the utmost to protect her from him."

"What are you saying, MacPhail?" cried Florimel, a tear issuing from her pale and dilated eyes. "You are mad!" But even as she uttered it, she sought a chair. The fight was ebbing from her body; something in her soul told her Malcolm's words were true.

"Proof!" exclaimed Liftore.

"To my sister I will give all the proof she may require," answered Malcolm. "But to you, my lord, I owe none. Stoat, order horses for Lady Bellair and his lordship."

"I will go with Lady Bellair," said Florimel. Then turning to Liftore, "Let us leave this place at once."

Malcolm took her by the arm. For a moment she struggled, but finding no one dared interfere, submitted and was led from the room like a naughty child.

"Keep his lordship there till I return," he said as they went.

He led her into an adjoining room and when he had shut the door, he said, "Florimel, I have striven to serve you the best way I knew. I loved my sister and longed for her goodness. But she has foiled all my attempts. She has not loved or followed the truth. She has been proud and disdainful and careless of right. You have cast from you the devotion of a gifted and large-hearted painter for a small and vile man. You have wronged the nature and the God of women. Once more, I pray you to give up this man—let your true self speak and send him away."

"Sir, I go with my Lady Bellair, driven from my father's house by one who calls himself my brother. My lawyer shall make inquiries."

She would have left the room but he prevented her.

"Florimel! You are casting the pearl of your womanhood before a swine. He will trample it under his feet and turn against you!"

"Let me go!"

"You shall not go until you have heard all the truth."

"What! More truth still? Your truth is anything but pleasant."

"It is more unpleasant than you yet think. Florimel, you have driven me to it. I would have prepared you a shield against the shock which must come, but you compel me to wound you to the quick. I would have had you receive the bitter truth from lips you loved, but you drove those lips of honor from you. Now there are left to utter it only lips that you hate. Yet you shall receive the truth. It may help to save you from weakness, arrogance, and falsehood. Our father married my mother; therefore I am the marquis. But, sister, your mother was never Lady Lossie."

"You lie! I know you lie! Because you wrong me, you would brand me with dishonor to take from me, as well, the sympathy of the world. But I defy you!"

"Alas, there is no help, sister. Your mother indeed passed as Lady Lossie, but my mother, the true Lady Lossie, was alive the whole time and only died last year. For twenty years my mother suffered in silence. In the eye of the law you are no better than the little child Liftore denied a short while ago. Give that man his dismissal, or he will give you yours when he learns of this. Never doubt that he would do it. Refuse me again, and I will go from this room to publish the fact that you are neither Lady Lossie nor Lady Florimel Colonsay. You have no right to any name but your mother's. You are Miss Gordon."

She gave a great gasp.

"All that is now left you," concluded Malcolm, "is the choice between sending Liftore away or being abandoned by him. That choice you must now make."

The poor girl tried to speak, but could not. Her fire was burning out, her strength fast failing her.

"Florimel," said Malcolm, and knelt on one knee and took her hand. "Florimel, I will be your true brother. I am your brother, your very own brother, to live for you, love you, fight for you, watch over you until a true man takes you for his wife." Her hand quivered.

"Send him away," she breathed rather than said and sank to the floor.

He lifted her, laid her on a couch, and returned to the drawing room.

"My Lady Clementina," he said, "will you oblige me by going to my sister in the next room?"

"I will, my lord," she said and went.

Malcolm walked up to Liftore. "My lord," he said, "my sister takes her leave of you."

"I must have my dismissal from her own lips."

"You shall have it from the hands of my fishermen. Take him away!"

As he turned from him, he saw Caley behind the little group of servants gathered just outside the door. He walked toward her. She attempted to slip inconspicuously away, but he laid his hand on her shoulder and whispered a word in her ear. She grew white and stood stock-still.

Just then, as the fishermen, with Liftore in tow, approached the top of the stairs, Mr. Morrison and Mr. Soutar entered the House and quickly made their way to the top.

"My lord!" said the lawyer coming up hastily to him, "surely there cannot be occasion for such—such—measures?"

But then catching sight of Malcolm's wounded forehead, he added a low exclamation of astonishment and dismay—the tone saying almost as clearly as the words, "How ill and foolishly everything is managed without a lawyer!"

Malcolm only smiled, went up to the magistrate whom he led into the middle of the room, saying, "Mr. Morrison, everyone here knows you. Tell them who I am."

"The marquis of Lossie, my lord," answered Morrison, "and from my heart I congratulate your people here that at length you assume the rights and honors of your position."

A murmur of pleasure arose in response. But before it ceased, Malcolm started and sprang to the door. There stood Lenorme! He seized him by the arm and without a word of explanation hurried him to the room where his sister was. He called Clementina, half drew her from the room, pushed Lenorme in, and closed the door.

He asked Mrs. Courthope to see that everyone was served luncheon, and then begged them to excuse him for a while and ran down the hill to his grandfather. He dreaded lest any other tongue than his own should tell him the opened secret. He was just in time, for already the town was in a tumult, and the spreading ripples of the news were fast approaching Duncan's ears.

Malcolm found him expectant and restless. When he disclosed himself, he showed little astonishment, only took him in his arms and pressed him to his bosom, saying, "Ta Lort pe praised, my son!" Then he broke out in fervent ejaculation of Gaelic, during which he instinctively turned to his pipes as the only sure way of escape for his imprisoned feelings.

While he played, Malcolm slipped out and hurried to Miss Horn.

One word to her was enough to unlock the months of pent-up emotion that had been hidden deep in Miss Horn's heart. The stern old woman burst into tears.

"Oh, Grizel! My Grizel! Look down from your house among the stars and see the great lad you left behind, and praise the Lord you have such a son!"

She sobbed for a moment and wept without restraint.

Then she stopped suddenly, dabbed her eyes indignantly, and cried, "Hoot! I'm an old fool. Somebody might think I had feelings after all!"

Malcolm laughed, and she could not help joining him.

On his way back to the House, he knocked at Mrs. Catanach's door and said a few words to her which had a remarkable effect on the expression of her plump countenance and deep-set black eyes.

When Malcolm reached the House, he ran up the main staircase, knocked at the first door, opened it, and peeped in. There sat Lenorme on the couch with Florimel on his knees nestling her head against his shoulder, like a child that has been very naughty but was fully forgiven. Her face was blotted with tears, and her hair was everywhere, but there was a light of dawning goodness all about her.

She did not move when Malcolm entered—more than to just bring the palms of her hands together and look up in his face.

"Have you told him all, Florimel?" he asked.

"Yes, Malcolm," she answered, "I told him *all*—and he loves me yet! He has taken the girl without a name to his heart."

"No wonder," said Malcolm, "when she brought it with her."

"Yes," said Lenorme, "I could dare the angel Gabriel to match happiness with me."

Poor Florimel, for all her worldly ways, was but a child. Bad associates had filled her with worldly maxims and words and thoughts and judgments. She had never loved Liftore; she had only taken delight in his flatteries.

"Will you come to your brother, Florimel?" said Malcolm tenderly, holding out his arms.

Lenorme raised her. She went softly to him and laid herself on his chest. "Forgive me, brother," she said, and looked up to him.

He kissed her and turned to Lenorme. "I give her to you," he said.

With that he left them and sought Mr. Morrison and Mr. Soutar. An hour of business followed in which, among other matters, they talked about the necessary arrangements for a dinner for his people, fishers and farmers and all. After the gentlemen took their leave, nobody saw him for hours. Till sunset approached he remained alone, shut up in the Wizard's chamber, the room in which he was born. Part of the time he occupied in writing to Mr. Graham.

As the sun fell behind the sea, Malcolm ascended the sandhill from the shore where he had been walking. From the other side, Clementina ascended but a moment later. On the top they met in the red light of the sunset. They clasped each other's hand and stood for a moment in silence.

"Ah, my lord," said the lady, "how shall I thank you that you kept your secret from me? But my heart is sore to lose my fisherman."

"My lady," returned Malcolm, "you have only found your groom."

35

· · · · · · · · · · · · · · · · · · ·

The Assembly

That same evening Duncan, in full dress, claymore and dirk at his sides and carrying the great Lossie pipes, marched first through the streets of the upper and then the lower town, followed by the bellman. At the proper stations Duncan blew a rousing pilbroch, after which the bellman proclaimed aloud that Malcolm, marquis of Lossie, desired the presence of each and every one of his tenants in the royal burgh of Portlossie, both Newton and Seaton, in the townhall of the same, at seven o'clock upon the evening following. The proclamation ended, the piper sounded one note three times, and they passed to the next station. When they had gone through the Seaton they entered a carriage waiting for them at the sea gate and were driven to Scaurnose, and from there again to the several other villages on the coast belonging to the marquis, making at each the same manner of announcement.

Portlossie was in a ferment of wonder, satisfaction, and pleasure. In the shops, among the nets, in the curing sheds, in the houses and cottages, nothing else was talked about. Stories and reminiscences innumerable were brought out to prove that Malcolm had always appeared likely to turn out somebody, the narrator not seldom modestly hinted at a glimmering foresight on his own part of what had now been revealed. His friends were jubilant. The men crowded around Duncan, congratulating him and asking a hundred questions. But the old man maintained a calm and stately pomp and grace and would not, by word or gesture or tone confess to any surprise, but behaved as if he had known it all the time.

Davy, in his yacht uniform, was the next morning appointed the marquis' personal attendant. Almost the first thing that fell to him in his office was to show into his master's room a pale, feeble man, bowed by the weight of a huge brass-clasped volume under each arm.

His lordship rose and met him with outstretched hand. "I am glad to see you, Mr. Crathie," he said, "but I fear you are out too soon."

"I am quite well since our talk of yesterday, my lord," returned the factor. "Your lordship's accession has made a young man of me again. I am here to render account of my stewardship."

"I want none, Mr. Crathie—nothing, that is, beyond a summary statement of how things stand with me."

"I should like to satisfy your lordship that I have dealt honestly"—here the factor paused for a moment, then with an effort added—"by you, my lord."

"One further word, then," said Malcolm, "the last of the sort, I believe, that will ever pass between us. Thank God we had it made up before yesterday. If you have ever been hard upon any of my tenants, not to say unfair, you have wronged me far more than had you taken from me. So now, if any man thinks he has cause of complaint, I leave it to you, with the help of the new light that has been given you, to reconsider the matter and, where needful, to make reparation. As to your loyalty to my family and its affairs, of that I never had a shadow of suspicion." And with that Malcolm held out his hand.

The factor's trembled in his strong grasp.

"Mistress Crathie is sorely vexed at herself, my lord," he said, rising to take his leave.

Malcolm laughed. "Give Mrs. Crathie my best wishes," he said, "and tell her that if she will, after this, greet every honest fisherman as if he might possibly turn out a lord, she and I will be more than even."

The next morning he carried her again a few mackerel he had just caught, and she never forgot the lesson given her.

When the evening came, the town hall was crammed to such an extent that Malcolm proposed they should occupy the square in front. A fisherman in garb and gesture, not the less a gentleman and a marquis, he stood on the steps of the hall and spoke to his people. They received him with wild enthusiasm.

"The open air is better for everything," he began. "Fishers, I have called you first, because you are my own people. I am and shall be a fisherman. How things have come about I will tell you later. I would like all of you to come and dine with me as soon as preparations can be made, and you shall then hear enough to satisfy your curiosity. At present my care is that you should understand the terms of what I intend to do. I would gladly be a friend to all and will do my best to that end.

"You of Portlossie shall have your harbor cleared without delay.

"You of Scaurnose shall hear the blasting necessary for your harbor commence within two weeks, and every house shall before long have a small piece of land allotted it. I feel bound to mention that there may be some among you whom I will have to keep an eye on. I give fair warning that whoever shall hereafter disturb the peace or liberty of my people shall assuredly be cast out of my borders.

"I shall take measures that all complaints shall be heard and all except foolish ones heeded. As much as lies in my power I will execute justice. Whoever oppresses or wrongs his neighbor shall have to do with me. And to aid me in doing justice I pray the help of every honest man. I am set to rule, and rule I will. He who loves right will help me to rule; he who does not love it shall be ruled or depart."

The address had been every now and then interrupted by a hearty cheer. At this point the cheering was greatly prolonged, and after it, he went on:

"And now I am about to give you proof that I mean what I say and that evil shall not come to light without being noted and dealt with.

"There are in this company two women. One of them is already well known to you all. Her name, or at least that by which she goes among you, is Barbara Catanach. The other is an Englishwoman by the name of Caley."

All eyes were turned upon the two. Even Mrs. Catanach was cowed by the consciousness of the universal stare.

"Well assured that if I brought a criminal action against them it would hang them both, I trust you will not imagine it revenge that moves me to thus expose them. In refraining from prosecuting them I bind myself of necessity to see that they work no more evil. In giving them time for repentance I take the consequences upon myself. Therefore, these women shall not go forth to pass for harmless members of society in some other place, but shall live here, in this town, thoroughly known and absolutely distrusted. That they may be thus known, I publicly declare that I hold proof against these women of having conspired to kill me. From the effects of the poison they succeeded in giving me, I fear I shall never altogether recover. There are also mischiefs innumerable upon their lying tongues. If I wrong them, let them accuse me. Only if they bring suit against me and lose, it will compel me to bring my accusations against them.

"Hear, then, what I have determined concerning them. The woman Catanach shall take to her cottage the woman Caley. That cottage they shall have rent free. I will appoint them also a sufficiency for life and maintenance, bare indeed, for I would not have them comfortable. But they shall be free to work if they can find any to employ them. If, however, either shall go beyond the bounds I set, she shall be followed the moment she is missed with a warrant for her apprehension. And I beg all honest folk to keep an eye on them. According as they live shall their lives be. If they come to repentance, they will bless the day I resolved upon such severe measures on their behalf. Now, let them go to their place."

I will not try to describe the devilish look of contempt and hate that possessed the countenance of the midwife as she obeyed the command. Caley, white as death, trembled and tottered, not daring once to look up as she followed her companion. Before many months had gone by, stared at and shunned by all, even Miss Horn's Jean, and totally deprived of every chance of indulging her dominant passion for mischievous influence, the midwife's face began to tell such a different tale that Malcolm began to hold a feeble hope that within a few years Mrs. Catanach might get so far as to begin to suspect that she was a sinner—that she had actually done things she ought not to have done.

Duncan was formally recognized as piper to the marquis of Lossie. His ambition reached no higher. Malcolm himself saw to his perfect equipment, heedful especially that his kilt and plaid should be of Duncan's own tartan of red and blue and green. His dirk and broadsword he had newly sheathed, with silver mountings. And whenever Malcolm had guests they had to endure, as long as Duncan continued able to fill the bag, as best they might, two or three minutes of uproar and outcry from the treble throat of powerful Lossie pipes between each course at every dinner. A lady guest would now and then venture to hint that the custom was rather a trying one for English ears. By his own desire, the piper had a chair and small table set for him behind and to the right of his chief, as he called him. There he ate with the family and guests, waited upon by Davy.

Malcolm was one of the few who understood the shelter of light, the protection to be gained by the open presentation of the truth. To Malcolm it was one of the promises of the Kingdom that there is nothing covered that shall not be revealed. He was anxious, therefore, to tell his people at the coming dinner the main points of his story, certain that such openness would also help to lay the foundation of confidence between him and them. The one difficulty in the way was the position of Florimel. But that could not fail to appear in any case; and he was satisfied that even for her sake it was far better to speak openly, for then the common heart would take her in and cover her. He consulted, therefore, with Lenorme, who went to find her. She came and begged him to say whatever he thought best.

This time the tables were not set in different parts of the grounds, but gathered upon the level of the drive and adjacent lawn spaces between the house and the trees. Malcolm, in full highland dress as chief of his clan, took the head of the central table, with Florimel in the place of honor at his right and Clementina on his left. Lenorme sat next to Florimel and Annie Mair next to Lenorme. On the other side, Mr. Graham sat next to Clementina, Miss Horn next to him, and Blue Peter next to Miss Horn. He set Mr. Morrison to preside at the farmers' table and had all the fisher-fold about himself.

When the main part of the dinner was over, he rose and, with as much circumstance as he thought desirable, told his story, beginning with the parts in it his uncle and Mrs. Catanach had taken. It was, however, he said, a principle in the history of the world that evil should bring forth good. Had he not been taken to the heart of one of the noblest and simplest of men who had brought him up in honorable poverty and rectitude? When he had said this he turned to Duncan who sat at his own table behind him with his pipes on a stool. "You all know my grandfather," he went on, "and all respect him."

At this rose a great shout.

"I thank you, my friends," he continued. "My desire is that every soul here should carry himself to Duncan MacPhail as if he were in blood what he is in deed and in truth—my grandfather."

A second great shout arose.

He went on to speak of the privileges he alone of all his race had ever enjoyed—the privileges of toil and danger, of human dependence and divine aid, the privilege of the confidence and companionship of honorable men and the understanding of their ways and thoughts and feelings, and the privilege of the friendship and instruction of the schoolmaster to whom he owed more than eternity could reveal.

Then he turned again to his narrative and told how his father, falsely informed that his wife and child were dead, married Florimel's mother; how his mother, out of compassion for both of them, held her peace, how for twenty years she had lived with her cousin Miss Horn and held her peace even from her; how at last, when having succeeded to the property, she heard he was coming to the House, the thought of his nearness yet un-approachableness so worked upon a worn and enfeebled frame that she died.

Then he told how Miss Horn, after his mother's death, came upon letters revealing the secret which she had all along known must exist which, from love and respect for her cousin, she had never inquired into.

Last of all he told how, in a paroxysm of rage, Mrs. Catanach had let thesecret of his birth escape her; how she afterward made affidavit concerning it, and how his father upon his deathbed, with all necessary legal obser-vances, acknowledged him as his son and heir.

"And now, to the mighty gladness of my soul," he said, looking on Florimel at his side, "my dearly loved and honored sister has accepted me as her brother. And I do not think she greatly regrets the loss of the headship of the house she has passed over to me. She will lose little else. And of all women, it may well be to her a small matter to lose a mere title, seeing she is so soon to change her name for one which will bring her honor of a more enduring reality. For he who is about to become her husband is not only a nobleman but a man of great talent whose praises she will hear on all sides. One of his works, the labor and gift of love, you shall see when we rise from the table. It is a portrait of your late landlord, my father, painted partly from a miniature, partly from my sister, and partly, I am happy to think, from my-self. And you will remember that Mr. Lenorme never saw my father. I say this not to excuse, but to enhance his work.

"My tenants, I will do my best to give you fair play. My friend and factor, Mr. Crathie, has confided to me his doubts whether he may not have been a little hard; he is prepared to reconsider some of your cases. Do no imagine that I am going to be a careless man of business. I want money, for I have enough to do with it, if only to set right much that is wrong. But let God judge between you and me.

"My fishermen, every honest man of you is my friend and you shall know it. Between you and me that is enough. But for the sake of harmony and right and order, and that I may keep near you, I shall appoint three men of yourselves in each village to whom any man or woman may go with request or complaint. If two of those three judge the matter fit to refer to me, the probability is that I shall see it as they do. If any man think them unjust toward him, let him come to me. Should I find myself in doubt, I have here at my side my loved and honored master to whom to apply for counsel. Friends, if we be honest with ourselves, we shall be honest with each other.

"And, in conclusion, I want you to hear from none but my own lips that this lady beside me, the daughter of an English earl of ancient house, has honored the house of Lossie by consenting to become its marchioness.

Lady Clementina Thornicroft possesses large estates in the south of England, but not for them did I seek her favor, and it was while my birth and position was yet unknown to her—she never dreaming that I was other than only a fisherman and a groom—that she accepted me for her husband."

With that he took his seat. After hearty cheering, a glass or two of wine and several speeches, all rose and went to look at the portrait of the late marquis.

36

•••••••••••••••••••••

The Wedding

*L*ady Clementina had to return to England to see her lawyers and arrange her affairs. So the *Psyche* was launched. Lady Clementina, Florimel, and Lenorme were the passengers; Malcolm, Blue Peter, and Davy the crew. There was no room for servants, yet there was no lack of service. They had rough weather part of the time and neither Clementina nor Lenorme was altogether comfortable, but they made a rapid voyage and were all well when they landed at Greenwich.

Knowing nothing of Lady Bellair's proceedings, they sent Davy to reconnoiter in Portland Place. He brought back word that there was no one in the house but an old woman. So Malcolm took Florimel there. Everything belonging to their late visitors had vanished and nobody knew where they had gone.

Searching the drawers and cabinets, Malcolm found, to his unspeakable delight, a miniature of his mother along with one of his father—a younger likeness than he had yet seen. Also he found a few letters of his mother—mostly were notes written in pencil—but neither these nor those of his father which Miss Horn had given him would he read. Lovingly he laid them together and burned them to dustflakes. "My mother shall tell me what she pleases when I find her," he said. "She shall not reprove me for reading her letters to my father."

They were married at Wastbeach, both couples in the same ceremony. Immediately after the wedding the painter and his bride set out for Rome, and the marquis and marchioness went on board the *Psyche*. As it was the desire of each to begin their married life at home, they sailed direct to Portlossie. After a good voyage, however, they landed, in order to reach home quietly, at Duff Harbor, took horses from there, and arrived at Lossie House late in the evening.

Before the return voyage Malcolm wrote to the housekeeper to prepare for them the wizard's chamber, but to alter nothing on walls or in furniture. That room, he resolved, should be the first he occupied with his bride, and it was there he told her the long story of his history which she hungered to hear. Mrs. Courthope was scandalized at the idea, but she had no choice and therefore contented herself with doing all that lay in the power of woman, under such severe restrictions, to make the dingy old room cheerful. Malcolm kept that chamber just as it was ever after, and often retired to it for meditation. He never restored the ruinous parts of the concealed stairway and kept the door at the top carefully closed. But he cleared out the rubbish that choked the place where the stairs had led lower down, came upon it again in tolerable preservation a little beneath, and followed it into a passage that ran under the burn. Doubtless there was some foundation for the legend of Lord Gernon.

There, however, he abandoned the work, thinking of the possibility of a time when employment would be scarce and his people in want of all he could give them. And when such a time did arrive within a couple of years, an even more important undertaking was in the making which was needful to employ the many who must either work or starve—the rebuilding of the ancient castle of Colonsay. Its vaults were emptied of rubbish and ruin, the rock faced afresh, walls and towers and battlements raised, until at last when its loftiest tower seemed to have reached its height, it rose yet higher, crowned by a splendid beacon lamp to shine far into the northern night to guide the fishermen when their way was unsure. Every summer for years, Florimel and her husband spent weeks in the castle and many a study the painter made there of the ever-changing face of the sea.

Malcolm had such a strong feeling for good and truth that nothing would suit him but that Mr. Graham be reinstated. He told the presbytery that if it were not done, he would himself build a schoolhouse for him, with the consequence that they reversed their former position. The young man they had put in his place was willing to act as his assistant, keeping the cottage and his same salary, with the understanding that when he found he could no longer conscientiously further the endeavors of Mr. Graham, the marquis would procure him another appointment.

Mr. Graham thenceforward lived in the House, a spiritual father to the whole family. There was an ancient building connected with the House, divided for many years into barn and dairy, but evidently originally the chapel of the monastery. This Malcolm soon set about reconverting. It made a lovely chapel—too large for the household, but not too large for its Wednesday evening congregation, when many of the fisher families, farm people from the neighborhood, and a number of the inhabitants of the upper town gathered to listen to the master.

Clementina adopted Lizza as her personal attendant. As Lizza's young boy was about her nearly always, by the time she had children of her own she had some notion of what could and ought to be done for the development of the divine germ that lay deep inside every human heart. Kelpie had a foal and apparently, in consequence, grew so much more gentle that at length Malcolm consented that Clementina should mount her. After a few attempts to unseat her, not of the most determined kind, however, Kelpie consented to carry her and ever after seemed proud of having a mistress that could ride.

It was not long before people began to remark that no one now ever heard the piper utter the name Campbell. An ill-bred youth once—it was well for him that Malcolm was not near—dared the evil word in his presence. A cloud swept across the old man's face, but he held his peace, and to the day of his death, which arrived in his ninety-first year, it never crossed his lips. He died with the Lossie pipes on his bed and Malcolm by his side.

Malcolm's relations with the fisher-fold, founded as they were in truth and open uprightness, were not in the least injured by his change of position. He made it a point to always be at home during the herring fishing. And when he was at home he was always out amongst the people. Almost every day he would look in at some door in the Seaton and call out a salutation to the busy housewife—perhaps go in and sit down for a minute. Now he would be walking with this one, now talking with that—oftenest with Blue Peter.

In the third year he launched a strange vessel. Her tonnage was two hundred, but she was built like a fishing boat. She had great stowage forward and below; if there was a large take, boat after boat could empty its load into her and go back and draw its nets again. But this was not the original design for her. The half of her deck, parted off with a light rope-rail, was kept as white as stone could make it and had a brass-railed bulwark. She was steered with a wheel, for more room; the top of the binnacle was made sloping, to serve as a lectern; and there were seats all round the bulwarks. She was called the *Clemency*.

For some time Malcolm had provided musical training for the most able of the youths he could find amongst the fishers, and now he had a pretty good band able to give back to God a shadow of His own music. And now, every Sunday evening the great fishing boat, with the marquis, and almost always the marchioness on board, led out from the harbor such of the boats as were going to spend the night on the water.

When they reached the ground, all the other boats gathered around the great boat and the chief men came on board. Malcolm then stood up to read, generally from the words of Jesus; talking to them, striving to get the truth alive into their hearts, after which a prayer and several numbers by the band sent the men dropping into their boats and the fleet scattering wide over the waters to search them for their treasure.

If ever a boat wanted help or the slightest danger arose, the first thing was to call the marquis. He was on deck in a moment, taking the situation in hand. In the morning, when a few of the boats had gathered, they would make for the harbor again, with a full blast of praising trumpets and horns, the waves seeming to dance to the well-ordered noise divine.

For such Monday mornings Malcolm wrote a little song for the band, the last stanza of which follows:

> Like the fish that brought the coin,
> We in ministry will join—
> Bringing what pleases Thee the best:
> Help from each to all the rest.

Taking You Places You'll Never Forget!

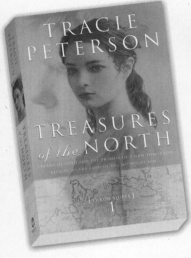

Yukon Quest: A Series of Renewed Hope

Torn between her desire to obey her parents and her terror of the man they've arranged for her to marry, young Grace decides to escape to Alaska. With "gold fever" and the call of the wild drawing a host of characters to the frozen north, she encounters others who believe they can build a future of hope and peace with the growing opportunities Alaska offers. Will they ever truly escape the pasts that threaten them?

Treasures of the North by Tracie Peterson

Caledonia: Experience the Romance and Excitement of Scotland

Part romance, part mystery, part spiritual quest, and all unforgettable, Michael Phillips' Caledonia books will have you on the edge of your seat.

Parliament member Andrew Trentham begins both a journey of faith as well as a rediscovery of his heritage when a scandal in the government overturns his life. His quest is not without obstacles and with shadowy enemies hounding his every move, Trentham must make one final stand. Seeking the same courage and vision granted to his ancestors in their fight for freedom, Trentham's quest culminates in a decision that could change his life...and the history of Scotland forever.

Legend of the Celtic Stone by Michael Phillips
An Ancient Strife

◆ BETHANYHOUSE
11400 Hampshire Ave. S. • Minneapolis, MN 55438 • 1-800-328-6109
www.bethanyhouse.com